Borneo in the Cold War, 1950–1990

It is an admirable virtue of Professor Ooi's most recent research . . . rather than immersing himself in the details of Borneo's recent history, which, in any case, he does with great skill, he examines the island as a whole and the increasing impacts of nation-building and the incorporation of constituent territories and peoples into regional and global movements.

[He] continued to draw attention to Borneo's position in a wider regional and . . . global history. . . . However, what struck me in Professor Ooi's ambitious study was the constant return to issues of political configuration, the struggle over the form and cultural content of the emerging nation-states involved in Borneo, and the position of constituent populations and ethnic groups in these multicultural national, and often uncertain adventures.

Victor T. King, *Professor of Borneo Studies*
Institute of Asian Studies,
Universiti Brunei Darussalam

Although by about 1950 both British Borneo, including the protected sultanate of Brunei, and Indonesian Borneo seemed settled under their different regimes and well on the way to post-war reconstruction and economic development, the upheavals which affected Southeast and East Asia during the Cold War period also deeply affected Borneo. Besides the impact of the Korean and Vietnam Wars and the Malayan Emergency and communist uprisings in other Southeast Asian states, there was within Borneo the attempted communist takeover of Sarawak from the 1950s, a failed coup d'état in Brunei in 1962, Sukarno's *Konfrontasi* (confrontation) with Malaysia, and the horrific purge of Leftists and ethnic Chinese in the late 1960s. This book details these momentous events and assesses their impact on Borneo and its people. It is a sequel to the author's earlier books, *The Japanese Occupation of Borneo, 1941–1945* (2011) and *Post-War Borneo, 1945–1950: Nationalism, Empire, and State-Building* (2013), collectively a trilogy.

Ooi Keat Gin, FRHistS, is Professor of History and Coordinator of the Asia Pacific Research Unit (APRU-USM) at the School of Humanities, Universiti Sains Malaysia, as well as editor-in-chief, *International Journal of Asia Pacific Studies* (IJAPS).

Routledge Studies in the Modern History of Asia

For a full list of available titles please visit: www.routledge.com/Routledge-Studies-in-the-Modern-History-of-Asia/book-series/MODHISTASIA

Borneo in the Cold War, 1950–1990

Ooi Keat Gin

Routledge
Taylor & Francis Group

LONDON AND NEW YORK

First published 2020
by Routledge
2 Park Square, Milton Park, Abingdon, Oxon OX14 4RN

and by Routledge
605 Third Avenue, New York, NY 10017

First issued in paperback 2021

Routledge is an imprint of the Taylor & Francis Group, an informa business

British Library Cataloguing-in-Publication Data
A catalogue record for this book is available from the British Library

Library of Congress Cataloging-in-Publication Data
A catalog record for this book has been requested

ISBN 13: 978-0-367-78489-8 (pbk)
ISBN 13: 978-1-138-91078-2 (hbk)

Typeset in Times New Roman
by Apex CoVantage, LLC

To Swee Im, my wife
And for our loved ones: Beannie, Mebs, and Boo Bee

Contents

Illustrations

Figure

Appendices

Foreword

I am pleased to provide these introductory comments on Professor Ooi Keat Gin's latest book, which completes his Routledge trilogy on the history of Borneo. *Borneo in the Cold War, 1950–1991* follows his *The Japanese Occupation of Borneo, 1941–1945* (2011) and *Post-War Borneo, 1945–1950: Nationalism, Empire, and Nation-Building* (2013). He has written much else on Borneo, including his earlier published work on education and economic development in Brooke Sarawak, which emerged from his postgraduate studies in Singapore and the UK, and a book which relates very closely to his developing interests in the Japanese period in Borneo, *Rising Sun over Borneo: The Japanese Occupation of Sarawak, 1941–1945* (1999).

I have frequently argued that Borneo Studies, if it is to establish a rationale for this field of research, requires a much more ambitious comparative perspective which embraces the several constituent regions of the island: Indonesian Kalimantan, Malaysian Borneo, and Brunei Darussalam. The established scholarly practices have exhibited the strong inclination to focus on one particular ethnic group or political unit; it is rare for those interested in Borneo to stray beyond, say, Sarawak or Sabah or Brunei Darussalam, or one of the Indonesian provinces. It is even more rare for a scholar of Malaysian Borneo to engage in research on the Indonesian regions to the south or for an Indonesian specialist to move farther north. There is an added need for the adoption of a wider perspective in that, with the exception of Brunei Darussalam, the major areas of Borneo have been incorporated into two nation-states, the Federation of Malaysia and the Republic of Indonesia, whose capital cities are located at some distance from the island. This politico-economic and cultural reality has acted to create a core-periphery relationship and one which gives to Borneo its marginal and dependent status. The process of marginalization and its consequences certainly need to be addressed in contextualizing the modern history of Borneo. Even Brunei, though an independent nation-state, also exhibits characteristics of regional marginality.

There is yet another requirement in the development of a research agenda, and that is to conceptualize the island in terms of its position, not only with regard to the nation-states of which it is part, but also to the wider region of Southeast Asia, which is following a path of continuous construction and re-formation – politically, economically, and culturally – within the Association of Southeast Asian Nations

(ASEAN) and to the region's engagement with globalizing processes. It is an admirable virtue of Professor Ooi's most recent research, particularly this latest book, that he has adopted this wider comparative approach, and rather than immersing himself in the details of Borneo's recent history, which, in any case, he does with great skill, he examines the island as a whole and the increasing impacts of nation-building and the incorporation of constituent territories and peoples into regional and global movements.

Professor Ooi has continued to draw attention to Borneo's position in a wider regional and, in this latest book, global history. Interestingly, he also indicates that, at certain moments, Borneo had assumed greater importance. During the Pacific War, for example, Japan, as a rapidly expanding imperial power, saw that the control of strategic coastal areas of Borneo was necessary not only for securing important resources such as oil in Miri, Brunei, and Tarakan, but also, during military operations, for gaining access to Singapore and Batavia/Jakarta from the airfields in Sarawak and Kalimantan. The resources from Borneo, especially petroleum, also played a later role in the Korean War. Professor Ooi's attention to the Cold War in Southeast Asia gives added prominence, and quite rightly so, to the recent history of Borneo.

In these concerns with centrality and marginality, the related issue is the interaction between local agency and external action, pressure, and influence. In the emerging post-war bipolar world, Professor Ooi poses the question of whether or not local political leaders in Borneo served as puppets, proxies, or satellites of Washington, Moscow, or Beijing. This is a complex issue to address, and to do so it requires the distillation of a wide-ranging body of information. Of course, there is no straightforward answer, and the question is rendered even more complex in Asia where two major agents of communism, the People's Republic of China and Soviet Russia, were at work.

After an introductory excursion into the experiences of Borneo under European colonialism, in the south under the Dutch, and in the north under the British-supported Brooke Raj in Sarawak, the Chartered Company in what was later to be renamed Sabah, and the Residency in Brunei, Professor Ooi discusses the underlying forces which gave rise to the Cold War and its expressions in conflicts in the Korean Peninsula and Vietnam/Indochina. In the period of post-war decolonization and nation-state formation in Southeast Asia, it is also necessary for him to examine a range of conflicts there: the Indonesian Revolution, the Malayan Emergency, and the Hukbalahap Rebellion in the Philippines, among others. In the context of Borneo, Professor Ooi focuses on a mixed set of local responses, some more clearly gaining inspiration from wider Cold War forces and others more concerned with local political, social, economic, and cultural issues, and in particular the configuration and identity of political units: these responses included the emergence of the 'Chinese Left' in Sarawak, elements of which were in evidence as early as the 1920s and 1930s, and which resulted in the eventual formation of the Sarawak United People's Party (SUPP) and the Sarawak Communist Organisation (SCO); the Brunei Rebellion engineered by the Partai Rakyat Brunei in 1962; the Dayak response to the Indonesian transmigration policy, which had a major impact on the economies, environments, and cultures of Kalimantan; the creation of the Dayak-dominated province of Central Kalimantan; the formation of Partai Dayak in West Kalimantan and the Muslim rebellion in South Kalimantan; Tunku Abdul Rahman's Malaysia, President Sukarno's 'Confrontation', and the extended communist guerrilla or 'low-key' conflict along the border between Sarawak and Kalimantan; and the Philippine claim to Sabah.

In his discussion of the forces and consequences of the 'igniting' of Borneo and the turbulent times which he so fluently and expertly describes and explains, it is evident that the diffuse reactions of local populations and their leaders (some nationally prominent, some provincial) brought the island into major focus, particularly in the 1960s. In his concluding chapter, Professor Ooi returns to the theme of the local and the global, and the agency exercised by local actors or their external manipulation by 'a hidden hand'. He proposes that there was 'a mixed bag of motives', which ranged from 'ideological commitment to personal ambitions and ethnic parochial interests'. Clearly, in his biographical excursions, Professor Ooi demonstrates that some Bornean actors were driven more by ideological commitments than by local concerns; others by the immediate issues which they faced rather than those on the grand stage of global tension, conflict, and political conviction. However, what struck me in Professor Ooi's ambitious study was the constant return to issues of political configuration, the struggle over the form and cultural content of the emerging nation-states involved in Borneo, and the position of constituent populations and ethnic groups in these multicultural national, and often uncertain adventures. In many respects, this book provides us with spectacle, excitement, tragedy, and, on occasion, the predictable, in equal measure. *The Cold War in Borneo* establishes Professor Ooi as a major historian of the history of Borneo and much more in the wider Southeast Asia. Perhaps we might, in hopeful anticipation in the years to come, welcome a tetralogy or quartet of books taking up the Borneo story from the early 1990s?

Victor T. King
Professor of Borneo Studies
Institute of Asian Studies
Universiti Brunei Darussalam

Preface

Kalah jadi abu, menang jadi arang

Traditional Malay saying

**The vanquished be ashes whilst the victor be coal;
in war, no one benefits, all parties suffer losses.**

Borneo, comprising the two East Malaysian states of Sabah and Sarawak, Negara Brunei Darussalam, and Indonesia's Kalimantan, during the Cold War decades from 1950 to 1990 completes the historiographical endeavour of the island in the latter half of the twentieth century. The present volume, *Borneo in the Cold War, 1950–1990*, complements two previous publications – *The Japanese Occupation of Borneo, 1941–1945* (2011) and *Post-war Borneo, 1945–1950: Nationalism, Empire, and State-building* (2013) – in taking forward the history of the island towards the close of the last century. This trilogy offers a holistic perspective of the island as a single entity with overlapping themes and interrelatedness. *Borneo in the Cold War, 1950–1990*, like its predecessors, demonstrates and emphasizes the interrelatedness of the island's history that, though divided along political boundaries, possessed shared experiences with cross-border activities, conflicts, and episodic developments.

The present work explores Borneo as a peripheral territory in the context of a global phenomenon, the Cold War, attempting to ascertain to what extent the historical drama that was played out on the Bornean stage was largely a 'local' production with 'local' actors acting in accordance to a 'local' script. If not, did influences and directives from without, especially from the Cold War 'big boys' – the U.S., USSR, or PRC – dictate the script for the 'local' players, or were the latter, not unlike puppets and pawns, being manipulated by puppet masters from afar, viz. Washington, Moscow, or Beijing, or from other quarters. In other words, the intention here is to demonstrate that developments in Borneo during the Cold War era were largely a consequence of local Bornean peoples acting independently in determining their own fate and destiny.

A point of departure of the present volume was the previous volume's closure at circa 1950. As a means of contextualizing the volume, a post-war geopolitical scenario is put into focus presenting the Soviet-U.S. split at the close of the

Second World War (1939–1945) that subsequently led to the phenomenon of what was referred to as the Cold War that many scholars and commentators placed its commencement from 1947 until 1990. Following the mandatory geographical and human factors of Borneo as the background setting, the volume opens with historical developments of the immediate post-war period. From there, a broad treatment presents the viewpoints from Moscow and Washington of this 'conflict' between them. Focus then shifts to East Asia and Southeast Asia as the theatres of the Cold War, from the Chinese Civil War to the Vietnam War, where the two major protagonists wielded a hand or two, directly or indirectly, involvement from within, or directing from without. Borneo then is brought into this Cold War scenario. The next three sections focus on northern Borneo, namely Sarawak, Brunei, and North Borneo/Sabah, as British crown colonies and protectorates. The seeds and growth of communism developed and nurtured in Sarawak, where the Chinese community, to some extent, had been marginalized. The disaffected within the community were susceptible to the ideology, but ethnic affinity to the mainland proved an even stronger 'pull' factor. *Republik Indonesia*'s romance with parliamentary democracy proved too problematic and intractable, prompting Sukarno's response with imposing his 'Guided Democracy'. Hitherto, the aforesaid developments were confined within the respective component territories. The 'spark' that literally and figuratively 'ignited' Borneo was the concept of 'Malaysia' that brought the hitherto disparate developments in confluence to one another. The proposal for the formation of a wider federation ('Malaysia'), first publicly mooted in mid-1961, sent reverberations across the region that kick-started a trajectory of rollercoaster-like developments, viz. from the outbreak of the Brunei Rebellion to the Indonesian Massacres. While Kalimantan was engulfed in a cauldron of violence and slaughter from the latter half of the 1960s, across the divide in Sarawak, a protracted communist insurgency characterized by guerrilla warfare in the midst of the thick rain forest tied down several battalions of government security forces.

There are compelling historiographic justifications for analyzing and evaluating developments in Borneo against the background of the global Cold War. No attempt had yet been attempted for an island-wide treatment of the period *per se*, regardless of relating to the Cold War or otherwise. Most of the literature tended to treat each of the political entities as a single unit confining discussion and analysis within its designated boundaries. Bringing all of the territories together and treating them as a single collective (island-wide) is the significance of this current volume, a pioneering undertaking. Like its two predecessors, Borneo is treated as a single entity, and though respecting the diversities, much commonalities have been discerned and much attention has been drawn to the interrelatedness of various developments therein. Such an approach offers a greater comprehension and deeper understanding of the historical narrative of Borneo as a whole as well as in its respective political component parts.

The conceptualization of this present work dates back a decade ago, but it proved prudent to adhere to the chronological progression upon the completion of the piece on the war and occupation (1941–1945), namely the post-war volume (1945–1950), the second in this trilogy. Only then could the embarkation of the present volume commence. On recollection, work on the previous two volumes had comparatively fewer distractions and/or interruptions than the present undertaking. Research and writing took up the bulk of the work, from conceptualization, collection of source materials from archives and libraries, and the writing stage, all time-consuming and pedestrian activities.

Upon reflection, the greatest challenge faced in the course of the present volume was time itself. Time was the essence, precious and uncompromising; each day passes without waiting for stragglers. More and more the dictum 'Time and tide waits for no man' rings its very truth without argument and/or qualification. The greatest hurdle faced was time.

Perusing the source materials, some hand-written, impressed on the fact that one's decisions as well as actions are determined by one's own deliberations and options decided upon. Not discounting external stimuli (influences, persuasions from other quarters, etc.), the ultimate decision made, and action taken, are solely determined by oneself. Hence, whatever consequences, implications, and/or repercussions thereof, one shall bear. In triumph or regret, one alone endures. To have spent more than two decades as a guerrilla in Sarawak's tropical rain forest, each day pursued and hunted down by security forces, succoured and sustained only and alone by ideological commitment, is fascinating, and at the same instance, admirable, of the human spirit of endurance and perseverance. Although far from endorsing their ideological leanings or condoning their actions, their endurance and perseverance are traits worth emulating.

Acknowledgements are due to several individuals and institutions that contributed directly or indirectly to the fruition of this present volume.

Appreciation is here rendered to all the staff and management of the various archives that were consulted on their respective collections of source materials, here listed in no particular manner of preferences: National Archives, Kew, Richmond, UK; Bodleian Library of Commonwealth and African Studies at Rhodes House, Oxford, UK; *Arkib Negara Malaysia*, Kuala Lumpur, Malaysia; Sarawak Museum and State Archives, Kuching, Malaysia; National Archives and Records Administration, College Park, Maryland, U.S. Others that have been visited and proved profitable as well included *Arsip Nasional Republik Indonesia*, Jakarta, Indonesia; *Dinas Perpustakaan dan Arsip Kota Banjarmasin*, Banjarmasin, Indonesia; *Dinas Perpustakaan, Arsip & Dokumentasi Pemerintah Kota Pontianak*, Pontianak, Indonesia; National Archives, Bandar Seri Begawan, Negara Brunei Darussalam; National Archives of Singapore, Singapore; National Archives of Australia, Canberra, Australia; *Nederlands Nationaal Archief*, The Hague, the Netherlands; Sabah State Archives, Kota Kinabalu, Sabah, Malaysia. Repositories and libraries that were consulted: *Perpustakaan Hamzah Sendut Universiti Sains Malaysia*, Penang, Malaysia; University of Malaya Library, Kuala Lumpur, Malaysia; Lee Kong Chian Reference Library, National Library, Singapore; CSEAS Library, Center for Southeast Asian Studies (CSEAS), Kyoto

University, Kyoto, Japan; Busan University of Foreign Studies Central Library, Busan, South Korea; British Library, London, UK; National Library of Australia, Canberra, Australia.

Funding for research was derived from various sources that I am indeed thankful for, notably as visiting professor, Academy of Brunei Studies, Universiti Brunei Darussalam, Negara Brunei Darussalam (2013–2014, 2014–2015); visiting scholar, Department of Sociology, University of Michigan, Ann Arbor, U.S. (2013); visiting research scholar, Center for Southeast Asian Studies, Kyoto University, Kyoto, Japan (2015, 2016); visiting professor, Institute for Southeast Asian Studies, Busan University of Foreign Studies, Busan, South Korea (2016); Sydney Southeast Asia Centre (SSEAC) Sabbatical Visitor, Asian Studies Program, School of Languages and Cultures, Faculty of Arts and Social Sciences, University of Sydney, Sydney, Australia (2016, 2017). I am indebted to all the aforesaid institutions for not only supporting my research but also accommodating my many sojourns for reflection and writing.

Individuals who played roles directly related to this present work in various capacities, I owe them a debt of gratitude for their invitation and playing host during my various visits as well as extended stays: Dr Stephen Druce (Universiti Brunei Darussalam), Emeritus Professor Gayle Ness (University of Michigan), Professor Caroline Hau (Kyoto University), Associate Professor Dr Yekyoum Kim (Busan University of Foreign Studies), and Professor Adrian Vickers (University of Sydney). Some individuals preferred to be behind-the-scenes; hence, I respect their wishes but take this opportunity to register my gratefulness for all that they have done for me. For testimonial support, I am indebted with gratitude to the late Emeritus Professor Nicholas Tarling (University of Auckland) and to Professor Victor T. King (Universiti Brunei Darussalam).

Emeritus Professor Victor T. King, who penned the Foreword, is gratefully acknowledged. Professor King is undoubtedly a scholar *par excellence* and one of the foremost authorities of Borneo. Our relations go back some three decades to Hull, England, of him as my doctoral supervisor, mentor, and friend. I am forever indebted to him (affectionately as Terry) in scholarship and friendship alike.

Special appreciation is accorded to Peter Sowden, senior editor at Routledge, who was supportive of my works on Borneo as well as other diverse themes that I was involved in over the years. His encouragement and 'nurturing' have been most helpful and invaluable. I treasure most our author-editor relations, not only in publications, but also in other scholarly endeavours, viz. review and evaluation of manuscripts, proposals, etc. I certainly look forward to further fruitful work together in the coming years.

The School of Humanities, Universiti Sains Malaysia, my present academic affiliation, has been most accommodating for two runs of sabbatical leave (2013, 2017) and equally supportive for other periods of leaves of absence for my scholarly pursuits *inter alia* the research and writing of this present book.

Close to home, as well as to heart, is my loving family – Swee Im (wife), Tan Ai Gek (mother), and Saw Lian and Saw Ean (elder sisters). All of their unqualified love, devotion, and support at all times are indispensable to a scholar's and writer's solitary preoccupation, which is almost always protracted and seemingly unending. I am indeed blessed to have them all as my loved ones.

War does not determine who is right – only who is left.

Bertrand Russell (1872–1970)

Ooi Keat Gin
The Pongo
Island Glades
Penang, Malaysia

Abbreviations and acronyms

ABL	Anti-British League
ABRI	*Angkatan Bersenjata Republik Indonesia* (Armed Forces of the Republic of Indonesia)
ADO	Assistant District Officer
AFP	Armed Forces of the Philippines
AIF	Australian Imperial Forces
ALRI	*Angkatan Laut Republik Indonesia* (Naval Forces of the Republic of Indonesia)
AMDA	Anglo-Malayan/Malaysian Defence Agreement
ANM	*Arkib Negara Malaysia*, Kuala Lumpur
APRIS	*Angkatan Perang* RIS/RUSI (Armed Forces of the Republic of the United States of Indonesia)
ARMM	Autonomous Region of Muslim Mindanao
ARVN	Army of the Republic of Vietnam; formerly Vietnamese National Army
ASA	Association of Southeast Asia
ASAS	*Angkatan Semangat Anaknegeri Sarawak* (Fervour of the Generation of Sarawak Natives)
ASEAN	Association of Southeast Asian Nations
ASPC	Anglo-Saxon Petroleum Company
AUREV	*Angkatan Udara Revolusioner* (Revolutionary Air Force)
AURI	*Angkatan Udara Republik Indonesia* (Air Force of the Republic of Indonesia)
BABINSA	*Bintara Pembina Desa* (NCOs for Village Development)
Baperki	*Badan Permusyawaratan Kewarganegaraan Indonesia* (Consultative Council on Indonesian Citizenship)
BARIP	*Barisan Pemuda Brunei* (Brunei Youth Front)
BARJASA	*Barisan Ra'ayat Jati Sarawak* (Sarawak Indigenous Peoples Front)
BBCAU	British Borneo Civil Affairs Unit
BBTC	British Borneo Timber Company
BCC	Brunei Commission Committee
BCOF	British Commonwealth Occupation Force

BFO	*Bijeenkomst voor Federaal Overleg* (Federal Consultative Assembly)
BMA	(BB) British Military Administration (British Borneo)
BMPC	British Malayan Petroleum Company Limited
BNB	British North Borneo
BNBCC	British North Borneo Chartered Company
BPPKT	*Barisan Pemuda Pembangunan Kalimantan Tengah* (Central Kalimantan Youth Front for Development)
BPS	*Barisan Pemuda Sarawak* (Sarawak Youth Front)
BPUPKI	*Badan Penyelidik Usaha Persiapan Kemerdekaan Indonesia* (Investigating Committee for Preparatory Work for Indonesian Independence)
BRD	(German) *Bundesrepublik Deutschland* (Federal Republic of Germany)
CAS	Colonial Administrative Service
CAT	Civil Air Transport (CAT)
CCO	Clandestine Communist Organization
CCP	Chinese Communist Party; also, Communist Party of China
CDB	*Comite Daerah Besar* (Provincial Committee)
CEFEO	*Expeditionnaire Francais en Extreme-Orient* (French Far-East Expeditionary Corps)
CHMS	Chung Hwa Middle School, Kuching
CHSC	Cambridge Higher School Certificate
CIA	(U.S.) Central Intelligence Agency
CICRED	Committee for International Cooperation in National Research in Demography, Paris
CO	Colonial Office, London, UK
COMUSMACV	Commander U.S. Military Assistance Command, Vietnam
CPK	Communist Party of Kampuchea
CPM	Communist Party of Malaya; also, Malayan Communist Party (MCP)
CPVA	Chinese People's Volunteer Army
CTs	communist terrorists
DAP	Democratic Action Party
DI	*Darul Islam* (Realm of Islam)
DIKB	*Daerah Istimewa Kalimantan Barat* (Special Region of West Kalimantan)
DK	Democratic Kampuchea
DMZ	Demilitarized Zone (Korea)
DO	district officer
DOBOPS	Director of Borneo Operations
DPA	*Dewan Pertimbangan Agong* (Supreme Advisory Council)
DPD	*Dewan Perwakilan Daerah* (Regional Representative Council)
DPR	*Dewan Perwakilan Rakyat* (People's Representative Council); also referred to as House of Representatives

DPR-GR	*Dewan Perwakilan Rakyat Gotong Royong* (People's Representative Council of Mutual Assistance)
DPRK	Democratic People's Republic of Korea, North Korea
DRKT	*Dewan Rakyat Kalimantan Tengah* (Central Kalimantan Peoples' Council)
EOKA	*Ethniki Organosis Kyprion Agoniston* (National Organisation of Greek Cypriot Fighters)
FLN	*Front de Libération Nationale*; Algerian nationalist political organization
FMS	Federated Malay States
FONI	*Fonds Nasional Indonesia* (Indonesia National Front)
FRG	Federal Republic of Germany
GAK	*Gerakan Anti-Komunis* (Anti-Communist Movement)
GBHN	*Garis-garis Besar Haluan Negara* (Broad Outlines of State Policy)
GERAKAN	*Gerakan Rakyat Malaysia* (Malaysian People's Movement)
GESTAPU/ G30S	*Gerakan September Tiga Puluh* (Thirtieth September Movement)
GESTOK	*Gerakan Satu Oktober* (First October Movement), interchangeably used with GESTAPU/G30S
GMTPS	*Gerakan Mandau Talawang Panca Sila* (Pro Pancasila Cutlass and Shield Movement)
GOC	General Officer Commanding-in-Chief
GOVPH	Government of the Philippines
GPII	*Gerakan Pemuda Islam Indonesia* (Indonesian Islamic Youth Movement)
GPK	*Gerakan Pembela Keadilan* (Movement for the Defence of Justice)
GTK	'Gerombolan Tjina Komunis' ('Chinese Communist Horde')
H.M	His/Her Majesty
HF	high frequency
HMB	*Hukbong Mapagpalaya ng Bayan* (People's Liberation Army)
HMS	His/Her Majesty's Ship
ICJ	International Court of Justice
IJA	Imperial Japanese Army
IJN	Imperial Japanese Navy
IKAD	*Ikatan Keluarga Dayak* (Dayak Communal League)
INI	*Ikatan Nasional Indonesia* (National Association of Indonesia)
INSAN	Institute of Social Analysis
IPKI	*Ikatan Pendukung Kemerdekaan Indonesia* (League of Supporters of Indonesian Independence)
IRASEC	*Institut De Recherche Sur L'Asie Du Sud-Est Contemporaine* (Research Institute of Contemporary Southeast Asia)

ISA	Internal Security Act
JCBC	Philippines-Malaysia Joint Commission for Bilateral Cooperation
KAMI	*Kesatuan Aksi Mahasiswa Indonesia* (Joint-Action Union of Indonesian Students)
KAP-Gestapu	*Komando Aksi Pengganyangan Gerakan September Tigapuluh* (Action Command to Crush the Thirtieth September Movement)
KAPPI	*Kesatuan Aksi Pelajar Pemuda Indonesia* (Joint-Action Union of Indonesian Youth and Students)
Katolik	*Partai Katolik* (Catholic Party)
KCP	Korean Communist Party
KDH	*Kepala Daerah* (Head of Region)
KELU	Kuching Employees and Labourers' Union
KESBAN	*Program Keselamatan dan Pembangunan* (Security and Development Programme)
KIM	*Komite Indonesia Merdeka* (Committee of Independent Indonesia)
KITLV	*Koninklijk Instituut voor Taal-, Land- en Volkenkunde* (Royal Netherlands Institute of Southeast Asian and Caribbean Studies)
KMT	Guomindang (Kuomintang)
KNIL	*Koninklijk Nederlands Indisch Leger* (Royal Netherlands [East] Indies Army)
KOANDA	*Komander Antara Daerah* (Commander-in-chief All Regions)
KODAM	*Komando Daerah Militer* (Regional Military Command)
KOPS	*Komando Perjuangan* Sarawak (Military Command for the Struggle of Sarawak)
KOSTRAD	*Komando Cadangan Strategis Angkatan Darat* (Army Strategic Reserve Command)
KPA	Korean People's Army, North Korea
KPM	*Koninklijke Paketvaart Maatschappij* (Royal Packet Navigation Company)
KRJT	*Kesatuan Rakjat jang Tertindas* (Union of the Oppressed People)
KSCB	Khe Sanh Combat Base
LA	local authority
MAAG	U.S. Military Assistance Advisory Group
MACV	U.S. Military Assistance Command, Vietnam
MAD	mutual assured destruction
MANIPOL	*Manifesto Politik Republik Indonesia* (Political Manifesto of the Republic of Indonesia)
Maphilindo	*Ma*laya, *Phil*ippines, *Indo*nesia
MCA	Malayan/Malaysian Chinese Association

MCP	Malayan Communist Party; also, Communist Party of Malaya (CPM)
MCS	Malayan Civil Service
MIB	*Melayu Islam Beraja* (Malay Islamic Monarchy)
MIRI	*Masyarakat Indonesia dan Revolusi Indonesia* (Indonesian Society and Indonesian Revolution)
MNLF	Moro National Liberation Front
MNU	Malay National Union of Sarawak
MOI	*Madjelis Oelama Islam* (Assembly of Islamic Ulamas)
MoU	memorandum of understanding
MPAJA	Malayan People's Anti-Japanese Army
MPR	*Majelis Permusyawaratan Rakyat* (People's Deliberative Assembly)
MPRS-S	*Majelis Permusyawaratan Rakyat (Sementara)* ([Provisional] People's Deliberative Assembly)
MSCC	Malaysia Solidarity Consultative Committee
MUTU	*Persekutuan Murid Tua Melayu Brunei* (Federation of Former Brunei Malay Students)
NAM	non-aligned movement
NATO	North Atlantic Treaty Organization
NAUK	National Archives, Richmond, UK; formerly, the Public Record Office
NCOs	non-commissioned (military) officers; generally, all ranks from sergeant and below
NEFF	North East Frontier Force
NEI	Netherlands East Indies
NICA	*Nederlandsche Indische Civil Administratie* (Netherlands Indies Civil Administration)
NII	*Negara Islam Indonesia* (Islamic State of Indonesia)
NIT	*Negara Indonesia Timur* (State of East Indonesia)
NKCP	North Kalimantan Communist Party
NKKU	*Negarabagian Kesatuan Kalimantan Utara* (Unitary State of North Kalimantan)
NKLL	North Kalimantan Liberation League
NKPA	North Korean People's Army
NKPA	North Kalimantan People's Army (*Pasukan Rakyat Kalimantan Utara* [PARAKU])
NKPGF	North Kalimantan People's Guerrilla Force
NLF	National Liberation Front; popularly referred to as Viet Cong, namely South Vietnamese communist guerrillas
NMM	*Nederlands Militaire Missie* (Dutch Military Mission)
NO	[Sarawak] Native Officer
NOC	(Federal) National Operations Council, Kuala Lumpur
NSA	National Security Archive, Washington, DC
NU	*Nahdatul Ulama*

NUS	National University of Singapore
NVA	North Vietnamese Army; also referred as the People's Army of Vietnam (PAVN)
NVS	Native Voluntary School (local authority)
PANAS	*Parti Negara Sarawak* (National Party of Sarawak)
PAP	People's Action Party
PARAKU	*Pasukan Rakyat Kalimantan Utara* (North Kalimantan People's Army [NKPA])
PARKINDO	*Partai Kristen Indonesia* (Indonesian Christian Party)
PAVN	People's Army of Vietnam
PD	*Partai Persatuan Dayak* (Dayak Unity Party)
PEPELRADA	*Penguasa Pelakana Peperangan Daerah* (Executive Authority of Regional Warfare)
PERMESTA	*Piagam Perjuangan Semesta Alam* (Universal Struggle Charter)
PERSUKAI	*Persatuan Suku Kalimantan Indonesia* (Indonesia Kalimantan Clan Association)
PESAKA	*Parti Pesaka Anak Sarawak* (Sarawak Native Heritage Party)
PGRS	*Pasukan Gerilya Rakyat Sarawak* (Sarawak People's Guerrilla Force [SPGF])
PIR	*Partai Persatuan Indonesian Raya* (Party of the Union of Great Indonesia)
PKI	*Partai Komunis Indonesia* (Indonesian Communist Party)
PKMS	*Persatuan Kebangsaan Melayu Sarawak* (Sarawak Malay National Union)
PLA	People's Liberation Army
PLAF	People's Liberation Armed Forces of South Vietnam
PNI	*Partai Nasional Indonesia* (Indonesian Nationalist Party)
POWs	prisoners of war
PPHRKT	*Panitia Penyalur Hasrat Rakyat Kalimantan Tengah* (Central Kalimantan People's Appellate Committee)
PPKD	*Panitia Penyelesaian Kekacauan Daerah* (Regional Peace Resolution Committee)
PPKI	*Panitia Persiapan Kemerdekaan Indonesia* (Preparatory Committee for Indonesian Independence)
PPM	*Pergerakan Pemuda Melayu* (Malay Youth Movement)
PPPKI	*Persatuan Pemuda-Pemudi Kristen Indonesia* (Indonesia Christian Youth Association)
PPTI	*Partai Persatuan Tharikah Islam* (Islamic Tharikah Unity Party)
PRB	*Partai Rakyat Brunei* (Brunei People's Party)
PRC	People's Republic of China; also Red China
PRG	Provisional Revolutionary Government (PRG)
PRN	*Partai Rakyat Nasional* (National People's Party)

PRRI	*Pemerintah Revolusioner Republik Indonesia* (Revolutionary Government of the Republic of Indonesia)
PSI	*Partai Sosialis Indonesia* (Socialist Party of Indonesia)
PSII	*Partai Sjarikat Islam Indonesia* (Indonesian Islamic Union Party)
PSK	*Pasukan Sipet Kanyawung* (Kanyawung Blowpipe Squad)
RAF	Royal Air Force
RASCOM	Rajang Area Security Command
RELA	*Ikatan Relawan Rakyat* (People's Volunteer Corps)
RI	*Republik Indonesia* (Republic of Indonesia)
RIS	*Republik Indonesia Serikat* (Republic of the United States of Indonesia [RUSI])
RMAF	Royal Malaysian Air Force
RMN	Royal Malaysian Navy
ROK	Republic of Korea, South Korea
RPKAD	*Resimen Para Komando Angkatan Darat* (Army Para-Commando Regiment)
RRI	*Radio Republik Indonesia* (Radio of the Republic of Indonesia)
RSF	Royal Security Forces of the Sultanate of Sulu and North Borneo
R-T	radio-telephone
RUSI	Republic of the United States of Indonesia
RVN	Republic of Vietnam
SAFL	Sarawak Anti-Fascist League
SAS	Sarawak Administrative Service
SAYA	Sarawak Advanced Youths' Association
SCA	Sarawak Chinese Association
SCC	Suez Canal Company
SCMSSU	Singapore Chinese Middle School Students Union
SCO	Sarawak Communist Organization
SCP	Sarawak Communist Party
SCS	Sarawak Civil Service
SDA	Sarawak Dayak Association
SEATO	Southeast Asia Treaty Organization
SERMI	*Serikat Muslimin Indonesia* (Indonesian Muslim Association)
SG	*Sarawak Gazette*
SGG	*Sarawak Government Gazette*
SJSC	Sarawak Junior School Certificate
SKDI	*Serikat Kaharingan Dayak Indonesia* (Union of Keharingan Dayaks of Indonesia)
SKI	*Serikat Kerakyatan Indonesia* (Populist Association of Indonesia)
SLL	Sarawak Liberation League
SMA	Sarawak Museum and State Archives, Kuching, Malaysia

SNAP	Sarawak National Party
SOC	State Operations Committee, Sarawak
SOL	Sarawak Oilfields Limited
SOPIK	*Sentral Organisasi Pemberontak Indonesia Kalimantan* (Indonesia Kalimantan Rebel Central Organization)
SPGF	Sarawak People's Guerrilla Force (*Pasukan Gerilya Rakyat Sarawak* [PGRS])
SPP	Sarawak People's Party
SRD	Services Reconnaissance Department
SRI	*Serikat Rakyat Islam* (Islamic People's Association)
SSEC	State Security Executive Council, Sarawak
SSOL	Sarawak Shell Oilfields Limited
SSR	Soviet Socialist Republics
SSSC	Sarawak State Security Committee
START	Strategic Arms Reduction Treaty
STUC	Sarawak Trade Union Congress
SUPP	Sarawak United People's Party
SWA	Singapore Women's Association
TKKB	*Tentera Komunis Kalimantan Barat* (Communist Army of West Kalimantan)
TMT	Turkish Resistance Organisation
TNI	*Tentera Nasional Indonesia* (National Armed Forces of Indonesia)
TNKU	*Tentera Negara Kalimantan Utara* (Army of the State of North Kalimantan)
UDP	United Democratic Party
UHF	ultra high frequency
UK	United Kingdom
UMNO	United Malays National Organization
UN	United Nations
UNC	United Nations Command
UNEF	United Nations Emergency Force
UNKO	United National Kadazan Organisation
UNMM	UN Malaysia Mission
U.S	United States
USDEK	*Undang-Undang Dasar 1945, Sosialisme Indonesia, Demokrasi Terpimpin, Ekonomi Terpimpin, dan Kepribadian Indonesia* (Basic Laws of 1945 [1945 Constitution], Indonesian Socialism, Guided Democracy, Commanded Economy, and Indonesian Identity)
USI	United States of Indonesia
USNO	United Sabah National Organization
USSR	Union of Soviet Socialist Republics, Soviet Union
UUD	*Undang-Undang Dasar*, denotes the 1945 Constitution of Indonesia

V-J	Day victory over Imperial Japan day
VE	Day victory in Europe day
VHF	very high frequency
VNAF	Republic of Vietnam Air Force, South Vietnam
VOC	*Vereenigde Oost-Indische Compagnie* (United [Dutch] East India Company)
VPA	Vietnam People's Army
W/T	wireless telegraph

Currencies

Pre-war British Borneo – Sarawak, Brunei, and North Borneo – the dollar ($), namely the Sarawak dollar, Brunei dollar, and British North Borneo dollar, were legal tender. All three currencies were tied to the Straits Settlements dollar (S$). From 1906, the Straits dollar was tied to British sterling, viz. S$1 was approximated as 2s. 4d., conversely S$ 8.57 to £1. Following agreement (January 1952) among the Crown Colonies of Singapore, Sarawak, and North Borneo, the Federation of Malaya, and the State of Brunei, the Board of Commissioners of Currency, Malaya and British Borneo was to be the sole currency-issuing authority in the aforesaid territories. In 1950 the Malayan dollar (M$) carried the same value as the SS$, equivalent to 1s. 2d., or £0.12. In 1953, coins bearing the new design of the Board of Commissioners of Currency, Malaya and British Borneo were released. The first coins bearing the new design – inscribed with "QUEEN ELIZABETH THE SECOND", and the reverse, "MALAYA AND BRITISH BORNEO" – were released in 1953.

Pre-war Dutch Borneo, present-day Kalimantan (common term from 1945), used the Dutch guilder (fl.) as currency. Nonetheless, Dayaks and other indigenous peoples in the interior and upland areas relied on the barter of goods and services. Post-war Kalimantan adopted the NICA gulden issued by the *Nederlandsche Indische Civil Administratie* (NICA, Netherlands Indies Civil Administration). Paralleling the gulden was the Indonesian rupiah (Rp.), unilaterally proclaimed by the *Republik* on 3 October 1946. The rupiah continued as the official currency following the establishment of *Republik Indonesia* in 1949, and as a unitary state from 1950, which Kalimantan was an integral part of both.

1 Introduction

The worst thing that colonialism did was to cloud our view of our past.

Barack Obama (b. 1961),
44th U.S. president (t. 2009–2017)

Although regarded as the world's third largest island, Borneo's location in the midst of archipelagic Southeast Asia is often overlooked or bypassed, with priority and attention focussing on far more prominent and/or interesting areas such as mainland territories like Thailand (Siam) or Vietnam, or neighbouring islands, Singapore, Java, and Bali. It is not surprising for people to question the whereabouts of Borneo, even in this day and age of the mid-first quarter of the twenty-first century, as it had been the case for more than the past two millennia. Therefore, it is necessary to offer a geographical and demographical portraiture of the island of Borneo as a prelude to its historical analysis vis-à-vis the Cold War.

Physical and human setting

Borneo, the world's third largest island, with an area of 427,500 square km, that is slightly bigger than California, is located at the heart of Southeast Asia (Map 1.1). Shaped like a sliced watermelon, its north and northwest shores are swept by the South China Sea, whereas the eastern part is washed by the Sulu and Celebes Seas, with the south and southeast portion fronting the Java Sea. Much of the island is hilly and mountainous, with a massive backbone of highlands running from the southwest towards the northeast, peaking at Mount Kinabalu (4,095 m). Thick tropical rain forest envelopes most of the island, with a vast assortment of flora and fauna of which the Rafflesia and the Orangutang are iconic representatives. The central mountainous spine acts as the watershed divide, with drainage patterns for the north and northwest (Rajang, 563 km) flowing towards the South China Sea, whereas the northeast (Kinabatangan, 560 km), east, and southeast (Mahakam, 980 km) drain into the Celebes Sea, and the southwest (Kapuas, 1143 km) and south into the Karimata Strait and Java Sea. With the equator slicing the island almost into two equal halves, Borneo experiences a year-round hot and wet climate with high temperatures (averaging between 27° C and 32° C) and equally

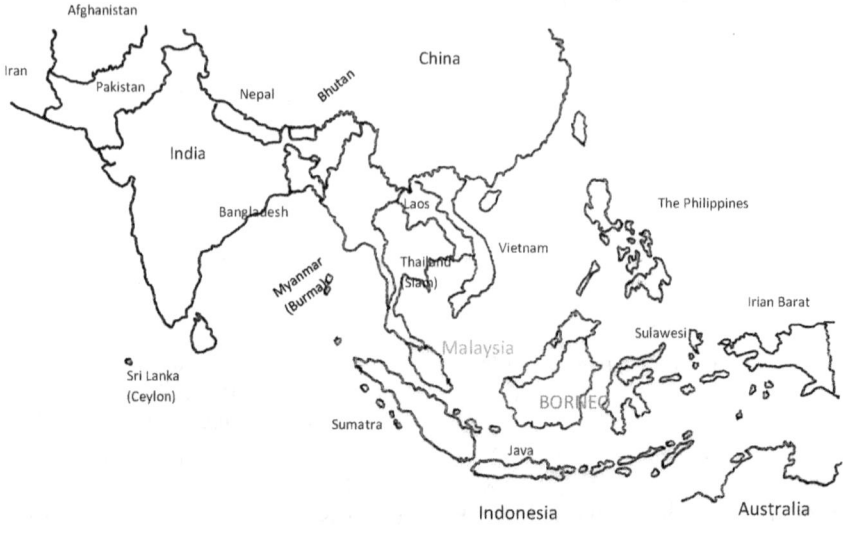

Map 1.1 Geopolitical Location of Borneo and Malaysia within South and Southeast Asia

Source: Author

high humidity (80 per cent). The lower reaches of the rivers enrich the coastal plains, whereby settlements and population tend to congregate.

Overall the population is sparse and characteristically rural and agrarian, with a sprinkling of towns and cities on the main rivers and coastal fringes. Notable urban areas include Kuching (617,887),[1] Sibu (247,995),[2] Miri (300,543),[3] Kota Kinabalu (199,742),[4] Sandakan (157,330),[5] Tarakan (178,900),[6] Banjarmasin (612,800),[7] and Pontianak (554,800).[8]

The contemporary political divide apportioned Borneo into four component parts (Map 1.2). East Malaysia comprises the states of Sabah and Sarawak and straddles the greater part of the north and northwest, occupying about a quarter of the island. Off the northwest coast of Sabah is the island of Labuan, a Malaysian federal territory. On Sarawak's northeast lies the twin-teardrop of the independent sovereign sultanate of Negara Brunei Darussalam (hereinafter Brunei). The remainder of the island's vast southeast and southern parts is Indonesia Kalimantan.

Within the four territories, the population is colourful and diverse, comprising a multitude of ethnic groups, each with its own defined language and/or dialect, socio-cultural customs and traditions, and lifestyle. More than 80 distinct ethnic communities reside in present-day Sabah and Sarawak. Sabah alone possesses 42 distinct ethnic groups, of which the Kadazandusun, Bajau, and Murut are the three largest indigenes. The Kadazandusun, a combination of two groups, Kadazan and Dusun, are the predominant peoples in Sabah. Other native communities include Orang Sungai, Rungus, Tidong, Lun Bawang/Lun Dayeh, Bruneian Malay, and

NOTES
BSB Bandar Seri Begawan
Sabah, formerly North Borneo before 1963, and Sarawak are the states of East Malaysia.
North Kalimantan was created in 2012 from East Kalimantan.
Central Kalimantan, carved out of South Kalimantan in 1957, was a means of providing the non-Muslim
Dayak communities greater autonomy from the Muslim-majority South Kalimantan.

Map 1.2 Contemporary Political Boundaries of Borneo

Source: Author

Suluks. The Bajau are divided into two groups geographically and by way of life, namely the West Coast horse culture land-based Bajau Darat and the East Coast sea-dwelling Bajau Laut. While Bruneian Malays originally came from neighbouring Brunei, likewise Suluks initially migrated from Sulu. The largest non-indigenous peoples are the Chinese, with pockets of Indian, Punjabi, Javanese, Bugis, and Eurasian minorities.

Out of the 40 ethnic groups in Sarawak, the Iban is the largest indigenous community, followed by Malay, Bidayuh, Orang Ulu, Melanau, and several minor groups like Penan, Kedayan, and Murut. Like in Sabah, Chinese comprise the largest non-native peoples in Sarawak.

Sunni Islam is the dominant religion of the Malays and Melanaus, whereas Christianity predominates among the Ibans, Kadazandusuns, Bidayuh, Kelabits, Kayans, Kenyahs, Muruts, Orang Hulu, and other indigenous communities. Traditional beliefs and practices in accordance to *adat* (customs, customary law) remain relevant to many non-Muslim native groups. The Chinese too embraced Christianity, but many still adhere to an eclectic combination of Confucianism, Daoism, and Buddhism. *Bahasa Malaysia*, basically the Malay language, is the *lingua franca* among the diverse peoples of Sabah and Sarawak, although each ethnic community possesses its own unique language and dialect. Hokkien, Teochew, Hakka, and Foochow *inter alia* are the disparate dialects spoken by the Chinese. Mandarin (Chinese language) furnishes the demands of a formal language (speech, text).

In Brunei, ethnic Malay is the umbrella term that includes Bruneian Malay, Tutong, Belait, Dusun, Murut, Kedayan, and Bisaya. Non-Malay ethnic groups are the indigenous Iban, Melanau, and Penan, among others. Chinese, Indian and Pakistani, and Europeans comprise the non-native residents. Islam, the sunni variant, is the predominant religion, and Brunei Malay is the main language of communication. Iban tended to embrace Christianity, whereas the Penan are animists and the Chinese adhere to a mixture of Buddhism juxtaposed with Daoism and Confucianism, the Chinese world of beliefs.

East Kalimantan, a territory that comprises the eastern portion of Borneo, is ethnically diverse as a result of transmigration being a major destination of origin for peoples from Java, Sulawesi, and South Kalimantan. Hence, Javanese and Bugis predominate as the major groups followed by Banjar. The indigenous Dayaks are found in the interior of central Borneo. Other minorities include Kutai, Torajan, Paser, Sundanese, Madurese, and Auto Buton. The majority ethnic community in South Kalimantan is Banjar with sub-groups of Banjar Kuala, Banjar Pahuluan, and Banjar Batang Banyu besides Javanese, Madurese, and Sundanese that comprise the migrant groups. Other migrants include Bugis Pagatan and Mandar, who occupy coastal areas. The native Dayak dwell around the Meratus mountains (Dayak Bukit) and the banks of the Barito River (Dayak Bakumpai). Other minorities include peoples of ethnic Arab descent and ethnic Chinese in Banjarmasin and Martapura, and Sungai Parit in Pelaihari (Cina Parit).

Indigenous Dayak and Malay are the predominant ethnic communities in West Kalimantan's hinterland and coastal areas, respectively. Javanese are mainly in transmigration areas, whereas the Chinese settled mainly in urban centres such as Singkawang and Pontianak. Minor groups include Bugis, Sundanese, Batak, Madurese, and Banjar.

Besides the multiethnic population, Kalimantan also possesses a multiplicity of languages and religions. Akin to Malay, *Bahasa Indonesia*, the national language of Indonesia, is the main means of communication. In West Kalimantan, Malay

Pontianak resembles and shares with Sarawak Malay and Johor/Riau Malay. *Bahasa Malaysia* is largely based on the Johor/Riau Malay variant. Hakka and Teochew dialects predominate among the Kalimantan Chinese communities. Overall the linguistic diversity extends over more than 200 dialects.

Religious-wise Islam is the majority belief followed by Christianity (both Catholic and Protestant), Buddhism, Daoism, and Confucianism. Whilst Malay, Javanese, Sundanese, Bugis, Banjar, and Madurese adhere to Islam, Dayak mainly embrace Christianity with some still practicing traditional beliefs (animism), and some Chinese Christians, though the majority of the Chinese practise a regime of Buddhism, Daoism, and Confucianism.

The provenance of political boundaries and governance

The current political configuration of four component territories – Sarawak, Brunei, Sabah, and Kalimantan – was a colonial legacy dating back to the nineteenth century. While the Dutch made tentative approaches to what is present-day Indonesia Kalimantan in the early part of the nineteenth century, the north and northeast were nominally the domain of the Malay Muslim Sultanate of Brunei. But Brunei, by the mid-century, was a waning political force, where factionalism at the court had greatly sapped its power and influence. During the sultanate's heyday that spanned the greater part of the fifteenth to seventeenth centuries, Brunei claimed hegemony over the entire expanse of the island and north-eastward across the Philippine archipelago extending as far north as Manila.

The arrival of an English gentleman adventurer, James Brooke (1803–1868), in 1839 literally injected 'life' to Borneo that was hitherto little known, largely neglected, and/or overlooked, both politically and economically. Ignorance was the main culprit but accentuated with gory tales of head-hunters and dangerous wildlife. On his way to Marudu Bay in the vicinity of present-day Sabah as part of his scientific expedition to the Celebes (Sulawesi), Brooke made a stopover at Kuching to deliver gifts to the local chief in appreciation for assistance to shipwrecked British sailors who were given a boat and provisions to return to Singapore. When the schooner *Royalist* sailed up the Saarawak River and Brooke and his English crew landed at Kuching in 1839, Pangeran Hashim, the uncle to the reigning Brunei sultan, was on hand to greet them. A friendship was struck between Brooke and Hashim. The latter was in Kuching, the downstream capital of the fiefdom of Sarawak then under Pangeran Mahkota, its *rajah* or governor, to address the issue of suppressing an anti-Brunei revolt (1836–1841) staged by the local Malays of Siniawan in league with the Bidayuh, then referred to as Land Dayaks. Owing to this uprising, Brooke was denied entry farther inland, but instead he was granted permission to visit a longhouse on the Lundu River. With his curiosity satiated, Brooke and the *Royalist* continued their journey to Marudu Bay and thence to the Celebes.

On his return voyage to Singapore in 1841, Brooke decided to re-visit his friend Hashim. Sarawak was still in the midst of a rebellion. Hashim offered Brooke a challenge: suppress the ongoing rebellion, and in return, be granted the rajahship of Sarawak. Brooke took up his friend's offer, and with his small crew, launched a daring assault on the rebels' defence perimeter. Taken by surprise, the rebels fled and thus ended the uprising. Brooke was rewarded with the fiefdom of Sarawak with the title of *rajah* or governor. Hence begun the era of the White Rajahs. Sarawak then was a territory between the river valleys of the Lundu in the west and Samarahan in the east, an area encompassing present-day Kuching District. Brooke (r. 1841–1868) and his successors – Charles Brooke (1829–1917; r. 1968–1917) and Charles Vyner Brooke (1874–1963; r. 1917–1946) – pushed Sarawak's boundaries eastwards to its current configuration encompassing both the Limbang and Trusan Rivers.

In response to the Englishman Brooke's exploits in Sarawak, the Dutch across the border to what is today Indonesia Kalimantan again took a more proactive role in this vast territory. In the 1820s, the *Koninklijk Nederlands Indisch Leger* (KNIL, Royal Netherlands [East] Indies Army) had moved against the Chinese *kongsi* in West Kalimantan in the first of many campaigns, collectively referred to as the Kongsi Wars (1822–1824, 1850–1854, 1884–1885).

The auriferous areas of West Kalimantan prompted local Malay rulers to import Chinese to work the gold and tin deposits in the late eighteenth century. Subsequently, the Chinese miners established mining companies called *kongsi* that not only served as a means of governance from within amongst their numbers but also as protection and defence from without, particularly encroachment from the imperialist Dutch. Then in 1777 several *kongsi* banded together to form a confederation known as the Lanfang Republic, an autonomous state, an *imperium in imperio*. Besides mining, the Chinese undertook farming mainly food crops and trading. The Lanfang Republic was allied with the Pontianak sultanate. KNIL launched a second expedition (1850–1854) targeting Montrado, while the third and final military campaign (1884–1885) in Mandor ended the rule and existence of the autonomous *kongsi*.

While the Dutch consolidated their governance over Kalimantan, the island's northeast portion witnessed a series of attempts by European individuals in acquiring concessions over the territory. The eastern half of what subsequently became known as North Borneo (Sabah from 1963) was under the nominal rule of the Sultanate of Brunei whilst its eastern portion was the Sultanate of Sulu. Rumours of supposed mineral and agricultural wealth prompted European concessionaires to the Brunei and Sulu courts in seeking and paying for territories. Short-lived settlements were established, but overall all endeavours ended in failures and losses.

Then in the late 1870s, a partnership between Baron Otto von Overbeck, the German consul in Hong Kong, and Edward Gent from the City of London succeeded in establishing an administration of North Borneo with a royal charter from Britain's Parliament in 1881. Overbeck sought and successfully secured written treaties with both the Brunei and Sulu sultanates granting legal concession over North Borneo. Armed with a royal charter, Dent and his partners inaugurated the British North Borneo Chartered Company (BNBCC) that administered North Borneo for some six decades (1881–1941).

In order to ensure the integrity and sustainability of Brunei, Britain granted protectorate status over the sultanate, Sarawak and North Borneo in 1888, hence was borne British Borneo. From 1906 Brunei came under a quasi-colonial governance whereby a British officer styled 'resident' became formal advisor to the sultan, not unlike the reigning rulers of the peninsular Malay states. Kalimantan was known as Dutch Borneo. The island then was clearly demarcated between two Western imperial and colonial powers and rivals, namely Britain and the Netherlands.

On the eve of the outbreak of the Pacific War (1941–1945), Borneo was divided into four territories, each under its own system of governance. Sarawak was under the personal and absolute rule of Brooke White Rajahs, whose form of paternalism protected and promoted the interests of the indigenous peoples from both European and Chinese capitalist entrepreneurs and investors. North Borneo, however, had a governor and a skeletal administrative corps that represented the BNBCC and its London-based Board of Directors. Whilst the Brookes governed Sarawak as a trusteeship of the native peoples, BNBCC was a capitalist enterprise that owed shareholders annual dividends; hence making profits from investments was the prime motivation of governance. Geographically situated between Sarawak and North Borneo was the Malay Muslim Sultanate of Brunei, where an absolute monarch reigned over a feudal form of governance. The Dutch brand of colonial rule governed the greater part of the island's eastern, southern, and southwest that was then referred to as Dutch Borneo and comprised a component part of the sprawling Netherlands East Indies (NEI) of what is present-day Indonesia.

The Pacific War (1941–1945) and Borneo

Borneo with its oilfields and installations was a prime military objective in Imperial Japan's southern push. The oilfields of Seria (Brunei), Miri (Sarawak), Tarakan (east Dutch Borneo), and refinery of Balikpapan (south Dutch Borneo) were attractive targets for seizure. Borneo's strategic location within air-striking distance to Singapore, the all-important British naval base, as well as Batavia, the administrative centre of NEI, made occupation an imperative for Tokyo's military planners.

Shortly following the assault on Pearl Harbor on 7 December 1941, a series of simultaneous invasions were launched across the region that later came to be referred to as Southeast Asia. Amphibious assault was targeted at the Brunei Bay area with landings at Miri for the capture of the oilfields and facilities, as well as the seizure of neighbouring Seria and Brunei. While a military unit headed northwards overland towards Jesselton, the then-administrative capital of North Borneo's West Coast Residency,[9] another unit steamed along the coast with landings on Sibu, Sarawak's main commercial port, and Kuching, the centre of the Brooke government. Units of the Imperial Japanese Army (IJA) on board patrol boats and barges made their way upstream the Sarawak River just as James Brooke did a century ago and landed at contemporary Kuching's Waterfront. Unopposed, the IJA literally marched into town on Christmas Eve 1941. Their counterparts, likewise, entered Jesselton and Sandakan with scant opposition.

Besides Kuching, IJA targeted the Bukit Stabar airfield to the southwest at the seventh milestone on the Kuching-Serian Road.[10] Together with Singkawang I and II airstrips across the border in Western Dutch Borneo, these airfields were essential for launching air strikes to Singapore and Batavia. It was here at Bukit Stabar that the only defence was staged by the 2/15 Punjabi Regiment against the invaders. The airfield was partially destroyed as part of denial plans carried out (also at the oil installations at Miri and Seria) by the only British military unit in British Borneo. Outnumbered, the remnants of the 2/15 Punjabi Regiment withdrew, seeking refuge across the border heading towards Pontianak.

Apart from scorched earth tactics as mentioned, both British Borneo and Dutch Borneo had no plans and/or intention to defend their respective territories. The stark reality was that in December 1941, Europe including the Netherlands was then overrun by Hitler's blitzkrieg. Island Britain stood alone in anticipation of a German invasion. Defence of the isle was undoubtedly of pivotal priority. Having faith in the impregnable 'Fortress Singapore', the self-fulfilling prophecy of its own propaganda, British military superiority was overestimated, at the same time underestimating the enemy (Imperial Japan). The Admiralty could only dispatch HMS *Prince of Wales* and HMS *Repulse* that arrived at Singapore just prior to the IJA landings at Kota Bahru on the northeast of British Malaya. Both ships were sunk off Kuantan by Japanese Zeroes, the most-up-to-date fighter planes then, as they steamed up the peninsula to oppose the landings. For British Borneo, the 1,000-strong 2/15 Punjabi Regiment was the only military unit.

The Dutch had simply no plans to defend their Bornean territory, neither KNIL ground troops or ships to spare. Dutch aircraft from Singkawang did stage bombing raids on the IJA amphibious landings at Miri, sinking a vessel that carried mainly civilian administrators. Across the border, no KNIL opposed the IJA that literally walked into towns in Dutch Borneo to jubilant Indonesian crowds that regarded Imperial Japan as both liberator and saviour.

Occupied Borneo was divided into two halves according to pre-invasion arrangements between the Imperial Japanese armed forces, namely the upper northern half of what was British Borneo came under the control of the IJA, and the lower southern half, pre-war Dutch Borneo, under the Imperial Japanese Navy (IJN). *Kita Boruneo* (Northern Borneo) was assigned to the IJA, as the population comparatively was larger, hence more personnel needed for its administration. *Minami Boruneo* (Southern Borneo) hitherto sparsely peopled came under the purview of the IJN. In accordance to the policy of *eikyu senryo* (permanent occupation or possession), the IJN was tasked to administer territories that were resource-rich with low and small population that considered incorporation as permanent possessions of Imperial Japan, a part of the imperial empire. Therefore, in contrast to military personnel helming the occupation administration like in IJA-governed territories of *Kita Boruneo*, civilian personnel seconded from the homeland bureaucracy undertook day-to-day administrative duties of *Minami Boruneo*.

For three years and eight months (1942–1945), regardless of IJA or IJN, occupied Borneo was ruled with an iron fist, where any infraction was severely dealt with, including capital punishment. Owing to Allied blockade, there were shortages in daily necessities from rice staple and foodstuffs, cooking oil to consumables such as matches, soap, and medicines and cloths. Deprivations of daily necessities became increasingly acute during the second half of the occupation. Urban areas where most items including foodstuffs were brought in from without were adversely affected. Agricultural produce including rice was seized by the occupation authorities that prioritized the garrisons over the common population. Hence, even native rice producers suffered scarcity of supplies if hoarding failed or was uncovered, whereby harsh punishments were meted for such capital offences. Comparatively, townspeople underwent a harsher existence than rural peasant communities across the island.

Wartime conditions of shortages were further worsened with the climate of fear and uncertainty. Fear was pervasive in the face of *hukum Jipun*, the Iban term for excessive punishment meted out in an unhesitating manner by the IJA. Punishment for small crimes such as the theft of chicken or bicycles was public beheading, which, even to the once head-hunting Ibans, was excessively harsh. Suspected subversives and anti-Japanese elements were swiftly eliminated. The ever-prevalent 'eyes' of the *Kempeitei*, the IJA's military police, and *Tokkeitai* (*Tokubetsu Keisatsutai*, Special Police Corps or Naval Secret Police), IJN's counterpart, struck terror and horror amongst the population. Utilizing a network of local informers, both the *Kempeitei* and *Tokkeitai*'s primary task was in seeking and eliminating anti-Japanese movements, groups, or individuals. Notorious for their *modus operandi* of torture preceding interrogation, comparable to the Nazi Gestapo, they were police agencies not to be taken lightly.

The Chinese community in Borneo, the most populous in Sarawak, was the especial target of the IJA and IJN. Singled out as the potential anti-Japanese group, the Chinese suffered more than any other community. Imperial Japan's invasion of China (1937–1945) was undoubtedly commonplace knowledge amongst Borneo's Chinese communities that contributed financial support to the homeland defenders against the invaders. A handful of youths returned to the mainland to fight the invaders. Hence, for such pre-war 'sins against Imperial Japan', the IJA exacted punishment in the form of *shu-jin* (life-redeeming money or blood money) amounting to Straits Dollar S$3 million on the Chinese residents of *Kita Boruneo*. Comparatively, the Chinese should be thankful that *only* pecuniary demands were imposed on them whilst in occupied Malaya and Singapore, not only were their brethren pressed with financial obligations[11] but also suffered from *sook ching* (purification, cleansing), a euphemism for mass killings whereby, "The total number of victims for the whole of Malaya is considered by Malayans to have been around 100,000".[12]

Subsequently there was an urban-rural Chinese wartime exodus to avoid direct contact with the occupying authorities. Flight was prompted by fear amongst male Chinese youths of being recruited into labour-gangs, whilst females were inducted into 'comfort stations' as 'comfort women', euphemisms for military brothels and prostitutes for soldiers, respectively. Chinese families from Kuching, for instance, fled northeastwards to the then-remote Santubong peninsula, where they subsisted off the land away from the Japanese.

Both the IJA and IJN in their respective Bornean territories focused on the oil industry, the oilfields in Seria and Miri, and the refinery at Lutong for the former, and Tarakan's Pamoesian and Djoeata oilfields and Balikpapan's Pandansari refinery for the latter. Apart from oil, agricultural products such as rubber, copra, and pepper were all of secondary concerns as far as Imperial Japan was concerned.

Unlike anti-Japanese forces in Malaya, notably the Malayan People's Anti-Japanese Army (MPAJA) that was initiated, dominated, and led by the Chinese-majority Malayan Communist Party (MCP), there was, however, a conspicuous absence of resistance movements in Borneo. Only three episodes, one in *Kita Boruneo* and two others in *Minami Boruneo*, rocked the Bornean quietness. All concluded in horrific tragedies.

On 10 October 1943, a Chinese-Suluk anti-Japanese revolt broke out, killing scores of Japanese in and around Jesselton. Led by Albert Kuok (Kwok), the rebels managed to seize and hold Jesselton for a day, and thereafter they fled to the mountainous interior. It was unclear what Kuok and his fellow rebels wanted; what was clear was that the revolt chose the symbolic Double Tenth of the Chinese Revolution of 1911 fame. On hindsight, this revolt appeared to be a show of foolhardiness on the part of Kuok and his comrades. The IJA backlash was merciless: the settlements on the offshore islands along the west coast were slaughtered, and likewise the villages that dotted the west coast from Kudat to Papar and Kimanis. Hundreds of natives, the majority oblivious to Kuok's anti-Japanese agenda, lost their lives. Kuok surrendered, and together with several others, were executed at Petagas.[13]

Meanwhile, in Minami Boruneo, more than 1,000 people of various ethnicity, of which the Chinese were the majority, were put to death as suspected plotters of an alleged conspiracy to overthrow the IJN administration.[14] Consequently, the *Tokkeitai* launched pre-emptive measures in swiftly rounding up in three waves (between 1944 and early 1945) so-called conspirators in Banjarmasin and Pontianak, subjected them to military tribunals, and subsequently had them disposed of in remote areas far from prying eyes.

Then in mid-1945, a Dayak uprising broke out around Sanggau on the Kapuas River. Retribution was undoubtedly swift and horrific, with massacres and destruction of many upriver longhouses suspected of involvement in the uprising. Hundreds perished in the IJN backlash.

Besides the death toll from revolts and alleged subversive activities, deaths of prisoners of war were also alarmingly high. The Batu Lintang Prisoners of War and Civilian Internment Camp on the outskirts of Kuching, the largest facility on Borneo, witnessed the death of hundreds of its inmates, victims of diseases, malnutrition, and maltreatment by prison guards (mainly Taiwanese and Koreans). It was estimated that out of 4,660 Allied prisoners of war and European civilian internees, only 1,387 were alive when the camp was liberated.[15] The infamous Sandakan Death March (1945) resulted in the survival of 6 out of 2,400 Allied POWs.[16] In the course of shifting inland towards Ranau from the Sandakan POW facility on the east coast, both Japanese soldiers and Allied POWs carrying supplies had to negotiate the harsh, thick tropical jungle and difficult mountainous terrain. Many of the latter were already weakened and/or sick during incarceration, succumbed to the intolerable heavy burden, and subsequently perished along the way, or their tardiness earned them the sharp end of a bayonet and death.

Transition period (1945–1946)

By mid-1945, implementation of the re-conquest of Borneo by Australian Imperial Forces (AIF) were underway, viz. the OBOE operations I – Tarakan (1 May), VI – Brunei Bay-Labuan (10 June), and II – Balikpapan (1 July). The U.S. Navy and Air Force provided support with pre-invasion naval and aerial bombardment. The AIF accomplished all of its military operations. Nonetheless, "there were questions raised as to the necessity of Australian involvement in the Bornean theatre, which posed little significance and/or relevance to the overall war situation, as U.S. forces headed towards the Japanese home islands".[17] It appears that political expediency overrode military strategy.

Prior to the actual AIF amphibious landings on Borneo, clandestine operations were deployed behind enemy lines, namely the covert operations of AGAS and SEMUT, 'sand fly' and 'ant' in the local Malay dialect, respectively.[18] Personnel of the Services Reconnaissance Department (SRD), a British covert outfit with Australian military participation, were parachuted into northern (AGAS) and north-central Borneo (SEMUT), whereby a score of Special Operations British and Australian officers and men were tasked for intelligence gathering, arming, and training native units to carry out guerrilla activities involving mainly acts of sabotage (of communication lines, supply depots) and the occasional swift hit-and-run assaults on enemy convoys and camps.

His Imperial Highness Emperor Hirohito's voice in archaic speech over radio waves announcing Imperial Japan's unconditional surrender on 15 August 1945 without prior hint or warning took everyone by surprise. Imperial Rescript on the Termination of the War read out at noon ended with the Emperor's call "to the dictates of time and fate that We [the Emperor] have resolved to pave the way for a grand peace for all the generations to come by enduring the unendurable and suffering what is unsufferable".[19] Although a mere four-minute address, the radio broadcast not only ended the Second Sino-Japanese War (1937–1945)[20] and the Pacific War (1941–1945) but also "obliterated the 20-year imperial ideology [worship of semi-divine emperor], and began Japan's rebirth into what it is today".[21] Some senior military officers could not believe His Imperial Highness's defeatist speech, and several opted for ritual suicide rather than "enduring the unendurable and suffering what is unsufferable".

The various OBOE operations notwithstanding, it was only in mid-September that the AIF had effectively re-occupied the entire island of Borneo. The Australian 9th Division was tasked to regain control of the northern half of the island (pre-war British Borneo; wartime *Kita Boruneo*), whereas the Australian 7th Division took responsibility for the southern or lower half (pre-war Dutch Borneo; wartime *Minami Boruneo*). Whether it was the British Borneo Civil Affairs Unit (BBCAU)/ British Military Administration (British Borneo) (BMA [BB]) or Australian 7th Division AIF with assistance from the *Nederlandsche Indische Civil Administratie*

(NICA, Netherlands Indies Civil Administration), they faced the immediate tasks of establishing civil public order and organizing the systematic distribution of essential materials to the local population, namely rice and other foodstuffs, medicines, daily essentials, and necessities.

Despite its name, NICA was a militarized colonial administrative corps whose primary objective was to re-instate Dutch colonial authority over re-occupied territories prior to the formal restoration of civil government. Realizing NICA's intention and not wanting to be embroiled in local (Dutch-Indonesian) political issues, the Australian 7th Division AIF conveniently withdrew following a brief month into its tenure (17 September to 24 October 1945), leaving and allowing NICA a free hand over southern Borneo.

BMA (BB), however, relinquished its responsibility to a civilian government only in mid-1946 following a nine-month tenureship. Handover was the earliest for Sarawak when Rajah Charles Vyner Brooke returned to Kuching on 15 April to re-commence the civil government. Brooke rule was reinstated. On 6 July, Sultan Ahmad Tajuddin of Brunei (1913–1950) re-assumed the reins of civil government of the sultanate. While Sarawak and Brunei witnessed the reinstatement of their pre-war regimes, on 15 July BMA (BB) handed over North Borneo to a civil government not of the pre-war BNBCC but instead to the Colonial Office (CO), as North Borneo had been ceded to His Majesty's Government, henceforth administered as a British Crown Colony headed by a governor.

The post-war period (1946–1950)

North Borneo was literally a wreck during the closing months of the war, and this was particularly conspicuous on the coastal fringes. Both aerial and naval bombardment laid waste to the greater part of its hitherto skeletal infrastructure, most coastal towns, and the few urban centres (mainly Jesselton on the west coast and Sandakan on the east coast) suffered massive destruction of properties and civilian casualties. It was not until 1949, four years after the end of the war, that any permanent building (offices and/or residences) were at last erected.[22]

Post-war physical reconstruction of public and private buildings, infrastructure, and rehabilitation of public services (health, education) were mammoth tasks and expensive undertakings. The pecuniary demands coupled with the feeling of anachronism, though secondary concerns, moved the Chartered Company's Board of Directors in London to take the decisive action to completely withdraw from its tropical territory that it had administered for some six decades (1881–1941). Cession of North Borneo from Chartered Company rule to Colonial Office administration was smooth, bureaucratic, and uneventful. Hence, on 15 July 1946, the Crown Colony of North Borneo came into being, joined by the Crown Colony of Labuan.[23]

The Malay Muslim Sultanate of Brunei happily resumed its pre-war status as a British protectorate, whereby defence and foreign relations were handled by His Majesty's Government while internal government was amply assisted by British civil officers headed by a Resident while the Sultan remained sovereign monarch. Like in the pre-war period, a British High Commissioner oversaw the general administration, but instead of the Colonial Governor of the Straits Settlements at Singapore, the post-war arrangement had the Governor of Sarawak as British High Commissioner for Brunei.

Both Brunei and North Borneo focused on the urgent and imperative undertaking of reconstruction and rehabilitation. Reviving the economy of both territories were urgent and undoubtedly challenging tasks, for which a weakened post-war Britain took responsibility.

The departure of the Australian military allowed NICA and the resuscitated KNIL a free hand over southern Borneo. Even while the AIF was present, NICA officers were re-instating Dutch colonial rule over the re-occupied territories, hereinafter referred to as Kalimantan.

Hiccup in Sarawak

In stark contrast, cession in Sarawak was neither smooth nor welcome, and in fact it turned ugly in 1949.[24] Within one and a half months of Rajah Vyner's return, Sarawak was handed over to the British Crown. On 1 July 1946, John Beville Archer (1993–1948), chief secretary (1939–1941, April-July 1946), and the last Brooke Officer Administering the Government[25] in lieu of the rajah did the last honours.

"In a few minutes", Archer stated in a telegram to Rajah Vyner dated 1 July 1946,

> I shall hand over your State to His Majesty's [R]epresentative with full honours and ceremony. I have impressed upon all [European Brooke officers, Native Officers, *datu*, and others] that the best way of showing their loyalty to you is to support the new Government fully and work for the rehabilitation of the State.[26]

British Governor-General Malcolm MacDonald (t. 1946–1948) undertook the formalities: he read out speeches from the Rajah and the King, and appointment of C. W. Dawson[27] as Chief Secretary (1946–1950) and Acting Governor (July–October 1946). The Malay version was delivered by newly elevated Datu Bandar Abang Haji Mustapha bin Abang Moasli (1906–1965).[28] As Archer recalled, "In twenty minutes it was all over".[29]

The Sarawak Malay elite, the *datu* (non-royal chieftains) and *perabangan* (male descents of *datu*) class that hitherto benefitted from Brooke rule with status and prestige, viewed cession to His Majesty's Government with suspicion and anticipated disadvantages. James Brooke, the first White Rajah, had installed the *datu* as advisers to his government. Although their comments and guidance were non-binding, the fact that the rajah consulted them on state matters related to native traditions and practices gave the *datu* immense prestige and respect from within the Malay community and from without in the wider Sarawak society. Sons of *datu*, the *perabangan*, were choice candidates as Native Officers, who, literally, acted as the indispensable 'right' hand of the European Brooke officer in dealing with native customs, traditions, and practices. As salaried members of the Brooke administration, the *perabangan* enjoyed status and prestige second only to the *datu*.

However, the Sarawak Malay elite was divided over the cession issue. One group led by the octogenarian Datu Patinggi Abang Haji Abdillah (1862–1946) regarded cession as a loss of especial rights, prestige, and honour for the Sarawak Malay elite. This anti-cession group faced a rival faction, the pro-secessionists, led by the youthful Datu Pahlawan Abang Haji Mustapha,[30] who argued that cession would offer an opportunity to uplift the socio-economic welfare of the Malay community that lagged behind other communities, notably the Chinese. To some extent, it was a rivalry between 'traditionalists' who stood for *status quo* and 'reformists' who sought change and progress.

Undoubtedly, those who opposed cession were conspicuously absent in the aforesaid handover ceremony of 1 July 1946. Present were British officers, procession *datu*, namely the Datu Bandar, Datu Menteri, and Datu Hakim, and non-native residents, notably Chinese communal leaders.

The immigrant Chinese community read advantages in cession, from greater economic growth and market expansion to accelerated infrastructure development. Their vested interests and direct involvement in trade and commerce and commercial cash cropping saw an expanded market in the event of cession. But more importantly, the Chinese, although not adversely discriminated as 'aliens' under the rather benign autocratic and paternalistic (to natives) Brooke rule, anticipated equal citizenship with native inhabitants that would enable them to enjoy all the concomitant rights and privileges befitting bona fide citizens of Sarawak.

But for the vast majority of the Ibans and other non-Malay native population (Kayans, Kenyahs, Bidayuh, Kelabit, Orang Hulu, and others), largely residing in the interior, the cession issue was a non-starter, simply, firstly, the remoteness of their habitat meant little news trickled through the thickly forested upriver and mountainous regions, and secondly, even if the goings-on of cession did reach the native ear in the *hulu* (upstream, interior), few would grasp the concept and its implications and consequences. Illiteracy and isolation in the interior worked against the bulk of the indigenous inhabitants.

The Sarawak cession controversy (1 July 1946 until March 1950) dates back to the pre-war period. Rajah Charles Vyner Brooke and Ranee Sylvia Brooke had three daughters – Leonora Margaret, Elizabeth, and Nancy Valerie. Without a male heir, the succession and sustainability of the rajahship was in predicament. Vyner had a younger brother, Captain Bertram Willes Dayrell Brooke (1876–1965), who carried the title of Tuan Muda of Sarawak, who, according to their father Rajah Charles Brooke's political will (1913), ruled in tandem with his elder brother when the latter was away for long periods in England. Although formally named as 'Rajah Muda' or 'Heir Presumptive', the dutiful and unassuming Bertram discarded this ambitious and loaded title for the simpler 'Tuan Muda' or 'Young Lord'. The marriage of Bertram to Gladys Milton Palmer (1884–1952) was blessed with three daughters and the fourth child, a son, Anthony.[31]

On the centenary of Brooke rule (1841–1941), Rajah Vyner presented to the people of Sarawak a written Constitution that for all intents and purposes placed himself as a constitutional monarch. It was unclear what was his *real* intention: fulfilling James Brooke's mission of trusteeship and handing back to the natives?

> Sarawak belongs to the Malays, the Sea Dayaks, the Land Dayaks, the Kayans and other tribes, not to us. It is for them that we labour not ourselves.[32]

As Bertram's health waned, Anthony took on his father's responsibilities to the extent of being accorded the title of 'Rajah Muda' by his uncle, Rajah Vyner. But Anthony had an estranged relationship with his uncle, at times in his favour and anointed heir, and a sudden turnaround, falling out of grace, disinherited.[33] The anti-cession activists turned to Anthony as their favoured 'Fourth White Rajah'.

Kuching-based groups that carried the anti-cession banner included the *Persatuan Kebangsaan Melayu Sarawak* (PKMS, Sarawak Malay National Union), *Angkatan Semangat Anaknegeri Sarawak* (ASAS, Fervour of the Generation of Sarawak Natives), while in Sibu, the *Pergerakan Pemuda Melayu* (PPM, Malay Youth Movement), that from the outset appeared to be more radical than the others. All gravitated and rallied to the doyen of the *datu*, Datu Patinggi Abang Haji Abdillah.

The dominant thesis of the anti-cession movement was over the issue of the *datu* and *perabangan* class losing their status and prestige in a CO administration, hence its opposition to cession.[34] Although the anti-cession movement was dominated by middle-aged conservatives, a minority group of much younger and better educated Malays, a so-called Young Turk's faction, saw an opportunity in the 1941 Constitution that paved the way for eventual self-government, and subsequently and ultimately, to attain political independence for Sarawak. The ascension of Anthony as the fourth White Rajah if Rajah Vyner was unwilling to resume his responsibility was deemed ideal, for it was hoped that subsequently through the Brooke regime, Sarawak would eventually attain its independence. A CO administration of Sarawak as a Crown Colony, the anti-secessionists believed, might be a rocky road towards independence, as there were too many variables to contend with: Foreign Office (FO) opinion, War Office (WO) consideration, Whitehall itself undoubtedly involving Number 11 (Chancellor of the Exchequer) and Number 10 (prime minister), literally involving the whole baggage of His Majesty's Government.

Although the 1 July 1946 handover ceremony occurred without any untoward incident apart from the non-presence of anti-cession *datu*, at the grassroots level in the various *kampung*, schism was conspicuous among the Malay community. The seriousness of the cession issue amongst the Malays could be seen as follows:

> public expressions of the anti-cession movement were exemplified in the boycott of the Malay mosque where the Mufti, Haji Nawawi who supported cession, presided; a different sighting of the moon to mark the end of Ramadhan (fasting month) by the opposing factions, hence Hari Raya Aidil Fitri (festivity

to celebrate the end of Ramadhan) commenced on a different date for the respective groups; widespread commemoration of Bertram Brooke's birthday on 8 August, which was a public holiday; social ostracism of the pro-cession *Datu* (Datu Bandar, Datu Amar, Datu Menteri, and Datu Hakim); and traces of anti-European feeling.[35]

Chief Secretary and Acting Governor Dawson took an accommodating approach towards the anti-secessionists, harbouring hope that he could win them over to reason and reality. Apart from the younger elements within them, the anti-secessionists were generally conservative to the extent of being rather embarrassed of participating in public demonstrations and/or protesting using placards and posters. They, instead, preferred constitutional means such as emphasizing the political wills of the Brookes and the British sense of justice and fair play.

But in contrast, the newly installed governor, Sir Charles Noble Arden-Clarke (1946–1949), who took office on 28 October, adopted a hardliner stance, "resolved to strangle the anti-cession movement . . . as soon as possible".[36] Not only did Governor Arden-Clarke have the police destroy all posters, placards, and oppose any street demonstrations, but he banned the entry, with CO approval, of Anthony Brooke from Sarawak. It was an unprecedented move that caught the anti-cession faction by surprise.

On 10 December, Governor Arden-Clarke issued Secretariat Circular No. 9/1946 that threatened dismissal of any civil servant associated and involved with the anti-cession movement and/or its activities. The Circular's clause (e) is explicit:

> Any Government servant in future [from 10 December 1946] who associates himself with any activity designed to keep open the question of cession or commits any act of deliberate disloyalty to the Government will render himself liable to instant dismissal.[37]

It hit a main nerve amongst the anti-secessionists, because the bulk of them were serving as civil bureaucrats. But instead of subjecting themselves to dismissal, 338 Malay civil servants readily handed in their resignations.[38] The governor was unmoved; all of the resignations, all willing departures on their own accord, affected a mere 12 per cent of the civil service, and within a short span, the positions were filled by other Malays.

Meanwhile, in England, Bertram and Anthony, who took legal proceedings against Rajah Vyner in his ceding Sarawak to His Majesty's Government, went all the way to the Privy Council. The protracted legal struggle did not contribute to the anti-cession cause; on the contrary, the failures that peppered along the steps to the Privy Council aggravated the frustrations of those on the ground in Sarawak.[39] The belated verdict of Bertram's case in the Privy Council was finally delivered on 30 November 1950 that favoured the Rajah.

Besides a sizeable number of Malays, almost half the community, involved in the anti-cession movement, a handful of mission-educated Ibans took to organizing themselves in anticipation of cession. Hence, on 23 February 1946, the Sarawak

Dayak Association (SDA) was established with Charles Mason as president, Edward Brandah as vice president, Philip Jitam and Andrew Jika as joint secretaries, and Robert Jitam as treasurer. Mason's SDA was non-committal at this early stage. But subsequently, the SDA decided to ally itself with PKMS owing to the 'ethnic factor'. The fear of these educated Ibans was that in the event of cession, there might be an influx of immigrants, especially Chinese, and their subsequent domination owing to their savviness that might lead to the marginalization and subsequent demise of the Iban. Malays within PKMS, likewise, shared this similar fear. On the other hand, the SDA was initially reluctant to commit to PKMS in the anti-cession struggle, as Malays too, as they had in the past, be the predominant ethnic group that similarly might see to the demise of the Iban. However, conservatives in PKMS turned the SDA's stance to cooperation between them in giving assurance and agreement,

> that in the event of the restoration of Brooke rule [objective of the anti-cession movement], political representation through Council Negri, Supreme Council, or whatever organ of government came into being, would be on the basis of the relative numerical strength of the Ibans and Malays.[40]

It was a dramatic turnaround on the part of Malay leaders, as hitherto both the Council Negri and the Supreme Council were Malay-dominated.

A PKMS-SDA alliance did not mean that Ibans throughout Sarawak supported the anti-cession struggle. The SDA predominantly comprised Kuching-based, educated Ibans whose numbers hardly attained more than a score of Ibans serving in the government bureaucracy. Moreover, the SDA was literally a dead letter since Secretariat Circular No. 9/1946 because none within the SDA resigned from their civil service jobs, hence adversely affecting its credibility, and in turn, jeopardized relations with PKMS. Coupled with its failure to garner mass support from the wider Iban community, the SDA became a mere footnote in the anti-cession movement.

Meanwhile, Governor Arden-Clarke's colonial administration embarked on a propaganda blitz, particularly amongst the Malay and Iban population. British Commissioner-General for Southeast Asia Malcolm MacDonald (1948–1955), then based in Singapore, took it upon himself to ensure that Sarawak's cession was successful and sustainable, and he paid repeated visits to longhouses in the upriver districts of the Third Division. In the Upper Rajang, MacDonald, the consummate diplomat, struck a friendship and won over two principle Iban leaders, notably Temenggong Koh anak Jubang (1870–1956) and Penghulu Jugah anak Barieng (1903–1981).[41] The former was paramount chief of the Sarawak Iban, who commanded respect, support, and influence beyond the Third Division. Penghulu Jugah then appeared to be the anointed heir of Temenggong Koh, subsequently assuming supreme leadership position.

By mid-1948, the anti-cession campaign from all indications seemed futile and fruitless due to numerous developments. Schism from within the movement became apparent after the demise of Datu Patinggi Abang Haji Abdillah (23

November 1946). The dramatic mass resignations of Malay civil servants (from 10 December 1946) had scant impact. But the ban of Anthony's entry into Sarawak (December 1946) was a major setback, and in lieu of his presence, his wife Kathleen in Sarawak had little impression, and likewise the numerous public demonstrations, including the unprecedented participation of Malay women (*Kaum Ibu* or Women's Wing of PKMS). Bertram's and Anthony's protracted legal proceedings and discouraging verdicts further aggravated the despair. Only the very faithful and hopeful remained optimistic. But others, especially the younger faction, harboured other ideas, much more radical and turning to the extreme.

Observing that constitutional and peaceful means appeared pointless, a strategic shift was made in resuscitating the anti-cession struggle. An extremist group known as the *Rukun Tigabelas* (Thirteen Principles), which subscribed to self-sacrifice including suicide for the cause, took up the challenge. A series of assassinations were planned for August 1949, targeting the Governor, various senior British officials, and the 'traitorous' pro-government *datu*. It was unclear what the schemers of these premeditated murderous acts had in mind to achieve with this calculated slaughter. Two young candidates – Rosli bin Dhobie (1932–1950) and Morshidi bin Sidek – were designated as the assassins, rationalizing that their youth, both in their late teens, might temper any punishment.

The targeted Governor Arden-Clarke, however, was reassigned, and left Kuching in July to assume the governorship of the Gold Coast (Ghana). The target then shifted to his successor, Duncan Stewart (1904–1949). Shortly after taking up office, Governor Stewart decided to go on an official tour to Sibu, Sarawak's second largest town and primary port. On that fateful day of 3 December, while moving amongst the crowd, Morshidi distracted Governor Stewart in requesting for a photograph, and when he stopped in his tracks to oblige, Rosli moved in to stab him in his abdomen. Both Rosli and Morshidi were immediately detained. Governor Stewart was flown to Singapore for treatment. A week later, the second colonial Governor to Sarawak succumbed to his wound, aged 45.

Their youthfulness notwithstanding, Rosli and Morshidi were given the death sentence, likewise Awang Ramli Amit and Bujang Suntong. The former pair were hanged on 2 March 1950, and the latter two, three weeks later. Several members of the proscribed *Rukun Tigabelas* were sentenced to prison terms between 5 and 15 years for various degrees of complicity.[42]

The government swiftly executed a state-wide clampdown on all anti-cession elements and suspected sympathizers, including raiding the offices of the PKMS, PPM, and other known groups, banning all public protests, and exerting pressure on Anthony to press his supporters to abandon the cause. His appeal to the PKMS, however, received this response, "[we] do not want to be a Colony but an independent state under the constitutional rule of the Brooke Rajahs within the British Commonwealth of nations".[43]

On hindsight, it could safely be surmised from the outset that the anti-cession cause was an uphill struggle with little hope for success. Practically all the odds were against the small knot of anti-secessionists, who were merely a section of the traditional Malay elite. In contrast to the contemporaneous but successful

Malay opposition to the Malayan Union (1946–1948) in Malaya, the anti-cession movement failed to garner all-out mass support from the Sarawak Malay community. "From the viewpoint of the colonial government", a scholar concluded, "the cession issue was but a hiccup that by the early 1950s had passed into history".[44] But it took more than two decades for the split in the Malay community to reconcile.

Kalimantan's dilemma

Across the border in Kalimantan, the drama only began after 20 August 1945, when news of Sukarno's famous *Proklamasi* of 17 August 1945 declaring Indonesia's independence appeared in the Kandangan edition of the Japanese-sponsored *Borneo Simboen*. Indonesians in Kalimantan, not unlike their brethren throughout the archipelago, were ecstatic. "It was as though", Republican Prime Minister Sutan Sjahrir described of the effect of the *Proklamasi*, "our Indonesian people had been electrified".[45]

It could be said that this '*Proklamasi* 17 August 1945' was *the* most significant pronouncement that, for all intents and purposes, fuelled and shaped the Indonesian Revolution (1945–1949) that subsequently led to the triumphant realization of *Republik Indonesia* in 1949. Owing to Sukarno's momentous proclamation, NICA personnel assisted by KNIL hurriedly, almost in desperation, reinstated Dutch colonial rule over Kalimantan as well as across territories of pre-war Netherlands East Indies (NEI). By mid-1946, when Dutch Lieutenant Governor-General Dr Hubertus Johannes Van Mook arrived in Batavia, he was able to assume the reins of a fully restored NEI colonial government. But it was an NEI administration lest large parts of Java and Sumatra that were then in Republican control, an untenable situation indeed.

Focus then for Van Mook was the Outer Islands (*Buitengewesten*), that of Netherlands Borneo, referring to Kalimantan, and Great East, namely the archipelago spread north and east of Java and Borneo (present-day Eastern Indonesia). The Dutch governor-general intended to garner support in these territories for his federal scheme as a counter poise to the unitary *Republik Indonesia Serikat* (RIS, Republic of the United States of Indonesia [RUSI]). "It appeared", as a scholar rightly surmised, "that 'federalism' was solely a Dutch agenda to ensure the continuity and sustainability of their influence and control over the archipelago" in the post-war period.[46]

Armed with this agenda, Van Mook embarked on a mission-relenting quest to create *negara* (political states) or *daerah istimewa* (autonomous or special territories). He proceeded to harness pre-war pro-Dutch elements – local aristocrats, indigenous elites, minorities including Christians, Chinese, Eurasians, and non-Muslim ethnic groups – to lend support in the establishment of new *negara*. "A United States of Indonesia [USI]", Van Mook announced of his proposed federal framework at the Malino Conference in late July 1946, to be established comprising "four principal states known as 'autonomous territories,' which would be Java, Sumatra, Netherlands Borneo, and Great East".[47]

The first of Van Mook's 'babies' was 'born' at the Den Pasar Conference (18–24 December 1946), namely *Negara Indonesia Timur* (NIT, State of East Indonesia) proclaimed at the conclusion of the week-long meeting of delegates from the Great East. Spurred by NIT's example, several *daerah istimewa* emerged in Kalimantan, but a singular *Negara Kalimantan* (State of Kalimantan) remained elusive. Hence, *Daerah Istimewa Kalimantan Barat* (DIKB, Special Region of West Kalimantan) (12 May 1947), *Federasi Kalimantan Timur* (Federation of East Kalimantan) (12 May 1947), and Greater Siak (3 June 1947), comprising south and central Borneo, resulted.

In Kalimantan, the peoples were divided over backing the Republican cause on the one hand and lending support to the federal proposal on the other. A dilemma emerged. Federalism lends credence to diverse multiethnic, multicultural, and multi-religious characteristics of Kalimantan, whereby the rights and interests, status and position, and identity of the disparately varied inhabitants be safe-guarded. In throwing their lot for the Republicans, the risk was of the emergence of a Java-centred and oriented centrist *Republik Indonesia* that might override and/or disregard the voices, interests, and rights of the Outer Islands including Kalimantan.

On the ground in Kalimantan, however, various opinions, expressions, and positions were found amongst the peoples. Observations in South Kalimantan, and likely to be representative elsewhere across Kalimantan, were that four categories of people were identified, viz.:

(1) Those that refused to accept the NICA and the Dutch and left South Kalimantan.
(2) Those that accepted the return of the Dutch and the NICA and were ready (and willing) to work as Dutch-NICA personnel.
(3) Those that opposed the return of the Dutch and the NICA that henceforth struggled through parliamentary means.
(4) Those that strongly opposed the return of the Dutch and the NICA to the extent of risking arrest and imprisonment, or of being forced to flee to the jungle to embark on an armed guerrilla struggle.[48]

Many of the émigré from the first category returned to Kalimantan as members of militia organizations on expeditionary missions to fight the colonial Dutch regime. The second grouping collectively was labelled '*andjing* NICA' (NICA [running] dogs), resented and despised by the other categories. Comprising this second category were the aristocrats like the sultans (*dokohs*) in the *swapraja* (self-governing autonomous territories), civil servants in pre-war NEI colonial government, war-time bureaucrats who served the IJN, and native members of NICA and KNIL. The third component comprised pro-republican individuals who numbered as members of political parties who took their opposition through parliamentary and legal means. The fourth group were the revolutionaries that removed to the interior to undertake their armed struggle, a guerrilla war of attrition against the restored NEI government.

Whilst the aforesaid first category of Kalimantan émigré fled mainly to Java were initiating, joining, and preparing armed expeditionary missions to return to unseat the hitherto NEI government in their homeland, the *pemuda*-cum-*pejuang* (youth fighters) that remained behind were translating their opposition in acts of sabotage, arson, and the occasional armed raids on NICA police posts, KNIL depots for weapons. Such small-scale acts, often uncoordinated, sporadic, and poorly planned, at times even foolhardy, ended fruitlessly with losses in lives on the part of the youthful perpetrators martyring themselves for the Republican cause. Hassan Basry, leader of the paramilitary *Lasykar Saifullah* (Saifullah Militia) based in Haruyan, South Kalimantan, attributed failures of pro-Republican *pemuda-pejuang* subversive activities to poor organization, the absence of effective and credible leaders, insufficient and reliable weaponry and other equipment, and without good operational coordination.[49]

A similar fate attended to the various military expeditionary missions of pro-Republican forces sent from Java to Kalimantan between 1945 and 1946 that ended in failures and disasters. The lack of coordination among the various expeditions, many acting unilaterally, and poor intelligence marred their success.[50]

Meanwhile, those that opted for pen and speech through legal constitutional means achieved gainful grounds, and in fact, were successful if success meant ensuring the non-emergence of a *Negara Kalimantan* (State of Kalimantan). *Komite Indonesia Merdeka* (KIM, Committee of Independent Indonesia), *Fonds Nasional Indonesia* (FONI, Indonesia National Front), *Ikatan Nasional Indonesia* (INI, National Association of Indonesia), *Gerakan Dokter Suwadji* (The Movement of Doctor Suwadji), *Serikat Kerakyatan Indonesia* (SKI, Populist Association of Indonesia), and *Serikat Muslimin Indonesia* (SERMI, Indonesian Muslim Association) were but some of the more prominent political organizations with pro-Republican agenda in Kalimantan.[51]

Van Mook and his officers appealed to pro-Dutch elements to rally to the federal plan. Not only did he succeed in winning over Sultan Hamid II (1913–1978) of Pontianak, but Van Mook also persuaded this lieutenant-colonel of the KNIL to sway his fellow sultans/*dokohs* to the Dutch cause. Van Mook's deputy, Dr Charles O. Van Der Plas, the pre-war Governor of East Java who was a reputed scholar of Islam, achieved a coup in winning over H. Abdulrahman Sidik, the founder-leader of SERMI, to not only switch to the Dutch side but also to set up a rival Muslim political party, namely *Serikat Rakyat Islam* (SRI, Islamic People's Association). In its inaugural congress (November 1947), SRI passed a resolution to work towards the creation of a *Negara Kalimantan*.[52] As a strategy and move to counter a SKI-SERMI alliance, the NEI government created the *Madjelis Oelama Islam* (MOI, Assembly of Islamic Ulamas) in October 1947 based in Kandangan. MOI in partnership with SRI were tasked to challenge the pro-Republican SKI-SERMI.

While *pemuda-pejuang* subversive activities from within and military expeditionary missions from without were overall ineffective and unsuccessful, a conglomeration of numerous militia groups came under a single command organization named *Batalyon Rahasia ALRI (Angkatan Laut Republik Indonesia) Divisi IV (A)*

Pertahanan Kalimantan [Covert Battalion ALRI (Naval Forces of the Republic of Indonesia) IV Division (A) Defence of Kalimantan]. Inaugurated in November 1946, based in Hulu Sungai, South Kalimantan ALRI *Divisi* IV (A) was the brain centre for all *perang gerilya* (guerrilla war) throughout Kalimantan.[53] It was headed by Lieutenant Colonel Hassan Basry as battalion commandant with Major H. Aberani Sulaiman as his chief of staff. While ALRI *Divisi IV* (A) coordinated guerrilla forces in South Kalimantan, ALRI *Divisi IV* (B) and ALRI *Divisi IV* (C) oversaw West Kalimantan and East Kalimantan, respectively. Centralized command was furthermore strengthened with the establishment of the *Sentral Organisasi Pemberontak Indonesia Kalimantan* (SOPIK, Indonesia Kalimantan Rebel Central Organization) based in Briyang, codename RX-8.

While the armed struggle continued with periodic and sudden guerrilla attacks by pro-Republican forces against NEI colonial government targets, Van Mook was on the diplomatic offensive with leaders from the Outer Islands. At Bandung (27 May to 17 July 1948), he called on the delegates, 18 altogether, with the purported purpose of discussing details of the internal administrative structure of the pro-posed federal state and its relationship thereafter with the Netherlands. But Van Mook's real intention was to garner the support of the delegates to lend credibility to the establishment of USI less the *Republik* territories of Java and Sumatra.

But this sly hand of Van Mook was rejected by the delegates. The mood among the delegates seemed to verge on "the ever-increasing desire . . . for national unity coupled with the retention of regional autonomy", or in other words, Indonesians increasingly wanted 'the best of both worlds', namely 'national integrity/unity' at the same time as 'regional autonomy'. Needless, Bandung was not at all lost on Van Mook. The *Bijeenkomst voor Federaal Overleg* (BFO, Federal Consultative Assembly), comprising leaders of *negara* and *daerah istimewa*, was constituted and tasked to establish an interim federal government.

Calculated to deliver the final annihilation of the *Republik*, the Dutch Second 'Police Action' (19 December 1948) backfired horribly.[54] On hindsight, in fact, on the contrary, it spelt the beginning of the end of the NEI colonial govern-ment (Table 1.1). Between 19 December 1948 and January 1949, Dutch colonial police apprehended leading figures of the *Republik*, notably Sukarno (president), Mohamad Hatta (vice president), and Sutan Sjahrir (prime minister), banishing them to Bangka Island, off southeast Sumatra. Throughout the archipelago, pro-Republican elements (from politicians to journalists) were rounded up and impris-oned. Jogjakarta, hitherto the capital and symbolic centre of the *Republik*, was occupied by KNIL.

Repercussions were adverse for Van Mook and the NEI. Many within the BFO deserted the Dutch. NIT and Pasundan (a *negara* in West Java) withdrew from BFO in protest. The Republicans swiftly established an emergency government, *Pemerintah Darurat Republik Indonesia* (Emergency Rule of the Republic of Indonesia), at Bukittinggi, West Sumatra headed by Sjafruddin Prawiranegara. Republican military forces launched an all-out *perang gerilya* on an archipelago scale from late December 1948. ALRI in Kalimantan, likewise, commenced offen-sives in early 1949.

Table 1.1 Second 'Police Action' to Round Table Conference at The Hague, 1948–1949

Date	Event
1948	
18–19 December	Second 'Police Action'; mass arrest of Republican leaders and supporters.
22 December	Republican Lieutenant-General Abdul Haris Nasution launched *Pertahanan Keamanan Rakyat Semesta* (Total Defence of the People's Security), literally transforming Java into a guerrilla battlefield.
1949	
January	Resignation in protest of some leaders in Dutch-sponsored *negara* and *daerah istimewa*.
14 April	United Nations Commission on Indonesia (UNCI) brokered a negotiation between the Dutch and the Republic.
7 May	Roem-Van Royen Accord called for, viz. a ceasefire, a round-table conference at The Hague, restoration of Republican rule in Jogjakarta, Dutch agreement to no new creation of *negara* in Republic-controlled territories (from 19 December 1948).
19–22 July	First *Konperensi Inter-Indonesia* (Inter-Indonesian Conference), Jogjakarta between Republicans led by Mohamad Hatta and BFO (federalist) headed by Sultan Hamid II to discuss the basic principles of the structure and administration of the future state, and deliberate over the transfer of political power and sovereignty.
30 July to 2 August	Second *Konperensi Inter-Indonesia*, Jakarta (Batavia).
23 August to 2 November	Round Table Conference at The Hague resulted in The Netherlands-Indonesian Union, comprising RUSI and the Netherlands with the Dutch queen as a symbolic Head of State, Sukarno as President of RUSI, with Hatta as both Prime Minister and Vice-president.
27 December	The Netherlands formally transfers sovereignty over Indonesia, excluding Dutch New Guinea, to the RUSI government.

Source: Ooi, *Post-war Borneo*, p. 137.

The writing was literally on the wall for the Dutch colonial regime that subsequently ended on 27 December 1949, when the Dutch monarch ceremoniously handed over sovereignty to Mohamad Hatta, RIS/RUSI vice-president-designate. This handover brought to a close the tumultuous chapter of the Indonesian Revolution, where the death toll of Indonesians, the bulk of fatalities, was some 200,000, a high price indeed for freedom.[55]

But within six weeks, there witnessed the dissolution of RIS/RUSI, a federation that comprised *Republik Indonesia* and 15 other constituent states (*negara* and *daerah istimewa*). One by one of the *negara*, *daerah istimewa* dismantled their governing apparatus to merge with the unitary *Republik Indonesia* that finally came into being on 17 August 1950, five long years after Sukarno's *Proklomasi*.

In Kalimantan, on 4 April 1950 was when *Daerah Bandjar* (Bandjar Region), *Daerah Dajak Besar* (Region of Greater Dajak), and *Federasi Kaliamantan*

Tenggara (Federation of Southeast Kalimantan) incorporated into *Republik Indonesia*. *Federasi Kalimantan Timur* (Federation of East Kalimantan) followed thereafter on 24 April.

Daerah Istimewa Kalimantan Barat (DIKB, Special Region of West Kalimantan) was the last to be incorporated into *Republik Indonesia*, undertaken only on 17 August 1950. This conspicuous tardiness owed to the situation whereby Sultan Hamid II headed DIKB. His implication in the Westerling Affair (January 1950) as the brainchild of the attempted coup to overthrow Mohamad Hatta's RIS/RUSI government saw him being sentenced to a ten-year imprisonment term.[56] Even without his arrest, Sultan Hamid II's position and that of DIKB were both untenable. His close affiliation with NICA and KNIL, undoubtedly labelled '*andjing NICA*', prompted massive anti-Hamid and anti-DIKB protests in most towns of West Kalimantan: Pontianak, Singkawang, Mempawah, Sambas, and Pemangkat. An unprecedented ten-day work stoppage in March 1950 literally paralyzed Pontianak. His imprisonment appeared to be a welcome relief. Following his incarceration, a federal commission was appointed by the central government in Jakarta and tasked to recommend the future of West Kalimantan; consequently, DIKB was replaced by a federal government-appointed Resident. Subsequently, West Kalimantan became a part of *Republik Indonesia*.

The intention

Meanwhile, between 1947 and 1990, a bipolar world emerged with two major camps of ideological orientation, namely communism and democracy, with the USSR and U.S. as respective champions. Described as a Cold War, based on the fact that both powers did not directly face one another in a battlefield, although there were proxy wars whereby each backed their respective ally, the tense global situation 'forced' nation-states to take sides. In Southeast Asia the newly decolonized nation-states and others in the process of decolonization were caught in this Cold War scenario of lending their support between the two colossus powers. Undoubtedly, directly or indirectly, overtly or covertly, Moscow and Washington, and from 1949, Beijing, intervened in the affairs of other nation-states as a means of garnering their support, not unlike two suitors courting the many maidens.

Borneo during the Cold War (1947–1991) endured a host of developments, from dramatic to horrific and barbaric, revolution, rebellion to protracted insurgency, pogroms and massacres.

Picking up from the immediate post-war period (1945–1950), the present volume, the third and final volume of a trilogy, commences from 1950 to the end of the Cold War.[57] The 1950s appeared to be pedestrian, somewhat a preparation stage for the following decade. The main 'act' was the explosive 1960s. Borneo then resembled a cauldron of violence that boiled over, claiming lives, inflicting hardships, and causing fear and panic, anguish and distress.

Were the local scenarios in Borneo a consequence of local decisions and local actions borne from within, or did causal factors derive from directives from without, the influence and intervention of Cold War players: Washington, Moscow, and/or Beijing? Were foreign puppeteers directing the show on the Bornean platform? Were regional and/or local players mere proxies of Cold War protagonists, advancing their agendas, their influence, and their fights on the Bornean stage?

Or were unfolding developments in Borneo during the Cold War simply a case of the proverbial mousedeer caught between duelling elephants, as in a traditional Malay expression, viz. "*Gajah sama gajah berjuang, pelanduk mati di tengah-tengah*", literally, "When two elephants fight, the mousedeer dies in the middle". In other words, when two colossus protagonists fight, bystanders and others die amidst the melee, the loss of innocents when nations wage war.

Notes

1 2010 Census. Sarawak Population. www.sarawak.gov.my/web/home/article_view/ 240/175/ Accessed 29 July 2017.
2 Ibid.
3 Ibid.
4 2010 Census. Sabah Population. www.statistics.gov.my/portal/download_Population/ files/population/04Jadual_PBT_negeri/PBT_Sabah.pdf Accessed 29 July 2017.
5 Ibid.
6 2010 Census. Tarakan Population. http://population.city/indonesia/tarakan/ Accessed 30 July 2017.
7 2010 Census. Banjarmasin Population. http://population.city/indonesia/banjarmasin/ Accessed 30 July 2017.
8 2010 Census. Pontianak Population. http://population.city/indonesia/pontianak/ Accessed 30 July 2017.
9 British North Borneo's administrative centre was Sandakan (1884–1945) following the abandonment of the initial Kudat (1881–1884). By 1922, there were established five administrative Residencies, viz. West Coast, Kudat, Tawau, Interior, and East Coast. While European officers held top positions such as residents and district officers, traditional native chiefs retained their pre-colonial status to continue to oversee the local inhabitants at the longhouse and village level.
10 Often the stretch between Kuching and Serian of some 50 kilometres is referred to as the Kuching-Serian Road, thereafter until Bandar Sri Aman (Simanggang), a distance of close to 197 kilometres, is the Kuching-Simanggang Road.
11 Straits Dollar S$50 million was demanded of the Chinese of Malaya through the Overseas Chinese Organisation tasked to raise this amount to atone the community for its 'sins' against Imperial Japan. See Cheah Boon Kheng, *Red Star over Malaya: Resistance and Social Conflict during and after the Japanese Occupation, 1941–1946*, 4th ed. (Singapore: National University of Singapore Press, 2012), p. 24.
12 Hara Fujio, "Sook Ching: A 'Cleansing' Exercise", in *Southeast Asia: A Historical Encyclopedia from Angkor Wat to East Timor*, edited by Ooi Keat Gin (Santa Barbara, CA: ABC-Clio, 2004), III: 1230.
13 A plaque at the Petagas War Memorial Garden stated that some 324 members of the "Kinabalu Guerrillas" were massacred by the Japanese at the present site on Jan 21, 1944.
14 See Ooi Keat Gin, "Calculated Strategy or Senseless Murder? Mass Killings in Japanese-Occupied South and West Borneo, 1943–1945", in *The Encyclopedia of Indonesia in the Pacific War*, edited by Peter Post et al. (Leiden and Boston: Brill, 2010), pp. 212–217.
15 Ooi Keat Gin, *The Japanese Occupation of Borneo, 1941–1945* (London: Routledge, 2011), p. 69.

16 Peter Stanley, "Sandakan Death March: A Tropical Hell", in *Southeast Asia: A Historical Encyclopedia from Angkor Wat to East Timor*, edited by Ooi Keat Gin (Santa Barbara, CA: ABC-Clio, 2004), III: 1172. Also, see Paul Ham, *Sandakan: The Harrowing True Story of the Borneo Death Marches 1944–5* (Melbourne: William Heinemann, 2012).

17 Ooi Keat Gin, *Post-War Borneo, 1945–1950: Nationalism, Empire and, Nation-Building* (London and New York: Routledge, 2013), p. 32. For the AIF re-occupation of Borneo, see ibid., pp. 32–38.

18 For a detailed study, see Ooi Keat Gin, "Prelude to Invasion: Covert Activities of SRD Prior to the Australian Re-Occupation of Northwest Borneo 1944–45", *Journal of the Australian War Memorial*, 37 (Oct 2002). www.awm.gov.au/articles/journal/j37/borneo Accessed 12 Oct 2017.

19 "Text of Hirohito's Radio Rescript", *The New York Times*, Aug 15, 1945. https://timesmachine. nytimes.com/timesmachine/1945/08/15/88279592.html?pageNumber=3 Accessed 12 Oct 2017.

20 Scholars on the Chinese mainland discarded the 'Second Sino-Japanese War', instead preferred 'China's War of Resistance against Japanese Aggression'. Similarly, the popularly accepted period between 1937 and 1945 was disputed; instead, a 14-year span dating back to the September 18 Mukden Incident in 1931 that saw the Japanese Kwangtung Army invading Manchuria. For instance, see Sun Jieqiong, "14-Year War of Resistance against Japanese Aggression a Consensus among Chinese Historians", *People's Daily Online*, Jan 11, 2017. http://en.people.cn/n3/2017/0111/c90000-9165703.html Accessed 12 Oct 2017.

21 Max Fisher, "The Emperor's Speech: 67 Years Ago, Hirohito Transformed Japan Forever", *The Atlantic*, Aug 15, 2012. www.theatlantic.com/international/archive/2012/08/the-emperors-speech-67-years-ago-hirohito-transformed-japan-forever/261166/ Accessed 12 Oct 2017.

22 See *North Borneo Annual Report 1949* (Jesselton: Government Printers, 1950), p. 5.

23 During the immediate post-war period, Labuan hosted BBCAU, and thereafter, BMA (BB) owing to its halfway strategic location off Brunei Bay between Sarawak, Brunei, and North Borneo. Labuan had a chequered past, viz. acquisition from Brunei to Britain (1846), British Crown Colony (1848), administered as a part of British North Borneo (1890–1906), and a component of the expanded Straits Settlements (1907–1941) that in fact reinstated its Crown Colony status.

24 Despite scores of works, the most detailed piece remained R. H. W. Reece, *The Name of Brooke: The End of White Rajah Rule in Sarawak* (Kuala Lumpur: Oxford University Press, 1982). Also, see Ooi, *Post-War Borneo*, pp. 82–99.

25 'Officer Administering the Government' was the title given to the most senior Brooke officer (the Resident of the First Division), later to the Chief Secretary when the post was created with the formation of the Secretariat at Kuching in 1923.

26 John Beville Archer, *Glimpses of Sarawak between 1912 & 1946: Autobiographical Extracts & Articles of an Officer of the Rajahs: John Beville Archer (1893–1948)*, comp. and introd. by Vernon L. Porritt (Hull: Special Issue of the Department of South-East Asian Studies, University of Hull, 1997), p. 64.

27 C. W. Dawson was seconded from the Malayan Civil Service (MCS) to be British Representative in Sarawak in April 1946 tasked to work with Archer, the Brooke Chief Secretary in preparing the bureaucratic passage for formal cession in July.

28 For the malleable character of Abang Haji Mustapha, see Ooi, *Post-War Borneo*, pp. 66–67. Also, see Bob Reece, *Datu Bandar: Abang Hj. Mustapha of Sarawak: Some Reflections of his Life and Times* (Kuala Lumpur: Sarawak Literary Society, 1993).

29 Archer, *Glimpses of Sarawak*, p. 64.

30 Rajah Vyner Brooke, in one of his last acts as monarch, elevated Datu Pahlawan Abang Haji Mustapha to the position of Datu Bandar, for his support of cession and the rehabilitation of the Sarawak Constabulary. However, it was at the displeasure of many

Malays, including Datu Patinggi Abang Haji Abdillah. Ooi, *Post-War Borneo*, pp. 91–92.

31 Christened as Anthoni Walter Dayrell Brooke (1912–2011), but to family members, he was affectionately referred to as 'Peter'.

32 Plaque at St Leonard's Church, Sheepstor, Devon, England, where the Brookes – James, Charles, Vyner, and Bertram – were buried in the church grounds, and nearby, Burrator House, where James spent his twilight years.

33 For the turbulent relations between uncle and nephew, see Ooi Keat Gin, "The Man Who Would Be King: The Tribulations of Anthoni Walter Dayrell Brooke (1912–2011) of Sarawak", Invited Speaker, 3rd Nicholas Tarling Conference on Southeast Asia Studies, Exalted Heroes, Demonized Villains, and Losers: Altering Perceptions and Memories of Leaders and Leadership in Southeast Asia, c. 1800-c. 2000, University of Malaya, Kuala Lumpur, 12–13 Nov 2013.

34 Ooi, *Post-War Borneo*, pp. 87, 90.

35 Ibid., p. 93.

36 This uncompromising position was mentioned by Kenelm Hutchinson Digby, Brooke Sarawak's first trained lawyer appointed as district officer in 1934. K. H. Digby, *Lawyer in the Wilderness* (Ithaca, NY: Cornell University Press, Cornell University Southeast Asia Program Data Paper No. 114, 1980), p. 213.

37 *Sarawak Government Gazette*, Dec 1946.

38 *Annual Report on Sarawak for the Year 1947* (Kuching: Government Printing Office, 1948), p. 47.

39 Anthony failed in his appeals, viz. to the Privy Council in early 1947, and another to the High Court of Brunei in mid-1948.

40 Reece, *The Name of Brooke*, p. 249.

41 See Malcolm MacDonald, *Borneo Peoples* (New York: Knopf, 1958).

42 *Sarawak Tribune*, Mar 3 and Mar 24, 1950.

43 *Sarawak Gazette*, Mar 1951.

44 Ooi, *Post-War Borneo*, p. 99.

45 Soutan Sjahrir, *Out of Exile*, trans. Charles Wolf (New York: New Day, 1949), p. 259.

46 Ooi, *Post-War Borneo*, p. 129.

47 David Wehl, *The Birth of Indonesia* (London: George Allen & Unwin, 1948), p. 129.

48 H. A. H. Budhigawis, "Laporan Perjuangan dari Munggu Raya", ms. Martapura, 1968, p. 36 cited in H. A. Ghazali Usman dan H. Ramli Nawawi, eds., *Sejarah Revolusi Kemerdekaan (1945–1949). Daerah Kalimantan Selatan [The History of Independence Revolution (1945–1949): Region of South Kalimantan]* (Banjarmasin: Departemen Pendidikan dan Kebudayaan, Direktorat Jenderal Kebudayaan, Direktorat Sejarah dan Nilai Tradisional, dan Proyek Inventarisasi dan Pembinaan Nilai-Nilai Budaya, 1991), p. 67.

49 H. Hassan Basry, *Kisah Gerila Kalimantan (Dalam Revolusi Indonesia) 1945–1949 [Guerrilla Stories of Kalimanatan (During the Indonesian Revolution) 1945–1949], Djilid Pertama: Kalimantan diachir Perang Dunia II – 1945 sehingga lahirnja ALRI Divisi IV – 1946 [Volume One: Kalimantan at the End of World War II-1945 to the Establishment of ALRI Divisi IV-1946]* (Bandjarmasin: Jajasan Lektur Lambung Mangkurat, 1961), pp. 76–77.

50 See ibid., pp. 50–51.

51 Ooi, *Post-War Borneo*, p. 127.

52 See M. Sanit Seman, "Sejarah Politik Pendudukan Belanda dan Perlawanan Rakyat di Kal-Sel [Political History of the Dutch Occupation and the People's Opposition in South Kalimantan]", thesis, Universitas Lambung Mangkurat (UNLAM), Banjarmasin, 1972, p. 65.

53 ALRI Divisi IV's main command post was in Tuban, East Java. Subsequently, it became Brigade XVI under the command of Major Firmansyah Tujan. Ghazali dan Ramli, *Sejarah Revolusi Kemerdekaan*, p. 111.

54 L. Zweers, *Agressi II: Operatie Kraai. De vergeten beelden van de tweede politionele actie* [*Aggression II: Operation Kraai: The Forgotten Images of the Second Police Action*] (The Hague: SDU Uitgevers, 1995).

55 The Indonesians literally paid in blood for their independence. Between 45,000 and 100,000 Indonesian military sacrificed their lives, and 25,000 and 100,000 Indonesian civilians were killed, and another seven million Indonesians displaced. Adrian Vickers, *A History of Modern Indonesia*, 2nd ed. (New York: Cambridge University Press, 2005), pp. 160–161.

56 For the Westerling Affair, see C. L. M. Penders, *The West New Guinea Debacle: Dutch Decolonisation and Indonesia, 1945–1962* (Leiden: Brill, 2002), pp. 185–191; Ooi, *Post-War Borneo*, pp. 140–141.

57 Previously published two volumes are Ooi Keat Gin, *The Japanese Occupation of Borneo, 1941–1945* (London: Routledge, 2011); Ooi Keat Gin, *Post-War Borneo, 1945–1950: Nationalism, Empire, and State-Building* (London: Routledge, 2013).

2 The global Cold War

Let every nation know, whether it wishes us well or ill, that we shall pay any price, bear any burden, meet any hardship, support any friend, oppose any foe to assure the survival and the success of liberty.

John F. Kennedy (t. 1961–1963),
Presidential inaugural address, 20 January 1961

A global Cold War enveloped the greater part of the second half of the twentieth century. Tensions between politico-military blocs and anxieties, fears, and apprehensions amongst peoples throughout the world of a possible, even imminent, Third World War holocaust marked situations and conditions for more than four decades. Here is presented the 'big picture' of this worldwide phenomenon in detailing the concept of a bipolar world and the emergence of camps of 'we' and 'they'. Developments in East and Southeast Asia, from the Chinese Civil War (1945–1949) to the protracted conflict in Vietnam, are detailed to set the tone from without. Attention then shifts to Borneo as to the unfolding of this global phenomenon as a preliminary start, setting out the focus and priorities of the present study.

A bipolar world

Even before the last war refugees could be settled satisfactorily or were able to return home, the world was confronted with the advent of another war, the Cold War (1947–1991) that, like the just-concluded Second World War (1939–1945), engulfed the entire world directly or indirectly. The Cold War was a state of tension and apprehension both politically and militarily in the post-war period between two colossus powers then, namely the United States (U.S.) and the Union of Soviet Socialist Republics (USSR, Soviet Union), each with their respective allies and satellites. It was designated 'cold' because throughout the entire period, the two main protagonists, the U.S. and the USSR, did not fight directly between one another. Instead they fought indirectly through proxy wars, and each supported – moral, materials, aerial, and naval military support, and deployment of ground forces – their candidate in regional conflicts such as the Korean War (1950–1953), the Vietnam War (1955–1975), and the Soviet–Afghan War (1979–1989).

The U.S. sought allies from Western Europe that subsequently formed NATO (North Atlantic Treaty Organization) in 1949, comprising Belgium, the Netherlands, Luxembourg, France, the United Kingdom (UK), the U.S., Canada, Portugal, Italy, Norway, Denmark, and Iceland. NATO was, and still is, an intergovernmental military alliance; in practical terms, it created a system of collective defence where each member formally pledged to mutual defence in the event of an attack or invasion by any external party on any of the members. In playground parlance, a band of children will literally come together to confront and beat up a bully who hit one of their numbers. This military alliance, whereby the U.S. appeared from the beginning as the leader, focused on collective defence in the face of a perceived belligerent and expansionist USSR.

The Soviet Union on its part had in the early stages of the Second World War annexed several states in Central and Eastern Europe following the Molotov-Ribbentrop Pact (1939),[1] whereby these states had been ceded to it by Nazi Germany, namely eastern Poland, Estonia, Latvia, Lithuania, eastern Finland, and eastern Romania.[2] Following liberation by the Soviet Red Army of Nazi-held territories in Central and Eastern Europe, these territories were incorporated as satellite states, viz. East Germany, the People's Republic of Bulgaria, the People's Republic of Poland, the People's Republic of Hungary, the People's Republic of Romania, the People's Republic of Albania, and the Czechoslovak Socialist Republic.[3]

By 1947, the stage was set for the play named the 'Cold War' to officially commence. One of the two principal protagonists, the United States and its allies in NATO, was collectively referred to as the so-called Western Bloc.[4] In opposition, the Soviet Union, with its annexed and satellite states of Central and Eastern Europe, was labelled the Eastern Bloc. The latter was often increasingly referred to as the Warsaw Pact.

In 1955, the Treaty of Friendship, Cooperation and Mutual Assistance was signed in Warsaw by the Soviet Union and seven other states, viz. Albania, Poland, Romania, Hungary, East Germany, Czechoslovakia, and Bulgaria. Like NATO, the Warsaw Pact was a mutual defence organization, whereby member states were committed to come to the defence of any member when attacked by a third party. A unified military command headed by the Soviet Union was established to oversee all military and defence matters.[5] The Warsaw Pact was Moscow's reaction to the entry of the Federal Republic of Germany (or West Germany) in NATO.[6]

Both protagonists conspicuously contrasted in ideological orientation: on the one hand, the U.S. represented a capitalist democracy where freedom, civil liberties, free market, and private property were highly valued, whereas on the other hand, the USSR was a communist totalitarian state, committed to the principle whereby the state possessed all power and emphasized centralized control. Both ideologies were starkly incompatible. Moreover, both protagonists believed that the opposing ideology posed a threat to their own way of life, and in order to sustain their own existence, it was a moral and dutiful responsibility that they needed to spread their ideology to the rest of the world lest the opposition gained ground in propagating their brand of ideology. Such firmly held beliefs from either side to a great extent influenced their foreign and international relations, and in turn, were a potent formula for conflict. There appeared an inevitability that the two colossi would somehow clash, whether directly or indirectly, but what remained was whence this would occur.

The blame game

The Cold War, a protracted 44-year-old state of tension and apprehension between the main protagonists and their respective allies and satellites, supporters and sympathizers, pawns and victims finally ended in 1991 with the dissolution of the USSR on Christmas Day, and thereafter the U.S. emerged as the undisputed singular most powerful nation in the world. Fortunately, there was no nuclear holocaust from a Third World War, as most quarters were worriedly foreseeing in witnessing the massive weaponry and arms stockpile on either side, particularly of their respective nuclear arsenals. The second half of the twentieth century was literally and largely consumed with the Cold War scenario, with flare-ups of conflicts that transformed into proxy wars across the globe, from the Korean peninsula (Korean War [1950–1953]), to the Caribbean (Cuban Missile Crisis, 1962), to the conflict in Vietnam (Vietnam War [1955–1975]), to Afghanistan (Soviet–Afghan War [1979–1989]). The world waited in fear with bated breath and reluctantly resigned to their fate as which of the unfolding events, crises, and various protracted armed struggles would lead to the Third World War and nuclear annihilation of our species.

But the terminology bandied around then – nuclear arms race, nuclear proliferation, policy of deterrence, doctrine of mutual assured destruction (MAD), nuclear triad, first strike, second strike – would make any rational-minded person-in-the-street shudder and cringe in fear and horror that presidents, prime ministers, heads of state, and national leaders would contemplate such murderous intents on their political foes, simply for the fact that the 'other' side subscribed to a philosophy, way of life, ideology, or belief different from theirs. But, happily for all that, the doomsday scenario did not materialize.

What brought about the deterioration of relations between the once wartime allies to transform into arch foes each intended to annihilate the other has been featured in the scholarly discourse. In perusing the historiography of the Cold War, there are three general trends or schools of thought of divided opinions: the 'traditional or orthodox' stance, 'revisionist' counter-arguments, and the 'post-revisionist' thesis.

The orthodox interpretation of the blame for the Cold War is from the U.S. perspective that attributed its own actions in the immediate post-war period as a response to the perceived expansionist agenda of the USSR.[7] Examples were aplenty that exhibited the Soviet Union strongman Josef Stalin's expansionist streak, viz. reluctance to leave Iran, the creation of satellites of the states of Eastern Europe with regimes dominated by communist parties loyal to Moscow, civil wars in Greece and China where communists were in pursuit of power, and the Soviet pressure on Turkey over the Dardenelles. In response, the traditionalist viewpoint argued, Washington pronounced the Truman Doctrine (12 March 1947) followed by the Marshall Plan (5 June 1947). The former committed the U.S. to contain (policy of containment) communism and to defend democracy and freedom in any corner of the world where it may be endangered or challenged. The Marshall Plan saw Washington's financial commitment – some USD $17 billion over a four-year period – in the reconstruction and rehabilitation of European economies and social fabric. Moscow's refusal for aid as well as denying any East European state to access this financial assistance, the orthodox view claimed, further demonstrated Stalin's hold on his satellites lest they become beholden to Washington. Both the Truman Doctrine and the Marshall Plan brought an end to the U.S. trademark isolationism; instead it took an active role either through overt and/or covert means to ensure that the spread of communism is contained or blocked. Washington's complete turnaround is evidenced in the following scenario:

> In 1938, the United States was without military alliances and had no troops stationed in non-U.S. territory; by 1989, military alliances were in effect with 50 countries, and 1.5 million U.S. troops were posted in 117 countries.[8]

Against the backdrop of the Vietnam War, scholars began to question and re-look at the position and role of the United States on the world stage. During this period of controversy over the involvement of the U.S. in Vietnam, the revisionist's viewpoint came to the fore. It marked the high point whence the orthodox standpoint was being scrutinized and criticized. The revisionist standpoint of the Cold War challenged and counter-argued the long-held traditionalist or orthodox school of thought that, for all intents and purposes in the Cold War environment, attempted to demonize and place the onus on the Soviet Union and its leaders, particularly the demagogue Stalin.

The first alternative view to the orthodox standpoint was in 1959 when William Appleman Williams published *The Tragedy of American Diplomacy*.[9] Williams argued that America's main aim in the immediate post-war period was to ensure an 'open door' for American trade, consequently fostering a foreign policy that promoted capitalism and that countries remained capitalist.[10]

The revisionist maintained that instead of expansionism from without, Moscow was struggling with post-war reconstruction from within. One of the worst war victims, the Soviet Union suffered 27 million deaths (8.7 million combat deaths and 19 million non-combat deaths).[11] Moreover, the economy had been devastated.

> Roughly a quarter of the country's capital resources had been destroyed, and industrial and agricultural output in 1945 fell far short of prewar levels. . . . By the time of Stalin's death in 1953, steel production was twice its 1940 level, but the production of many consumer goods and foodstuffs was lower than it had been in the late 1920s.[12]

In order to effect reconstruction, political stability needed to be maintained, hence the pivotal concern of Stalin, the revisionist argued, was not so much in promoting and expanding communism abroad but to ensure that communism at home was safeguarded and maintained.

In response to Moscow's creation of an 'Iron Curtain', equivalent to a *cordon sanitaire*, in Eastern Europe, the revisionist attributed it as a security need along its western borders lest a repeat of incursions such as the invasion of Nazi Germany in mid-1941 occur. At the Yalta Conference (4–11 February 1945), U.S. President Franklin Delano Roosevelt (t. 1933–1945) and UK Prime Minister Winston Churchill (t. 1940–1945, 1951–1955) had viewed Stalin's control over Eastern Europe (then occupied by the Red Army) as a defensive strategy in protecting the Soviet Union's southwest flank. Interestingly, however, Roosevelt's successor, President Harry S. Truman (t. 1945–1953), in contrast, insisted that the propped-up Moscow-sponsored communist regimes in Eastern Europe demonstrated Stalin's expansionist ambition in Europe and the world.

This turnaround, the revisionist maintained, was necessary to feed the myth created by Washington "of limitless communist expansion [in order] to mobilize domestic support for America's global hegemonic role".[13] In continually requesting that American citizens make sacrifices in order to defend democracy and freedom throughout the world in the face of the Soviet Union's expansionism,

> the answer lies in America's new role as *hegemon* within the capitalist world economy for which the Bretton Woods conference in July 1944 laid the groundwork. At this conference, the International Monetary Fund and the World Bank were founded as multilateral institutions designed to regulate economic challenges *under American control and guidance*. The U.S. dollar became the most important international currency and thus became a *crucial pillar* of the postwar global financial system. *The United States thus committed itself to becoming a global power well before the war ended.*[14]

Furthermore, the successful application of Fordism, or continuous-flow production (involving synchronization, precision, and specialization) across industries that made American manufacturers highly competitive in the international markets, prompted the U.S. government to adopt an interventionist foreign policy that could ensure the maintenance of safe and sustainable access to raw materials, global markets, and investment opportunities.

American anti-communism dates back to President Woodrow Wilson (t. 1913–1921), who refused to acknowledge recognition of the Soviet Union on moral grounds: "Bolshevism is a mistake and it must be resisted as all mistakes must be resisted. . . . It cannot survive because it is wrong".[15] Therefore, any leader or regime, irrespective of dictators, megalomaniacs, homicidal murderers, or oppressors, from Benito Mussolini (1883–1945), Adolf Hitler (1889–1945), and Chiang Kai-shek (1887–1957) to Rhee Syngman (1875–1965), Ferdinand Marcos (1917–1989), and Ngo Dien Diem (1901–1963), who steadfastly opposed communism were supported. Viewed from this standpoint, the 'appeasement' of Hitler at Munich (30 September 1938) by British Prime Minister Neville Chamberlain (t. 1937–1940) was not at all surprising, in fact consistent with the principle that worked towards the elimination of Bolshevism and communism to which Nazi Germany was committed.

The revisionist, therefore, blames the post-war deterioration of U.S.–USSR relations between 1945 and 1947 on Washington's leaders and government. Besides, as the sole possessor of the atomic bombs that were effectively demonstrated on Hiroshima and Nagasaki, that made the U.S. not only the instigator but also the villain of the piece of the post-war Cold War scenario.[16]

On the other hand, the post-revisionist viewpoint appears to be non-partisan, neither fault-finding nor finger-pointing at any party as the perpetrator.[17] It argued that a more impartial and realistic approach was needed to comprehend the Cold War from a *longue durée* lense, including the long-term agenda of each of the main protagonists, the United States and the Soviet Union. In a crux, the U.S. as the champion of the capitalist free market, democracy, and freedom vis-à-vis the USSR communism and planned-centralized economy and communist-totalitarianism, were like water and oil, diametrically opposite, incompatible. The ultimate goal or agenda of a world order from Washington's perspective was a free world, with the U.S. as the doyen as well as champion. To Moscow, a future world order was a communist utopia headed by the USSR as the undisputed leader. From this viewpoint, the clash between them appeared inevitable and/or even predictable, only that the latter was unable to zero in on the specific time and place of conflict.

Nonetheless, pragmatism overrode the disparate ideological and long-term aspirations of both the United States and the Soviet Union. Their wartime alliance was a temporary measure, simply a necessity of the time. Nazi Germany's invasion (22 June 1941) of the Soviet Union not only shattered the German-Soviet Nonaggression Pact (23 August 1939) but forced the latter to turn to the Western democracies, namely the United States and Britain. The United States entered the fray when Imperial Japan launched its stealth attack on Pearl Harbor on 7 December 1941. Subsequently, the Grand Alliance among the USSR, Britain, and the U.S. came to be forged.

> [But the Grand Alliance] did not consist of a long period of working together for common aims, as most successful alliances do. [Instead] It was a set of shotgun marriages brought by real need, at a time when each of them had to find help to defeat immediate threats [from Nazi Germany].[18]

The breakdown of the Grand Alliance shortly after the "immediate threats" had been averted was unsurprising given the divergent future course that the U.S. and the USSR had unilaterally chartered for themselves. In other words, "Given that both profoundly disagreed in terms of their respective images of a future world order, *conflict was inevitable*" between them.[19]

Drawing from newly accessible materials from Russian archives, post-1991 works tended to view the Cold War as an ideological struggle between capitalism and communism.[20] Moreover, in recent years, focus has shifted to other than the political, economic, and/or military aspects of the Cold War, instead on the analysis of its memory and representation, the socio-cultural perspectives from an international angle.[21]

Between Moscow and Washington

> Competing across an ideological divide symbolized by the "Iron Curtain", they sought allies, trading partners, military bases, strategic minerals, and investment opportunities in Asian, African, Middle Eastern, and Latin American countries. Diplomatic maneuvering, economic pressure, selective aid, intimidation, propaganda, assassinations, low-intensity military operations, and full-scale proxy wars were used as instruments of influence and control from about 1947 until the decline of the Warsaw Pact . . . in the late 1980s.[22]

As the chronological snapshot of momentous events in Appendix 2.1 shows, the Cold War enveloped almost all corners of the world, with notable flashpoints on the Chinese mainland, Cuba in the Caribbean, Berlin, the Korean peninsula, Eastern Europe, Malaya, Egypt, Vietnam, and Afghanistan. Before turning specifically to the island of Borneo, developments on the Asian continent, especially in East Asia and Southeast Asia, are exemplary by way of a preamble and contextualization.

East Asia

Chinese Civil War (1945–1949) and Occupied Japan

The outbreak of the Second Sino-Japanese War (1937–1945) manifested Imperial Japan's expansionist agenda. The all-out war against the Nationalist regime of Generalissimo Chiang Kai-Shek even managed to draw erstwhile rivals, the Guomindang (KMT) and the Chinese Communist Party (CCP), for a temporary truce and military alliance to address the national threat of invasion and military occupation of the fatherland. Imperial Japan was the targeted enemy that needed to be defeated. But once Imperial Japan's unconditional surrender set in, the wartime allies turned on one another for the ultimate prize, the Chinese fatherland. The Chinese Civil War (1945–1949), to a certain extent, was a dress rehearsal of more protracted proxy wars to follow during the Cold War proper. Chiang's Nationalist regime received moral and material support from the U.S. in particular and from other Western democracies. Until 1927, Moscow supported Chiang and the KMT, but following Chiang's purge in 1927 of the CCP, Mao and his comrades received moral support and material aid from the Soviet Union. But on a personal basis, Stalin was distrustful of Mao, seeing in him a potential rival.[23]

A combination of reasons led to the triumphant victory of the CCP and the disgraceful defeat of the KMT.[24] Chiang and his band of supporters fled to Taiwan. Drawn from the CCP's perspective as expressed in 1951, four pivotal causal factors decided in favour of a Communist victory, viz. "the complete rottenness and collapse of Chiang's regime", "Chiang finally deserted by American imperialism", "the CCP's subjective strength", namely the peasantry, and "aid from the Soviet Union" to the CCP.[25] In other words, Chiang's corrupt-ridden KMT had estranged itself from the people, who in turn embraced Mao and the communists as defenders and champions of the masses.

Mao Zedong at Tiananmen Square declared the People's Republic of China (PRC), commonly known as Red China or Communist China. Mao's historic pronouncement on 1 October 1949 marked the end of a century of humiliation for China and the Chinese people resulting from foreign incursions and domestic strife since the mid-nineteenth century.[26] The country was literally in tatters and the masses in dire straits; reconstruction, rehabilitation, and all-round developments literally in every sector were urgently needed in rebuilding the country.

While civil war enveloped the Chinese mainland, the unconditional surrender of Imperial Japan saw the country occupied by Allied forces, primarily U.S. military as an army of occupation headed by General Douglas MacArthur, the Supreme Commander of the Allied Powers (SCAP).[27] As a counterpart to the American occupying forces was the British Commonwealth Occupation Force (BCOF) drawn from Australia, Britain, India, and New Zealand. Demilitarization and the removal of the country's war industries were under the purview of the BCOF as well as responsible for occupation of several western prefectures.[28]

Engrossed with shame and guilt, humiliation and remorse, the Japanese people together with their emperor, Hirohito, steadfastly committed their whole self in rebuilding their nation from the ashes of war. The Yoshida Doctrine, named after Shigeru Yoshida (t. 1946–1947, 1948–1954), Japan's first post-war prime minister, was a national strategy that was wholeheartedly adopted that prioritized economics in the reconstruction of the country's domestic economy whilst the country's security was entrusted to the U.S.[29] Therefore, throughout the Cold War period, Tokyo relied heavily on Washington for defence, and in turn, tolerated U.S. military bases that dotted across the islands.

Korean War (1950–1953)

War that broke out on the Korean peninsula on 25 June 1950 had antecedents some five decades ago. Having defeated Tsarist Russia in the Russo-Japanese War (1904–1905), Imperial Japan turned Korea into its protectorate with the Ulsa Treaty (Japan–Korea Protectorate Treaty) of 1905, and thereafter, annexed the country with the penning of the Japan–Korea Annexation Treaty of 1910. Korea under colonial rule was harsh and oppressive.[30] Then a wartime meeting in Cairo (22–26 November 1943) was held to consider the Allied stance towards Imperial Japan, the fate of its colonies, and the shaping of post-war Asia. Decisions during the Cairo Conference were borne from discussions among U.S. President Franklin Delano Roosevelt, British Prime Minister Winston Churchill, and China's Generalissimo Chiang Kai-shek. It was agreed that Imperial Japan should be deprived of all the territories that it had conquered by force, notably Manchuria, Formosa (Taiwan), and the Pescadores, and shall be restored to the Republic of China, lest it (Japan) might become too powerful. Korea, on the other hand, "mindful of the enslavement of the people . . . are determined that in due course Korea shall become free and independent".[31]

At the Yalta Conference (4–11 February 1945), Roosevelt raised the issue of Korea again, proposing a 20- to 30-year trusteeship involving the United States, China, and the Soviet Union. But Soviet leader Stalin preferred a shorter mandate. No clear or concrete resolution was made on Korea then. Shortly after the atomic bombing of Hiroshima on 6 August 1945, the Soviet Red Army entered Manchuria in accordance to the agreement at Yalta that the Soviet Union would enter the war against Imperial Japan once the war ended in Europe. By then, the Truman administration was uneasy over the Soviet military advance lest it consumed the entire Korean peninsula as well as Japan. The scenario then appeared to be heading towards an apocalypse climax: Red Army advancing southward down the peninsula head-on directly towards U.S. forces proceeding northward. Interestingly, a settlement was made:

> On August 10, 1945 two young colonels, Dean Rusk and Charles Bonesteel, supervised by Brigadier General George Lincoln, working on extremely short notice, proposed the 38th parallel as the administrative line for the two armies. They used a small *National Geographic* map of Asia to decide on the 38th parallel, dividing the country approximately in half while leaving the capital Seoul under American control, a prime consideration. The two men had been unaware that forty years previous, [Imperial] Japan and [Tsarist] Russia had discussed splitting Korea along the same parallel. The officers forwarded their recommendation which was incorporated into General Order No. 1 for the administration of postwar Japan. More interested in obtaining the northern Japanese island of Hokkaido, Stalin agreed to the dividing line.[32]

Hence, the 38th Parallel divided 'North' and 'South' Korea. The former with backing from the Soviet Union established the Democratic People's Republic of Korea (DPRK), although the term 'North Korea' was, and still is, popularly used. U.S.-supported 'South Korea' was, and still is, known as the Republic of Korea (ROK). From the military standpoint, U.S. forces were withdrawn in 1949, with only a token knot of military advisers to assist the ROK Army. Meanwhile, there were thousands of Soviet Red Army personnel on the ground as trainers to the North Korean People's Army (NKPA).

At Moscow in December 1945, the U.S., UK, and the Soviet Union discussed a plan for a four-power trusteeship of Korea over a five-year period.[33] While South Koreans objected and demanded immediate independence, the Soviet Union, intended to prop up the Korean Communist Party (KCP) headed by Kim Il Sung to gain overall power, was reluctant.

Then in August 1947, the U.S. and UK together with Nationalist China revived the four-power trusteeship to facilitate Korean unification. Again, this proposed trusteeship failed to materialize owing to non-cooperation from the Soviet Union. Washington then suggested the UN oversee elections on either side of the 38th parallel divide, and subsequently the formation of a national government for the peninsula. In May 1948, South Koreans cast their ballot for representatives of a National Assembly of the new Republic of Korea. Syngman Rhee (1875–1965) was Head of State of the Provisional Government of the Republic of Korea. In July 1948, the National Assembly produced a constitution and elected Syngman Rhee as president (1948–1960). The U.S. military administration hence concluded and withdrew (late June 1949), leaving a skeletal military advisory group. Shortly thereafter, in September, the Democratic People's Republic of Korea was established, led by Kim Il Sung (1912–1994),[34] who claimed authority over all of Korea. It was Kim's ambition to helm Korean reunification that brought forth the outbreak of hostilities.

Since the early part of 1947, agitations and provocations were launched by the North Koreans to destabilize the South Korean regime. Then on 3 May 1949, they launched the first assault across the 38th parallel in the vicinity of Kaesong but were pushed back. Thereafter, during the first half of 1950, small-scale attacks and skirmishes were commonplace across the divide. Concurrently North Korean communist guerrillas' subversive activities on the island of Cheju-do spilled over to the mainland towards the end of 1948. Whether clashes across the divide or guerrilla activities, the ROK Army succeeded in facing these challenges.

Who fired the first shot?

> Whether 17th Regiment soldiers may have occupied Haeju on June 25, or even initiated the fighting on Ongjin, is still inconclusive, with the existing evidence pointing both ways. There is no evidence, however, to back up the North's claim that the South launched a general invasion; at worst there may have been a small assault across the [38th] parallel, as happened many times in 1949. Whatever transpired, the North met it with a full invasion.[35]

The three-year (25 June 1950–27 July 1953) Korean War was an all-out armed conflict that was waged on land and on sea as well as in the air over and in the vicinity of the Korean peninsula. The full invasion launched by Kim Il Sung's regime with support from the Soviet Union and the neighbouring PRC managed to capture Seoul and push UN forces into a small crook of southeast Korea, near the port-city of Pusan (Busan) (July–September 1950). A 140-mile defence line, which came to be known as the Pusan Perimeter, partially defined by the Nakdong River, appeared to be the last bulwark for UN forces. Led mainly by U.S. military forces, the UN forces comprised military personnel drawn from some 20 countries, viz. the UK, Canada, Turkey, Australia, Philippines, New Zealand, Thailand, Ethiopia, Greece, France, Colombia, Belgium, South Africa, the Netherlands, Luxembourg, and others. The United Nations Command (UNC) managed to drive the enemy back across the 38th parallel but stopped short of heading towards Pyongyang (September–October 1950). At this juncture, Mao Zedong unleashed the Chinese People's Volunteer Army (CPVA), a force of 200,000, that entered North Korea on 25 October.[36]

The initial year (1950) witnessed a pendulum-like struggle for domination of the peninsula. Thereafter, another two years of positional warfare took place as a background to extended ceasefire negotiations. The armistice negotiations were characterized by its 'on-again, off-again' peace talks. Finally, the Korean Armistice Agreement was concluded on 27 July 1953 among all belligerents, namely the UNC, Korean People's Army (KPA), and the CPVA. The Armistice was *merely a ceasefire agreement* that established the Korean Demilitarized Zone (DMZ), a *de facto* new border between the two nations that runs close to the 38th parallel, and finalized repatriation of prisoners of war (POWs). Until today, since no peace resolution was ever finalized, technically both Koreas remain at war with one another.

Undoubtedly the Korean War was the Cold War's first 'hot' war, a semi-proxy war. Washington's direct involvement, with commitment of ground combat troops with naval and aerial support under the umbrella of the UNC that it led, fought alongside their ally the ROK Army. The entry of the PVA, with full blessing of the Soviet Union, on the side of the KPA 'balanced' the seesaw between the opposing parties.

The turmoil in East Asia within a short lull following Imperial Japan's unconditional surrender thus set the stage for the Cold War in this part of the world. Much was to unfold as the focus shifted to another corner of Asia, its southeast realm. A revolution, an emergency, a rebellion, a conference, and a war summed up the forthcoming 'acts' on the Cold War stage in Southeast Asia. Having cognizance of the surrounding happenings allows a better grasp of the internal situation in Borneo during this Cold War era, contextualizing from within against the background from without.

Southeast Asia

In emerging, underdeveloped nation-states, collectively referred to as the Third World, whether in Asia, Africa, or Latin America, then undergoing the throes of decolonization, the major Cold War protagonists, each in their respective ways and means, sought to entice these nations over to their camp.

Blood, tears, and triumph: Indonesian Revolution (1945–1949)

The Indonesian Revolution (1945–1949), which has been touched in some details in the preceding chapter, is here viewed from the global Cold War scenario. The post-war scenario across the vast Indonesian archipelago saw the returning Dutch attempting in the fastest manner the reinstatement of their pre-war colonial regime, namely the Netherlands East Indies. But in Java, the main island, the Dutch did not expect to confront a *Republik Indonesia* replete with most apparatus of a nation-state. Consequently, the Dutch sought to offer the federal-based United States of Indonesia (USI) as an alternative to the unitary *Republik Indonesia Serikat* (RIS, Republic of the United States of Indonesia [RUSI]).

Meanwhile, from amongst Indonesians themselves, the *Partai Komunis Indonesia* (PKI) strongly urged Republican leaders to seek assistance from the Soviet Union against the Dutch imperialist. The PKI expressed its pro-Soviet stance:

> The Soviet Union is an indispensable ally of the Indonesian people against imperialism, for the Soviet Union is the vanguard of the struggle against

the imperialist bloc, which is led by the United States. It is clear enough that the United States is helping and making use of the Netherlands to smash our democratic Republic . . . that Soviet recognition [of the Republic] is unmixed blessing, for the Soviet Union as a workers' state cannot have other than an *anti-imperialist* standpoint. The Soviet Union therefore has no interests as regards Indonesia other than helping it in its anti-imperialist struggle.[37]

On 18 September 1948, pro-PKI troops in the city of Madiun were ordered by the Republican government to demobilize, but instead they revolted and together with the Indonesian Socialist Party (PSI) declared a National Front government known as the Indonesian Soviet Republic. This declaration drew PKI leaders including Musso (1897–1948), Amir Sjarifuddin (1907–1948), and others to Madiun to lend their support. Madiun, about 120 kilometres slightly to the southwest of Jogjakarta, the capital of the Republican government, could be the rallying point for PKI and its sympathizers against the Sukarno-Hatta clique that appeared to be the lackeys of Imperial Japan and the U.S.[38] But poor organization easily led to its suppression by Republican forces within a month; most of the participants including Musso were killed in the backlash.

The Madiun Affair,[39] as the aforesaid events came to be known, made the Republican government a worthwhile cause to support, as its anti-communist stance clearly placed it in the U.S. camp. Initially, where stood Sukarno and his Republican government in the Cold War scenario was unclear, but Madiun established decisively their stance, and subsequently drew political currency from the suppression of the PKI.

Impatient with progress, the Dutch employed strong-arm tactics to press their ambition, notably launching the Second 'Police Action' (19 December 1948) that, instead of accomplishing their ultimate objective of eliminating the *Republik* through the detention of its core leaders, viz. Sukarno, Mohamad Hatta, and Sutan Sjahrir (president, vice president, and prime minister, respectively), brought forth the intervention of the U.S. and the UN.

Dean Acheson,[40] undersecretary of state since 1945, assumed the position of U.S. Secretary of State on 21 January 1949. Convinced of the anti-communist stance of the Republican government, Acheson pressed the Netherlands government to the negotiating table. As a result of pressure from Washington, as well as general concern of the world community, the UN Security Council on 28 January 1949 passed 'Resolution 67' calling for an end to the Dutch military offensive against Republican forces in Indonesia and demanded that the Republican government be restored. The UN strongly urged that both parties resumed talks to seek a peaceful settlement. Subsequently, the Round Table Conference was held at The Hague between 23 August and 2 November 1949. A settlement was attained. Sovereignty was formally transferred on 27 December 1949, and the new state – *Republik Indonesia Serikat* (RIS, Republic of the United States of Indonesia [RUSI]) – received formal recognition by the U.S.

Winning hearts and minds: Malayan Emergency
(1948–1960, 1968–1989)

The Malayan Communist Party (MCP)[41] sought to overthrow the government of the day, from the British colonial administration (1948–1957), government of independent Malaya (1957–1963), to the Malaysian government (from 1963). This armed insurrection played out in two stages that came to be referred to as the Malayan Emergency (1948–1960) and the Second Malayan Emergency (1968–1989).[42] Military resources and personnel from the British Commonwealth – Australia, New Zealand, the UK, and Fiji – lent support in suppressing the insurgency. They continued their participation and contribution even after *merdeka* (independence).[43] Confidently, Malayan Prime Minister Tunku Abdul Rahman Putra Al-Haj (t. 1957–1963) declared the end of the conflict in 1960. But in less than a decade, the struggle was revived, viz. the Second Malayan Emergency. On both counts, the communist insurgents[44] were defeated and forced further inland into the thick jungle. A score of hard-core communists led by Secretary General Chin Peng (t. 1947–1988) took refuge in the hilly and forested borderlands on the Thai-Malaysia boundary where the Thai authorities were apparently much more tolerant.

The MCP's primary intention was to overthrow the incumbent government, and in its place, established a communist republic aligned with Beijing that had provided moral support as well as material aid since the 1950s. The pro-Beijing stance was as much as of ethnic comraderies as of ideological orientation. Ethnic Chinese formed the backbone of MCP membership with a handful of Malays and Indians. MCP supporters and sympathizers were also Chinese, where many, despite in the diaspora, possessed and maintained close affinity with the fatherland. On the government side – British Malaya, independent Malaya, Malaysia – alliances were forged with the U.S. and other Western democracies. Tunku was pro-British and staunchly anti-communist, and had no qualms in crushing the MCP. At the Baling Talks (1955), Tunku flatly refused to recognize the MCP as a legitimate political organization, hence the meeting failed, and Chin Peng and his colleagues returned to the jungle to continue the struggle.

A combination of military action, deprivation and collective punishment, propaganda and psychological warfare in 'winning the hearts and minds' of the masses, engaging the Orang Asli, and Briggs' Plan of resettlement collectively managed to turn the tide against the MCP. Conventional warfare was eschewed by the MCP fighters, who prudently waged a guerrilla jungle war that they had honed during the wartime Japanese occupation.[45] Malayan police and British army together with military personnel from Australia, New Zealand, and Fiji engaged in deadly 'hide-and-seek' games in the tropical jungle, outsmarting and outmanoeuvring one another. Meanwhile concerted efforts in 'winning the hearts and minds' of the multiethnic population were undertaken in earnest; this psychological war was as important as the jungle skirmishes and battles engaged by military forces with the guerrillas.[46] The latter, who had since the wartime period enticed the Orang Asli, the aboriginal peoples, to assist in terms of foodstuff, routes through the jungle maze, and intelligence, again revived their relationships for survival. But government material aid to the Orang Asli increasingly denied the guerrillas their traditional helpers. Likewise, the removal of squatter settlers, mainly of Chinese peasant farmers from the jungle fringes to 'New Villages', denied the guerrillas their major sources of recruits, foodstuffs, medicines, and intelligence. Again, Chinese farmers who lent the MCP assistance were as much persuaded by common ethnicity rather than by ideological appeal.

Whether in the initial insurgency (1948–1960) or the second (1968–1989) outing, the MCP was decisively unsuccessful largely because of their inability to win over non-Chinese participants, sympathizers, or supporters. No less than a score of Malays and Indians joined the side of the MCP. Failure to garner non-Chinese recruits and/or support was pivotal in the MCP's struggle. MCP propaganda of marginalization, neglect, or 'hollow' independence was countered by government development projects that effectively raised the socio-economic status of rural peoples. Tunku's unqualified success in attaining *merdeka* declared on 31 August 1957 proved MCP claims of fighting an anti-imperialistic war to be false. *Merdeka*, in effect, won over the people's 'hearts and minds'.

Development, especially in the rural areas, was the Malaysian government's main thrust in addressing the second insurgency phase (1968–1989), namely *Program Keselamatan dan Pembangunan* (KESBAN; Security and Development Programme). In combining security and development, KESBAN produced concrete benefits in the alleviation of poverty, through infrastructure developments ranging from supplying piped water and electricity to construction of schools and clinics and hospitals that directly benefitted the multiethnic population, especially in rural areas. In short, security and stability provided the ambience for economic development, leading to improved overall prosperity amongst the populace that in turn succeeded in denying the MCP all forms of support.

At the same time, the Orang Asli Senoi Praaq Regiment, hitherto a unit of its own, was formally incorporated into the Royal Malaysian Police in September 1974.[47] This official recognition was indeed an invaluable boost to morale. Headquartered in Kroh, Perak, the Senoi Praaq was expanded with a full battalion created based in Bidor. As jungle trackers who knew the jungle like the back of their hand, they managed to outmanoeuvre the MCP guerrillas.

The Malayan Emergency was undoubtedly one of the first of the Cold War's proxy wars. Beijing, then an ally of the Soviet Union, supported the MCP's anti-imperialist struggle against the British colonial administration, thereafter following *merdeka* (in 1957), the independent Malayan government, and from 1963, the Malaysian government. From the colonial administration to the Malaysian government, support came from the UK, a staunch ally of the U.S. The MCP's failure owed to its inability to garner support from the multiethnic population, even amongst the Chinese, but it also failed due to various political alternatives, viz. the Malayan/Malaysian Chinese Association (MCA),[48] People's Action Party (PAP), Democratic Action Party (DAP),[49] and *Gerakan Rakyat Malaysia* (Gerakan; Malaysian People's Movement).[50]

'Agreement Between the Government of Malaysia and the Malayan Communist Party to Terminate Hostilities', or simply the Peace Agreement of Hat Yai, was signed on 2 December 1989 and ratified by the MCP, and the governments of Malaysia and Thailand effectively ended the second phase of the communist insurgency in Malaysia (1968–1989). Thereafter, the MCP was dissolved, and its former members were resettled across the border.

Struggle for socio-economic reforms: Hukbalahap Rebellion (1946–1954)

The Hukbalahap Rebellion (1946–1954) was a Filipino peasant revolt against the independent Philippines Republic. *Hukbalahap* or *Hukbo ng Bayan Laban sa Hapon* (People's Army against the Japanese) was initially organized as an armed guerrilla force against the IJA, which was then occupying the Philippines. Despite admiring the Chinese Red Army fighting in the Sino-Japanese War, Huk leaders remained steadfast to Marxist-Leninist doctrines and fought the fascist IJA, who had treated the Filipino peasantry harshly. The wartime anti-Japanese armed struggle was successful to the extent that Huk leaders could build a functioning democracy in Huk areas, whereby social and economic reforms were implemented for the benefit of the peasantry. Land rents were abrogated and pro-Japanese landlords were executed as collaborators. Huk wartime activities and successes forewarned the U.S. armed forces and Filipino politicians that they were a force to reckon with in the post-war era.

When the government of the Commonwealth of the Philippines was re-established following the surrender of Imperial Japan, U.S. Army and anti-communist Filipino guerrillas apprehended Huks, charging them with subversion, murder, or being communist. In February 1945, rival guerrilla groups slaughtered more than 100 Huks in Malolos, Bulacan. Nonetheless, in the post-war election for the Philippine Congress, Luis Taruc (1913–2005) and Jesus Lava (1914–2003) contested under a Huk ticket. Their campaign manifesto was socio-economic reforms and strong opposition to granting the U.S. parity rights in the exploitation of natural resources in the country. Both won but were denied their seats. Then when one of the Huk leaders was kidnapped and allegedly murdered, Taruc declared opposition against the government in Manila. At this juncture a new name was adopted, viz. *Hukbong Mapagpalaya ng Bayan* (HMB, People's Liberation Army). Between 1946 and 1954, the Huks fought against the government; the latter in turn declared HMB an illegal organization. From central Luzon, the Huk rebellion spread to the Visayas and Mindanao.

The fear of the Huks was not so much as their struggle for socio-economic reforms, a peasant-landlord dispute, but to their leanings towards the Soviet brand of communism. It was also unclear if the Huks received material aid from the Soviet Union in their armed opposition to the Manila government, and if so, it was an apparent proxy war that Moscow was involved. It appeared then that U.S. intelligence were feeding Manila a diet of information implicating complicity of the Soviet Union with the Huks.[51]

On the Philippine government side, various strategies and tactics were employed in countering the Huks from President Manuel Roxas' (t. 1946–1948) tough military offensive, President Elpidio Quirino's (t. 1948–1953) olive branch of amnesty in June 1948, to Secretary of National Defense Ramon Magsaysay's (t. 195o-1953) unconventional strategy in combating the Huk guerrillas. Hitherto the Philippine Army was perceived as distrustful, feared, and even with indifference from the wider populace. But in utilizing soldiers in distributing various forms of aids and relief materials to isolated villages and marginalized communities, the image of the army immediately had a facelift. As president (t. 1953–1957), Magsaysay's agrarian reform that included offering land to landless peasants, providing availability of rural credit, and initiating vast irrigation projects collectively brought relief, hope, and improved well-being of the rural peoples. At the same time, government efforts debunked Huk propaganda of alleged neglect and marginalization of rural communities. On the part of the Huks, their seemingly merciless treatment of the peasantry that did not acquiesce to their cause and internal struggles from within led to their downfall. By 1954 when Taruc surrendered to the authorities, the Huk threat had subsided. Many Huks had also surrendered following the outlawing of the HMB from 17 June 1957.

The following indictment of the Philippines' chief ally, the U.S., is not only revealing but also underscores the indifference and revealed the many oversights in addressing the rebellion:

> Without American economic and military assistance to the Philippine governments after 1950, the Huks might well have succeeded in their rebellion. But . . . U.S. neglect and short sighted helped put the government in jeopardy. Before 1950, U.S. policy makers concentrated their attentions on Europe, were tired of war in the Pacific, and seemed blind to the many problems that tore at the islands. The land-tenure question had been present since the days the nation became an American protectorate and very little had been done to ease its burden on the Filipino farmer. Although land-tenure was a major factor in the years preceding WWII, after the war, U.S. policy ignored it and was intent on divestiture of responsibility for the islands.
>
> Economic aid was made available to the government after the war but the programs were poorly managed and did little other than increase the size of many Filipino elite's bank balances. . . . American foreign policy makers simply did not understand Filipino concerns and aspirations and therefore chose to ignore them. Many incisive and worthwhile reports on conditions in the Philippines . . . went unheeded until the government in Manila nearly fell in 1950.
>
> Luckily, once the American government realized how close to collapse the Quirino administration was in 1950, Washington reacted.[52]

Neither East nor West: Bandung (1955)

A week-long (18–24 April 1955) deliberation amongst 29 Asian and African nations at Bandung, Indonesia set the momentum that subsequently led to the establishment of the Non-Aligned Movement (NAM). *Konferensi Asia-Afrika* or

Asian–African Conference, also popularly known as the Bandung Conference, was a gathering of mainly newly independent Asian and African nations that had tasted the bitter colonial experience and hence collectively and roundly opposed colonialism, neither East nor West. The major concerns of the delegates that were tabled for open discussions *inter alia* political self-determination (or the independence struggle), mutual respect for sovereignty, non-aggression, non-interference in internal affairs, and equality amongst sovereign states.

The Conference closing communique set out several concrete and practical objectives, viz.:

> the promotion of economic and cultural cooperation, protection of human rights and the principle of self-determination, a call for an end to racial discrimination wherever it occurred, and a reiteration of the importance of peaceful coexistence . . . the potential for collaboration among the nations of the third world, promoting efforts to reduce their reliance on Europe and North America.[53]

Jointly sponsored by Burma, India, Indonesia, Pakistan, and Sri Lanka, the newly independent nations of the Third World came together to express solidarity with one another in the hope that each could avoid being forced or bounded to support either camp in the bipolar Cold War setting. But amongst the Asian–African leaders, there were great diversities in backgrounds and experiences, concerns and aspirations, prejudices and predispositions, personalities, attitudes, and idiosyncrasies.[54] Nonetheless, the Bandung Conference became a harbinger for the establishment of NAM at the gathering in Belgrade in 1961.

The long, long war: Vietnam (1946–1955, 1955–1975)

Across the South China Sea westwards is a narrow strip of land hugging the Asian continent, like a long fence enclosing within known as Indochina. The narrow strip is today what is officially known as the Socialist Republic of Vietnam. But throughout the greater part of the second half of the twentieth century, Vietnam was a partition country perennially at war for more than three decades. From the mid-nineteenth century, Vietnam under the Nguyen dynasty was gradually absorbed as colonial territories in realization of the French Emperor Napoleon III's (r. 1852–1870) pursuit of 'a place in the sun', aspiration of a colonial empire vis-à-vis other European powers. Subsequently, on the eve of the Pacific War (1941–1945), French Indochina comprised the Colony of Cochin-China, the protectorates of Annam and Tonkin, and of Cambodia and Laos. Vichy signed the Protocol Concerning Joint Defense and Joint Military Cooperation on 29 July 1941 with Imperial Japan, whereby Hanoi and Saigon were ceded to the latter, and towards the end of 1941, control across French Indochina. From the Vietnamese coastal base of Cam Ranh Bay, the IJA launched an amphibious invasion of Hong Kong, Malaya, Singapore, and Borneo in concert with the stealth attack of the IJN on Pearl Harbor in the mid-Pacific on 7 December 1941.

Aggravating wartime conditions, a combination of causes from crop failures, delinquency in the maintenance of dikes and damages owing to U.S. bombing, and unusually heavy rainfall (August-September 1944) that inundated rice fields and losses all compounded to bring forth a severe famine to the northern part of Vietnam from October 1944 to May 1945. The death toll ranged between a conservative quarter of a million to two million people.[55] It was a prelude for much more woes and sufferings about to unfold on the Vietnamese masses.

When Imperial Japan pronounced its unconditional surrender in August 1945, within a short time, Vietnamese revolutionary leader Ho Chi Minh (1890–1969) declared on 2 September 1945 the Declaration of Independence of Vietnam, pronouncing the birth of the Democratic Republic of Vietnam. But independence was denied as British and Nationalist Chinese troops that entered Vietnam helped the returning French to reinstate their colonial regime.

Before 1949, the U.S. appeared to be partial towards the Việt Minh and rather apprehensive of the imperialist French and the reinstatement of their colonial empire over Vietnam and Indochina. But Mao's proclamation of the People's Republic of China in October 1949 made Washington re-consider its stance of the Việt Minh and Ho Chi Minh in a communist cloak (possibly a gift from Beijing) rather than his nationalist cotton garment. The U.S. viewpoint was from a wider geopolitical perspective. Therefore, although anti-imperialist in nature, the U.S. much preferred a re-instatement of French colonial rule over Indochina rather than a communist alternative, initially a communist-ruled Vietnam might also dominate Laos and Cambodia. U.S. President Harry Truman was distrustful of Ho Chi Minh and the Việt Minh, which were outwardly nationalist but inwardly communist. Hence, by 1947, Washington was putting its bet on France, from an initial USD$160 million in 1954 to USD$3 billion in 1957.[56]

By December 1945, the lines were drawn; on one side was the French colonial military force, the *Corps Expeditionnaire Francais en Extreme-Orient* (CEFEO, French Far-East Expeditionary Corps), and on the other was the *Việt Minh* (*Việt Nam Độc Lập Đồng Minh Hội*, League for the Independence of Vietnam). Established in May 1941, the Việt Minh was a nationalist coalition formed at Pác Bó by Ho Chi Minh. The First Indochina War (December 1946 to August 1954) had commenced. Its proceedings were aptly described by Ho Chi Minh utilizing a tiger–elephant dueling analogy:

> If the tiger [Việt Minh] ever stands still, the elephant [French] will crush him with his mighty tusks. But the tiger will not stand still. He will leap upon the back of the elephant, tearing huge chunks from his side, and then he will leap back into the dark jungle. And slowly the elephant will bleed to death. Such will be the war in Indochina.[57]

Then at Dien Bien Phu, a former Japanese airstrip located 300 kilometres west of Hanoi close to the Laotian border, the CEFEO suffered a decisive defeat on 7 May 1954. Consequently, the French pulled out of Vietnam and Indochina. Signed on 21 July 1954, the Geneva Accords set the 17th parallel as a '*provisional* military demarcation line' between the North (Democratic Republic of Vietnam, DRV/ North Vietnam) and South (State of Vietnam, subsequently the Republic of Vietnam, RVN/South Vietnam).[58] Two implications were clear: firstly, the demarcation was not permanent, pending elections for a unified country and government scheduled for 1956, and secondly, the Accords only addressed the military issue that concluded a ceasefire to end armed hostilities and not a political settlement. An unsigned Final Declaration, Article 6, was as follows:

> The [Geneva] Conference recognizes that the essential purpose of the agreement [Geneva Accords] relating to Vietnam is to settle military questions with a view to ending hostilities and that the military demarcation line [17th Parallel] is provisional and should not in any way be interpreted as constituting a political or territorial boundary.[59]

The signatories included France, the DRV, the PRC, the Soviet Union, and the UK.[60] The last French Union forces left Vietnam on 28 April 1956, ending nine decades of colonial rule and influence.

Although the guns were silent, albeit a temporary lull, many 'unfinished businesses' remained. Firstly, despite having won a decisive victory over the French at Dien Bien Phu, Ho Chi Minh failed to see his beloved country united. It appeared to be a hollow triumph, the DRV being short-changed. Apparently, Moscow and Beijing, the principal backers of the DRV, were concerned or even feared Washington's full-scale involvement, hence they pressed Hanoi to agree to the Accords.[61] Since then, Ho Chi Minh and General Vo Nguyen Giap (1911–2013) and their comrades were determined to strive for a united Vietnamese nation.

Secondly, the State of Vietnam (South) and the U.S., both non-signatories, were steadfast in their respective stance to the Geneva Accords. The former forthrightly rejected the agreement. The Eisenhower administration (1953–1961) registered its acknowledgement of the ceasefire Accord that would "refrain from the threat or use of force to disturb them".[62] But what was troubling was President Dwight D. Eisenhower's (t. 1953–1961) statement at a press conference on the day the Accords were signed, stating that since the U.S. was not a party to the Accords, hence it was not bound by its terms that his administration could not support.[63]

The aftermath of the Accords, for all intents and purposes, led to the Second Indochina War, or better known as the Vietnam War (1955–1975). National elections scheduled for 1956 were *never* staged. RVN President Ngo Dinh Diem and U.S. President Eisenhower were convinced that Ho Chi Minh and the Việt Minh would win. Ho Chi Minh then did not press for the elections as he was preoccupied with the implementation of the collectivization policy. Moreover, abiding by the Geneva Accords, the NVA had withdrawn northwards beyond the 17th parallel, hence Hanoi was in no position to assert military pressure for the scheduled elections. Beijing then was cautious, fearing that further pressure for elections might force Washington's hand to push for a UN intervention not unlike the Korean situation. In Moscow, Soviet leader Nikita Khrushchev (1953–1964) was then preoccupied with domestic politics, consolidation of his position, and from without, instability in Poland and Hungary.[64]

Post-Geneva developments subsequently proceeded along these lines. Ho Chi Minh's regime, in pursuit of reunification, set up a political organization known as Việt Cộng, or the National Liberation Front, in South Vietnam as well as in neighbouring Cambodia. Its main objective was Vietnam's reunification through armed struggle. To this end, its militant arm was the People's Liberation Armed Forces of South Vietnam (PLAF). Its counterpart and source of support was the North Vietnamese Army (NVA), also referred to as the Vietnam People's Army (VPA). Meanwhile, U.S. military advisers continued their roles within the armed forces of South Vietnam, namely the Army of the Republic of Vietnam (ARVN), previously the Vietnamese National Army. Both sides were more than ready for a showdown, with the entire country of Vietnam and its 28 million population as the ultimate prize.[65] Significant developments in the Vietnam War (1955–1975) are presented in Appendix 2.2.

Borneo and the Cold War

Into this cauldron of revolutions, 'police actions', 'emergencies', rebellions, protracted conflicts, and conventional wars, Borneo too was party to geopolitical manoeuvrings, revolts, insurgencies, 'confrontations', and temper of violence. Despite being on the periphery of the main theatres of Cold War conflicts – Malayan Emergency (1948–1960), First Indochina War (1946–1954), Korean War (1950–1953), and Second Indochina War or Vietnam War (1955–1975) – Borneo had its share of Cold War struggles and conflicts that impacted on its four territories.

Here, Borneo is utilized as a case study to ascertain and evaluate the extent of the influence and impact of a global phenomenon (Cold War) on a peripheral territory (Borneo). At the same time, the intention is to demonstrate the independence of the Bornean players who were not proxies, satellites, or agents of Moscow, Washington, or Beijing, the 'big boys' of the Cold War, but instead, each were striving for their respective agendas, viz. attaining political ascendancy over the island, navigating the decolonization process, struggling for political independence, attempting the creation of a communist state, establishing ethnic hegemony and domination, resisting political centralization, decentralization, and democratization. Support, moral or material, from any quarter, however, was welcome as long as local agendas remained the focus and were not hijacked or sidelined.

Notes

1 It was officially known as the Treaty of Non-aggression between Germany and the Union of Soviet Socialist Republics that was penned in Moscow on 23 August 1939 by foreign ministers Joachim von Ribbentrop and Vyacheslav Molotov, respectively. See David Zabecki, *Germany at War: 400 Years of Military History* (Santa Barbara: ABC-Clio, 2014), p. 536.

2 Each of the annexed states became Soviet Socialist Republics (SSR), hence Polish People's Republic, Latvian SSR, Estonian SSR, Lithuanian SSR, Karelo-Finnish SSR, and Moldavian SSR. See Geoffrey Roberts, *Stalin's Wars: From World War to Cold War, 1939–1953* (New Haven, CT: Yale University Press, 2006), pp. 43, 55; Gerhard Wettig, *Stalin and the Cold War in Europe* (Lanham, MD: Rowman & Littlefield, 2008), p. 21; Alfred Erich Senn, *Lithuania 1940: Revolution from Above* (Amsterdam, NY: Rodopi, 2007), pp. 7–26, 85–102; William L. Shirer, *Rise and Fall of the Third Reich: A History of Nazi Germany* (New York: Simon and Schuster, 1990), p. 794.

3 See Wettig, *Stalin and the Cold War in Europe*, pp. 96–100; Ruud Van Dijk, ed., *Encyclopedia of the Cold War* (New York: Routledge, 2008), vol. 1: 200; John Ashley Soames Grenville, *A History of the World from the 20th to the 21st Century* (London: Routledge, 2005), pp. 370–371; Miranda Vickers, *The Albanians: A Modern History*, rev. ed. (London: I. B. Tauris, 2014), pp. 163–184.

4 Washington, London, or Paris, and others preferred the term 'Free World or 'Western World', and these terms were readily picked up by the media, hence gaining wide currency in usage.

5 The Warsaw Pact complemented the economic agreement that was established in 1949 known as the Council for Mutual Economic Assistance or COMECON that comprised the Soviet Union, Bulgaria, Czechoslovakia, Hungary, Poland, and Romania. The primary objective of COMECON was to strengthen the socialist relationship at an economic level between the Soviet Union and the less progressive states of Central Europe. See Robert Bideleux and Ian Jeffries, *A History of Eastern Europe: Crisis and Change* (London: Routledge, 1998), pp. 534–536.

6 David S. Yost, *NATO Transformed: The Alliance's New Roles in International Security* (Washington, DC: U.S. Institute of Peace Press, 1998), p. 31.

7 For the orthodox line, see George Keenan, *Russia and the West under Lenin and Stalin* (New York: Atlantic Monthly Press, 1961); Jeane J. Kirkpatrick, *The Withering Away of the Totalitarian State* (Washington, DC: The American Enterprise Institute [AEI] for Public Policy Research, 1990). For more recent works, see Stephen E. Ambrose, *Rise to Globalism: American Foreign Policy Since 1938*, ed. Douglas G. Brinkley, 9th ed. (New York: Penguin, 2010); Alan Brinkley, *American History: A Survey*, 13th ed. (New York: McGraw-Hill, 2008).

8 Craig Calhoun, ed., *Dictionary of the Social Sciences* (Oxford: Oxford University Press, 2002), p. 76.

9 Published by World Publishing Company, Cleveland, Ohio. See 50th Anniversary paperback edition, William Appleman Williams, *The Tragedy of American Diplomacy* (New York: W. W. Norton & Company, 2009). For recent works on similar lines of argument, for instance, see Walter LaFeber, *America, Russia and the Cold War 1945–2006*, 10th ed. (New York: McGraw-Hill Education, 2006).

10 For works by revisionists, see Joyce Kolko and Gabriel Kolko, *The Limits of Power: The World and United States Foreign Policy* (New York: Harper & Row, 1972); Gar Alperovitz, *The Decision to Use the Atomic Bomb and the Architecture of an American Myth* (New York: Knopf, 1995).

11 See Michael Ellman and S. Maksudov, "Soviet Deaths in the Great Patriotic War: A Note", *Europe-Asia Studies*, 46, 4, Soviet and East European History (1994): 671–680.

12 Glenn E. Curtis, ed., *Russia: A Country Study* (Washington: GPO for the Library of Congress, 1996). http://countrystudies.us/russia/ Accessed 5 Nov 2017.

13 Brigette H. Schulz, "Cold War", in *Encyclopedia of Violence, Peace, Conflict*, edited by Lester Kurtz (San Diego, CA: Academic Press, 1999), I: 322.

14 Ibid., pp. 321–322. Emphasis added.

15 Quoted in ibid., p. 323.

16 See Alperovitz, *The Decision to Use the Atomic Bomb*.

17 For proponents of the post-revisionist views, see John Lewis Gaddis, *The United States and the Origins of the Cold War 1941–1947* (New York: Columbia University Press,

1972), and his more recent works, *We Now Know: Rethinking Cold War History* (Oxford: Oxford University Press, 1997); *The Cold War: A New History* (London: Penguin, 2005).

18 Odd Arne Westad, *The Cold War: A World History* (New York: Hachette Book Group, 2017), p. 44.

19 Graham Evans and Jeffrey Newnham, *The Dictionary of World Politics: A Reference Guide to Concepts, Ideas and Institutions* (New York: Harvester Wheatsheaf, 1992), p. 43. Emphasis added.

20 For instance, see Vladislav Zubok and Constantine Pleshakov, *Inside the Kremlin's Cold War: From Stalin to Krushchev* (Cambridge, MA: Harvard University Press, 1997); Timothy J. White, "Cold War Historiography: New Evidence behind Traditional Typographies", *International Social Science Review*, 75, 3/4 (2000): 35–46.

21 For instance, see Konrad H. Jarausch et al., eds., *The Cold War: Historiography, Memory, Representation* (Berlin and Boston: Walter de Gruyter GmbH, 2017).

22 William A. Darity, ed., *International Encyclopedia of the Social Sciences* (Detroit, MI: Thomson Gale, 2008), II: 4.

23 See Helen Rappaport, *Joseph Stalin: A Biographical Companion* (Santa Barbara, CA: ABC-Clio, 1999), p. 36.

24 Odd Arne Westad, *Decisive Encounters: The Chinese Civil War, 1946–1950* (Stanford, CA: Stanford University Press, 2003), pp. 215–258.

25 Peng Shuzi, "The Causes of the Victory of the Chinese Communist Party over Chiang Kai-Shek, and the CCP's Perspectives", Report on the Chinese Situation to the Third Congress of the Fourth International, AugustSeptember 1951. *International Information Bulletin*, Socialist Workers Party, February 1952, from Tamiment Library microfilm archives, transcribed & marked up by Andrew Pollack. www.marxists.org/archive/peng/1951/nov/causes.htm Accessed 16 Nov 2017.

26 For instance, see Jonathan D. Spence, *The Search for Modern China*, 3rd ed. (New York: W. W. Norton & Company, 2012); Jonathan Fenby, *The Penguin History of Modern China: The Fall and Rise of a Great Power, 1850 to the Present*, 2nd ed. (London: Penguin, 2013).

27 See Seymour Morris, Jr., *Supreme Commander: MacArthur's Triumph in Japan* (New York: HarperCollins, 2014). For a personal, contemporaneous and insightful perspective, see William J. Sebald, *With MacArthur in Japan: A Personal History of the Occupation* (New York: W. W. Norton, 1965).

28 See Peter Bates, *Japan and the British Commonwealth Occupation Force 1946–52* (Lincoln, NE: Potomac Books Inc., 1994).

29 For instance, see Aaron Forsberg, *America and the Japanese Miracle: The Cold War Context of Japan's Postwar Economic Revival, 1950–1960* (Chapel Hill, NC: University of North Carolina Press, 2000).

30 See Carter J. Eckert et al., *Korea Old and New: A History* (Seoul: Ilchokak Publishers for Korea Institute, Harvard University, 1990), pp. 260–275, 306–326. Also, see Hildi Kang, *Under the Black Umbrella: Voices from Colonial Korea, 1910–1945* (Ithaca, NY: Cornell University Press, 2001).

31 First Cairo Conference, 1943. Communique Released Dec 1, 1943. www.loc.gov/law/help/us-treaties/bevans/m-ust000003-0858.pdf Accessed 17 Nov 2017.

32 Division of Korea. New World Encyclopedia. www.newworldencyclopedia.org/entry/Division_of_Korea Accessed 17 Nov 2017.

33 Nationalist China was the fourth trustee.

34 Kim held the posts of premier (1948–1972) and thence president (1972–1994).

35 Bruce Cumings, *The Korean War: A History* (New York: Modern Library, 2011), p. 10.

36 Barbara Barnouin and Yu Changgeng, *Zhou Enlai: A Political Life* (Hong Kong: Chinese University Press, 2006), pp. 147–148. The CPVA was in fact the People's Liberation Army's (PLA) North East Frontier Force (NEFF). Fearing an official war with the U.S., the CPVA was separately constituted.

37 Ruth T. McVey, *The Soviet View of the Indonesian Revolution: A Study in the Russian Attitude towards Asian Nationalism* (Jakarta and Kuala Lumpur: Equinox Publishing, 2009), p. 86.

38 See Theodore Friend, *Indonesian Destinies* (Cambridge, MA: The Belknap Press of Harvard University Press, 2003), p. 32.

39 See Ann Swift, *The Road to Madiun: The Indonesian Communist Uprising of 1948* (Jakarta and Kuala Lumpur: Equinox Publishing, 2010); Ruth McVey, "Early Indonesian Communism", in *Born in Fire: The Indonesian Struggle for Independence, an Anthology*, edited by Colin Ward and Peter Care (Athens, OH: Ohio University Press, 1988), pp. 22–27.

40 Dean Acheson, who played pivotal roles in designing U.S. foreign policy during the Cold War era, viz. the Truman Doctrine, Marshall Plan, and establishment of NATO, was often regarded as the primary architect of the Cold War. See Robert L. Beisner, "Patterns of Peril: Dean Acheson Joins the Cold Warriors, 1945–46", *Diplomatic History*, 20, 3 (1996): 321–355.

41 Officially the MCP was known as the Communist Party of Malaya (CPM). MCP, on the other hand, was a popular term used by the media as well as the government. Communist guerrillas were labelled 'communist terrorists' or CTs.

42 See Robert Jackson, *The Malayan Emergency* (Barnsley, UK: Pen and Sword, 2008); Noel Barber, *The War of the Running Dogs: The Malayan Emergency: 1948–1960* (New York: Weybright and Talley, 1972); Richard Clutterbuck, *Riot and Revolution in Singapore and Malaya, 1945–63* (London: Faber and Faber, 1973). For the second phase, see Ong Weichong, *Malaysia's Defeat of Armed Communism: The Second Emergency, 1968–1989* (London: Routledge, 2014); Gerry van Tonder, *Malayan Emergency* (Barnsley, UK: Pen and Sword, 2017) appears to be the most recent work. Utilizing a different approach, is Souchou Yao, *The Malayan Emergency: Essays on a Small, Distant War* (Copenhagen: Nordic Institute of Asian Studies (NIAS), 2016).

43 Set up in 1957, the Anglo-Malayan Defence Agreement (AMDA) between newly independent Malaya and the UK facilitated the continued military involvement of the latter together with Australia and New Zealand in the fight against the communist insurgency. When Malaysia was constituted in 1963, AMDA was renamed the Anglo-Malaysian Defence Agreement with similar purpose. See Chin Kin Wah, *The Defence of Malaysia and Singapore: The Transformation of a Security System, 1957–1971* (Cambridge: Cambridge University Press, 1983).

44 Initially regarded as communist 'bandits', the MCP guerrillas came to be termed 'communist terrorists' or CTs. The former label was once attributed to the Chinese communist guerrillas, hence, in order to avoid any untoward diplomatic issue with Beijing, the British colonial Malayan government dropped the brigand label.

45 The MPAJA that undertook a guerrilla war of attrition against the IJA provided invaluable experience for MCP fighters who comprised the bulk of the fighting force. The MCP, in fact, initiated the formation of the MPAJA as a means of garnering support under an anti-Japanese banner.

46 See Paul Dixon, "'Hearts and Minds'? British Counter-Insurgency from Malaya to Iraq", *Journal of Strategic Studies*, 32, 3 (2009): 353–381. www.tandfonline.com/doi/abs/10.1080/01402390902928172 Accessed 3 Dec 2017.

47 See Roy Davis Linville Jumper, *Death Waits in the "dark": The Senoi Praaq, Malaysia's Killer Elite* (Westport, CT: Greenwood Publishing Group, 2001).

48 Initially a welfare organization established in 1949 to aid settlers in New Villages, thereafter in 1951, the MCA transformed into a political party that comprised the *towkay* elite and officers from the *Guomindang* (KMT, Kuomintang).

49 Following the secession of Singapore from Malaysia on 9 August 1965, the PAP was deregistered as a political party in the country. Subsequently the DAP, successor to the PAP, was established on 11 October 1965 to continue the struggle for the principle of 'Malaysian Malaysia', namely equality of all ethnic communities without privileges and special rights to any particular ethnic group.

50 Constituted in Penang in 1968 from members of the proscribed left-leaning United Democratic Party (UDP) and the Labour Party, Gerakan positioned itself as a noncommunal political party with a multiethnic membership. It subsequently evolved into a Chinese-dominated political party with socialist leanings.

51 Benedict J. Kerkvliet, *The Huk Rebellion: A Study of Peasant Revolt in the Philippines* (Lanham, MD: Rowman & Littlefield, 2002), pp. 191–192. Also, see Geoffrey Jukes, *The Soviet Union in Asia* (Berkeley, CA: University of California Press, 1973), p. 187.

52 Lawrence M. Greenberg, *The Hukbalahap Insurrection: A Case Study of a Successful Anti-Insurgency Operation in the Philippines, 1946–1955* (Washington, DC: U.S. Army Center of Military History, 1987), pp. 147–148. https://history.army.mil/books/coldwar/huk/huk-fm.htm Accessed 23 Nov 2017.

53 "Bandung Conference (Asian-African Conference), 1955", Office of the Historian, Department of State, United States of America. https://history.state.gov/milestones/1953-1960/bandung-conf Accessed 3 Dec 2017.

54 For an insightful look, see Dipesh Chakrabathy, "The Legacies of Bandung: Decolonization and the Politics of Culture", in *Making a World after Empire: The Bandung Moment and Its Political Afterlives*, edited by Christopher J. Lee (Athens, OH: Ohio RIS Global Series, Ohio University Press, 2010), pp. 45–68.

55 Geoffrey Gunn, "The Great Vietnamese Famine of 1944–45 Revisited", *The Asia Pacific Journal*, 5, 5, 4 (Jan 24, 2011). http://apjjf.org/2011/9/5/Geoffrey-Gunn/3483/article.html Accessed 24 Nov 2017.

56 J. Llewellyn et al., "US Involvement in Vietnam", *Alpha History* http://alphahistory.com/vietnamwar/us-involvement-in-vietnam/ Accessed 25 Nov 2017.

57 Attributed to Ho Chi Minh. www.quotesinternet.com/author/minh-ho-chi/ Accessed 24 Nov 2017.

58 Commonly referred to as South Vietnam during the Vietnam War (1955–1975), this southern portion of Vietnam went through several name changes. Between 1949 and 1955, it was known as the 'State of Vietnam', a self-governing entity with a constitutional monarchy within French Indochina. Bao Dai (1913–1997), the thirteenth and last emperor (r. 1926–1945) of the Nguyễn Dynasty, was its reigning monarch (r. 1949–1955). Following the Geneva Conference (1954), non-communist Vietnam south of the 17th parallel was formally known as the 'Republic of Vietnam' (RVN) (1955–1975). The term 'South Vietnam', however, was popular and widely used within the international media circles, likewise 'North Vietnam'.

59 *The Final Declaration of The Geneva Conference: On Restoring Peace in Indochina*, 21 July 1954. https://sourcebooks.fordham.edu/mod/1954-geneva-indochina.html Accessed 25 Nov 2017.

60 At the same time, separate accords were penned by the aforesaid signatories with the Kingdom of Cambodia and the Kingdom of Laos related to Cambodia and Laos respectively. Both Cambodia and Laos gained their political independence.

61 See Fredrik Logevall, *Embers of War: The Fall of an Empire and the Making of America's Vietnam* (New York: Random House, 2014), pp. 607–609.

62 Ibid., p. 606.

63 Ibid., p. 612.

64 Khrushchev delivered his 'Secret Speech' behind closed doors to Soviet delegates to the 20th Party Congress on 25 February 1956 that, in unprecedented fashion, denounced his predecessor Stalin for shortcomings. This 'Secret Speech' provoked stirrings in Poland and ignited the Hungarian Revolution.

65 Population Division of the Department of Economic and Social Affairs of the United Nations Secretariat, World Population Prospects: the 2010 Revision, quoted in Demographics of Vietnam. https://en.wikipedia.org/wiki/Demographics_of_Vietnam#cite_note-WPP_2010-3 Accessed 25 Nov 2017.

3 British Crown Colonies of Sarawak and North Borneo

The first circle for us [Britain] is naturally the British Commonwealth and Empire, with all that that comprises. Then there is also the English-speaking world in which we, Canada, and the other British Dominions and the United States play so important a part. And finally there is United Europe. These three majestic circles are co-existent and if they are linked together there is no force or combination which could overthrow them or even challenge them. Now if you think of the three inter-linked circles you will see that we are the only country which has a great part in every one of them. We stand, in fact, at the very point of junction, and here in this Island at the centre of the seaways and perhaps of the airways also, we have the opportunity of joining them all together. If we rise to the occasion in the years that are to come it may be found that once again we hold the key to opening a safe and happy future to humanity, and will gain for ourselves gratitude and fame.[1]

Winston Churchill, 9 October 1948

Churchill's envisioned sketch of the place of Britain in the post-war world sparked of self-importance and imperialistic grandeur. The world and the peoples have changed since the worldwide conflict aptly referred to as the Second World War. Churchill, however, seemed not to have taken cognizance of a transformed world and thinking of peoples.

In northern Borneo, while the immediate post-war cession controversy engulfed the Malay community of Sarawak much to the community's disadvantage, the task of rehabilitation and reconstruction were initiated from the onset when the Crown Colonies of Sarawak and North Borneo came into being from 1 July and 15 July, respectively. North Borneo suffered much physical damage to properties, both public and private. Being situated a distance away from the various OBOE operations, Sarawak escaped as targets of bombardments as well as battlegrounds during the Australian reoccupation. The multiethnic peoples of Sarawak and North Borneo were traumatized by the wartime experiences, and all quarters overall welcomed the new status and administration.

Post-war Britain and the global scenario

When the Colonial Office (CO) assumed the administration of Sarawak and North Borneo, its agenda of governance was influenced by several considerations from within as well as threats and pressure from without. The latter came from the communist threat of an armed takeover from across the Sarawak-Kalimantan border, and during the late 1950s and early 1960s, the increasing UN emphasis that independence be given to colonies. Clement Atlee's (t. 1945–1951) post-war Labour government of Britain faced internal issues (wartime debts and depreciating currency) and challenges (the creation of a welfare state). Likewise, developments in the 1950s from without had impacts on Sarawak and North Borneo, including the Korean War (1950–1953), and shortly thereafter, the Suez Crisis (1956). The former brought into question and context of the geopolitics of the Cold War; in fact, the conflict on the Korean peninsula was the first major 'hot' war of the Cold War era. The Suez Crisis, on the other hand, exposed not only Britain's vulnerability but also its fall from grace as a world power. By then, the 'Great' in Britain had been rendered anachronistic.

Ironically, victorious Britain in the post-war period (late 1940s to the 1960s) was on the verge of bankruptcy, severely drained, and crippled by the war. If not for the timely, in fact, *crucial*, Anglo-American Loan Agreement whereby the U.S. extended a massive USD$ 3.75 billion (US$57 billion at 2015 rates) at a low 2 per cent interest rate, and an additional USD$ 1.19 billion from Canada, Britain would have literally collapsed financially.[2] There were undoubtedly 'strings', subtle at least, attached to this helping hand from Britain's distant Anglo-Saxon cousins. Nonetheless, both the U.S. and the newly established UN (October 1945) were exerting pressure on empires, the British Empire being the largest, to disengage and decolonize. Furthermore, an additional element as far as Washington was concerned was the expansion of communism, the single largest threat to the capitalist 'free' world, that had to be contained. In line with this agenda, the U.S., despite upholding anti-imperialism and anti-colonialism, for the time being, not only tolerated but lent a helping hand to London in maintaining its vast empire, that to a certain extent acted as a bulwark fending against the extending tentacles of communism.[3]

The Labour-led government of Britain had in fact started the decolonization process with India (18 July 1947) and Burma (4 January 1948), but Prime Minister Clement Attlee's (t. 1945–1951) forward-looking policy of disengagement was greatly criticized by wartime prime minister Winston Churchill. The imperialist and empire-builder, Churchill, had famously declared that he had "not become the King's First Minister [prime minister] to preside over the liquidation of the British Empire". He was determined to retain the pre-war *status quo* of colonies and empire; hence post-war efforts were to be expanded in the recolonization process, the reinstatement of colonialism, and its attendant oppression and enforced backwardness, viz. in the political, economic, and social fields. Hence, when he returned as prime minister (t. 1951–1955), Churchill 'halted', albeit temporarily, "the liquidation of the British Empire". His successor to the premiership, Anthony Eden (t. 1955–1957), failed miserably in his imperialistic goals.

Harold Macmillan's (t. 1957–1963) Conservative government revived decolonization following a seven-year hiatus with his historic 'Wind of Change' speech to the South Africa Parliament on 3 February 1960 in Cape Town:

The *wind of change* is blowing through this [African] continent, and whether we like it or not, this growth of national consciousness is a political fact. We must all accept it as a fact, and *our national policies must take account of it*.[4]

Cold War politics was undoubtedly one of the major determinants in Macmillan wishing to dismantle the empire at an increasing pace. Decolonization by metropolitan Britain could to a great extent pre-empt nationalist leaders and movements in turning to communism, Moscow in particular and also Beijing, in pursuit of independence.[5] At the same time, the U.S. sought decolonization in order to exploit alternate sources of raw materials and new markets.[6]

Accordingly, Britain launched a policy of disengagement through negotiations, the pen for the rifle, from its colonies when a stable, non-communist government was in place to hand over sovereignty and political power. The 1960s witnessed the granting of independence to some 27 former colonies in Asia, Africa, and the Caribbean, altogether an unprecedented phenomenon in the annals of history. Malaya, excluding Singapore, obtained *merdeka* (independence) on 31 August 1957, five months later than the Gold Coast Colony (Ghana) attaining its independence (6 March 1957).

Against this backdrop of decolonization, Sarawak and North Borneo came under the wing of a progressive-minded Britain albeit for a brief 'imperialist' interregnum (1951–1957) during the premierships of Churchill and Eden. Prime Minister Eden's misadventure in the Middle East (West Asia), intending to turn the clock back to its imperial setting, backfired with implications across the British Empire. But before turning to Eden's Suez debacle, the Korean War vis-à-vis Sarawak and North Borneo needs some comments in setting the background.

Notwithstanding the political and military instability that the conflict on the Korean peninsula brought forth in the early 1950s and the untold human sufferings from the ravages of war, the economic demands for strategic raw materials created boom times for Sarawak and North Borneo, both producers then of commodities (rubber, pepper, petroleum). Owing to fresh recollections of the problematic supply situation and acute shortages of industrial materials during the Second World War (1939–1945), global insecurity pushed up commodity prices. A widespread build-up of strategic inventories pressured demand and pushed up prices. War operations of the belligerents in the conflict over the Korean peninsula in turn spurred economic growth and industrial output. Therefore, between the onset of the Korean War to the latter part of 1952, there was a surge in Sarawak and North Borneo's exports, particularly pronounced for rubber, pepper, and petroleum products. Although the boom was a transient phenomenon, the uptake of production for exports and foreign exchange earnings undoubtedly contributed to the strengthening of the economy.

The Suez Crisis (1956), on the other hand, on hindsight was construed as Downing Street's miscalculation and misreading of U.S. President Dwight D. Eisenhower's (t. 1953–1961) stance on the issue vis-à-vis the then geopolitical situation. In retaliation to Egyptian President Gamal Abdel Nasser's (t. 1956–1970) anti-imperialistic policy of the nationalization of the Suez Canal Company (SCC) on

26 July 1956, an Anglo-French entity that owned and operated the passageway since its construction in 1869, as an instrument to perpetuate their colonial influence and domination of the region, Britain, France, and Israel secretly conspired on a military plan to reinstate and assert their respective agendas. Nasser intended the nationalization to fund his Aswan dam project to irrigate the Nile valley, hence boosting Egypt's economy. Notwithstanding Cairo's commitment to economic compensation for SCC, in October 1956, the conspirators, notably British Prime Minister Eden, joined his French and Israeli counterparts Guy Mollet (t. 1956–1957) and David Ben-Gurion (t. 1955–1963) at a clandestine meeting at Sèvres near Paris, whereby they agreed on a concerted military action against Nasser's Egypt.[7]

Each came with their respective concerns and motives. Mollet was troubled with Nasser's support for the Algerian nationalists, namely the *Front de Libération Nationale* (FLN, [Algerian] National Liberation Front), and feared the possibility of intervention on the latter's behalf. The nationalists' revolt threatened a million French residents in the country. Ben-Gurion felt threatened by Cairo's rearmament and border skirmishes, and in turn, was negotiating arms including aircrafts from Paris.

Eden, on his part, had a direct hand in Anglo-Egyptian affairs since the early 1950s when the nationalist upsurge then had threatened British interests, lives, and properties. In July 1952, General Mohammed Neguib (as inaugural president of the republic, t. 1953–1954) seized power, dethroning King Farouk. The latter had just dismissed Prime Minister Mostafa el-Nahhas Pasha (t. 1950–1952), who had revoked the Anglo-Egyptian Treaty of 1936. Instead of reinstating Pasha, then British Foreign Secretary Eden attempted to negotiate a new agreement with President Neguib. On 19 October 1954, a treaty was signed between then Premier Nasser and Anthony Nutting, British minister of state for foreign affairs.[8] This seven-year agreement (1954–1961) maintained that British troops were to be withdrawn from Egypt by June 1956; British military bases were to be jointly managed by British and Egyptian civilian technicians. While Egypt agreed to respect the freedom of navigation through the Canal by all nations, there was an understanding that British troops would be allowed to return to defend the Canal when threatened by a third party.

But in November 1954, President Neguib was forced to resign, making way for the elevation of Nasser as president. When the last British troops left Egypt, Nasser was finalizing procurement of Soviet-made aircrafts, tanks and arms from Czechoslovakia, which might help him to realize one of his major goals, the destruction of Israel. Washington was particularly concerned over this arms transaction.

In January 1956, Washington and London had pledged funding to help finance Nasser's High Dam project at Aswan. But by mid-July, Cold War fear clouded decision-making. Consequently, both sponsors backtracked on their initial promise. Eisenhower's administration was uneasy over Nasser's rearmament drive, especially with Soviet arms. By then, British Prime Minister Eden too was concerned that Nasser might be crossing over to Moscow's camp. At the same time, the World Bank also withdrew its earlier promise of advancing USD$ 200 million to Cairo. It was apparently the proverbial last straw for Nasser, who proceeded with the nationalization of the SCC, justifying that the revenue from the Canal would be channelled to fund his dam project.

The outcome of the clandestine meeting was the Protocol of Sèvres, whereby Israel shall launch an attack on Egypt, thereby furnishing the pretext (under the Anglo-Egyptian Treaty of 1954) for an Anglo-French invasion of Suez. The play was well-staged, and all actors acted according to the prescribed script. The reception from the audience, however, was unanticipated.

According to the tripartite invasion plan, Israel launched a military assault on Egyptian Sinai on 29 October 1956. Promptly, London and Paris issued a joint ultimatum for a ceasefire but conveniently disregarded Tel Aviv. Consequently, the latter's pre-planned snub facilitated British and French paratroopers landing along the Suez Canal on 5 November. Despite being defeated, Egypt's forces managed to block and deny all shipping on the Canal. From the military standpoint, the seizure of parts of Sinai, Gaza Strip, and Port Said, and the northern sector of the Canal itself, was an unqualified accomplishment.[9] But politically, it was disastrous. The military action was roundly criticized and condemned by the international community that applied diplomatic pressure in demanding immediate withdrawal.

Eisenhower's hands were tied. On the one hand, he could not point the accusing finger at Moscow intervening in Hungary, while on the other hand condoning the actions of Tel Aviv, London, and Paris in Egypt. It would certainly be a case of double standards. If Washington showed support for the Anglo-French-Israeli action, it might give a wrong signal to the Arab states, and they in turn might turn to Moscow. Timing was uncanny, *as if staged*, between the aggressors. On 4 November, Soviet armoured forces rolled into Budapest; the following day, 5 November, Anglo-French paratroopers occupied the northern end of the Suez Canal.

Consequently, Eisenhower demanded an immediate withdrawal from the aggressors, to the extent of threatening Britain with financial repercussion in the event that part of the U.S.-held Sterling Bond was sold that would lead to the devaluation of the pound.[10]

On 2 November, the UN General Assembly adopted the U.S. proposal that called for an immediate ceasefire, the withdrawal of all forces behind the armistice lines, an arms embargo from all quarters, and the reopening of the Suez Canal, which was then blocked by Egyptian forces. By 22 December, the Anglo-French Task Force withdrew and was replaced by Colombian and Danish personnel of the United Nations Emergency Force (UNEF). The Israelis withdrew from the Sinai in March 1957, but prior to departure, executed a systematic destruction of the infrastructure (roads, railroads, and communications lines). The Suez Canal was again operational to international shipping from 24 April 1957.

As far as Britain was concerned, the Suez Crisis brought about the resignation of Eden as prime minister and the elevation of his colleague in the Conservative Party, Harold Macmillan (t. 1957–1963). The unshackling of colonial relations across the British Empire took on a hastened pace under Macmillan's stewardship, particularly pronounced following his pivotal 'Wind of Change' speech (3 February 1960).

"There is little doubt", a commentator of the liberal broadsheet, *The Guardian*, recalled of the Suez Crisis, "that the end of the imperial era was greatly accelerated by the squalid little war in Egypt".[11] Fifty years since, *The Economist* handed down a scathing verdict:

> The British were hurt most by [the] Suez [Crisis]. [Prime Minister] Eden resigned soon afterwards, his health wrecked, his reputation in tatters, his lies and evasions damaging the country's always tendentious reputation for fair play. The crisis exploded Britain's lingering imperial pretensions, and hastened the independence of its colonies. . . . The major lesson of Suez for the British was that the country *would never be able to act independently of America again.* Unlike the French, who have sought to lead Europe, most British politicians have been content to play second fiddle to America.[12]

The debacle at Suez marked the dawn of a new era, a shifting of the loci of power in the world. Since then, Britain had to be content to withdraw further backstage.

A caretaker government: the agenda of the Colonial Office (CO) administration

The post-war temper of the times was for imperialist powers such as Britain, France, and others to disengage and dismantle their respective colonial empires and possessions. The Suez Crisis (1956) had shown that Britain, like the other imperial powers, still harboured pretentions of 'continuity' of empire, rather than disengagement and withdrawal. Pressing circumstances, however, had witnessed Britain granting independence to India and Burma shortly after the war; mayhem and slaughter following partition (Hindu India and Muslim Pakistan) in the former, and a determined 'closed door' to the outside world in the latter. Decolonization at this early stage appeared not at all auspicious in outcome.

In the context of Sarawak and North Borneo, were there indications, covert as well as overt, of 'continuity', a reluctance to withdrawal, a lingering intention for extending their welcome? Was there a hidden agenda to prolong the 'continuity' of empire? Or did sincerity predominate and noble actions encompassed efforts in preparation for subsequent self-government, a prelude to full independence when circumstances deem propitious and/or agreeable?

When CO assumed the reins of administration of Sarawak and North Borneo, it was clearly a case of a 'caretaker government' role. The UN Charter, specifically 'Chapter XI: Declaration Regarding Non-Self-Governing Territories – Articles 73 and 74', clearly outlined the guidelines for the task ahead in terms of governance and political development (Appendix 3.1). Specific to Sarawak, there was the 'Nine Cardinal Principles of the Rule of the English Rajah' (Appendix 3.2) that originally appeared as a Preamble to Order No. C-21 (Constitution), 1941.[13]

Chapter XI Article 73 of the UN Charter emphasized to the governing authority (CO in the case of Sarawak and North Borneo) "which have or assume responsibilities for the administration of territories whose peoples have not yet attained a full measure of self-government [to] *recognize the principle that the interests of the inhabitants of these territories are paramount*".[14] This principle that prioritizes "the interests of the inhabitants of these territories are paramount" was in fact consistent with predecessor regimes of Sarawak and North Borneo, namely the Brooke White Rajahs and the British North Borneo Chartered Company (BNBCC),[15] respectively. James Brooke, the first White Rajah, reminded his successors that, "Sarawak belongs to the Malays, the Sea Dayaks, the Kayans, and other tribes; not to us. *It is for them that we labour*; not ourselves".[16] The BNBCC, likewise, in accordance to its Royal Charter (1881) *inter alia*,

> shall not in any way interfere with the religion of any class or tribe of the people of [North] Borneo, or of any of the inhabitants thereof.
>
> In the administration of justice . . . careful regard shall always be had to the customs and laws of the class or tribe or nation to which the parties respectively belong, especially with respects to the holding[,] possession[,] transfer and disposition of lands and goods, and testate or intestate succession thereto, and marriage, divorce, and legitimacy, and other rights of property and personal rights.[17]

Therefore, it was apparent that predecessor regimes had safeguards in place for the interests and welfare of the native peoples.

Furthermore, Chapter XI Article 73 of the UN Charter enjoined the 'governing authority':

a   to ensure, with due respect for the culture of the peoples concerned, their political, economic, social, and educational advancement, their just treatment, and their protection against abuses;

b   *to develop self-government*, to take due account of the political aspirations of the peoples, and to assist them in the progressive development of their free political institutions, according to the particular circumstances of each territory and its peoples and their varying stages of advancement;

The aforesaid, namely 'b.', was in line with the 8th Principle of 'Nine Cardinal Principles of the Rule of the English Rajah' that reads:

8   *That the goal of self-government shall always be kept in mind*, that the people of Sarawak shall be entrusted in due course with the governance of themselves, and that continuous efforts shall be made to hasten the reaching of this goal by educating them in the obligations, the responsibilities, and the privileges of citizenship.[18]

As is clearly spelt out, "to develop self-government", preparation for self-government and eventual independence was in the agenda; in other words, the 'governing authority' possesses a trusteeship role.

Therefore, the following sections shall examine the CO-era administration of Sarawak and North Borneo. Focus shall be on developments in the political and administrative spheres with the ultimate goal of preparation towards self-government, advancements in the economic and social services including laying the infrastructure groundwork, and intervention and changes in education and schooling. Paralleling these efforts were labours undertaken in streamlining the wide spectrum of laws (from Brooke Orders, Ordinances to native *adat* or customary law, traditional practices), the restructuring of the judiciary and the court system, and strengthening the arm of the law and enforcement agencies.

Political and administrative intervention

Britain's two Crown Colonies underwent a series of political as well as administrative changes and developments. The most conspicuous could be witnessed in Sarawak, whereas interventions in North Borneo were less fundamental or sweeping. Since Sarawak's accelerated development outpaced North Borneo, it shall take the lead in discussion and evaluation.

Sarawak: transformation from apex to grassroots

By the Instrument of Cession on 1 July 1946, the Rajah's sovereignty over Sarawak was handed over to the British Crown. In practical terms, final and overall authority in Sarawak thereafter was with the British Parliament in Westminster, specifically in the office of the Secretary of State for the Colonies. More precisely, all matters dealing with the Crown Colony of Sarawak (hereinafter, Sarawak) were channelled to the CO, literally to a specific 'desk' created along geographical lines covering every corner of the British Empire. This 'desk' addressed all routine matters between the respective Crown Colony's governor and the CO.[19] The CO-designated governor held a whole range of powers, even almost absolute authority, for all intents and purposes acting as the delegated authority of the British monarch, hence vested in his office were the supreme civil and military authority in the colony. No other authority except the CO could remove the governor, technically to withdraw his (governor's) commission.

In order to facilitate politico-administrative organization, harmonization and rapport amongst British colonial possessions in post-war Southeast Asia, the post of governor-general, and from 1946, commissioner-general for Southeast Asia, was created linking British key personnel in the region. Malcolm MacDonald was initially designated as British Governor-General for Southeast Asia (t. 1941–1946), and thereafter Commissioner-General for Southeast Asia (t. 1946–1955).[20] Based in Singapore, MacDonald held regular meetings or conferences with the governors of Sarawak and North Borneo and the residents of Brunei. Through regular face-to-face consultation between key officials, British policy towards the region as a whole and to its respective colonial territories in particular, viz. British Malaya and British Borneo, viz., Sarawak, Brunei, and North Borneo, benefitted from better coordination and superintendence.[21]

Between 1946 and 1963, the CO tenure, Sarawak had four governors, all of whom had no relations with this part of the world prior to their assuming office. The foremost scholarly authority of this period summarizes each governorship:

> The first, Sir Charles Arden Clarke [t. 1946–1949], is associated with the development of local government and his determination to crush the anti-cession movement that resulted in the resignation of 13 per cent of the civil service. His successor, Duncan Stewart [1949], was assassinated shortly after arriving in Sarawak. Anthony Abell's [1950–1959] period was one of constitutional reform, economic development, and growing preoccupation with controlling communism. Alexander Waddell's [1960–1963] main concern was the smooth transfer of power to a locally born governor and an indirectly elected state government.[22]

Overall, the structure of administration under the Brooke Raj was inherited intact by the CO administration, the governor in place of the Rajah at the apex. The post and title of chief secretary was retained, and altogether five served during the colonial era, three of whom had no association with Borneo prior to appointment.[23] Sarawak Administrative Service (SAS) that comprised British and European officers were absorbed into the Colonial Administrative Service (CAS). Each of the five Divisions retained the office of Resident whilst the six districts continued with their respective District Officer (DO), and likewise, the five sub-districts, Assistant District Officer (ADO).[24] Each DO and ADO had a 'right-hand' man in the person of a Native Officer (NO), traditionally drawn mainly from the *perabangan*. The NO was crucial, literally the 'native' face of the colonial administration, whose pivotal function was in liaising with the local leaders on behalf of their European DO/ADO.

Consequent of Sarawak's Governor acting as High Commissioner of Brunei from 1948 until 1959, senior officers and personnel from technical departments were routinely removed to serve in Brunei whenever necessary. This practice, however, was discontinued following the conclusion of a new treaty between Brunei and Britain in 1959.[25]

Borneanization – the replacement in the civil administration of a British or European officer by a suitably qualified local officer – began early in 1948 in line with the CO policy of *only* supplying administrative staff for posts where no local officer was suitably qualified. Despite the positive political will of the indigenization of the administration, progress was at best sluggish owing to the reality of the paucity of local candidates for senior positions. Whether Sarawak Chinese or natives, the highest schooling attained was limited to a third year of secondary schooling, more common amongst the former than the latter. The number of natives who benefited from schooling was small vis-à-vis the Chinese, and of those who did, only a handful managed to complete the three years of lower secondary education.[26] Nonetheless, by mid-1951, an encouraging 12 local officers were elevated to the Senior Service.[27]

Although structurally the administration was unchanged, there were undoubtedly and inevitably changes in terms of roles and functions of the administrative staff, not to mention the type and character of the officers who served in the post-war regime. Constitutional changes in the mid-1950s and early 1960s transformed the role of the senior officers. Between 1946 and 1956, the initial decade of the Crown Colony period, senior officers of the administration – Governor, Residents, official members (government nominees) – dominated (absolute majority) in both the Supreme Council and the Council Negri, the executive and legislative arms respectively of the government of Sarawak. The roles then of the Governor and his senior officers were basically to *represent* and *act* on behalf of the peoples. It was a form of paternalism that, to some extent, was not unlike their predecessor the Brooke Raj, with the Governor in lieu of the Rajah.

But the amended Constitution of August 1956 brought forth a reconstituted Supreme Council (10 members) and Council Negri (42 members). In the former, unofficial members (5) equalled *ex officio* members (3) combined with the nominees (2) of the Governor, hence removing the hitherto dominance of the government administrators. In the Council Negri, unofficial members (24) formed the majority vis-à-vis the combined total from the standing or life members (3), *ex officio* members (14), and nominated members (4).[28] Such changes transformed the role of the Governor and his senior officers in both the executive and legislative councils to that of *defending* the government's policies and actions vis-à-vis the 'representatives' of the peoples. Moreover, Sarawak (Constitution) Order in Council, 1962, reduced *ex officio* members from 14 to 3, hence resulted in the removal of all five Residents of having any voice in the legislature.

The ascendancy of local authorities was another transformation in the administration during the CO period.[29] Within an eight-year span (1948–1956), local authorities dominated the length and breadth of Sarawak. These local councils were initially chaired by the DO while the NO addressed secretarial matters. This transition of handing over responsibilities from the government administration to local authorities was overseen by the DO and NO in their changed roles from direct administrators to advisers. Following local elections of 1959, elected councillors took over the responsibilities of the councils from the DO and NO. The latter assumed the liaison role as the go-between, the state secretariat (government bureaucracy) at Kuching on the one hand, and the various Local Councils across the territory on the other.

The outstation administrators – DO, ADO, and NO – the officers in the field with direct face-to-face and daily contacts with the peoples, gradually saw their traditional role and authority diminished. Post-war developments witnessed improved infrastructures, especially in road transportation and telecommunications (telegraph, telephone, etc.), that in turn facilitated centralized control from the state secretariat. The personal touch, once the forte of Brooke officers, and initially enjoyed by the colonial administrators, had to give way to government dictates from afar (Kuching state secretariat).

The last word on this transformation is succinctly presented in these words:

> All these factors underlined the marked change in the role of the Administrative Service, from governing and administration to advisers to local government bodies and proponents of government policies through the local Councils, the District Advisory Councils, and the Divisional Advisory Councils. Administrative officers were of course expected not to question government policies in those forums.[30]

Such measures, from apex to grassroots, were in line towards preparation for self-government, the ultimate goal of the CO as a caretaker government.

North Borneo: continuity and pedestrian developments

Turning northeastwards, the North Borneo Cession Order in Council and the Labuan Order in Council, both similarly dated on 10 July 1946, witnessed the proclamation of the Crown Colony of North Borneo (hereinafter North Borneo) comprising the former British North Borneo (BNB) and the Settlement of Labuan. To some measure, the former structure of administration of BNB was retained, but the CO-appointed governor wielded more power and wider leverage than his predecessor. Although there was constituted an Advisory Council, its composition included *ex officio* the Chief Secretary, the Attorney-General, and the Financial Secretary, and other Governor nominees (official and non-official), to advise the Governor on matters of the state including legislation, but he could disregard its recommendations altogether. Moreover, the Governor alone could summon the Advisory Council.

On 15 July 1946, the Advisory Council had its inaugural meeting with 20 attendees including *ex officio* members. Two additional nominees brought membership to 22 towards the end of 1947; the following year there were 23 members.[31]

As a means to curb the vast executive and legislative powers of the Governor, two institutions were created in October 1950: the Executive Council and the Legislative Council. For all intents and purposes, the Executive Council replaced the Advisory Council. Its composition included the aforesaid three *ex officio*, two official members, and four nominated members (indigenes, or if non-native, it has to be a non-civil servant). Acting on instructions from the Secretary of State for the Colonies, the Governor appointed the latter two categories (official and nominated) of membership for a three-year term. Additionally, if circumstances dictate, the Governor could invite any individual for consultation by the Executive Council. If the Governor disagreed or was not in favour of the opinions expressed by the Executive Council, he had the prerogative to act on the contrary. However, unlike previously, the Governor was required to report in writing directly to the Secretary of State for the Colonies for his non-compliance.

The Governor presided over the Legislative Council that comprised the usual three *ex officio*, nine official members, and ten nominated members. Entitlement either as official members or nominated members was British citizenship, the former to be a civil servant while the latter a non-government employee; both categories of membership was a three-year tenure. All decisions on legislation were decided by a majority of votes of members present; if a tie, the Governor held the casting vote. The Governor, in the name of the Crown, or the Crown, through the Secretary of State for the Colonies, gave assent, and a bill became law by a proclamation published in the *Government Gazette*.

The day-to-day administration of North Borneo during the CO era was no different from the pre-war days. Headquartered in Jesselton (present-day Kota Kinabalu), the territory's administrative and political capital, the state administration was headed by the Chief Secretary, who presided over the Secretariat and a small army of civil bureaucrats, who carried out the will of the Governor and decisions of the Executive Council and the Legislative Council. The bureaucracy was organized along the lines of departments, each headed by a director or commissioner, viz. agriculture, forest, civil aviation, public works, posts and telecommunications, lands and surveys, inland revenue, police, labour and immigration, and others. Changes were made when functions changed or re-organization took place, for instance, the Agriculture Department was created in 1946 when agriculture was taken out of the Forest Department (established 1921), or when the Land Office and the Survey Department combined in 1954 to become the Lands and Surveys Department.[32]

Meanwhile, the Attorney-General and the Financial Secretary dealt with legal and legislative matters and financial administration, respectively. Like the Secretariat, both the Attorney-General's chambers and the Financial Secretary's office were at Jesselton.

Similar to the situation in neighbouring Sarawak, senior positions were dominated by British/European officers while local-born served in the lower rungs of the government bureaucracy. Likewise, the process of Borneanization was sluggish at best, owing to the low level of educational attainment of indigenes; the first appointment of a local-born as an Administrative Officer was in 1957, and by 1963, on the eve of Malaysia, there were only 11 local-born Administrative Officers in the entire public service.[33]

In the initial decade of the CO period, the pre-war administrative divisions were retained in essence with some re-configurations and downsizing. The Labuan and Interior Residency was added to the existing West Coast Residency and East Coast Residency with Beaufort, Jesselton, and Sandakan respectively as administrative centres, each headed by a Resident. The 17 districts of the pre-war era were downsized to only 11, viz. Jesselton, Papar, Kota Belud, and Kudat Districts under West Coast Residency; Sandakan and Lahad Datu Districts under East Coast Residency; and Labuan, Beaufort, Tenom, and Keningau Districts under Labuan and Interior Residency.[34]

In the later part of 1954, after decentralization by the CO administration, the East Coast Residency was divided into two parts, one residency was centred at Sandakan and the other at Tawau, each with their respective Resident.[35] The following year there was a change in the headquarters of the Labuan and Interior Residency, from Labuan to Keningau; hereinafter, Labuan was dropped from the designation, hence simply Interior Residency. Labuan was placed under a DO who reported directly to the Chief Secretary.

Sub-districts came under the purview of ADOs who, unlike Residents and DOs, were local indigenes. Meanwhile, at the district and sub-district level, grassroots level, headmen continued to address minor local administrative matters reporting to the native chiefs who were answerable to the DO/ADO. Native courts were presided by native chiefs who dealt with issues pertaining to native customs and the *syariah* (Islamic jurisprudence).

Apart from minor changes, the foregoing demonstrates the dominant force of continuity between the CO era and the Chartered Company period. It was apparent that natives were formally incorporated into the local administration that to some extent paved the way towards efforts of self-government. The Rural Government Ordinance of 1951 created local authorities (LA), and the first was in Kota Belud District. It comprised 47 members, all natives including chiefs and headmen, and was presided over by the DO.[36] Like other LAs to follow, its primary local concerns dealt with "building regulations, public hygiene, firefighting, water supply and traffic control", but without financial control.[37] Moreover, the LA was "specifically authorised to make by-laws for such purposes as improvement of agriculture, movement of livestock, control and development of communal grazing grounds, fencing of land, control of markets, and measures to promote public health".[38] The LA derived its revenue from various sources but primarily drawn from "poll taxes, rates and cesses, grants-in-aid from the Government, profits and rents".[39]

Comparatively, the CO era in North Borneo lagged behind Sarawak's progress in laying the groundwork towards self-government. The following overview encapsulates the dire situation:

> The seventeen years under Colonial rule had therefore seen very little, if any, radical change to the system of administration. The years immediately following the war were reconstruction years. Significant progress had been made in education which meant that an increasing number of local people were beginning to fill Government posts which, during the Chartered Company days were the reserve of expatriate officers.[40]

The economy

Both the war and military occupation period (1941–1945) brought much baneful impact on Sarawak and North Borneo in terms of physical destruction, social and economic dislocation, and the psychological and covert scars of horror and brutality. Physically, North Borneo suffered the worst, "not even Burma, had been so utterly devastated", that "In some respects the country was back to pre-1881 standards".[41] First and foremost, the economy across all territories was hard hit, and the infrastructure though already sparse and minimal was badly damaged with many roads, bridges, and harbours completely destroyed and likewise the skeletal telecommunications networks. Therefore, the early part of the CO era was largely devoted to reconstruction and rehabilitation of most aspects and sectors of the economy. Development and expansion had to wait until at least from the mid-1950s for implementation, and results and gains only becoming apparent in the later part of the decade.

Secondly, in terms of overall policy direction, the CO administration did not introduce many changes, radical or otherwise, in the economic landscape, and the Bornean territories pre-war array of economic activities, means of production, consumption, and livelihood continued into the post-war period. Agriculture-based economy remained predominant despite the substantial contribution of the oil and petroleum industry in Brunei and Sarawak. One report, for instance, declared thus:

> In North Borneo, in 1953, three agricultural products [rubber, timber, and copra] accounted for half the value of all exports. In Sarawak 70 per cent of the value of all exports (reshipped oil excluded) was accounted for by the products of agriculture [viz. rubber, pepper, sago, copra].[42]

The third shared characteristic across the two territories was the elusive attainment of self-sufficiency in rice, the staple food; hence throughout the CO era, rice imports were the norm, a crucial commodity, not unlike the Chartered Company period. Family-owned and managed smallholding agricultural farms predominated in all Sarawak and North Borneo at the expense of large plantations or estates.[43] The Iban, Sarawak's largest indigenous ethnic group, and the Kadazandusun, North Borneo's main ethnic community, were smallholding agriculturalists working on between one and three acres of self-owned land, largely focusing on subsistence rice farming and cash cropping of rubber and/or coconut as supplementary sources of income. But the cultivation of export crops of rubber, pepper, and coconut were the norm amongst ethnic Chinese smallholders, a non-native community. Sarawak possessed the largest number of Chinese settlers.

The twin features, the destruction of virgin timber forests and the low yield of swidden agriculture of mainly hill rice and other food crops, were primary concerns of the colonial authorities in both Kuching and Jesselton. Official negativity and widely adverse perception towards swidden agriculture and its practitioners that persisted throughout post-colonial periods to contemporary times was, as James Scott surmised, more of its 'illegibility' from the perspective of the state authorities in efforts of control and extraction than for any other reasons.[44]

The subsequent section will examine the economic situation and challenges in each of the territories, viz. Sarawak and North Borneo, highlighting peculiarities, if any, to help further enlighten our understanding of developments during this period.

Status quo in Sarawak

In line with the Nine Cardinal Principles of the Rule of the English Rajah, namely the latter part of the second principle, that is "the standard of living of the people of Sarawak shall steadily be raised",[45] the colonial administration of Sarawak undertook measures throughout its tenure to attain this objective. But, as far as the economy was concerned, *continuity* with past (Brooke) practices was the guiding principle. The Brooke preference for indigenous smallholders farming their own land focusing on subsistence food crops, primarily rice, supplemented by cash crops (rubber, coconut) continued to be fostered by the post-war colonial government. Family-owned and worked farmland was the norm and the ideal idyllic scenario where serenity reigned amidst the verdant backdrop of rice fields and coconut palms with the occasional tropical breeze. At the same time, large Malayan-style plantations with hundreds of coolies toiling under the tropical sun were largely eschewed. Also, like the Rajah's government, agriculture was acknowledged and encouraged as the mainstay of Sarawak 's economy. The mining of minerals, including the lucrative but capital- and expertise-intensive oil and petroleum industry, recognized as a wasting asset that was depleting in production in the post-war period, was discouraged as unreliable.

Acting Colonial Governor C. W. Dawson in addressing the Council Negri on 16 May 1949 highlighted three pressing economic issues confronting the state, viz. the lack of communications, the necessity of diversification as a move away from overdependence on rubber as the main cash crop, and the baneful impact of swidden agriculture to be curtailed.[46] Moreover, the ever-elusive attainment of rice self-sufficiency was reiterated, suggesting that swampland be drained and cleared for rice cultivation. By the mid-1950s, food crops especially rice and the concomitant need to be self-sufficient in this staple food were greatly emphasized.[47]

As mentioned earlier, the native practice of the slash-and-burn method of cultivation of hill rice in virgin jungle clearings on a cyclical basis that had been the traditional subsistence mainstay since time immemorial was highly criticized by various quarters, including members of the colonial administration. Chief amongst the criticisms were that it was a wasteful form of farming and the low output. Nonetheless, the consensus of 'experts' decrying native practice of swidden agriculture was overruled by the colonial administration that had pledged, like its predecessor, to uphold *adat lama* (old customary traditions, practices). Consequently, in order not to radically change the indigenous peoples' traditional way of life, colonial officers, especially those in the Department of Agriculture, had to, albeit reluctantly, overlook swidden agriculture practices in the interior, upriver regions. In adhering to native sensitivity, the Department of Agriculture admitted that it had made little advancement and/or development during the 1950s.[48]

Likewise, despite continuous and persistent exhortations to encourage and implement efforts to increase domestic rice production, rice self-sufficiency remained unattainable throughout the CO era. Paralleling this dismal performance was the encouragement of cash crop diversification. Tobacco, coffee, and cocoa, the three newly introduced cash crops as alternatives to rubber, had not made any significant contribution to export earnings over the 17-year tenure of the colonial administration.[49]

Unlike North Borneo that suffered much physical devastation to its infrastructure, Sarawak's skeletal infrastructure managed to carry over the post-war period. It was therefore imperative that infrastructure development was given great emphasis by the colonial government in order to facilitate much-needed economic growth and development. Post-war Sarawak witnessed the formulation and implementation of a series of development plans, viz. 1951–1957, revised version 1955–1960, and 1959–1963.

The radial system of roads within townships, namely Kuching, Sibu, and Miri, suffered little damage from the war, but road construction in the outstations was negligible apart from an unmetalled, non-all-weather, 40-kilometre stretch from Kuching to the mining centre of Bau to the southwest, and another 64-kilometre partially metalled road eastwards to Serian. The former dated to 1901 whilst the latter to 1930. Owing to negligence, both roads were in disrepair in the immediate post-war period to the extent that the Kuching-Serian Road was impassable, particularly during the *landas* season,[50] where heavy downpour rendered roads into rivers of mud. Between 1946 and 1952, the colonial government emphasized road rehabilitation and maintenance, but the increasing traffic exerted a heavy burden whereby the former could not keep pace with the latter. An unflattering comparison was hurled at the urban roads in and around Sibu to "buffalo fields".[51] Meanwhile, despite earnest attention to repairs and maintenance, the Bau Road had to be temporarily closed to traffic periodically.[52] Moreover, work (1952–1954) on the Bau Road was particularly expensive to transform to all-weather bitumen standard at the rate of M$150,000 per kilometre, three-fold in cost in comparison to the 7th Mile road to the Bukit Stabar airport.[53]

The 1951–1957 Development Plan allocated M$12.7 million for the construction of a 130-kilometre trunk road between Serian and Simanggang. It was Rajah Vyner's intention back in the late 1920s to foster economic development via a road that not only facilitated the opening of new agricultural lands but also provided farmers a way to market their produce. But the global-wide Depression (1929–1931) dismissed all such intentions then. Work commenced from 1955, and by 1959, the costs had escalated to M$22 million. Three years later, when it was opened albeit to restricted traffic, the road surface was at best temporary, and only 2 out of 14 permanent bridges had been completed.[54]

The 1959–1963 Development Plan shifted emphasis from envisaging a network of trunk and secondary roads to establishing a system of feeder roads as a means of opening up undeveloped regions for agricultural development. To this end, an ambitious feeder network was to connect Sematan, on the west, northwest of Lundu, to Durin on the east, on the outskirts of Sibu.[55] By 1962, the projected 810 kilometres of roads to be built saw only less than half fulfilled, namely 348 kilometres or 43 per cent completed.[56] Against much physical odds of difficult terrain and less than agreeable weather conditions, the colonial government did accomplish a commendable achievement.

Sarawak's only railway was a 13-mile (21-kilometre) line from Kuching southwards to the 13th Mile, the maximum reach attained in 1925. Rajah Charles had anticipated that a railroad would connect the capital to Simanggang, his favourite outstation, some 160 kilometres eastwards.[57] In 1949 the colonial government resuscitated the railway but only until the 7th Mile to carry stone and gravel from the quarries to Kuching, and thence to Bukit Stabar for the airport.

Miri alone possessed an open sea port whilst Sibu, the territory's main port, and Kuching, the capital, were on rivers or in shallow inlets, hence limitations of access to oceangoing vessels. Under the 1951–1957 Development Plan, a 150-metre concrete wharf was erected for Sibu, with work commencing from 1956. Kuching's new 246-metre wharf was built 4 kilometres downstream at Tanah Putih under the aegis of the 1955–1960 Development Plan and completed in mid-1961.[58] Besides coastal shipping with neighbouring territories, there was a regular shipping traffic between Kuching and Singapore before the war that was revived in the post-war period.

Pre-war air travel was limited to military and defence purposes, utilizing grass airstrips at Kuching (740-metre), Lutong, and Miri (330-metre). But during the war, all of the landing strips were destroyed via bombings and/or scorched-earth tactics undertaken by both sides as the fortunes of war shifted dramatically. But owing to pressures of necessity, by 1946 both the Kuching and Miri airstrips were serviceable for light aircrafts.[59] As a temporary measure, between 1945 and 1949, the Royal Air Force (RAF) maintained air communications among Labuan, Kuching, and Singapore. Malayan Airways assumed this responsibility thereafter with regular flights for civilian patronage. Kuching's Bukit Stabar airport's grass runway was extended to 1,110 metres in 1948. Shortly thereafter, in order to accommodate larger aircrafts, a new airport was erected north of the existing venue. In 1950, Kuching boasted a 1,380-metre runway of international standing.

The 1951–1957 Development Plan prioritized an airfield at Sibu, whereby a 1,110-metre gravel runway was operational in 1952. At the same time, the Bintulu airstrip was extended to a 950-metre all-weather grass strip.[60] Lutong's 330-metre runway was owned and managed by the oil concessionaires. Lutong was incorporated into the feeder service that linked Labuan, Sarawak, and Brunei. As far as communications was concerned, the colonial government intended that airstrips and aircrafts be utilized for economic development.[61]

The postal services literally collapsed during the wartime occupation period, but with restoration of shipping and air connectivity in the immediate post-war period, thanks to Sarawak Steamship vessels and RAF Sunderland flying crafts, overseas postal services were resuscitated. Internal postal services, however, needed more time to attain pre-war standards and efficiency. As progress developed in road transport and internal air services from the mid-1950s, postal services improved, too. An additional six post offices were added to the revived 36 post offices across the territory servicing practically all urban centres and townships.[62]

Telecommunications was completely overhauled in the post-war period, firstly the existing wireless telegraph (W/T) technology were dated, as well as much of the equipment in the 19 W/T stations were in dire straits of repair. Therefore, two phases were planned in the replacement of the old with new very high frequency (VHF) radio-telephone (R-T) systems and new telephone exchanges. Phase one, funded under the 1951–1957 Revised Development Plan, involved the replacement of W/T stations at the divisional headquarters and outstations and connecting police stations with lighthouses. By early part of 1957, Kuching was in telecommunications with most outstations, likewise Sibu and Miri were similarly linked. By then 55 VHF stations were in place.[63]

Under the 1955–1960 Development Plan, the second phase was implemented from 1960, whereby a VHF multichannel system (public telephone system, telegraphs, and broadcasting) replaced the W/T links between divisional headquarters and the outstations. Following the installation of a new High Frequency (HF) transmitter in late 1960, Kuching was in telecommunication link with Singapore and Kuala Lumpur. In 1963 HF sideband circuits were in place, facilitating around-the-clock service transmission for the Kuching-Miri and Kuching-Jesselton links.[64]

Concurrently, the telephone network was expanded quantitatively, from 12 exchanges in 1948 to 51 in 1962, with larger exchanges being automated. Advanced automated telephone exchanges replaced the pre-war switchboards: Kuching and Sibu in 1955; Miri, 1958; Binatang, 1959; 7th Mile Penrissen Road, Kuching, and Sungai Merah, Sibu, 1961.[65]

Initially radio broadcasting was sidelined as some quarters felt that other infrastructure projects were much more urgent and should be prioritized, but the colonial government felt that radio broadcasting was an essential tool in combating subversive propaganda from Leftist elements. Funds were allocated that subsequently brought forth Radio Sarawak in June 1954. Interestingly, the colonial authorities allowed the radio station freedom of expression, including criticism of government policy.[66] Beginning from 1959, Radio Sarawak broadcast regular educational programmes to rural primary schools; by 1961, aided by receivers donated by the Asia Foundation and the Australian government, 400 schools benefitted from the educational services. Holders of radio licenses jumped dramatically from 7,000 in 1954 to 45,000 in 1961.[67]

The Korean War presented fiscal opportunities for Sarawak's commodities (Table 3.1). When the conflict erupted on the Korean peninsula, rubber exports jumped more than three-fold, likewise sago flour and copra with a two-fold increase and one-half increase, respectively. Pepper exports registered an

Table 3.1 Sarawak Exports during the Korean War (1950–1953)

	1949	1950	1951	1952	1953	1954
Rubber	31,545,400* [38,902]†	113,941,617 [55,475]	158,865,402 [42,521]	65,182,029 [31,471]	31,616,358 [23,188]	31,087,822 [23,958]
Pepper	38,437 [313]	4,107,166 [267]	17,925,184 [165]	16,931,835 [4,013]	49,444,086 [8,997]	43,706,513 [15,465]
Sago Flour	4,699,629 [27,082]	9,277,842 [28,243]	7,988,232 [23,945]	5,954,774 [22,619]	4,371,384 [16,073]	2,828,635 [12,543]
Copra	1,676,702 [3,418]	2,651,451 [4,330]	2,654,196 [3,864]	1,106,541 [2,612]	1,275,837 [1,635]	N.A. [2,994]

* Exports in value (M$)
† Exports in tonnage (tonnes)

Sources: Sarawak Government, *Annual Report on Sarawak for the Year, 1948–52*; SAR, 1953–54.

astonishing spurt, from merely 38,437 tonnes in 1949 to 4,107,166 tonnes when hostilities begun in 1950. While rubber and copra prices peaked in 1951, pepper continued to surge beyond the ceasefire that earned invaluable foreign exchange for development.

Transformation in North Borneo

Although understandably the North Borneo Reconstruction and Development Plan (1948–1955) prioritized the territory's war-damaged infrastructure, efforts at resuscitating the economy were also given due concern. According to this post-war plan, the agricultural sector would undergo a 'major transformation' under the stewardship of a new Agriculture Department. This leadership change for agricultural activities, from the pre-war charge of the Conservator of Forests to the Agriculture Department, was in itself a radical move, a recognition of agriculture as being separated from forestry. At the same time, efforts by the Agriculture Department "towards the betterment and improvement of the 'peasant' agriculturalists with the object of making them as nearly self-supporting as possible" was a departure from pre-war practices that gave scant attention to native farmers.[68] Furthermore, the colonial government intended to "make the country self-sufficient in foodstuffs", in entrusting the Agriculture Department to provide "improved and selected seeds and the demonstration of better methods of cultivation".[69] The latter in terms of high-yielding seeds and efficient methods of cultivation were applied to the rubber sector, the major export crop, whereby war ravages impacted to the extent of reducing production to half of the pre-war output.

Moreover, there were plans in agricultural extension to create and develop model *kampung* (village) and the selection of 'progressive' farmers. Both were to be utilized as role models in the expectation that the demonstration effect might encourage other villages and their inhabitants to adopt forward-looking methods of cultivation, hence improving their livelihood.

Like Sarawak, rice self-sufficiency was an objective for North Borneo. Fortuitously, the war had not unduly affected rice output, hence in order to attain domestic self-sufficiency, it necessitated an additional 15,000 acres of wet rice to complement the existing 85,000 acres, as well as introducing mechanized methods of production. Targeted areas for this expansion were Bandau in the Marudu Bay area of 40,000 acres, Klias Peninsula of some 30,000 acres, and in the vicinity of Beluran, another 30,000 acres.[70] An assortment of new crops was also considered to further boost the agriculture sector, viz. cane sugar, tobacco, coffee, coconuts, tea, and palm oil. Other cash crops include mulberry (for silkworm industry), maize, cotton, jute, hemp, groundnuts, cocoa, fruit, and vegetables, all to be encouraged to further improve the livelihood of indigenous peoples.

Like with rubber, the all-important livestock industry had suffered the consequences of war; post-war cattle figures had dropped to less than half that of the 1930s. The buffalo population needed to be quadrupled, hence creation of a central stud farm in the main cattle-rearing area of Kota Belud to be complemented with smaller stud centres in the many model *kampung*. Rearing of sheep, poultry, goats, and pigs and establishment of a state-of-the-art dairy farm were all in the pipeline for consideration. Enclosed grazing land was introduced on a 6,000-acre area known as the Sorob Farm, the first in the territory.

It took more than a decade to witness improvements in the livestock industry. In comparing livestock in terms of quantity between 1938 and 1963, there were overall increases with the exception of cattle, thus water buffalo (46,959 to 66,800), pigs (34,959 to 81,100), and goats (9,613 to 17,600).[71] Figures for cattle were of concern: from 23,110 in 1938, a severe plunge to 11,401 in 1951, a recovery to 20,000 in 1955, and another drastic decline to 14,535 in 1961 and 14,500 in 1963.[72]

Little was resolved in the fisheries sector as pre-war issues of poorly equipped native fishermen (vessels without outboard engines) and indebtedness to the middleman remained throughout the tenure of the colonial administration. The 1948–1955 plan proposed the establishment of fishermen cooperatives to bypass the middleman. Refrigerated plants were aimed at further facilitating marketing. Freshwater fish-breeding ponds would further boost inland fisheries. By 1955, 550 fish ponds were created.[73] A re-introduction of tuna fishing and canning was another commercial agenda besides the promotion of high-quality products such as sharks' fins, prawns, turtle eggs, pearls, and trochus shells for the export market.[74] In this initiative, the Chinese with their oceangoing trawlers targeted tuna and prawns for the lucrative foreign market. Japanese companies returned to embark on pearl cultivation in Labuk Bay and tuna fishing and canning utilizing a 3,000-ton factory ship.[75] Native inshore fishermen, "among the poorest in the land", were apparently marginalized.[76]

While collection and gathering of forest products was a traditional form of activity undertaken by most indigenous communities for domestic subsistence-level consumption, logging for timber as an export commodity undertaken by companies achieved leaps and bounds beyond expectations during the CO era. In 1940, 4.9 million cubic feet were valued at S$2.2 million; in comparison, 1955 registered 13 million cubic feet valued at M$21 million. By 1960, exported amounts had attained 50.2 million cubic feet valued at M$61 million.[77] Sandakan emerged as one of the wold's major timber-exporting ports.

By 1961, timber had surpassed rubber as the major export earner: M$41.2 million earned from rubber compared to M$102.8 million of timber receipt.[78] Two years later, timber attained M$149.6 million in export revenue; rubber suffered a drop to M$32.1 million.[79] The bulk of the timber (some 80 per cent) went to Japan.

The timber industry, however, largely benefitted foreign companies as well as foreign labour drawn from neighbouring Indonesia and the Philippines. The local indigenous peoples were generally not keen as workers, and neither were they favoured vis-à-vis foreign labour. The sole pre-war concessionaire was Sarawak and North Borneo Timber Company (BBTC) whose contract terminated in 1954; thereafter, BBTC and three other companies (Bombay Burmah Trading Company, North Borneo Timbers, and Kennedy Bay Company) were each granted 21-year leases. Besides these, the Forest Department issued annual licences to smaller operators, allowing more players and competition in the field. The east coast, in particular the hinterland of Sandakan, were major logging areas.

Under the North Borneo Development Plan (1959–1964), the initial allocation for 'Agriculture' was revised from M$ 1.25 million to M$ 7.96 million in 1963 consequent of a policy shift from "development of agricultural research, training and educational facilities . . . towards smallholders . . . resettlement and development schemes".[80] Notwithstanding the political will as well as efforts on the part of the colonial government "to boost domestic supplies and stocks by the padi purchasing scheme, and efforts to improve yields and milling conversion rates – no impact had been made on the level of rice imports".[81]

Rubber, however, proved otherwise. Resulting from steadfast efforts at promoting re-planting of high-yielding variety, within the plan's six-year period, smallholders expanded acreage to over 75,000 acres and another 20,000 acres by estates. On the eve of joining 'Malaysia' in 1963, high-yielding rubber comprised 231,000 acres, of which 60 per cent was in the hands of family-owned smallholdings.[82] But producers failed to reap returns owing to the depressed world prices, and hence exports were reduced to 21,200 tons in 1963 in comparison to 24,000 tons in 1950.

Boom times were during the Korean War when commodity prices surged owing to high demand. Rubber, copra, and timber, North Borneo's main exports, benefitted from boom prices.

Rubber exports increased from 19,500 tons in 1949 to 24,000 tons in 1950 and amounted to about 21,000 tons in 1951. Exports of copra increased from 19,000 tons in 1949 to 31,700 tons in 1950. Production of timber during 1950 amounted to 6,237,558 cubic feet of which 3,750,507 cubic feet were exported.[83]

Of the introduction of various new crops, palm oil appeared to be the most promising, from a mere 30-acre spread in 1958, expanded to 6,500 acres in 1963 undertaken by six plantations. The two major players were Unilever Estate and Mostyn Estate on the Labuk River. Meanwhile, trials for smallholders were successfully undertaken in 1963 in the vicinity of Beaufort as well as in the Klias Peninsula, and subsequently, the following year witnessed the commencement of six smallholder schemes, each of 8,000-acre coverage.[84]

Infrastructure reconstruction was undoubtedly the highest priority for post-war North Borneo. Both plans, 1948–1955 and 1959–1964, allocated the majority of funds (more than half) for reconstruction, rehabilitation, and development of transport, communications, and public utilities.[85] Progress was commendable as far as airports and air travel were concerned. In 1947, only the Labuan airfield was operational; others at Jesselton, Sandakan, and Tawau had suffered severe war damage. Nonetheless, by 1960, Labuan and Jesselton at least enjoyed tarmac-surface runways (6,074 feet / 1,851 metres and 5,100 feet / 1,554 metres, respectively).[86] While Sandakan's was gravel-surface, other airstrips at Kudat, Keningau, Tanau, Tawau, and Lahad Datu were either grass or sand. In 1963, Jesselton, as the territory's administrative centre, was favoured to be the principal air hub, hence an extension was made to the runway to 6,300 feet / 1,920 metres to facilitate Comet jet aircraft. International air services then connected North Borneo with neighbouring Sarawak and Brunei, daily flights to Singapore and Kuala Lumpur, and weekly connections with Hong Kong and Manila.

In the immediate post-war period, North Borneo was literally isolated as there were non-existent shipping connections with the outside world. In 1949, a port development plan was implemented with U.S. funding that witnessed the construction of new wharfs in Labuan (1953, 600 feet / 182 metres), Sandakan (1954, 750 feet / 229 metres), and Jesselton 1953, (650 feet / 198 metres).[87] The wharfs could barely handle the increase in tonnage traffic. Sandakan had a 31 per cent increase over a three-year period (1960–1963) accommodating 205,000 tons, while Jesselton, a 66 per cent increase during the same period barely being able to service 177,906 tons.[88]

Against the war-damaged scenario, it was decided in 1949 by the post-war colonial government that the 30-lb rails be replaced with 60-lb, concomitantly all bridges would not only be repaired but also needed to be strengthened to accommodate the change, and a line would be extended to Jesselton's new harbour. At the same time, diesel and petrol replaced the old coal and wood-fired steam engines. Freight tonnage doubled, from 22,069 in 1947 to 48,810 in 1960; even more spectacular was the increase in passenger traffic, 124,776 in 1947 to a jump to 706,600 in 1960.[89] Then in the plan (1959–1964), a pro-road lobby won over, whereby the Tenom/Melalap and Beaufort/Weston branch rail roads were to be replaced with gravel road. Subsequently in mid-1963, the 20-mile/32-kilometre Beaufort/Weston line was closed after six decades of operation.

Road repairs, reconstruction, and the building of new roads were undertaken in earnest, as such arteries of connectivity not only necessitated but spurred economic growth and development. On the eve of the war, the territory had only 103 miles (166 kilometres) of metalled roads with asphalt surface, mainly radial networks within the confines of the five major towns of Jesselton, Sandakan, Beaufort, Tawau, and Kudat. There were also 600 miles (966 kilometres) of bridle paths (6ft to 8ft [1.8m to 2.4m] wide) to accommodate ponies as pack animals transporting rubber sheets, rice, rattans, and other products. In 1949, therefore, a new road network was initiated: Jesselton-Tambunan-Papar, Tuaran-Kota Belud, and from Sandakan inland to the Labuk River. But the difficult hilly terrain, the perennial problem of labour shortages, and the lack of machinery for road-building delayed and hampered desired rates of progress. It took more than a decade to at least witness some semblance of improvement. Meanwhile, bridle paths were increasingly converted into jeep tracks (gravel and earth roads). Consequently, all-weather macadamised roads rose from 125 miles (201 kilometres) to 209 miles (336 kilometres) between 1948 and 1955. Gravel and earth networks expanded from 241 miles (387 kilometres) in 1950 to 536 miles (863 kilometres) in 1960.[90]

Progress in communications witnessed the development of a radio-telephone network that linked Jesselton with Sandakan in 1949, and the following year, Labuan was included. The major towns – Jesselton, Sandakan, Tuaran, Kota Belud, and Papar – received very high frequency (VHF) and automatic exchanges. By the mid-1950s, overseas links were made via Singapore and Hong Kong, enabling telephone connections with Europe and Australia. By 1960, the territory possessed 3,320 telephone subscribers, a growth described as "modest with delays in equipment deliveries limiting the number of lines and exchange capacities".[91]

The most notable transformation in the postal services was the introduction of feeder air facilities that revolutionized the movement and distribution of mail and parcels. Rural areas benefitted through the establishment of ten postal agencies by 1960, whilst urban centres were better served with erection of new post offices in Jesselton, Sandakan, Tenom, Kota Belud, and Keningau. Taking advantage of the aforesaid developments, there was a 40 per cent increase in posted articles, from 2.89 million in 1960 to 4.05 million in 1963.[92]

North Borneo in 1963 was radically different from that of 1941, thanks to the positive outcomes borne from the plans of 1948–1955 and 1959–1964. Both the economy and the territory's infrastructure benefitted from the steadfast efforts and commitment of the colonial government in reconstruction and rehabilitation as well as development and expansion.

Oil and petroleum industry: mixed fortunes

Oil was initially struck at Sarawak's Miri in 1910, and four years later, a refinery was constructed at Lutong, some 9.5 kilometres to the northeast. The Miri oilfield peaked during the mid-1920s, declined and briefly stabilized in the early 1930s, and had a slight revival towards the late 1930s.[93] Owing to the capital-intensive operations that necessitated a corps of highly skilled and specialized personnel, the oil and gas industry of Sarawak were in the hands of private companies, namely SSOL.[94] Crude oil from Seria was piped to the Lutong refinery, 56 kilometres to the southwest.

Across the border in Sarawak, the Miri oilfields had witnessed a gradual but steady decline from the late 1920s. For instance, SSOL in 1929 recorded crude oil output exceeding 5.5 million U.S. barrels, but in 1940, less than 700,000 U.S. barrels were reported.[95] By the time the CO era begun, oil and petroleum were no longer the 'star' foreign exchange earner; in fact, output was a mere one-tenth of peak production of the late 1920s. The refinery at Lutong during the post-war period almost exclusively served Brunei's Seria oilfields that were then experiencing booms after booms from the late 1940s and early 1950s. SSOL turned to exploration in the immediate vicinity and afar, on land and in the coastal waters along Sarawak's long shoreline as far as offshore Bintulu.

> However, the exploratory wells drilled both on land and offshore . . . did not uncover any commercially viable oil deposits to replace the Miri oilfield, although gas deposits found off Bintulu later proved of significant economic benefit. By 1960, SSOL oil royalties, export duty, company tax, and mining rents had fallen to [M]$792,298, about 1 per cent of total state revenue.[96]

Nonetheless, the oil industry in Sarawak, where SSOL engaged a workforce of more than 1,000, remained one of the largest industrial employers. Resurgence from offshore oil and gas fields only began in the 1970s.

Education and schooling

Although there were commendable advances in public health, the main thrust in the social services sector was in the field of education, in which the colonial government exerted tremendous effort and investment, resulting in much significant impact. In this section, education and schooling are given especial focus, relating them to the ultimate goal of the colonial government in preparing the people of Sarawak and North Borneo for eventual self-government in the foreseeable future.

Sarawak: direction and vision in education

During the CO era, the colonial authorities built on and expanded the existing educational infrastructure of their predecessors, but more importantly, they provided much-needed direction and vision for the education and schooling of the masses. Besides the provision of schools and other related facilities, the curriculum was revisited and thereafter revised to better serve the objectives mapped out by the colonial government.

Educational development in Sarawak throughout the CO era was planned and executed in accordance to the objectives laid out:

> the Colonial Government from the start set in motion an education programme with two objectives: to *close the wide disparity in education* between the native peoples and the Chinese, and to bring the existing plural school systems . . . into a *national education system*. Educational parity among the multi-racial population was politically essential in the light of the overall objective . . . to prepare the Colony for eventual self-government.[97]

One outstanding shortcoming of the previous Brooke administration was the dire shortage of indigenous peoples, particularly of non-Malay natives, in the government bureaucracy as well as in the private sector, owing to the low level of education. As mentioned, Malays of the *perabangan* class literally monopolized the lower echelons of government offices, namely in their position as NO assisting the ADO/DO. Thanks to their schooling to the Junior Cambridge level in Christian mission schools in Kuching and Sibu, a handful of Malays served in the civil service as *kerani* (clerk) alongside their Chinese, Eurasian, and Indian colleagues. Therefore, the colonial government strived to address this inadequacy through better provision of schooling for indigenous peoples, enabling their future participation in the workforce. At the same time, attention was also provided for human resource development in terms of producing technical expertise and professionals, for serving both the public and private sectors.

The ultimate goal that the colonial government steadfastly worked to attain was the creation of a national education system:

> with the aim of developing among all the peoples a sense of common citizenship, identity, brotherhood and undivided loyalty . . . without unduly interfering with cultures inherited from overseas, to orient the interests and attachments

of the children of immigrant peoples towards Sarawak, the country of their birth and upbringing.[98]

The last passage was undoubtedly targeted at the Chinese community. The major concern was the distance and built-in insularity of the hitherto Chinese community, as well as its self-funded, self-managed vernacular school system. The latter, owing to language particularization and ample dosage of ethnocentrism courtesy of the imported China-born teachers, curriculum and textbooks imported wholly from the Chinese mainland, isolated the young and the Chinese community as a whole from the wider mainstream society. An insular Chinese community was one issue, but a more pressing matter, not unlike a threat, was the spread of subversive Leftist/communist influence within the community from the Chinese mainland. The Chinese vernacular schools, in fact, were nurseries for the nurturing and recruitment of communists, as young as middle school graduates (15- or 16-year-olds).

Compounding the situation was the non-recognition of Chinese vernacular school certificates by the Brooke and CO administrations for civil service entry and in the private sector (European firms, banks, shipping companies, insurance agencies, etc.). Specifically, Chinese school graduates' inability in the English language, the *lingua franca* in both the government bureaucracy and the Western-dominated commercial sector, denied them entry. Owing to the prioritization of blood and/or clan relations in the recruitment of workers in Chinese businesses, many young Chinese vernacular school graduates found themselves rejected by practically all quarters, hence they became susceptible and easy prey to subversive propaganda and persuasive communist activists-cum-recruiters.

The answer was in the dismantling of the plural school system, and in its place, a national education system at the secondary level, whereby Chinese vernacular schools would be transformed into national schools adopting English as the medium of instruction together with locally oriented national curriculum and textbooks. Such a transformation would create parity among all secondary schools, viz. government, Christian missionary, and Chinese (Tables 3.2 and 3.3).

Table 3.2 Sarawak: Schools at Elementary Level (7–12-year-olds), 1946–1955

Management	Medium of Instruction	Locality
Government	Malay; English as a single subject	Coastal districts
	Iban; English as a single subject	Interior, upriver districts
Mission	Iban; English as a single subject	Interior, upriver districts
	English	Urban
Chinese	Chinese dialect†, *Guo-yu**;	Coastal districts; Urban
	English as a single subject	

† Chinese vernacular schools in Kuching and Miri utilized the Hokkien dialect; also, Cantonese and Hakka in the former. In Bau, Hakka was used, in Sibu, Foochow (Hock-chiu).

* Following the May Fourth Movement of 1919, or the First Cultural Revolution, *guo-yu* or Standard Chinese (Mandarin) was adopted on the mainland. Its written form utilizes traditional Chinese characters.

Table 3.3 Sarawak: Schools at Secondary Level (13–17-year-olds), 1955–1963

Management	Medium of Instruction^	Locality
Government	English Pupils' mother tongue as a single subject	All localities
Mission	English Pupils' mother tongue as a single subject	Interior, upriver districts Urban
Chinese	English Chinese (*Guo-yu*)* as a single subject	Coastal districts; Urban

^ The National Education System pronounced English as the medium of instruction for all secondary education. Hence, the Conversion Plan, namely from Chinese to English, was carried out in Chinese vernacular secondary schools (up to middle school or lower secondary, the highest level) from the late 1950s and early 1960s.
* *Guo-yu* is Standard Chinese or Mandarin. Its written form utilizes traditional Chinese characters. It was adopted following the May Fourth Movement of 1919, or the First Cultural Revolution.

In the mid-1950s, as a measure to bring about greater control over the hitherto plural school system, particularly with regards to the Chinese vernacular schools, the colonial government introduced a grants-in-aid policy known as the Grant Code (Regulations) of 1956. The latter was aimed at re-organizing the financing of education, whereby the colonial government henceforth commencing from 1956 would assume responsibility for all approved recurrent expenditure and an equal share in capital expenditure divided with the schools' management.[99] This financial input serves two objectives: firstly, it narrowed the wide disparity between the indigenous peoples and the Chinese in terms of offering greater access to schooling, including assisting the poorer quarters. Moreover, the new financing system also contributed to improvement and upgrading of educational infrastructure particularly to rural native schools. Consequently, native student enrolment rose dramatically, from 15,121 in 1954, to 34,452 in 1958, to an estimated 57,700 in 1961.[100] The increased participation of indigenous peoples in schooling contributed to the closing of the educational gap amongst the natives and the Chinese.

Since most schools participated in this financial assistance, including the Chinese vernacular schools, it ensured that the colonial authorities possessed a greater control over the schools and at the same time weeded out subversive influences.

Equally important was the training of teachers, vital not only to keep pace with the programme of expanding native elementary schools in the interior districts but also to complement the locally oriented curriculum and textbooks. The pressing demand for teachers led to the establishment in mid-1948 of the Batu Lintang Teacher Training Centre and School, located about five kilometres to the southeast of Kuching.[101] This new facility added to the existing Sarawak Malay Teachers' Training College, Kuching that was found wanting as newly established native schools in the interior required teachers conversant in English, notwithstanding that the medium of instruction was in the vernacular (Malay or Iban). A lower secondary school was attached to the Centre catering to selected native boys drawn from elementary schools for training as teachers or for the civil service. In 1950, Sarawak Malay Teachers' Training College closed down, and its trainee teachers continued at the Centre.[102]

Besides the provision of more native elementary schools throughout the territory, various programmes were implemented to improve education of the indigenous peoples, *inter alia* group headmaster scheme, schools broadcasting, local scholarship scheme, school mothers programme, boarding subsidy scheme, and the construction of more government junior secondary schools.[103] Initiated from 1957, the group headmaster scheme focused on addressing the perennial issue of low-quality instruction borne of teachers of low morale serving in rural schools through more regular and closer supervision by experienced and qualified personnel. Under the aegis of the Colombo Plan, experienced and seasoned teachers and head teachers from Canada, Australia, and New Zealand were recruited on a short-term basis (often a five-year tenure or less) to provide the much-needed professional guidance and assistance to selected groups of native elementary schools in these districts, viz. Saratok (Iban), Kanowit (Iban), Mukah (Melanau), and Baram (Kayan, Kenyah, Orang Ulu).[104]

Beginning in 1959, schools broadcasting – educational programmes over the air – basically focused on improving English mastery amongst children of native schools in the interior. Thanks to radio sets made available by the Asia Foundation and the governments of Australia, New Zealand, and Japan, by 1960, more than 770 schools comprising some 60,000 pupils benefitted from this initiative.[105] It was another three years before schools broadcast was expanded to secondary schools, likewise focusing on English proficiency.

Local scholarship scheme, school mothers programme, and boarding subsidy scheme were interrelated support. The fact that at rural native schools the majority of the serving teachers had barely acquired schooling beyond Primary V, many possessed schooling until Primary IV. Hence, higher elementary classes (Primary V and VI) were only available at the few mission-managed native central schools. Likewise, this similar situation was evident in Malay elementary education, namely unqualified teachers, and the availability of Primary V and VI only at the few Malay central schools managed by local authorities. Therefore, the colonial government resolved this dire situation by providing scholarships for promising pupils to attend higher elementary classes at native/Malay central schools, and the boarding subsidy scheme addressed the children's boarding needs. In order to allow these promising pupils to fully focus on their studies, women with the title 'School Mother' under the school mothers programme undertook the daily task of preparing meals for their boarding charges and oversee their general well-being.[106]

Students who performed well in the higher elementary classes would be sent to one of the four existing government junior secondary schools in 1960, viz. Maderasah Melayu (Kuching), Tanjong Lobang School (Miri), Kanowit Government School (Kanowit), and Dragon School (24th Mile Kuching-Simanggang Road). In the pipeline to be implemented by 1963 were the construction of six more government junior secondary schools at Bau, Bintulu, Saratok, Mukah, Baram, and Limbang.[107]

As a result of the ongoing developments in uplifting the education and schooling of the multiethnic population, it appeared opportune to create and attain a national education system "with the aim of developing among all the peoples a sense of common citizenship, identity, brotherhood and undivided loyalty".[108] The objective of a national education system was in line with the ultimate goal of preparation towards eventual self-government, thereby "by educating them in the obligations, the responsibilities, and the privileges of citizenship" as spelt out in the 8th Principle of 'Nine Cardinal Principles of the Rule of the English Rajah'.[109]

Public opinion as well as the temper amongst members of the Council Negri appeared to be amiable to the concept of a national education system. "It [a national education system] springs", according to Sarawak Colonial Governor Sir Alexander Waddell (1960–1963) in a speech in December 1960, "not only from the desire to provide equality of opportunity but from the need to promote a truly inter-racial society – an objective which we all sincerely desire and work for".[110]

Striving for a national education system, however, entailed the attainment of several basic objectives, viz. the implementation of English as a common medium of instruction at the secondary level of schooling, common curriculum and common examinations, usage of Sarawak-centric textbooks, and instruction in civics.[111] A national education system envisaged the creation of multiethnic secondary school with English as the medium of instruction. The choice of the English language vis-à-vis other native languages (Malay, Iban) as the medium of instruction for education at the secondary level was motivated and justified by its general acceptability across the multiethnic population, its economic utility in terms of marketability in the employment sector, and the opportunities for tertiary education.[112] Hence, a changeover to English as the medium of instruction implemented at stages and over a reasonable period of years, overall referred to as the Conversion Plan, was for all intents and purposes an ingenious strategy to phase out the divisive plural school system that ran on communal lines. Implementation of the Conversion Plan appeared unobtrusive for government Malay junior secondary schools and their mission-managed counterparts. The stumbling block was with the 16 independent Chinese vernacular middle schools. Although subsequently the majority acquiesced, it was not before much drama of heated debates, public protests and demonstrations, and closed-door intense deliberations by school management committees.

Adoption of a common Sarawak-centric curriculum and common examinations complemented the common medium of instruction. Only through such measures coupled with Sarawak-centric textbooks could the aim of developing a common identity, a sense of belonging, and hence loyalty among the multiethnic peoples be achieved. Additionally, the incorporation of formal instruction in civics in the higher elementary school curriculum, and thereafter, likewise at the junior secondary level, was a practical approach in inculcating a sense of belonging. Identification with the land of their domicile was the first step in nurturing patriotism among the young. Undoubtedly, classroom instruction in civics had constraints and limitations in comparison with the reality from without, which was particularly telling amongst Chinese youths.

North Borneo: education as second fiddle

During the period of Chartered Company administration, education and schooling played secondary roles to economic development. The CO era likewise similarly treated education as less urgent and/or important, instead prioritizing repairs, reconstruction, and development of infrastructure facilities such as roads and communications. Nonetheless, there were much-desired progress and improvements in the educational field, as evidenced by the statistics as shown in Table 3.4, where the number of schools quadrupled and there was close to a seven-fold increase in student enrolment. As for female education, an almost eight-fold increase in enrolment occurred between 1947 and 1963, but the gender gap remained.

In recounting the educational development of North Borneo during the period of colonial government, between 1946 and 1963, several major milestones were attained, namely the appointment of the first director of education and three senior officers, a five-year plan, key legislations, establishment of the first teacher training facility, creation of Local Authority Native Voluntary Schools, key documents like the Woodhead Report (1955), and administrative reform including the setting up of a Board of Education.

Shortly after the colonial government assumed the reins of administration, a post of Director of Education was created. The first appointee, R. E. Perry, laid the groundwork and set the direction in producing the first five-year plan (1947–1951) for educational development.[113] Perry's ultimate goal was uplifting the education of the entire population, both the young and adults, making education and schooling as a community undertaking requiring cooperation and participation at all levels.[114]

The Education Ordinance (1947) defined the various types of schools, established an Advisory Committee for Education, and registered and inspected schools

Table 3.4 North Borneo: Schools and Student Enrolment, 1947 and 1963

Year	Schools	Total Student Enrolment	Male Students	Female Students
1947	165	14,052	10,579	3,473
1963	520†	70,057	42,881	27,176

† The figure for number of schools in 1963 was 519, according to *State of Sabah: Annual Summary Report of the Department of Education, 1963*, p. 33. However, a figure of 520 was cited by the *Statistics Division of the Education Department* [1963].

Source: K. M. George, "Historical Development of Education", *Commemorative History of Sabah, 1881–1981*, edited by Anwar Sullivan and Cecilia Leong (Kota Kinabalu: Sabah State Government Centenary Publications Committee, 1981), pp. 490 n. 70, 491, 506.

and teachers.[115] Besides the Director, three senior officers were appointed, viz. a Senior Education Officer, a Woman Education Officer, and an Education Officer to oversee the inspection of schools and teachers. Additionally, three Supervisors of vernacular Schools and two for Chinese schools were appointed.

Initially, the Teacher Training College, the first in the territory, was temporarily accommodated in the Trade School at Menggatal; it later shifted to its permanent venue in Tuaran. On 18 October 1952, the Duchess of Kent formally opened the Teacher Training College or Kent College to train teachers for government schools. Although recruits were expected from graduates of Primary V and Primary VI government schools for a two-year course, circumstances decided otherwise. The initial intake instead comprised experienced head teachers and teachers of more than five years' experience for a shortened one-year course. From 1957, this one-year course was replaced with a three-year programme of study offered to graduates of government primary schools. Meanwhile, in mid-1953, Chinese-medium students who possessed a minimum three-year secondary education were recruited for a training course. In 1958, candidates with a North Borneo Junior Certificate were selected for courses to enable them entry as teachers in English-medium schools.

The following year, 1953 marked the entry of a new concept of educational facility, viz. Local Authority Native Voluntary School (NVS). The forward-looking Kota Belud Local Authority erected three new schools complemented with five teachers' quarters.

> The uniqueness of this system was that building materials were partly from central [government] and partly from local funds . . . local inhabitants supplied voluntary labour for the construction work. The [colonial] government provided grants for books and equipment and sometimes provided government trained teachers. To raise the standard of the teachers . . . the government initiate training courses.[116]

It was only in mid-1962 that a training centre was set up in Jesselton to train teachers in NVS. Following an intensive six-month course, the teachers were incorporated into the public civil service and returned to their respective NVS.

Educational Survey of North Borneo, a commissioned work by E. W. Woodhead, chief Education Officer for the County of Kent, England, was submitted in 1955. Educational advances thus far were defined in these words:

> Between 1954 and 1956 a new education ordinance [Education (Amendment) Ordinance], an educational survey [by Woodhead] of the State, an education policy committee and an amended ordinance between them effectively initiated a procedure whereby the schools of the country were brought under one control, and which began to produce citizens with a broadly similar education, outlook and language ability; and, one hoped, a common loyalty to the State.[117]

The Education (Amendment) Ordinance that came into operation from 1956 introduced a noted development in the establishment of a Board of Education and Local

Education Committee. Composition of this Board of Education included the Director of Education, the Financial Secretary, the Secretary for Local Government, the Residents, three nominated members from the Legislative Council,[118] and another three Representatives drawn from the Christian missions.[119] The Board of Education oversaw all matters relating to educational planning and expansion. At the grassroots level, Local Education Committees were formed in each of the 14 designated School Areas, whereby its members (Native Chiefs, headmen, volunteers) addressed educational issues at the respective localities.

By the late 1950s, the plural school system inherited from the pre-war Chartered Company period remained intact, as shown in Table 3.5 of the five types of schools, their management, and medium of instruction. By the early 1960s, there apparently was a public call for a wider usage of English as the medium of instruction. In response, the Board of Education recommended that instruction in English in Government Malay Schools should commence not in Primary III but from Primary I.

Therefore, not unlike neighbouring Sarawak, North Borneo too worked towards a single education policy whereby the hitherto disparate plural school system would ultimately come under one education system with a common medium of instruction (namely, English), common curriculum, common usage of locally centric textbooks, and staffed by locally trained teachers. Some measures were undertaken from the late 1950s to this end. For instance, in 1957, pupils wishing to enter English-medium secondary schools shall go through a transition stage or 'bridge class' where they upgraded their proficiency in English. In the context of Chinese schools that had until middle school (equivalent with the junior secondary school in the English-medium school), they were allowed to attend a one-year 'Remove Class', and thereafter, presumably that their English proficiency would have improved, hence they would be eligible for English-medium upper secondary classes.[120] The Board of Education also submitted recommendations to the colonial government in 1960, *inter alia* enumeration of teachers, grant-in-aid scheme, and

Table 3.5 North Borneo: Plural School System, 1950s

Type	Funded and Management	Medium of Instruction
Government Malay Schools	Colonial Government	Malay
Christian Mission Schools	Christian Missions	English
Chinese Schools	Chinese community subscription, clan houses, philanthropists	*Guo-yu* (Mandarin)
Native Voluntary Schools	Colonial Government	Non-Malay native languages
Estate Schools	Plantation owners	Malay or *Guo-yu* (Mandarin)

Source: K. M. George, "Historical Development of Education", *Commemorative History of Sabah, 1881–1981*, edited by Anwar Sullivan and Cecilia Leong (Kota Kinabalu: Sabah State Government Centenary Publications Committee, 1981), p. 497.

the levying of education rates paid to a Central Education Fund to finance elementary education.

Progress in secondary education was at best sluggish. The pre-war Chartered Company administration had a prejudicial view of secondary education. As late as mid-1937, the governor, in an address to native chiefs, criticized mission schools of "producing more boys fitted for clerkships than the country required".[121] Only the Christian mission schools and Chinese schools provided lower secondary education, namely to the level for attaining the Cambridge Overseas Junior Certificate and the Middle School Certificate, respectively. Both mission schools and Chinese schools resumed their lower secondary education during the CO era. From 1952, a five-year secondary programme was mandatory in order to create full-fledged secondary schools, leading to the Cambridge Overseas School Certificate. Then in 1957 the colonial government established the first Government Secondary School in Jesselton that subsequently became the Sabah College. It had a Form VI class with an initial intake of 21 students (15 boys and 6 girls).[122]

Making sense of the law

Initially, the incoming CO administration adopted a judicial system from its predecessor in Sarawak and North Borneo, namely a pattern composed of a Supreme Court, Resident's Courts, District Courts, Police Courts, and the Native Courts. Added to this overall judicial system was the complicated as well as sensitive issue of customary law and traditional native practices, Islamic jurisprudence, and Chinese customary norms. Succinctly presented as follows is the situation in Sarawak that confronted the colonial government then and was similarly applicable to its counterparts in North Borneo:

> The many indigenous tribes have their own *adat* or customary law, and in some cases native customs have been embodied in Codes [viz.] . . . the Malay *Undang-undang* and the *Tusun Tunggu*, the latter being a Code of the Sea Dayak [Iban] Fines in use in the Third Division. Chinese customary law, chiefly in matrimonial matters and in relation to inheritance, is recognised to a limited extent, but only in so far as such recognition is expressly or by implication to be found in a local Ordinance. Where Sarawak law is silent, the Courts are required to apply English law "in so far as it is applicable to Sarawak having regard to native customs and local conditions".[123]

Towards the later part of 1949, senior British officials 'on-the-spot', notably Malcolm MacDonald, the Commissioner-General for South-East Asia, Governors Duncan Stewart and Edward Twining of Sarawak and North Borneo, respectively, and Resident Eric Ernest Falk Pretty of Brunei, discussed the possibilities of a closer association among the three territories, within a five-year framework.[124] In line with this aspiration, Sarawak, North Borneo, and Brunei (Courts) Order in Council of 1951 unified the judicial system of all three territories from 1 December 1951 (Chart 3.1). The Brunei monarch as the supreme Islamic authority in the sultanate was complemented by the Court of Kathis.[125]

Chart 3.1 Judicial Structure of Sarawak, Brunei, and North Borneo, 1951–1963

Supreme Court of Judicature *Court of Appeal* *High Court of Justice*					
Sarawak		*Brunei*		*North Borneo*	
1st Class Magistrate	Governor	1st Class Magistrate	Sultan-in-Religious-Council		Native Court of Appeal†
2nd Class Magistrate	Resident	2nd Class Magistrate	Court of Kathis		Resident's Native Court
3rd Class Magistrate	District Officer	3rd Class Magistrate		District Court	District Native Court
	Native Officer			Court of Small Causes and Police Court	Native Officer's Court
				Petty Court	Headman's Court

Sources: SAR, 1953, pp. 113–116; *North Borneo Annual Report 1953* (Jesselton: Government Printers, 1954), pp. 103–104; Colonial Office, *Brunei, Annual Report on Brunei, 1952*, pp. 68–69.

† Justices of the Supreme Court serve in the Native Court of Appeal.

Overall, the judicial system served the basic needs of Sarawak and North Borneo. Undoubtedly there remained minor hitches and issues, especially pertaining to the rather perplexing meaning and/or interpretation of native customary practices. Common sense of 'pragmatic justice' appears to be the practical panacea as the situation in CO-era Sarawak illustrates, and it was likewise applicable to North Borneo with its multiethnic peoples. The reality was thus as the situation in Sarawak illustrates:

> The excesses of *adat lama* had been removed by 1946, thus enabling the British colonial administration to adopt a policy of non-interference, although the tensions between English law, customary law, and the Brooke heritage of informal justice remained. In the rural areas where the majority of the indigenous peoples lived and the lower courts dealt with most cases, many of the SCS [Sarawak Civil Service] officers were veterans of the Brooke era and carried on the Brooke tradition of administering pragmatic justice rather than applying the intricacies of statutory law.[126]

Security issues and enforcement agencies

Undoubtedly present but less apparent in the pre-war period, the post-war CO era faced the threat of subversion from within, especially in the context of Sarawak. Following several tumultuous events, the police and constabulary were strengthened and expanded to meet the various security challenges that were increasingly compromising the safety, peace, and sovereignty of Sarawak and North Borneo.

Following the assumption of civil administration, all Sarawak and North Borneo literally had to reassemble a police force or a constabulary for law enforcement to ensure peace and order from within. The organization of the police was similar in both territories. Police bases were in Kuching and Jesselton, the administrative centres of Sarawak and North Borneo, respectively.

The regular police force, field force, and a special force constituted the three branches of the police force. Besides routine police responsibilities, the regular police force also enforced customs and immigration regulations, passport control, and traffic duties. Owing to the ongoing jungle war with communist terrorists (CTs) in British Malaya,[127] it was deemed appropriate and timely that a police field force was constituted to be a mobile para-military unit primarily tasked to suppress civil unrest in any corner of the territory under its jurisdiction.[128] Hand-picked and trained in jungle warfare, police field force personnel were primed to face any internal threat. Members of the field force were trained to supplement the army in times of emergency. The special force was specifically geared and armed to counter political subversion, especially from communist elements. Besides gathering political intelligence, special force officers also investigated criminal organizations and their activities.

SSOL engaged its own security team for maintaining the vast installations and facilities from theft, arson, and/or sabotage. Despite the porous border between Sarawak and Kalimantan, there was a conspicuous absence of a border police unit. Instead, the army was called in during *Konfrontasi* (1962–1966).

Although recruitment of police personnel from the various ethnic groups that mostly possessed martial traditions was a non-issue, the major obstacle was over Chinese enlistment. Aversion to the army or police was an age-old Chinese tradition, whereby sons were groomed to be scholars, not soldiers or policemen.

> Despite recruitment efforts, Chinese enlistments have not been proportionated to the size of the Chinese population. . . . The lack of Chinese-speaking detectives is a particular handicap to the anti-communist campaign of the special force since the communist subversive potential centers in the Chinese segment of the population.[129]

The aforesaid situation was most intractable in the case of Sarawak, where communist subversive activities were the most threatening vis-à-vis other neighbouring territories.[130] Besides the traditional disinclination that prompted parental disapproval, the Chinese were put off of having to go through the ranks (for promotion), an aversion to discipline and conformity, and Malay being the *lingua franca*.[131] Additionally, the fact that Sarawak constabulary was notoriously tarred with unpunished wartime collaborators, the Chinese people as a whole shunned it as they had suffered the most during the dark days of the Japanese military occupation.[132]

Although the crime rate plummeted dramatically during the greater part of the CO era, there was a climate of instability owing to the volatile political situation.[133] The rather vociferous protests and demonstrations staged by the anti-cession movement between 1946 and 1949 were at best disconcerting, and at worst, threatening eruption of chaos and riots.[134] Meanwhile, the global Cold War became apparent from 1947, and within months, the Malayan Emergency (1948–1960) was declared in mid-June 1948. In response to a possible outbreak of civil disorder from within the Bornean territories, the Special Branch was formed, headed by an officer specially recruited in 1949 in gathering political intelligence and detecting subversive activities.[135]

But the newly formed Special Branch failed in anticipating the political assassination of Duncan Stewart, the second colonial governor, during his inaugural visit to Sibu in early December 1949. Consequently, security measures were hastened and tightened, *inter alia* 'spot checks' were carried out on the civilian population, riot control was inserted into the training programme in anticipation of outbreaks of civil unrest, and a Special Branch office was set up in Kuala Belait to oversee security in northern Sarawak as well as Brunei. Additionally, a Marine Police Unit was established to patrol coastal waters and shipping, and a Radio Branch utilized UHF/VHF communications links to hasten quicker exchange of intelligence.[136]

Undoubtedly deemed a serious 'wake-up call' was the fatal shooting of a police lance-corporal and the wounding of two of his colleagues while manning a routine roadblock at the 27th Mile Kuching-Simanggang Road in the early hours of 6 August 1952 by alleged communist guerrillas from Kalimantan. Dubbed the Batu Kitang Incident,[137] this daring assault on security personnel sparked a series of developments that subsequently led to overall improvements to Sarawak Constabulary. On 9 August, the First Division came under a state of emergency that armed the colonial authorities with draconian powers, viz. imposition of curfew, detention without trial up to 12 months, and death sentences for those in possession of unlicensed firearms.[138] Patrols were undertaken along the thickly forested and porous Sarawak-Kalimantan border areas. Sweeps on suspected communist and/ or sympathizers were carried out, likewise arms checks. The former action was fruitful, leading to 25 detentions and 5 deportations, all of ethnic Chinese.[139]

Doubtless as a means to allay fears and panic among the masses, the Deputy Director of Operations of Malaya declared at a press conference on 1 September 1952 that there was no evidence of an organized communist party or overall plan of communist activities in Sarawak. But confidentially, this senior Malayan official confided otherwise with Governor Sir Anthony Abell, who promptly put forth various security measures, notably expanding the Constabulary, including improving conditions of service to attract recruits especially among the Chinese, strengthening of the Special Branch, and building more police stations, all of which entailed greater allocation of expenditure.[140]

Targeted improvements were focused on the Special Branch. Not only did it receive an Assistant Commissioner as its head in 1953, but its operations besides in Kuching were also extended to Simanggang, Sibu, Miri, and Kuala Belait.[141]

Investment in the Special Branch was justifiable. A coup of sorts was achieved in the aftermath of the Brunei Revolt on 8 December 1962, whereby over an eight-day period, 49 suspects of the Clandestine Communist Organization (CCO) were detained.[142] The sweep of detention of communists continued thereafter with astonishing results: detained under 'public security or emergency', 79 persons in 1962 and 803 in 1963; 'detention pending deportation', 49 in 1961 and 157 in 1963.[143]

Interrogation of detainees revealed invaluable intelligence of the CCO including its *modus operandi*, depth of infiltration in various organizations, and movements (education, political parties, labour, farmers'). Information gathered was published as a Government White Paper titled *The Danger Within*.[144]

Moving forward

A new era emerged in the aftermath of the Second World War whereby there was a realignment of power that became more pronounced from the late 1940s. While imperial powers of the pre-war period faced declining fortunes, a shifting of the loci of power – political, military, and economic – from London, Paris, Berlin, and Tokyo to Washington and Moscow, and a gradually emergent Beijing.

Britain, in the post-war scenario, found itself worn, tired, almost bankrupt, and increasingly dependent on its transatlantic wartime ally, the U.S. Nonetheless, British premiers Churchill and Eden still harboured aspirations of resuscitating the old British Empire, not realizing or simply in denial that 'the empire on which the sun never sets' was increasingly declining, entering its twilight years. Prime Minister Eden miscalculated and misread Washington's reaction and response to the Suez Crisis (1956) vis-à-vis the Cold War climate. Suez marked the turning point of post-war Britain as a 'has-been', no longer dictating the temper and pace of world affairs, instead having to bow to the agenda of others, in particular the U.S. The Suez debacle, or 'the squalid little war in Egypt' to borrow *The Guardian*'s Derek Brown's phrase, was the undoing of Britain and that of Eden.

Immediate post-war British Prime Minister Attlee's Labour government had no illusion of grandeur of old empires. Although pressing circumstances of the local situation pushed for a hurried exit from the Indian sub-continent, once 'the jewel in the crown of the British Empire', likewise Burma, in 1947 and 1948 respectively, Whitehall too was equally anxious for colonial disengagement.

But Sarawak and North Borneo were premature for disengagement. On the contrary, in fact, from 1946, the CO assumed administrative responsibility of two crown colonies (Sarawak and North Borneo). The CO colonial administration in Sarawak and North Borneo, for all intents and purposes, were 'caretakers' entrusted with initiating and laying the groundwork preparation for self-government leading to eventual independence. Once rehabilitation and reconstruction from war damages were completed, developments and expansion followed through in the economic and social services in tandem with political and constitutional advances.

All sectors of the economy were resuscitated, rebuilt, developed, and expanded alongside investments in infrastructure build-up. After the Korean War, commodity prices surged that brought forth some measure of prosperity to rubber smallholders, pepper farmers, sago cultivators, and copra producers. Similarly, timber concessionaires and the oil companies also benefited from the brief but lucrative boom period.

Education was the key, not only in preparing the multiethnic peoples of the three territories but also in preparing them as responsible citizens for self-government and subsequent independence. Accordingly, investments in capital, funding, facilities, and training of teachers were expended for this pivotal social service, for inculcating political consciousness, and for producing expertise for economic development.

In large measure, it necessitated the dismantling of the plural school system of the pre-war era that sowed the seeds of separatism and disparity. Moreover, the pace of progress among the government vernacular native schools (coastal and interior), Christian mission schools (urban and rural), plantation schools, and Chinese schools were likewise disparate, the most advanced being the urban Christian mission schools followed by the Chinese schools, and the most backward were the vernacular native schools in the interior. Most conspicuous was the ethnic educational gap, as a wide gulf existed between urban Chinese and upriver natives; the former armed with a Cambridge Senior Certificate could further his tertiary studies abroad (mainly in the UK and Hong Kong), whereas the latter possessing barely the 3Rs was in no better position than his unschooled parents or grandparents in the longhouse.

Between Sarawak and North Borneo, Sarawak attained the most in educational advances. The colonial government in Sarawak from the outset had outlined the educational goals, viz. to close the ethnic educational gap between natives and Chinese, and to establish a national education system. Various programmes and support were channelled to native education in terms of quantitative expansion and qualitative uplift. Implementation of the national education system at the secondary level through a single medium of instruction (English being chosen), adoption of a common locally oriented curriculum and textbooks, and locally trained teachers was set in motion towards the late 1950s and early 1960s.

The Conversion Plan – English to replace the vernacular as the medium of instruction in secondary education – faced the most difficult hurdle with the Chinese middle schools (lower secondary). On the one hand, advocates of *status quo*, that is the retention of *quo-yu* (Mandarin), argued for the preservation of the age-old heritage of Chinese culture, history, and language, the very essence of Chinese ethnic identity. On the other hand, supporters of the Conversion Plan saw in English and the concomitant attainment of the Cambridge Junior and Senior Certificate *the* 'passport' to a clerical career and for tertiary studies abroad. But some advocates of *quo-yu* harboured more sinister motives. Left-leaning agitators possessed political designs in demanding that the Chinese school system remained untouched, lest interfering with their political agenda.

The third protagonist of the Cold War – the Chinese communists – had entered the Bornean stage, specifically in Sarawak. In fact, the trajectory of the Cold War for Sarawak stretched back to the late 1920s and 1930s, when the Brooke regime attempted to contain and stem Leftist influences that had seeped into the classroom and playground. It became conspicuous, threatening from the early 1950s. The Batu Kitang Incident (1952) was a communist assault, the first salvo of an impending armed struggle. The Cold War's 'hot' war had reached the Bornean soil.

Notes

1 Winston Churchill, 'Speech at a Conservative Mass Meeting, Llandudno, 9 October 1948', reprinted in *Europe Unite-Speeches: 1947 and 1948 by Winston S. Churchill*, edited by Randolph S. Churchill (London: Cassell, 1950), pp. 417–418.
2 Britain made the final repayment of USD$ 83 million in 2006, finally closing an account, and a chapter, with its transatlantic war ally. Finlo Rohrer, "What's a Little Debt between Friends?", *BBC News Magazine*, Wednesday, May 10, 2006. http://news.bbc.co.uk/2/hi/uk_news/magazine/4757181.stm Accessed 21 Dec 2017.
3 Philippa Levine, *The British Empire: Sunrise to Sunset*, 2nd ed. (London: Routledge, 2013), p. 208.
4 "Wind of Change": A speech made to the South Africa Parliament on 3 February 1960 by Harold Macmillan, *South Africa History Online: Towards a People's History*. www.sahistory.org.za/archive/wind-change-speech-made-south-africa-parliament-3-february-1960-harold-macmillan Emphasis added. Accessed 21 Dec 2017, Emphasis added.
5 See Ritchie Ovendale, "Macmillan and the Wind of Change in Africa, 1957–1960", *The Historical Journal*, 38, 2 (June 1995): 455–477; Carl Peter Watts, "The 'Wind of Change': British Decolonisation in Africa, 1957–1965", *History Review*, 71 (2011): 12–17.
6 Levine, *The British Empire*, pp. 208–209.
7 Avi Shlaim, "The Protocol of Sèvres,1956: Anatomy of a War Plot", *International Affairs*, 73, 3 (1997): 509–530.
8 Elie Podeh, "The Drift towards Neutrality: Egyptian Foreign Policy during the Early Nasserist Era, 1952–55", *Middle Eastern Studies*, 32, 1 (Jan 1996): 159–178.
9 Dona J. Stewart, *The Middle East Today: Political, Geographical and Cultural Perspectives* (London: Routledge, 2013), p. 133; David Tal, ed., *The 1956 War: Collusion and Rivalry in the Middle East* (London: Frank Cass Publishers, 2001), p. 203.
10 Keith Kyle, *Suez: Britain's End of Empire in the Middle East* (London: I. B. Tauris, 2003), p. 464.
11 Derek Brown, "1956: Suez and the End of Empire", *The Guardian*, Mar 14, 2001. www.theguardian.com/politics/2001/mar/14/past.education1 Accessed 28 Dec 2017.
12 "The Suez Crisis: An Affair to Remember", *The Economist*, July 27, 2006. Emphasis added. www.economist.com/node/7218678 Accessed 28 Dec 2017.
13 Later, the 'Nine Cardinal Principles' were featured in the First Schedule to Sarawak (Constitution) Order in Council, 1956, and adopted into the *Report of the Commission of Enquiry, North Borneo and Sarawak, 1962.*
14 Emphasis added.
15 Often referred to as the 'Chartered Company', or simply, the 'Company'.
16 Emphasis added. This principle of trusteeship became the so-called Brooke tradition that was steadfastly abided by the Brooke's successors. The aforesaid words are enshrined in a plaque in the Anglican St Leonards Church, Sheepstor, Dartmoor, England. In the nearby cemetery are the graves of the Brookes: James, Charles, Charles Vyner, and Bertram.
17 British North Borneo, 1881. Charter granted to the British North Borneo Company, Westminster, Nov 1, 1881, p. 6. www.lawnet.sabah.gov.my/Lawnet/SabahLaws/Treaties/CharterGrantedToTheBritishNorthBorneoCompany.pdf Accessed 29 Dec 2017.
18 Emphasis added.
19 See Cosmo Parkinson, *The Colonial Office from within* (London: Faber and Faber, 1947), pp. 55–56.

20 MacDonald was succeeded by Robert Scott (t. 1955–1959) and George Nigel Douglas-Hamilton, Earl of Selkirk (1960–1963). Following the formation of Malaysia in September 1963, the office was dissolved.

21 See Ooi Keat Gin, ed., *The Works of Nicholas Tarling on Southeast Asia, Vol. I: The Superintendence of British Interests in Southeast Asia* (London and New York: Routledge, 2012).

22 Vernon L. Porritt, *British Colonial Rule in Sarawak, 1946–1963* (Kuala Lumpur: Oxford University Press, 1997), pp. 121, 124.

23 Ex-Brooke officers, R. G. Aikman (t. 1950–1955) and J. C. H. Barcroft (t. 1958), served as chief secretary during the post-war CO administration.

24 The five Divisions were simply designated First, Second, Third, Fourth, and Fifth. Districts included Sibu, Lower Rajang, Oya, Mukah, Kanowit, and Kapit, and sub-districts were Sarikei, Binatang, Daro, Matu, and Rajang. See B. A. Hepburn, *The Handbook of Sarawak* (Singapore: Malaya Publishing House, 1949), pp. 46–60.

25 See Chapter 5 of this volume.

26 With regard to the education of natives and Chinese, see Ooi Keat Gin, "Mission Education in Sarawak during the Period of Brooke Rule, 1841–1946", *Sarawak Museum Journal*, 42, 63 (New Series) (Dec 1991): 283–373; Ooi Keat Gin, "Chinese Vernacular Education in Sarawak during Brooke Rule, 1841–1946", *Modern Asian Studies*, 28, Part 3 (July 1994): 503–531; Ooi Keat Gin, "Sarawak Malay Attitudes towards Education during the Brooke Period, 1841–1946", *Journal of Southeast Asian Studies*, 21, 2 (Sep 1990): 340–359.

27 *Sarawak Tribune*, 5 May 1951.

28 Porritt, *British Colonial Rule in Sarawak*, p. 23.

29 See John Woods, *Local Government in Sarawak: An Introduction to the Nature and Working of District Councils in the State* (Kuching: Sarawak Government Printing Office, 1968).

30 Porritt, *British Colonial Rule in Sarawak*, p. 131.

31 V. Gabriel William, "The General State Administration of Sabah, 1881–1981", in *Commemorative History of Sabah, 1881–1981*, edited by Anwar Sullivan and Cecilia Leong (Kota Kinabalu: Sabah State Government Centenary Publications Committee, 1981), p. 17, n. 40.

32 For other examples of department configurations and name changes, see ibid., p. 20.

33 Ibid., p. 21.

34 Ibid., p. 70 Appendix B2.

35 *Colony of North Borneo Annual Report 1954* (London: H.M. Stationery Office, 1954), p. 145.

36 William, "Administration", p. 23, n.50.

37 M. H. Baker, *Sabah: The First Ten Years as a Colony, 1946–1956* (Kuala Lumpur: Malaysia Publishing House for the Department of History, University of Singapore, 1965), p. 50.

38 William, "Administration", p. 23.

39 Ibid. Under the Local Government Ordinance of 1962, bolstered with additional public funding from the colonial government, the LA could extend into building minor roads, raising the quality of agriculture, further developing the public services and amenities, and improving and promoting public health. Ibid., pp. 23–24.

40 Ibid., p. 25.

41 K. G. Tregonning, *A History of Modern Sabah (North Borneo, 881–1963)* (Singapore: University of Malaya Press, 1965), p. 23. Burma (present-day Myanmar) had the unfortunate fate of being fought twice over. Imperial Japanese forces launched a northward advance in 1942 from the south to the northeast, and the British reconquest in 1945, reoccupying from the north/northeast towards the southeast. For instance, see Louis Allen, *Burma: The Longest War, 1941–1945* (New York: St Martin's Press, 1985).

42 *North Borneo, Brunei, Sarawak (Sarawak and North Borneo)*, p. 171.

43 In the mid-1950s, there were in existence 69 estates, out of which 60 were rubber. North Borneo had the lion's share, whereby 49 estates accounted for half the acreage for rubber. Other plantation crops were tobacco, hemp, and coconuts. Ibid., p. 172.

44 See James Scott, *Seeing Like a State* (New Haven, CT: Yale University Press, 1998), pp. 282–283. On the contrary, as Michael Dove and others have empirically demonstrated, swidden agriculture "is well suited to its tropical ecosystems with high rainfall and poor soils", and "it may indeed be the only sustainable form of agriculture yet devised for tropical rain forest habitats". Michael Dove, "Swidden Agriculture", in *Southeast Asia: A Historical Encyclopedia from Angkor Wat to East Timor*, edited by Ooi Keat Gin (Santa Barbara, CA: ABC-Clio, 2004), III: 1284, 1285). Also, see Peter Kelinman et al., "The Ecological Sustainability of Slash-and-Burn Agriculture", *Agriculture, Ecosystems and Environment* 52 (1995): 235–249; Michael Dove, "Theories of Swidden Agriculture, and the Political Economy of Ignorance", *Agroforestry Systems*, 1 (1983): 85–99.

45 See Appendix 3.2.

46 British Information Services, "General Surveys", in *Commonwealth Survey: A Record of United Kingdom and Commonwealth Affairs* (London: HMSO, 3 [Aug 6, 1949]), p. 25.

47 *Sarawak Annual Report* (SAR), 1962, p. 83; SAR, 1958, p. 39.

48 SAR, 1962, p. 82.

49 Porritt, *British Colonial Rule in Sarawak*, pp. 196–197.

50 The northeast monsoon season, locally referred to as the *landas* between November and February, experienced gale-strength winds and choppy seas often with big waves and heavy rains. Floods were not uncommon. Hence, travel on land and especially along the coasts was inadvisable lest courting untoward incidents, even outright disasters.

51 See *Sarawak Gazette* (hereinafter SG) Mar 1951.

52 SAR, 1951, p. 135.

53 See *Report of the Proceedings of the Council Negri held in the Main Court House*, Kuching, 1, 2 and 4 Dec 1953.

54 See Sarawak Development Board, *Sarawak Development Plan, 1959–1963*, pp. 6, 18; SAR, 1962, pp. 252–253.

55 SAR, 1959, p. 145; SAR, 1962, p. 252.

56 SAR, 1962, p. 254.

57 Ooi Keat Gin, *Of Free Trade and Native Interests: The Brookes and the Economic Development of Sarawak, 1841–1941* (Kuala Lumpur: Oxford University Press, 1997), pp. 206–207.

58 See *Straits Times*, 6 July 1961.

59 SAR, 1948, p. 72.

60 SAR, 1955, p. 111.

61 SAR, 1956, p. 115.

62 SAR, 1962, p. 262.

63 SAR, 1957, p. 121.

64 SAR, 1962, p. 261.

65 Porritt, *British Colonial Rule in Sarawak*, p. 262, n. 44.

66 SAR, 1954, pp. 154–156.

67 SAR, 1961, p. 267.

68 Peter Spence Gudgeon, "Economic Development in Sabah, 1881–1981", in *Commemorative History of Sabah, 1881–1981*, edited by Anwar Sullivan and Cecilia Leong (Kota Kinabalu: Sabah State Government Centenary Publications Committee, 1981), p. 206.

69 Ibid.

70 Ibid., p. 207.

71 Ibid., p. 221, Table 10.
72 Ibid.
73 Ibid., p. 222.
74 Ibid., pp. 207–208.
75 Ibid., p. 222.
76 Ibid.
77 Lee Yong Leng, *North Borneo (Sabah): A Study in Settlement Geography* (Singapore: Donald Moore for Eastern Universities Press, 1965), p. 38, Table 6. A figure of M$ 90.7 million for 1960 was unlikely. See Gudgeon, "Economic Development in Sabah", p. 236; Tregonning, *A History of Modern Sabah*, p. 229.
78 Tregonning, *A History of Modern Sabah*, p. 229.
79 Ibid., p. 228.
80 Gudgeon, "Economic Development in Sabah", p. 233.
81 Ibid., p. 234.
82 Ibid.
83 "North Borneo", *The Economic Weekly*, Feb 16, 1952, p. 184. www.epw.in/system/files/pdf/1952_4/7/north_borneo.pdf Accessed 28 Mar 2018.
84 Gudgeon, "Economic Development in Sabah", p. 235.
85 Ibid., p. 205, Table 3; p. 229, Table 12.
86 Ibid., p. 234.
87 Ibid., p. 223.
88 Ibid., p. 240.
89 Ibid., pp. 224, 226, Table 11.4.
90 Ibid., pp. 224, 225, Table 11.1.
91 Ibid., p. 239.
92 Ibid.
93 G. E. Wilford, *The Geology and Mineral Resources of Brunei and Adjacent Parts of Sarawak with Descriptions of Seria and Miri Oilfields*, Geological Survey Department, British Territories in Borneo, Memoir 10 (Brunei: Brunei Press Limited, 1961), p. 148.
94 SSOL was only adopted in 1958, but to avoid confusion, this term/abbreviation is used throughout to refer to this oil company. The Anglo-Saxon Petroleum Company (ASPC), the British partner in the Royal Dutch Shell Group, originally was granted the prospecting license by Rajah Charles Brooke of Sarawak in 1909. The London-based ASPC continued to be the sole operator when oil was struck in Miri the following year, responsible for production, processing (Lutong refinery), and export. All infrastructure facilities including roads, wharfs, pipeline, etc. were undertaken by ASPC. In 1921, the locally (Kuching) registered Sarawak Oilfields Limited (SOL) assumed the reins of ownership and operations from ASPC. SOL was also a subsidiary of the Royal Dutch Shell Group. Ooi, *Of Free Trade and Native Interests*, pp. 138–139, 140; Sarawak Shell Oilfields Limited (SSOL), *Oil in Sarawak 1910–1960* (Kuala Belait, Brunei: Brunei Press, 1961), p. 2.
95 Sarawak Shell Oilfields Limited (SSOL), *Oil in Sarawak*, p. 8.
96 Porritt, *British Colonial Rule in Sarawak*, p. 236.
97 Ooi Keat Gin, *World beyond the Rivers: Education in Sarawak From Brooke Rule to Colonial Office Administration, 1841–1963* (Special Publication Series, Hull, England: Department for South-East Asian Studies, University of Hull, 1996), p. 111. Emphasis added.
98 Sarawak Education Department, *Triennial Survey 1955–1957* (Kuching: Government Printing Office, n.d.), p. 6.
99 'The Grant Code (Regulations) 1956', SGG, 1955, pp. 19, 173. In special cases, especially involving schools catering to indigenous peoples, the colonial government assumes a greater share of the capital expenditure burden (contributing more than the stipulated 50 per cent). Ibid., 174. Also, see Sarawak Education Department, *Annual Summary for 1959* (Kuching: Government Printing Office, 1960), p. 23.

100 Sarawak Information Service, *A Guide to Education in Sarawak* (Kuching: Government Printing Office, 1960), p. 9.

101 This facility occupies the site of the wartime notorious Batu Lintang Prisoners of War and Civilian Internment Camp set up by the occupying Imperial Japanese Army (IJA), where were incarcerated throughout the occupation all Europeans including women and children, British, Indian, Australian, and Dutch army personnel, Brooke officers, and Dutch colonial officers. See Ooi Keat Gin, *Rising Sun over Borneo: The Japanese Occupation of Sarawak, 1941–1945* (London and Basingstoke: Macmillan; New York: Saint Martin's Press, 1999), pp. 58–60.

102 SAR, 1950, p. 53.

103 See Ooi, *World Beyond the Rivers*, pp. 125–130.

104 Sarawak Education Department, *Triennial Survey 1958–1960* (Kuching: Government Printing Office, n.d.), p. 34; Ooi, *World Beyond the Rivers*, pp. 126–127.

105 See Alan Moore, "Instruction by Radio in Sarawak", *Overseas Quarterly* (Sep 1963): 212–213.

106 Hitherto, children prepare their own meals with their own utensils utilizing food supplies brought from home. See Knight, "School Mothers", SG, 20 Nov 1966.

107 Sarawak Council Negri, "Secondary Education", Sessional Paper No. 2 of 1960.

108 *Triennial Survey 1955–1957*, p. 6.

109 See Appendix 3.2.

110 *His Excellency the Governor's Address to Council Negri on 6th December 1960* (Kuching: Government Printing Press, 1961), p. 3.

111 See Ooi, *World beyond the Rivers*, pp. 130–135.

112 See *Governor's Address to Council Negri on 6th December 1960*, p. 3.

113 R. E. Perry, *The Colony of North Borneo: A Five-Year Plan of Educational Development for the Year 1947–51* (Jesselton: Government Printing Office, Aug 28 1946).

114 K. M. George, "Historical Development of Education", in *Commemorative History of Sabah, 1881–1981*, edited by Anwar Sullivan and Cecilia Leong (Kota Kinabalu: Sabah State Government Centenary Publications Committee, 1981), pp. 488–489.

115 *Colony of North Borneo: The Education Ordinance 17/4/1947*.

116 Ibid., pp. 489–490.

117 Tregonning, *A History of Modern Sabah*, p. 236.

118 Appointed by the Governor.

119 The head of each mission shall submit a candidate, and the Governor shall make the formal appointment.

120 See Francis Wong Hoy Kee and and Gwee Yee Hean, *Perspective: The Development of Education in Malaysia and Singapore* (Kuala Lumpur: Heinemann Educational Books (Asia), 1972), p. 48.

121 Extract of H. E.'s [Governor] Address to native Chiefs, Council held on 11/5/1937, quoted in George, "Historical Development of Education", p. 507.

122 *Colony of North Borneo*, p. 42.

123 SAR, 1948, p. 58.

124 See Minutes of the 13 Commissioner-General's Conference held in Singapore on Nov 1, 1949. CO 954 5/3 Item 3 (National Archives, UK; hereinafter NAUK).

125 Variously rendered as *kathi* or *kadi*, it is derived from the Arabic *qadi*, which carries the meaning, 'to judge' or 'to decide'.

126 Porritt, *British Colonial Rule in Sarawak*, p. 153.

127 Between 1948 and 1960, the colonial government, and after 1957, the Malayan government, engaged in a protracted war with the Malayan Communist Party (MCP) that sought to establish a 'Republic of Malaya', after the image of the People's Republic of China (PRC). For insurance claims purposes, the all-out war was referred to as an 'emergency', hence the Malayan Emergency. The second phase (1968–1989) was fought out not only on the peninsular but also in Sarawak. See, Ooi Keat Gin, *Historical Dictionary of Malaysia*, 2nd ed. (Lanham, MD: Rowman & Littlefield, 2018), pp. 268–273.

128 In North Borneo, the field force was referred to as the mobile force. *North Borneo, Brunei, Sarawak (Sarawak and North Borneo)*, p. 103.

129 *North Borneo, Brunei, Sarawak (Sarawak and North Borneo)*, p. 104.

130 See *Annual Report on Sarawak for the Year 1949*, pp. 9, 76.

131 See SAR, 1961, p. 127; SAR, 1962, p. 204.

132 As many as two-thirds of the Malay officers were collaborators, and chief among them was Abang Haji Mustapha bin Abang Haji Moasili, who was even made Datu Bandar by Rajah Vyner Brooke because he supported cession. See R. H. W. Reece, *The Name of Brooke: The End of White Rajah Rule in Sarawak* (Kuala Lumpur: Oxford University Press, 1982), p. 152; K. H. Digby, *Lawyer in the Wilderness* (Ithaca, NY: Cornell University Press, Cornell University Southeast Asia Program Data Paper No. 114, 1980), pp. 75–76.

133 For the drop in crime, see Sarawak Constabulary, *Annual Report on Sarawak Constabulary, 1947–63*, and Sarawak Statistics Department, *Annual Bulletin of Statistics*, 1964.

134 See *Straits Times*, Jan 10, 1947; *Sarawak Tribune*, Sep 15, 1948.

135 *Annual Report on Sarawak for the Year 1949*, p. 78.

136 Sarawak Constabulary, *Annual Report on Sarawak Constabulary, 1950*, pp. 2, 7; ibid., 1951, p. 10; ibid., 1961, pp. 19, 23.

137 For the Batu Kitang Incident, see SG, Dec 12, 1952; *Straits Times*, Aug 12, 1952; *Sarawak Tribune*, 8 Aug 1952. See Chapter 4.

138 See *Sarawak Tribune*, Aug 11, 1952.

139 S*arawak Tribune*, Aug 15, 1952.

140 *Report of the Proceedings of the Council Negri held in the Main Court House*, Kuching, on 2, 3 and 5 Dec 1952.

141 Sarawak Constabulary, *Annual Report on Sarawak Constabulary, 1953*, p. 3; ibid., *1954*, p. 4.

142 *Sarawak Tribune*, Dec 19, 1962.

143 Sarawak Statistics Department, *Annual Bulletin of Statistics*, 1964, Table 9.5.

144 See Sarawak Information Service, *The Danger within: A History of the Clandestine Communist Organization in Sarawak* (Kuching: Government Printing Office, 1963). Tim Hardy, a Special Branch officer compiled and authored this revealing piece that allowed the colonial government, and the Malaysian government an insightful grasp of the communist threat.

4 Bitterness and intrigue

The Chinese Left in Sarawak

The young people are the most active and vital force in society. They are the most eager to learn and the least conservative in their thinking. This is especially so in the era of socialism.[1]

Mao Zedong (1893–1976)

Underlying the quiet façade of Sarawak Chinese society in the post-war decades, there was a simmering feeling of bitterness, which was particularly apparent among the lower rungs of the community. Enduring and surviving the war years and the Japanese military occupation took a heavy toll on the Chinese. Strained inter-ethnic relations, resentment towards the reinstated *towkay* leadership by the newly established British colonial government (from 1946), and the limited educational and employment opportunities among Chinese middle school graduates were predicaments confronting the Chinese community. Leftist/communist elements exploited the community's 'bitterness', transforming it into 'intrigues' that were manipulated in "striving for the establishment of a new democratic society, then a socialist society and finally a communist society".[2] The communist stealth organization utilizing the 'united front' tactic worked through the student movement, labour and peasant movement, and a legitimate political party to achieve its agenda. Chinese language newspapers were utilized as a means in politicizing the wider masses. The colonial government literally had its hands full in tackling the covert and overt subversive activities of the Chinese Left, a struggle for their respective survival.

The Sarawak Chinese

Demographically, Sarawak vis-à-vis neighbouring Brunei and North Borneo has the highest number of Chinese settlers, both in the pre-war Brooke period and during the post-war tenure of the British colonial administration. For all three years shown in Table 4.1, Sarawak has more than twice the number of Chinese inhabitants as North Borneo. In 1960, the Sarawak Chinese comprised almost one-third of the total population.

Comparatively, the Brooke regime in Sarawak was more successful in attracting Chinese immigrants in contrast to the Chartered Company administration.[3] Hence,

Table 4.1 Comparative Ethnic Breakdown of Population in Sarawak, Brunei, and North Borneo, 1939–1960

	Year	Indigenous	Chinese	Others	Total
Sarawak	1939[†]	361,585 (74%)[#]	123,626 (25%)	5,283 (1%)	490,585
	1947	395,417 (73%)	145,158 (26%)	5,810 (1%)	546,385
	1960*	507,252 (68%)	229,154 (31%)	8,123 (1%)	744,529
North Borneo	1931	205,218 (74%)	50,056 (18%)	22,202 (8%)	277,476
	1951	243,009 (73%)	74,374 (22%)	16,758 (5%)	334,141
	1960	306,498 (67%)	104,542 (23%)	43,381 (10%)	454,421
Brunei	1931	26,746 (89%)	2,683 (9%)	706 (2%)	30,135
	1947[◊]	31,161 (77%)	8,300 (20%)	1,196 (3%)	40,657
	1960	59,203 (71%)	21,795 (26%)	2,879 (3%)	83,877

† Head count conducted by the Food Control Department.
# Figures in parentheses denote percentage of total population.
* 1960 census was undertaken by a pan-British Borneo Census Department.
◊ Part of the census of Sarawak.

Source: (Adapted from) After L. W. Jones, *The Population of Borneo: A Study of the Peoples of Sarawak, Sabah and Brunei* (London: University of London, The Athlone Press, 1966), p. 63.

Chinese communities were resident in the major towns, viz. Kuching, Sibu, and Miri, owing largely to trade and other commercial activities, besides rural areas such as in and around Bau (mining) and the lower Rajang and delta (rubber). Every bazaar throughout Sarawak had a congregation of Chinese businesses, whether as rubber and rice dealers and/or as retailers of sundry goods. Chinese economic predominance in the import/export sector and the distribution retail network was commonplace and sustainable to present times.

Typically, where any Chinese community settled, characteristic features included a row of shophouses housing businesses (dealers in local commodities, medicines, eateries, retail of sundry goods), a Daoist-Buddhist temple, *huaiguan* (clan, descendants of common ancestry) building, schoolhouse, and residential housing (of brick in urban settings and of wood and thatch in rural areas). Economically, Chinese traits of adaptability and pragmatism sustained an assortment of livelihoods from import/exporters, retailers, miners (gold), commercial agriculture as peasant smallholders (pepper, rubber, market gardening) to artisans, schoolteachers, and clerks in the public and private sectors.[4]

Owing to the Confucian tradition of education and reverence to scholars, the schoolhouse was an indispensable building no different from the Buddhist-Daoist temple or *huaiguan*. Schooling was prioritized for the young even among illiterate peasants, who ensured that the next generation be lettered. Moreover, education and schooling were the channel for the transmission of socio-cultural traditions, history, and heritage and the all-important language. Hence, from one generation to another, language and culture were transmitted through the classroom where rote learning, conformity, and discipline were the norms.

Fragmented community

Outwardly and physiologically, in the eyes of indigenous peoples, all Chinese appeared as alike. A Malay or an Iban would be clueless in differentiating a Hokkien *towkay* or a Cantonese carpenter from a Henghua fisherman, because all appeared simply as Chinese to them. The Chinese in Sarawak, like those in neighbouring North Borneo or their brethren in Malaya and Singapore, were in fact highly fragmented along dialect lines. As listed in Table 4.2, there were seven main Chinese dialect communities in Sarawak. Particular dialect groups tended to live in close proximity and to have a predilection for a particular sector of the economy as livelihood. Consequently, the Chinese in Sarawak in fact appeared as segregated communities.

Although numerically the Hakka was twice and more than three and a half times the Hokkien and Teochew populations, respectively, the latter two communities were significantly more important as members of the mercantile elite of *towkay*. The Brooke system of indirect rule relied on Kapitan China appointees who ensured peace and stability within the Chinese community. The first rajah Brooke relied on the counsel of three Chinese community leaders, namely the Hokkien Ong Ewe Hai, the Chaoan[5] Chan Ah Ko, and the Teochew Law Kian Huat.[6] Charles Brooke, the second rajah, appointed Ong Tiang Swee (1864–1950), son of Ong Ewe Hai, as Kapitan China, essentially as the sole representative and voice of the Chinese community of Sarawak. The *towkay* elite leadership survived the war and continued to be influential and significant during the postwar years.

On first appearance, the Chinese in immediate post-war Sarawak might appear to be better endowed materially in comparison with the indigenous inhabitants, particularly in the big towns of Kuching, Sibu, and Miri. Undeniably there were wealthy families among their numbers in the major urban areas as well as in smaller towns in the interior such as the *towkay* rubber and rice dealers, rice and sago millers, proprietors of mines, wholesalers and major retailers, and owners of medium-sized rubber smallholdings and pepper orchards. The *towkay* elite class of capitalists were undoubtedly better off than the proletariats of the community, namely the mine workers, family-sized smallholders of rubber, peasant farmers particularly in market gardening (vegetables, poultry, pigs, freshwater fish), petty traders, itinerant coolies, shophouse assistants, hawkers, and artisans. Middle-level merchants, English-educated civil servants, clerks in European

Table 4.2 Main Dialect Communities of Chinese in Post-war Sarawak

Dialect	Spatial Distribution/Livelihood
Hakka[†] 45,409* (31.1%)	Interior of First and Second Divisions; outskirts of Kuching especially in Upper Sarawak centering around Bau; Serian district; Batu and Riam in Miri district of Fourth Division/mainly mining (gold); market gardening; tin-smithing
Foochow[□] 41,946 (28.9%)	Predominant community in the Third Division within the triangular area bounded by Igan, Kanowit and Sarikei in the Lower Rajang; Sebauh to the southeast of Bintulu; Poyut in Baram district/rubber smallholders and pepper cultivators; distribution trade in local produce; timber industry and trade
Hokkien 20,289 (14.0%)	Largest group in Kuching; predominant in Oya and Mukah in the Third Division; Limbang, Trusan, and Lawas in the Fifth Division/traders and merchants; import and export and wholesaling; shipping and banking
Cantonese 14,622 (10.1%)	Mainly settled in Kanowit district of the Lower Rajang/timber industry and trade; pepper cultivators; goldsmithing; artisans such as carpentering, furniture-makers, clockmakers
Teochew 12,892 (8.9%)	Small but significant presence in Kuching and outskirts; in urban areas of Second Division; small numbers in Bintulu/ traders and merchants; green grocers in towns; gambier and pepper cultivators in the interior districts
Henghua 4,356 (3.0%)	Found in major urban areas, particularly focused on Sibu/ cornered the coffee-shop business; fishermen; bicycle shops; bus, taxi, and boat transportation sector
Hainanese[◊] 3,871 (2.6%)	Settled in the major urban centres such as Kuching, Sibu and Miri/food catering business; proprietors of restaurants and eateries
Others[°] 1,773 (1.2%)	Mainly in towns like Kuching, Sibu, and Miri/mostly unskilled labourers; odd jobs

† Also known as Khek or Kheh.
* Population according to 1947 census where the total population of the Chinese stood at 145,158 out of Sarawak's 546,385; in parentheses shows percentage of total population of the Chinese.
□ Also referred to as Hockchiu.
◊ Hailam is another designation.
° Unlike the seven named dialect groups that originated mainly from the southern Chinese provinces of Fujian and Guangdong, there was a trickle of immigrants from other parts of the mainland, including wartime coolies brought over from Shanghai and other northern provinces.

Sources: J. L. Noakes, *Sarawak and Brunei: A Report on the 1947 Population Census* (Kuching: Government Printing Office, 1959), p. 93; James C. Jackson, *Sarawak: A Geographical Survey of a Developing State* (London: London University Press, 1968), pp. 52–61; Richard Outram, "The Chinese", *The Peoples of Sarawak*, edited by Tom Harrisson (Kuching: Sarawak Museum, 1959), pp. 116–126; Ooi Keat Gin, *Of Free Trade and Native Interests: The Brookes and the Economic Development of Sarawak, 1841–1941* (Kuala Lumpur: Oxford University Press, 1997), pp. 251– 288; Ju-K'ang T'ien, *The Chinese of Sarawak: A Study of Social Structure*, Monographs on Social Anthropology no. 12 (London: Department of Anthropology, the London School of Economics and Political Science, 1953), pp. 11–15.

firms and banks, schoolteachers, and the handful of professionals comprised the middle-class bourgeoise in Sarawak's colonial society. Therefore, it was apparent that the *towkay* elite class was at the apex of the economic and social pyramid not only in the pre-war Brooke period but also during the post-war British colonial administration era.

Clan house and schoolhouse

Following an horrific episode in the early years of the Brooke regime, Sarawak had scant issues with intra-ethnic rivalry within the Chinese community. Although they were far more antagonistic in the peninsular Malay states during the nineteenth century, with outright armed clashes over tin mining fields, Chinese dialect particularism did not create trouble in Sarawak. The Hakka goldminers' abortive attempt in 1857 to unseat Rajah James Brooke that almost killed him forced the adoption of a hard-line policy in proscribing Chinese *hui* (society, association, clan; also, brotherhoods, clandestine societies).[7] Eliminating and outlawing *hui* since 1857, and thereafter, Brooke officers were ever wary and suspicious of Chinese activities, which ensured that Sarawak was not troubled by Chinese intra-rivalry or conflict, as was commonplace in the Malay states and Straits Settlements in the late nineteenth and early twentieth centuries.[8]

Nonetheless, the *huiguan* (clan association) or clan house set up along dialect lines, geographical origin (location of ancestral village, district), and clan group that was established by Chinese immigrants remained vibrant and sustainable, having survived the anti-*hui* Brooke period, the Pacific War and Japanese occupation, and the post-war British colonial administration era. In the early 1950s, Kuching possessed eight major *huiguan*, where the largest boasted a membership of 2,389 and the smallest, 93.[9]

> A Chinese who comes as an immigrant to join an already existing community of overseas Chinese makes his first contacts with others [in a *huiguan*] who not only speak his own dialect . . . but also come from his own locality, often his own home town or village. This kind of shared experience is especially significant for those who feel themselves exiles in a foreign land and the closer the original geographical proximity the more intense the sentiments of mutual sympathy are likely to be.[10]

In addition to common dialect, common locality, and clanship in the establishment of a *huiguan* was added common occupational niche. For instance, "all the members being Hainan speaking cooks and domestic servants in European employ, most of them coming from contiguous districts in Hainan island and many of them linked by clanship", namely having shared family name and related through genealogical relationships, typified a *huiguan*.[11] The shared common features of *huiguan*, viz. dialect, origins, clanship, and occupation, further accentuated the gulf between the different groupings. In other words, the *huiguan* contributed to the state of a fragmented Chinese community.

The Chinese possessed a long tradition of emphasizing the importance of literacy, whereby traditional society placed the scholar at the apex of the social hierarchy.[12] Thanks to Confucianism, the traditional social stratification has the scholar-bureaucrats at the top because of their knowledge and wisdom, thereby ensuring social order. Below them were the farmers who produced foodstuff for sustenance, followed by the artisans owing to their necessary and essential skills. Merchants, who apparently did not produce anything apart from selling the farmers' and artisans' goods to others, occupied the lowest strata of the social division.

The imperial examinations were organized at three levels or tiers, namely district, provincial, and the imperial court.[13] Holders of the initial or first degree, *shengyuan*, often owing to surplus, were unable to receive an official appointment, nonetheless as a consolation, they were granted social privileges and respected in the wider society. Successful candidates of the civil service examinations at the highest degree, the *jinshi*, of the imperial court examinations would secure a position in the palace bureaucracy as a scholar-bureaucrat.

Consequently, every Chinese family would aspire for a son to attain *jinshi* and become a scholar-bureaucrat. Rich or poor families, even illiterate peasant farmers, all valued education for the young, for the latter as a vehicle of social mobility while the well-to-do regarded it as the guarantee to the sustainability of their wealth and influence. At the same time, through education knowledge of the spoken and written language, history, culture, traditional practices, and heritage were handed down from one generation to another. Therefore, it was commonplace to find the schoolhouse as a permanent fixture, not unlike the *huiguan* building in every community. Likewise, for the Chinese diaspora in any corner of the world where they had settled and a community developed, priority was given through public subscription and collective effort to realize the erection of a schoolhouse, engaging schoolteachers, furnishing materials such as chairs and desks, and providing textbooks, brush, ink, paper, pen, and all the paraphernalia of the classroom. And in common practice, the wealthy donated funds while others supplied their labour and/or materials. Generally, it was a communal effort to ensure that the children of the community benefited from the written word.

In pre-war Sarawak, Chinese vernacular education developed, with schools proliferating in every community from major urban centres such as Kuching to upriver bazaar small towns like Kapit, Marudi, Sebauh, and others.[14] The non-committal and *laissez faire* stance of the Brooke regime on education and schooling allowed a free hand for other agencies including Christian missions, private philanthropists, and community organizations to take on an active role in the provision and management of the schools. The Chinese *huaiguan* assumed the role of catering to the educational needs of the community, hence from public subscriptions and private donations, schoolhouses were built. Management and financing were the responsibilities of the local Chinese community. Wealthy merchants and philanthropists, often the same individuals, initiated the set-up of a school board of management, where they served as voluntary members to oversee the running of the school including engaging the headteacher and teachers, being responsible for financial obligations, and determining overall policy and settling outstanding issues. Curriculum, textbooks, and teachers were imported from China. Sustainability of the Chinese vernacular schools depended heavily on donations by the local Chinese community, philanthropists, and school fees (often nominal). The Brooke government extended minimal assistance, financial or otherwise, and likewise had scant involvement with Chinese vernacular education and its schools.

Nomenclature of Brooke-era Chinese vernacular education was a six-year elementary or primary schooling (Year 1 to 6) to be followed by a three-year lower secondary programme (Junior Middle Standard 1 to 3). The absence of a three-year senior or upper secondary programme was conspicuous. Hence, those who sought to continue Senior Middle Standard had to return to the Chinese mainland, and likewise for those who intended to further their studies at the tertiary level. Avenues and opportunities were thus limited.

Moreover, owing to the imported materials including teachers from China, the Chinese mainland flavour was undoubtedly all over the education platter. The struggles on the mainland between the -isms (nationalism, republicanism, communism, totalitarianism, democracy) too spilled over into the Chinese schools through imported educational materials. But the most influential was undeniably the China-born and trained imported teaching personnel.

Considering that the *huiguan* in general were the primary agents for Chinese vernacular education and the setting up of schools, and the importance of dialect groups, dialects played a pivotal function as the medium of instruction. Despite the adoption of *Guo-yu* (Standard Chinese or Mandarin) since the May Fourth Movement (1915–1921) on the mainland and similarly adopted in the Straits Settlements and Malay States from the 1920s, Sarawak Chinese vernacular schools retained their respective dialects as the medium of instruction.[15] Notwithstanding the fact that the Chinese in Sarawak remained in touch with their brethren in the homeland, and through newspapers and broadcast media were informed of developments on the mainland, there appeared to be scant conspicuous nationalism among the various dialect groups. Dialect parochialism remained dominant and particularly apparent in the education field.

Through educational materials like curriculum and textbooks, and especially teachers, all imported from the mainland, the influences were pervasive. In this connection, the Cold War had a longer trajectory in the context of Sarawak, for in the struggles between the nationalist Guomindang (KMT) and the Chinese Communist Party (CCP) during the late 1920s and 1930s that had percolated into the Chinese vernacular schools, the Brooke government took sides.[16] The KMT was preferred over the CCP, labelling the latter as subversive, justifiable by its anti-colonialist and anti-imperialist stance in its propaganda and literature. Leftist activists and agitators targeted Chinese vernacular schools as nurseries for recruitment. Children of the working class were the most vulnerable and susceptible to subversive propaganda. As a result, stern measures were taken against alleged Leftist elements and/or sympathizers including repatriation to the mainland. In the 1920s greater surveillance over the Chinese vernacular schools was stepped up, *inter alia* registration of schools and teaching personnel; suspected Leftists or sympathizers were promptly detained and subsequently deported for propagating subversive propaganda and literature.

At the same time, in order to ensure that more Chinese vernacular schools were registered and hence monitored, Brooke government grants-in-aid were gradually increased from the mid-1930s. Nonetheless, "in 1938 less than half the number of registered Chinese schools received such financial assistance, and the amount given was often small".[17]

Overall, however, the Chinese in Sarawak appeared less passionate about either KMT or CCP efforts at garnering their support and recruiting their involvement. One particular indicator can be seen from the dormant existence of a KMT chapter in Kuching.[18] The inward-looking dialect parochialism might have contributed to the Sarawak Chinese's less than enthusiastic nationalistic fervour, as they instead displayed interest in locally centred *huiguan* issues.

Bitterness

In outward appearances the Sarawak Chinese seemed contented with their well-being during the immediate post-war years of the late 1940s and early 1950s. Materially the Chinese in general were much better off than the indigenous peoples, where the majority continued to eke out a subsistence existence as in pre-war times. Nonetheless, under the stoic look of the Chinese in the bazaar coffeeshop, or among chattering Chinese housewives with Chinese vendors in the marketplace, there were undercurrents of bitterness within the community, particularly pronounced among the lower rungs of the working class. Sullenness and resentment ranged from strained inter-ethnic relations as a result of the war, to disappointment in the community's *towkay* leadership, dissatisfaction over the scant opportunities for Chinese to further their studies after attaining the Junior Middle Three Certificate, and frustration of unemployed Chinese vernacular school graduates.

Strained inter-ethnic relations and the quisling issue

The Brooke Rajahs were famously champions of native interests and well-being, and legislation was enacted to protect the indigenes from exploitation from both Europeans and Chinese, the latter considered worldly wise and tended to be unscrupulous.[19] Land ownership was a native prerogative, although any unworked or uncultivated land within a stipulated period, reverts back to the government. Consequently, the bulk of Chinese peasant farmers tilled land illegally but were generally overlooked by the authorities. Being non-native, the Chinese as a community was excluded from the shelter of the paternalistic Brooke protective umbrella. For the upper echelons of Chinese society, this exclusion did not pose an issue, but to the working class barely eking out a subsistence existence, they felt marginalized and discriminated.

Prior to the war, there was no doubt that each ethnic group was aware of its differences in terms of privileges enjoyed under the Brookes (that tended to be pro-Malay), social standing, and economic opportunities. The wartime Japanese military occupation with apparently ethnic-based policies that was anti-Chinese strained Sino-native relations in the post-war period.[20] The Malay *datu*, and the *perabangan*, the favoured class of the Brooke regime, appeared to have become turncoats overnight; once *tabek* (salute) to the Tuan and Mem were now bowing and brownnosing the Japanese invaders and occupiers. Public displays in towns like Kuching, Sibu, and Miri of such Malay antics, including that of *mata-mata* (policemen) and government *krani* (clerks), brought a bitterness to others, especially the Chinese. To most Chinese, Malay disloyalty and treacherous behaviour were unforgivable.

Indigenous peoples in the interior were equally unforgiving to Chinese *towkay* who brought Japanese soldiers to their longhouses, who confiscated invaluable rice stores and hunting rifles. The Ibans, in particular, were waiting for the first chance to exact vengeance on the traitorous Chinese.

Furthermore, consequent of the monetary demand (*shu-jin*, lit. 'life-redeeming') imposed on the Chinese community in Sarawak and North Borneo totalling some S\$3 million,[21] many Chinese businesses became insolvent, which further aggravated the wartime conditions of deprivations, shortages, and an overall sense of fear, hopelessness, and helplessness. Then, in viewing the Malays in particular, and other indigenous peoples that in general appeared not to have been deprived and were apparently living well and unmolested (financially or physically), this further added to Chinese resentment. To be fair, the Malays and other natives were overall subsistence peasant farmers and, in fact, were no worse or better off than their pre-war existence. Only the Malay elite (*datu*, *perabangan*) and the mere handful of clerks and police personnel were seemingly 'doing well'.

When the war ended, therefore, because of perceptions, real or otherwise, inter-ethnic relations were strained. Being eyewitness to some people being reinstated, some even elevated, and recognized by the incoming British colonial administration, knowing the wartime behaviour and activities of such individuals, was exasperating and frustrating for many Chinese. Furthermore, injustice was undoubtedly felt by Chinese communities in the lower Rajang when the British colonial administration did not prosecute Iban perpetrators for decapitating some Chinese during the interregnum (between the Japanese surrender and the arrival of Australian Imperial Forces (AIF), a period of about a fortnight).[22]

Over the issue of cession to the British government, a sector of the Malay community opposed on grounds that they feared the privileges they had enjoyed during the Brooke era would be abrogated.[23] Others within the community, however, felt that cession would improve the hitherto socioeconomic backwardness vis-à-vis the Chinese. The Chinese saw the anti-cession movement to be reactionary, arguing for *status quo*, and when cession was realized in mid-1946, restoring the Brooke Raj. To the Chinese, cession could open new opportunities, new markets for trade and commerce. Notwithstanding their stance on cession, the Chinese as a community witnessed from the sidelines the public demonstrations and other anti-government behaviour staged by the Malay anti-cession advocates, abstaining from involvement and/or comments. To some extent, the controversy over cession further add to the hitherto strained inter-ethnic relations.

Meanwhile, the quisling issue, provoked troubles within the Chinese community. During the occupation years, the Chinese people-in-the-street witnessed their *towkay* leaders appearing to work hand-in-hand with the Japanese enemy; these antics were unpalatable to watch with unease and/or even tinged with embarrassment. Worst scenarios were to come. Expecting such turncoat *towkay* to be punished after the war, instead these individuals were reinstated as the community's leaders by the new British colonial administration.[24] It was certainly a bitter scene to swallow for the Chinese community in seeing the continuation of the communal leadership by the same *towkay* elite.

Limited opportunities

Recipients of Chinese vernacular education faced two predicaments: limited opportunities for further studies and limited prospects of employment. Bitterness over their dilemmas made Chinese vernacular school students susceptible to various quarters, easily swayed by persuasive subversive literature and activities of activists. Their vulnerability was exploited by Leftist elements who were seeking recruits and sympathizers to their cause.

Chinese middle school graduates, 16- and 17-year-olds, armed with their newly attained achievement, to their utter dismay faced rebuff. Their Junior Middle Three Certificates were worthless paper in the eyes of the Brooke government, likewise the private sector comprising British and European firms (agency houses, shipping, insurance, banks), owing to the fact that English was conspicuously absent from the transcript. Being untutored in the English language put the Chinese school graduates at a grave disadvantage because of the reality then whereby all government and private-sector businesses (excluding Chinese companies) utilized English as the medium of communication and documentation. Hampered by both oral and written English, Chinese school graduates faced rejection in the colonial-dominated employment marketplace.

Alternatively, working-class Chinese school graduates could seek employment at the many Chinese businesses. But here again, they too faced rejection. Entry into Chinese businesses of whatever nature was founded on family ties; most businesses were family concerns relying on immediate family members as the workforce, and if circumstances necessitated, relatives were brought in. For bigger establishments, such as rice milling and rubber processing, where a larger workforce was required, fellow clansmen were relied on as labourers and other employees. Hence, children of peasant farmers, coolies, neither possessing familial ties or clanship connections, were turned down, their Middle School Certificates notwithstanding. These youngsters had little choice but to return to their family farm with nothing to show despite the pains of their schooling. They were ideal candidates for Leftist activists and recruiters for their 'higher cause'. Many easily fell prey and embarked on the socialist-communist road. Such a scenario, although apparent in the pre-war period, became more pronounced, numerous, and active in the 1950s and early 1960s.

Intrigue

Bitterness among the Chinese, especially the educated youths from working-class backgrounds, was exploited by Leftist/communist elements in the post-war decades. Chinese vernacular schools became nurseries for recruitment. Leftists/

communists utilized 'united front' tactics with student and labour movements, and a legal political party to move forward their agenda.

Political exiles

Fleeing abroad to escape persecution at home was not an uncommon phenomenon over the ages and across all lands and peoples. Political refugees flee across borders literally for their lives. Thus, the flight abroad of the Chinese intelligentsia in the twentieth century was not unique. However, their fleeing the homeland to the Nanyang brought implications to their host destinations. In the case of Sarawak, the presence of Left-wing educated Chinese refugees to a great extent stirred the political consciousness of the local Chinese community, which was hitherto unenthusiastic and unduly moved by developments on the mainland.

Political upheavals, economic instability, armed conflicts, social chaos, and natural calamities (earthquakes, floods, famines) marked the last quarter of the nineteenth century and the first half of the twentieth century in China, viz. the Yellow River floods (1887, 1931, 1938), the Boxer Rebellion (1899–1901), famine (1907), Chinese Revolution (1911), warlord era (1916–1928), and Haiyuan earthquake (1920). Against this disastrous and chaotic backdrop, many Chinese intelligentsia, began to search for solutions and panaceas, therefore experimenting with various political thoughts, philosophies, and systems including democracy, republicanism, constitutional monarchy, socialism, and communism. The pivotal May Fourth Movement witnessed a surge in Chinese nationalism, but more significantly it was a tipping point in terms of Chinese intellectual thought. The Versailles Treaty (1919), whereby Imperial Japan, an ally of Britain and France in the Great War (1914–1918), was rewarded with German-held territories in Shandong, was regarded as a betrayal to China by the Western powers. Consequently, not only did Chinese intellectuals begin to doubt the viability of Western-style liberal democracy and/or Woodrow Wilson's Fourteen Points as hypocritical since the U.S. appeared not to have done enough in Chinese eyes to persuade its acceptance by the imperialist allies (namely Britain, France, and Japan), but they also turned to Marxism as a possible viable ideological alternative. Subsequently, within a two-year window, between 1919 and 1921, the latter year marked the coming together of Left-leaning intellectuals in establishing the Chinese Communist Party (CCP) in Shanghai.[25]

Nonetheless, communists who were members of the KMT remained within the ambit of this nationalist party, occupying its left wing in direct opposition to its right wing. But even before attaining the ultimate objective of his Northern Expedition (1926–1928), namely defeat of the Beiyang government (1912–1928), the legitimate and internationally recognized government of the Republic of China at Beijing, KMT leader Generalissimo Chiang Kai-shek turned on the communists from within the KMT. The White Terror broke out in August 1927, purging communists within the KMT and thereby terminating the First United Front (1923–1927).[26] The slaughter forced many communists and other Left-leaning intellectuals to flee. Many fled abroad to the Nanyang to escape persecution and death.

The Left-wing Chinese intelligentsia sought asylum mainly in the Straits Settlements of Penang and Singapore, where some had familial ties. Similarly, others fled to Sarawak, where they joined their brethren who had settled earlier. While abroad in the Nanyang, the Chinese-educated émigré continued their studies in Marxism-Leninism, for Lenin and the Bolshevik Revolution (1917) had a positive impact. At the same time, this Left-leaning Chinese-educated group actively invested efforts in garnering support and followings, especially among the youths. They became particularly conspicuous in their activist work when hostilities broke out following the Marco Polo Bridge Incident (7 July 1937) between the Republic of China's National Revolutionary Army and the Imperial Japanese Army (IJA). The Incident sparked the Second Sino-Japanese War (1937–1945).[27]

During the conflict, the Left-wing Chinese intelligentsia not only was able to spread anti-Japanese and anti-imperialistic propaganda that stirred Chinese nationalism among the Chinese diaspora in the Nanyang but also managed to mobilize resources (funds, materials, and volunteers) in the defence of the motherland. Both efforts paid dividends, and the fact that the activists were communists or sympathizers raised the profile and appeal of the CCP in the eyes of the overseas Chinese in Southeast Asia. The outbreak of the war also forced a KMT-CCP Second United Front (1936–1945) against Imperial Japan, the common enemy.

In Sarawak, the hitherto inert Chinese community was also nudged in their prolonged political slumber by the Left-wing Chinese-educated activists. Appeal to Chinese patriotism and nationalism, together with anti-colonialism and anti-imperialism propaganda aimed at Imperial Japan, roused the local Chinese communities in contributing funds and materials during anti-Japanese campaigns staged by local organizers drawn from both Nationalists (KMT) and Communists (CCP) of the China Relief Fund movement.[28] Volunteers too were recruited. Known as Nanyang Volunteers, they served as truck drivers and mechanics, conveying supplies to China via the Burma Road. Some 100 Sarawak Chinese volunteered their services as drivers and mechanics.[29] Political consciousness and activism were increasingly fermented among the local Chinese communities across dialect groups that were once dormant and indifferent. Further developments from without of rumours of war gradually gained traction within the Sarawak Chinese community.

Following the atomic bombings of Hiroshima and Nagasaki, Emperor Hirohito announced the unconditional surrender of Imperial Japan. The surrender that marked the end of the war immediately saw both the KMT and CCP actively consolidating their respective areas of control and at the same time seeking to expand their territorial hegemony and garner support from the masses. The Chinese Civil War (1927–1950) that took a hiatus during the Second United Front resumed in earnest between the Nationalists of Generalissimo Chiang Kai-shek and the Communists led by Mao Zedong for the ultimate prize, China.[30] This immediate post-war conflict was also often referred to as the Chinese Communist Revolution (1945–1949), which concluded with Mao's declaration of the People's Republic of China (PRC) on 1 October 1949 at Tiananmen Square. Generalissimo Chiang and the top echelon of the KMT fled to Taiwan, where a Nationalist government was established.

Left-wing influence

> Achieve self-government and independence . . . striving for the establishment of a new democratic society, then a socialist society and finally a communist society.
>
> *The Danger Within*, p. 3.

The ultimate aim of the Chinese communist activists and agitators in Sarawak was the overthrow of Sarawak's colonial regime and, in its place, to set up a communist state. The establishment of the PRC offered the impetus to push forward their agenda in recruitment and garnering support. 'A communist society' after the model of the mainland and aligned to the PRC was the penultimate struggle. Left-ist/communist organizations active in Sarawak in the early 1940s through the early 1960s are featured in Table 4.3. Owing to their subversive nature and activities, most of these organizations functioned covertly and in secrecy.

Table 4.3 Leftist/Communist (Mainly) Clandestine Organizations in Sarawak, c. Early 1940s and c. Early 1960s

Name/Date of Establishment	Key Personalities	Activities
Sarawak Anti-Fascist League (SAFL)* / 1941; also known as North Borneo Anti-Japanese Alliance, and (Sarawak) Races Liberation League (RLL)	Wu Chan; Chin Shaw Tung	Members mainly Chinese schoolteachers; on settlements along the Sarawak River, viz. Kuching, Siniawan, Bau; dissolved Aug 1945.
Overseas Chinese Youth Associations (OCYA) / 1943	Lim Kong Gan (chairman); Chin Shaw Tung	Established in Bau (1943); Kuching (1945); various branches throughout Sarawak; indoctrination through supplying reading materials and cultural activities for Chinese youths; proscribed on 13 Feb 1952 following CHMS student strikers staging anti-imperialism and anti-colonialism protests on its Kuching premises.
Chung Hwa Education Society / 17 Oct 1945	Wu Chan (chairman); Hsu Yaw Tong; Ban Tao Kui; Lin Lixin; Wu Xiaoyuan; Tan Tze Min	Convened a meeting of 17 Chinese intelligentsia (from all persuasions and dialect groups) to discuss the future of Chinese education; *Guo-yu* (Mandarin) adopted as medium of instruction discarding dialects; Chung Hwa Primary Schools and Chung Hwa Middle Schools (CHMS) to be jointly managed by the Kuching Chung Hwa Schools Board of Management.
Chung Hwa Association (CHA) / 1 July 1946	Lim Kong Gan; Wu Chan; Jian Changbo	Constituent members comprised all Chinese dialect groups and clan associations; aspired to be the supreme authority of Sarawak Chinese.
Kuching Overseas Chinese Preparatory Committee / 7 Jan 1950	Lim Kong Gan (head); Yang Zhanmou (secretary)	Organized celebrations of the declaration of the People's Republic of China (PRC) and the establishment of Sino-British diplomatic ties; featuring carnivals, mass rallies, *yangko* dance.

Name/Date of Establishment	Key Personalities	Activities
Overseas Chinese Progressive Youth Associations (OCPYA)* / 1950; also known as Overseas Chinese Young Men's Youth Associations (OCYMA)	Yun Dafeng; Ye Qiuxia; Huang Huibai	Focused on disseminating Marxist-Leninist-Maoist ideas and training of cadres among students; codenamed 'Y'; proscribed 13 Feb 1952.
Chung Hwa Middle School (CHMS) Students' Self-Governing Society (SSGS)*/c. 1951	Wen Ming Chyuan (head)	*Hsueh hsih* (study for action) set up by pro-communist students in Kuching CHMS; organized activities such as concerts, picnics where communists songs were sung; proscribed 30 June 1951.
Sarawak New Democratic Youth League (SNDYL)* / 21 Oct 1951; also known as Sarawak Overseas Chinese Democratic Youth League (SOCDYL)	Huang Jinmao; Qiu Liben; Tay Chok Chong	Faction within OCPYA supporting the thesis that the Chinese had become an integral part of Sarawak society, hence should shoulder the responsibility of leading local revolutionary activities; to initiate the mobilization of the masses beginning from the Kuching CHMS and OCYA; code-named 'X'; dissolution during the 1952 Emergency.
Progressive Teachers' Association (PTA)*/c. 1952; Students' Society (SS)*/c. 1952	Chin Shaw Tung (head of PTA); Wen Ming Chyuan (head of SS in Kuching CHMS); Bong Kee Chok (SS member)	Dissolution of SNDYL during the 1952 Emergency whence ex-members set up PTA and SS; PTA organized young teachers for service in rural schools, real task was to initiate the peasants' movement; SS took charge of students' movement in Kuching CHMS, and initiate students' movement in the Third and Fourth Divisions.
Sarawak Liberation League (SLL)*/July 1953	Teo Yong Jim (1953–1954); Wen Ming Chyuan (head from 1954); Lin Yonglun (non-student; discipline teacher; peasant movement); Wang Fuk Ing (married Wen in 1960); Bong Kee Chok (2nd leader, 'open front' leader); Bong Kee Siaw; Fong Moi Kee; Tan Lee Seng; Ang Cho Teng; Lai Jieyuan; Chen Jinmei; Lui How Ming (Sibu); Guo Weizhong (3rd leader); Lim Ho Kui (labour movement)	Modelled after the Anti-British League (ABL), a satellite organization of the Malayan Communist Party (MCP); a local Sarawak organization conducting a revolutionary agenda; comprised Kuching CHMS students who were highly versed in Marxist-Leninist theories; Wen, Bong. and Guo dominated SLL Organization Bureau that determined policy, direction, and strategy.
Sarawak Advance Youth Association (SAYA)*/late 1955		Satellite of SLL under its leadership, but SAYA members unaware of the existence of SLL; referred to as 'O' members.

(*Continued*)

Table 4.3 (Continued)

Name/Date of Establishment	Key Personalities	Activities
Sarawak United People's Party (SUPP) / 4 June 1959	Ong Kee Hui (president; English-educated moderate); Stephen Yong (secretary general; English-educated moderate); Bong Kee Chok (central [Kuching] assistant secretary general – organization); Wen Ming Chyuan (central [Kuching] assistant secretary general – publicity)	Facilitated communists' access to and garnered support from grassroots and indigenous peoples (mainly Dayak) support through SUPP.
Borneo Communist Party (BCP)*/c. 1960	Stanley Wong	Based in Sarikei; small membership, loosely organized in structure; individual members joined SLL during the armed revolutionary phase (1962–1990).

* Clandestine organization

Sources: "Political Intelligence Reports from Sarawak and Brunei", Feb 1951, CO 537/7349; "Political Intelligence Reports from Sarawak and Brunei", June-July 1951, CO 537/7340; *Sarawak Tribune*, 14 Apr 1951; Seng Guo Quan, "The Origins of the Socialist Revolution in Sarawak (1945–1963)", MA thesis, National University of Singapore, 2007, passim; Hara Fujio, "The North Kalimantan Communist Party and the People's Republic of China", *The Developing Economies*, XLIII-4 (Dec 2005), p. 495; Sarawak Information Service, *The Danger Within: A History of the Clandestine Communist Organization in Sarawak* (Kuching: Government Printing Office, 1963), p. 2; Vernon L. Porritt, *The Rise and Fall of Communism in Sarawak 1940–1990* (Clayton, Vic.: Monash Asia Institute, 2004), pp. 10, 11, 17, Appendix 12; Sarawak Government, Subversion in Sarawak, Sessional Paper no. 3, July 1960, p. 1; *Straits Times*, 13 Oct 1961; *Straits Times*, 18 Oct 1961; Ooi Keat Gin, "The Cold War and British Borneo: Impact and Legacy, 1945–63", *Southeast Asia and the Cold War*, edited by Albert Lau (London: Routledge, 2012), p. 113.

Since the last quarter of the 1930s, Leftist elements had been politically active, especially involvement in the activities of the China Relief Fund. When the Pacific War (1941–1945) broke out followed by the swift invasion and occupation by the IJA, covert anti-Japanese organizations were set up. Established in 1941, the Sarawak Anti-Fascist League (SAFL) that comprised schoolteachers of Chinese vernacular schools propagated anti-colonialism and anti-imperialism propaganda aimed at Imperial Japan as an occupier. SAFL was active in Bau, Siniawan, and Kuching. Another wartime clandestine Leftist organization was the Overseas Chinese Youth Associations (OCYA), initially established in Bau (1943), with a branch in Kuching (1945) and other chapters across the state. It was a recruiting platform for Chinese youths in supplying them with Leftist literature and organizing cultural activities. Unlike the Malayan People's Anti-Japanese Army (MPAJA), both SFL and OCYA did not engage militarily with the IJA, instead focussed on indoctrination and recruitment to their cause. While SAFL ceased when the war ended, OCYA continued until it was proscribed in 1952 following the incident with student strikers.

At the same time, in the post-war period (1940s to 1960s), several Leftist/communist organizations were set up, mainly as overt non-political establishments to avoid arousing untoward attention by the colonial authorities. But covertly subversive and communist activities were carried out, particularly among the educated Chinese youths. It was the classic communist practice of the 'united front' tactic.

The wartime hiatus witnessed an explosion of increment in school registration in the immediate post-war period. Enrolment figures for Chinese vernacular elementary schools were more than doubled from 13,416 in 1941 to 18,222 in 1946, and 28,222 in 1953.[31] As a result, there was pressure to increase the demand for secondary education, both Junior Middle Standard and Senior Middle Standard, but the latter was conspicuously absent. The former was only available at a limited number of schools in the major towns, such as Kuching, Sibu, and Miri. Hence, when the Kuching Chung Hwa Middle School (CHMS) opened its Senior Middle Standard classes in 1951, many from as far as neighbouring Brunei sought entry. The Chinese demand for education and schools was phenomenal. By 1953, the figure for Chinese vernacular secondary school enrolment outpaced that of Christian mission English-medium schools and Malay Government schools by a ratio of 27:10:1, respectively.[32]

Another momentous post-war development on the Chinese vernacular education landscape was the ending of the divisive system of dialect-based schools. On 17 October 1945, the Chung Hwa Education Society that was inaugurated convened a group of 17 Chinese intelligentsia (from all political persuasions and dialect groups) to deliberate on the future of Chinese vernacular education and schools. The outcome was indeed a breakthrough. *Guo-yu*, the Chinese National Language or Mandarin, was finally adopted (after some 26 years) as the medium of instruction for all Chung Hwa schools. At the same time, it was agreed that all Chung Hwa primary and middle schools would be jointly managed by a Kuching Chung Hwa Schools Board of Management that would draw voluntary members from all the *huiguan*.

The growth in student numbers meant a larger pool for Leftist activists to garner support and induct recruits to their cause. Therefore, the Chinese vernacular schools continued to be prized recruitment grounds. Schoolyard recruitment resumed in earnest in the post-war period. Many of the teachers were born, bred, and trained on the mainland, and many supported the CCP. Egged on by the Left-wing Chinese intelligentsia, both teachers and middle school students (13- to 15-year-olds) became enthusiastic supporters and sympathizers of the communists.

With the establishment of the PRC in 1949, national and ethnic pride took on a new flavour: Mao and the CCP were the saviours of China and the Chinese people. The 'Century of Humiliation', from the mid-nineteenth century to the mid-twentieth century when China suffered foreign intervention and pseudo-colonialism in the form of foreign concessions and spheres of influence from European imperialist powers and Imperial Japan, ended with the proclamation of the PRC. Communist activists and recruiters called on Sarawak Chinese youth to join hands and together build a 'New China'.

Following the Tiananmen proclamation of the PRC, numerous communist organizations were set up in Sarawak (Table 4.3). Britain's recognition of the PRC and the establishment of Sino-British diplomatic relations in 1950 prompted the convening of the Kuching Overseas Chinese Preparatory Committee that was tasked to organize celebrations of these momentous events. Carnivals, mass rallies, and parades featuring *yangko* dance were staged in Kuching and on a lesser scale in other towns. The last-named item, the *yangko* dance, is a traditional folk dance performed by peasants that features a unique collective singing and dancing art. In the early 1950s, the *yangko* dance was symbolic and representative of the 'New China' as it gained popularity in communist-liberated areas; the peasants were the vanguard of the Chinese Communist Revolution, and their wholehearted support, participation, and sacrifice attained the realization of the PRC.

Meanwhile, the Overseas Chinese Progressive Associations (OCPYA), which existed clandestinely from 1950, focussed on dissemination of Marxist-Leninist-Maoist literature and training of cadres among middle school students (Table 4.3).[33] The following year, another two prominent organizations were constituted. The Chung Hwa Middle School (CHMS) Students' Self-Governing Society (SSGS) came into being as a *Hsueh hsih*, a study for action cell. Concerts were staged and picnics were organized, whereby interspersed in these activities were the propagation of communist ideas and ideals, storytelling sessions of heroic tales of peasants and workers, and singing of martial songs, all channelled to indoctrinate adolescents' impressionable minds. Songs such as 'The East is Red', adapted from an old Shaanxi folk song about love but transformed into an idolatrous tribute to Mao Zedong, was sung at student gatherings, picnics, and campfires in the early 1950s.

Later in the year saw the emergence of the Sarawak New Democratic Youth League (SNDYL), which was set up on 21 October by students of CHMS. It was born from the outcome of a tight debate between two factions within the OCPYA. One faction had argued that the Chinese in Sarawak were not part of the wider local society, regarding themselves as 'outsiders', hence they should only lend a hand in the local revolution as Overseas Chinese sojourners in the spirit of internationalism. The opposing faction strongly denounced this thesis and counter-argued that the Chinese communities in Sarawak were part and parcel of the local wider society, hence as an integral member of local society they should eschew from the sojourner mentality, reject the 'Go Back North [to China]' line, and instead mobilize the local masses. The latter group finally prevailed.

The starting point for SNDYL in mobilizing the local masses was to begin from the Kuching CHMS and OCYA. Two major strike actions were undertaken: one failed, the other succeeded (see Tables 4.4 and 4.5).

Table 4.4 First Strike Action by Students of Chung Hwa Middle School, Kuching, Sarawak, 29 October 1951: Chronology of Events/Activities

Date	Events/Activities
30 June 1951	Following a police raid on the Chung Hwa Middle School (CHMS) Students' Self-Governing Society (SSGS) where 'prohibited books' were found, the Secretary of Chinese Affairs Tom Pearson Cromwell proscribed CHMS SSGS. Both Lim Chong Chew, the principal, and Wu Chan, discipline master of CHMS, tendered their resignations. Kuching Chung Hwa Schools Board of Management brought in numerous ex-KMT government officials from Hong Kong to serve as teachers.
14–15 Oct 1951	A majority of students in two classes failed in their English-language papers. Several grievances were voiced: appeal for uplifting of their grades, criticism of the teaching methodology, and examination questions. Commencement of daily confrontation between students and school authorities over the issue of alleged unfair evaluation of the English examination and accusations over the alleged ineptitude of Ralph Yang, the English teacher. Zhang Jun, the principal, did not respond and neither was any action taken.
25 Oct 1951	Two student leaders confronted Principal Zhang regarding the outcome of the students' appeal. Principal Zhang claimed that he had no power to grant their requests. Confrontation turned violent when students wrecked the principal's living quarters. Principal Zhang turned to Secretary of Chinese Affairs Cromwell for assistance.
29 Oct 1951	Police intervened and detained 18 student leaders. In response, some 100 students besieged Principal Zhang in his office. Police dispersed the crowd with tear gas. At this juncture, under the initiative of the Sarawak New Democratic Youth League (SNDYL), a 19-member 'Strike Directing Group' was convened, drawing representatives from each class in CHMS. The leaders Huang Jinmao, Qiu Liben, and Tay Chok Chong declared the commencement of a school-wide strike action that subsequently prolonged to 103 days until 9 Feb 1952.
1 Dec 1951	The student strikers' original demand for the replacement of the allegedly incompetent principal and teachers was discarded, instead switching to a clarion call for defeating British colonialism and imperialism.
Dec 1951	The Court was lenient, whereby six of the detained student leaders were let off with fines between M$50 and M$250 without demanding any apology. The presiding magistrate described the students as misguided young men; the students felt that they were righteous in correcting an injustice, and their strike continued.
17 Jan 1952	The newly elected Kuching Chung Hwa Schools Board of Management took the decision to dismiss both Principal Zhang and expel the 18 detained student leaders. The students stepped up their opposition, chanting anti-imperialism and anti-colonialism slogans on the premises of the Kuching Overseas Chinese Youth Associations (OCYA), a popular meeting place of student leaders.
28 Jan 1952	Cromwell together with the police launched a raid on the students at OCYA where they were in the midst of staging a performance of 'Oppose U.S.A., Assist Korea'. OCYA was proscribed.

(Continued)

Table 4.4 (Continued)

Date	Events/Activities
9 Feb 1952	Strike of CHMS ended. Many of the expelled student leaders, fearing re-arrest, crossed over to West Kalimantan.
Apr 1952	Appointment of Hsu Yaw Tong as principal of CHMS. Hsu, a local Chinese, was formerly a school inspector in the Sarawak Education Department; swift and decisive actions were implemented: mandatory re-registration of all students; abolishment of the entire Senior Middle Section responsible for the strike action; expulsion of another 15 students, and altogether 33 students were struck off the school's register; parents' pledge for their children's good behavior.

Source: Seng Guo Quan, "The Origins of the Socialist Revolution in Sarawak (1945–1963)", MA thesis, National University of Singapore, 2007, pp. 43–45; *Sarawak Tribune*, 21 Nov 1951, 1 Dec 1951, 14 Feb 1952; Vernon L. Porritt, *The Rise and Fall of Communism in Sarawak 1940–1990* (Clayton, Vic.: Monash Asia Institute, 2004), pp. 10–11.

Table 4.5 Second Strike Action by Students of Chung Hwa Middle School, Kuching, Sarawak, 30 March 1955: Chronology of Events/Activities

Date	Events/Activities
26 Feb 1955	Wong Chock Yin and Zhuang Jin Ming, monitors of Class B, Junior Middle Two (Lower Standard), Chung Hwa Middle School (CHMS), Kuching at the weekly school assembly called upon Chia Yun Chee, mathematics teacher, to improve his teaching methodology. Wong and Zhuang discussed the matter with the school authorities.
5 Mar 1955	During the weekly school assembly, Chia prevented monitors Wong and Zhuang from delivering an update on the issue. The students then demanded an explanation from Principal Huang Zhong Jin, setting 10 March as the deadline for a response.
10 Mar 1955	Principal Huang responded, but to the students, it was unacceptable, "incomplete and ambiguous".
11 Mar 1955	Principal Huang issued a notice giving "black marks" or demerits to the monitors Wong Chock Yin and Zhuang Jin Ming, and another student Zhang Benren, who had "expressed opinions and doubts", accusing them of "creating trouble on the pretext of improving pedagogy", "bullying the class into the blackmail action", "setting the principal a deadline".
14 Mar 1955	Following the rejection of several appeals, Class B, Junior Middle Two (Lower Standard), submitted a petition to Principal Huang as well as the Kuching Chung Hwa Schools Board of Management for the retraction of penalties and to "uphold justice". Principal Huang summoned the entire class, where each student was interrogated individually in an attempt to identity the "culprits".
16 Mar 1955	Class B, Junior Middle Two (Lower Standard) went on strike when their appeals on behalf of their monitors were ignored. At the same time, monitors and chairmen from all classes in CHMS met to elect an eight-member All Students' Representative Delegation. Led by Bong Kee Chok, Yap Choon Ho, and Chen Sheng Xin, the Delegation demanded "justice" from the Board of Management. The latter issued a guarantee against any punishment for the students, but this was objected to by Principal Huang.

Date	Events/Activities
21–23 Mar 1955	Principal Huang, instead of abiding by the summon by the Board of Management to hearings, issued a public statement giving his side of the standoff, and led his teachers on a three-day strike, 21–23 March.
26 Mar 1955	The Delegation countered Principal Huang's public statement and called for his resignation.
27 Mar 1955	Principal Huang responded in demanding that "2 students be expelled, 13 temporarily suspended and 16 to write letter of apology". The Board of Management affirmed the demands, but at the same time, announced that CHMS would resume on 30 March. At this juncture, the Delegation forewarned all of the 13 Chinese associations that constituted (through representatives) the Board of Management of a possible boycott.
30 Mar 1955	Commencement of a 47-day boycott when the Delegation's warning was ignored. Out of a total student enrolment of 1,300, only 157 attended classes while the remainder stayed away. During the boycott period, tuition classes were organized to ensure that students did not miss their lessons, picnics and excursions were held for entertainment, and regular meetings were held to update the strikers on developments.
27 Apr 1955	Chaired by Stephen Yong Kuet Tze and Ong Kee Hui, an Enquiry Meeting was held by the 13 Chinese associations that decided on the motion that called on the resignation of Principal Huang on the basis of "guilty of immoral conduct and had been biased and unfair in his treatment of the students". Principal Huang had refused to attend the Enquiry. Thereafter, the strike/boycott was called off.

Source: Seng Guo Quan, "The Origins of the Socialist Revolution in Sarawak (1945–1963)", MA thesis, National University of Singapore, 2007, pp. 56–57; Chin Ung-Ho, *Chinese Politics in Sarawak: A Study of the Sarawak United People's Party* (Kuala Lumpur: Oxford University Press, 1997), pp. 42–43; Stephen K. T. Yong, *A Life Twice Live: A Memoir* (Kuching: author, 1998), pp. 134–135; Vernon L. Porritt, *The Rise and Fall of Communism in Sarawak 1940–1990* (Clayton, Vic.: Monash Asia Institute, 2004), p. 24.

'Heaven on Earth'

> You, young people, full of vigour and vitality, are in the bloom of life, like the sun at eight or nine in the morning. Our hope is placed on you.
> *Mao Zedong, discussion with Chinese students in Moscow, 17 Nov 1957*

Through delving into Left-wing literature – school textbooks, newspapers, books, novels, magazines, cartoons – Chinese youths and especially middle school students began to discover the Marxist theory of historical materialism. Simply presented, Marx viewed history developing in stages, whereby each stage brought forth a new class that subsequently would lead to its downfall owing to internal contradictions and class conflicts.[34] The downfall, however, would not be adverse, since with each stage, man in general would benefit and progress forward. The stages are: (1) primitive communism, (2) slave society, (3) feudalism, (4) capitalism, (5) socialism, and (6) communism.

Both Left-wing Chinese intelligentsia and middle school students were equally persuaded by Marxist theory. They greeted the establishment of the PRC in 1949 enthusiastically as a realistic achievement of a communist state. They too, in the local context of Sarawak, would strive to attain such a similar goal. Therefore, middle school students sought to put theory into practice in the Kuching CHMS with a protracted strike action that stretched to 103 days from 29 October 1951 over the issue of an alleged unfair evaluation of an examination owing to the alleged incompetency of the schoolteacher.

Table 4.4 details the student strike action that was undoubtedly an unprecedented phenomenon considering the hitherto well-known disciplined nature of Chinese students and their reverence for teachers. But upon hindsight, the strike appeared inevitable when the school's principal and disciplined master, both covert communists, if not, at least active sympathizers, handed in their resignation consequent of the police raid on the CHMS Students' Self-Governing Society (SSGS) in June 1951. The replacement academic staff were former KMT government officials brought over from Hong Kong. The student–teacher feud over teaching methodology and evaluation might be a mere pretext as the pro-communist student body came face-to-face with KMT faculty.

Although the civil court acted leniently towards the detained student leaders described by the presiding judge as "misguided young men", the incoming members of the Kuching Chung Hwa Schools Board of Management in its determination to cleanse the school of problematic elements of whatever persuasion decided to dismiss both the principal and the detained student leaders. This hard-line stance further spurred the student strikers to continue their action, which was seen as "righteous in correcting an injustice".

If the strikers had remained faithful to their initial demand for the removal of the alleged incompetent principal and teacher, they might have attained a viable and favourable outcome. Instead, they lost their moral compass and abandoned altogether their "righteous" demand to veer toward a typical Leftist/communist rhetoric of calling for the defeat of British colonialism and imperialism.

This switch in the strikers' demand was revealing and, as a result, served as a pretext for stern action on the part of the colonial authorities. The anti-colonialism and anti-imperialism protest slogans unmasked the covert Leftist/communist involvement, undoubtedly long suspected by the Special Branch from the outset. Communist agitators and activists certainly had instigated, or even had a hand in, orchestrating the entire strike drama. It was just the ripe pretext needed by the police, if at all, to once and for all smash the student strikers and end the strike action.

The aftermath of the strike witnessed a hardliner being appointed principal, who without hesitation executed draconian measures to clean CHMS of recalcitrant elements, viz. through re-registration of all students, a parents' pledge for the good behaviour of their children, and expulsion of an additional 15 students, totalling 33 altogether. The expelled students, whether communists or sympathizers, to avoid future detention, fled across the border to Indonesia West Kalimantan.

Youthful enthusiasm and idealism exposed the underlying purpose as well as the involvement of the communists in the students' strike action of 1951–1952.

The colonial government that had harboured suspicion of the dark hand of communist intervention had earlier (June 1951) moved against CHMS SSGS in a police raid that had uncovered tell-tale prohibited *(read*: communist) literature on its premises, leading to the Society being proscribed.

In the eyes of the colonial government, the first strike action at Kuching CHMS confirmed its suspicion of direct communist involvement in the Chinese vernacular school system. The harsh manner employed by the colonial authorities was justifiable in eliminating subversive elements that were undermining the peace and order of Kuching and its multiethnic inhabitants.

'Stamped with a five-star seal,' and said, 'that they were not robbers'

> Late in the evening of 5 August 1952, three men and one woman, all armed and in khaki uniforms, commandeered a bus parked between the 23rd and the 26th Mile of the Kuching to Serian Road. The group ordered the bus driver to take them to the Batu Kitang bazaar some 20 miles away, the bazaar being on the Kuching to Bau Road some ten miles from the capital, Kuching. On arrival, the group fired a few shots in the air, pounded on the doors of ten shophouses in the bazaar, and demanded that the shopkeepers open their doors. At the time of night all the shops were closed and shuttered. The raiders, who were fluent in Hokkien, Teochew, and Malay, told the shopkeepers that they were members of the Sarawak People's Liberation Army from Sangaw in Kalimantan and that there were about 1,000 of them who were all living in the jungle. Demanding a loan of [M]$10,000 from each shopkeeper, the raiders made them open their safes and produce their account books for inspection.
>
> Under duress, each shopkeeper handed over all the ready cash in the shop's safe and in return the raiders gave each shopkeeper a written statement showing the amount of cash taken and the amount still to be paid to make up the [M]$10,000 loan originally demanded. Each statement was *stamped with a five[-]star seal* and signed by Commanding Officer Lee and his deputy Ng. . . . One shopkeeper offered the raiders a gold bangle to convince them that there was no money in her shop, but the raiders refused to accept the bangle, saying *that they were not robbers.*[35]

While the CHMS drama was played out in the later part of 1951 and ended in early February 1952, a much more serious occurrence that came to be known as the 'Batu Kitang Incident' jolted both the general public of hitherto peaceful Sarawak and the colonial government. Demanding money as extortion was nothing new, as in the past 15 months the authorities encountered reports of Chinese youth involved in extortion threats to shopkeepers as well as reports of other illegal activities in the same vicinity. But what followed thereafter at Batu Kitang Bazaar and later at the 27th Mile was fearfully unusual and cause for great concern.

> The sound of a whistle at about 2:30 am, that is three and a half hours after the raiders arrived, served as a signal for the group to withdraw from the bazaar. . . . Using the bus on which they had arrived, the raiders returned to the area on the Kuching to Serian Road where the bus had been

commandeered and boarded an unregistered taxi. By coincidence, at that time a detachment of the Sarawak Constabulary was investigating allegations of communist extortion threats in the 27th Mile area and had set up a road block at the 27th Mile, but the main body of the detachment was searching an area some distance away. . . . Routinely, the police manning the 27th Mile road-block challenged the unregistered taxi as it approached the road block, but the passengers in the taxi opened fire with automatic weapons without warning, killing police Lance Corporal Natu and wounding two constables. The police in turn fired 30 rounds, possibly wounding one of the raiders and damaging the taxi. Although badly damaged, the taxi managed to run through the road-block, but had to be abandoned about a mile further on. The raiders were last seen running into the jungle and were never caught.[36]

The killing of Lance Corporal Natu at the 27 Mile Kuching-Serian Road was the first salvo and first fatality of a protracted 40-year armed conflict between the Sarawak government (initially colonial thereafter independent Malaysian) and the communists.

Meanwhile, the contemporaneous scenario from without was less than encouraging: in Vietnam, colonial French forces were battling with the Việt Minh in the First Indochina War (1946–1954); the Malayan Emergency (1948–1960) was ongoing in the tropical jungle of the peninsula; and in the Philippines, the Manila government was facing the Hukbalahap Rebellion (1946–1954), a communist uprising. Taking cognizance of the regional situation then, the Sarawak colonial government on 8 August 1952 proclaimed a state of emergency, subjecting the First Division under Emergency Regulation 1952. The proclamation enabled the colonial administration to wield unlimited powers, including imposing the death sentence for illegal possession of a firearm, his/her accomplice could be imprisoned up to a maximum of ten years, and any individual could be detained for 12 months without charges and/or trial, besides imposition of curfews, restricting movements and assemblies of people, and a ban on military-style uniforms and flags.[37] The hitherto open and unsecured border with Kalimantan was closed while the death penalty awaited anyone gaining illegal entry.

Furthermore, aware that Sarawak was unprepared for a communist insurgency as in the peninsula, the colonial government sought assistance from Singapore and North Borneo. On 16 August saw the arrival of airlifted materials by the Royal Air Force (RAF) of materials and supplies of jungle warfare, viz. camouflaged uniforms, jungle boots, and food packs. The following day, two platoons of police personnel of 68 men arrived from North Borneo to assist the Constabulary to undertake patrols along the porous Sarawak-Kalimantan border and in and around the Serian area. At the same time, General Sir Robert Lockhart, deputy director of operations in Malaya, accompanied by two senior officers of the Malayan Police, called on Kuching. Sir Robert projected an optimistic outlook that Sarawak was unlikely to face trouble or unrest, citing the absence of any large trade unions and the undue difficulty to acquire firearms. Nonetheless, 'forewarned is to be forearmed', and the Batu Kitang Incident served as a harbinger, hence prepared-ness in strengthening security were put in place.[38]

One major casualty of the Batu Kitang Incident was the dissolution of the SNYDL after Emergency Regulation 1952. With scant hesitation, ex-members proceeded to establish two underground organizations, viz. Progressive Teach-ers' Association (PTA) and Students' Society (SS), some time at the end of 1952 (Table 4.3). The former arranged for young teachers to be posted to serve in the interior districts; the real intention, however, was for them to organize the peas-ants into a viable movement. The SS took over the students' movement in the Kuching CHMS, and from there initiated students' movement in the Third and Fourth Divisions. To a large extent, mainly through stealth, the communist tenta-cles reached every corner of Sarawak territory and every sector of its population.

But it was apparent that the students (SS), rather than the teachers (PTA), who proved more single-minded with fewer distractions like familial obligations, were better suited for the revolutionary struggle ahead. It was from the SS that emerged the names of Wen Ming Chyuan (head) (b. 1932) and Bong Kee Chok (member) (b. 1937), two personalities who were to orchestrate the communist movement in Sarawak for the next several decades.

A turning point

Between 1952 and 1954, the groundwork was laid for Sarawak's communist orga-nization, namely the shadowy Sarawak Liberation League (SLL), that subse-quently would 'mobilise the masses . . . [and] launch revolution'. SLL was established under the leadership of Wen Ming Chyuan, who would set the agenda and direction. Not knowing of its existence, the colonial authorities attached vari-ous labels when referring to the communists, initially, 'Clandestine Communist Organization (CCO)', later changed to 'Sarawak Communist Organization (SCO)', and finally to the 'North Kalimantan Communist Party (NKCP)'[39] that was for-mally inaugurated in 1971. In whatever name and/or manifestations, Wen Ming Chyuan was the undisputed leader at the helm throughout.

Sarawak Liberation League (SLL)

Teo Yong Jim, a Kuching-born former student and ex-schoolteacher of CHMS while in Singapore in the early 1950s, had been in contact with Chin Peng's Malayan Communist Party (MCP). Upon his return to Kuching in mid-1953, Teo together with Wen Ming Chyuan set up the Sarawak Liberation League (SLL) after the template of the MCP's satellite organization in Singapore, the Anti-British League (ABL).[40] SLL's primary undertaking was in mobilizing the masses in preparation for the revolutionary stage. The triangular clandestine cell organization system was instituted by Teo, whereby each small group of members only knew the identities of their fellow cell members, direct subordinate, and their immediate superior. Adherence to secrecy was strictly enforced, whereby cell members only utilized a *nom de guerre* or pseudo name. Hence, its cell system could effectively resist penetration by the authorities. In the event of a cell member being apprehended and interrogated, revelations would be limited to the few people the detainee was in direct contact with, hence safeguarding exposing the entire organization.

From 1954, following the departure of Teo, Wen Ming Chyuan became the undisputed leader of SLL and, in turn, the arbiter of Sarawak's communist revolution.[41] The formative years of the SLL were devoted to recruitment and indoctrination. The initial core members were CHMS students who were all adept at Marxist-Leninist theory (Table 4.3). With Wen as the leader, other notable members included Lin Yonglun[42] (peasant movement), Bong Kee Chok (No. 2 leader, 'open front' or public leader), Guo Weizhong (No. 3 leader), Lim Ho Kui (labour movement), and Lui How Ming (Sibu). The triumvirate of Wen, Bong, and Guo, who dominated the Organization Bureau of SLL, was the arbiter of policy and strategy.[43]

By 1955, Wen considered SLL poised to put into action its policy line of "Set our hands free to *mobilise the masses*. Actively *launch revolution*".[44] The litmus test was a 47-day student strike action at Kuching CHMS that by all estimates the SLL was triumphant in successfully mobilizing the masses, in this context, Chinese middle school students.

To 'mobilise the masses . . . [and] launch [the] revolution'

The second student strike (1955)

Table 4.5 shows the chronology of the second strike by students of Chung Hwa Middle School, Kuching, that commenced from 30 March 1955 but with an antecedent in late February. Unlike the previous failed student strike action (1951–1952), the SLL orchestrated student strike action consistently and persistently held on to its demand to "uphold justice" for the resignation of the CHMS principal. This strategy paid dividends. The enquiry meeting organized by 13 Chinese associations chaired by lawyer Stephen Yong Kuet Tze (1921–2001) and businessman Ong Kee Hui (1914–2000) decided on the removal of the principal.

During the 47-day strike/boycott, 1,143 students were tutored by their seniors, and picnics and excursions were organized for entertainment. Throughout these activities, the SLL managed to politicize the students and trained a large number of cadres. The *ultimate and real objective* was "to mobilise the masses", and the SLL attained an unqualified success. The strike action was merely a façade.

Treading cautiously, the SLL did not absorb the more than 1,000 students who were politicized, had "turned progressive", or in other words, were ideologically indoctrinated. Until each individual had proven himself/herself, viz. fully grasping Marxist-Leninist theory and commitment to the revolution, they were in the interim enrolled as members of the Sarawak Advanced Youths' Association (SAYA). Covertness was strictly maintained. Those who joined SAYA referred to themselves as members of 'O', denoting the 'Organization'. Like SLL members, SAYA members were also subjected to an oath-taking: commitment to "the democracy and freedom of Sarawak", to master the "theories of Marxism/Lenin-ism and the ideology of Mao Tse Tung, and make use of what I have learnt to educate the masses", and to offer their "whole li[ves] without the slightest hesita-tion for the service of the organization [SAYA] and the great enterprise [that is, the communist revolution]".[45] Members of SAYA were unaware of the existence of SLL. Wen ensured that SLL remained in the shadows.

The student standoff tested SLL's organizational network, operational deploy-ment, and commitment of its members, which had resulted in a satisfactory out-come. Learning from past failure (first strike) had been profitable in seeing that determination, perseverance, and singlemindedness were pivotal ingredients for success. As pointed out, the politicizing of the masses, in this context Chinese middle school students, was the underlying aim and had been achieved with unex-pected success. The large numbers of "progressive" youths had achieved success to the extent that SAYA had to be specifically constituted to serve the interim needs prior to subsequent induction into SLL.

Having succeeded in mobilizing the students, the labour movement was next on the agenda. Conducted in parallel was the mobilizing of the masses, the general public albeit the Chinese-educated group, through the print media.

Labour, media, and Dayak

Lim Ho Kui was assigned the task of mobilizing the labouring masses. Meanwhile, upon graduation from CHMS, SLL/SAYA members infiltrated labour organiza-tions and trade unions as clerks and secretaries, allowing them access to members, and through the latter, influenced policies that adopted a pro-communist agenda. Through interviews, including Lim Ho Kui and other SLL/SAYA members directly involved in mobilizing the labour movement, an insightful scenario is thus revealed. Lim, for instance, steered the labour movement in four directions:

> First . . . made the material needs of the workers top priority for the unions: pushing for shorter working hours, negotiating better wages, and providing unemployment benefits and funeral services. Second, . . . introduced cultural activities to educate and entertain the workers . . . from choral singing, mass dancing, . . . free education in the Trade Unions Free Night School (est. 1959). Third . . . [Lim himself] presided over a period of expansion and consolidation [of the trade unions]. . . . [Fourth] instituted two communications systems – one official, the other underground – modelled after the pyramidal hierarchy of SLL/SAYA.[46]

Through the dedicated and focused efforts of Lim and his fellow comrades in SLL/ SAYA, the communist-influenced labour movement controlled "more than 4,000 workers in [Kuching] [and] a stand-by army ready to be mobilised whenever num-bers and manpower were needed".[47] Table 4.6 shows the extent of SLL infiltration in the leadership of six trade unions, some as high as almost 70 per cent, as in the Kuching Employees and Labourers' Union (KELU, estb. 1957) that represented

Table 4.6 Communist Infiltration of Labour Unions in Sarawak

Trade Union Executive Committee	Members	Chinese	Native	CCO[†]
Sarawak Trade Union Congress (STUC) % infiltration of total – 65%	28*	28	–	13°
Kuching Building Workers % infiltration of total – 28% % infiltration of Chinese – 31%	21	19	2	6
Kuching Bus Workers % infiltration of total – 41%	17	17	–	7
Kuching Employees and Labourers % infiltration of total – 69% % infiltration of Chinese – 76%	23	19	2	16
Kuching Printing Workers % infiltration of total – 41%	17	17	–	7
Sibu All Trades Employees % infiltration of total – 57% % infiltration of Chinese – 60%	21	20	1	12

† Clandestine Communist Organization (CCO) was the term initially used by the colonial/Malaysian government to refer to the communists, later Sarawak Communist Organization (SCO), and finally to the North Kalimantan Communist Party (NKCP) that was formally established in 1971.

* Figures do not include communist activists and/or sympathizers, hence influence in these committees is much greater than presented.

° Communists held key posts including secretary, thus making their influence even more dominant. Similar infiltration was also found in smaller unions.

Source: After CO 1030/1105, cited in Vernon L. Porritt, *The Rise and Fall of Communism in Sarawak 1940–1990* (Clayton, Vic.: Monash Asia Institute, 2004), p. 265, Appendix 5.

shophouse assistants. As has been pointed out, SLL members more often held key positions, hence their influence in these executive committees was much more dominant, especially in matters of policy formulation.

With mainly Chinese students and workers in its grasp, SLL/SAYA moved toward further mobilizing the wider masses. In this connection, the commencement on 1 August 1956 of *Sin Wen Pau*, the first Left-wing Chinese-medium, Sarawak-based-and-oriented newspaper, was a promising start. Wen Ming Chyuan assumed the editor position of the international news desk of *Sin Wen Pau*. His tenure between 1957 and 1960 witnessed his mark on editorial policy. *Sin Wen Pau*, for all intents and purposes, served as the public mouthpiece of SLL. In the early 1960s, SLL generated *Min Chong Pau* (25 April 1960, Sibu) and *Sa Min Pau* (11 February 1961, Miri) to widen the readership in the Third and Fourth Divisions, respectively. The provision of daily newspapers that even reached the interior districts thanks to the overall improvement in land transport was a radical phenomenon, because hitherto dailies were limited to readership among the townspeople. The combined circulation of all three SLL 'mouthpieces' was 7,000 copies daily, but arguably it reached a readership beyond the subscribed copies as it was commonplace for each copy to be re-circulated and/or read by more than one individual.[48] Through these print media, SLL could to a large extent politicize and mobilize the Chinese literate group, in other words helped to galvanize them to a pro-communist persuasion.

Unlike the encouraging outcomes of work in the labour movement and the mass influence enjoyed by the dailies in reaching to the grassroots, albeit limited within the Chinese-educated community, the efforts in politicizing and mobilizing the indigenous peoples were less than positive. Enticing the Dayak peasantry into a 'united front' peasant movement was considered pivotal, and SLL 'big guns' themselves took to the field, viz. a Minzu Works Sub-Committee under the Central Committee was constituted in 1958 comprising Wen as the head, and committee members included Bong Kee Chok, Liu How Ying,[49] and Yap Choon Ho.

Consequent of the fieldwork in the First Division focusing on the Sarawak-Kalimantan border areas, it was admitted that there were "real 'historical' barriers" between the Chinese cadres and the Dayak peasantry that were "attributed to the colonial policy of 'divide and rule'".[50] Communication was the initial hurdle, as few Chinese then were conversant in indigenous languages (Malay, Iban), and likewise natives speaking Hokkien or Foochow, or *Guoyu*. Mutual ignorance between Chinese and indigenes of each other's culture and way of life made them literally 'like fish out of water' in one another's socio-cultural environment. In addition, there was also undeniably an air of 'cultural superiority' among the Chinese vis-à-vis indigenous cultures and peoples.

As proposals for the formation of a political party gained momentum in the early part of 1959, Wen, Bong, and Yap returned to Kuching, leaving others to carry on the work with the indigenous peoples.

SLL and the Sarawak United People's Party (SUPP)

Wen and his comrades turned to the communist 'united front' strategy of working through a legitimate political party. The Sarawak United Peoples' Party (SUPP) as an SLL 'front' bona fide political party was evident from its gestation to its formation in mid-1959.

Although SUPP, formed on 4 June 1959, was acknowledged as the first formal political party in Sarawak, there was a preceding but stillborn entity, the Sarawak People's Party (SPP). As early as July 1955, when Ong Kee Hui was appointed an unofficial member of Council Negri, Colonial Chief Secretary J. H. Ellis suggested to him "that the unofficial members . . . should take the initiative and form their own political party".[51] It was barely two months prior (27 April) that Ong, together with Stephen Yong Kuet Tze, successfully resolved the Chinese student strike action that both believed "were caused by communist agitators fomenting unrest amongst the students".[52] "These [student] problems", Ong recalled, "clearly showed the need for an organization to lead the young in the right direction and provide a constructive outlet for their aspirations".[53]

Following further deliberations, Ong and his circle of colleagues agreed that Malayan-style communal political parties should be eschewed. The provisional name of the proposed party was the SPP, that would be spearheaded by Ong and Stephen Yong. The latter was tasked to gain the support of the Chinese-educated community.

Meanwhile, Ong received encouraging backing from Temenggong Jugah anak Bariang, whom Governor Sir Anthony Abell had urged to support him (Ong). Temenggong Jugah was an influential figure of the Dayaks (Ibans) of the Third Division, and his support was important.[54] But there was a less than enthusiastic response from other quarters, namely senior Malay government servants who were "more cautious", the Malay National Union of Sarawak (MNU) preferred "communal political parties", while the Sarawak Dayak Association (SDA) then was prioritizing "raising [Dayak] standard of education and living and that forming a political party . . . was premature".[55]

In 1956, nominated (by the colonial governor) members of the Kuching Municipal Council were replaced by elected members, a progressive constitutional development implemented by the colonial government. Locals were hopeful that Sarawak's independence was imminent, hence political alliances began to be negotiated and forged. According to Stephen Yong, the initiative of the formation of a multiethnic political party was from Stanley Wong Cheng Ting of Sibu.[56] Stanley Wong, together with Chan Siaw Hee, deliberated the idea with Chin Shou Tong, Koo Choon Hui, and Wen Ming Chyuan from the Chinese-educated community. Chan Siaw Hee, a Kuching Municipal Councillor and brother-in-law to Stephen Yong, approached the latter to garner support from the English-educated Chinese group for such a political party.

A further impetus was the appearance in the local English-medium daily, *Sarawak Tribune*, 4 March 1959 of an article entitled "Democracy, National Unity, People's Party: Essential Ingredients" penned by Safri Awang, a Sarawak Malay then furthering his studies in New Zealand. The article's title was self-explanatory. Stephen Yong, Chan Siaw Hee, and Ong worked on the draft of the party constitution of the 'Sarawak United Peoples' Party' replacing the stillborn SPP, in Ong's words, "giving greater emphasis to unity amongst our multi-racial nation to achieve our aims and goals together".[57]

Then on 4 June 1959, SUPP came into being. Ong was elected as chairman, and Stephen Yong as secretary-general of the Central Committee, which according to the party constitution both held the reins of the party. The daily affairs of SUPP were delegated to the Central Working Committee comprising appointees made by the Central Committee. Altogether there were 34 founding members with an ethnic composition of Chinese (24), Iban (5), Melanau (2), Bidayuh (2), and Malay (1).[58] Appearance-wise and in reality, SUPP was a Chinese-dominated political entity.

Rather troubling for both Ong and Stephen Yong was a turnaround on the part of the colonial governor. Just a week earlier it seemed that Governor Abell changed his mind and expressed reservations regarding the formation of political parties. On the occasion of the opening of the Fourth Division Advisory Council meeting in Miri on 28 May 1959, Governor Abell noted, "I frankly doubt if political parties at the present stage of development will spell faster progress in this small country".[59] It became clear to Ong the reason why earlier that February, Temenggong Jugah withdrew his involvement with the SPP. Nonetheless, Temenggong Jugah, the gentlemen, attended the inaugural meeting of SUPP at Stephen Yong's residence on Tabuan Road, Kuching but abstained from signing the declaration of the formation of SUPP.[60] Moral support was what Temenggong Jugah, Pengarah Montegrai, and Pengarah Banyang, the Dayak unofficial members of Council Negri, could offer then.[61]

The realization of SUPP literally played into the cards of Wen and the SLL. During the fieldwork of the Minzu Works Sub-Committee in the First Division in 1958, Wen was targeting the integration of the Dayak peasantry into the 'united front'. But as earlier mentioned, there were "real 'historical' barriers" between the Chinese cadres and the Dayak peasantry, specifically in terms of linguistic and cultural barriers. What was crucially wanting was a legitimate political party whereby the Dayak peasantry (native masses) could be politicized and mobilized openly without hindrance. The formation of SUPP thus fulfilled this end.

In the early part of 1959, an essay titled "On the Formation of an Open Political Party and the Struggle for Independence" set out the argument for the need of a political party as a vehicle in mobilizing the masses.[62] Governor Abell's turnaround in February 1959 was understandable following the capture of the aforesaid essay by Special Branch:

> The revolution is now [early 1959] at a low-ebb, a passive atmosphere exists not only in the masses but even in our organization [SLL]. What can be done about it? . . . the only way open to us is to form an open [legal] political party. If we persist in secret work and fail boldly to organize a political party, we shall crawl along as before. We must readjust our ranks, propagate amongst the masses and create favourable conditions for the formation of a political party.[63]

Although greatly aware of the existence of underground communist activities amongst the Chinese community, it did not anticipate a 'united front' with a bona fide political party. The colonial government then became hesitant. Consequently, Governor Abell's cautionary speech in Miri on 28 May 1959:

> essential that party politics should not cause further divisions in our community but should have a unifying and binding effect. If a party tends to be dominated by one race or class. . . . it may have a disintegrating effect on our community.[64]

Governor Abell's speech was hinted at the soon-to-form SUPP that might see a surge of overwhelming Chinese participation. Surprisingly, the governor's cautionary note notwithstanding, SUPP formally received its letter of approval from the colonial government on 18 June 1959.[65] It was unclear regarding the haste in approval; Special Branch might have assured that the situation was under control and, if needed, emergency regulation could again be imposed to counter any untoward exigencies.

The emergence of SUPP opened the floodgates for the formation of political parties. Not unlike SUPP, all of the parties were established on communal lines. *Parti Negara Sarawak* (PANAS, National Party of Sarawak), registered on 9 April 1960, initially was multiethnic with a spread of Malays, Ibans, Chinese, and Melanaus but subsequently moved towards a Malay predominance in both leadership and rank-and-file members.[66] In all appearances, *Barisan Ra'ayat Jati Sarawak* (BARJASA, Sarawak Indigenous Peoples Front) was a counterweight to PANAS in that it comprised the Malay faction that was the backbone of the anti-cession movement. Understandably, BARJASA campaigned for special privileges for indigenous *(read*: Muslim natives) peoples.[67] Unexpectedly, the Iban-based Sarawak National Party (SNAP) was inaugurated on 10 April 1961. It was a surprise move by founding members who were not the least connected to the colonial government and/or were noted Ibans. Exclusively the initiators were from the Saribas district of the Iban heartland of the Second Division.[68] Comparatively, the Saribas Ibans were the most forward looking, as they had shown in their reception to education at an early stage.[69]

A further impetus to political party formation was the public mooting of the 'Malaysia' concept by Malayan Prime Minister Tunku Abdul Rahman Putra Al-Haj on 27 May 1961.[70] A wider federation of a federal constitutional monarchy was proposed to comprise independent Malaya, the British colonies of Singapore, Sarawak, and North Borneo, and the protectorate of Brunei. Rumours, however, were in the air though details remained speculative until Tunku's pronouncement at a meeting of foreign correspondents in Singapore.

What later followed was the inauguration of PESAKA and SCA, both in July 1962. Parti Pesaka anak Sarawak (PESAKA, Sarawak Native's Heritage Party) was an attempt to bring the hitherto fragmented Ibans of the Third Division, notably of the Rajang, under one single political umbrella and "thus create a bond that would enable them to be politically potent and stand on their own feet".[71] The concept and initial 'push' for PESAKA was from a senior British officer.[72] As SUPP was increasingly seen as leaning to the political Left in harping on a socialist agenda, an alternative for the Chinese appeared in the form of the Sarawak Chinese Association (SCA). Urged by the Malayan Chinese Association (MCA), which was a counterweight to the MCP, it was no surprise that SCA had a mirror copy of the former's constitution with minor amendments.[73] Like its promoter, SCA was a *towkay* party drawing from the Kuching Teochew and Sibu Foochow, as well as from English-educated Chinese. The latter was rather estranged from the Chinese middle school–dominated SUPP, likewise the older conservative Chinese too were disillusioned with SUPP's youthful membership and their socialist agenda.[74]

From the mushrooming of communal-based political parties, it was apparent that political consciousness was fomenting in the respective ethnic communities; each was aware of their interests, well-being, rights, and status vis-à-vis the other groups. The differentiation between native and Chinese too was pronounced, and similarly past histories too had their role, such as BARJASA's insistence on special privileges for indigenes.

Despite Ong's intention of inserting 'United' in SUPP, "thus giving greater emphasis to *unity* amongst our multi-racial nation [Sarawak] to achieve our aims and goals *together*", SUPP in all appearances was regarded by the colonial administration as anti-government. PESAKA and PANAS, on the other hand, were seen as pro-government. In Stephen Yong's words:

> The primary reason that SUPP was considered as the opposition party was due to the simple fact that we were more vocal and critical and demanded accountability on the part of the Colonial Officers. As Party spokesman, I was considered a thorn on their side.[75]

It was certainly more than Stephen Yong's outspoken and critical approach that coloured the colonial government's perception of SUPP. Special Branch had gathered much intelligence by the late 1950s and early 1960s.

Moreover, when David McLelland, Adviser on Education to the Commissioner General for the United Kingdom in South-East Asia, was commissioned to review secondary education, he was also instructed to prepare a confidential report on the state of subversion in Chinese schools.[76] His report dated 6 November 1959 provided an insightful and troubling scenario of the penetrating reach of the communists in both Chinese primary and middle schools. Then, in July 1960, Council Negri discussed a sessional paper titled *Subversion in Sarawak* (Sessional Paper no. 3, July 1960), followed a year later by another government White Paper, *Communism and the Farmers*, and three years on, in 1963, Sarawak Information Service produced an abridged version of Tim Hardy's *The Danger Within: A History of the Clandestine Communist Organization in Sarawak*.

Hardy arrived in Kuching in December 1961 to assume the post of deputy head of Special Branch; within a fortnight, he became acting head. Concerned about the communist threat in Sarawak, the colonial government wanted a definitive report, and this task fell on Hardy, who commenced collating the intelligence hitherto collected and wrote out the paper, completing it by November 1962. *The Danger Within* was literally an exposé of SLL intentions, objectives, activities, structure and network, and much other useful information in between, enabling the colonial government to fully comprehend the communist threat. In this work, SLL was identified as CCO.

The communist 'cancer' literally engulfed the entire body polity of SUPP, as Table 4.7 reveals. Highly successful penetration could be seen in the Kuching and Sibu branches and less effect in the Fourth and Fifth Divisions. Furthermore, many of the communists held key positions such as secretary, hence making their influence even more effective. Besides infiltration at the higher echelons of SUPP, the rank-and-file too were many communists or sympathizers as ordinary members of this legitimate political party.

As with the Minzu Works Sub-Committee, SLL 'big guns' were prominently placed in the SUPP hierarchy. Wen Ming Chyuan, SLL leader and later as

Table 4.7 Communist Infiltration of the Sarawak United People's Party (SUPP)

Committee* (% of communist infiltration)	Chinese	Native	Total members	CCO°
Central Executive Committee (25% of whole; 50% of Chinese)	20	20	40	10◊
Central Working, Kuching (30% of whole; 40% of Chinese)	15	5	20	6
Sibu Branch (69% of whole; 76% of Chinese)	16	4	20	8
Simanggang Branch (14% of whole; 41% of Chinese)	12	23	35	5
Miri Branch (8% of whole; 13% of Chinese)	23	12	35	3
Limbang Branch (4% of whole; 16% of Chinese)	6	16	22	1

* Excludes communist activists and/or sympathizers, hence influence in these committees is much greater than presented.
° Clandestine Communist Organization (CCO) was the term initially used by the colonial/Malaysian government to refer to the communist, later Sarawak Communist Organization (SCO), and finally to the North Kalimantan Communist Party (NKCP) that was formally established in 1971.
◊ Communists held key posts of secretary in most cases, thus making their influence even more dominant. Similar infiltration is also found in the smaller branches and sub-branches.
Source: After CO 1030/1105, cited in Vernon L. Porritt, *The Rise and Fall of Communism in Sarawak 1940–1990* (Clayton, Vic.: Monash Asia Institute, 2004), p. 267, Appendix 6.

chairman of the North Kalimantan Communist Party (NKCP), held the post of Central Assistant Secretary General (Publicity). Bong Kee Chok, second in command in SLL and later as founder-leader of *Pasukan Gerilya Rakyat Sarawak* (PGRS, Sarawak People's Guerrilla Force [SPGF]), assumed as Central Assistant Secretary General (Organization). Then there were Yang Chu Chung and Yap Choon Ho, both commanders of 3rd Company PGRS, as members of the SUPP Central Committee.

Moreover, the repeated confluence of objectives and agendas of SUPP and SLL was unlikely to be mere coincidences. Both steadfastly opposed the colonial government's second thrust of pursuing a national education system that envisaged the creation of multiethnic secondary schools with a common medium of instruction, namely the English language.[77]

The 'Conversion Plan'

Governor Sir Alexander Waddell announced to Council Negri on 6 December 1960 the implementation of the Conversion Plan. To be implemented in stages over several years, the Conversion Plan was a strategic ploy to phase out the hitherto plural school system that operated on communal lines. It was made a mandatory criterion under the Grant Code, the colonial government's financing of education programme. No communal-based school was allowed, and any new school should welcome pupils from all ethnic groups. The Sarawak Junior School Certificate (SJSC) and the Cambridge Higher School Certificate (CHSC) were to replace the Chinese Junior Middle and Senior Middle examinations, respectively. In any case, as mentioned, the certificates of the latter two were not recognized by the colonial government or by the private sector, namely European commercial firms, shipping lines, insurance agencies, and banks. Misgivings of the loss of ethnic cultural heritage and language were assured that adequate provision was instituted in the school curricula for Chinese and other native languages and cultures. Neither mission-managed secondary schools nor government Malay junior secondary schools opposed the changeover to English as the sole medium of instruction. The 'obstacle' seemed to be only with the 16 independent Chinese vernacular middle schools. Accordingly, Chinese-medium secondary schools were issued a 15 April 1961 deadline to furnish their conversion plan for approval by the colonial education department. Failing that, all colonial government financing would cease from 1 April 1962.

Acting as the *de facto* representative of the Sarawak Chinese community, SUPP immediately responded with an alternative proposed education programme. The gist was over the language medium: a common syllabus was accepted but schools were to be given the choice of language of instruction, and the question of a national language should be postponed until Sarawak gained independence from Britain.[78]

The Left-wing print media waded into the war of words. *Sin Wen Pau* contended that:

> the same set of principles that reinforce Sarawak nationalism can be taught in different language-medium schools, to inform children from every race that the children and adults of other races are just like their own siblings and parents, who need our care and concern.[79]

Sibu's *Min Chong Pau* was even more forceful, concluding in its editorial that the "nationalization" of secondary schools was not unlike "a second round of 'colonization'". Moreover, the same editorial criticized the choice of English as the chosen medium of instruction:

> those who knew English were in the absolute minority in this country; [advocates of the Conversion Plan] also fail to recognise that a common language should be selected from among the [language of the] three major races [Malay, Dayak, and Chinese] of this country. . . . A genuine national system [of education] or common language could only be decided by a self-governing and independent people, on the basis of equality and mutual benefit.[80]

On point of fact and rational reasoning, *Min Chong Pau* was difficult to challenge. The English-educated cohort across ethnic groups was undoubtedly a small fraction of the overall population. In pushing for a national education system and its concomitant Conversion Plan, for all intents and purposes the colonial government was forcefully imposing its will on a colonized people, hence rightly regarded as "a second round of 'colonization'".

Moreover, a contemporary critical opinion regards the Conversion Plan as "essentially a plan to buy out the sixty-year-old [Chinese] private school system with four years of state funding, the finances of which in any case had been drawn mainly from taxing Chinese economic activities".[81] In other words, *it was outright bullying on the part of the colonial government.*

The SLL in opposing the Conversion Plan was in fact fighting a war for its survival and sustainability. The Chinese vernacular school system was no less than the platforms for ideological indoctrination and a major source of their recruitment. The 47-day student strike/boycott action at CHMS, as mentioned, was not so much the demands for rectifying injustice but the *real* intention was "to mobilise the masses", all 1,143 student strikers. The SLL through SUPP and the Chinese print media employed various arguments to ensure they staved off conversion by all 16 independent Chinese vernacular middle schools:

> Appealing to Chinese sentiments that played on the preservation of Chinese socio-cultural heritage, the all-important perpetuation of Chinese language from one generation to another was the communists' stratagem to win over the Chinese community and to fortify its resistance to the change in the medium of instruction. Moreover, Chinese ethnic identity as manifested in the Chinese school system, the bastion of Chinese socio-cultural heritage, had to be defended at all costs. The communists threw in the patriotic trump card: those who supported the Conversion Plan were labelled unpatriotic and traitors to the motherland.[82]

In countering claims that the Conversion Plan might compromise the teaching and learning of Chinese language and literature, McLellan drew examples from Penang's Chung Ling High School and Hong Kong's Anglo-Chinese secondary schools where quality of achievement in Chinese studies (language and literature) was "as high as those reached in the ordinary middle schools".[83]

A captured document entitled "Outline of the Summary Report in the Struggle against the 10-Year Conversion Plan" demonstrated without a shadow of a doubt of SLL direct and explicit instigation to derail the colonial government's ultimate aim of creating a national education system for Sarawak:

> The Conversion Plan seriously conflicts with the racial concepts of the Chinese people. Correct leadership [of the SLL] provides us with favourable terms to control and make use of the anti-conversion struggle. By convincing and winning the support of the [Chinese] school management boards who fought shoulder to shoulder with us despite pressure by the British Imperialists, only 3 out of 16 middle schools agreed with the [P]lan.[84]

On the contrary, 11 out of 16 independent Chinese vernacular middle schools undertook the conversion.[85] Pragmatism finally won the day.

> The obvious economic advantages by way of better and wider employment opportunities and the possibilities open for further education motivated both parents and students in wanting to acquire and English education.[86]

Out of those that refused to bow were the three middle schools in Kuching that were hotbeds of student activism.

On course with its 'united front' tactic

Thus far, the scorecard between the SLL and the colonial government appeared to be favouring the latter with the victory over the Conversion Plan. Undoubtedly it was a great disappointment, a setback, but SLL did not lose hope as it persevered with its 'united front' tactic through SUPP to continue the struggle through constitutional means.

Oblivious to the moderate leadership of SUPP, SLL's top echelons, as pointed out, held strategic positions within the political party's set-up, such as the office of Central Assistant Secretary General (Publicity) and Central Assistant Secretary General (Organization), held by Wen Ming Chyuan and Bong Kee Chok, respectively, pivotal positions to subtly and covertly influence policy directions 'behind-the-scenes'. Within SUPP, recruitment of supporters and sympathizers, if not converts, was continuously undertaken by SLL personnel. Farther afield, from without, utilizing the cloak of SUPP, work was carried out in enlisting enthusiasts to the cause, garnering adherents to the ideology.

The next major challenge was the idea of 'Malaysia'.

Notes

1 Mao Zedong, *Quotations from Chairman Mao Tse-tung (The Little Red Book) & Other Works* (Morrisville, NC: Lulu Press Inc., 2017), p. 147.
2 Sarawak Information Service, *The Danger Within: A History of the Clandestine Communist Organization in Sarawak* (Kuching: Government Printing Office, 1963), p. 3.
3 For Brooke immigration policy mainly targeting Chinese, see Ooi Keat Gin, *Of Free Trade and Native Interests: The Brookes and the Economic Development of Sarawak, 1841–1941* (Kuala Lumpur: Oxford University Press, 1997), pp. 30–31, 33–38, 40–41, 56–57.
4 See ibid., pp. 83–106, 120–122, 251–288.
5 Chan Ah Ko's home country was Chao'an county, a district of Chaozhou City in eastern Guangdong Province. Chan's compatriots spoke a particular strain of Cantonese. Formerly, Chao'an was known as Haiyang until 1914.
6 See Ooi, *Of Free Trade and Native Interests*, p. 31.
7 It included the death penalty for a leader of a "secret *hueh*". See ibid., pp. 123, 262, 282 n. 55. Although it should be *hui*, British colonial documents mistakenly attributed *kongsi* in referring to covert so-called secret societies. The term *kongsi* literally means to share, hence a partnership, a cooperative. Also refers to a Chinese clan house on the basis of a shared progenitor, or from the same (common) country or district on the

mainland. Ooi Keat Gin, *Historical Dictionary of Malaysia*, 2nd ed. (Lanham, MD: Rowman & Littlefield, 2018), pp. 191–192, 233–234.

8 For instance, see Wilfred Blythe, *The Impact of Chinese Secret Societies in Malaya: A Historical Study* (London: Oxford University Press, 1969); Mak Lau Fong, *The Sociology of Secret Societies: A Study of Chinese Secret Societies in Singapore and Peninsular Malaysia* (Kuala Lumpur: Oxford University Press, 1981).

9 T'ien Ju-K'ang, *The Chinese of Sarawak: A Study of Social Structure*, Monographs on Social Anthropology No. 12 (London: Department of Anthropology, the London School of Economics and Political Science, 1953), p. 16 Table 3.

10 Ibid., p. 17.

11 Ibid., p. 19.

12 See Li Yi, *The Structure and Evolution of Chinese Social Stratification* (Lanham, MD: University Press of America, 2005), pp. 33–36.

13 See ibid., pp. 38–40.

14 See Ooi Keat Gin, "Chinese Vernacular Education in Sarawak during Brooke Rule, 1841–1946", *Modern Asian Studies*, 28, 3 (July 1994), pp. 503–531.

15 Ooi Keat Gin, *World beyond the Rivers: Education in Sarawak From Brooke Rule to Colonial Office Administration, 1841–1963* (Special Publication Series, Hull, England: Department for South-East Asian Studies, University of Hull, 1996), pp. 58–61.

16 Ibid., pp. 72–73.

17 Ibid., pp. 63, 64. Also, see ibid., p. 64 Table 6.

18 By 1926, the KMT's quest to canvass support from the Chinese diaspora in Southeast Asia saw the establishment of some 300 branch or chapter offices across the region: British Burma, British Malaya, French Indochina, American Philippines, and Netherlands East Indies. Collectively, a 31,000-strong membership base was attained that apparently doubled within eight years. Yoji Akashi, *The Nanyang Chinese Salvation Movement, 1937–1941* (Lawrence, KS: Center for East Asian Studies, University of Kansas, 1970), pp. 6–8.

19 See Ooi, *Of Free Trade and Native Interests*, pp. 238–239, 277–278.

20 See Ooi Keat Gin, *Rising Sun Over Borneo: The Japanese Occupation of Sarawak, 1941–1945* (London and Basingstoke: Macmillan; New York: St Martin's Press, 1999), pp. 96–100.

21 See Ooi Keat Gin, *The Japanese Occupation of Borneo, 1941–1945* (London: Routledge, 2011), pp. 65–66.

22 See Ooi, *Rising Sun over Borneo*, pp. 98–101.

23 See Ooi Keat Gin, *Post-War Borneo, 1945–1950: Nationalism, Empire, and State-Building* (London: Routledge, 2013), pp. 90–91.

24 See ibid., p. 145.

25 See Peter Zarrow, *China in War and Revolution, 1895–1949* (London: Routledge, 2005), pp. 149–169.

26 Ibid., pp. 237–240.

27 Ibid., pp. 299–323. In contemporary Chinese scholarship, it is often referred to as the Eight-Year War of Anti-Japanese Resistance, or the War Against Japanese Aggression.

28 Ching-Hwang Yen, *The Chinese in Southeast Asia and Beyond: Socioeconomic and Political Dimensions* (Singapore: World Scientific Publishing, 2008), p. 353.

29 See Julitta Lim Shau Hua and Hon Kah Fong, *The Intrepid Sarawak Volunteer Mechanics 1937–1945* (Kuching: Author, 2013).

30 See Zarrow, *China in War and Revolution*, pp. 337–357.

31 E. W. Woodhead, *Report upon Financing of Education and Conditions of Service in the Teaching Profession in Sarawak* (Kuching: Sarawak Government Printing Press, 1955), pp. 43, 47.

32 Ibid., p. 7.

33 In order to differentiate from the OCYA, codename 'Y' was attributed to OCPYA while 'X' for the former.

34 See Raju J. Das, *Marxist Class Theory for a Skeptical World* (Leiden: Brill, 2017).
35 Vernon L. Porritt, *The Rise and Fall of Communism in Sarawak 1940–1990* (Clayton, VIC: Monash Asia Institute, 2004), pp. 12–13. Emphasis added.
36 Ibid., pp. 13–14.
37 See *Sarawak Tribune*, Aug 11, 1952.
38 See *Straits Times*, Aug 25, 1952; *Sarawak Tribune*, Sep 2, 1952.
39 NKCP's military wing was the North Kalimantan People's Army (NKPA) or *Pasukan Rakyat Kalimantan Utara* (PARAKU).
40 For the disparity of the date of establishment of SLL, see *The Danger within*, p. 3; Douglas Arnold Hyde, *The Roots of Guerrilla Warfare* (London: The Bodley Head, 1968), pp. 64–67; Porritt, *The Rise and Fall of Communism in Sarawak*, p. 17; Seng Guo Quan, "The Origins of the Socialist Revolution in Sarawak (1945–1963)", MA thesis, National University of Singapore, Singapore, 2007, pp. 52–53.
41 It was unclear why Teo Yong Jim left SLL. See Seng, "The Origins of the Socialist Revolution in Sarawak", p. 54.
42 The only non-student, Lin was a discipline master at the 17-Mile (Simanggang Road) Chung Hwa Public School. Seng, "The Origins of the Socialist Revolution in Sarawak", p. 55.
43 Seng, "The Origins of the Socialist Revolution in Sarawak", p. 63.
44 Wen Ming Chyuan, "A Historical Outline of the Struggles of the Sarawak Liberation League, SLL" (1965?), quoted in Seng, "The Origins of the Socialist Revolution in Sarawak", p. 55. Emphasis added.
45 *The Danger Within*, p. 56.
46 Seng, "The Origins of the Socialist Revolution in Sarawak", pp. 64–65.
47 Ibid., p. 65.
48 *The Danger Within*, pp. 36–37.
49 Bong and Lui were husband and wife.
50 Seng, "The Origins of the Socialist Revolution in Sarawak", p. 68.
51 Ong Kee Hui, *Footprints in Sarawak: Memoirs of Tan Sri Datuk (Dr) Ong Kee Hui, 1914 to 1963* (Kuching: Research & Resource Centre, SUPP Headquarters, 1998), p. 416.
52 Ibid., p. 415.
53 Ibid.
54 Ibid., p. 416.
55 Ibid., p. 417.
56 Tan Sri Datuk Amar Stephen K. T. Yong, *A Life Twice Lived: A Memoir* (Kuching: Author, 1998), p. 155.
57 Ong, *Footprints in Sarawak*, pp. 422–423.
58 Yong, *A Life Twice Lived*, p. 158.
59 Sarawak Information Service, *Sarawak by the Week*, Week No. 21, 1959 (May 24–30).
60 For this declaration, see Ong, *Footprints in Sarawak*, pp. 644–645.
61 Apparently, there was some sort of misunderstanding on the issue of 'support'. It seemed that Temenggong Jugah and Pengarah Montegrai "claimed that they had simply agreed not to oppose formation of [SUPP]"; however, the Ong-Yong leadership "felt that a commitment to lead the party [SUPP] had been made and were bitterly disappointed by the failure of these two important Dayaks to join SUPP". Michael B. Leigh, *The Rising Moon: Political Change in Sarawak* (Sydney: Sydney University Press, 1974), p. 14, n. 28.
62 *The Danger Within*, p. 25. Although the document did not cite any source or authorship, it was plausible that Wen, as head of SLL, penned the essay. See Seng, "The Origins of the Socialist Revolution in Sarawak", p. 70.
63 *The Danger Within*, pp. 25–26.
64 *Sarawak by the Week*, Week No. 21, 1959 (May 24–30).
65 While Ong cited 12 June 1959 as the formal date of registration, Stephen Yong stated it to be four days later, that is, 16 June. Porritt, on the other hand, mentioned an earlier

date of 10 June. See Ong, *Footprints in Sarawak*, p. 427; Yong, *A Life Twice Lived*, p. 158; Porritt, *The Rise and Fall of Communism in Sarawak*, p. 59.

66 See Leigh, *The Rising Moon*, pp. 26–27.
67 See ibid., pp. 30–31.
68 See ibid., pp. 34–35.
69 See Ooi, *World beyond the Rivers*, pp. 93–94, 103.
70 See Chapter VII.
71 See Leigh, *The Rising Moon*, p. 36.
72 Ibid.
73 See ibid., p. 22.
74 Ibid.
75 Yong, *A Life Twice Lived*, p. 160.
76 See D. McLellan, "Notes on Subversion in Chinese Schools", Sarawak Government, Nov 5, 1959. Pertinent details are reproduced in Porritt, *The Rise and Fall of Communism in Sarawak*, pp. 261–263, Appendix 4.
77 See Chapter III.
78 See *Straits Times*, Jan 17, 1961.
79 *Sin Wen Pao Editorials*, June 2, 1960, pp. 75–76, quoted in Seng, "The Origins of the Socialist Revolution in Sarawak", p. 74.
80 *Min Chong Pau Selected Editorials and Features*, Mar 9, 1961, pp. 61–62, quoted in Seng, "The Origins of the Socialist Revolution in Sarawak", p. 74.
81 Seng, "The Origins of the Socialist Revolution in Sarawak", p. 74.
82 Ooi Keat Gin, "The Cold War and British Borneo: Impact and Legacy, 1945–63", in *Southeast Asia and the Cold War*, edited by Albert Lau (London: Routledge, 2012), p. 109.
83 D. McLellan, *Report on Secondary Education* (Kuching: Government Printing Office, 1960), p. 6.
84 *The Danger Within*, p. 24.
85 SAR, 1962, p. 151.
86 Ooi Keat Gin, "Education in Sarawak during the Period of Colonial Administration, 1946–1963", *Journal of the Malaysian Branch of the Royal Asiatic Society*, 63, 2 (Dec 1990), p. 60.

5   British protectorate of Brunei
Discontentment amidst wealth

Juga Malaya, Singapore dan mulai pula kita di Brunei dan Borneo. Nah! kalau kita sudah dapat meninjau demikian, kita pula perchaya satu waktu nanti pemerintahan British juga akan mengembalikan hak Melayu kepada bangsa Melayu, sebab pemerintahan British yang adil itu akan terus adil.
   [Also Malaya, Singapore and beginning with us in Brunei and Borneo. Well! If we have been able to see this, we believe in the foreseeable future the British government will also restore Malay rights to the Malays, because the fair British government will continue to be fair.][1]

A. M. Azahari, speech at inaugural meeting of
Partai Rakyat Brunei, 22 January 1956

In the post-war era, Brunei opted for *status quo*, to remain a British protectorate as in pre-war days. On 6 July 1946, it witnessed the handover of civil government from BMA (BB) to Sultan Sir Ahmad Tajuddin Akhazul Khairi Waddien ibn Sultan Sir Muhammad Jamalul Alam II (1913–1950), who was reinstated on the throne of this Malay Muslim sultanate.

Wartime neglect and devastation took a heavy toll on Brunei, not unlike its neighbour, North Borneo, a victim of U.S. bombings prior to the AIF reoccupation.

By the time Allied forces [AIF] landed at Muara Beach on 10 July 1945, most of the development work of the pre-war years had been neglected or destroyed during the three and a half years of Japanese occupation. By 1943, the supplies of food stockpiled before the war had run out and the population faced a state of starvation which was compounded by the abandonment of anti-malaria work and other health programmes. In the year that followed [1944], all the main areas of Brunei were flattened by the almost daily strafing raids of Allied bombers. Brunei Town's newly completed hospital was razed to the ground; only the famous Water Village [Kampong Ayer] escaped destruction, though many houses bore the marks of machine gun bullets.[2]

The hitherto skeletal infrastructure of Brunei Town, present-day Bandar Seri Begawan,[3] were obliterated. As a result, the immediate post-war years from the second half of the 1940s and early 1950s were dedicated to reconstruction and rehabilitation work that was carried out in earnest. By mid-1953, efforts expanded on reconstruction, and rehabilitation had almost been accomplished, and the next step, that of development, was ready for initiation. Paralleling socio-economic developments were advances in constitutional progress that culminated in a new constitution and a fresh Anglo-Brunei treaty.

Nonetheless, despite a more than healthy coffer derived from oil revenue thanks to high demand as a result of conflict on the Korean peninsula in the early 1950s, there were rumblings amongst the *rakyat* (peoples, masses). The *Partai Rakyat Brunei* (PRB, Brunei People's Party) and its leader Sheikh Azahari bin Sheikh Mahmud (1928–202), or better known as A. M. Azahari, harboured future plans for the sultanate.

Brunei in the 1950s and early 1960s, especially the latter decade, experienced turbulent times when the sultanate was at a crossroads, a defining period faced with the dilemma between change and continuity. In this connection, therefore, a twin-pronged approach is adopted, viz. advancements in the political and administrative sphere and the economy and social services are detailed on one hand, while grass-roots discontentment with Azahari and his PRB as the activists and agitators amongst the *rakyat* on the other.

Protectorate to internal self-government

Status quo ante bellum

Administrative-wise, pre-war and post-war Brunei's situation was *status quo ante bellum*. All authority of state rested with the Sultan-in-Council. Eleven members mainly from the nobility and appointed by the sultan constituted the State Council, where all legislations were made and fundamental executive policies were deliberated and sanctioned. Chaired by the sultan himself, the State Council, for all intents and purposes, merely functioned as a formal advisory body. In 1906, consequent of the Anglo-Brunei Treaty, a British officer, styled "Resident", was accredited to the royal court as well as appointed as a member to the State Council. The Resident, like his counterparts in the Federated Malay States (FMS), in practical terms, was the *real* power-behind-the-throne, as his *advice* had to be "asked and acted upon" on all matters of the state apart from questions affecting Malay customs and the religious faith of Islam.[4]

Under the aegis of the throne, the Resident presided over the sultanate's government. Another British officer, titled "Assistant Resident", headed the administrative machinery in Brunei Town, the capital of the sultanate, and another "Assistant Resident" was stationed at Kuala Belait, some 89 kilometres (55 miles) westward from the capital in proximity to the oil-producing centre of Seria. Local Malay DOs were in charge of the four administrative districts of Muara, Temburong, Tutong, and Belait, all answerable directly to the Resident. Technical departments in the government bureaucracy consisting of public works, medical, agriculture, forest, police, customs, and education were headed by expatriates, mainly British and some Europeans.

After Sarawak's colonial governor acting as high commissioner of Brunei between 1948 until 1959, senior officers and technical personnel from Kuching were routinely seconded to serve in Brunei whenever necessary. This practice, however, was discontinued in the wake of a new treaty penned by Brunei and Britain in 1959.

An American assessment of the British protected state of Brunei of the mid-1950s was surmised in these words:

> The government has obviously been very drastically revised since 1906 [introduction of the residency system], and the Malay officials of Brunei carry out their functions under tight British control. For all practical purposes, *Brunei is ruled as a colony rather than as a protected state.* .... The British evidently are attempting to introduce their own government standards and system into the extensive Brunei bureaucracy. ... The Malay aristocracy has probably lost many of its former feudal privileges, but it probably *still* dominates the village by virtue of prestige and official positions.[5]

With regards to local government, there was little progress relative to its neighbours, Sarawak or North Borneo. Local control too remained static as in pre-war times. Whilst Brunei Town, Tutong, and Kuala Belait retained their sanitary boards, Muara and Temburong possessed municipal or town boards in the pre-war period. In all boards, government-appointed native members, drawn from various native ethnic groups and Chinese, were entrusted with public responsibilities for sanitation, street lighting, and other municipal matters.

Notwithstanding the sluggish development in the preparation of the *rakyat* for eventual self-government, the *istana* (palace) on its part possessed plans in this direction sometime in mid-1953. Though absolute monarchs, Bruneian sultans were paternal rulers that had the interests and well-being of the *rakyat* in accordance with Islamic principles. A paternalistic welfare kingdom, Brunei afforded a cradle-to-grave scheme ensuring that the welfare of the *rakyat* were well cared for. In the political sphere, however, empowering the peoples was not on the throne's agenda.

Meanwhile, Sultan Ahmad Tajuddin, who was the reigning monarch since 1924, suddenly died of a haemorrhage in Singapore on 4 June 1950. Without an heir, it fell upon his younger brother, then Pengiran Bendahara (First/Prime Minister), to ascend the throne as Sultan Haji Omar Ali Saifuddien Sa'adul Khairi Waddien ibni Sultan Muhammad Jamalul Alam II (hereinafter, Sultan Omar Ali; 1914–1986) (r. 1950–1967). A year later on 31 May 1951, the official elaborate coronation ceremony took place that showcased ancient rituals of the Malay world.

Semblance of change: 1959 constitution

Not unlike the neighbouring crown colonies of Sarawak and North Borneo, Whitehall too has plans for self-government leading to eventual independence for Brunei. The sultanate's oil wealth was an attractive prize hence British military protection was deemed imperative in the midst of the Cold War environment from the late 1940s.

The idea of a merger of the three protectorates of Britain – Sarawak, Brunei, and North Borneo – had been discussed since the 1930s. Then in 1948, Sultan Ahmad Tajuddin had signed an agreement whereby colonial personnel from Sarawak could be seconded to the sultanate since the colonial governor of Sarawak also took on the duties as high commissioner of Brunei. It appeared to be an unsettling situation for Brunei, physically sandwiched between two large neighbours, Sarawak to the southwest and North Borneo to the northeast, that had in the past, especially the former, expanded territorially at the expense of Brunei.[6]

A closer union or merger again resurfaced among colonial mandarins in Whitehall in the early 1950s. The plan for a merger of the three territories

> appealed to the British as a way to establish a political grouping large enough to stand on its own and eventually be given independence, thus allowing them to bow out gracefully having done their duty by introducing democratic government to a once "uncivilized" part of the world.[7]

But Brunei, took exception to it being 'bundled' together with the two other crown colonies, for the sultanate was not of similar status but a protectorate of Britain, whereby its sovereignty and dignity remained intact.

Nonetheless, Sultan Omar Ali, who was conscious of the writing on the wall – the surge of nationalism and struggle for self-determination in neighbouring territories, the Cold War scenario that was increasingly unfolding in the region (notably the conflict on the Indochinese peninsula, the Malayan Emergency [1948–1960] and the Hukbalahap Rebellion [1942–1954] among others) – and Whitehall's long-term intention and ultimate objective of disengagement, knew that the democratization agenda was inevitable. It was better for him as ruler to make the first move rather than being 'forced' or 'imposed' from without.

Typical of the sultanate, decision-making was a top-down mechanism, from the palace to the peoples. Hence, in 1953, Sultan Omar Ali initiated preparation for a written constitution in composing a *Tujuh Serangkai*, a committee of seven members tasked to gather the views amongst the *rakyat*. The following year (1954), the committee's findings were discussed among the Sultan, the British resident, and the British high commissioner.[8]

Running parallel to the preparation of a constitution was the setting up of District Advisory Councils in 1954, whereby members were appointed by the monarch. Through them, representatives were sent to the State Council to air the grassroots viewpoint. Although the throne retained the sole prerogative of appointment, at least some semblance of the *rakyat*'s voice could be channelled through representatives to the State Council. It was a small voice undoubtedly, but a big step towards the rudiments of participatory governance.

At the same time, Sultan Omar Ali brought forth the concept of '*Melayu Islam Beraja*' (MIB), simply translated as 'Malay Islamic Monarchy'. Its genesis, it was claimed, dates back to the founding of the sultanate that predated fifteenth-century

Malay Muslim Melaka by at least a century. MIB's fundamental basis was premised on three foundations: firstly, Malay ethnicity and 'Malayness' that comprises the Malay language, culture, customs and traditions; secondly, Islam as the principal religious faith; and thirdly, the sultanate as the monarchical form of governance. The three foundations or pillars – Malay-Islam-Monarchy – are mutually interrelated and complemented one another. Collectively, the three pillars moulded to form Brunei's socio-political and national identity.[9]

In this connection, several developments sought to boost the importance, relevancy, and especial and integral status of Islam in the monarchical system of governance. Following his coronation in May 1951, Sultan Omar Ali embarked on the Hajj pilgrimage, one of the five Pillars of Islam,[10] in September as a demonstration of piety.[11] Several religious bodies were set up within the government, viz. *Majlis Ugama Islam* (Islamic Religious Council) and *Adat Istiadat Negeri* (Customary Practices of the State).[12] From 1955, the legal system was divided among jurisdictions under English common law courts and the Islamic *Syariah*.[13]

The outcome of the discussion of the findings of the *Tujuh Serangkai*[14] committee led to the drafting of a written constitution. The process was rather pedestrian, finally completed only in early 1959. An Anglo-Brunei meeting was held in London in March; Sultan Omar Ali held discussions over the draft constitution with Sir Alan Lennox-Boyd (t. 1954–1959), Secretary of State for the Colonies. Finally, Whitehall gave its green light, and on 29 September, the Constitution Agreement was penned in Brunei Town between Sultan Omar Ali and Sir Robert Scott (t. 1955–1959), the British Commissioner-General for Southeast Asia. As a result, the 1906 treaty was revoked.

The 1959 Constitution was the first written constitution for the sultanate. There were four significant provisions, notably: (1) the Sultan was the Supreme Head of State; (2) Brunei was responsible for its internal administration, internal self-government; (3) the British Government was only responsible for foreign relations, defence, and internal security; and (4) the post of Resident was replaced by a (newly appointed) British High Commissioner. Armed with full executive authority, the Sultan received advice as well as assistance from five state councils, namely the Religious Council, the Privy Council, the Council of Cabinet Ministers, the Legislative Council, and the Council of Succession.[15]

The 1959 Constitution designated the post of the Sultan-appointed Chief Minister as the highest administrative official.[16] The British High Commissioner acts as adviser to the government on all state matters except those relating to Islam and Malay customs.[17]

The positions of Islam and the *Syariah* were further strengthened with the promulgation of the 1959 Constitution. Provision was afforded to the Sultan as the Head of the Islamic religion to enact laws in direct relation to Islam (Article 3 [4]). In this respect, the Religious Council played its advisory role in guiding the Sultan in exercising the power to promulgate laws pertaining to the Islamic faith (Articles 3 [3] and [4]).

The Constitution notwithstanding, the Brunei monarch in reality was an absolute ruler, but significantly the Constitution further enhanced and strengthened the power of the throne. In a nutshell, an opinion surmised as follows:

> This [the 1959 Constitution] was no victory for parliamentary democracy, but it was a victory for the Sultan. *The British had granted internal self-government to the Sultan, not to the people.* There was no elective majority in the Legislative Council and no direct elections to that Council.[18]

The economy

Oil production and the exports of oil products had, since the 1930s, been the mainstay of Brunei's foreign exchange earner and played the predominant role in the sultanate's economy. The post-war scenario was literally a continuity of the pre-war situation where the oil and petroleum industry dominated almost the entire economic landscape. Besides peasant subsistence rice growing, family-owned rubber smallholdings contributed for export to foreign markets. Infrastructure development was prioritized over social services, and the latter particularly focused on education and schooling. The perennial unresolved issue of economic diversification to offset the overreliance on oil, a wasting asset, remained a major challenge in the post-war period.

Oil and petroleum industry

> The importance of the area's oil industry to the British can hardly be overestimated. The industry provides the largest share of Sarawak and North Borneo's export income and of government revenues as well as affording employment income for other sectors of the economy. It is also significant for the entire [British] Commonwealth since it is based on the only developed oil reserves under British control in Southeast Asia or Australasia.[19]

It was only in 1929 that Brunei's Seria oilfields, situated in the remote western district of Belait near the border with Sarawak, became operational recording a slight increase, and thereafter stabilized throughout the next two decades. Overshadowed by Miri during the pre-war days, Seria's star started to shine from the late 1940s and early 1950s, and since then, literally did not have to look back. The 1950s and 1960s saw Seria's output dwarfing Miri's diminishing decline.[20] Owing to the highly capital-intensive operations that necessitated a corps of highly skilled and specialized personnel, the oil and gas industry of Brunei was in the hands of a private concern, the British Malayan Petroleum Company Limited (BMPC). Crude oil from Seria were piped to the Lutong refinery, 56 kilometres to the southwest.

The refinery at Lutong during the post-war period almost exclusively served Brunei's Seria oilfields that were then experiencing booms after booms from the late 1940s and early 1950s. In 1952, Seria had a daily output of 105,000 barrels, "making it the largest producing field in the colonial territories".[21] Throughout the decade, "oil supplied some 90 per cent of [Brunei's] revenues, [oil] exports rising to over 5 million tons worth almost M$290 million in 1955", undoubtedly a boon that enabled post-war reconstruction as well as development.[22]

Oil production was boosted by the high demand posed by the outbreak of the Korean War (1950–1953). Revenue surged more than ten-fold between pre-conflict (1949) and towards the end of the war (1953), as shown in Table 5.1.

Agriculture-based economy remained important despite the substantial contribution of the oil and petroleum industry in Brunei. One report, for instance, declared: "Even in Brunei, where other export commodities were subordinate to oil shipments, rubber was second in value".[23] Natives involved in agriculture were subsistence rice cultivators, and increasing numbers also planted commercial crops, especially rubber on their own land, as supplementary income. However, an official study in 1960 had discerned the trend whereby, "Three-fifths of all workers . . . have left their traditional small enterprise activities, and all but a small number of those in employment have left agriculture altogether".[24] The decreasing number of rice farmers in the inter-censal period (1947 and 1960) was half, namely from 32 per cent to 15 per cent.[25]

Interestingly, only a small proportion of the economically active were engaged in industry. The oil and petroleum industry, in fact, in 1960 engaged "no more than one in seven of all workers".[26] Within this industry that brought exceptional wealth to the sultanate, half of the employees were indigenes, but alas due to their want of education were found in the lower echelons of the workforce. Although comprising half of the workforce, many of them were indirectly involved, viz. 'services' (included civil service), 'building and construction', 'transport', 'manufacturing', and 'commerce', sectors that played supporting roles to the oil

Table 5.1 Brunei Oil Exports during the Korean War (1950–1953)

	Oil exports (metric tons)/Value (M$m)°	Total exports (M$m)	Govt revenue (M$m) OR*/IT†	Total revenue (M$m)
1949^	3.2 / 60.1	62.1	5.6 / Nil	8.7
1950	4.0 / 198.2	205.4	0.0 / Nil	17.3
1951	4.9 / 262.8	271.8	24.2 / 40.0	69.4
1952	5.0 / 270.7	275.6	26.8 / 41.6	75.7
1953	4.8 / 264.0	282.6	25.5 / 61.0	99.0

° Malayan dollar (M$) in millions
* oil royalty
† income tax introduced from 1951
^ devaluation of pound sterling (£) by 30% against the U.S. dollar in Nov 1949

Source: (Adapted from) After A. V. M. Horton, " 'So Rich as to be Almost Indecent': Some Aspects of Post-war Rehabilitation in Brunei, 1946–1953", *Bulletin of the School of Oriental and African Studies*, 58, 1 (1995), p. 99.

Table 5.2 Brunei: Economically Active Population by Industries, 1960 – Percentages

Status and Industry Sectors of Employed Persons	Percentages of Economically Active Population
Employed in:	
Agriculture, forestry	5
Services†	18
Oil production	15
Building, construction	13
Transport	3
Manufacturing	3
Commerce	3
Other industries	1
All employed	61
Employers	
Self-employment	25
Family workers*	11

† Both public and private sectors
* Worked as assistants in shops and coolies on farms

Source: (Adapted from) After L. W. Jones, *The Population of Borneo: A Study of the Peoples of Sarawak, Sabah and Brunei* (London: University of London, The Athlone Press, 1966), p. 162.

industry (Table 5.2). Expatriates, especially British, Europeans, and Australians, with specialized skills and expertise staffed the higher sectors, both technical and managerial.

In 1960 the employees of Brunei's large, mechanized, capital-intensive oil industry, were 51 per cent indigenous, 32 per cent Chinese and 17 per cent 'Others' [mainly British, Europeans, Australians, Indonesians]. We may be certain that different sectors of this particular industry depend on]people [from] different groups, it [is] only because local men have not so far [possessed] the education or skill to become engineers and managers, while hardly any expatriate [Westerners] would come to Brunei to work at the level of, say truck driving.[27]

National development plans

Although it appears to be *status quo ante bellum* with regards to post-war fiscal policy, namely meeting current expenditures with funds from oil revenue, such as customs tariffs, there was an urgency that oil, being a wasting asset that inevitably might run out, seek alternative sources of revenue. Furthermore, the Colonial Office was anxious about the geopolitical situation of an emergence of an increasingly Leftist influence in the region – the Malayan Emergency, First Indochina War

(1946–1954), Hukbalahap Rebellion, the establishment of the People's Republic of China (1949) – and it became increasingly imperative that the sultanate should be economically strengthened, hence to undertake surveys to ascertain the potential of non-oil natural resources. Then in October 1948, Sir Charles Arden-Clarke,[28] the High Commissioner to Brunei, chaired a conference of senior officers of the sultanate. The outcome of the deliberations was an ambitious ten-year projection of a development plan for 1948 to 1957 (Table 5.3). Four sectors – rural development, internal communications, education, and public health – between them took the lion's share (80 per cent) of the M$10 million allocated. Prioritization of the aforesaid sectors was prudent and rightfully strategized to impact favourably on the sultanate benefitting the *rakyat*.

Paralleling the aforesaid proposed ten-year plan were five-year plans, the first comprised the period between 1953 and 1958, and followed by the second, 1962 to 1966. An impressive budget of M$100 million was dedicated to the inaugural five-year plan (1953–1958). Its importance was further enhanced, whereby a newly created post of 'Commissioner of Development' was to oversee its implementation. E. R. Bevington was appointed, and he laid out the details of executing the plan.[29]

Almost identical between the first and the second plans,[30] the following were the 14 objectives outlined:[31]

(1) Diversify the economy to reduce dependency on oil; (2) Reduce and avoid marked disparities in the prosperity and growth of different areas and regions in the country; (3) Maintain a high level of employment; (4) Raise per capita income through the increase of productivity; (5) Maintain a relatively stable price level; (6) Encourage and foster good industrial labour relations to

Table 5.3 Brunei: Projected Ten-Year Plan, 1948–1957

Sector	Allocation (M$m)^ (Percentage of Total)
Economy	
Rural development (agriculture, forestry)	2.0 (20%)
Fisheries	1.0 (10%)
Other economic development	0.5 (05%)
Infrastructure	
Internal communications (roads, posts, telegraphs)	2.0 (20%)
Ports and harbours	0.5 (05%)
Social services and facilities	
Education	2.0 (20%)
Medical and health	2.0 (20%)
Total	10.0 (100%)

^ Malayan dollar (M$) in million

Source: After [Acting High Commissioner] C. W. Dawson to [Colonial Secretary] A. C. Jones, Brunei (no. 5) 24 Sept 1949, CO 943/1/18, Item 1, para 3 (NAUK).

achieve increased efficiency and higher productivity; (7) Achieve a more equitable income distribution; (8) Develop an adequate and comprehensive national system of education; (9) Develop a comprehensive system of national health services to provide facilities adequate to raise the levels of all aspects of public health; (10) Provide adequate public services through: *(a) improve communication means; (b) adequate water, sewage and sanitation facilities to all areas of the country; (c) drainage and irrigation facilities for agricultural development, proper industrial zoning, town and country planning*; (11) Community development; (12) Provision of adequate power facilities; (13) Cultural development; and, (14) Encourage and promote private sector participation in all aspects of national development projects.

On paper, the 14 objectives appeared to be all-encompassing, a great departure from the previous ad hoc manner that development works were undertaken by the administration. Discounting the hyperbole, the *Borneo Bulletin* in 1958, the year the second National Development Plan concluded, offered this impressive observation: "rarely has a place changed its appearance so quickly as quickly as Brunei Town"; "Gone are most of the shacks – apart from the seemingly permanent hovels of Kampong Ayer – of former years, and in their places, have arisen the steel and concrete buildings of a more modern age – offices, shops, restaurants and similar enterprises".[32] Erection of 'modern' buildings literally transformed the streetscape of the capital.

Nonetheless, the overall reality was less upbeat. A critic of Brunei's national agenda for development surmised as follows:

> Common to all [first] three plans [(1953–1958), (1962–1966), and (1975–1979)] are brevity and a lack of coherence. There is also little precision in the plans' objectives. Indeed, in all three development plans, the same fourteen points have been repeatedly stressed as the objectives for development. . . . *The main problem with all Brunei's national development plans is that they neither suggest how nor at what pace the objectives can be met.* Also missing from the plans are the essentials: capital formation, the structure and characteristics of the economy, important development data, and designation of responsibilities. . . . [Moreover] It is impossible to keep track of Brunei's development plans in the absence of development reviews.[33]

Furthermore, despite being prioritized as the first of the fourteen objectives, '(1) Diversify the economy to reduce dependency on oil', economic diversification for non-oil resources appeared to be elusive and unfulfilled. "Despite a long-standing pledge to diversify the economy", a study of the late 1970s revealed that, "Brunei is becoming *increasingly dependent* on oil and gas exports".[34]

Education and schooling

On the eve of the Japanese military occupation in 1941, there were in total 24 government-managed elementary schools providing very basic education (3 Rs, viz. *r*eading, w*r*iting and a*r*ithmetic). Consequent of Brunei's pre-war neglect of education, efforts were hastened in the immediate post-war period. Moreover, the high illiteracy rate was cause for concern by the Colonial Office and the sultanate's administration, lest the people were susceptible to Leftist propaganda that preyed on shortcomings to garner political mileage. The increasing Leftist influence, espe-cially from neighbouring Sarawak, to some extent reinvigorated measures to improve education and schooling as a countermeasure. Therefore, the projected ten-year plan (1948–1957) allocated M$2.0 (or 20 per cent of the total budget) to the education sector (Table 5.3).

Dismal progress

Notable advances were witnessed in the late 1940s and early 1950s, namely a quali-fied head of education was appointed in 1949, and two years later, the first English-medium secondary school was opened in Brunei Town and another in Kuala Belait in 1952. Previously those in Brunei who sought secondary education either in the English- or Chinese-medium had to proceed to Kuching for their studies.

Then, under the sultanate's inaugural Five-Year Plan (1953–1958) with a budget of M$100 million, infrastructure continued to be allocated the lion's share of some 80 per cent while social services received 20 per cent. But within the latter, educa-tion enjoyed a 20-fold increase in expenditure. Significant improvements included free elementary education, promotion of elementary education for females, open-ing of the Sultan Omar Ali Saifuddin College (1954) and the Raja Isteri's School for Girls (1957), government subsidy to cover half of the operating cost of the eight Chinese schools, and professional training for the petrol sector was provided in Seria.[35] Before 1956, teachers for Brunei were either recruited directly from the UK or were Brunei students who graduated from Sarawak's Batu Lintang Teacher Training Centre and School (Kuching) and/or from Malaya's Sultan Idris Teacher's Training College (Tanjung Malim). Then in January 1956, the Brunei Teach-er's Training Centre located in Brunei Town was established. Three years later it moved to its permanent facility in Berakas, on the outskirts of the capital, renamed Brunei Malay Teacher's Training College.

Towards the close of the 1950s, some 90 per cent of boys and 37 per cent of girls of school-going age were partaking education from the 52 Malay elementary schools, three secondary government schools, eight Anglican mission schools, and eight Chinese schools.[36] Nonetheless, educational progress had been dismal.

> Yet education remained mediocre in quality, with overflowing classes at the primary level, limited access to secondary schools and a lack of professional training for teachers. And since 52% of those over ten years were still illiterate in 1960, most of the posts of responsibility continued to be held by Westerners and technical jobs by Asians who were not *bumiputera* [native].[37]

But unlike neighbouring Sarawak, where the Chinese vernacular schools were hotbeds for Leftist agitation and activism, Brunei's eight Chinese-medium schools did not witness subversive activities to that extent. Close surveillance by the authorities on the schools, as well as the small Chinese community (Table 4.1), ensured stability and dispelled any untoward civil disruption.

Rule of Law

Towards the later part of 1949, senior British officials 'on-the-spot', notably the Commissioner-General for South-East Asia Malcolm MacDonald, Governors Duncan Stewart, and Edward Twining of Sarawak and North Borneo, respectively, and Resident Eric Ernest Falk Pretty of Brunei, discussed the possibilities of a closer association between the three territories, within a five-year framework. In line with this aspiration, Sarawak, North Borneo, and Brunei (Courts) Order in Council of 1951 unified the judicial system of all three territories from 1 December 1951 (Chart 3.1). The Brunei monarch as the supreme Islamic authority in the sultanate was complemented by the Court of Kathis.

In Brunei the *Syariah* appeared rigorous and consistent. However, owing to a dual legal system, the Islamic courts were to a certain extent marginalized. Commencement of the British residential system (from 1906) marked the start of a dual legal system, namely the parallel existence of the Islamic legal system (*Syariah*) and a common law system derived from the English legal system, each having its own separate judicial courts. However, in 1908, an amendment to the Courts Enactment of 1906 brought about the constitution of five courts for the administration of civil and criminal justice into the country.[38] As a result there was a significant reduction in the application of Islamic laws from its previously wide application to only confined to the Islamic religion (theological issues), marriage, and divorce.[39] In countering this unfavourable state of affairs, therefore, from 1955 administration of the Islamic courts was disengaged from the ambit of the British colonial authorities, and instead came directly under the purview of the *Syariah* system.

Islam and the *Syariah* were further strengthened by the embracing of MIB as well as the adoption of the 1959 Constitution, as have been pointed out. The former, in fact, established and elevated Islam to the position of core philosophy and national identity of the sultanate.

'Still waters run deep': the question of security

Brunei was confronted with a serious security issue in the early 1960s, subsequently referred to as a 'revolt'. Brunei, owing to its physical size, possessed a less elaborate security set-up than both its neighbours. Moreover, by the early 1950s, when reorganization had been settled, the Brunei police force, for all intents and purposes, was an appendage to Sarawak's larger establishment. A police base was established at Kuala Belait, the centre of the oil industry. Targeted improvements were focused on Special Branch thanks to the Batu Kitang Incident (5 August 1952).[40] Not only did it receive an assistant commissioner as its head in 1953, but Kuala Belait too benefitted with a Special Branch office.[41] Being an appendage of the Sarawak constabulary has numerous advantages, viz. in terms of additional personnel in the event if a situation necessitated, access to a wider netting of intelligence, and tapping of expertise that was available in a bigger establishment. The oil company engaged its own security personnel for maintaining installations and facilities from theft of materials or equipment, arson, and/or sabotage.

Meanwhile, the Malayan Emergency and similar communist-led conflicts in the region made authorities in small and vulnerable Brunei nervously concerned. Understandably, security authorities in the sultanate looked to the Malayan situation for 'lessons' to be learnt or applicable, if any. According to a 1957 report by Malayan Director of Operations Lieutenant-General R. H. Bower, there were indeed 'lessons' as guidelines.[42] He emphasized preventive measures through good intelligence-gathering in the pre-insurgency stage. Immediate and/or timely intervention should be the rule if intelligence failed. But once insurgency was in full swing, the Templer model should be adopted, notably to combine the posts of high commissioner and director of operations in one individual, as was held by General Gerald Templer during his tenure from 1952 to 1954. In this unified command structure, the High Commissioner-cum-Director of Operations assumed the role as supreme commander with full control over all military and civil resources and personnel. In this dual capacity, this Templer-style supreme commander ensured that some ineffectual or underperforming personnel, either military or civilian, could be swiftly replaced. The removal of this 'weak link' was pivotal in the overall anti-insurgency operation, lest the enemy exploit this liability.

At the same time, this dualistic appointment recognized that the armed conflict against the Malayan Communist Party (MCP) was not only a military effort per se but also a political battle in winning over the 'hearts-and-minds' of the wider population. General Bower outlined the three phases at the operational level of counter-insurgency in the context of Malaya's experiences: the initial stage was in controlling the general population; the second stage was in taking the fight to the enemy (CTs) deep in their jungle hideaway; and the third stage was in winning the 'hearts-and-minds' of the people. The gathering and analysis of intelligence and the execution of psychological warfare were equally important in counter-insurgency measures.

At the same time, flexibility in approach was another Templer guideline, namely possessing four operational scenarios: (1) 'framework' operations in target areas, (2) intelligence-led priority operations, (3) 'mopping-up' pacified areas, and (4) deep jungle operations to not only flush out CTs but also to deny sanctuaries. This flexible approach was explained in a Templer-Walker training booklet.[43] Incidentally, General Walter Walker would feature prominently as director of operations during the Brunei Revolt.[44]

Apparently Special Branch was aware of the Brunei Revolt, "even its approximate timing", but alas, senior administrators, neither in Kuching nor Brunei Town, took serious cognizance of such intelligence.[45] In fact, in the wake of the Cyprus Emergency (1955–1959),[46] the Colonial Office was rather anxious and urged overseas colonial administrators to undertake an evaluation of intelligence-gathering mechanisms in foreseeing the potential outbreaks of insurgencies.[47] Meanwhile, a state of discontentment was brewing among some sectors of Brunei society.

Discontentment

Ever since the Seria oilfields became operational from the 1930s, Brunei was never wanting for material wealth. The post-war period continued to witness the prosperity brought by oil exports that enjoyed additional boost in demand during the Korean War (1950–1953) (Table 5.1). But there was dissatisfaction amidst the fabulous richness. Despite being the reigning monarch, the Brunei sultan had to be cautious of British political and economic manoeuvrings in gaining the upper hand of control over the sultanate. In order not to be transformed into a puppet-on-a-string or as a mere rubber stamp, the sultan had to outmanoeuvre his British protector to be able to turn the tables in his favour and Brunei's as well.[48]

From without the palace grounds, there were rumblings amongst the *rakyat* that were already apparent from the 1930s but became even more acute in the late 1940s and 1950s. With the emergence of the Partai Rakyat Brunei (PRB, Brunei People's Party) in the mid-1950s with its charismatic founder-chairman A. M. Azahari, ripples of discontentment within the *rakyat* were channelled towards the palace seeking a resolution.

Reign but not rule

A 'Sixth division of Sarawak?'

With little input from the then Brunei Sultan Ahmad Tajuddin, an administrative fusion was executed in 1948, bringing into closer rapport between the sultanate and Sarawak, whereby the governor of the latter also posed as high commissioner of Brunei. A regular half-yearly meeting between the colonial governors of Sarawak and North Borneo together with the British Resident of Brunei facilitated cooperation in various sectors, viz. personnel, justice, public health, police, customs, and shipping. Since the Brunei Resident was junior in rank to the high commissioner, there was little or even a semblance of Bruneian voice at such gatherings.

It was most unpalatable that Brunei could be treated as a 'Sixth division of Sarawak'. Adopting a non-confrontational stance, typical of Malay-style etiquette, Sultan Ahmad Tajuddin instead gave his blessings to several nationalistic movements to assume the opposition position vis-à-vis the British. In the second half of the 1940s, three movements emerged – the *Barisan Pemuda Brunei* (BARIP, Brunei Youth Front), the *Persekutuan Murid Tua Melayu Brunei* (MUTU, Federation of Former Brunei Malay Students), and the Brunei Malay Women's Association. Among their discontentment, directed both at the British colonials and the throne, were *inter alia*, a greater share in governance by indigenous Malays (recruitment of high-ranking officials, non-religious, to the State Council) and educated Malays to serve in the government bureaucracy hitherto dominated by Anglophile Chinese. Haji Muhammed Salleh bin Haji Masri (Salleh Masri), president of BARIP, in May 1947 submitted a petition to the high commissioner for the independence of Brunei. BARIP even insisted that all Chinese shops be closed as a mark of respect during the dowager's funeral. BARIP expounded the pre-eminence of Malays.[49]

The ascension of Sultan Omar Ali ushered in a new era for Brunei. Having his schooling (1932–1936) at the prestigious Malay College[50] in Kuala Kangsar, Perak, he was the first Brunei monarch to have an education outside the sultanate, which undoubtedly offered him a wider worldview than that of his predecessors. Although young then, he had at least witnessed fellow Malay sultans interacting with their British protectors. Hence, when it was his turn, he was well-prepared. He possessed two trump cards: the all-powerful State Council that literally administered the sultanate was dominated by native Bruneians, and revenue from oil ensured that the sultanate did not have to rely on Britain or others for financial aid whether in development and/or modernization. Consequently, he not only reigned but also ruled.

In terms of stamping his mark but more in attaining the higher goal of the sustainability of the Brunei sultanate system, Sultan Omar Ali brought forth the MIB concept as an identity marker. 'Malayness' was in tandem with Islam and monarchy; collectively the three pillars denoted Brunei's sense of purpose, existence, and identity. It was clear in his goal about what he intended for the throne (his personal ambition) and for the sultanate as a whole, namely political independence for Brunei as a Malay Islamic Monarchy where all power (executive and legislative) laid in the hands of the sultan.

Since the 1930s, there had been the idea or concept of a closer union of the three British Bornean territories, that in the post-war era comprised two crown colonies (Sarawak and North Borneo) and a protectorate (Brunei). The colonial governors of Sarawak and North Borneo harboured the creation of a federation of the Bornean territories, as an interim step towards eventual full independence.[51] This 'closer union' concept was initially mooted by Sir Cecil Clementi in 1930 when he was governor of the Straits Settlements and High Commissioner to the Malay States and Brunei. In line with such plans, an Inter-Territorial Conference (1953–1961) was held to hear arguments of the pros and cons of such a possibility, *inter alia* administrative co-ordination and efficiency in policies and governance, and cost-cutting earned from dispensing with duplication were but some of the supportive opinions.

But, Sultan Omar Ali was not having any of those plans of union or federation. In fact, "*It was rather unpalatable, even demeaning*, to equate Brunei, a sovereign state, with the two British Crown Colonies of Sarawak and North Borneo", but he "favoured Malaya, intending to foster closer ties following the latter's independence from Britain in 1957".[52]

The carrot that was not

In order to participate in a closer relationship with Malaya, Sultan Omar Ali initiated constitutional steps towards eventual independence for the sultanate: firstly, the election of unofficial members of district councils hitherto appointed by the throne; secondly, a majority of elected members to the Legislative

Council in a proposed constitution; and, thirdly, the first written constitution for the sultanate. The third step was accomplished with the 1959 Constitution. The second step, however, was problematic, which led to much disaffection amongst the *rakyat*.

The second step was 'problematic' on two counts. In accordance to the 1959 Constitution, the Legislative Council comprised a membership list of eight *ex officio* members, six sultan-nominated official members, three sultan-appointed non-official members, and 16 elected members from the district council. Plainly it was apparent that the sultan had the edge, his 17 members against 16 elected members. It renegaded Sultan Omar Ali's second constitutional steps. This could be regarded as the first 'royal slap' in the *rakyat*'s face.

Secondly, again according to the 1959 Constitution, elections to the 16 district councils were scheduled to be held two years after the promulgation of the Constitution, that is, in 1961. Procrastination on the government's side in delaying the elections led to frustrations and discontentment amongst the hopefuls, notably members of the PRB as electoral candidates. It could be construed as the second 'royal slap'. Finally, in late August 1962, a one-year delay, when elections to district councils were held, PRB candidates swept 54 out of the 55 contested seats. Hence, all of the 16 elected members (one from each district council) to the all-important Legislative Council – responsible for overall control of state financial expenditure and enactment of legislations – were PRB members. But, as pointed out, 16 against the sultan's 17 was but an 'empty' triumph. The *rakyat* was literally short-changed, cheated – another painful (third) 'royal slap'.

An 'empty' triumph

Capturing the imagination and support of the *rakyat*, Azahari garnered support for his PRB that was anxious to establish some representative voice in the Legislative Council. Through such constitutional channels, Azahari and the PRB wanted a share in the governance of the sultanate. But, as it appeared then, it was not to be. The delays in the election to the district councils proved disheartening. And when PRB representatives finally attended the Legislative Council, the arithmetic was totally against their efforts in seeking change through constitutional means.

Azahari was an ambivalent character. Of mixed parentage (Arab-Malay) and born in Labuan, he was in fact not even a citizen of Brunei in legal terms. Nonetheless, he was a man with a vision, for Brunei and for himself. Azahari possessed grandiose visions and equally grandiose ambitions. His visions were almost having millenarian attributes: a return of Brunei to its 'Golden Age', circa sixteenth/seventeenth century, whereby the sultanate claimed to have political hegemony as far north as Manila, implying hegemony over the greater part of the Philippine archipelago, and as far south as Banjarmasin, likewise control over the entire island of Borneo.[53] Brunei's 'Golden Age' might have command of a sphere of influence, not direct politico-military domination, of the aforesaid realm. Even such a vast sphere of influence could only be translated to be nominal at best.

In the mid-1950s, Azahari expressed the intention to create a *Negarabagian Kesatuan Kalimantan Utara* (NKKU, Unitary State of North Kalimantan), at least comprising a part of the realm of the 'Golden Age', in taking in Sarawak, North Borneo with Brunei at the centre of governance, whereby the Brunei monarch would be head of state, and he, Azahari, would be prime minister. In consequence of such an ambition, Azahari and his PRB was defiantly opposed to any other formation, viz. 'closer union', 'wider federation' for northern Borneo, as such proposed configurations worked against his vision and plans. Therefore, understandably, when Tunku in 1961 mooted the 'Mighty Malaysia' concept that envisaged a wider federation bringing together independent Malaya, the British crown colonies of Singapore, Sarawak, and North Borneo, and the protectorate of Brunei, it was wholly anathema to Azahari and the PRB that strongly opposed such a proposal. As a result, PRB gathered with other anti-Malaysia elements such as Ong-Yong's SUPP and Donald Stephens' United National Kadazan Organization (UNKO).

But at first glance, constitutional means to effect change or at least in possession of a voice in the governance of the sultanate might appear to be PRB's intention. But, as it turned out, Azahari had other plans in mind when a military wing of the PRB was created, viz. the *Tentera Nasional Kalimantan Utara* (TNKU). Is an armed uprising on Azahari's and the PRB's agenda?

Turning to the Legislative Council that held its inaugural sitting on 5 December 1962, PRB presented several demands:

> (1) a motion rejecting the concepts of the Federation of Malaysia; (2) a motion asking the British Government to restore the sovereignty of the Sultanate of Brunei over the former territories of Sarawak and North Borneo; and, (3) a motion urging the British Government to federate the three territories of Sarawak, Brunei and North Borneo under the Unitary State of Kalimantan Utara with Sultan Omar Ali Saifuddin III as its constitutional and parliamentary Head of State and the granting of complete and absolute Independence too this new State not later than 1963.[54]

The speaker dismissed all of PRB's motions, citing that it was beyond the jurisdiction of the Legislative Council. This blatant rejection seemed to be the proverbial 'straw that broke the [PRB's] camel's back'. The next move, for Azahari and the PRB, appeared to be armed revolt to achieve the aim of the creation of NKKU. It could be construed that the rebuff at the Legislative Council forced PRB's hand to turn to non-constitutional means in pursuing its vision of the establishment of a new state.

Therefore, when Sarawak police uncovered military uniforms and detained several individuals in Lawas close to the border with Brunei, Special Branch immediately sensed that something underground and big was brewing in the sultanate. The uncovering of military fatigues and weaponry by Sarawak authorities were telltale signs of an army on the move. In fact, Special Branch, through intelligence, even knew of the impending revolt, but thanks to the indifference of higher authorities in Kuching, Special Branch's intelligence was filed away in the bureau-cratic maze. A missed opportunity, indeed.

Amidst a bipolar world

Against the backdrop of an increasingly bipolar world of the 1950s and 1960s, was the advent of NKKU an idealistic dream or a plausible realistic goal in the rejuve-nation of Brunei's past glory over northern Borneo? Rightly, both Sarawak and North Borneo were once part of the territorial domain of the sultanate, although admittedly the *pangeran* (chieftain) in possession of the fiefdoms were negligent in actively exercising their rights as overlords. Although at best, Sarawak and North Borneo were feudal territories held by various *pangeran*, James Brooke in 1841 received his credentials as *rajah* (governor) of Sarawak from the Brunei monarch, and Baron Gustav von Overbeck in 1877 had to negotiate and struck an agreement with the Brunei court as well as with the Sulu court for the territorial rights over what became North Borneo, Brunei, and also, Sulu, possessed rights over the aforesaid territories of northern Borneo. Hence, having the intention to create NKKU was not at all idealistic or far-fetched to comprehend. NKKU could be a counter-argument to the 'Mighty Malaysia' concept. The latter, despite Tunku's pronouncement, was undoubtedly a British concoction, its strategic agenda to remain relevant, if not influential, in the post-decolonization period. In fact, NKKU possessed more commonality and shared historical baggage than the wider federation of Malaysia that intended to bring under its umbrella Malaya and Singapore on the western fringe of the South China Sea and Sarawak, Brunei, and North Borneo on the eastern side of the same sea. In terms of physical features and demographic composition, the 'west' and the 'east' were worlds apart. NKKU from this viewpoint and reasoning was more plausible and more realistic.

But, in observing the company that PRB fraternized with, namely SUPP and UNKO, particularly the Left-leaning former, the colonial mandarins at the Colonial Office, Foreign Office, War Office, and Whitehall would have fits if NKKU came to fruition. Furthermore, Azahari and the PRB being also friendly with the renegade Sukarno of Indonesia, who was then increasingly influenced and/or moving closer to the Partai Komunis Indonesia (PKI), literally sent shivers down the spine of most British colonial officials in Kuala Lumpur and Singapore, and Kuching, Brunei Town, and Jesselton. Azahari, who had fought alongside republicans in the Indonesian Revo-lution (1945–1949), and had named 'Partai', and not 'Parti' Brunei Rakyat, the former an Indonesian phrase, might even contemplate NKKU as a republic ala-*Republik Indonesia*, and himself as 'president', another Sukarno or Castro-in-the-making (of the Cuban Revolution, 1953–1959). Sukarno's *Republik Indonesia* then was proven to be a headache; Azahari's *Negara Kesatuan Kalimantan Utara* might spark a migraine for the British, who were then trying hard to counter the anti-imperialist and anti-colonialist communists already increasingly menacing in Sarawak.

Therefore, *Negara Kesatuan Kalimantan Utara*, or whatever Azahari had in his mind, had to be crushed at all costs. A friendly 'Mighty Malaysia', on the other hand, had to be supported by all means. Against this mindset of British colonial officials, the Brunei Revolt broke out on 8 December 1962.

A revolt in the making

Like neighbouring Sarawak and North Borneo, the post-war British residency system in Brunei, for all intents and purposes, was a 'caretaker' administration entrusted in initiating and laying the groundwork preparation for self-government leading to eventual independence. The democratization agenda hence became imperative. The ascension of Sultan Omar Ali in 1950 as the 28th monarch of Brunei took the sultanate to the next level, that of development and self-rule. Post-war reconstruction and rehabilitation proceeded without untoward delays or obstacles that by 1953, development plans were on the agenda for implementation. After the Korean War, the oil industry benefited from the brief but lucrative boom period. Paralleling advancement in the socio-economic field was progress in the political sphere. Plans were underway since 1953 for the drafting of the sultanate's first written constitution. Finally, the 1959 Constitution was promulgated that established internal self-rule and formed part of the design towards subsequent British decolonization in northern Borneo and the region in general.

In pursuit of the sustainability of the sultanate, Sultan Omar Ali propounded the concept of 'Melayu Islam Beraja' (MIB), thereby sanctioning the three fundamental pillars of the sultanate, notably 'Malay', 'Islam', and 'Monarchy'. The interconnectedness of the three pillars Malay-Islam-Monarchy collectively established and conveyed the sultanate's socio-political and national identity.

But there was discontentment amidst the wealth. The charismatic and ambitious personality of Azahari and his PRB stirred the grassroots. Azahari harboured grandiose visions of resurrecting Brunei's heyday, the sultanate's 'Golden Age', whereby its imperial realm held sway over not only the island of Borneo but also the Philippine archipelago as far north as present-day Manila. He intended to establish a 'Negara Kesatuan Kalimantan Utara', or NKKU, that comprised Brunei, Sarawak, and North Borneo, in fact what encompassed British Borneo. NKKU was not what the British had in mind when it came to a closer relationship between post-war British Borneo territories. Likewise, PRB's choice of 'friends', particularly the Left-leaning SUPP, and Azahari's past links, and even current proximity with Sukarno and his *Republik Indonesia* that was then (early 1960s) increasingly leaning towards the PKI, sent shudders across British colonial circles. Thus, the Anglophile Tunku's announcement of a 'Mighty Malaysia' was indeed a welcoming respite.

The fact that the PRB possessed a militia wing, the TNKU, complete with military fatigues and firearms, pointed to the possibility that more than constitutional means were planned in the attainment of NKKU. Therefore, when the speaker of the Legislative Council refused to address PRB's three proposals during the 5 December 1962 sitting, Azahari and the PRB turned to more radical measures – the launching of a revolt three days later on 8 December.

Notes

1 'Pidato A. M. Azahari dalam pembukaan meshuarat pembentukan Party Rakyat Chabang di Brunei dan sekitarnya yang diadakan pada 22.1.1956 [Speech of A. M. Azahari at the opening of the formation of a branch of the People's Party in Brunei and surrounding areas held on 22.1.1956]'. Haji Zaini Haji Ahmad, *The People's Party: Selected Documents* (Petaling Jaya: INSAN, the Institute of Social Analysis, 1987), p. 81.

2 Lord Chalfont, *By God's Will: A Portrait of the Sultan of Brunei* (London: Weidenfield and Nicolson, 1989), p. 49.

3 Upon the abdication of Sultan Haji Omar Ali Saifuddien Sa'adul Khairi Waddien ibni Sultan Muhammad Jamalul Alam II in 1967 in favour of his eldest son and heir, Sultan Haji Hassanal Bolkiah Mu'izzaddin Waddaulah ibni Sultan Haji Omar 'Ali Saifuddien Sa'adul Khairi Waddien (b. 1946), the former took the title 'Seri Begawan', from the Sanskrit meaning the 'Blessed One'. Since the emergence of modern Brunei owed much to him, on 5 October 1970 the hitherto state capital of Brunei Town was renamed 'Bandar Seri Begawan'.

4 The British introduced an effective as well as cost-effective system of indirect rule through a binding clause in the Pangkor Engagement (1874) with the Malay chiefs of Perak, whereby a British officer styled 'Resident' served as adviser to the ruler at his court; all advice relating to all matters of state including revenue collection was incumbent on the ruler to abide. Only issues related to Malay customs and traditions, and the Islamic faith escaped the Resident's 'advisory purview'. The system was 'effective' as the Malay ruler kept to the binding terms, and was 'cost effective' simply for the fact that a single British officer was involved, and his salary and residence were borne by the Malay ruler. Pangkor-like treaties were contracted with Selangor, Sungai Ujong (subsequently Negeri Sembilan) in the same year, and Pahang in 1888. Then in 1895, to further consolidate their control, the aforesaid four Malay states came under a closer union named the Federated Malay States, where a Resident-General presided with a bureaucracy at Kuala Lumpur. See Ooi Keat Gin, *Historical Dictionary of Malaysia*, 2nd ed. (Lanham, MD: Rowman & Littlefield, 2018), pp. 96–97, 160–161.

5 *North Borneo, Brunei, Sarawak (Sarawak and North Borneo)* (New Haven, CT: Human Relations Area Files, 1956), pp. 87–88. Emphasis added.

6 See Nicholas Tarling, *Britain, the Brookes, and Brunei* (Kuala Lumpur: Oxford University Press, 1971); L. R. Wright, *The Origins of British Borneo* (Hong Kong: Hong Kong University Press, 1970).

7 Michael B. Leigh, *The Rising Moon: Political Change in Sarawak* (Sydney: Sydney University Press, 1974), p. 45.

8 Brunei British Resident John Coleraine Hanbury Barcroft (t. 1951–1954), and Sarawak Governor Anthony Abell (t. 1950–1959) who acted as British High Commissioner for Brunei.

9 Although proponents of MIB placed the concept, implementation, and practice to Brunei's early years of establishment, its legal references originated in the 1959 Constitution whereby the Malay language was declared as the national language (Bab 82 [1]), Islam as the official religion (Bab 3 [1]), and the sultan as the head of state and government (Bab 4 [1]). Thereafter, MIB appeared in the royal *titah* (proclamation) during independence in 1984. Then, in July 1990, on the occasion of his forty-fourth birthday, Sultan Haji Hassanal Bolkiah Mu'izzaddin Waddaulah ibn Al-Marhum Sultan Haji Omar Ali Saifuddien Sa'adul Khairi Waddien, Sultan and Yang Di-Pertuan of Brunei Darussalam (hereinafter, Sultan Hassanal Bolkiah) formally enunciated the MIB concept. Graham Saunders, *A History of Brunei* (Kuala Lumpur: Oxford University Press, 1994), p. 187.

10 Considered basic and mandatory, the Five Pillars comprised *Shahada*, a declaration of faith, a declaration that there is only one God (Allah) and that Muhammad is His messenger; *Salah* that consists of five daily prayers; Zakāt or alms-giving; *Sawm* or ritual fasting during the month of Ramadan, ninth month of the Islamic calendar; and, performing the *Hajj*, a pilgrimage to Mecca obligatory for all able-bodied faithful at least once in their lifetime.

11 Apparently, the last reigning monarch to undertake the pilgrimage was Sultan Muhammad Ali (r. 1660–1661). See A. V. M. Horton, *Turun-Temurun: Dissection of Negara Brunei Darussalam* (Bordesley, Worcestershire, UK: Author, 1995), p. 60.

12 Iik Arifin Mansurnoor, "Socio-religious Changes in Brunei during the British Residency (1906–1959)", 13 Conference of the International Association of Historians of Asia, Sophia University, Tokyo, 3–9 Sep 1994.

13 See below.

14 Literally, 'seven [a] series', a seven-men committee.

15 Laws of Brunei, *Constitutional Matters I: Constitution of Brunei Darussalam* [1959]. rev. ed. 2011.

16 Pehin Datu Perdana Menteri Dato Laila Utama Haji Awang Ibrahim bin Mohammad Jaafar (1902–971) was the first Chief Minister or Menteri Besar (t. 1959–1961). The next appointee was Haji Marsal bin Maun (1913–2000) whose tenure of office, 1961 to 1962, was when the Brunei Revolt (8 December 1962) broke out. The third and last to hold the post was Pengiran Muhammad Yusuf bin Abdul Rahim (1923–2016) who served between 1967 and 1972.

17 The incumbent Resident then, Dennis Charles White assumed the post of British High Commissioner (t. 1959–1963).

18 Saunders, *A History of Brunei*, pp. 137–138. Emphasis added.

19 *North Borneo, Brunei, Sarawak (Sarawak and North Borneo)*, p. 132.

20 Ibid.

21 Ibid, p. 193.

22 Saunders, *A History of Brunei*, p. 126.

23 *North Borneo, Brunei, Sarawak (Sarawak and North Borneo)*, p. 171.

24 L. W. Jones, *The Population of Borneo: A Study of the Peoples of Sarawak, Sabah and Brunei* (London: University of London, the Athlone Press, 1966), p. 162.

25 Ibid., p. 163.

26 Ibid., p. 157.

27 Ibid., p. 159.

28 Arden-Clarke was then the colonial governor (t. 1946–1949) of Sarawak. Between 1948 and 1959, Sarawak's governor also acted as high commissioner to Brunei.

29 See E. R. Bevington, *The Economy and Development of the State of Brunei* (Brunei: Government Report, June 1953).

30 See Brunei, *[First] National Development Plan, 1953–1958* (Kuala Belait: Brunei Press, 1958); Brunei, *[Second] National Development Plan, 1962–1966* (Kuala Belait: Brunei Press, 1962).

31 Extracted from B. A. Hamzah, *Oil and Economic Development Issues in Brunei* (Singapore: Institute of Southeast Asian Studies, 1980), pp. 5–6. Similarly, present in the third National Development Plan, 1975–1979. See Brunei, *Ranchangan Kemajuan Negara, 1975–1979 [National Development Plan, 1975–1979]* ([Bandar Seri Begawan: Brunei Government, 1975]), pp. 34–36.

32 Quoted in Rozan Yunos, "Town and Country Planning in Brunei: The History and Development of Planning in Brunei", *The Brunei Times*, Mar 3, 2008.

33 Hamzah, *Oil and Economic Development Issues in Brunei*, pp. 5–6, 7. Emphasis added.

34 Ibid., p. 6. Emphasis added.

35 Marie-Sybille de Vienne, *Brunei: From the Age of Commerce to the 21st Century* (Singapore: National University of Singapore (NUS) Press in Association with Institut De Recherche Sur L'Asie Du Sud-Est Contemporaine (Research Institute of Contemporary Southeast Asia) (IRASEC), 2015), p. 108.

36 Ibid., p. 113.

37 Ibid., p. 114.

38 Ahmad Basuni Haji Abbas and Dy Hasnah Hassan, "The Legal System of Brunei Darussalam", in *ASEAN Legal Systems*, edited by ASEAN Law Association (Singapore: Butterworths Asia, 1995), p. 3.

39 Ibid., p. 5.

40 See Chapter IV.

41 Sarawak Constabulary, *Annual Report on Sarawak Constabulary, 1953*, p. 3; ibid., *1954*, p. 4.

42 Review of Emergency in Malaya, June 1948–Aug 1957 by Director of Operations, Sep 12, 1957. WO 106/5990 (NAUK).

43 See *The Conduct of Anti-Terrorist Operations in Malaya*, 3rd ed, 1958. WO 279/241 (NAUK).

44 See Tom Pocock, *Fighting General: The Public and Private Campaigns of General Sir Walter Walker* (London: Collins, 1973).

45 Porritt, *British Colonial Rule in Sarawak*, p. 165.

46 An armed conflict in British-occupied Cyprus waged by the Greek Cypriot militant group, the *Ethniki Organosis Kyprion Agoniston* (EOKA, National Organisation of Greek Cypriot Fighters), intent on ejecting the British colonialist from Cyprus in order that it could be amalgamated with Greece. At the same instance, both the British and the EOKA were rejected by the Turkish Cypriot group, the Turkish Resistance Organisation (TMT), who opposed union with Greece. See Robert Holland, *Britain and the Revolt in Cyprus, 1954–1959* (Oxford: Oxford University Press, 1999).

47 See Letter from Reginald Maudling (Secretary of State for the Colonies to [Sarawak Colonial Governor Sir Alexander] Waddell, Nov 1, 1961. FCO 141/12701 (NAUK).

48 Contemporary Malay sultans in the peninsular Malay States, particularly in the FMS, suffered the fate as mere rubber stamps consequent of the reality whereby the British resident controlled all powers – executive, legislative, and judicial – who wielded such powers in the name of the sultan. See Emily Sadka, *The Protected Malay States 1874–1895* (Kuala Lumpur: University Press of Malaya, 1968), p. 178; Barbara Watson Andaya and Leonard Y. Andaya, *A History of Malaysia*, 3rd ed. (London: Palgrave, 2017), p. 175.

49 BARIP, however, was short-lived, having disbanded two years after its establishment in 1946.

50 Established in 1905, MCKK as it was favourably known, was to all intents and purposes an English public school in the tropics aimed at educating and preparing Malay princes and sons of chieftains for their future roles in the governance of their country. Its sobriquet 'Eton of the East' spoke of its high quality as well as its elitism. See Khasnor Johan, *Educating the Malay Elite: The Malay College Kuala Kangsar, 1905–1941* (Kuala Lumpur: Pustaka Antara, 1996).

51 See Porritt, *British Colonial Rule in Sarawak*, pp. 58–61.

52 Ooi Keat Gin, ed., *Brunei: History, Islam, Society, and Contemporary Issues* (London: Routledge, 2016), p. 9. Emphasis added.

53 See Ooi Keat Gin, "Borneo in the Early Modern Period, c. Late Fourteenth to c. Late Eighteenth Centuries", in *Early Modern Period of Southeast Asia, 1350–1800*, edited by Ooi Keat Gin and Hoang Anh Tuan (London: Routledge, 2016), pp. 88–102.

54 Haji Zaini Haji Ahmad, ed., *Partai Rakyat Brunei/The People's Party of Brunei: Selected Documents/Dokumen Terpilih* (Petaling Jaya: INSAN [Institute of Social Analysis], 1987), p. 198.

6 Kalimantan

From parliamentary democracy to guided democracy

This country, the Republic of Indonesia, does not belong to any group, nor to any religion, nor to any ethnic group, nor to any group with customs and traditions, but the property of all of us from Sabang to Merauke!

Sukarno, speech in Surabaya,
24 September 1955

Following the round-table conference at The Hague (23 August to 2 November 1949), a transfer of sovereignty to the newly created and fully independent *Republik Indonesia Serikat* (RIS, Republic of the United States of Indonesia [RUSI]) was realized on 27 December 1949 when the Netherlands' Queen Juliana formally handed over the instrument of transfer to RIS/RUSI Vice-president-designate Mohammad Hatta. This official ceremony at the civic hall of the Amsterdam Palace witnessed by more than 330 invited dignitaries and the international media signified the formal closure of 340 years of Dutch colonial rule and the end of the almost five-year *Revolusi* (Revolution).[1] The estimated death toll of military and civilian was between 45,000 and 100,000, on the Indonesian side, and more than 15,000 casualties on the opposing side (namely Dutch, British), as well as 1,000 Japanese lives.[2]

When RIS/RUSI came into being, Kalimantan was a hotchpotch of *federasi* (federal state), *daerah istimewa* (special region), and *daerah* (region). But by 17 August 1950, all of Kalimantan from Tarakan to Banjarmasin to Pontianak was incorporated into the unitary state of the *Republik Indonesia* (RI, Republic of Indonesia). Kalimantan underwent an administrative restructuring during the first half of the 1950s. Meanwhile, there was a shifting of power between social groups, with the emergence and subsequent assertion of the Dayaks culminating in the creation of Central Kalimantan. But the inaugural parliamentary general elections to the *Dewan Perwakilan Rakyat* (DPR, People's Representative Council) (29 September 1955) and the elections to the *Konstituante* (Constitutional Assembly) (15 December 1955) at the local level (Kalimantan) sprung several surprises in contrast to the national scenario. While elections were underway, a long-drawn-out rebellion by ex-*pejuang* flared up in the interior of South Kalimantan, touted at the grassroots level as a righteous struggle of the oppressed. Such uprisings and others in the provinces ironically strengthened the Army, both at the central government and in the regional territories. Kalimantan was one of the host territories of the central government's transmigration policy, an attempt at addressing the issue of overpopulation and dense population in certain areas, whereas other places possessed a sparse population.

But before scrutinizing the local micro-scenario within Kalimantan, an overall picture at the national stage is needed to allow the contextualization of local developments. Moreover, cognizance of the then geopolitical situation against the backdrop of the Cold War is needed in examining the unfolding of the 1950s, its last quarter as a prelude to the early 1960s.

The big picture: the national stage

If one was impressed with the drama and action of the latter half of the 1940s, the following decades of the 1950s and first half of the 1960s was no less impregnated with theatrics, tensions, crisis to fear, and subsequently untold tragedy. The 1950s posed as the setting of the stage or scene for the subsequent development of events that ended rather tragically in the mid- and latter part of the 1960s. It could be cast as a prelude to *vivere pericolosamente*, the Italian phrase meaning 'of living dangerously', ironically upon hindsight, used by Indonesian President Sukarno as the title of his Independence Day speech of 1964. Within a year, the strongman president fell from his pinnacle of power (president-for-life declared in May 1963) and pedestal of public adoration in the face of the unfolding of a series of events that overtook and outmanoeuvred the ever-cunning Javanese puppeteer (Sukarno), who apparently ran out of tricks for an uncompromising audience.

The realization of the *Republik Indonesia* witnessed the play of party politics during the beginnings and workings of parliamentary democracy throughout the 1950s. It was considered an experiential period for the newly independent country that hitherto had scant encounter with constitutional arrangements and parliamentary democracy. The far-flung archipelago, from the Muslim Achenese sultanate to the overlordship of the Sultan of Tidore over pre-colonial Irian Jaya, had only known of strong, dictatorial governance. The three-and-a-half centuries of Dutch colonial rule did not differ much from their indigenous predecessors, comparable in being exacting, exploitative, at times harsh and uncompromising, but at other times, paternalistic and patronizing. The authoritarian tradition of governance had been the norm, the rule rather than the exception. To a great extent then, parliamentary democracy of elected governments seemed to be an alien concept to the elite as well as to the grassroots.

Therefore, although the formation of political parties was not a post-independent phenomenon, forming a government and governing through a cabinet (executive) and parliament (legislative), adhering to the concept of collective responsibility, were nonetheless all novel and untried undertakings. Moreover, the clarion call of *merdeka* (independence) has, to a large extent, served as a unifying factor for the coming together of a very disparate people divided along ethnicity, culture, language, way of life, beliefs and religions, geographical diversity, and social norms.

But the post-independent period witnessed a host of cleavages amongst the peoples that were increasingly apparent. Besides religious traditions, Islam and Christianity, political ideologies, notably Marxism, liberalism, and democracy, were divisive elements that further contributed to disunity, factionalism, and parochialism. Meanwhile, Outer Islanders harboured fears of Javanese political domination as in the past, that increasingly became particularly pronounced as the decade (1950s) progressed.

Within the country there were groups opposed to the establishment of *Republik Indonesia*. *Darul Islam* (DI), or Realm of Islam, which unilaterally set up a *Negara Islam Indonesia* (NII, 'Islamic State of Indonesia') in West Java, had since 1949 waged a guerrilla war against the central government at Jakarta. The proclamation of the Republic of South Maluku by disaffected Ambonese who were ex-*Koninklijk Nederlands Indisch Leger* (KNIL, Royal Netherlands [East] Indies Army) was in defiance of the central government. Between 1955 and 1961, rebellions erupted in Sumatra – Acheh Rebellion (1953–1957), *Pemerintah Revolusioner Republik Indonesia* (PRRI, Revolutionary Government of the Republic of Indonesia) (1956–1958), and in Sulawesi – PERMESTA (*Piagam Perjuangan Semesta Alam* [Universal Struggle Charter]) (1957–1961). In South Kalimantan, DI manifested in the Ibnu Hadjar Rebellion (1950–1963).[3]

Newly independent Indonesia was characterized by widespread poverty, high illiteracy, and perpetuation of authoritarian traditions. In 1961, some 60 per cent of males and 77 per cent of females were illiterate.[4] The economy was in shambles, thanks to the military occupation by Imperial Japan (1942–1945), and thereafter, the protracted armed struggle for independence from Dutch colonial rule (1945–1949). Merely to supply food and other basic necessities were huge challenges that were further aggravated by a burgeoning population growth that the economy could barely sustain. Its population in 1955 stood at 77,327,794, and in 1960 was 87,792,515.[5] Rampant inflation and widespread smuggling across the archipelago were other economic woes. The latter problem, in particular, adversely impacted on the national coffers at Jakarta.

Between 1950 and 1957, Indonesia's governance was fashioned after a Western-style constitutional democracy under the purview of the 1950 Provisional Constitution that was in place from 17 August 1950 until its abrogation on 5 July 1959. Under this Constitution, provision was made for the convening of a unicameral parliamentary form of government, with an executive of a cabinet headed by a prime minister, who was collectively responsible to Parliament.[6] Although the office of a president existed, the position accrued no executive powers. However, the president could dissolve the House of Representatives, and in doing so, he could instruct the holding of general elections within 30 days. Through election by secret ballot, members would serve the constituent assembly that would deliberate on legislation, including the heavy task of producing a definitive constitution that required a two-thirds majority for approval. Out of the 146 articles of the 1950 Provisional Constitution, 28 articles dealt with fundamental human rights and freedoms, viz. equality before the law, proscription of all forms of slavery, freedom of movement, freedom of religious adherence, freedom of opinion and expression, freedom of assembly, and the right to hold public demonstrations and strikes that drew extensively from the 1948 Universal Declaration of Human Rights.[7]

Parliamentary democracy era

During the period of parliamentary democracy, because no single political party could command support in forming a majority government, there was at best a series of coalition governments, each holding tenuously to power until a crisis that prompted the next round of musical chairs of prime ministers and cabinets to assume their turn in this political merry-go-round. As Table 6.1 shows, the helm of the premiership, hence the government, alternated between the *Masyumi* Party (*Partai Majelis Syuro Muslimin Indonesia*; Council of Indonesian Muslim Associations), and *Partai Nasional Indonesia* (PNI, Indonesian National Party). The latter was closely associated with President Sukarno, one of the founder-members since its establishment in 1927.

Against the bipolar Cold War world then, the governments of Indonesia during the 1950s tended to lean toward the Western bloc, notably that of Mohammad Natsir and Sukiman Wirjosandjojo. A modernist Muslim leader, Natsir's government held the reins of power for some seven months in which he emphasized national reconstruction with support from the Western democracies. Also a modernist Muslim leader, Wirjosandjojo, as prime minister, took an anti-Army and anti-PKI stance and was particularly partial towards the West, especially the U.S. His downfall came when it was revealed that his foreign minister, Achmed Subardjo, had secretly accepted assistance from Washington under a mutual security agreement.[8]

Wilopo of the PNI, on the other hand, opposed aid from the U.S., instead favoured trade with Eastern bloc countries. Ironically, within the country, he neither favoured the PKI nor the Army; the latter, in fact, attempted an abortive coup ('17 October [1952] Affair') to topple his government.[9]

The first Ali Sastroamidjojo government (1953–1955) witnessed a shift to one of neutrality or non-alignment, as demonstrated in the hosting of the Asia-Africa Conference in 1955, famously referred to as the Bandung Conference, and in the public expression of revoking the Netherlands-Indonesian Union. It was tasked to the succeeding government of Burhanuddin Harahap (*Masyumi*) to prepare the legal and legislative requirements in taking Indonesia out of the Union that symbolically severed all ties with its former colonial master.

On 29 September 1955, independent Indonesia's inaugural parliamentary general election to the 257-seat DPR[10] was held to replace the existing provisional legislature as well as for the *Konstituante* election to draft a permanent constitution. Despite pre-election rumours of tensions and impending troubles, nothing untoward marred the auspicious day, with a high voter turnout of 91.54 per cent, of which 87.65 per cent served valid votes.[11] It was a remarkable achievement, for in the short span of time, the diverse multiethnic population with high illiteracy

Table 6.1 Governments in Indonesia under Constitutional Democracy, 1950–1959

Prime Minister	Deputy Prime Minister	Tenure	Remarks
Mohammad Natsir (*Masyumi*) *	Sultan Hamengkubuwana IX	7 Sept 1950–21 Mar 1951	The first cabinet of the (Unitary) Republic of Indonesia (RI) after the dissolution of the Republic of the United States of Indonesia (RUSI); pro-Western orientation; emphasis on national reconstruction.
Sukiman Wirjosandjojo (*Masyumi*)	Suwirjo (PNI)	27 Apr 1951–25 Feb 1952	Adopted a pro-Western stance; not only was anti-Army but also anti-PKI.
Wilopo (PNI)	Prawoto Mangkusasmito (*Masyumi*)	1 Apr 1952–3 June 1953	The Korean War boom that benefitted the Natsir government was at its tail end and posed a bane; the demobilization of troops was a major predicament.
Ali Sastroamidjojo (PNI)	1st DPM: Wongsonegoro (PIR) 2nd DPM: Zainal Arifin (NU)	1 Aug 1953–24 July 1955	Oversaw the Asia-Africa Conference at Bandung; revoked the Netherlands-Indonesian Union. An increase in incidences of corruption and smuggling.
Burhanuddin Harahap (*Masyumi*)	1st DPM: R. Djanoe (PIR) 2nd DPM: Harsono Tjokroaminoto (PSII)	11 Aug 1955–3 Mar 1956	Oversaw the first general elections in September 1955; prepared legislation to take Indonesia out of the Netherlands-Indonesian Union.
Ali Sastroamidjojo (PNI)	1st DPM: Mohammed Roem (*Masyumi*) 2nd DPM: Idham Chalid (NU)	26 Mar 1956–14 Mar 1957	Bogged down by scandals and regional rebellions; Ali's stepping down as prime minister signaled the end of parliamentary democracy.
Djuanda Kartawidjaja	1st DPM: Hardi (PNI) 2nd DPM: Idham Chalid (NU) 3rd DPM: Johannes Leimaena (PARKINDO)	9 Apr 1957–5 July 1959	President Sukarno appointed Djuanda to preside over a cabinet comprising mainly qualified individuals who had no affiliation to any political parties; headed the first *Kabinet Karya* (Working Cabinet).

* Political party affiliation

PNI   *Partai Nasional Indonesia* (Indonesian National Party)
PIR   *Partai Persatuan Indonesian Raya* (Party of the Union of Great Indonesia)
PSII   *Partai Sjarikat Islam Indonesia* (Indonesian Islamic Union Party)
NU   *Nahdatul Ulama*
PARKINDO   *Partai Kristen Indonesia* (Indonesian Christian Party)

Sources: Robert Cribb, *Historical Dictionary of Indonesia* (Metuchen, NJ, and London: The Scarecrow Press, 1992), pp. 11, 182, 319, 449, 494; P. N. H. Simanjuntak, *Kabinet-Kabinet Republik Indonesia: Dari Awal Kemerdekaan Sampai Reformasi [Cabinets of the Republic of Indonesia: From Early Independence until Reformation]* (Jakarta: Djambatan, 2003), pp. 108–116, 116–124, 125–133, 133–148, 160–180; Herbert Feith, *The Wilopo Cabinet, 1952–1953: A Turning Point in Post-Revolutionary Indonesia*, reprint ed. (Singapore: Equinox Publishing, 2009; first published in 1958 by Cornell University); Herbert Feith, *The Decline of Constitutional Democracy in Indonesia*, reprint ed. (Singapore: Equinox Publishing (Asia) Pte Ltd, 2009; first published in 1962 under the auspices of the Modern Indonesia Project, Southeast Asia Program, Cornell University), pp. 339, 469–470, 418–419.

and widespread poverty had, to a certain extent, transformed into a responsible electorate aware of their rights, turning out in droves to cast their votes. Electoral results (Table 6.2) showcased the success of the 'Big 4' – PNI, *Masyumi*, NU, and PKI – that between them won almost 80 per cent of the votes. Although all the 'Big 4' gained additional seats, the greatest beneficiary was NU, which gained a five-fold increase in seats, from 8 (Provisional Parliament) to 45 in the DPR. The 1955 Parliamentary General Elections to some extent was a symbolic triumph for parliamentary democracy.

Within six months, elected members took their seats in the DPR on 26 March 1956. The *Konstituante* was convened later that year on 10 November. Once again PNI's Ali Sastroamidjojo set up a cabinet, his second thus far, flanked by two deputy premiers, the first being R. Djanoe (PIR) and the second, Idham Chalid (NU). To a certain extent, the elections of 1955 did serve its primary purpose with a sitting DPR, a cabinet, and its constitutional government, and at the same time, the *Konstituante* managed to convene with its paramount role of drafting a new and permanent constitution. Sastroamidjojo's second cabinet and government faced rather insurmountable odds, namely rebellions had begun to foment in Sumatra and Sulawesi, whereby recalcitrant colonels declared alternatives to the governing authority of the central government at Jakarta. Within a year, on

Table 6.2 Indonesia's Inaugural Parliamentary General Elections and Constituent Assembly, 29 September 1955 and 15 December 1955

Electoral Results of the 'Big 4' that between them garnered almost 80 per cent of total votes casted in both elections.

Political Party	Parliamentary General Elections Votes Won	Parliamentary General Elections % of Total Votes	Seats in DPR#	Constituent Assembly (Konstituante) Votes Won
Partai Nasional Indonesia (PNI, Indonesian National Party)	8,434,653	22.3	57 (42)*	9,070,218 [+635,565]^
Masyumi	7,903,886	20.9	57 (44)	7,789,619 [−114,267]
Nahdatul Ulama (NU)	6,955,141	18.4	45 (8)	6,989,333 [+34,192]
Partai Komunis Indonesia (PKI, Indonesian Communist Party)	6,176,914	16.4	39 (17)	6,232,512 [55,598]

Dewan Perwakilan Rakyat (People's Representative Council), Indonesia's Parliament
^ Difference between Parliamentary General Elections Votes and Constituent Assembly Votes.
* Seats held at the dissolution of the Provisional Parliament.

Source: Herbert Feith, *The Indonesian Elections of 1955* (Ithaca, NY: Cornell Southeast Asia Program 1957; 2nd printing 1971), pp. 58–59, 65; A. van Marle, "The First Indonesian Parliamentary Elections", *Indonesia*, 9 (June 1956): 257–264.

14 March 1957, Sastroamidjojo stood down as prime minister, and this momentous action marked the end of parliamentary government and democracy in Indonesia. Notwithstanding the creation of the so-called *Kabinet Karya* (Working Cabinet) headed by the Sukarno-appointed prime minister, Djuanda Kartawidjaja, a series of events of highhanded actions on the part of Sukarno in addressing challenges from within and from without, inevitably lead to one-man rule.

The Bandung Conference (1955)

The inaugural Asia-Africa Conference hosted by Indonesia in the cool tropical clime of Bandung, located about 150 kilometres southeast of Jakarta, was a diplomatic triumph for the nation's reputation as a pioneering force of neutrality on the international stage.[12] In the then post-war world dictated by Cold War politics of 'with-us-or-with-them', the leaders of Indonesia, Burma (Myanmar), Ceylon (Sri Lanka), Pakistan, and India took the lead in organizing a meaningful meeting of newly independent Asian and African nations. The objective was to promote Afro-Asian economic and cultural cooperation, and collectively, to oppose colonialism or neo-colonialism by any party. More specific concerns and issues, *inter alia*, a response to the disregard and neglect shown by Western powers regarding decisions affecting their (Asian-African nations) fate and future; apprehension over the then-strained relations between Washington and Beijing; desiring cordial and peaceful relations with the People's Republic of China (PRC); and uncompromising rejection of any manifestation of imperialism and colonialism. The majority of the 29 participating nation-states that had recently unshackled their colonial chains did not wish to be again in harness to either 'camp' or 'bloc' then emerging in the Cold War environment; instead, they wished to be independent of either group, the Western democracies or the Communist states. Neither Washington nor Moscow, the opposing Cold War protagonists, were represented at Bandung. Sukarno, on his part, wanted to use the gathering as a means of soliciting support for Indonesia's case against the Netherlands over the possession of the western portion of New Guinea.[13]

Following deliberations during the weeklong (18–24 April) conference, the outcome was that all parties unanimously proclaimed the promotion of world peace and cooperation among nations and the adoption of the principles of the United Nations Charter.[14] The Bandung Conference, as it came to be known, was undoubtedly Sukarno's finest hour on the world stage when he emerged triumphant. The conference at Bandung set the stage and provided the impetus for the subsequent formation of the Non-Aligned Movement (NAM).[15]

Notwithstanding the accomplishment of staging the first general elections of independent Indonesia in 1955, the electoral results were inconclusive, with no single political party gaining a clear majority, hence settling for another coalition government with its tenuous hold on power. Bickering amongst politicians of various shades was the norm rather than addressing the business of governance. Meanwhile, divisive forces in the form of rebellions in the Outer Islands (Acheh, West Sumatra, northern Sulawesi, South Kalimantan) were tearing the nation asunder. Moreover, the support and participation of politicians from *Masyumi* and PSII in the PPRI and PERMESTA rebellions further discredited the central government's inability to maintain control over the provinces from without and political parties from within. The situation was entering crisis phase, and Sukarno, as president, felt that he had to act.

Guided democracy

It was not so much a situation of Sukarno wanting to seize power and bolster his ineffectual presidency but more of a thoughtful father-figure intending on saving his children (people) and family (nation) from being dragged down into the abyss of chaos and anarchy. Sukarno criticized the practitioners of parliamentary democracy, namely politicians and political parties that held steadfast to ideologies and -isms, the latter bringing forth bloody clashes between opposing parties. In January 1956, he warned:

> [that] the number of victims among the Indonesian people killed by the nation itself is far greater than the victims of the previous struggle against the Dutch. Let us not contend over ideology which just spills blood.[16]

He emphasized that the Indonesia project was an inclusive venture: "Remember that we are building a big house *for all ethnicities, all groups, all religions*".[17] In contrast to Western practices of decisions based on majority votes, Sukarno suggested the application of traditional decision-making mechanisms of "Indonesian gotong-royong democracy which is based on consensus".[18] His "bury the parties" (October 1956) statement was undoubtedly a direct criticism of politicians and political parties, but at the same time, a venting of his frustration and disappointment with the problematic workings of parliamentary democracy that had plunged the nation onto the brink of disaster.[19]

The peaceful transition from constitutional democracy to Guided Democracy is surmised as follows:

> The critical events in this [transition] process were the announcement of Sukarno's 'Konsepsi' in February 1957, the installation of the extra-parliamentary Kabinet Karya in April 1957 and establishment of the National Council a month later [May 1957], the proclamation by Presidential Decree of the 1945 Constitution and concomitant dissolution of the Constituent Assembly in July 1959, and finally the dissolution of the elected parliament in March 1960 and its replacement by an appointed Gotong-Royong Parliament in June [1960].[20]

Implementation of Guided Democracy took up momentum following Sukarno's '*Konsepsi*' speech of 21 February 1957, whereby he lamented on the rather woeful situation that Indonesia was facing then owing to the system of governance.

> Every cabinet in this period of eleven years . . . has experienced difficulties of this kind. A lack of authority and always facing strong opposition so that not

one Cabinet is able to last for any length of time, and every Cabinet finally fell into crisis and must be replaced with another Cabinet. For eleven long years we have tried to overcome those difficulties with complete integrity of heart, with complete sincerity of heart, but every time we have precisely the same experience. Because of this . . . I ponder why [do] we always have these experiences, these unpleasant experiences? And I finally arrive at the conviction that *we have used a wrong system, a wrong style of governance, a style which we call Western democracy.*[21]

Sukarno's '*Konsepsi*' is surmised as follows: the system of Western parliamentary democracy was not appropriate for the nature and character of Indonesia and thus should be replaced by Guided Democracy. For the implementation of the system of Guided Democracy, it necessitates the establishment of a *gotong royong* Cabinet, whose members are drawn from all political parties and organizations based on the balance of power within society then. The president's '*Konsepsi*' emphasized the need to form a 'Four-legged Cabinet', which meant the participation of all four main political parties, the 'Big 4', namely PNI, *Masyumi*, NU, and PKI, to *create* national mutual cooperation. The establishment of a National Council, which comprised representatives from functional social groups from society, was to offer counsel to the Cabinet regardless if such advice was solicited or otherwise.

About three weeks following the '*Konsepsi*' speech, Prime Minister Ali Sastroamidjojo rendered his resignation on 14 March 1957, which marked the close of the constitutional democracy phase and ushered in a new era of Guided Democracy. Owing to the failure of any viable 'Four-legged Cabinet' to be constituted from the four principal political parties, Sukarno then called on cabinet veteran, Djuanda Kartawidjaja, to head the first *Kabinet Karya* comprising mainly, but not exclusively, professionals without political party affiliation to work alongside politicians. Djuanda was not affiliated with any political party. It was the first 'test' for the subsequent implementation of Guided Democracy. Djuanda's Cabinet drew members that represented functional groups from society, hence the moniker, 'Working Cabinet'.

Crucially, on 5 July 1959, Sukarno, through presidential decree, proclaimed the reinstatement of the 1945 Constitution[22] and the dissolution of the Constituent Assembly (*Konstituante*). Formally convened on 10 November 1956, *Konstituante* witnessed protracted disagreements over the choice, of whether Islam or *Pancasila*, should be adopted as the primary foundation of the nation-state, hence retarding progress in the drafting of the new permanent constitution.[23] Sukarno was exasperated with this deadlock among elected politicians, that *inter alia*, drove him to dismiss the *Konstituante*; its last session was on 2 July 1959. On 9 July, in addition to the presidency, Sukarno assumed the title and post of prime minister. Later, in May 1963, he declared himself president-for-life.

The preamble of the 1945 Constitution explicitly spelled out the five principles of the *Pancasila*, namely (1) *Ketuhanan yang Maha Esa* (belief in the One and Only God); (2) *Kemanusiaan yang adil dan beradab* (just and civilised humanity);

(3) *Persatuan Indonesia* (the unity of Indonesia); (4) *Kerakyatan yang dipimpim oleh hikmat kebijaksanaan dalam permusyawaratan/perwakilan* (democratic life led by wisdom of thoughts in deliberation amongst representatives of the people); and (5) *Keadilan sosial bagi seluruh rakyat* (achieving social justice for all the people of Indonesia).[24]

By invoking the 1945 Constitution, Sukarno strengthened his capacity as president, as laid out in Articles 4 and 5, notably:

Article 4

(1) The President of the Republic of Indonesia shall hold the power of government in accordance with the Constitution.
(2) In exercising his duties, the President shall be assisted by a Vice President.

Article 5

(1) The President is entitled to submit bills to the DPR [*Dewan Perwakilan Rakyat*, People's Representative Council].
(2) The President shall issue government regulations to implement laws as needed.

It was apparent that the president possessed sweeping powers. Although sovereignty lies with the people, it was "*dilakukan sepenuhnya oleh Majelis Permusyawaratan Rakyat* (MPR) [fully exercised by the People's Deliberative Assembly]".[25] The MPR comprised members of the DPR, who were elected via general elections, and additionally with "*utusan-utusan dari daerah-daerah dan golongan-golongan, menurut aturan yang ditetapkan dengan undang-undang* [representatives from the provinces and other groups as laid out by the law]".[26] The MPR convened once every five years at the national capital (Jakarta), and decisions were made in accordance with majority vote.

Notwithstanding the existence of the MPR and DPR, it was apparent that *real* executive power was in the hands of the person of the president. Sukarno hence became a strongman, often administering the nation through decrees in implementing his *Demokrasi Terpimpin* or Guided Democracy, he as the predominant 'Guide'.

Was Sukarno's reckoning, "And I finally arrive at the conviction that we have used a wrong system, a wrong style of governance, a style which we call Western democracy", correct that necessitated an alternative – Guided Democracy – form of governance that apparently was more suited to Indonesia? Was Western-style democracy anathema to the socio-cultural background of Indonesia then that saw such a form of governance inappropriate for its setting? Or was the collapse due to a power struggle among proponents of constitutional democracy and their detractors, ending with the triumph of the latter? Or was it simply the unfolding of a series of events that dictated the transition from one form of governance to another form, that appeared more appropriate under the emerging circumstances?

Analysis and interpretation for the causality of the fall from grace of parliamentary democracy of 1950s Indonesia began in the early 1960s and continued throughout the following decades. Recalling the critical events that subsequently led to its demise that ushered in a new form of governance – Guided Democracy – could uncover and discern some of the reasons contributing to this changeover.

Sukarno's '*Konsepsi*' speech of 21 February 1957 was sparked, as pointed out, by his disappointment in the workings of parliamentary democracy that to him proved inappropriate and unsuitable in the context of Indonesia. His alternative was guidance from above, hence Guided Democracy. But the reappointment of General A. H. Nasution as Army Chief of Staff in October 1955 could be regarded as a crucial turning point. Hitherto, the Army elite, on the one hand, and the President, on the other, each in their respective ways, had been criticizing the parliamentarians for ineffectual governance. With Nasution at the helm, a Sukarno-Army anti-politician alliance was in place to ensure the demise of parliamentary democracy.

Disaffection in the Outer Islands

Meanwhile, in the provinces there was increasing disaffection with the Java-based central government at Jakarta. Rumblings in Sumatra and Sulawesi gravitated to Vice President Mohammad Hatta, who was from Sumatra, culminating in an ultimatum followed by proclamation in mid-February 1958. Inability of the cabinet and government in countering and suppressing dissent in the provinces revealed their weaknesses and vulnerability.

Earlier, Hatta was increasingly 'uncomfortable' in his working relationship with Sukarno, who was showing signs of turning into an autocrat. Prior to the 1955 Parliamentary General Elections, Hatta wrote to Sukarno of his intention to step down once the DPR was convened and the *Konstituante* (Constitutional Assembly) set up to draft a permanent constitution. As promised, on 1 December 1956, Hatta stood down as vice president.

Two significant events, one in faraway New York and another in a Jakarta neighbourhood, spurred President Sukarno to adopt a tough stance on outstanding issues. On 29 November 1957, the much-awaited outcome over the West New Guinea/Irian Barat issue at the UN turned to disappointment that contributed to the push for drastic measures. Indonesia's foreign ministry had been working tirelessly in garnering support among UN members in backing its claim over West New Guinea that hitherto remained under Dutch colonial administration. But a UN General Assembly vote to place the Netherlands-Indonesia dispute on the agenda failed as it fell short of the required two-thirds majority.[27] An exasperated President Sukarno put into action his veiled threats, made several weeks earlier leading up to the vote, in ordering the expulsion of Dutch citizens from Indonesia and authorizing labour unions and the Army to assume control of Dutch properties, plantations, and businesses.[28] A government-sanctioned strike by Indonesian workers paralyzed the Dutch-owned *Koninklijke Paketvaart Maatschappij* (KPM, Royal Packet Navigation Company) and, in turn, stalled inter-island shipping. Faced with militant nationalization, KPM shifted its base and international shipping assets to Singapore in the following year.

Only a day after the pivotal UN decision, on the evening of 30 November, an assassination attempt was made on the president's life that claimed 11 deaths and no less than 30, mainly children, who were severely injured from a grenade attack.[29] Sukarno was attending a night fair at his children's school in the Cikini neighbourhood of Jakarta when several youth members of the *Gerakan Anti-Komunis* (GAK, Anti-Communist Movement), a Jakarta-based radical organization (established July 1956), seemingly acting on a spontaneous decision having witnessed the president's presence in the vicinity, decided to act. Sukarno barely escaped with his life. Many GAK members also belonged to the *Gerakan Pemuda Islam Indonesia* (GPII, Indonesian Islamic Youth Movement), an officially sanctioned youth arm of the *Masyumi*. Such a treacherous act, though perpetrated by members of GAK, tainted *Masyumi* through affiliation with GPII.

The Cikini Affair undoubtedly had shaken the president, and to a great extent, heartened him to lean towards the Left, the PKI, and also the Army. Fearing imminent arrest, several *Masyumi* leaders took flight, notably ex-premiers Mohammad Natsir and Burhanuddin Harahap, Sjafruddin Prawiranegara, then Governor of Bank Indonesia, Sumitro Joyohadikusumo, ex-cabinet minister, and Colonel Zulkfli Lubis, all finally ending up in Padang to be with the rebellious colonels led by Lieutenant-Colonel Ahmad Husein.[30] Lubis was widely regarded to be the *dalang* (lit. puppeteer, mastermind) of the attempt on Sukarno's life. A former army intelligence chief, Lubis, in 1955 then deputy army chief of staff, was in contention for the top post when, to everyone's consternation, Nasution was reappointed. Apparently, Lubis claimed he advised the youths who undertook the attempted assassination to refrain from such a radical move; they, however, acted on the contrary. The leader of GAK, Saleh Ibrahim, an aide of Lubis, managed to escape following the horrific incident.

Events in mid-February 1958 witnessed the increasing strengthening of the Sukarno-Army hand vis-à-vis rebellious regimes in the provinces. On 10 February 1958, the dissident colonels in Padang, the administrative centre of Western Sumatra, issued an ultimatum to the central government at Jakarta to meet its three demands: firstly, that Sukarno re-assume his role as a figurehead president; secondly, that a cabinet and government be headed by ex-Vice President Hatta; and thirdly, that Nasution be replaced as Army Chief of Staff.[31] When the five-day deadline expired, an alternative new government, *Pemerintah Revolusioner Republik Indonesia* (PRRI, Revolutionary Government of the Republic of Indonesia), was proclaimed on 15 February with Sjafruddin Prawiranegara as prime minister.[32] Two days later, on 17 February, Lieutenant-Colonel H. N. Ventje Sumual's PERMESTA rebel group in North Sulawesi declared its alliance with PRRI in their defiance to Jakarta.[33] Hence, a military showdown existed between PRRI-PERMESTA and the Sukarno-Army alliance.

Although U.S. covert involvement in the Cikini Affair was doubtful, it was apparent that the PRRI-PERMESTA alliance did receive U.S. military aid. The latter, however, backfired in that Sukarno moved further Left in the wake of the provincial challenge. Nasution mobilized the Army to suppress the opposition in Sumatra and Sulawesi. Government forces moved against the dissident colonels in Sumatra, earning a significant victory on 12 March 1958 that prevented PRRI troops from destroying the Caltex oilfields and refinery in Pekanbaru. Washington's complicity was evident from the substantial haul of American-made military equipment and materials abandoned by the retreating rebel forces. Nasution ordered the launch of numerous surprise amphibious invasions on rebel cities in Sumatra during March 1958. Overwhelmed by superior government forces, Lieutenant-Colonel Husein had little choice other than to order a tactical withdrawal, turning to a strategy of attrition and protracted guerrilla warfare.[34]

Towards the close of 1960, in his efforts to not only save the loss of lives, both military and civilians, but more importantly to win over officers and men to the government side, Nasution offered an olive branch, namely *Operasi Pemanggilan Kembali* (Operation Call Back), in hopes of voluntary surrender rather than capture or casualties on the part of the rebels. By mid-1961, PRRI entered the pages of history, and Natsir's surrender on 28 September closed the chapter on this military misadventure of Hatta's supporters.[35]

While ground military operations were underway in Sumatra, *Angkatan Udara Republik Indonesia* (AURI, Air Force of the Republic of Indonesia) struck the PERMESTA rebel stronghold at Manado in North Sulawesi, succeeding in destroying AUREV B-26 aircrafts. Having accomplished the latter, *Operasi Merdeka* (Operation Independence) was launched in mid-1958. An ambitious assault – amphibious landings and aerial bombardments – on Manado forced rebel forces to withdraw inland southeast towards Lake Tondano to continue the insurgency through guerrilla warfare. However, similar to the tactic utilized for PRRI, offers of amnesties to encourage voluntarily surrenders succeeded in drawing out many rebels from their hideouts and ceasing their struggle and return to the fold.

A twist of fate struck a roadblock on the international, diplomatic stage with the capture of Allen Lawrence Pope, an American pilot serving in the Civil Air Transport (CAT), a U.S. Central Intelligence Agency (CIA) front organization.[36] Pope carried out sorties for the *Angkatan Udara Revolusioner* (AUREV, Revolutionary Air Force) of PERMESTA since April 1958. When his B-26 bomber was downed and he and his crew were captured (18 May 1958), Pope was in possession of incriminating documents that confirmed undisputed evidence of the complicity of the Eisenhower administration (1953–1961) with anti-Jakarta forces bent on toppling what appeared to be a pro-communist Sukarno regime.[37] Although sentenced to death by a military court (20 April 1960), Pope was clandestinely packed off to the U.S. in mid-1962.

The Pope debacle and Lieutenant-Colonel Husein's tactical shift signalled a policy shift by Washington in a turnaround that literally spelt the death knell of PRRI-PERMESTA. Nasution's offensives in both Sumatra and Sulawesi proved decisive, and the pendulum swung towards Sukarno and the Jakarta central government. By the time Natsir surrendered on 28 September 1961, practically all rebel military officers and the rank-and-file had already switched sides in support of Nasution. Likewise, following amphibious and airborne assaults on Manado, the capital and headquarters of PERMESTA, the rebels retreated to continue with

guerrilla resistance. Similar to PRRI in Sumatra, the government offered amnesties, and many military personnel crossed over. By the later part of 1961, PER-
MESTA was but a memory of a vain struggle.

The Pope debacle saw the U.S. switching support to the Jakarta central government, and coupled with Nasution's military offensive from mid-1958, the PRRI-
PERMESTA rebellion ended in defeat and surrender of the rebel opposition.
Military triumph over the insurgent forces in Sumatra and Sulawesi fortified physically and symbolically Nasution's and the Army's hand in the political arena.

With the 1945 Constitution in place for more than a year, Sukarno moved to
disband DPR in March 1960 when it defiantly refused to approve the national
budget. In its place, was established in June the *Dewan Perwakilan Rakyat Gotong
Royong* (DPR-GR, People's Representative Council of Mutual Assistance), where
membership was by presidential appointment, and their service subject to the
whims and fancies of the president. For all intents and purposes, the DPR-GR was
nothing more than a formal rubber stamp institution for Sukarno's policies. Guided
Democracy was firmly entrenched.

Turning to indigenous recourse of governance

In his Independence Day speech on 17 August 1959 entitled '*Penemuan Kembali
Revolusi Kita* [Rediscovery of Our Revolution]', Sukarno called for social justice
and a rejuvenation of the spirit of (Indonesian) Revolution. This calling was
adopted by the *Dewan Pertimbangan Agong* (DPA, Supreme Advisory Council).
A DPA Working Committee chaired by PKI's chairman D. N. Aidit[38] translated the
president's wishes into *Garis-garis Besar Haluan Negara* (GBHN, Broad Outlines
of State Policy). In short, the 'Broad Outlines' was referred to as MANIPOL,
namely *Manifesto Politik Republik Indonesia* (Political Manifesto of the Republic
of Indonesia). The systematization of MANIPOL was based on PKI's thesis of
Masyarakat Indonesia dan Revolusi Indonesia (MIRI, Indonesian Society and
Indonesian Revolution) that was formulated back in 1957.[39]

In 1960, added to MANIPOL was USDEK, that was drawn from *Undang-Undang
Dasar 1945*, *Sosialisme Indonesia*, *Demokrasi Terpimpin*, *Ekonomi Terpimpin, dan
Kepribadian Indonesia* (Basic Laws of 1945 [1945 Constitution], Indonesian Social-
ism, Guided Democracy, Commanded Economy, and Indonesian Identity).

On closer scrutiny, MANIPOL (1959) appears to be a close semblance to
the blueprint of MIRI (1957) (Table 6.3). Therefore, it came as no surprise that
the PKI was relentless in its support, propagation, and realization. MANIPOL-
USDEK was popularized through the slogan of *Pancasila* in its implementation.
Opposition to MANIPOL-USDEK meant anti-*Pancasila* and anti-NASAKOM.
The latter was an acronym for *NASionalisme, Agama, KOMunisme*, Sukarno's
recipe of cooperative blending of nationalism-religion-communism. Furthermore,
a PKI ploy was in labelling those opposed to NASAKOM as anti-Sukarno.

With the advantage of hindsight and drawing from a historical analysis perspective, Sukarno's Guided Democracy is succinctly encapsulated in four developments, notably Sukarno-centric, applying indigenous concepts to governance, the

Table 6.3 MANIPOL (1959): A Mirror to MIRI (1957)

MANIPOL (1959) Manifesto Politik Republik Indonesia [Political Manifesto of the Republic of Indonesia]	MIRI (1957) Masyarakat Indonesia dan Revolusi Indonesia [Indonesian Society and Indonesian Revolution]
II. Persoalan-persoalan pokok Revolusi Indonesia [Questions of the Principles of the Indonesian Revolution].	Bab II. Revolusi Indonesia, Pasal 2 [Chapter II. Indonesian Revolution, Article 2]
5. Musuh-musuh Revolusi [Enemies of the Revolution]	Soal-soal pokok Revolusi Indonesia [Principle Question of the Indonesian Revolution]
(1) Dasar/tujuan dan kewajiban Revolusi Indonesia [Policy/aim and responsibility of the Indonesian Revolution]	Tentang sasaran pokok atau musuh Indonesia [About principal targets or enemies of Indonesia]
(2) Kekuatan-kekuatan sosial Revolusi Indonesia [Social strength of the Indonesian Revolution]	Pokok daripada Revolusi Indonesia [Principles of the Indonesian Revolution]
(3) Sifat Revolusi Indonesia [Character of the Indonesian Revolution]	Tentang tugas-tugas Revolusi Indonesia [About the tasks of the Indonesian Revolution]
	Tentang tenaga-tenaga penggerak [About the driving forces]
(4) Hari depan Revolusi Indonesia [Future of the Indonesian Revolution]	Atau kekuatan pendorong Revolusi Indonesia [Or the strength of the driving force of the Indonsian Revolution]
	Tentang watak Revolusi Indonesia [About the character of the Indonesian Revolution]
	Tentang perspektif daripada Revolusi Indonesia [About the perspective from the Indonesian Revolution]

Source: Nugroho Notosusanto, ed., Tercapainya Konsensus Nasional/1966–1969 [Achievement of National Consensus/1966–1969] (Jakarta: Balai Pustaka, Cetakan Ketiga, 1985), pp. 50, 51, 69.

various struggles in addressing the question of national unity amidst the nation's myriad diversity, and the ascendancy of the Army. The various developments were undoubtedly interlinked and overlapped one another. In short, Guided Democracy could be referred to as an Indonesian style or way of governance that was deemed appropriate by the local actors, Sukarno in principal.

As has been alluded to, in early 1957, Sukarno took the bull by the horns with his '*Konsepsi*' speech, presenting himself in paternal fashion of 'saving' the people (children) and the nation (family) from the ineffectual governance of parliamentary democracy. The presidency, whom Sukarno had held since the declaration of independence of 17 August 1945, and since the establishment of the unitary state of *Republik Indonesia* in 1950, proved to be an impotent institution. In reinstating the 1945 Constitution that provided sweeping powers for the president, the pivot of almost all political power dwelled on him, Sukarno, the 'hero' of the *Revolusi* (Revolution). Once again, the spotlight shone on him, the grandstanding leader of the Indonesian people, of the Indonesian nation. In his hands were the twin sources of political power and political ideology, the latter termed 'Guided Democracy'. With fiery speeches, brinkmanship together with bravado showmanship, Sukarno, the consummate orator, was at his best when playing to the gallery.

Meanwhile, while the public image of Sukarno as a strongman created an aura of invincibility thanks to creative public relations coupled with media hype, the reality in the offices and departments of administration and on the ground amongst the populace was a far cry from the grandiose speeches and forceful gesturing of the president. Never diligent nor possessing an aptitude for day-to-day administrative duties and responsibilities, Sukarno shoved all the burden of governance literally on the shoulders and lap of Djuanda Kartawidjaja, his chief or main minister,[40] who diligently carried out the functions of government through a series of so-called *Kabinet Karya* in the name of the president. The non-partisan, party-less Djuanda worked until his death on 7 November 1963. Thereafter, it was increasingly obvious that the central government at Jakarta was falling apart.

Having concluded that Western-style democracy was inappropriate for Indonesia, Sukarno turned to indigenous recourse of governance. Hence, invoking such concepts as *musyawarah* (deliberate), *mufakat* (consensus), corporatism, and *gotong-royong* (mutual self-help, cooperation). From the Arabic root word *syawara*, *musyawarah* refers to the act of deliberating and negotiating. In practical terms, it refers to a concerted effort by all parties, adopting a humble attitude, to resolve a problem or find a solution, subsequently adopting a collective decision on the agreed-upon solution. Hand-in-hand with *musyawarah* is *mufakat*, the latter denoting consensus or collective agreement. Apparently, in local village society, *musyawarah* and *mufakat* were cornerstones of governance of the community. Such a practice appeared to be more advantageous in comparison to what Sukarno often referred to as '50% +1 democracy', the basis of Western democratic principles of the triumph of the majority. He pointed out that a majoritarian system in fact oppressed minorities.

Having paid witness to the divisiveness of political parties often encountering difficulties in coming to an agreeable solution, Sukarno turned to the workings of corporatism as an alternative. Corporatism refers to the permanent representation of well-organized hierarchical interest groups – corporate, agricultural, labour, military, intellectual – in the state apparatus, serving as organs of political representation. Corporatism it seemed had been an integral component of indigenous thought that emphasized the harmonious interaction of an assortment of functional groups within society. Corporatism was favoured over competition, because the latter promoted divisiveness. In order to further nurture harmonious interaction amongst social groups, the traditional spirit of *gotong-royong* was invoked, again in contrast to competition. Therefore,

> in 1959, [Sukano] appointed 200 functional group representatives (representing workers, peasants, women, intellectuals, youth, and so on) and 94 presidential nominees to sit alongside the existing 281 members of Parliament in the new Provisional People's Deliberative Council (Madjelis Permusyawaratan Rakjat-Sementara, MPRS), which formally became the central legislative body of Guided Democracy.[41]

The third development saw Guided Democracy utilizing corporatism, functional groups working together with political parties, as the basic structure in addressing political issues of the 1950s and 1960s, notably the nature of the independent nation-state of Indonesia, national unity amidst the diversity, the question of regional autonomy, Islam vis-à-vis *Pancasila*, socialism and communism, social and economic reform to tackle poverty, illiteracy, corruption, and smuggling. By the second half of the 1950s, it was apparent that parliamentary democracy as a form of governance appeared to have been ineffectual in addressing the aforesaid issues, hence corporatism as embraced by Guided Democracy might be the panacea. But could Guided Democracy address and resolve "the question of national unity amidst the nation's myriad diversity"?

While recalcitrant elements were active in the provinces (Sumatra, Sulawesi, etc.), on Java itself the central government's authority at Jakarta had been challenged by DI since 1949. Having declared NII in West Java, DI aimed for the implementation of *Syariah*, and subsequently, transforming the entire archipelago to be an Islamic state. DI had been in existence since 1942, a group of Muslim radicals headed by Sekarmadji Maridjan Kartosoewirjo (1905–1962), a radical Muslim politician. The group recognised only *Syariah* as a valid source of law. The movement to some extent had spread its influence and/or inspired uprisings in Acheh (led by Daud Beureu'eh [1899–1987]), South Sulawesi (headed by Kahar Muzakkar [1921–1965]), and Banjarmasin (under Ibnu Hadjar [1920–1963]).

On the opposite side of the scale was the increasing influence of the PKI. Having garnered 16.4 per cent of the vote that delivered 39 seats (of 257 parliamentary seats), PKI was among the 'Big 4' parties alongside PNI (22.3%, 57 seats), *Masyumi* (20.9%, 57 seats), and *Nahdatul Ulama* (18.4%, 45 seats) (Table 6.2).[42] Some 80 per cent of the vote was garnered by the 'Big 4'. During the 1957 local elections for representations on provincial and regency and city councils, PKI among the 'Big 4', attained the most progress since the 1955 Parliamentary General Elections, as can be seen in Table 6.4, with greater support, ranging from a

Table 6.4 Local Elections in Indonesia, 1957

Local elections were held in the second half of 1957 to elect provincial and regency and city councils. Focus is on the 'Big 4' political parties, that between them garnered the majority of the votes, namely *Masyumi, Partai Komunis Indonesia* (PKI), *Partai Nasional Indonesia* (PNI), and *Nahdatul Ulama* (NU).

Jakarta (22 June)

Political Party	Number of Votes	% of Votes	% change from 1955
Masyumi	153,709	22.0	−4.1
PKI	137,305	19.7	+7.1
PNI	124,955	17.9	−1.9
NU	104,892	15.0	−0.7

Central Java (17 July)

Political Party	Number of Votes	% of Votes	% change from 1955
PKI	2,706,893	31.8	+5.9
PNI	2,235,714	26.3	−8.8
NU	1,771,556	20.8	+0.1
Masyumi	714,722	8.4	−1.2

East Java (29 July)

Political Party	Number of Votes	% of Votes	% change from 1955
NU	2,999,785	30.4	−3.7
PKI	2,704,523	27.4	+4.1
PNI	1,899,782	19.2	−3.6
Masyumi	977,443	9.9	−1.3

West Java (10 Aug)

Political Party	Number of Votes	% of Votes	% change from 1955
Masyumi	1,841,030	26.1	+0.8
PKI	1,087,269	15.4	+3.5
PNI	1,055,801	15.0	−7.8
NU	597,356	8.5	−1.5

Jogjakarta (7 Nov)

Political Party	Number of Votes
PKI	298,257
PNI	164,568
Masyumi	118,985
NU	94,012

South Sumatra (1 Dec)

Political Party	Number of Votes	% of Votes	% change from 1955
Masyumi	553,276	38.0	−5.1
PKI	228,965	15.7	+3.6
PNI	187,042	12.9	−1.8
NU	113,888	7.8	−0.2

Source: Daniel S. Lev, *The Transition to Guided Democracy: Indonesian Politics 1957–1959* (Singapore: Equinox Publishing, 2009; first published in 1966 by Cornell Southeast Asia Program Publications), pp. 111–117; W. F. Wertheim, *Indonesian Society in Transition: A Study of Social Change*, 2nd ed. (The Hague: W. van Hoev, 1959), p. 355.

high 7.1 per cent in Jakarta to a respectable increase of 3.5 per cent in West Java. Despite the influence and base of DI in West Java, PKI (15.4%) managed a second placing to *Masyumi* (26.1%). In the capital city of Jakarta, PKI, although in a distant second behind *Masyumi*, achieved a 3.6 per cent increase in support compared to the 1955 outing. But PKI's support in Jogjakarta, accumulating 298,257 votes leaving far behind its opponents, viz. PNI (164,568), *Masyumi* (118,985), and NU (94,012), was significantly symbolic as the city was the heartland of the *Revolusi Indonesia*.[43]

At the pace of electoral progress attained by PKI, another scheduled general election in 1959 (it was never held) might elevate the communists into the seat of government, a dire prospect loathed by many including within military circles, particularly the Army. The Guided Democracy era was likened to a political *sandiwara* (stage play) between the main protagonist, Sukarno, and two pretenders or heirs apparent to the presidential 'throne', PKI holding the left stage and the Army, the right stage, both ever eager to occupy centre stage when the principal protagonist takes his exit.

The fourth trajectory was the military, notably the Army. Martial law was declared by Sukarno in March 1957 in response to the numerous armed uprisings and rebellions in the provinces. Under martial law, the Army took centre stage in day-to-day dealings with the common peoples across the archipelago, thereby elevating its power and prestige at the grassroots level as the guardian of the realm. Military authority hence became commonplace. In the wake of nationalization of Dutch properties and businesses from December 1957, the Army again seized possession from the labour unions and workers.

The armed forces, prominently the Army and other branches, the Navy and the Air Force, since the days of *Revolusi* had partook roles in politics and government, hence justifying its formal doctrine of *Dwifungsi*, or 'dual function':

the official doctrine which authorizes the armed forces' extensive participation in politics and government. The army's territorial structure, a military hierarchy distinct from the combat commands and running parallel to the civilian bureaucracy from provincial (KODAM, Komando Daerah Militer, Regional

Military Command) to village (BABINSA, Bintara Pembina Desa, NCOs [non-commissioned officers] for Village Development) level, provides military personnel with day-to-day involvement in the running of the country. The typical career pattern of an officer is alternating stints in the territorial and combat commands followed by 'retirement' into a post in the civil bureaucracy.[44]

As a means of countering its foe, namely the PKI, the Army lent moral and material support to various non-Leftist functional groups, including Islamic organizations, and subsequently became identified as the champion-cum-leader of an anti-communist front. It seemed inevitable that a showdown between the Army and the communists (PKI) would occur.

The foregoing outline of the four main developments comprised the internal situation of Guided Democracy (1959–1965). A closer scrutiny revealed a dire polity of internal conflicts between two formidable forces (PKI and the Army) with a besieged president, desparately grappling with a balancing act to stave off the Left (PKI) against the Right (the Army), and vice versa, with himself as the playmaker and arbiter of power. On the international stage, Sukarno portrayed himself as the robust champion of anti-imperialism and anti-colonialism, adopting an aggressive confrontational approach to the West New Guinea dispute (1950–1963) with the Netherlands and to the 'Malaysia' proposal (1963–1965), including military campaigns that were planned in the former and actively launched in the latter. Not only was Sukarno able to garner Moscow's political support in his row with the Dutch, but he also secured military support to bolster the planned amphibious invasion of the disputed territory. Cross-border skirmishes characterized *Konfrontasi*, with the launching of the '*Ganyang Malaysia*' ('Crush Malaysia') military campaign on the Kalimantan-Sarawak divide.

Kalimantan: the local scenario

The decade of the 1950s and beginning of the 1960s saw changes in the administrative structure across Kalimantan, including the realignment of divisional boundaries to create new regions. Dayak ascendancy in the post-war decades and political assertion subsequently led to the establishment of a new region, namely Central Kalimantan, that they could recognize as their heartland and ethnic identity. South Kalimantan, on the other hand, experienced a rebellion of disaffected revolutionary fighters who were marginalized in the post-independent period by the Army. The Ibnu Hadjar Rebellion was linked to DI, regarded as a branch in South Kalimantan, that intended to establish an Islamic State.

Elections in 1955 at the regional (Kalimantan) level for the DPR and the *Konstituante* to some extent mirrored the national outcome but with some surprises that reflected the local priorities. The political stage witnessed the appearance of 'new players', the Dayaks, which were hitherto politically insignificant and marginalized, asserting their rights and pressing their interests.

Meanwhile, resource-rich Kalimantan with a sparse population was regarded as the ideal territorial host for the central government's transmigration policy, an organized and concerted attempt at population redistribution, relocation of people from overpopulated regions to less peopled territories. Therefore, as a means to alleviate the population pressure from densely populated regions, such as Java or Madura, migrants were officially relocated to other parts of the far-flung archipelago to territories that were less populated with ample land and natural resources awaiting exploitation. Kalimantan, likewise Sumatra, played host to transmigrants. Accommodation and co-existence between indigenous and transmigrants were more problematic than envisaged. Tensions and strained relations were increasingly undermining the socio-economic structure between locals and newcomers, as the former resented the presence of the latter, intending to rid their homeland of foreign interlopers, as transmigrants were generally perceived by indigenes.

Administrative division

Contemporary Kalimantan's delineation of *provinsi* (provinces), *daerah* (region), and *kabupaten* (district) was undertaken mainly during the first half of the mid-1950s.[45] Table 6.5 indicates the background origins of each of the main provinces of Kalimantan and the sub-divisions (into districts) within each respective province (also see Map 1.2).

The pre-war colonial Dutch Borneo, as Kalimantan was then known,[46] had only two administrative divisions, viz. *Residentie Westerafdeeling van Borneo* (Residency of Western Division of Borneo) and *Residentie Zuider en Oostafdeeling van Borneo* (Residency of Eastern Division of Borneo). During the immediate post-war period (1945–1946), amidst the struggle between the returned Dutch colonial authorities and Republican forces, Kalimantan was apportioned into five 'states', namely *Satuan Kenegaraan Daerah Istimewa Kalimantan Barat* (State of Special Region of West Kalimantan), *Satuan Kenegaraan Kalimantan Tenggara* (State of Southeast Kalimantan), *Satuan Kenegaraan Kalimantan Timur* (State of East Kalimantan), *Satuan Kenegaraan Dayak Besar* (State of Greater Dayak), and *Satuan Kenegaraan Daerah Banjar* (State of Region of Banjar) (Table 6.5).

It was a Dutch scheme in the creation of a federal system, but it had subsequently failed. When the unitary state of RI came into being in 1950, the five so-called states were reduced to three provincial residencies of *Wilayah Karesidenan Kalimantan Barat* (Provincial Residency of West Kalimantan), *Wilayah Karesidenan Kalimantan Selatan* (Provincial Residency of South Kalimantan), and *Wilayah Karesidenan Kalimantan Timur* (Provincial Residency of East Kalimantan). It was unclear whether Banjarmasin in *Wilayah*

Table 6.5 Kalimantan: Genesis of the Division of Provinces and Districts

Authority/Legal Ruling	Hitherto Structure	New Structure
KALIMANTAN (ADMINISTRATION) I (1945–1946)		
Decision of *Panitia Persiapan Kemerdekaan Indonesia* (Preparatory Committee for Indonesian Independence), 19 August 1945	Kalimantan Province of Dutch East Indies (*Residentie Westerafdeeling van Borneo* [Residency of Western Division of Borneo] and *Residentie Zuider en Oostafdeeling van Borneo* [Residency of Eastern Division of Borneo]) (pre-1941); *Daerah Kaigun* (1941–1945) [District of Imperial Japanese Navy]; *Tentera Nasional Indonesia* (TNI) *Angkatan Laut* (1945–1946) [National Armed Forces of Indonesia Navy] Administrative Centre: Banjarmasin (?)	From 1946: *Satuan Kenegaraan Daerah Istimewa Kalimantan Barat* (State of Special Region of West Kalimantan); *Satuan Kenegaraan Kalimantan Tenggara* (State of Southeast Kalimantan); *Satuan Kenegaraan Kalimantan Timur* (State of East Kalimantan); *Satuan Kenegaraan Dayak Besar* (State of Greater Dayak); *Satuan Kenegaraan Daerah Banjar* (State of Region of Banjar) Administrative Centre: Banjarmasin
KALIMANTAN (ADMINISTRATION) II (1950–1953)		
Peraturan Pemerintah (PP, Government Regulation) *Republik Indonesia Serikat* (RIS, Republic of the United States of Indonesia) No. 21 1950 (formulated: 14 Aug 1950; announcement: 16 Aug 1950; implementation: 17 Aug 1950)	*Wilayah Karesidenan Kalimantan Barat* (Provincial Residency of West Kalimantan); *Wilayah Karesidenan Kalimantan Selatan* (Provincial Residency of South Kalimantan); *Wilayah Karesidenan Kalimantan Timur* (Provincial Residency of East Kalimantan) Administrative Centre: Banjarmasin (?)	From 1953: *Provinci Otonom Wilayah Karesidenan Kalimantan Barat* (Autonomous Provincial Residency of West Kalimantan); *Provinci Otonom Wilayah Karesidenan Kalimantan Selatan* (Autonomous Provincial Residency of South Kalimantan); *Provinci Otonom Wilayah Karesidenan Kalimantan Timur* (Autonomous Provincial Residency of East Kalimantan) Administrative Centre: Banjarmasin

KALIMANTAN (1953–1956) Undang-undang (UU, Laws) Darurat (Drt, Emergency) No. 2 Tahun (Year) 1953 (approved: 7 Jan 1953; gazetted: 13 Jan 1953; implementation: 7 Jan 1953); Dissolution with Undang-undang (UU, Laws) No. 25 Tahun (Year) 1956	*Wilayah Provinsi [Administratif]* Kalimantan (Provincial Region [Adminstrative] of Kalimantan) comprising the regions of: 1. *Karesidenan Kalimantan Barat* (Residency of West Kalimantan) 2. *Karesidenan Kalimantan Selatan* (Residency of South Kalimantan) 3. *Karesidenan Kalimantan Timur* (Residency of East Kalimantan) Administrative Centre: Banjarmasin	From 1956: *Provinsi Kalimantan Barat* [Province of West Kalimantan]; *Provinsi Kalimantan Selatan (dan Provinsi Kalimantan Tengah)* [Province of South Kalimantan (and Province of Central Kalimantan]; *Provinsi Kalimantan Timur* [Province of East Kalimantan] Administrative Centre: Banjarmasin
WEST KALIMANTAN PROVINCE (1956–present) UU No. 25 Tahun 1956 approved: 19 Nov 1956; gazetted: 7 Dec 1956); also, UU Drt No. 10 Tahun 1957 (confirmed as UU No. 21 Tahun 1958)	1. *Kabupaten* [District] Sambas; 2. *Kabupaten* [District] Pontianak; 3. Kabupaten [District] Ketapang; 4. *Kabupaten* [District] Sanggau; 5. *Kabupaten* [District] Sintang; 6. *Kabupaten* [District] Kapuas-Hulu; and, 8. *Kota Besar* Pontianak (as stated in UU Drt No. 3 Tahun 1953). Administrative Centre: Pontianak	Status quo: 1. *Kabupaten* [District] Sambas; 2. *Kabupaten* [District] Pontianak; 3. *Kabupaten* [District] Ketapang; 4. *Kabupaten* [District] Sanggau; 5. *Kabupaten* [District] Sintang; 6. *Kabupaten* [District] Kapuas-Hulu; and, 8. *Kota Besar* Pontianak Administrative Centre: Pontianak

(Continued)

Table 6.5 (Continued)

Authority/Legal Ruling	Hitherto Structure	New Structure
SOUTH KALIMANTAN PROVINCE (1956-present)		
UU No. 25 Tahun 1956 (approved: 19 Nov 1956; gazetted: 7 Dec 1956); also, UU Drt No. 10 Tahun 1957 (confirmed as UU No. 21 Tahun 1958); also, UU No. 27 Tahun 1959	1. *Kabupaten* [District] Banjar; 2. *Kabupaten* [District] Hulusungai-Selatan; 3. *Kabupaten* [District] Hulusungai-Utara; 4. *Kabupaten* [District] Barito; 5. *Kabupaten* [District] Kapuas; 6. *Kabupaten* [District] Kotawaringin; 7. *Kabupaten* [District] Kotabaru; and, 8. *Kota Besar* Banjarmasin (as stated in UU Drt No. 3 Tahun 1953). Administrative Centre: Banjarmasin	Status quo: 1. *Kabupaten* [District] Banjar; 2. *Kabupaten* [District] Hulusungai-Selatan; 3. *Kabupaten* [District] Hulusungai-Utara; 4. *Kabupaten* [District] Barito; 5. *Kabupaten* [District] Kapuas; 6. *Kabupaten* [District] Kotawaringin; 7. *Kabupaten* [District] Kotabaru; and, 8. *Kota Besar* Banjarmasin (as stated in UU Drt No. 3 Tahun 1953). Administrative Centre: Banjarmasin Part of territory appropriated to Central Kalimantan Province (1957–1958) as well as East Kalimantan Province.
CENTRAL KALIMANTAN PROVINCE (1957-present)		
UU Drt No. 10 Tahun 1957 (approved: 7 May 1957; gazetted: 23 May 1957); confirmed as UU No. 21 Tahun 1958 (approved: 17 June 1958; gazetted: 2 July 1958); also, UU No. 25 Tahun 1956	1. *Daerah Swatantra Tingkat II* Barito [Barito Tier II Autonomous Area]; 2. *Daerah Swatantra Tingkat II* Kapuas [Kapuas Tier II Autonomous Area]; 3. *Daerah Swatantra Tingkat II* Kotawaringin [Kotawaringin Tier II Autonomous Area] (as stated in UU Drt No. 3 Tahun 1953). Administrative Centre (albeit temporary): Banjarmasin	Status quo: 1. *Daerah Swatantra Tingkat II* Barito [Barito Tier II Autonomous Area]; 2. *Daerah Swatantra Tingkat II* Kapuas [Kapuas Tier II Autonomous Area]; 3. *Daerah Swatantra Tingkat II* Kotawaringin [Kotawaringin Tier II Autonomous Area] (as stated in UU Drt No. 3 Tahun 1953). Administrative Centre: Pahandut (1956); Palangkaraya (1957)

EAST KALIMANTAN PROVINCE (1956–present)

UU No. 25 Tahun 1956 (approved: 17 June 1958; gazetted: 2 July 1958; also, UU Drt No. 10 Tahun 1957 (confirmed as UU No. 21 Tahun 1958); also, UU No. 27 Tahun 1959; also, UU No. 20 Tahun 2012 (approved: 16 Nov 2012; gazetted: 17 July 2012)

1. *Daerah Istimewa* Kutai [Kutai Special Area]; 2. *Daerah Istimewa Berau* [Berau Special Area]; 3. *Daerah Istimewa* Bulongan [Bulongan Special Area] (as stated in UU Drt No. 3 Tahun 1953).

Administrative Centre: Samarinda

1. *Daerah Istimewa* Kutai [Kutai Special Area]; 2. *Daerah Istimewa Berau* [Berau Special Area]; 3. *Daerah Istimewa* Bulongan [Bulongan Special Area] (as stated in UU Drt No. 3 Tahun 1953); 4. *Daerah Swatantra Tingkat II* Pasir [Pasir Tier II Autonomous Area] (appropriated to South Kalimantan Province, 1959)

Administrative Centre: Samarinda

Part of territory appropriated to North Kalimantan Province.

Source: *Profil Propinsi Republik Indonesia – Kalimantan Tengah* [*Provincial Profile of the Republic of Indonesia – Central Kalimantan*] (Jakarta: Yayasan Bhakti Wawasan Nusantara, 1992), pp. 116–118; *Profil Propinsi Republik Indonesia – Kalimantan Selatan* [*Provincial Profile of the Republic of Indonesia – South Kalimantan*] (Jakarta: Yayasan Bhakti Wawasan Nusantara, 1992), pp. 135–136; *Profil Propinsi Republik Indonesia – Kalimantan Timur* [*Provincial Profile of the Republic of Indonesia – East Kalimantan*] (Jakarta: Yayasan Bhakti Wawasan Nusantara, 1992), pp. 134–135; *Profil Propinsi Republik Indonesia – Kalimantan Barat* [*Provincial Profile of the Republic of Indonesia – West Kalimantan*] (Jakarta: Yayasan Bhakti Wawasan Nusantara, 1992), pp. 000; Undang-Undang Darurat Nomor 2 Tahun 1953. Tentang: PEMBENTUKAN DAERAH OTONOM PROPINSI KALIMANTAN[www.hukumonline.com/pusatdata/detail/21733/node/964/undang-undang-darurat-no-2-tahun-1953-pembentukan-daerah-otonom-propinsi-kalimantan Accessed 19 June 2018]]

Karesidenan Kalimantan Selatan retained its status as Kalimantan's overall administrative centre.

Arguing for greater internal control over local administrative matters, three autonomous regions were then created from 1953, hence *Provinci Otonom Wilayah Karesidenan Kalimantan Barat* (Autonomous Provincial Residency of West Kalimantan), *Provinci Otonom Wilayah Karesidenan Kalimantan Selatan* (Autonomous Provincial Residency of South Kalimantan), and *Provinci Otonom Wilayah Karesidenan Kalimantan Timur* (Autonomous Provincial Residency of East Kalimantan). But between 1953 and 1956, autonomy was abrogated, and the three provinces were mere residencies by the provincial administrative centre based at Banjarmasin that conveyed directives from the central government at Jakarta. Thus, *Wilayah Karesidenan Kalimantan Barat* (Provincial Residency of West Kalimantan), *Wilayah Karesidenan Kalimantan Selatan* (Provincial Residency of South Kalimantan), and *Wilayah Karesidenan Kalimantan Timur* (Provincial Residency of East Kalimantan). Then from 1956, following the 1955 Parliamentary General Elections, full provincial status was reinstated, viz. *Provinsi Kalimantan Barat* (Province of West Kalimantan), *Provinsi Kalimantan Selatan dan Provinsi Kalimantan Tengah* (Province of South Kalimantan and Province of Central Kalimantan), and *Provinsi Kalimantan Timur* (Province of East Kalimantan).

Owing to the ascendancy of the Dayaks and their assertion of identity and demands for greater autonomy, *Provinsi Kalimantan Tengah* (Province of Central Kalimantan) was created in 1958, carved out from *Provinsi Kalimantan Selatan* (Province of South Kalimantan). The latter originally comprised *Kotawaringin*, *Dayak Besar* (Great Dayak), *Daerah Banjar* (Banjar Region), and *Federasi Kalimanatan Tenggara* (Federation of Southeast Kalimantan). Then in 1957, Pasir Regency, a part of *Federasi Kalimanatan Tenggara*, was transferred to *Provinsi Kalimantan Timur* (Province of East Kalimantan). *Kotawaringin* and *Dayak Besar* broke away to create *Provinsi Kalimantan Tengah*. By 1958, *Provinsi Kalimantan Selatan* comprised only *Daerah Banjar*. However, in 1959, *Daerah Swatantra Tingkat II Pasir* (Pasir Tier II Autonomous Area) of *Provinsi Kalimantan Timur* was appropriated to South Kalimantan Province.

Ascension of the Dayaks

The term *Dayak* or *Dyak*, also *Dayuh*, is the generic term attributed to the native inhabitants of Borneo that encompassed some 20 different ethnic groups clustered under three main groupings, specifically the Dusun and Murut that settled in the northern parts of the island, the Kenyah, Kayan, and Iban of the central areas, and the Ngaju in the southern regions.[47] Traditionally, the Dayaks' means of economic sustenance was through the practice of swidden or shifting agriculture of rice and root crops supplemented by hunting for game. Typically, Dayaks settled in the interior in the middle and upper reaches of rivers, living in communal multi-apartment longhouses, where each *bilek* (apartment) settled a two-generation nuclear family. They were animists by tradition, but as a result of proselytizing by

Western missionaries, some Dayaks had been converted to Christianity during the nineteenth century, and a handful embraced the Muslim faith in the middle and later part of the twentieth century. A sizeable number remained with the traditional beliefs termed *Kaharingan*.

Head-hunting was a traditional socio-cultural practice amongst Dayaks that served as markers of great warriors, hence as leaders and progenitors. Taking a human head was a vital pre-condition in terminating the period of mourning. Other impetus for this gory practice was a result of intra- and inter-ethnic conflicts, acquisition of material wealth, and territorial expansion. During colonial times, head-hunting was proscribed by the Brooke White Rajahs in Sarawak.[48] Dutch colonials too outlawed such traditional practices within their half of the island, but enforcement was at best problematic.

Although the Dayaks of the interior and upriver regions traditionally carried out trade with Banjar Malays on the coasts, there was strained relations and animosity between settlers of the hinterlands and coastal groups. At times, suspicions and mistrust marred relations between the two groups.

Dayak ascendancy in the post-war period was a result of wartime tragedies.[49] In a series of arrests, show trials, and mass executions, the actions of the Imperial Japanese Navy (IJN) literally almost eliminated the majority of West and South Borneo's elite, with the conspicuous exception of the Dayaks. The majority of the educated and propertied elite across ethnic groups, indigenous and Chinese, in Banjarmasin and Pontianak were implicated in a perceived anti-Japanese conspiracy. The *Tokkei Tai*, the Special Naval Police, in a series of pre-emptive measures wiped out the core leadership of the indigenous peoples and the Chinese. Thus, a leadership vacuum existed in the post-war period that opened opportune prospects for Dayaks to exploit.

Pre-war Dayak articulation of their identity and political interests was initially represented in the *Sarekat Dayak* (Dayak League) in 1919 based in Banjarmasin, and thereafter in the *Partai Persatuan Dayak* (Dayak Unity Party; hereinafter *Partai Dayak*) during the 1930s and 1940s. The colonial Dutch regime, however, took scant interest of Dayak organizations, political or otherwise. Likewise, the IJN too exhibited little interest in the Dayaks, where the majority lived in the interior regions. It was indeed a blessing as the Dayak elite alone survived unscathed from the IJN pogroms.

During the post-war tussle for power between the returned Dutch in reinstating their pre-war colonial rule and pro-Republican forces in Kalimantan equally determined to deny the Dutch and dissuade pro-Dutch elements from asserting political domination, the Dayaks were caught in the middle, facing a dilemma. It was a case not unlike the proverbial 'between the devil and the deep blue sea' scenario that the largely (economically, educationally) backward Dayak as an ethnic community faced.

It was unclear whether the delegation sent by the *Daerah Dajak Besar* Council to the republican capital of Jogjakarta in mid-1947 sought a constitution of their own, similar to what had been initialled for West Kalimantan, was rejected, denied, or simply ignored. But what was apparent was the dire circumstances the Dayaks found themselves in. For the Dayaks, their independence and ethnic survival were at stake. In the event that:

> Negara Kalimantan [State of Kalimantan] materialized, the Dayaks feared that they might be subsumed under the dominance of the coastal Malays. [At the same time] [d]espite seeking a constitution from the republican government in Java, the Dayaks were also apprehensive of the pro-republican groups in neighbouring Banjarmasin and Hulu Sungai that might also wish to assert control in the event of a republican ascendancy.[50]

Dayak disaffection and insecurity persisted following the establishment of the unitary state of *Republik Indonesia* on 17 August 1950 that subsequently led to them demanding the creation of their own province, namely Central Kalimantan Province (1958).

But even prior to August 1950, Sahari Andung, who hailed from a farming family from Tewah Pajangan, Kahayan, set up *Serikat Keharingan Dayak Indonesia* (SKDI, Union of Keharingan Dayaks of Indonesia) in July to demand for the Dayaks an autonomous region or province, detached from the South Kalimantan Province. It was hoped that this proposed 'Central Kalimantan Autonomous Province' would comprise *Kabupaten Barito*, *Kabupaten Kapuas*, and *dan Kabupaten Kotawaringin* hitherto part of the South Kalimantan Province. *Ikatan Keluarga Dayak* (IKAD, Dayak Communal League) initiated a move to appeal to the central government at Jakarta. The creation of a 'Central Kalimantan Autonomous Province' was one of the main points raised that gained traction amongst delegates at the SKDI Congress at Desa Bahu Palawa, 22–25 July 1953. This gathering of adherents of traditional Dayak *Kaharingan* sought an autonomous homeland to ensure the sustainability of the community's creed and belief system, ethnic identity, and way of life. But the central government dismissed the SKDI petition based on the premise that the regional economy was too weak, as well as that the local educated group was too small. Such a basis for rejection was challenged by the Dayaks.

To further encapsulate their demand, a *Panitia Penyalur Hasrat Rakyat Kalimantan Tengah* (PPHRKT, Central Kalimantan People's Appellate Committee) was set up in 1954 headed by Mahir Mahar, and drew support from PNI, *Partai Sosialis Indonesia* (PSI, Indonesia Socialist Party), *Partai Murba*, *Partai Rakyat Nasional* (PRN, National People's Party), *Persatuan Pemuda-Pemudi Kristen Indonesia* (PPPKI, Indonesia Christian Youth Association), and *Persatuan Suku Kalimantan Indonesia* (PERSUKAI, Indonesia Kalimantan Clan Association).

On 3 February 1954, the central government at Jakarta stipulated that Kalimantan was to have no more than three provinces – West Kalimantan, South Kalimantan, and East Kalimantan. In response, a meeting of PPHRKT on 17 April 1954 produced an agreement calling on Jakarta to enact a fourth province, namely *Provinsi Otonom Kalimantan Tengah* (Central Kalimantan Autonomous Province).

J. M. Nahan in a speech during a meeting between PPHRKT and Minister of the Interior Hazairin on 25 June 1954 in Banjarmasin presented the Dayak viewpoint:

> Central Kalimantan with a population of about 400,000 and an area of 158,828 square kilometres and renowned for the largest timber factory in Southeast Asia currently located in Kota Sampit with a 90 per cent capital owned by *Republik Indonesia* with the capacity of 400 m³ of daily output with customers from Africa, Australia, West Germany, and others. Generating income from gold, diamonds, coal, famous rattan, resin, rubber, jelutong [a specie of lightweight timber], candle, tengkawang [Borneo tallow nut], and others, and not including other incomes that remained concealed in the natural environment in the forest that presents potential in the future. Surely if East Kalimantan is entitled to become a province, then Central Kalimantan is also ENTITLED to be a province.[51]

In another statement by PPHRKT of 10 August 1955, the plea for *Provinsi Otonom Kalimantan Tengah* was articulated thus:

> In awarding provincial status for Central Kalimantan will raise the possibility and confidence and strengthen the trust of "the most afflicted groups in Kalimantan"; whereas the realization that their fate is given attention unlike in colonial times in accordance with national and our government's aspirations; whereas in their fate they are given great attention despite their great backwardness; whereas the national plan of our current government convinces us to believe that our demands are being given due consideration.[52]

Regardless of the appeals and lobbying by various groups, including representations by the *Partai Dayak* in the *Dewan Perwakilan Daerah Kalimantan Barat* (West Kalimantan Regional Representative Council),[53] it seemed that Dayak voices were muted, as shown by the action of the Jakarta central government. The second Ali Sastroamidjojo cabinet approved and ratified Law Number 25 of 1956 that sanctioned the creation of *Daerah Swatantra* (Self-governing Region) of West Kalimantan, South Kalimantan, and East Kalimantan that came into being on 1 January 1957. In the case of *Provinsi Otonom Kalimantan Tengah*, the central government alluded to its formation at the end of three years.

Undoubtedly the Dayak community was disheartened. It appeared that the diplomatic road and persuasive strategy had disappointingly failed. Amongst advocates for the establishment of a *Provinsi Otonom Kalimantan Tengah*, there were militant groups, *inter alia Gerakan Pembela Keadilan* (GPK, Movement for the Defence of Justice) and *Pasukan Sipet Kanyawung* (PSK, Kanyawung Blowpipe Squad) headed by Sikoer Patoes, and *Gerakan Mandau Talawang Panca Sila* (GMTPS, Pro Pancasila Cutlass and Shield Movement), that clashed with government security forces. GMTPS were uncompromising in its goals and militantly aggressive befitting its namesake. Members were drawn from Muslims, Christians,

Buddhists, and Kaharingan. Established in 1952, GMTPS claimed a 42,000-strong membership, accounting for some 10 per cent of Nagaju-speaking Dayaks.[54] The movement operated in three areas: a Kahayan-Kapuas sector under Sahari Andung (founder-leader of SKDI), a Barito section headed by Charles Simbar (Uria Mapas), and a Kotawaringin area led by William Embang. On 21 November 1953 in Buntok on the Barito river, GMTPS was involved in an armed clash resulting in several fatalities among government forces.[55]

Leaders and members of GMTPS subscribed to *jalan bahandang* or *jalan merah*, meaning advocating violence and/or war as the course of action. The latter term, *jalan merah*, literally and symbolically refers to a 'trail of blood'. The GMTPS will meet any opposition with violent action, "*tidak segan-segan membakar rumah, kantor instansi, dan membunuh orang yang dianggap tidak mendukung perjuangannya* [will not hesitate to burn houses, offices, and kill people who are considered not supportive of their struggle]".[56] Taking its cue from a November 1956 meeting in Tangkahen on the Kahayan River, GMTPS launched a series of raids and demonstrations in various sites, including Dayu, Tumbang, Samba, Kasongan, Masaran, and Tangkahen as well.

While the militant factions were perpetrating acts of violence against the government, PPHRKT organized *Kongres Rakyat Kalimantan Tengah* (Central Kalimantan Peoples' Congress) in Bajarmasin, 2–5 December 1956. A 600-strong delegation pledged their commitment to the aspiration of creating *Provinsi Otonom Kalimantan Tengah*, and passed a resolution (5 December) urging the Jakarta government as soon as possible before local elections (to provincial and regency and city councils) scheduled for mid-1957. The resolution was handed over to the then governor of Kalimantan, R. T. A. Milono.

Another outcome of the congress was the constitution of a *Dewan Rakyat Kalimantan Tengah* (DRKT, Central Kalimantan Peoples' Council). DRKT acted on behalf of the government in negotiating a series of peace talks throughout May 1957 with the militant GMTPS, viz. at Madara, Tehang (Sampit), Pahandut, and Dayu. Following the peace settlement at Madara, GMTPS was disbanded, and its members organized into *Barisan Pemuda Pembangunan Kalimantan Tengah* (BPPKT, Central Kalimantan Youth Front for Development). Members of the newly formed BPPKT were channelled to participate in *Panitia Penyelesaian Kekacauan Daerah* (PPKD, Regional Peace Resolution Committee).[57]

Following the peace settlements, the central government established *Kantor Persiapan Pembentukan Provinsi Kalimantan Tengah* (Preparatory Office for the Establishment of Central Kalimantan Province), headed by Milono as Governor of Central Kalimantan Province. A temporary office was based in Banjarmasin, where day-to-day workings were directed by Tjilik Riwut as Resident, assisted by G. Obos, and 25 supporting staff. This set-up was the most positive development to the realization of the Dayaks' aspiration of the creation of their own home province of Central Kalimantan.

Finally, the passing of *Undang-Undang Darurat No. 10 Tahun 1957* (UU Drt No. 10 Tahun 1957, Emergency Law No. 10 1957), that gained approval on 7 May 1957, and officially gazetted on 23 May 1957, brought forth *Daerah Swatantra*

Provinsi Kalimantan Tengah or Self-governing Region of Central Kalimantan Province, with Milono as provincial governor. Pahandut, later renamed as Palangka Raya, was designated as its administrative centre.[58]

Party politics and the vote

While it had been convincingly demonstrated in both electoral results of the DPR and the *Konstituante*, whereby the 'Big 4', viz. PNI, *Masyumi*, NU, and PKI, were the big winners at the nationwide-level, it was a different scenario at the electoral districts in Kalimantan (Table 6.6). The electoral outcome in West, South, and East Kalimantan was indeed interesting vis-à-vis the national results. PNI could only convincingly capture East Kalimantan; in both West and South Kalimantan, it only

Table 6.6 Results of Parliamentary and Constituent Assembly Elections according to Electoral Districts in Kalimantan, 29 September 1955 and 15 December 1955

Featuring political parties and organizations garnering more than 5,000 votes.

West Kalimantan

Political Parties	Parliamentary Vote	Constituent Assembly Vote
Masyumi	155,173	152,715
PD	146,054	157,490
PNI	64,195	74,123
NU	37,945	37,123
PSI	15,909	13,848
PKI	8,526	8,680
IPKI	7,289	5,993

PSII (3,030 / 1,863) and *Katolik* (2,505 / 2,259) obtained less than 5,000 votes.

South Kalimantan

Political Parties	Parliamentary Vote	Constituent Assembly Vote
NU	380,874	390,561
Masyumi	252,296	236,513
PNI	46,440	60,860
IPKI	19,383	13,997
PKI	17,210	20,092
PPTI	16,429	14,074
PD	11,641	11,732
Parkindo	10,642	13,221
PSII	6,717	4,916
PSI	5,307	4,664

Baperki (2,152 / 1,981) and *Katolik* (484 / Nil) obtained less than 5,000 votes.

Table 6.6 (Continued)

East Kalimantan

Political Parties	Parliamentary Vote	Constituent Assembly Vote
PNI	43,067	50,940
Masyumi	44,347	38,610
NU	20,793	24,304
PSI	13,029	12,008
PKI	8,209	8,762
PSII	7,401	5,521

Katolik (4,153 / 4,025) and PARKINDO (2, 585 / 4,223) obtained less than 5,000 votes.

NU *Nahdatul Ulama*; IPKI *Ikatan Pendukung Kemerdekaan Indonesia* (League of Supporters of Indonesian Independence); PKI *Partai Komunis Indonesia* (Indonesian Communist Party); PPTI *Partai Persatuan Tharikah Islam* (Islamic Tharikah Unity Party); PSII *Partai Sjarikat Islam Indonesia* (Indonesian Islamic Union Party); PSI *Partai Sosialis Indonesia* (Indonesian Socialist Party); PNI *Partai Nasional Indonesia* (Indonesian Nationalist Party); *Partai Persatuan Dayak* (PD, Dayak Unity Party); PARKINDO *Partai Kristen Indonesia* (Indonesian Christian Party); Katolik *Partai Katolik* (Catholic Party); *Baperki Badan Permusyawaratan Kewarganegaraan Indonesia* (Consultative Council on Indonesian Citizenship)

Source: Herbert Feith, *The Indonesian Elections of 1955* (Ithaca, NY: Cornell Southeast Asia Program 1957; 2nd printing 1971), pp. 69–70.

managed a third placing. *Partai Dayak, Ikatan Pendukung Kemerdekaan Indonesia* (IPKI, League of Supporters of Indonesian Independence), *Partai Persatuan Tharikah Islam* (PPTI, Islamic Tharikah Unity Party), and *Partai Sosialis Indonesia* (PSI, Indonesian Socialist Party) presented a relatively good performance.[59] On the other hand, *Partai Sjarikat Islam Indonesia* (PSII, Indonesian Islamic Union Party), PARKINDO (*Partai Kristen Indonesia*, Indonesian Christian Party) and *Partai Katolik* (Catholic Party), which were placed at fifth, sixth, and seventh respectively at the national level, had disappointing outings in Kalimantan.[60]

In West Kalimantan, although the big winner in the parliamentary vote was *Masyumi*, it was a mere 9,119 vote difference with the *Partai Dayak* as runner-up (Table 6.6). *Partai Dayak* even peaked *Masyumi* in the *Konstituante* vote, 157,490 to 152,715 (difference of 4,775). PNI and NU, however, performed fairly well in third and fourth placing, respectively. PKI, one of the 'Big 4' in the national line-up, was relegated to sixth placing in West Kalimantan. Meanwhile, PSII and *Partai Katolik* displayed a poor showing. Interesting to note, that while many Dayaks embraced Christianity, *Partai Katolik* that had enjoyed relatively good support nationwide failed to gain Dayak backing. Likewise, West Kalimantan, that had a sizeable Chinese population in the so-called Chinese Districts, would have given the socialists and communists much support. But the electoral results displayed a contrary picture: PSI and PKI lagged far behind PNI and NU. It might be a question of eligibility for the ballot box, for the greater part of the Chinese population were not regarded then as citizens.[61] Also, surprisingly, there was a no-show in

West Kalimantan of Baperki (*Badan Permusyawaratan Kewarganegaraan Indonesia*, Indonesian Citizenship Consultative Body), apparently the largest ethnic Chinese socio-political organization then.[62]

The scenario in South Kalimantan witnessed the electoral ascendency of the two Muslim-oriented parties – NU and *Masyumi* – clinching first and second place, respectively (Table 6.6). The outcome was predictable considering the region being traditionally coastal Malay Muslim and Banjar Malay Muslim enclaves. Both NU and *Masyumi* featured among the 'Big 4'. IPKI (*Ikatan Pendukung Kemerdekaan Indonesia*, League of Supporters of Indonesian Independence) trailed very far behind in third place but still outpaced PKI. *Partai Dayak* had some token support. Understandably, Baperki and *Partai Katolik* did not perform well in this indigenous Muslim region.

The electoral performance in East Kalimantan almost mirrored the national outcome, with the triumph of Sukarno's PNI, closely trailed by *Masyumi* and NU in third place (Table 6.6). PKI, the fourth runner in the nationwide stage, was here overtaken by PSI (*Partai Sosialis Indonesia*, Indonesian Socialist Party) by a wide margin of 4,820. PARKINDO and *Partai Katolik* both had poor outings.

The euphoria of the elections impregnated hopes among the populace of more political stability with the convening of the DPR and the *Konstituante*. But as was mentioned, within a short span of 18 months, consequent of a host of events and developments, the DPR was rendered impotent with the first of the extra-parliamentary establishment of the *Kabinet Karya* (Working or Business Cabinet) in April 1957.

Disaffection: the Ibnu Hadjar Rebellion (1950–1963)

For more than a decade, a group of ex-*pejuang* in South Kalimantan, who had fought the Dutch during the revolutionary period, waged a protracted guerrilla war against the central government at Jakarta. The armed opposition began in 1950 shortly following the round-table conference at The Hague (1949) that brought about Indonesian independence and the creation of RUSI. With high hopes and anxiousness, many armed revolutionaries who had risked their lives challenging the colonial Dutch forces (KNIL) applied for induction into the newly created *Angkatan Perang* RIS/RUSI (APRIS, Armed Forces of the Republic of the United States of Indonesia). Apparently, the ex-*pejuang* of South Kalimantan were turned down by APRIS,[63] owing to their illiteracy, which appeared to be unreasonable and unjustifiable against the context of the overall low literacy rate in Kalimantan during the pre-war and immediate post-war period.[64] Ex-guerrilla leaders also received the short end of the straw.[65]

In accordance to conclusions reached at The Hague round-table conference (1949), citizens of RIS/RUSI were eligible for recruitment into APRIS. Emergency Law No. 4/1950 (State Gazette No. 5/1950) provided the authority for the induction of citizens regardless of their past affiliation, whether they were ex-*pejuang*, ex-KNIL, or ex-NICA (*Nederlandsche Indische Civil Administratie* [Netherlands Indies Civil Administration]). RIS Vice-president/Prime Minister Mohammad

Hatta intended that the armed forces of the newly independent nation be a professional army modelled after Western examples. In this connection, the *Nederlands Militaire Missie* (NMM, Dutch Military Mission) was engaged to train APRIS.

Without doubt, Hatta's intention and the inclusiveness of recruitment were for the sake of professionalism and modernization based on the Western model. Imperial Japan during the last quarter of the nineteenth century undertook a similar practice in moulding its army after the *Wehrmacht* of Germany and its navy after the Royal Navy of Britain, both the foremost forces then.

But overlooked by policy makers was the psychological aspect of such a ruling. Ex-*pejuang* who had fought the KNIL and NICA during the revolutionary years were now expected to be brothers-in-arms with their former *enemy*. Besides, the ex-*pejuang* were also expected to undergo training under NMM officers, again their *enemy*. It was an unpalatable situation for many ex-*pejuang* who were absorbed into APRIS. Besides, when compared with ex-KNIL, ex-*pejuang* who were guerrilla fighters were generally outranked, hence occupied low-ranking positions, whereas their former *enemy* (ex-KNIL) held higher ranks such as troop commanders. Furthermore, with the arrival of military personnel from Java, local ex-*pejuang* and others felt that chances for military appointments were greatly compromised vis-à-vis the better educated newcomers.

Those who failed to be inducted into APRIS, as was the fate of many ex-*pejuang* in South Kalimantan, each were awarded severance pay of Rupiah (Rp.) 50 and a piece of cloth measuring 1.3 metres. Many felt a sense of injustice despite their sacrifices for the *Revolusi*.

Among the legion of disaffected was Ibnu Hadjar, a native of Hulu Sungai, who, during the struggle against the Dutch, had led bands of guerrillas in Kandangan and Hulu Sungai. He was a platoon commander of Hassan Basry's ALRI *Divisi IV* (A) that was active in South Kalimantan. Ibnu Hadjar held the rank of second lieutenant. Prior to his revolutionary days, he was a honey collector, hence was well-versed in the forest environment of his home district of Hulu Sungai that came as an invaluable asset during his years as a guerrilla commander in the jungle.

Consequently, the 30-year-old Ibnu Hadjar organized and led *Kesatuan Rakjat Jang Tertindas* (KRJT, Union of the Oppressed People) in 1950 with an initial membership of 50.[66] But following an assault of a military post in March 1950, the numbers in KRJT increased five-fold to 250. Having been a platoon commander, Ibnu Hadjar was unprepared to lead a guerrilla force of the aforesaid scale. Furthermore, the raid led to the seizure of only 50 firearms, which was wholly inadequate to equip a 250-strong force.

Understandably, the untenable situation led Ibnu Hadjar to take up the olive branch extended by the government in October 1950. He proceeded to Banjarmasin. However, he was treated in a patronizing manner by the local commandant and allowed to return to his base, tasked with persuading his followers to surrender. His reaction was to the contrary: he returned to the jungle, more determined than ever, and for the next 13 years conducted a guerrilla war against the Jakarta government.

Towards the close of 1954, Hadjar was offered a position, albeit a secondary appointment, in Kartosoewirjo's NII cabinet. He was to be a minister of state but without any specific portfolio, and also designated as *Panglima Angkatan Perang Tentera Islam* (Commander of the Islamic Armed Forces) of Kalimantan. The dangling of such 'carrots' convinced Hadjar and his KRJT to align with DI. Expectedly, the pursuit of the realization of a *Negara Islam* (an Islamic State) was the penultimate goal, but Hadjar's decision (to associate with DI) was not solely for Islam *per se*.

> Ibnu Hadjar's decision to join the Darul Islam movement was much more motivated by disappointment with the government policy towards former guerilla [sic.] armies rather than by the Islamic ideology. Nevertheless, Islam as a political identity was quite strong among the Banjarese, and therefore, Islamic ideology certainly attracted them.[67]

The aforesaid alignment with DI "amounted to nothing more than an Islamisation of Ibnu Hadjar's political rhetoric", and, in fact, "he carried out no substantial [Islamic] reforms in the territory he controlled".[68] There was clearly no declaration of any semblance of an Islamic State in South Kalimantan akin to the 'metropolitan' NII in West Java.

The protracted struggle took its toll. Over the decade, many aborted the struggle to surrender. The authorities alternated amnesties for surrender and concerted military offensives against the insurgents in the interior. By 1959, the military phase of the rebellion could be said to have concluded. It was, however, another three years before Hadjar finally surrendered to the authorities. Towards the end of July 1963, Hadjar and a small band of guerrillas formally laid down their weapons and surrendered at Ambutan, his birthplace in South Hulu Sungai. He was brought to Banjarmasin, and thence flown to Jakarta. Commissioner Tengku Abdul Aziz, Commander-in-Chief of Police, South Kalimantan, who was instrumental in engineering Hadjar's surrender, thus bringing to an end the more than a decade-old rebellion, worked towards securing an amnesty from President Sukarno. The outcome was to the contrary. On 11 March 1965, a military court sentenced Second Lieutenant Ibnu Hadjar to death.

Ibnu Hadjar's initial struggle in leading the disaffected people who felt that they were being 'wronged' and 'oppressed' was undoubtedly noble and moral. In allying with DI and fighting for a bigger cause, viz. the establishment of an Islamic state, it appeared that Hadjar had adopted the righteous struggle, although apparently it was not his intention. Nonetheless, armed rebellion through a protracted guerrilla war was neither the strategy nor the panacea. For his pains, he faced the firing squad in Jakarta.[69]

'Welcome to Kalimantan': *transmigrasi* policy

For past centuries as well as in the post-independent decades of the 1950s and 1960s, Indonesia possessed a conspicuously uneven geographical distribution of its large population. Mal-distribution was undoubtedly a bane, with the distinct

Table 6.7 Indonesia: Phenomena of Mal-distribution of Population, 1920–1971

Region	1920 % of total population	1930 % of total population	1961 % of total population	1971 % of total population	% of total area
Java	70.9	68.7	**64.9**	64.2	6.64
Sumatra	12.8	13.6	**16.2**	17.6	26.69
Kalimantan	3.3	3.6	**4.3**	4.4	27.17
Sulawesi	6.3	7.0	**7.3**	7.2	11.23
Other Islands	6.8	7.1	**7.3**	6.6	28.25

Bolded terms are the reference points.

Source: After CICRED Series, *The Population of Indonesia*, World Population Year 1974 (Paris: Committee for International Cooperation in National Research in Demography (CICRED), 1974), p. 40. www.cicred.org/Eng/Publications/pdf/c-c24.pdf Accessed 18 Aug 2018

disparity shown in Table 6.7. Drawing from statistics of 1961, it is obvious that Java had an issue with population: it possessed about 64.9 per cent of the nation's overall population but only occupied 6.64 per cent of the total land area. Conversely, Kalimantan's situation was the exact opposite: a mere 4.3 per cent of the total population with 27.17 per cent of the overall total land. Such disparity necessitated a solution in addressing the question of mal-distribution.

Owing to various reasons – historical, climate, soil type and fertility, land use – Java and Madura, despite their high population, were able to manage a large population, although barely surviving and likely to be unsustainable. Hence, the solution was to move people from overcrowded Java and Madura to sparsely populated territories such as Sumatra and Kalimantan in particular, and also Sulawesi and Maluku. This strategy was referred to as 'colonization' during the colonial Dutch era; the term adopted in the post-independent period was '*transmigrasi*' or 'transmigration'.

An effort to improve one's economic status (*read*: higher income) was the main motive of transmigrants embarking on the government-initiated transmigration programme. Other extenuating circumstances also pushed others to consider transmigration, viz. socio-cultural, political, and demographic pressure; the last mentioned was the stark reality of untenable overcrowding in some neighbourhoods. Nonetheless:

Transmigration . . . is a government program but it is not completely executed by the government [itself]. There is also specific transmigration, that is transmigration which is implemented in cooperation with projects, whether national, regional or private, and spontaneous transmigration which is financed by the individual and the destination is also determined by the individual. In 1964, as a consequence of inflation, a new self-help system of transmigration was instituted . . . [whereby] each family is provided [by the government] with facilities including two hectares of agricultural land and agricultural tools, but the transmigrants have to pay their own way.[70]

Table 6.8 Kalimantan: Transmigration according to Settlement Area, 1951–1972

Settlement Area	Number of Transmigrants outbound from Java	% of Total
Kalimantan Barat (West Kalimantan)	12,912	2.72
Kalimantan Selatan (South Kalimantan)	14,623	3.08
Kalimantan Tengah (Central Kalimantan)	8,006	1.69
Kalimantan Timur (East Kalimantan)	20,199	4.26
Kalimantan (overall)	55,740	11.77

Source: After CICRED Series, *The Population of Indonesia*, World Population Year 1974 (Paris: Committee for International Cooperation in National Research in Demography (CICRED), 1974), p. 47. www.cicred.org/Eng/Publications/pdf/c-c24.pdf Accessed 18 Aug 2018

Between 1951 and 1972, Kalimantan as a whole hosted 55,740, accounting for nearly 12 per cent of the total number of transmigrants (Table 6.8). East Kalimantan took the lead as the top destination, followed by South Kalimantan, West Kalimantan, and Central Kalimantan. Nevertheless, the top destination area during this two-decade span was Sumatra, accounting for 77 per cent of trans-migrants outbound from Java.[71]

Transmigrants faced a host of issues in their new environment, undoubtedly the worst was not being welcome by the native inhabitants. The latter often viewed the newcomers as competitors for local resources, employments, or opportunities. Such socio-economic rivalry, whether based on factual reality or mere perception, when coupled with socio-cultural traits (ethnicity, religious adherence, cultural norms, etc.) and political affiliation, might lead to open clashes. Dayak–Madurese ethnic violence flared up in Kalimantan during the latter part of the 1990s but had antecedents in the 1960s.[72]

The army and KODAM

Rebellion in the Outer Islands strengthened Nasution's and the Army's hand. Under his leadership and strategic military manoeuvres, Nasution succeeded in defeating rebellious colonels and winning over their rank-and-file to his fold. Insurgencies in the provinces further strengthened the Army's justification for the establishment of KODAM across the archipelago to ensure stability as well as to thwart any recalcitrant elements.

In the context of Kalimantan, KODAM's genesis was in the revolutionary *Batalyon Rahasia* ALRI (*Angkatan Laut Republik Indonesia*) *Divisi IV Pertahanan Kalimantan* (Covert Battalion ALRI [Naval Forces of the Republic of Indonesia] IV Division [A] Defence of Kalimantan).[73] Following the attainment of independence, ALRI *Divisi IV* became a single military unit styled *Divisi Lambung Mangkurat* (Lambung Mangkurat Division) with responsibility for the whole of Kalimantan. On 5 January 1950, a name change was made whereby *Divisi Lambung Mangkurat* was renamed *Teritorium Kalimantan* (Kalimantan [Military] Territory) comprising three Sub Teritorium, I, II, and III. Later, Sub Teritorium I, II, and III became Brigade G, F, and E, respectively. Then, on 20 July 1959, Nasution established *Komando Tentara Teritorium VI Tanjungpura* (Army Command Military Territory VI Tanjungpura) based at Banjarmasin.

The physical presence of *Tentera Nasional Indonesia* (TNI, National Armed Forces of Indonesia)[74] in practically every corner of the far-flung archipelago ensured two certainties. Firstly, in the eyes of the people, the Army, in particular, as the hero of the *Revolusi*, was on hand to protect and safeguard the nation from within and from without. Secondly, on the part of the Army, its presence on the ground would ensure that its interests were not compromised in any way by others, notably the communists. Nasution warranted the workings of *dwifungsi* would maximize the Army's leverage vis-à-vis all other quarters, the communists in particular.

In Kalimantan, homegrown communists or their sympathizers appeared not to be a threat. The electoral performance of the PKI had demonstrated that its influence among the populace was insignificant. Consequently, the predominance of *Masyumi* and *Partai Dayak* in West Kalimantan, NU and *Masyumi* in South Kalimantan, and PNI and *Masyumi* in East Kalimantan ensured the suppression of PKI in the region.

Setting up the Kalimantan stage

Although not moving at the pace of events and developments as at the central government in Jakarta and across Java, Kalimantan, for its part, was progressing forward. The Dayaks had shown their assertive nature in successfully lobbying for a region (and homeland) of their own, namely Central Kalimantan. Mirroring the national stage, parliamentary elections and elections to the *Konstituante* were executed without any untoward incidences. PNI, the leading party at the national level, only managed to clinch East Kalimantan, and in third placing in both West and South Kalimantan. The electoral outcome witnessed the ascendancy of Dayaks through the success garnered by the *Partai Dayak* in West Kalimantan. The Muslim NU and *Masyumi* performed commendably in the elections of 1955. The PKI, on the other hand, had made scant inroads in Kalimantan despite being one of the 'Big 4' on the national stage. An assortment of Republican *pejuang*, pro-Republican aristocrats, Dayaks, Malay, and Banjarese Muslims collectively formed a bulwark against the penetration of Marxist thoughts and communist ideology.

The end of the 1950s in Kalimantan witnessed the conclusion of the long-drawn Ibnu Hadjar Rebellion, consolidation of the Army at Banjarmasin with the set up of the *Komando Tentara Teritorium VI Tanjungpura*. For the greater part of the decade, Kalimantan had played the supporting role to the Jakarta protagonist. Admittedly, the Ibnu Hadjar Rebellion was a sideshow to the big-stage PRRI-PERMESTA. Unlike the latter that at one time received foreign support, the rebels in Kalimantan neither had support nor publicity from without; it was a domestic issue. Even within the DI struggle, Hadjar's uprising was secondary to the rebellion erupting across West Java, whereby NII was declared.

As Indonesia moved into Sukarno's Guided Democracy phase, in unprecedented fashion, the focus converged on Kalimantan. For once, the bipolar world took cognizance of this thickly forested territory where an assortment of unlikely groups out of expediency set up an armed alliance, trained and supported by TNI generals, politicized by PKI cadres, received more than moral support from Indonesia's Foreign Minister and Foreign Ministry, and the Beijing factor also came into the equation, not discounting Moscow's adept hand. Manila too claimed a role with its territorial claim of the northeastern portion of the island, North Borneo (later Sabah). Others – London, Washington, Canberra, Wellington – threw in their lot, making more than cameo appearances. Sukarno, the showman, was the main 'star' as the 1960s rolled out its play.

Notes

1 Although the armed struggle between Indonesians and the Dutch during the period 1945 to 1949 is often referred to as the 'Indonesian Revolution', the term is challenged by various quarters. During the period of Guided Democracy (1959–1965), Sukarno insisted that the *revolusi* had yet to end until the recovery of West New Guinea (Irian Barat; renamed Irian Jaya from 1963), as well as the complete transformation of the country's political, economic, and social spheres, arguing forcefully for a *continuing revolution*. The *Orde Baru* (New Order) regime (1966–1998), on the other hand, preferred the term '*perang kemerdekaan*' or 'war of independence' in referring to the 1945–1949 era in order to not only emphasize the significant role and contribution of the Army but also to dissuade belief that revolutions were acceptable phenomena. Some non-Indonesian scholars, on the other hand, considered 'revolution' as a misnomer as the transformations and changes consequent of the 1945–1949 period were not significantly adequate to justify the ushering of a 'new' social order as there were too many continuities that persisted. See Robert Cribb, *Historical Dictionary of Indonesia* (Metuchen, NJ and London: The Scarecrow Press, 1992), p. 405; Benedict R. O'G Anderson, *Java in a Time of Revolution: Occupation and Resistance, 1944–1946* (Ithaca, NY: Cornell University Press, 1972); Anthony J. S. Reid, *The Indonesian National Revolution, 1945–1950* (Hawthorn, VIC, Australia: Longmans, 1974).

2 Drawn from a host of sources, cited in Woodburn S. Kirby, *War Against Japan, Volume 5: The Surrender of Japan* (London: Her Majesty's Stationery Office, 1969), p. 258; *Overzicht Nederlandse Grevelden in Indonesie* [Overview Dutch Grieved/Deaths in Indonesia], Nov 10, 2013. www.1945-1950ubachsberg.nl/site/erevelden.htm Accessed 11 July 2018.

3 See section 'Disaffection: The Ibnu Hadjar Rebellion (1950–1963)'.

4 CICRED Series, *The Population of Indonesia*, World Population Year 1974 (Paris: Committee for International Cooperation in National Research in Demography (CICRED), 1974), p. 33. www.cicred.org/Eng/Publications/pdf/c-c24.pdf Accessed 18 Aug 2018.

5 For 1955 and 1961, the population growth rate was 2.14 per cent and 2.57 per cent, respectively. Worldometers: Indonesia Population. www.worldometers.info/world-population/indonesia-population/ Accessed 11 July 2018.

6 The Provisional Constitution of the Republic of Indonesia. Promulgated on 15th of Aug, 1950 (Act No. 7, 1950, Gazette No. 37, 1950). www.worldstatesmen.org/Indonesia-Constitution-1950.pdf Accessed 2 Aug 2018.

7 'Section V. Fundamental human rights and freedoms', ibid., pp. 373–375. See Universal Declaration of Human Rights. Proclaimed by the United Nations General Assembly in

Paris on Dec 10, 1948 (General Assembly resolution 217 A). www.un.org/en/universal-declaration-human-rights/ Accessed 2 Aug 2018.

8 See P. N. H. Simanjuntak, *Kabinet-Kabinet Republik Indonesia: Dari Awal Kemerdekaan Sampai Reformasi* [*Cabinets of the Republic of Indonesia: From Early Independence until Reformation*] (Jakarta: Djambatan, 2003), pp. 116–124.

9 See Ulf Sundhausen, "Indonesia", in *The Political Role of the Military: An International Handbook*, edited by Constantin P. Danopoulos and Cynthia A. Watson (Westport, CT: Greenwood Press, 1996), p. 192.

10 DPR, also referred to as the House of Representatives, together with the *Dewan Per-wakilan Daerah* (DPD, Regional Representative Council), comprises the legislative body termed, the *Majelis Permusyawaratan Rakyat* (MPR, People's Consultative Assembly).

11 Herbert Feith, *The Decline of Constitutional Democracy in Indonesia*, reprint ed. (Singapore: Equinox Publishing (Asia) Pte Ltd., 2009; first published in 1962 under the auspices of the Modern Indonesia Project, Southeast Asia Program, Cornell University), pp. 436–437.

12 See Kweku Ampiah, *The Political and Moral Imperatives of the Bandung Conference of 1955: The Reactions of the US, UK and Japan* (Folkestone, UK: Global Oriental, 2007); Christopher J. Lee, ed., *Making a World after Empire: The Bandung Moment and Its Political Afterlives* (Athens, OH: Ohio University Press, 2010); Jamie Mackie, *Bandung 1955: Non-Alignment and Afro-Asian Solidarity* (Singapore: Editions Didier Millet, 2005).

13 Referred to as Irian Barat to the Indonesians; later it was renamed Irian Jaya upon (re-)possession by Jakarta in 1963.

14 For the conference's long-term legacy, see Tan See Seng and Amitav Acharya, eds., *Bandung Revisited: The Legacy of the 1955 Asian-African Conference for International Order* (Singapore: National University of Singapore Press, 2008).

15 Follow-up conferences included the Afro-Asian People's Solidarity Conference in Cairo (1957) and the pivotal Belgrade Conference (1961) that led to the establishment of NAM.

16 *Suluh Indonesia*, 23 Jan 1956, quoted and translated and paraphrased in R. E. Elson, *The Idea of Indonesia: A History* (Cambridge: Cambridge University Press, 2008), p. 180.

17 Ibid. Emphasis added.

18 *Suluh Indonesia*, 3 Apr 1956, quoted and translated in Elson, *The Idea of Indonesia*, p. 180. The term *gotong-royong* refers to the traditional communal practice of working together or mutual cooperation for collective benefit, akin to farming communities like in *padi* (rice) cultivation. Also, written as *gotong-rojong*.

19 Sukarno lambasted politicians that while they bickered among themselves, "ignoring the needs and wishes, the hopes and disappointments of millions of [the Indonesian] people". *Suluh Indonesia*, 18 Jan 1957.

20 Greg Fealy, "'Rowing in a Typhoon': Nahdatul Ulama and the Decline of Parliamentary Democracy", in *Democracy in Indonesia, 1950s and 1990s*, edited by David Bourchier and John Legge (Clayton, VIC: Centre of Southeast Asian Studies, Monash University, 1994), p. 92.

21 *Suluh Indonesia*, 23 Feb 1957, quoted and translated in Elson, *The Idea of Indonesia*, p. 181. Emphasis added.

22 The 1945 Constitution, the nation's first constitution, *Undang-Undang Dasar Republik Indonesia 1945* (UUD 1945), was based on work undertaken by the wartime *Badan Penyelidik Usaha Persiapan Kemerdekaan Indonesia* (BPUPKI, Investigatory Body for Preparatory Work for Indonesian Independence) (March–August 1945), and *Pani-tia Persiapan Kemerdekaan Indonesia* (PPKI, Preparatory Committee for Indonesian Independence) (7–15 August, 1945). BPUPKI incorporated Sukarno's 1 June 1945 pronouncement of Pancasila when it drafted the constitution (10–17 July 1945).

Following the Sukarno-Hatta proclamation of independence on 17 August 1945, PPKI formally ratified the constitution, thereinafter as the 1945 Constitution or UUD.

23 For an analysis and evaluation of the *Konstituante*, see Adnan Buyung Nasution, *The Aspiration for Constitutional Government in Indonesia: A Socio-Legal Study of the Indonesian Konstituante, 1956–1959* (Jakarta: Pustaka Sinar Harapan, 1992).
24 Undang-Undang Dasar Republik Indonesia 1945; Konstitusi 1945 asli dan pertama (1999), kedua (2000), ketiga (2001) dan keempat (2002) amandemen. www.humanrights.asia/countries/indonesia/laws/uud1945 Accessed 26 July 2018.
25 Ibid.
26 Ibid.
27 Nicholas Tarling, *Britain and the West New Guinea Dispute, 1949–1962* (Lewiston, NY: Edwin Mellen Press, 2008).
28 Ibid., pp. 114–119.
29 Audrey Kahin, *Rebellion to Integration: West Sumatra and the Indonesian Polity, 1926–1998* (Amsterdam: Amsterdam University Press, 2014), pp. 204–205.
30 Ibid., p. 205.
31 Ibid., p. 210.
32 For PRRI, see Kenneth Conboy and James Morrison, *Feet to the Fire: CIA Covert Operations in Indonesia, 1957–1958* (Annapolis, MD: Naval Institute Press, 1999); Kahin, *Rebellion to Integration*; Audrey R. Kahin and George McTurnan Kahin, *Subversion as Foreign Policy: The Secret Eisenhower and Dulles Debacle in Indonesia* (Seattle and London: University of Washington Press, 1997).
33 For PERMESTA, see Barbara S. Harvey, *Permesta: Half a Rebellion* (Ithaca, NY: Cornell Modern Indonesia Project, 1977).
34 Kahin, *Rebellion to Integration*, p. 215.
35 Ibid., pp. 225–228.
36 See Conboy and Morrison, *Feet to the Fire*, pp. 100–162; Kahin and Kahin, *Subversion as Foreign Policy*, pp. 173, 180–182.
37 Conboy and Morrison, *Feet to the Fire*, pp. 132–133.
38 Dipa Nusantara Aidit but better known as D. N. Aidit, was born Ahmad Aidit.
39 Nugroho Notosusanto, ed., *Tercapainya Konsensus Nasional/1966–1969* [Achievement of a National Consensus/1966-1969] (Jakarta: Balai Pustaka, Cetakan Ketiga, 1985), p. 3.
40 In mid-1959, besides holding the presidency, Sukarno also assumed the premiership as well.
41 Robert Cribb, "Guided Democracy (*Demokrasi Terpimpin*): Indonesian Style of Governance", in *Southeast Asia: A Historical Encyclopedia from Angkor Wat to East Timor*, edited by Ooi Keat Gin (Santa Barbara, CA: ABC-Clio, 2004), I: 555.
42 Feith, *The Decline of Constitutional Democracy in Indonesia*, pp. 436–437.
43 Daniel S. Lev, *The Transition to Guided Democracy: Indonesian Politics 1957–1959* (Singapore: Equinox Publishing, 2009; first published in 1966 by Cornell Southeast Asia Program Publications), p. 113.
44 Cribb, *Historical Dictionary of Indonesia*, p. 133.
45 In more recent times, *Provinsi Kalimantan Utara* (North Kalimantan Province) was created in 2012 by drawing territories from East Kalimantan Province, mainly appropriating *Daerah Istimewa Bulongan* (Bulongan Special Area). It comprised Kabupaten (District) Bulungan, Kota Tarakan, Kabupaten (District) Nunukan, Kabupaten (District] Malinau), and Kabupaten (District) Tana Tidung. Tanung Selor serves as its administrative centre.
46 'Kalimantan Province of Dutch East Indies' was the lesser used term referring to the Dutch-controlled portion of Borneo, namely the western, southern, and eastern portion of the island.
47 For detailed information on the various Dayak groups, distribution, language, and salient characteristics, see Tjilik Riwut, *Kalimantan Membangun* [*Kalimantan Rises*] (Jakarta: P. T. Jayakarta Agung, 1979), pp. 212–241.

48 Ooi Keat Gin, *Of Free Trade and Native Interests: The Brookes and the Economic Development of Sarawak, 1841–1941* (Kuala Lumpur: Oxford University Press, 1997), pp. 22, 35–36.

49 See Ooi Keat Gin, *The Japanese Occupation of Borneo, 1941–1945* (London: Routledge, 2011), pp. 102–117.

50 Ooi Keat Gin, *Post-War Borneo, 1945–1950: Nationalism, Empire and, State-Building* (London and New York: Routledge, 2013), pp. 132–133. In fact, the Dayaks were desperate to the extent of willing to establish some form of relations with the Netherlands if they failed to attain autonomous status in the proposed *Negara Kalimantan*. For instance, see David Wehl, *The Birth of Indonesia* (London: George Allen & Unwin, 1948), p. 366, n. 504.

51 Cited in Tjilik Riwut, *Kalimantan Memanggil* [*Kalimantan Calls*] (Jakarta: Penerbit Endang, 1958), p. 118. Translation by present author.

52 Cited in ibid., p. 109.

53 *Partai Dayak* managed to secure 33.1 per cent of the votes in West Kalimantan, attaining 9 out of 29 seats in the *Dewan Perwakilan Daerah Kalimantan Barat*, second only to Masyumi.

54 Anne Schiller, *Small Sacrifices: Religious Change and Cultural Identity among the Ngaju of Indonesia* (New York: Oxford University Press, 1997), p. 137.

55 Ibid. Also, see *45 Tahun Kiprah dan Pengabdian DPRD* (*Dewan Perwakilan Rakyat Daerah*) *Kalteng* (*Kalimantan Tengah*) [*45 Years of Progress and Service of Central Kalimantan DPRD* (*Regional People's Representative Council*)] (Jakarta: Penerbit Indomedia, 2004), p. 14.

56 P. M. Laksono et al., *Pergulatan Identitas Dayak dan Indonesia: Belajar dari Tjilik Riwut* [*Identity Struggle of the Dayaks and Indonesia: Learning from Tjilik Riwut*] (Yogyakarta: Percetakan Galangpress, 2006), p. 53.

57 Ibid., p. 54.

58 For details relating to the choice of Pahandut (Palangka Raya), see ibid., pp. 57–62.

59 See Herbert Feith, *The Indonesian Elections of 1955* (Ithaca, NY: Cornell Southeast Asia Program 1957), p. 65.

60 Ibid.

61 See Leo Suryadinata, *Elections and Politics in Indonesia* (Singapore: Institute of Southeast Asian Studies, 2002), p. 133.

62 For the electoral performance of Baperki, see ibid., pp. 132–134.

63 Following the declaration of the unitary state of the *Republik Indonesia*, APRIS had a name change to *Tentera Nasional Indonesia* (TNI, National Armed Forces of Indonesia).

64 In Kalimantan, a mere 9.61 per cent of males were able to read and write (considered as literate) in 1930; three decades later, in 1961, nearly 40 per cent were literate. Most of the ex-*pejuang* fall into the illiterate category of 60 per cent. CICRED Series, *The Population of Indonesia*, p. 33.

65 Instead of being offered a position of rank, the leader of ALRI *Divisi IV* (A) Brigadir Jenderal Hassan Basry was shipped off to Cairo to pursue studies at al-Azhar University and also at the American University. Undoubtedly, he was being marginalized in favour of newly arrived Republicans from Java. See Mujiburrahman, "Historical Dynamics of Inter-Religious Relations in South Kalimantan", *Journal of Indonesian Islam*, 11, 1 (June 2017), p. 158.

66 For the Ibnu Hadjar rebellion, see Muhammad Iqbal, "Kesatuan Rakjat yang Tertindas (KRjT): Pemberontakan Ibnu Hadjar di Kalimantan Selatan 1950–1963 [Union of the Oppressed People (KRjT): Ibnu Hadjar Rebellion in South Kalimantan 1950-1963]", MA thesis, Department of History, University of Indonesia, Indonesia, 2014; C. van Dijk, *Rebellions under the Banner of Islam: The Darul Islam in Indonesia* (Leiden: Koninklijk Instituut voor Taal-, Land- en Volkenkunde, KITLV, Royal Netherlands Institute of Southeast Asian and Caribbean Studies, 1981).

67 Mujiburrahman, "Historical Dynamics of Inter-Religious Relations in South Kalimantan", p. 158.

68 Remy Madinier, *Islam and Politics in Indonesia: The Masyumi Party between Democracy and Integralism*, trans. Jeremy Desmon (Singapore: National University of Singapore Press, 2015), p. 159.

69 Commissioner Aziz rendered his resignation upon hearing the verdict. See Petrik Matanasi, "*Kekecewaan Ibnu Hadjar, Sang Pemberontak* [The Disillusionment of Ibnu Hadjar, the Rebel]". https://tirto.id/kekecewaan-ibnu-hadjar-sang-pemberontak-cpMj Accessed 8 Aug 2018. Also, see Petrik Matanasi, *Para Jagoan: Dari Ken Arok sampai Kusni Kasdut [The Heroes: From Ken Arok to Kusni Kasdut]* (Yogyakarta: Trompet Book, 2011), pp. 66–73. In the past decade, there were efforts on the part of revisionist writers to rehabilitate the 'rebel' label of Ibnu Hadjar citing the malice of the central government towards this regional personality. For instance, see Wajidi [Amberi], "Ibnu Hadjar dan Stigma Pemberontak [Ibnu Hadjar and the Rebel Stigma]", 14 Jan 2012. https://bubuhanbanjar.wordpress.com/2012/01/14/ibnu-hadjar-dan-stigma-pemberontak/ Accessed 20 Aug 2018.

70 CICRED Series, *The Population of Indonesia*, p. 47.

71 Ibid. Also, see Dietrich Kebschull, *Transmigration in Indonesia: An Empirical Analysis of Motivation, Expectations and Experiences* (Piscataway, NJ: Transaction Publishers, 1986); J. Hardjono, "The Indonesian Transmigration Program in Historical Perspective", *International Migration*, 26 (1989): 427–439.

72 See Nancy Lee Peluso, "A Political Ecology of Violence and Territory in West Kalimantan", *Asia Pacific Viewpoints*, 49, 1 (Apr 2008): 48–67; Jamie S. Davidson, "The Politics of Violence on an Indonesian Periphery", *South East Asia Research*, 11, 1 (Mar 2003): 59–89.

73 While ALRI *Divisi IV* (A) headquartered in Hulu Sungai had its field of guerrilla operation in South Kalimantan against the Dutch, ALRI *Divisi IV* (B) covered West Kalimantan, and ALRI *Divisi IV* (C), East Kalimantan. Ooi, *Post-War Borneo*, p. 134.

74 TNI comprised the Army (*Angkatan Darat*), the Navy (*Angkatan Laut*), and the Air Force (*Angkatan Udara*). Then, in 1962, owing to the cumbersome and decentralized character, President Sukarno created *Angkatan Bersenjata Republik Indonesia* (ABRI, Armed Forces of the Republic of Indonesia) that combined TNI and the police (*Polisi Negara*, or *Angkatan Kepolisian*) as an overarching security central body. Ironically, until the establishment of *Orde Baru* (New Order), ABRI had little control or influence over the various armed services. Instead, it was Sukarno's intention to play one against the other, balancing them off, he, as the main arbiter of power, the consummate *dalang* (puppeteer). ABRI was put in place as a means of neutralizing and subsequently eliminating the increasingly powerful head of the Army, Nasution, once a Sukarno ally vis-à-vis the PKI. See Nugruho Notosusanto, *The National Struggle and the Armed Forces in Indonesia* (Jakarta: Centre for Armed Forces History, Department of Defence and Security, 1975), pp. 152–153.

7 Igniting Borneo

*The great smash and grab that failed [referring to the Brunei Rebellion] . . . the
knowledge of the millions he [A. M. Azahari] could make if he could capture the
country [Sultanate of Brunei] and set up a government.*

Alex Josey, journalist, *The Straits Times*, 21 January 1963

The plot thickens as the early 1960s commenced optimistically with new beginnings
from Kuala Lumpur's and London's standpoint with the public announcement by independent Malaya's Prime Minister Tunku Abdul Rahman (hereinafter as the Tunku)[1] of
a proposal for a wider federation. The concept of 'Malaysia', a larger federation to
encompass the hitherto independent Malaya together with the British Crown Colonies
of Singapore, Sarawak, and North Borneo, and the British protectorate of the Sultanate
of Brunei mooted by the Tunku on 27 May 1961 in Singapore triggered a chain of
events and developments that within four years and five months stood witness to the
start in the early morning hours of 1 October 1965 of one of Southeast Asia's most
horrific carnages of the twentieth century. The Tunku's suggestion of creating a new
political entity sent reverberations across the region: Singapore, Kuala Lumpur, Kuching, Jesselton, Brunei Town, Jakarta, and Manila, as well as beyond to London, The
Hague, Washington, Moscow, Beijing, Canberra, and Wellington.

The Tunku's public announcement of the 'Malaysia' proposal was made against
a heightening of tensions among the main Cold War players, namely the U.S. and
USSR. The year 1961 had its share of eventful happenings on the world stage. Moscow successfully detonated (October) 'Tsar Bomba', also dubbed the 'Kuzkina mat'
or 'Big Ivan', over the Novaya Zemlya island in the Arctic. Reputedly the largest
and most powerful weapon ever created, the accomplished test literally sent shivers
amongst the political elite as well as people-in-the-street in the West. The Soviet
Union's technological prowess had earlier been demonstrated when in April, *Vostok
1* was launched with a human passenger, Yuri Alekseyevich Gagarin, who became
the first man in space. The space race had begun between the Cold War's main rivals.
Shortly thereafter, in early May, Alan Shepard on the *Freedom 7* became the first
American in space. Newly inaugurated (January) 44-year-old President John F. Kennedy, the 35th President of the United States, and the youngest to hold the presidency, immediately urged Congress to allocate USD $531 million to put a man on

the moon by the end of the 1960s, an ambitious call indeed.[2] In April, the notoriously disastrous failed attempt to unseat Fidel Castro of Cuba, known as the Bay of Pigs, embarrassed Kennedy and the White House.[3] Meanwhile, in Europe, in mid-August, a new phenomenon was emerging: foundations for the soon-to-be notorious Berlin Wall had begun. The year 1961 was not the most auspicious of times.

Borneo was an eyewitness to a series of stupendous developments, from accusations and (political) quarrels over the airwaves and print media across the region, between Jakarta and Kuala Lumpur, Manila and Kuala Lumpur, a so-called rebellion in Brunei, fugitive groups fleeing from Sarawak and Brunei across the Sarawak-Kalimantan border, thereby creating an uneasy congregation of groups sharing the common ground of opposition to Malaysia on the Kalimantan side of the border that proved to be inconvenient bedfellows, and the waging of a low-key war called *Konfrontasi* (1963–1966).

Tunku's 'Malaysia'

The Tunku's 27 May 1961 speech on the idea of 'Malaysia' was made on the occasion of the Conference of Foreign Journalists' Association of Southeast Asia at the Adelphi Hotel in Singapore.[4] The British colonials were duly concerned about the increasing Leftist wave then engulfing Singapore and Sarawak. Several Leftist-instigated disturbances had broken out in Singapore in the past five years, notably the Anti-National Service Riots (May 1954), whereby Chinese school students demonstrated in opposition to the National Service proposal; the Hock Lee bus riots (May 1955); and Chinese middle schools riots (October 1956) as a reaction to the government's proscription of the Singapore Women's Association (SWA), the Chinese Musical Gong Society, and the Singapore Chinese Middle School Students Union (SCMSSU).[5] Similarly, in Sarawak, the stealth involvement of communist agitators was behind the Chung Hwa Middle School's strike actions (October 1951 and March 1955), the Batu Kitang Incident (February 1952), suspected infiltration of Leftist elements in labour and trade unions, and the increasing influence of Left-wing Chinese-medium Sarawak-based and -oriented newspapers promoting anti-imperial and anti-colonial editorials and viewpoints, the suspected 'united front' tactic utilized by Leftists working within the *bona fide* political organization of the Sarawak United Peoples' Party (SUPP).[6]

Malaya, on the other hand, had just concluded containing a 12-year insurgency by the Malayan Communist Party (MCP) in 1960, and was understandably apprehensive of developments in neighbouring Singapore and Sarawak. Hence, a merger with Singapore, the British impressed upon the Tunku, could arrest the Leftist wave. But the Tunku was hesitant that the self-governed island (full self-government attained in June 1959[7]), that had a predominantly Chinese population, might not be agreeable to his Malay colleagues within his political party, the United Malays National Organization (UMNO). At *Merdeka* (Independence) in 1957, the ethnic breakdown in Malaya is shown in Table 7.1. Statistically, if non-Malays combined, they slightly edged Malays. Hence, with the populations of Malaya and Singapore combined (Tables 7.1 and 7.2), a cursory glance

Table 7.1 Ethnic Breakdown of Population of Malaya in 1957

	Malay	Chinese	Indian	Others	Total Population
1957	3,125,474	2,333,756	696,186	123,342	6,278,758
% of total population	49.77	37.16	11.08	1.96	±100

Source: H. Fell, *1957 Population Census of the Federation of Malaya*, Report No. 14 (Kuala Lumpur: Department of Statistics, Federation of Malaya, 1960), pp. 1, 12, 51–52.

Table 7.2 Ethnic Breakdown of Population of Singapore in 1957

	Malay	Chinese	Indian	Others*	Total Population
1957	197,059	1,090,596	124,084	34,190	1,445,929
% of total population	13.62	75.42	8.58	2.36	±100

* Include Europeans, Eurasians, Cafres (from Malagasy), Siamese, Parsis, Jews.

Source: Lim Peng Han, "The History of an Emerging Multilingual Public Library System and the Role of Mobile Libraries in Postcolonial Singapore, 1956–1991", *Malaysian Journal of Library & Information Science*, 15, 2 (Aug 2010): 85–108.

shows that the Chinese (3.4 million) outnumbered the Malays (3.3 million), an untenable scenario indeed. When taken into account the population of 1960 (Table 4.1), Sarawak's, North Borneo's, and Brunei's native populations were 507,252 (68%),[8] 306,498 (67%), and 59,203 (71%), respectively, and collectively numbered 872,953 compared to 355,491 Chinese inhabitants from the three territories. Therefore, the native inhabitants of Sarawak, Brunei, and North Borneo could offset the ethnic demography of the new federation in favour of indigenes.

Besides addressing the Leftist element, Britain's decolonization process could also be settled when its remaining three crown colonies and a protectorate could in a single stroke merge with Malaya into a larger and wider federation of 'Malaysia'. From the Cold War geopolitical standpoint, 'Malaysia' would have command of the southern portion of the South China Sea, and the all-important East-West maritime route of the Straits of Melaka[9] would continue to be friendly with Britain and remain within the Western camp. If Britain's three Borneo territories and Singapore were to fall into communist's hands, regardless of whether Moscow's or Beijing's, independent Malaya would find itself surrounded by Leftist and unfriendly neighbours, a disastrous scenario considering the developments on mainland Indochina.

The French had been defeated by the communist Việt Minh at Dien Bien Phu (1954), which brought a close to its colonial regime and an end to the First Indochina War (1946–1954). In 1960, the ongoing Second Indochina War or the Vietnam War (1955–1975) was escalating with greater U.S. commitment of ground personnel (mainly acting as military advisors) under the Military Assistance Advisory Group (MAAG) programme, from less than a thousand in 1959 to 16,000 within four years.[10] U.S. President Kennedy was determined that Vietnam and

Indochina do not fall into communist hands like the colossus to the north, Red China (People's Republic of China, PRC).

British Prime Minister Winston Churchill (1940–1945, 1951–1955) and American President Franklin Delano Roosevelt (1933–1945) differed in their opinions as to the shaping of the post-war world in the event of the defeat of the fascist regimes in Nazi Germany, Italy, and Imperial Japan. Roosevelt's 'Grand Design' envisaged "the post-war world must see the former colonies developed economically with American System methods and technology".[11] By "American System methods and technology", he meant that the founding principles of the U.S. Republic that 'all men are created equal, with certain inalienable rights' and economic development and modernization through the utilization of technology be adopted following the unshackling of the colonial yoke. But the empire-builder Churchill was steadfast in upholding his imperial design, namely in maintaining and strengthening the pre-war *status quo* of empire and colonial possessions whereby post-war endeavours should focuss on recolonization, the reinstatement of colonial rule inclusive of its associated oppression and imposed backwardness in the political, economic, and social realms. On 10 November 1942, Prime Minister Churchill at the Lord Mayor's luncheon at the Mansion House delivered a speech on Britain's victory in Egypt:

> We have not entered this war for profit or expansion. Let me, however, make this clear: we mean to hold our own. (Cheers.) *I have not become the King's First Minister in order to preside over the liquidation of the British Empire.* (Cheers.)[12]

Meanwhile, adamant in reasserting their colonial power, the Dutch harboured the conviction of the "manifest incompetence of the Indonesians to rule themselves".[13] Such a conviction expounded by the Dutch was undoubtedly shared by other Western colonialists, viz. the French, Belgians, Portuguese, Spanish, as well as the British among some mandarins in the Colonial Office, and to a much lesser extent, the Americans.

This *British colonial worldview* was to dominate the post-war geopolitical scenario following the sudden demise of Roosevelt on 12 April 1945. Succeeding U.S. presidents, Harry S. Truman (1945–1953) and Dwight D. Eisenhower (1953–1961), were persuaded and/or manipulated into endorsing, supporting, and implementing Churchill's British colonial worldview.[14] However, President John F. Kennedy (1961–1963), an enemy of both Western imperialism and colonialism as well as both Soviet- and Chinese-sponsored subversion and terrorism, favoured the 'Spirit of Bandung' (Inaugural Asia-Africa Conference, Bandung, Indonesia, 1955) and the Non-Aligned Movement (NAM, 1961):

> the core of NAM member nations were dedicated to the New International Economic Order, based on peace between the East and West as well as North and South, and global collaboration to industrialize the sovereign nations in the South. John F. Kennedy believed such collaboration was both *possible and necessary.*[15]

Kennedy, in fact, possessed a good rapport with Sukarno, who he invited to visit shortly after his inauguration. The U.S. president's supportive attitude was translated in three concrete ways, viz. sending an American team of economists to study Indonesia's needs whereby their report proposed significant development aid that the White House agreed to provide; secondly, Robert Kennedy (1961–1964), the U.S. Attorney General and brother of the president, embarked on a special mission to Indonesia and the Netherlands whereby he succeeded in convincing the Dutch to hand over West/Dutch New Guinea to Jakarta; and thirdly, presidential endorsement was given to the Maphilindo concept.

Maphilindo, an acronym comprising *Ma*laya, the *Phil*ippines, and *Indo*nesia, was originally envisaged by Filipino national hero Dr José Rizal (1861–1896) of the unity of the ethnic Malay peoples that had been separated by American, Dutch, and British colonial boundaries, namely U.S. Philippines, Dutch Indonesia, and British Malaya. The realization of Maphilindo envisaged the coming together of all the lands and peoples of Malay descent and heritage.[16] Post-independent Philippine President Diosdado Macapagal too favoured such a concept.

But Maphilindo would jeopardize British geopolitical strategy in Southeast Asia, namely the economic powerhouse of Malaya and the strategic and trading base of Singapore. By then, the former had attained independence (1957) but the latter remained a British colony. A Malaya-Singapore merger, Malaysia, though an independent sovereign nation, would still be within the British sphere of political, military, and economic influence and control. Independent Malaya's economy, based on the production and export of primary commodities of tin and rubber, were largely owned, managed, and dictated by London-based firms and agency houses.[17]

Therefore, Maphilindo had to be blocked. In playing the communist bogeyman card, the pro-British Singapore Chief Minister Lee Kuan Yew succeeded in convincing the staunchly anti-communist Tunku to agree to merger. But the Tunku had reservations as his wholly ethnic Malay-dominated United Malays National Organization (UMNO) would not agree to such a merger with Chinese-dominated Singapore. An influx into the proposed wider federation by ethnic Chinese who were generally ahead socioeconomically and educationally vis-à-vis Malays would certainly be unpalatable to the rank-and-file of the UMNO. The British Borneo colonies of Sarawak and North Borneo, and the protectorate of the Brunei sultanate, all populated by indigenous peoples regarded as part of the Malay ethnic family, to be incorporated as components of Malaysia might be the appropriate panacea. The ethnic demographic equation – Malay and other indigenes to offset the ethnic Chinese deluge of Singapore – appeared to be the winning hand for the realization of Malaysia.

Perceptive Sukarno saw through the British guise of subterfuge of Maphilindo through the Malaysia scheme. Sukarno was not an enemy of Malaya, nor against the formation of Malaysia, but he adamantly opposed what he labelled as a 'neo-colonialist' plan of the British, namely sustaining its power and influence in the region through Malaysia. Hence, this 'neo-colonialist' plan should be overturned through a policy of '*Konfrontasi*' or 'confrontation'.

Notwithstanding British attempts at derailing the realization of Maphilindo, July 1963 witnessed the penning of the Manila Declaration by the Tunku, Macapagal, and Sukarno. It appeared to be a peaceful solution to the formation of Malaysia. But prior to Malaysia, the views of the inhabitants of Sarawak, Brunei, and North Borneo needed to be ascertained, and the best way was through a UN-conducted opinion survey. All parties, including Sukarno, agreed to abide by the UN verdict.

UN Secretary General U Thant (1961–1971) agreed to the task with a time-frame of completion by mid-September 1963. All seemed calm with the UN time-table. But for whatever justifiable reason other than to derail the 'peaceful solution' to the formation of Malaysia, Whitehall instructed British Minister of Commonwealth Relations Duncan Sandys, and again, Lee Kuan Yew, to pressure the Tunku "to agree to an announcement in August [1963] that the merger [to form Malaysia] would proceed with or without a satisfactory result of U Thant's survey [of public opinion]".[18] It remained uncertain as to the reasons behind the British action, other than to hasten the formation of Malaysia, but the repercussions were certainly clear: Sukarno was livid and subsequently launched '*Konfrontasi*', and Macapagal proceeded with the territorial claim over North Borneo (Sabah). U Thant and the UN appeared 'irrelevant' and impotent at the twist of developments.

Regardless, Kennedy maintained his support for Sukarno. But in November, Kennedy was assassinated in Dallas, Texas. Thereafter, when U.S. aid to Jakarta was accompanied by 'conditions', Sukarno angrily rebuked, "To hell with your aid". From then onwards, Sukarno increasingly turned towards the East, to Beijing specifically.

Wooing the four maidens

For the fruition of 'Malaysia', the Tunku had to persuade and convince the political leadership of Singapore, namely Prime Minister Lee Kuan Yew,[19] the British colonial governors of Sarawak (Sir Anthony Foster Abell) and North Borneo (William Allmond Codrington Goode), and the ruler of Brunei (Sultan Omar Ali) and the British Resident of Brunei (Sir Dennis Charles White) that merger with independent Malaya was their best option in unshackling colonial rule from Britain. 'Malaysia', from Whitehall's viewpoint, was intended as a bulwark against the communist wind then prevailing across the region, viz. Vietnam (Viet Cong), Indonesia (PKI), the Philippines (Hukbalahap), and the British colonial possessions, in particular, Singapore and Sarawak. Malaya, under the Tunku's leadership, had confidently ended the so-called Emergency in 1960, a communist insurgency that had been fought since 1948 at various levels and fronts, psychological warfare to direct military operations to the campaign of 'winning hearts and minds'. The latter strategy proved the most viable, whereby the populace rejected the communist terrorists and communism as an ideology.[20] Having both faith and confidence in the anti-communist Tunku to helm 'Malaysia', the mandarins at the Foreign Office (FO) and Colonial Office (CO) gave their full backing for the wider federation proposal.

Having attained internal self-government for Singapore in 1959, Prime Minister Lee Kuan Yew's next agenda was *obtaining full independence* from Britain. Merger with Malaya was a rational and logical move considering the shared historical background of both territories. Undeniably, most families in Singapore, whether Chinese, Malay, Indian, Eurasian, or others, possessed familial ties across the Causeway, and vice versa for those in Malaya. Rapport between Singapore and Johor, the southernmost state of Malaya, before and during the colonial period, had been close. The former components of the Straits Settlements – Penang and Melaka – had historical ties with Singapore, a fellow component until 1948; the former two territories in that year became a part of the Federation of Malaya while Singapore remained a British crown colony.

Merger with Malaya and others might provide greater resources in addressing the Leftist threat then sweeping across island Singapore. Timely action on the part of the party leadership to expel communists or sympathizers within Lee's ruling People's Action Party (PAP) saved the ruling party from subversion from within. The *Barisan Sosialis* (Socialist Front) that comprised Leftist elements who were ousted from Lee's PAP embarked on its agenda of subversion that ultimately aimed at the seizure of power. In anticipation of eliminating the communist menace, Lee favoured the Tunku's 'Malaysia' proposal.

Furthermore, while the Tunku, as mentioned, saw ethnic demography in the short-term, Lee took the *longue durée* perspective:

> My theme in the last forum [themed "Merger & Malaysia"] was the absolute necessity of racial harmony and peace and co-operation between the communities, if we are going to make a reasonably happy society. I want to take that theme one step further and say to you tonight, with facts and figures, that merger and Malaysia will make that more likely. Let me explain the obvious.
>
> Today, in the Federation, with more than 50% of the population Malays, it is theoretically possible and practically possible for any single party to rely only on Malay votes and win power. That you know as a fact. With Singapore 70% Chinese, the opposite holds true – that you can make your appeal completely to one section of the community and win power to the utter disregard of the other sectors.
>
> My theme to you is this, that with merger and Malaysia, the whole complexion undergoes a subtle but a vital change. Over a period of five, 10, 15 years, and with every year it will become more and more marked as everybody is local-born and no longer an immigrant, *he or the party that desires to assume power by the democratic process, must win the support of more than one community.* To rely on one community alone, it is impossible to assume power.[21]

Meanwhile, in British Borneo, the colonial governors of Sarawak and North Borneo, and the British resident of Brunei favoured a closer union among their three territories.[22] A step in that direction had already been put in place, namely the fact that Sarawak's colonial governor was acting as high commissioner of Brunei, unlike in the past whereby the colonial governor at Singapore was officiating in that capacity. The proximity of the three northern Bornean territories to re-configure as a single political entity was not only a logical conclusion but also presented a common-sense approach in containing the heightened Leftist activities then engulfing Sarawak, especially within its Chinese community. It was to this end that local British officials were deliberating and working for such an eventuality.

The ruler of Brunei, Sultan Omar Ali, was initially keen on 'Malaysia'. To be united with his brethren of the Malayan peninsula was an opportunity for the ascendancy of the Malays. The Anglophile, anti-communist Tunku was, to a certain extent, not too dissimilar from Sultan Omar Ali. Nonetheless, there were concerns and reservations. Firstly, the oil wealth of the sultanate would have to be shared with other component states within the proposed wider federation. Understandably, Sultan Omar Ali was not exactly keen on such a prospect as the wealth accrued from the oil and petroleum industry had given him financial independence as well as a major bargaining chip in Anglo-Brunei relations and negotiations. Secondly, Sultan Omar Ali would merely be *one among ten Malay monarchs* in the new federation. Comfortable on his throne as the absolute ruler who not only reigned but also ruled over his kingdom, sharing the royal spotlight with nine other rulers might not be palatable. Furthermore, his fellow Malay rulers were constitutional monarchs, who commanded moral and religious authority, not executive and legislative power, unlike his royal person.

Deep down, Sultan Omar Ali quite likely harboured anti-'Malaysia' feelings for the aforementioned reasons. Publicly, however, at best he appeared ambivalent on the issue, and he showed himself neither affirmative nor dismissive of the idea. Instead, he turned to his subjects for a decision on the proposed merger. On 10 August 1962, he voiced his opinion in a diplomatic vein to members of the Legislative Council:

> One aspect of the ['Malaysia'] proposal which interests me most is the close cooperation and relationship which existed between my Government and those of the Federation of Malaya, Singapore and the Borneo territories. . . . The recent proposal was put forward by Tunku Abdul Rahman, the Prime Minister of Malaya in the form of closer ties between the Federation of Malaya, Singapore, North Borneo and Brunei, the plan for the formation of Melayu Raya. . . . The proposal was well received by the British Government. . . . In my opinion, *it's an interesting proposal since there was already a common and strong bond of religion, race, custom and culture among the countries mentioned in the proposal.*[23]

Thereafter, the Brunei Commission Committee on the Malaysia Proposal was established on 16 January 1962, headed by the then Menteri Besar Dato Marsal bin Maun.[24] Intriguingly, out of the five members of the Committee appointed by the throne, none expressed any pro-'Malaysia' sentiment. A. M. Azahari, the Brunei Malay representative, was a known dissenting voice, and likewise the chairman, Dato Marsal bin Maun, and other members, Orang Kaya Gimang anak Perait (Iban representative), Orang Kaya Lukan bin Uking (Dusun representative), Pehin Bendahari China, and Mr Hong Kok Tien (representative of the Chinese community), were all not in favour of merger. It appeared that Sultan Omar Ali wanted a non-affirmative outcome to the 'Malaysia' proposal. Nonetheless, delegates were sent to participate in the Malaysia Solidarity Consultative Committee (MSCC).[25] Events, subsequently, were to overtake Sultan Omar Ali's hesitation and understandable reservations.

From the Tunku's vantage from Kuala Lumpur, Sarawak and North Borneo posed a non-issue in the proposed merger as the colonial governors would have to adhere to the priorities set by the CO, FO, and ultimately, Whitehall's call. Local leaders among the Ibans, Malays, and other indigenes of Sarawak might need some coaxing for their agreement to 'Malaysia'. Likewise, a similar situation existed in North Borneo with the Kadazandusun and other native leadership. Singapore, however, appeared to be the most amicable and agreeable to 'Malaysia'. The communist challenge and threat was, without a doubt, a *real* threat. Sultan Omar Ali of Brunei, however, comparatively was the most problematic to persuade and convince. Brunei then did not face any Leftist threat, and it was unlikely to face one in the foreseeable future. Wealth from oil and petroleum seemed sustainable. Sultan Omar Ali also appeared comfortable and contented with the *status quo* with a British adviser and British pledge of security from third-party aggression. Hence, there was little bargaining leverage on the part of the Tunku in convincing the Brunei monarch that merger with 'Malaysia' would accrue advantages either to him personally or to his kingdom. It was, indeed, a tough call and a challenge for the Malayan premier.

Dissenting voices

The Tunku's 'Malaysia' proposal sent ripples across the region: from Singapore across the South China Sea to Kuching, Brunei Town, and Jesselton through the Visayas to Manila. In the southeast, Jakarta was severely distraught. There were dissenting voices from various quarters.

Others, indeed, did not view 'Malaysia' in a favourable light, and in fact, some quarters vehemently opposed its creation. The far Left in Sarawak, the SCO, that looked to Beijing for inspiration, guidance, and support, strongly rejected the proposed wider federation. Instead, Sarawak, according to the SCO, should prioritize seeking full independence from Britain. To the SCO, the establishment of a communist republic of Sarawak in the Beijing mould was the ultimate goal, hence the communists preferred independence from Britain and discounted any other alternatives. Once colonial rule had been unshackled, a communist takeover would be the next step, either through SUPP via the constitutional path of the ballot box or, if circumstances necessitated, through an armed seizure of power. The realization of 'Malaysia' represented a stumbling obstacle, whereby a federal government at Kuala Lumpur would assert its control and influence, thereby dispelling any possibility of a communist ascendency in Sarawak. Moreover, a Malay-dominated administration was unlikely to favour a Chinese-based SUPP, what's more a pre-dominantly Chinese communist organization such as the SCO. Besides, with the anti-communist Tunku at the helm of 'Malaysia', the extermination of the com-munists in Sarawak was both imminent and inevitable. Therefore, from the SCO's standpoint, 'Malaysia' had to be subverted at all costs for its (SCO's) very survival.

Working through the bona fide political party of SUPP with its moderate leader-ship, the camouflaged communists within the party's organization persuaded and convinced non-communist members to reject 'Malaysia' and, in turn, strive for securing independence from Britain. In placating SUPP members, the communists argued that following attaining independence, then SUPP and Sarawak could con-sider other options, including merger with 'Malaysia'. The SUPP moderates, Presi-dent Ong Kee Hui and Secretary-General Stephen Yong Kuet Tze, played into the SCO's 'independence-from-Britain-first' agenda, literally both were played into the latter's covert scheme.

The United National Kadazan Organization (UNKO), led by the Eurasian, Don-ald Stephens, also favoured the 'independence-from-Britain-first' strategy, and thereafter, to consider other alternatives, viz. a federation-style closer union of the three north Borneo territories of Sarawak, Brunei, and North Borneo, or the Tunku's 'Malaysia' proposal. To a certain extent, Stephens and his fellow Kada-zans felt that independence from Britain should be prioritized rather than joining some form of federation scheme. Once North Borneo untied its colonial shackles, then UNKO and others could ponder the future of their state. Being a component of 'Malaysia' would mean 'control' from a faraway central federal government at Kuala Lumpur, which was not too dissimilar in negating North Borneo's indepen-dence. Hence, Stephens and UNKO initially adopted an 'independence-from-Britain-first' stance like their counterpart SUPP in Sarawak. Later, Stephens was to reverse his stance.[26]

Meanwhile, in Brunei, Sultan Omar Ali, as mentioned previously, was person-ally partial to 'Malaysia', but he wholly dismissed the closer union scheme whereby Brunei joined Sarawak and North Borneo for a federation of northern Bornean territories. To Sultan Omar Ali, it was demeaning to even equate a sov-ereign and independent state of Brunei, though a British protectorate, with two British crown colonies. 'Malaysia', in fact, was more palatable was the ruler's initial response. But his '*rakyat*' had other opinions.

Azahari and his PRB strongly opposed 'Malaysia'. Instead, Azahari harboured a grander vision for the sultanate. He intended to resurrect the past glory of the sultanate of a bygone age, circa fifteenth and sixteenth centuries, whence Brunei was the preeminent power in the region. The Brunei sultanate then oversaw an imperial realm that encompassed the entire island of Borneo as far south as Ban-jarmasin and as far north as Manila and Luzon. Borneo and the greater part of the Philippines were then under the sway of Brunei's rulers. But more realistic and pragmatic, Azahari, in the late 1950s and early 1960s, demanded a restoration to Brunei of territories of northern Borneo, principally Sarawak and North Borneo that during the course of the second half of the nineteenth century were partitioned and annexed in creating colonial territories by the Brookes and the British North Borneo Chartered Company (BNBCC). Britain, which had assumed the aforesaid two territories in the post-war period, should rightly return them to Brunei, their original overlord. Azahari envisioned the establishment of a *Negarabagian Kesatuan Kalimantan Utara* (NKKU, Unitary State of North Kalimantan) comprising Brunei, Sarawak, and North Borneo.

Having legitimately won representations to the Legislative Council, the PRB submitted three motions at the August assembly's inaugural sitting on 5 December 1962: (1) rejecting the 'Malaysia' proposal, (2) requesting Britain to restore to Brunei its former territories of Sarawak and North Borneo, and (3) urging Britain to establish the federation of the three territories of Sarawak, Brunei, and North Borneo "under the Unitary State of Kalimantan Utara with Sultan Omar Ali Saifuddin III as its constitutional and parliamentary Head of State and the granting of complete and absolute Independence to this new State not later than 1963".[27]

But the speaker responded that it was beyond the purview and jurisdiction of the Legislative Council to consider all three motions put forth by the PRB. Azahari took this as a rebuff, in other words, evidently a failure of pursuing his agenda through constitutional means. Therefore, it necessitated alternative action.

In the meantime, in Jakarta, President Sukarno sensed the 'hidden hand' of Britain in the 'Malaysia' proposal. Labelling the wider federation as a 'neo-colony', Sukarno accused London of perpetuating its influence over the region notwithstanding its decolonization. British 'Malaysia' was considered a challenge to *Republik Indonesia* and to Sukarno, who was rightly the predominant power in the archipelago. Therefore, Jakarta unequivocally opposed Kuala Lumpur's agenda of creating a wider federation seen as a 'usurper', an attempt to 'usurp' Indonesia as the major power in the region. Sukarno openly regarded the Tunku as a British stooge, a puppet, who colluded in perpetuating Britain's influence and power in the region. Stern measures, therefore, were needed to be taken to ensure that 'Malaysia' would not be 'born'.

President Diosdado Macapagal (t. 1961–1965) of the Philippines registered disagreement to Tunku's 'Malaysia' plan in staking a claim over North Borneo that was regarded as a part of his country's territorial realm. The fact that Baron Gustav von Overbeck, in 1878, had to negotiate with the Sulu court for the territorial rights over what subsequently became North Borneo clearly demonstrated the fact that the latter was a territory belonging to the Philippines when it attained independence from the U.S. in 1946 where the Sultanate of Sulu was incorporated into the Republic of the Philippines. Consequently, therefore, North Borneo should be reinstated to the Philippines and should not merge or be part of the proposed wider federation of 'Malaysia'. That was the stance that Manila had reasoned. This 'Sabah Claim',[28] as this territorial reinstatement came to be known, remained unresolved to the present and had since marred Kuala Lumpur–Manila relations.

Thus far, a war of words appeared to be the only means utilized among detractors to the 'Malaysia' proposal. Undoubtedly the exchanges between Jakarta and Kuala Lumpur, between Sukarno and the Tunku, with accusations and counter-accusations, were the most attractive with colourful language to effect. While harsh and demeaning words as well as name-calling were exchanged on a daily basis – entertaining fodder for the print media and air waves (radio), on either side of the Straits of Melaka – there were concerns of an escalation beyond mere words. But the first action came not from Jakarta, Kuala Lumpur, Kuching, or Manila, but surprisingly, from traditionally peaceful and serene Brunei Town.

The spark

The 'order of battle' was set. On one side of the divide was the pro-'Malaysia' camp, those that supported the Tunku's proposal for a wider federation, which comprised the Lee-led self-governing Singapore, the colonial governors of Sarawak and Brunei, and Sultan Omar Ali of Brunei. In opposition to the advocates were the detractors, notably the SCO-infiltrated SUPP, Stephen's UNKO, and Azahari's PRB. Further afield were Sukarno's denouncement of the proposed scheme and Macapagal's statement of claim over North Borneo (Sabah).

Azahari's coup d'état, the so-called Brunei Rebellion

In December 1962, nationalists in Brunei, the hugely wealthy small kingdom on the North Coast of Borneo, formed the Army of North Kalimantan (TNKU) and, demanding greater democracy, engineered a rebellion against the Sultan and seized a large number of hostages. Perceived to be an attempt by communists to destabilize the Sultanate and seize power, within twelve hours of its outbreak, British forces were dispatched by ship and aircraft from Singapore to restore order, the first unit to arrive being 1/2nd Gurkhas, who entered the capital [Brunei Town]. Within the week, the 1st Queens Own Highlanders had recaptured the strategically important oil fields and occupied Seria, 42 Commando, Royal Marines attacked Limbang and 1st Green Jackets landed in west Brunei. The next six months were spent rounding up TNKU and, since there were major concerns that Indonesia could be behind the Revolt, the charismatic Major General Walter Walker, then commanding 17th Gurkha Division, was sent to Brunei to command operations. By mid-May 1963, the surviving TNKU had been captured. While rapidly suppressed, the Revolt was the catalyst for the three year Confrontation with Indonesia 1963–66.[29]

In a nutshell, that sums the whole episode of the so-called Brunei Revolt, as Nick van der Brijl, author of one of the most recent works, preferred to call it rather than the 'Brunei Rebellion'. Originally planned for Christmas Eve 1962, a misstep forced the PRB to launch a series of concerted armed action two weeks earlier on 8 December. Azahari and Zaini Ahmad,[30] one of the vice presidents of PRB, were in Manila when the PRB executed its armed action across the sultanate and neighbouring territories of Sarawak and North Borneo. Surprisingly, while members of the PRB armed wing, *Tentera Nasional Kalimantan Utara* (TNKU, Northern Borneo National Army), held sway over most parts of the sultanate, Brunei Town remained in government hands including the palace, and the all-important telecommunications (telephone and telegraph) centre and networks, the radio station as well as the airport. Such a phenomenon says a lot of PRB/TNKU planning and strategy that appeared seemingly ad hoc, clumsy, and even hesitant.

TNKU's tenuous hold on the kingdom was, however, short-lived, for within a week, the government managed to wrest back the state. Swift action by Sultan Omar Ali, who invoked the Anglo-Brunei Treaty (1959), called for British military assistance, which saw the arrival from Singapore contingents of British military units in the likes of Gurkhas, Royal Marines, Green Jackets, and Queen's Own Highlanders. Upon landing, British forces fanned out throughout the kingdom, recapturing the main towns and regaining control of the sultanate. On the day of the outbreak, when the sultan made his distress call for assistance, police from North Borneo were hastily rushed to secure Brunei Town.

On 12 December, with the presence of British military units on the ground, a state of emergency was proclaimed.[31] An emergency council presided over by the sultan and assisted by the British high commissioner administered the sultanate through decrees. The Legislative Council and all District Councils were suspended. The PRB was proscribed. It was not until the detention of Yassin Affandy,[32] PRB secretary-general and general officer commanding TNKU, at his *kampung* in Serdang, on 18 May 1963, that the so-called rebellion was officially concluded.

The actions of the PRB, executed by lightly armed uniformed members of TNKU, were unprecedented happenings in peaceful Brunei. It was wholly unexpected and literally caught many by surprise. It seemed that Special Branch, through its intelligence-gathering network in Sarawak and Brunei, claimed knowledge of the impending PRB revolt, "even its approximate timing", but for sceptical senior administrators, both in Kuching and Brunei Town, who took such intelligence lightly, there were scant preparations to meet such an eventuality.[33]

The outbreak of armed hostilities occurred when Azahari was abroad. If not for his failure to secure a U.S. visa, Azahari was scheduled to travel together with SUPP Secretary-General Stephen Yong to New York to present a PRB-SUPP joint opposition to 'Malaysia' to the United Nations Decolonization Committee. Fate appeared to have intervened as the SUPP delegation was held back at Kuching airport on 7 December when one of its delegates from Miri was delayed. The entire delegation failed to proceed to Manila the following day (8 December) when hostilities broke out.

Interestingly, whilst Azahari and his SUPP colleagues were embarking to present their joint opposition to 'Malaysia', PRB-TNKU had made preparations for armed hostilities for 24 December. But what exactly did Azahari have in mind? While pleading a case against 'Malaysia' with the UN, his colleagues would wrest power in Brunei through force of arms, undoubtedly to fulfil his vision of establishing NKKU. Was this his premeditated inauguration of NKKU through violent means in the wake of the Speaker's rebuff merely three days ago?[34]

However, the chance discovery by the Sarawak police in Lawas, the northernmost district bordering with Brunei, of two military training camps with 35 TNKU uniforms, and the detention of ten people, pushed PRB to act lest the detainees reveal the planned agenda. Hence, the plan for action was hurriedly brought forward to 8 December.

Although the action of the TNKU appeared to be a rebellious act, hence a *rebellion* ('an act of armed resistance to an established government or leader'), it was interesting to note that Azahari's NKKU envisaged Sultan Omar Ali as its head of state, and Azahari as prime minister. Therefore, when Sultan Omar Ali made a radio broadcast denouncing the outbreak, many PRB-TNKU personnel surrendered as they thought that they were fighting on the sultan's behalf, or in his name, against the colonial British presence. It became apparent that there was confusion and/or misunderstanding among members of PRB-TNKU as to their role and the goals that they were supposedly pursuing. Therefore, were members of PRB-TNKU rightly labelled 'rebels' and Azahari the 'arch rebel'? Or was Azahari a reformist, intending to reform the sultanate through force of arms since constitutional means that were attempted had failed.

The outbreak apparently was "[p]erceived to be *an attempt by communists to destabilize the Sultanate and seize power*" might be the justification that Sultan Omar Ali seized upon in his call for military assistance, invoking the newly penned Anglo-Brunei Treaty of 1959. Against the backdrop of the Cold War, the bogeyman was the communists, a profanity within colonial circles, from London to Singapore, Kuching to Jesselton. Signalling this 'red' alert undoubtedly activated a swift response from colonial authorities. But labelling Azahari and the PRB to be 'communists' seemed to be rather an underhanded tactic of the sultan and appeared to be a desperate measure. Nonetheless, it served the purpose of the throne, in that Azahari and his cohorts in the PRB, seen as a threat, an alternative to the monarchy, were swiftly removed with the assistance of British military forces.

Whether the hostile outbreak in early December 1962 in Brunei was a rebellion, a communist plot for armed takeover, or otherwise, it was the 'spark' that literally ignited Borneo. Events in Brunei set off a chain of reactions and concomitant developments. The British colonial authorities in neighbouring Sarawak and North Borneo launched a swift campaign of eliminating all subversive elements, particularly targeting the Chinese community where the SCO thrived. The cleansing literally denuded the membership of SUPP, whereby communists were uncovered at every level of the party hierarchy and in every branch.[35] Disappointed with such infiltration, Ibans and other native members of SUPP, who did not subscribe to this foreign ideology, dissociated themselves from the party.

The government witch-hunt forced many hard-core SCO members to flee across the border to Kalimantan seeking sanctuary. Hundreds of Chinese youths, male and female, negotiated the tropical jungle and endured hardships for their ideological commitment to settle on the Kalimantan side of the border. In camps, manned by the *Tentera Nasional Indonesia* (TNI, National Armed Forces of Indonesia),[36] SCO members met up with PRB-TNKU fugitives. The young men and women from Sarawak and Brunei subjected themselves to military training by Army instructors. Liew Min Jaw, a farmer from Bau who joined the SCO, recalled the training at Serikin astride the border with Kalimantan: "The intensive training included swimming, tree climbing, blind-folded assembly, disassembly of guns and TNT explosive handling".[37]

Moral and material support were provided by the Indonesian host, especially *Partai Komunis Indonesia* (PKI, Indonesian Communist Party) cadres. Hence, in the hot and humid, mosquito-infested tropical rain forest of West Kalimantan in particular, anti-'Malaysia' elements congregated, undertook military training, ideologically fortified by PKI cadres, and prepared themselves physically and ideologically to cross over to their respective homeland for the ultimate struggle, viz. the 'Communist Republic of Sarawak' for SCO adherents and NKKU for PRB-TNKU members.

Despite being military trainers for the aforesaid 'guests', the Army was distrustful of them, especially the SCO members. Likewise, the Army was equally suspicious of PKI intentions and agenda. Although the generals took instructions from Jakarta, they were cautious of the political tide and generally assumed a 'wait-and-see' attitude.

Following the clampdown in Brunei and neighbouring Sarawak and North Borneo, on 20 January 1963, Indonesian Foreign Minister Dr Subandrio proclaimed the adoption of a policy of *Konfrontasi* (Confrontation) towards 'Malaysia', in line with President Sukarno's hostility towards the concept of a wider federation.[38] In this context, activities on the Kalimantan side of the border with Sarawak was consistent with Jakarta's policy, regardless of whether TNI generals and officers were apprehensive and/or uneasy of their 'guests', as well as having to work alongside PKI cadres.

In order to assuage the escalation of tension or outright hostilities, there were intermittent attempts at resolving the standoff among Kuala Lumpur, Jakarta, and Manila. All diplomatic efforts, however, were inconclusive failures.

Earlier in May 1963, Sukarno and the Tunku met up in Tokyo for talks. The Tunku agreed that a referendum would be held in the three territories – Sarawak, Brunei, and North Borneo – prior to the formation of 'Malaysia'. In turn, Sukarno pledged that he would not oppose the new federation if the peoples of northern Borneo supported it. Despite this mutual understanding, the Tunku proceeded to sign the London Agreement on 9 July 1963, whereby the Federation of Malaysia would be formed on 31 August 1963 that would comprise Malaya, Singapore, North Borneo, and Sarawak. As a result, a livid Sukarno announced a '*Ganyang Malaysia*' or 'Crush Malaysia' campaign on 27 July 1963 that further intensified the ongoing *Konfrontasi*.

Following the penning of the Malaysia Agreement (9 July 1963), further talks were held to attain a sort of political understanding among the estranged parties, notably Malaya, Indonesia, and the Philippines. Thus, between 30 July and 5 August 1963, acting on the invitation of Philippine President Macapagal, a three-way meeting was held in Manila with invitees Malayan Prime Minister Tunku and Indonesian President Sukarno. The agenda was to address issues over the wishes of the inhabitants of Sarawak and North Borneo relating to 'Malaysia' through a referendum in accordance with the United Nations General Assembly Resolution 1541 (XV), Principle 9 of the Annex. Initially, on 30 July, Maphilindo – *Ma*laya, *Phil*ippines, *Indo*nesia – a loose consultative body tasked to resolve mutual issues, was constituted, an attempt at bringing the three leaders in closer rapport to one another. Then on 31 July 1963, all three parties penned the Manila Accord. The Tunku, in affixing his signature, agreed that the Philippine's claim over Sabah remained relevant despite the creation of the Federation of Malaysia on 16 September 1963.

Sukarno's Konfrontasi

> Kuala Lumpur, Monday. Tengku Abdul Rahman said tonight that the speech by Indonesian Foreign Minister, Dr. Subandrio, in Jogjakarta yesterday [20 January 1963], was a "direct attack" against Malaya. Dr. Subandrio had said the Indonesian Government was adopting a policy of "confrontation" towards Malaya, which he claimed, was "neo-colonialist" and "neo-imperialist" hostile to Indonesia. . . . "It is regrettable that we have to adopt such a policy against our neighbour, which we always regarded as a friend and brother", he said.[39]

Although Dr Subandrio regarded 'Malaysia' as unacceptable and described Indonesia's policy as one of '*konfrontasi*' in January 1963, and Sukarno declared his '*Ganyang Malaysia*' campaign in late July, the official declaration of 'confrontation' only began following the formation of the Federation of Malaysia in mid-September 1963 with the assault on the British embassy in Jakarta and the breaking off of diplomatic relations with London and Kuala Lumpur. For all intents and purposes, *Konfrontasi* was a low-key border war, notably along the Sarawak-Kalimantan divide, whence the Army occasionally launched small-scale raids into Sarawak territory. As mentioned, the Army was involved in the military training of SCO and offered support when the latter returned across the border to conduct its armed struggle against the Malaysian-Sarawak government.

But from a military standpoint, the Indonesian Army had begun infiltration into Sarawak as early as April 1963. Tebedu, on Sarawak territory, slightly more than 3 kilometres from the Sarawak-Kalimantan border, witnessed a raid by a 60-strong force on its police station on 12 April.[40] Having killed a police corporal, the uniformed raiders escaped across the border carrying a quantity of carbines and automatic weapons as their loot. The raid on Tebedu could be taken as the military commencement of *Konfrontasi*.[41] Later in the month, another assault struck Kampung Gumbang, Bau, southwest of the capital Kuching.

The causality of Sukarno's *Konfrontasi* could be viewed from without as well as from within Indonesia. In looking from the regional perspective, the proposed 'Malaysia' federation comprising Malaya, Singapore, Sarawak, Brunei, and North Borneo from a simple glance at the map literally sees this wider federation controlling a greater part of the southern portion of the South China Sea and the eastern stretch of the Straits of Melaka. The scope of coverage is undoubtedly large and, at the same time and more importantly, strategic in its layout. In other words, Kuala Lumpur would have a greater direct control and influence over a large portion of real estate (territorial and maritime) of Southeast Asia, placed as a centre piece in the region. With little doubt, the new wider federation had the full support of its past colonial power, notably Britain, and the post-Malaysia stage would certainly see a continuous close rapport between Kuala Lumpur and London. In geopolitical terms against the context of the Cold War, independent Malaysia would be in the Anglo-American camp. Malaysia would continue with the Westminster system of constitutional monarchy and parliamentary democracy, ingratiating itself in the heartland of the Western democracies. Moreover, in newly created Malaysia there would be continuity with Malaya's commodities-based economy with direct connectivity to the Western capitalist market infrastructure that sustained capitalism. Although Malaya attained independence in 1957, the greater part of its economy of primary commodities (from production, processing, to export) remained in British corporate hands. The opposing communist camp considered 'Malaysia' to be a hostile and threatening political entity.

Sukarno, on the other hand, intended to introduce a paradigm shift away from the hitherto imperialistic and colonial framework that had predominated the region for more than the past century. Building on the momentum of the Bandung Conference (1955), he brought forth a new ideology aptly called 'New Emerging Forces', as an alternative to the UN as well as to 'old established forces', the latter comprising Britain, France, Germany and also included the main Cold War players of the U.S. and the USSR. Sukarno's New Emerging Forces would prioritize and promote the interests of the Third World and posit a non-partisan stance towards the Cold War, neither supporting any camp. Against such an ideological mindset, it was imperative that Jakarta fervently oppose the establishment of 'Malaysia', seen as a neo-colonial entity that was specifically designed to perpetuate the influence of Britain, one of the 'old established forces'.

Furthermore, the fact that 'Malaysia' would continue with the institution of the Malay sultanate, all nine sultans to remain intact, in fact, creating a system of rotating monarchs with a supreme sovereign, *Yang Di-Pertuan Agong* (King),[42] reigning for a five-year tenure, was at best feudalistic and at worst retrogressive. Besides the Yogyakarta sultanate that originated in the Sultanate of Mataram (1587–1755), *Republik Indonesia* had done away with all monarchs and princelings, including the royal houses of Kalimantan.[43] In other words, 'Malaysia' was, in fact, an anachronism.

Another external factor of Indonesia's opposition to 'Malaysia' was the issue of pride. As an emerging power in the region, a colossal newly independent nation (1949), Sukarno regarded *Republik Indonesia* to be a major player in Southeast Asia, if not in the greater part of its archipelagic realm. The fact that London practically disregarded Jakarta, formally and informally, over the intention of supporting a wider federation ('Malaysia') that would occupy a central and strategic location in the region enraged Sukarno for this diplomatic snub.[44] Personally offended, he intended to 'crush' the proposed new federation if it came into fruition.

Jakarta was clearly knowledgeable of Azahari and the PRB in favouring an independent nation, NKKU, of which Brunei would play the leading role. Educated in Java and who had fought the Dutch alongside the Republicans, Azahari had harboured his NKKU concept and ambition back in the late 1940s. The fact that PRB utilized the Indonesian term '*partai*', in lieu of the Malay '*parti*', exhibited his affinity and partiality. Therefore, Indonesia's rejection of 'Malaysia' could be taken as lending support for Azahari's NKKU.

From within Indonesia, *Konfrontasi* served three foci of power, each vying with one another for leverage and ultimate domination, viz. Sukarno the president, the Army, and the PKI. Sukarno, the consummate Javanese *dalang*, was hard-pressed in balancing two increasingly threatening (to his power and position) forces: the Army on one hand, and the PKI on the other. In the early 1960s, he appeared to be running out of 'tricks' in arresting the Army's and PKI's respective ascendancy. Hence, an external issue, or foreign threat, could be played up to camouflage his almost empty bag of 'tricks'; moreover, it would at least buy time, until events and developments shifted in his favour. *Konfrontasi* fitted Sukarno's scheme, pivoting himself as the anti-imperial, anti-colonial champion, resurrecting his role as the 'hero' of the *Revolusi*. At the same time, involving the Army, and other branches of the armed forces, in a foreign war (*Konfrontasi*) would 'distract' the generals from moving against him and the presidency. For the populace, a foreign threat ('Malaysia') and *Konfrontasi* in addressing it could be a welcome distraction from the fast-deteriorating and near-collapsing domestic economy.[45] The *Karya Kabinet* was incapable of overcoming economic woes.

Konfrontasi, not unlike the regional rebellions in Sumatra and Sulawesi of the late 1950s, to the Army necessitated military action, which meant justification for demanding greater allocation of resources. The additional resources and weaponry further strengthened the power and the arsenal of the Army in particular, which bore the brunt of the *Konfrontasi* campaign, as well as other branches (navy and air force), but to a lesser extent. The savvy generals, however, being consciously aware and alerted to their rival's (mainly PKI) positioning and manoeuvring, retained their best personnel and military divisions on Java, the arena for a probable and inevitable showdown, only awaiting the time and place.

The PKI, on its part, exploited *Konfrontasi* in the mobilization and radicalization of the masses, because in the latter laid its strength and support base. Portraying *Konfrontasi* and the '*Ganyang Malaysia*' campaign as measures to address aggression from without – the presence of British and Commonwealth forces alongside Malaysian military units – justified that *Republik Indonesia* was being threatened, hence the people must rise up to its defence. The PKI called upon Sukarno and the government to sanction the formation and arming of a people's (workers and peasants) militia, a 'Fifth Force'. D. N. Aidit, leader of the PKI, at a public speech on 17 January 1965 proclaimed the formation of such a militia:

> I have submitted a proposal to President Sukarno to arm immediately the workers and peasants, the pillars of the revolution. No less than 5 million organized workers and 10 million organized peasants are ready to take up arms. This is the only correct reply to the British and American aggression.[46]

The Army, in particular, strongly opposed such a move of creating a communist 'army'.

Apparently, in order to strengthen itself vis-à-vis the PKI, the Army only dispatched less-than-competent military units to the Sarawak-Kalimantan border, where most of the *Konfrontasi* skirmishes occurred. Understandably and unsurprisingly, Indonesian troops performed poorly against Malaysian forces ably assisted by British, Australian, and New Zealander units. Indonesian commandos sent as raiding parties to the southern part of the Malaysian peninsula – Pontian (17 August 1964), Labis (2 September 1964), Terendak, Malacca (9 October 1964) – were an embarrassment, a handful were killed, and the majority were captured.[47]

Konfrontasi towards 'Malaysia' had a precursor in a similar military campaign named for the seizure of West New Guinea from the Netherlands. Having landed some 1,500 paratroopers and marines near Merauke, by mid-1962, Sukarno had instructed preparations for Operation Jayawijaya scheduled for August. But intervention on the part of the Kennedy administration (1961–1963) in Washington averted a full-blown war. Owing to the Eisenhower administration's (1953–1961) support for the PRRI-PERMESTA rebels, Sukarno had turned to Moscow for military aid, which had facilitated the amphibious landings on West New Guinea. Hence, in order to woo Sukarno over to the U.S. side, President Kennedy decided to play peacemaker behind the scene. The result was the New York Agreement penned on 15 August 1962 by Indonesia and the Netherlands that concluded the West New Guinea dispute (1949–1963).[48] The disputed territory, renamed Irian Barat (thereafter Irian Jaya), was handed over to Indonesia on 1 May 1963. Buoyed by this diplomatic success, Sukarno again applied *Konfrontasi* to the case of 'Malaysia', with expectations to secure another coup.

Events, however, intervened with adverse consequences for Sukarno. *Gerakan September Tiga Puluh* (30 September Movement), or GESTAPU, that commenced on the evening of 30 September 1965, sparked a series of rollercoaster events that in its wake ended up (1966) with the wholesale massacre of a staggering figure of between 200,000 and 500,000 people.[49] The ascension of General Suharto, as acting president (12 March 1967–27 March 1968) in place of Sukarno (placed under house arrest), and as president (7 March 1968–21 May 1998), closed a chapter on an iconic charismatic leader with all his aspirations, ambitions, ideologies, and policies.

Macapagal's 'Sabah Claim'

Opposition of Manila to Tunku's 'Malaysia' proposal was a consequence of a case of historical precedence and legacy. North Borneo, renamed Sabah following the merger into the wider federation of Malaysia in September 1963, was originally a territory that was claimed to be part of the Sulu sultanate (Appendix 7.1). As mentioned, the fact that Overbeck sought out the Sulu court in relation to the eastern portion of what later became a part of North Borneo proved the latter had a legitimate claim over the territory. (A similar agreement relating to the western portion was undertaken with the Brunei court.) However, there was uncertainty as to the terminology used in the agreement, whether *a lease* or *a cession*, depending on the translation used, whereby an annual payment of S\$5,000 was made in return (Table 7.3). This ambiguity on the transaction status, 'leased' or 'ceded', apparently was not given much issue when, in 1881, the BNBCC, registered and based in London, assumed the concession and, accordingly, established British North Borneo (or

Table 7.3 Ambiguity over the Status of North Borneo (Sabah)

On 22 January 1878, an agreement was signed between the Sultanate of Sulu and Gustavus Baron van Overbeck, who represented a British commercial syndicate (Dent Brothers and Co.). The question was to the status of North Borneo, whether it was *ceded* or *leased*, according to two versions, to the said British syndicate in return for a yearly payment of S$5,000.

British version	Sulu version
"WE Sri Paduka Maulana Al Sultan Mohamet Jamal Al Alam Bin Sri Paduka Al Marhom Al Sultan Mohamet Fathlon Sultan of Sulu and the dependencies thereof on behalf of ourselves our heirs and successors and with the consent and advice of the Datoos in council assembled hereby **grant and cede** of our own free and sovereign will to Gustavus Baron de Overbeck of Hong Kong and Alfred Dent Esquire of London . . . and assigns for ever and in perpetuity all the rights and powers belonging to us over all the territories and lands being tributary to us on the mainland of the island of Borneo commencing from the Pandassan River on the north-west coast and extending along the whole east coast as far as the Sibuco River in the south and comprising amongst other the States of Paitan, Sugut, Bangaya, Labuk, Sandakan, Kina Batangan, Mumiang, and all the other territories and states to the southward thereof bordering on Darvel Bay and as far as the Sibuco river with all the islands within three marine leagues of the coast".	"do hereby **lease** of our own freewill and satisfaction to . . . all the territories and lands being tributary to [us] together with their heirs, associates, successors and assigns forever and until the end of time, all rights and powers which we possess over all territories and lands tributary to us on the mainland of the Island of Borneo, commencing from the Pandassan River on the west coast to Maludu Bay, and extending along the whole east coast as far as Sibuco River on the south, . . . , and all the other territories and states to the southward thereof bordering on Darvel Bay and as far as the Sibuco River, . . . , [9 nautical miles] of the coast".

Sources: British North Borneo Treaties. British North Borneo, 1878. (Translation) 'GRANT by Sultan of Sulu of Territories and Lands on the Mainland of the Island of Borneo.' Dated 22nd January, 1878. www.lawnet.sabah.gov.my/Lawnet/SabahLaws/Treaties/GrantBySultanOfSuluOfTerritoriesAndLands OnTheMainlandOfTheIslandOfBorneo.pdf Accessed 4 Sept 2018; 'Grant by the Sultan of Sulu of a Permanent Lease covering his Lands and Territories on the Island of Borneo.' Dated January 22, 1878. Translation by Prof. Harold C. Conklin done in 1946; original text in Arabic script, see "letter from Francis B. Harrison . . .", infra, at p. 333. Government of the Philippines Official Gazette – The Philippine Claim to a Portion of North Borneo. www.officialgazette.gov.ph/1878/01/22/grant-by-the-sultan-of-sulu-of-a-permanent-lease-covering-his-lands-and-territories-on-the-island-of-borneo/ Accessed 5 Sept 2018

simply, North Borneo) that was administered by the servants of the BNBCC between 1881 and 1941. Then, in 1888, as a pre-emptive measure for fear of foreign interference, Britain granted protectorate status over North Borneo together with the Brunei sultanate and Sarawak. During the Pacific War (1941–1945), North Borneo, like the territories across Southeast Asia, came under military rule of Imperial Japan. Owing to the enormous wartime devastation, BNBCC ceded all of its duties, rights, sovereignty, and responsibilities to the British Crown in mid-1946. North Borneo then became a British Crown Colony, until 1963, when it became a component of the Federation of Malaysia.

Basically, Manila's claim over Sabah was based on the fact that the territory, or more specifically, the eastern portion, was a region of the Sulu sultanate. Since the Sulu sultanate became a part of the Republic of the Philippines following independence from the U.S. in 1946, Manila had legitimate claim over this aforesaid territory in northern Borneo. Two issues arise from this line of reasoning. Firstly, the ambiguity on the transaction status, 'leased' or 'ceded' in the 1878 agreement between Overbeck and the Sulu court, necessitated a clear confirmation of the terms of transaction. Secondly, a more fundamental issue relates to the disputed territory's ownership.

Owing to the different translations, it is difficult to ascertain whether the British version or the Sulu wording is the legal document to which to adhere. From other examples of treaties made between Britain and native rulers, in the event of any issues arising thereof, the English-language version of the treaty or agreement was the legal document for reference. In other words, if a legal matter relating to the treaty/agreement was brought to a British court that had jurisdiction over such a case, reference relating to documentation was based on documents in the English language and not on the non-English version. According to this convention, then the eastern portion of North Borneo was 'granted or ceded' to Overbeck by the Sulu court.

However, there is still the question of 'for a yearly payment of S$5,000'. The annual amount of the initial 'S$5,000' in the post-war era was rendered as Malayan dollars M$5,000, both having the same value. In a grant or cession, often a one-time payment of compensation or cost was made, not an annual payment. If it was the latter, there was no stipulation as to the duration of such a payment, or was such a yearly compensation to be 'for ever and in perpetuity'? Both – transaction status and payment issue – remained unclear, and any conclusion, at this juncture, is at best tentative until further evidence reveals otherwise.

Secondly, the question of the disputed territory's ownership needed to be addressed. Drawing from a sixteenth-century Portuguese source, Brunei's power extended as far northwards to the island of Luzon and southwards to the southern parts of Borneo.[50] Towards the last quarter of the sixteenth century, owing to Spanish assaults on Brunei, the latter was rendered weak, thereby allowing one of its vassals, namely Sulu, to stray away from control and influence. Furthermore, over a period of strife during the seventeenth century (1661–1673), Brunei appeared seemingly impotent, allowing its erstwhile vassal, Sulu, to severe vassalage ties and, in turn, declare its independence as a sovereign sultanate of its own. Moreover, Sulu gained territory from its former overlord:

> Owing to the supposed assistance of Sulu one of the claimants to the Brunei throne was killed; the triumphant claimant became Sultan Muhyiddin (1673–1690). The upshot was, however, in return for their assistance Sulu was given the territories north of Brunei Bay.[51]

Far more significant was the development whereby Sulu asserted itself as "an independent power with its ruler no longer an *adipati* [viceroy] of Brunei but claiming the title of Sultan of Sulu".[52]

Hence, "given the territories north of Brunei Bay", plausibly refers to the eastern half of what later in the 1870s and 1880s was the territory that was 'granted or ceded or leased' to Overbeck. But the plot further thickened on the issue of Sulu's acquisition of territory supposedly given by Sultan Muhyiddin of Brunei.

According to Hugh Low (1880) and H. R. Hughes-Hallett (1940), Sulu did receive territory from Brunei, viz. the former declared, "the land from the North as far as westward as Kimani[s] should belong to Soolook [Sulu]", and the latter indicated that, "by the beginning of the 18th century, the kingdom (Brunei) had been territorially diminished by the cession to the Sultan of Sulu in the north", respectively.[53] Lending further credence, Cesar Adib Majul (1999) cited a letter of 17 September 1879 from Sultan Jamalul Azam of Sulu to the Governor General of Spain in Manila that the coastal strip from Kimanis to Balikpapan was to pay tribute to the Sultan; therefore, he surmised that the said territory that faced Suluk was ceded to Suluk.[54]

Although it is apparent from the aforesaid, a Brunei author dismissed such assertions, insisting that no territory was ever ceded to Sulu. Not denying the promise of Sultan Muhyiddin to Sulu, Pehin Jamil Umar (2007) claimed that during the battle for Pulau Cermin, instead of providing assistance, the Sulu forces only appeared when the battle had been won. In consequence, Sultan Muhyiddin denied the Sulu his promise. The area that was supposedly to be ceded, according to Pehin Jamil Umar, was later 'claimed' by Sulu to be in their possession. Pehin Jamil Umar's contention, to a certain extent, found support in the observations of Stamford Raffles: "On the north-east coast of Borneo Proper [Brunei] lies a very considerable territory, the sovereignty of which has long been *claimed* by the Sulu government".[55]

Furthermore, Raffles' comments continued as follows:

and a very considerable part of which, together with the islands of the coast, has been for upwards for forty years regularly ceded to the English by the Sulus, and has, also, at different periods been occupied by the English, without any objection on the part of the government of Borneo Proper [Brunei]. This ceded district, which extends from the river Kiomanis on the north-west, which forms the boundary of Borneo Proper, to the great bay of Towsan Abia [north of Sandakan] on the north-east is undoubtedly a rich and fertile country, though in a rude and uncultivated manner; and it is admirably suited for commerce.[56]

Could Raffles' "for upwards for forty years regularly ceded to the English by the Sulus" be a reference to the settlement of Balambangan, an island off the northeast tip of present-day Sabah, which was initiated by Alexander Dalrymple of the English East India Company (EEIC)? Dalrymple contracted an agreement with Sultan Bantilan Muizzud-Din (1748–1763) of Sulu on 12 September 1762, whereby the island of Balambangan was ceded to the EEIC.[57] Five months later, on 22 January 1763, Dalrymple landed and formally took possession of the island. According to Raffles, the cession went beyond the island where it "extends from the river Kiomanis on the north-west, which forms the boundary of Borneo Proper, to the great bay of Towsan Abia on the north-east", where there were intermittent settlements by the EEIC "without any objection on the part of the government of Borneo Proper [Brunei]".

Therefore, if Raffles' testimony was to be taken as fact, then the Sulu sultanate had *ceded* territories to a third party (EEIC) notwithstanding that the said territory was in fact not of its (Sulu's) possession but which it (Sulu) *claimed* to be. Moreover, EEIC's intermittent occupation of the *ceded* territory did not draw any objections from Brunei, the *real* owner.

Dalrymple, on the other hand, cited '1704' as the year that Brunei ceded Balambangan, and presumably also the territory that "extends from the river Kiomanis on the north-west, which forms the boundary of Borneo Proper, to the great bay of Towsan Abia on the north-east".[58]

Clarification by Leigh R. Wright, a historian of Borneo and the vicinity, appeared to be the most cogent. Firstly, she surmised in this vein:

> Indeed, the legitimacy of the Sulu claim to the territory is in considerable doubt partly because of the unreliability of *tasilas* [genealogy, ancestry] such as 'Selesilah', which in many cases are nothing more than written-down legends to enhance the status of the royal house which produced them. Succeeding Sultans of Brunei have denied that northern Borneo was given to Sulu, and *only the weight of Sulu tradition supports the claim. The weight of Brunei tradition challenges it.*[59]

But the most telling and compelling evidence thus far that literally dismissed altogether Macapagal's 'Sabah Claim' is the Protocol of 1885, also referred to as the Madrid Protocol of 1885, a tripartite agreement among Spain, Britain, and Germany "for the purpose of obtaining from these two Powers [Britain and Germany] the formal recognition of the sovereignty of Spain over the Archipelago of Sulu (Jolo)".

Article III

> The Spanish Government *renounces*, as far as regards the British Government, all claims of sovereignty over the territories of the continent of Borneo, which belong, or which have belonged in the past to the Sultan of Sulu (Jolo), and which comprise the neighbouring islands of Balambangan, Banguey, and Malawali, as well as all those comprised within a zone of three maritime leagues from the coast, and which form part of the territories administered by the Company styled the "British North Borneo Company".[60]

Hence, it is emphatically clear as laid out in the Madrid Protocol of 1885. If the Sulu sultanate had no claims whatsoever over northern Borneo or present-day

Sabah, then the issue of the 'Sabah Claim' raised by President Macapagal of the Philippines therefore has no merit, and is in fact, a non-issue.

On the matter of an annual payment of Malayan dollars M$5,000 made to the Sulu sultanate, Wright opined, thus:

> Britain and Malaysia have never denied *a financial obligation to the descendants of Sultan Mohammad Jamalul Alam with regard to the "cession" money*. This is undoubtedly the true issue pending at the present time. It involves questions such as, which of the heirs of the Sultan are entitled to money, should it continue to be paid annually or should a lump sum settle the question. Once the Borneo issue ceases to be a highly charged political question, perhaps the Philippines and Malaysia can settle down to resolving this financial claim, which is *the only real point of contention* in the Borneo dispute.[61]

Reflecting on the Philippines' claim over North Borneo, initially with Britain, and from 1963, referred to as the 'Sabah Claim', with Malaysia, there were several pivotal developments, although none appeared to be a breakthrough in resolving the dispute (Appendix 7.1). The whole dispute formally began with Malayan Prime Minister Tunku Abdul Rahman's public announcement of the 'Malaysia' proposal in Singapore (May 1961). Then Philippines' President Diosdado Macapagal responded with a claim over North Borneo that featured as one of the five component territories of the proposed wider federation.

Public opinion

The Malaysia Solidarity Consultative Committee (MSCC) was set up (July 1961), chaired by Donald Stephens[62] and comprising representatives from each of the proposed constituents of the wider federation. MSCC was tasked: (1) to collect and collate views and opinions concerning the creation of Malaysia consisting of Brunei, North Borneo, Sarawak, Singapore, and the Federation of Malaya; (2) to disseminate information on the question of Malaysia; (3) to initiate and encourage discussions on Malaysia; and (4) to foster activities that would promote and expedite the realization of Malaysia.[63] Altogether, the MSCC convened on four occasions.[64]

Besides the MSCC's task "to collect and collate views and opinions concerning the creation of Malaysia", there were two other missions to ascertain the public opinion of the peoples of North Borneo and Sarawak, namely the Cobbold Commission (February-April 1962) and the UN Malaysia Mission (UNMM) (September 1963).

Headed by Lord Cobbold, former governor of the Bank of England, there were two representatives from Malaya, namely Wong Pow Nee, chief minister of Penang, and Ghazali Shafie, permanent secretary to the Ministry of Foreign Affairs, and two other members from the UK, Anthony Abell, former governor of Sarawak, and David Watherston, former chief secretary of Malaya. The Commission's report surmised the gathered public opinion:

> About one-third of the population of each territory strongly favours early realisation of Malaysia without too much concern about terms and conditions. Another third, many of them favourable to the Malaysia project, ask, with varying degrees of emphasis, for conditions and safeguards varying in nature and extent: the warmth of support among this category would be markedly influenced by a firm expression of opinion by Governments that the detailed arrangements eventually agreed upon are in the best interests of the territories. The remaining third is divided between those who insist on independence before Malaysia is considered and those who would strongly prefer to see British rule continue for some years to come. If the conditions and reservations which they have put forward could be substantially met, the second category referred to above would generally support the proposals. Moreover[,] once a firm decision was taken quite a number of the third category would be likely to abandon their opposition and decide to make the best of a doubtful job. There will remain a hard core, vocal and politically active, which will oppose Malaysia on any terms unless it is preceded by independence and self-government: this hard core might amount to near 20 per cent of the population of Sarawak and somewhat less in North Borneo.[65]

The Commission confronted three viewpoints, viz. one-third of the peoples of the two northern Bornean territories agreed to 'Malaysia', and another one-third were favourable but subject to conditions and safeguards being met. The final one-third was split between two divergent views: on the one hand, there were those who preferred 'independence-then-consider 'Malaysia'', and on the other, those who would rather settle for the *status quo* of colonial rule.

Both Indonesia and the Philippines rejected the report of the Cobbold Commission as it was not a referendum. Unlike the referendum on 'Malaysia' held in Singapore (September 1962), between February and April 1962, the Commission

> met more than 4,000 people and received 2,200 memorandums [sic.] from the various groups that consisted of political parties, members of Government and Legislative Assemblies, the chiefs, the natives and the leaders of the country, municipal councils, religious leaders, trade unions and members of the public who gave their views.[66]

The memorandum of the MSCC was one of the many memoranda that the Commission took into consideration.

The conclusion of the UNMM, likewise, was favourable:

> Bearing in mind the fundamental agreement of the three participating Governments in the Manila meetings, and the statement by the Republic of Indonesia

and the Republic of the Philippine that they would welcome the formation of Malaysia provided that the support of the people of the territories was ascertained by me [UN Secretary General U Thant] and that, in my opinion, complete compliance with the principal of self-determination within the requirements of General Assembly resolution 1541 (XV), Principal IX of the Annex, was ensured, my conclusion, based on the findings of the Mission, is that on both of these counts *there is no doubt about the wishes of a sizeable majority of the peoples of these territories to join in the Federation of Malaysia.*[67]

Prior to the UNMM taking place, between 30 July and 5 August 1963, a meeting was held in Manila among the Tunku, Sukarno, and Philippines' Macapagal. This summit produced two outcomes: the first was the creation of Maphilindo (*Ma*laya, *Phili*ppines, *Indo*nesia), a loose consultative body tasked to resolve mutual issues, and the second was the signing of the Manila Accord. Clause 12 of the Accord is the most pivotal:

> 12. The Philippines made it clear that its position on the inclusion of North Borneo in the Federation of Malaysia is subject to the final outcome of the Philippine claim to North Borneo. The Ministers took note of the Philippine claim and the right of the Philippines to continue to pursue it in accordance with international law and the principle of the pacific settlement of disputes. They agreed that *the inclusion of North Borneo in the Federation of Malaysia would not prejudice either the claim or any right thereunder.* Moreover, in the context of their close association, the three countries agreed to exert their best endeavours to bring the claim to a just and expeditious solution by peaceful means, such as negotiation, conciliation, arbitration, or judicial settlement as well as other peaceful means of the parties' own choice, in conformity with the Charter of the United Nations and the Bandung Declaration.[68]

A Joint Statement issued by the foreign ministers of the Philippines, Malaya, and Indonesia on 5 August 1963 reiterated the following:

> 8 . . . . The three Heads of Government take cognizance of the position regarding the Philippine claim to Sabah (North Borneo) after the establishment of the Federation of Malaysia as provided under paragraph 12 of the Manila Accord, that is, *that the inclusion of Sabah (North Borneo) in the Federation of Malaysia does not prejudice either the claim or any right thereunder.*[69]

Therefore, when the Federation of Malaysia finally came into being on 16 September 1963, the Philippines withheld recognition pending formal assurances from Kuala Lumpur that Clause 12 of the Manila Accord (July 1963) would be upheld. Moreover, despite being party to the UNMM, including the participation of observers (from the Philippines), the report of the Mission, like that of the Cobbold Commission's findings, was rejected by both Manila and Jakarta. Consequently, the Philippines and Indonesia severed diplomatic relations with the newly inaugurated Malaysia on 17 September 1963. The Philippines intended to bring its 'Sabah Claim' to the International Court of Justice (ICJ) for settlement.

At this juncture, it is prudent to re-visit the Brunei Commission Committee (BCC) (January 1962) and the outcome of its opinion survey in Brunei. By 3 February 1962, the BCC had completed its entrusted responsibility. Notwithstanding pressure from the PRB to publish its report, the BCC withheld public consumption of its findings. Instead, a summary of the report was prepared by the *Menteri Besar*, the chair of the Commission, and was delivered twice, on 18 July and on 23 September: the former read to the members of the Legislative Council and the latter at the Investiture Ceremony. On both occasions, a rosy positive outcome was presented, whereby the majority of the inhabitants of Brunei favoured 'Malaysia'.[70] It was in direct contrast to the original Commission's report.[71] In fact, Lord Selkirk, Commissioner-General for Southeast Asia (1959–1963), revealed that:

> [the] Brunei Government Fact Finding Commission had recorded stiff and almost 100 percent opposition from sections of the population to Malaysia. . . . The exact figures are not available for the whole State of Brunei, but *some hundreds of people spoke against Malaysia*, while literally one or perhaps two persons spoke in favour. In Kuala Belait and Seria 78 persons spoke against and 1 in favour; the two meetings here were attended by 700 or 800 people.[72]

Such a devastating outcome, a voracious public rebuff of the 'Malaysia' proposal, was manipulated, undoubtedly by the Brunei government in collusion with British officials lest it impacted adversely on neighbouring Sarawak and North Borneo.

Post-1963 'Sabah Claim'

In the post-1963 period, the Philippines that had hitherto pursued the claim over North Borneo with Britain now turned directly to Malaysia. The Malaysian government regarded the 'Sabah Claim' by the Philippines government as *a non-issue*. As a result, Kuala Lumpur did not heed Manila's attempts to bring the dispute to the ICJ. At the same time, the federal government of Malaysia appeared to be ambivalent towards the Manila Accord; at times the government ignored it, and at other times, reiterated its commitment. Even with the establishment of the Association of Southeast Asian Nations (ASEAN) in 1967, where both Malaysia and the Philippines were two of the five founding members, there was little headway as far as the dispute was concerned.

In April 1967, Sabah held its first post-independent elections to its 32-seat State Legislative Assembly.[73] Observers from both the Philippines and Indonesia were invited, but only the latter complied. Of the 31 victorious candidates, all stood on the platform of rejecting the Philippines' claim over Sabah. Honouring the electoral results, Jakarta formally recognized Sabah and Sarawak as legitimate states of the Federation of Malaysia. Manila acted to the contrary; not only did it reject the outcome of the elections, but it also continued to pursue its 'Sabah Claim'.

During the presidency of Ferdinand E. Marcos (1965–1986) of the Philippines, there were dramas and conspiracies related to the 'Sabah Claim'. A covert mission, *Oplan Merdeka* (Operation Merdeka), whereby a team of Moro Muslim militants were to infiltrate Sabah, destabilized the state through sabotage, hence setting the stage for a military intervention by the Armed Forces of the Philippines (AFP).[74] But, while under training on Corregidor Island, members of the AFP allegedly killed the Muslim trainees, a tragic incident referred to as the Jabidah Massacre (18 March 1968).[75] President Marcos was alleged to be the mastermind of the abortive *Oplan Merdeka*. This clandestine affair that implicated Malacañang Palace was shrouded in mystery and rife with speculations.

Marcos severed diplomatic relations with Malaysia (July 1968), and thereafter advocated that the Philippines should bring its claim to the ICJ. Moreover, he passed Republic Act RA No. 5446 (September 1968), whereby the baselines of the Philippines proclaimed "the territory of Sabah, situated in North Borneo, over which the Republic of the Philippines has acquired dominion and sovereignty". Both London and Washington, however, assured Kuala Lumpur of their support in the dispute.[76] The fact that the U.S., former colonial master and post-independent close ally of the Philippines, stood by Malaysia in the dispute brought a bank of disappointments from Filipino politicians.

Philippines' Senator Benigno S. Aquino, Jr., an arch critic of Marcos and of his regime, disapproved of the way the 'Sabah Claim' was hitherto handled. Voicing a contradictory viewpoint, Aquino gave a speech (October 1968) wherein he drew strength from President Macapagal, who first championed the territorial claim and who also upheld the principle of self-determination. Aquino cited the April 1967 Sabah elections *as evidence of the exercising of their right to self-determination.* He quoted Macapagal, who in 1963 proclaimed the following, viz.:

> In laying claim to North Borneo [Sabah] in pursuance of the legal and historic rights and security interests of the Philippines, we recognize the cardinal principle of self-determination of which the Philippines has been a steadfast adherent. In the prosecution of our valid claim, it is agreeable to us that at an appropriate time, the people of North Borneo should be given an opportunity to determine whether they would wish to be independent or whether they would wish to be part of the Philippines or be placed under another state. Such [a] referendum, however, should be authentic and bona fide by holding it under conditions, preferably supervised by the United Nations, that would insure effective freedom to the people of North Borneo to express their true and enlightened will.[77]

In other words, Aquino urged that the Philippines' government should withdraw its territorial claim.

At the UN General Assembly (October 1968), the Philippines drew attention to the Manila Accord and expressed its intention to refer the dispute to the ICJ for adjudication. Malaysia, however, quashed the Philippine claim simply to the fact that the inhabitants of Sabah had shown their intention, through the April 1967 state elections, to be with the Federation of Malaysia, and the latter had upheld the British title to Sabah. In a nutshell then, *as far as Malaysia was concerned, there is no Philippine claim*; therefore, there is nothing to discuss.

Despite its brash and uncompromising stance at the UN, Kuala Lumpur proposed the normalization of diplomatic relations between Malaysia and the Philippines, but accompanied by a precondition, namely that the Philippines should recognize Malaysia's sovereignty over Sabah but without prejudice to the Philippines' pursuit of its claim. In December 1969, formal resumption of diplomatic relations between Malaysia and the Philippines was realized.

Then on 4 August 1977, at the Second ASEAN Summit in Kuala Lumpur, President Marcos announced that the Philippines had given up its claim to Sabah.[78] Although it was welcome news, Malaysia requested that the Philippines overturn two pending matters, viz.: (1) that amendment to the Philippines' 1973 Constitution relating to its broad definition of national territory expunge the clause, "territories belonging to the Philippines by historic right or legal title"; and (2) that the Philippines' government proceed to repeal Republican Act RA 5446, particularly Section 2.[79]

It took another three decades for the aforesaid 'second request' of Malaysia's to be finally fulfilled, when on 10 March 2009, Philippines President Gloria Macapagal-Arroyo penned Republic Act RA 9522, amending RA 5446 that removes mention of Sabah in the Archipelagic Baselines of the Philippines law. It remained to be seen for the fulfilment of Malaysia's 'first request'. It came *almost* full circle: President Gloria Macapagal-Arroyo is the daughter of President Diosdado Macapagal, who initiated the 'Sabah Claim' back in April 1962.

Besides Malaysia's 'first request', Wright had surmised the whole dispute, indicating that what was pending is the question of "a financial obligation to the descendants of Sultan Mohammad Jamalul Alam with regard to the 'cession' money".[80] The 2013 demise of self-proclaimed Sultan Jamalul Kiram III of Sulu, the purported heir to Sultan Mohammad Jamalul Alam, left possible claimants to the throne, notably the late sultan's two brothers, Esmail and Agbimuddin, the latter designated as *raja muda* or heir apparent, and also another claimant in the person of his brother-in-law, Bantilan.

As a postscript, in mid-February 2013, Raja Muda Agbimuddin Kiram led a 235-strong Royal Security Forces (RSF) of the Sultanate of Sulu and North Borneo, which laid siege to a small village, Kampung Tanduo in Lahad Datu, Sabah. On 1 March, the Aquino administration (2010–2016) urged the Sulu militants to withdraw; they, however, disregarded Manila's call.[81] Consequently thereafter, Malaysian security forces launched an assault on 1 March, killing 56 militants with 10 losses. Agbimuddin, heir apparent to the Sulu sultanate, together with the RSF remained on the terrorist list of the Malaysian government.[82]

'Malaysia' proposal: from the Cold War perspective

The intention to create a wider federation that encompassed then-independent Malaya, and the remaining British colonial possessions in Southeast Asia, notably Singapore, Sarawak, Brunei, and North Borneo, would result in a reconfiguration of the regional geopolitical setting. It would re-confirm that the territories of the Malay Peninsula, including the island off its southern tip (Singapore) and northern Borneo, would remain pro-UK, and by extension, in the U.S. camp of the so-called free world of Western democracies. Such a new state (Malaysia), strategically located in the sea lanes (South China Sea and the Straits of Melaka) of East-West trade and commerce, undoubtedly boosted the pro-Western camp in being able to safeguard pivotal international trade routes that were essential to the workings of the capitalist market-oriented world economic system. At the same time, this new state that stretched from the Straits of Melaka to the west, across the South China Sea, and to the Sulu Sea to the east posed a barrier to the communist wave that was then (1950s and early 1960s) sweeping across the region. But importantly and much more specifically, if not more urgent and pressing, the creation of the Federation of Malaysia that subsequently comprised Malaya, Singapore, Sarawak, and North Borneo (renamed Sabah) arrested the increasing ascendancy of the far Left in Singapore (*Barisan Sosialis* [Socialist Front]) and in Sarawak (SUPP that had been thoroughly infiltrated by the SCO).

This new state of Malaysia that came into being on 16 September 1963 triggered significant events and developments prior to its formal formation and immediately following its establishment. The pre-Malaysia period witnessed the initiation of the 'Sabah Claim' by the Philippines (1961–present), the outbreak of the Brunei Rebellion (December 1962), and the onset of the Sarawak Communist Insurgency (1962–1990). The former and the latter were protracted affairs, whereas the uprising was a short-lived explosion of activities. In the wake of Malaysia's formation, *Konfrontasi* was launched, subsequently leading to the GESTAPU Affair (1965) and its horrific and tragic aftermath, the Indonesian Massacres (1965–1966). The 1960s were aptly and prophetically referred to as years 'of living dangerously',[83] whereby developments unfolded rollercoaster-style, unceremoniously and rudely, one event overtaking another.

'Malaysia' and its aftermath

The period between the late 1950s and the mid-1960s could be regarded as turbulent times for Borneo. The once laid-back ambience against the humid tropical heat, the buzzing of mosquitos during the twilight hours, and the sounds from the nocturnal jungle in close proximity was rudely disrupted. Excitement was in the air, with newspapers and radio broadcasts repeatedly mentioning the word Malaysia, so that even upriver folks were getting curious about the latest happenings downstream. Word-of-mouth spread to the *hulu* (interior regions), alerting brethren that 'outsiders', 'foreigners', 'Big Tuans' are intending to have a stopover at this longhouse or that *kampung*. Indeed, top colonial brass such as the likes of Malcolm MacDonald, Britain's Commissioner-General for South-East Asia (1948–1955), did share meals and *tuak* (local alcoholic rice drink) with Iban leaders including Temenggong Koh, paramount chief of the Ibans, and others like Penghulu Jugah.

Then, the 'troubles' in Brunei impacted on neighbouring Limbang and Lawas on the Sarawak side of the border. Thereafter followed the witch hunts, with detentions and deportations of Sarawak Chinese communists and suspected sympathizers across the British Borneo territories. As a result, the communists in Sarawak abandoned their united front tactics and turned to armed revolution, signalling the commencement of the protracted decades-long Sarawak Communist Insurgency. Months prior to 16 September 1963, when Malaysia came into being, North Borneo and Sarawak hosted two fact-finding survey teams, notably the Cobbold Commission (February-August 1963) and the UN Malaysia Mission (August-September 1963), that were tasked to ascertain the views of the local peoples regarding the proposed merger. Once Malaysia was formalized, Indonesia embarked on *Konfrontasi*, and the Philippines pressed on its territorial claim over Sabah. Borneo then was *ignited*, figuratively and literally.

Within two years of the formation of Malaysia, Singapore seceded on 9 August 1965 to become an independent, sovereign republic. Vested intractable political and economic differences that aggravated Sino-Malay relations sparking racial riots in July and September 1964 forced the inevitable secession. Seven weeks later witnessed the GESTAPU Affair, an abortive seizure of power in Jakarta by young officers of the Thirtieth September Movement, whence during the early hours of 1 October, six senior Army generals were killed. Just before noon, the officers claimed to have President Sukarno in their custody, and they claimed possession of the city's media and communication facilities. But before dusk, all was over as government forces re-took Jakarta. The backlash was horrific. Since the GESTAPU Affair was blamed on the PKI, communists and their sympathizers were slaughtered; it was estimated that more than half a million lost their lives.[84] There emerged in Indonesia a new strongman, Suharto. Under his *Orde Baru* (New Order) regime, Suharto dismantled his predecessor's works and policies; notably, PKI was proscribed, *Konfrontasi* was abandoned (August 1966), and diplomatic relations between Indonesia and Malaysia were normalized (August 1967). Thereafter, from October 1967, the Army, that had once trained SCO cadres, launched an elimination and annihilation campaign against all Leftists (PKI, SCO). Army units hunted PKI remnants and SCO members in the vast jungle of West Kalimantan and along the porous Sarawak-Kalimantan border and its vicinity.

The SCO was forced to abandon its safe havens in West Kalimantan and crossed back to Sarawak to carry on its armed struggle for the realization of a communist republic for the next three decades – the Sarawak Communist Insurgency (1962–1990) – with the Lower Rajang as the main battleground. It paralleled the MCP's armed struggle on West/Peninsular Malaysia, namely the Second Malayan Emergency (1968–1989). The ramifications of the SCO's protracted revolutionary struggle were domestic, limited to within the confines of Sarawak with unclear and doubtful foreign aid and/or intervention.

Borneo on the world stage

When the concept of 'Malaysia' was first mooted by the Tunku in late May 1961 in Singapore, a flurry of developments took place in the proposed component territories and beyond. In Tunku's Malaya, there was concern regarding the demographic balance between indigenes and immigrant groups. UMNO, Tunku as its president, was apprehensive of a Chinese deluge and domination from Singapore. Across the Causeway, 'Malaysia' created a rupture in the PAP, with one faction led by Lee Kuan Yew in favour of merger and an opposing faction of Left-wing elements. The latter, forced to exit the PAP, formed the *Barisan Sosialis* that took on an anti-'Malaysia' stance. In the Bornean territories of Sarawak and North Borneo, the small knot of the educated elite from the various ethnic communities hurriedly formed political organizations to ensure that the interests and rights of their respective communities were safeguarded in the context of the proposed wider federation. Only Sarawak's SUPP established in 1959, and a year earlier (1960), Abang Haji Mustapha set up the Malay-Muslim *Parti Negara Sarawak* (PANAS) or National Party of Sarawak predated 'Malaysia', while others were constituted after the Tunku's public announcement. Stephen Kalong Ningkan initiated Sarawak National Party (SNAP) (1961) for the Dayaks. In North Borneo, Tun Datu Haji Mustapha bin Datu Harun convened the United Sabah National Organization (USNO) (1961) while Donald Stephens formed the United National Kadazan Organisation (UNKO) (1961). Despite readying themselves with political parties, the majority of the indigenous peoples, where the illiteracy rate was relatively high, were generally clueless of the proposed wider federation and its impacts and implications thereof.

Only the SCO-infiltrated SUPP seemed to be aware of 'Malaysia' and vehemently opposed its realization; instead, this Chinese-dominated political party held strongly to the 'independence-from-Britain-first' strategy. Likewise, in Brunei, the PRB appeared to be clear about 'Malaysia', unhesitant in rejecting the concept of a wider federation. Owing to other intractable domestic issues and aggravated by the 'Malaysia' proposal, the PRB launched an uprising (December 1962). The Brunei Rebellion set in motion a series of interrelated developments: Sarawak Communist Insurgency, *Konfrontasi*, the 'Sabah Claim', and subsequently, the GESTAPU Affair with its aftermath, the Indonesian Massacres.

Except for the latter two mentioned, the others were Borneo-centred front-page news. The media, local and foreign news agencies, had a field day reporting on a rebellion, a communist insurgency, an armed confrontation, and a territorial dispute. 'Borneo', together with other exotic-sounding names/terms, 'Brunei', 'Kuching', Tebedu', 'Sulu sultanate', and little-known personalities like A. M. Azahari, Ong Kee Hui, and Donald Stephens, and the likes of *Partai Rakyat Brunei*, Clandestine Communist Organization (later, Sarawak Communist Organization), *Negarabagian Kesatuan Kalimantan Utara* (NKKU), and Sarawak United People's Party (SUPP) were accorded print space and air time. *Konfrontasi* entered the media vocabulary.

For better, or for worse, developments on Borneo were accorded front-page treatment. The limelight had been the exception for Borneo, where hitherto the backstage had been the norm. Not only had developments impacted on the island from within, but they also had repercussions from without, rippling across the region with geopolitical implications for major protagonists of the Cold War. Borneo, then, mattered.

Notes

1   In his later years following his retirement, the Tunku, as he was often referred to by the mass media from within and from without, came to be known as Tunku Abdul Rahman Putra al-Haj.

2   Excerpt from the 'Special Message to the Congress on Urgent National Needs – Section IX: Space', President John F. Kennedy speaks before a joint session of Congress, May 25, 1961. NASA History, May 25, 2004. www.nasa.gov/vision/space/features/jfk_speech_text.html Accessed 15 Sep 2018.

3   For a most detailed study, see Jim Rasenberger, *The Brilliant Disaster: JFK, Castro, and America's Doomed Invasion of Cuba's Bay of Pigs* (New York: Scribner, 2012).

4   For a detailed analysis of the formation of Malaysia, see Matthew Jones, *Conflict and Confrontation in South East Asia, 1961–1965: Britain, the United States, Indonesia and the Creation of Malaysia* (Cambridge, UK: Cambridge University Press, 2002). From a Singapore viewpoint, see Tan Tai Yong, *Creating "Greater Malaysia": Decolonization and the Politics of Merger* (Singapore: Institute of Southeast Asian Studies, 2008). For an insightful account from an eyewitness, *Ghazali Shafie, Memoir Ghazali Shafie – Penubuhan Malaysia* [*Ghazali Shafie's Memoir on the Formation of Malaysia*] (Bangi: Penerbit Universiti Kebangsaan Malaysia, 2015).

5   See Bilveer Singh, *Quest for Political Power: Communist Subversion and Militancy in Singapore* (Singapore: Marshall Cavendish, 2015).

6   See Chapter IV.

7   Singapore's external relations remained in the hands of the British colonial administration as well as important domestic policies such as internal security.

8   Figures in parentheses indicate percentage of the total population.

9   Also rendered as 'Straits of Malacca'.

10 Vietnam War (1960–1975). The Oxford Companion to American Military History 2000 (Originally published by Oxford: Oxford University Press, 2000). www.encyclopedia.com/history/asia-and-africa/southeast-asia-history/vietnam-war Accessed 15 Sep 2018.

11 Michael O. Billington, "Britain's Cold War against FDR's Grand Design: The East Asian Theater, 1943–63", EIR Feature, *Executive Intelligence Review* (EIR), 26, 41, Oct 15, 1999, p. 14. https://larouchepub.com/eiw/public/1999/eirv26n41-19991015/eirv26n41-19991015_014-britains_cold_war_against_fdrs_g.pdf Accessed 10 Jan 2019.

12 'From the Archive: Mr. Churchill on Our One Aim', *The Guardian*, Nov 11, 1942. www.theguardian.com/theguardian/2009/nov/11/churchill-blood-sweat-tears Accessed 1 Feb 2019. Emphasis added.

13 Rolf Tanner, *"A Strong Showing": Britain's Struggle for Power and Influence in South Asia 1942–1950* (Stuttgart: Steiner Franz Verlag, 1994), p. 91.

14 In the context of Southeast Asia, see ibid., pp. 21–29, 34–36.

15 Ibid., p. 39. Emphasis added.

16 Commonwealth President of the Philippines Manuel L. Quezon resurrected Rizal's idea, and Wenceslao Quinito Vinzons (1910–1942), a Filipino politician and a leader of the armed resistance against the Japanese occupying forces, conceived a united nation-state of ethnic Malays; these were forerunners of the idea of Maphilindo.

17 For instance, see Nicholas J. White, *British Business in Post-Colonial Malaysia, 1957–70: Neo-Colonialism or Disengagement?* (London: RoutledgeCurzon, 2004).

18 Billington, "Britain's Cold War against FDR's Grand Design", p. 41.

19 Until 1959 when Singapore was granted self-government, Lee was designated 'Chief Minister', a position appointed by the British colonial governor of Singapore in lieu of he being the leader of the largest party, namely the People's Action Party (PAP) in the Legislative Assembly. The position was abolished in June 1959.

20 For instance, see Kumar Ramakrishna, *Emergency Propaganda: The Winning of Malayan Hearts and Minds 1948–1958* (London: Routledge, 2015); Richard Stubbs,

Hearts and Minds in Guerrilla Warfare: The Malayan Emergency 1948–1960 (Singapore: Oxford University Press, 1989).

21 Lee Kuan Yew, "Speech by the Prime Minister, Mr. Lee Kuan Yew, at the Public Forum on 'Merger & Malaysia'", Organised by the University of Singapore Students Union at the University on Monday, Aug 27, 1962. For Broadcast on Sep 25 at 7.10 p.m. www. nas.gov.sg/archivesonline/data/pdfdoc/lky19620827a.pdf Accessed 16 Sep 2018. Also, see Lee Kuan Yew, *The Battle for Merger* (Singapore: Government Printing Office, 1961), pp. 4–8.

22 See Ooi Keat Gin, *Post-War Borneo, 1945–1950: Nationalism, Empire and State-Building* (London: Routledge, 2013), pp. 79–80.

23 *Titah, 1959–67, kebawah DYMM Paduka Seri Baginda Maulana Al-Sultan Sir Omar Ali Saifuddin Sa'adul Khairi Waddin [(Royal) Command, 1959–67, kebawah DYMM Paduka Seri Baginda Maulana Al-Sultan Sir Omar Ali Saifuddin Sa'adul Khairi Waddin]* (Brunei: Dewan Bahasa dan Pustaka, 1971), pp. 106–107.

24 Marsal bin Maun was Brunei's second *menteri besar* or chief minister. His tenure was between Aug 1, 1961 and Sep 1, 1962.

25 See below.

26 Ibid.

27 Haji Zaini Haji Ahmad, ed., *Partai Rakyat Brunei: The People's Party of Brunei: Selected Documents/Dokumen Terpilih* (Petaling Jaya: INSAN [Institute of Social Analysis], 1987), p. 198.

28 North Borneo was renamed Sabah following its merger into Malaysia in 1963. Apparently the etymology of 'Sabah' was unclear. A plausible origin was that the term derived from Brunei Malay referring to 'upstream', that practically describes its location vis-à-vis Brunei. See Allen R. Maxwell, "The Origin of the name 'Sabah'", *Sabah Society Journal*, 7, 2 (1981–1982): 91–105.

29 Nick van der Bijl, *The Brunei Revolt: 1962–1963*, Kindle ed. (Barnsley, UK: Pen and Sword, 2012), blurp.

30 Zaini Ahmad's full designation, viz. Dr Haji Zaini bin Pehin Orang Kaya Shahbandar Dato Setia Haji Ahmad.

31 Interestingly, this state of emergency was never lifted, and since then to the present, the sultan ruled by decree. The Executive Summary of Brunei 2016 Human Rights Report commences with the following: "Brunei Darussalam is a monarchy governed since 1967 by Sultan Haji Hassanal Bolkiah under *emergency powers in place since 1962* that place few limits on his authority". Brunei 2016 Human Rights Report. www.state.gov/documents/organization/265534.pdf Accessed 2 Sep 2018. Emphasis added.

32 Haji Muhammad Yasin bin Abdul Rahman.

33 See Vernon L. Porritt, *British Colonial Rule in Sarawak, 1946–1963* (Kuala Lumpur: Oxford University Press, 1997), p. 165.

34 Alex Josey, a journalist, portrayed Azahari as a money-grabbing "bum and liar", who intended the uprising as a means to seize the country, government, and all the wealth therein. He claimed that Azahari was in cohort with Nicasio Osmena, his legal adviser, who was also the president and treasurer of the Kiram Corporation, a company set up by the descendants of Sultan Jamalul Kiram III of Sulu to lay claim to North Borneo (Sabah). "The Great Smash and Grab That Failed . . . ", *The Straits Times*, Jan 21, 1963. http://eresources.nlb.gov.sg/newspapers/Digitised/Article/straitstimes19630121-1.2.71 Accessed 24 Jan 2019.

35 See Ooi Keat Gin, "The Cold War and British Borneo: Impact and Legacy, 1945–63", in *Southeast Asia and the Cold War*, edited by Albert Lau (London: Routledge, 2012), pp. 112–114; and, Vernon L. Porritt, *The Rise and Fall of Communism in Sarawak 1940–1990* (Clayton, Vic: Monash Asia Institute, 2004), Appendices 6 and 12.

36 Until 1962, following the creation of ABRI, TNI, or more appropriately, the Army, shall be used interchangeably. For the creation of ABRI, see Chapter VI.

37 Francis Chan and Phyllis Wong, "Saga of Communist Insurgency in Sarawak", *The Borneo Post*, Sep 16, 2011. www.theborneopost.com/2011/09/16/saga-of-communist-insurgency-in-sarawak/ Accessed 26 Dec 2018.
38 Dr Subandrio was, in fact, not Sukarno, the architect behind *Konfrontasi*. In pursuing an anti-Chinese policy, Dr Subandrio's intention was aligned to British intelligence, namely to eliminate the communist cancer in West Kalimantan and Sarawak. See Greg Poulgrain, *The Genesis of Konfrontasi: Malaysia, Brunei, Indonesia, 1945–1965* (Barthurst, NSW: Crawford House Publishing and London: C. Hurst & Co., 1998), pp. 297–298.
39 *Straits Times*, Jan 22, 1963. Also, see *Straits Times*, July 10, 1963. http://eresources.nlb.gov.sg/newspapers/Digitised/Article/straitstimes19630122-1.2.6 Accessed 17 Sep 2018.
40 Indonesian raid on Tebedu police station in Sarawak, 1963. FO 371/169739 (NAUK).
41 See Peter Dennis, et al., *The Oxford Companion to Australian Military History*, 2nd ed. (Melbourne: Oxford University Press, 2008), p. 152.
42 For details of this institution of rotating kingship, see Ooi Keat Gin, *Historical Dictionary of Malaysia*, 2nd ed. (Lanham, MD: Rowman & Littlefield, 2018), p. 58.
43 The Pontianak sultanate, Pontianak, West Kalimantan, and the Sultanate of Banjar, Banjarmasin, South Kalimantan, all possessed only cultural and heritage significance. The Kutai Kartanegara sultanate in East Kalimantan met its demise at the hands of the Dutch in the mid-1840s, when the last ruler was exiled.
44 For instance, see Robert Cribb and Colin Brown, *Modern Indonesia: A History Since 1945* (Harlow, UK: Longman Publishing Group, 1996), p. 86.
45 The economic situation was dire. Runaway inflation pushed up the cost-of-living index from 100 in 1958 to an astronomical 18,000 in 1965, and an absurd 600,000 in 1967. See Willard A. Hanna, "Sukarno: President of Indonesia", *Encyclopædia Britannica*. www.britannica.com/biography/Sukarno Accessed 4 Sep 2018.
46 *Harian Raklat*, Jan 19, 1965.
47 See Christopher Tuck, *Confrontation, Strategy and War Termination: Britain's Conflict with Indonesia* (London: Routledge, 2016), p. 31; David Easter, *Britain and the Confrontation with Indonesia, 1960–1966* (London: I. B. Tauris, 2004), pp. 98–99.
48 Audrey R. Kahin and George McTurnan Kahin, *Subversion as Foreign Policy: The Secret Eisenhower and Dulles Debacle in Indonesia* (Seattle and London: University of Washington Press, 1997), pp. 217–221.
49 While editors of the *Encyclopaedia Britannica* placed a figure for fatalities between 80,000 and 1,000,000, Robert Cribb suggested "perhaps 500,000 people died". See "September 30th Movement: Indonesian History", *Encyclopaedia Britannica*. www.britannica.com/event/September-30th-Movement Accessed 18 Sep 2018; and, Robert Cribb, "GESTAPU Affair (1965): Annihilation of the Left", in *Southeast Asia: A Historical Encyclopedia from Angkor Wat to East Timor*, edited by Ooi Keat Gin (Santa Barbara, CA: ABC-Clio, 2004), I, p. 544.
50 "Pigafetta's Description of Brunei: July 1521", in *European Sources for the History of the Sultanate of Brunei in the Sixteenth Century*, edited by Robert Nicholl (Bandar Seri Begawan: Muzium Brunei, Penerbitan Khas Bil. 9, 1975), pp. 10–11.
51 Ooi Keat Gin, "Borneo in the Early Modern Period ca. Late Fourteenth to ca. Late Seventeenth Centuries", in *Early Modern Southeast Asia, 1350–1800*, edited by Ooi Keat Gin and Hoang Anh Tuan (London: Routledge, 2016), p. 95.
52 Graham Saunders, *A History of Brunei* (Kuala Lumpur: Oxford University Press, 1994), p. 64.
53 Hugh Low, "Selesilah (Book of Descent) of the Rajas of Bruni", *Journal of the Straits Branch of the Royal Asiatic Society*, 5 (June 1880): 1–36; and, H. R. Hughes-Hallett, "A Sketch of the History of Brunei", *Journal of the Malayan Branch of the Royal Asiatic Society*, 18, 2 (137) (Aug 1940): 23–42.

54 Cited in Rozan Yunos, "Sabah and the Sulu claims", *The Brunei Times*, Mar 7, 2013. It refers to Cesar Adib Majul, *Muslims in the Philippines* (Manila: University of Philippines Press, 1999).

55 Lady Sophia Raffles, *Memoir of the Life and Public Services of Sir Thomas Stamford Raffles, Particularly in the Government of Java, 1811–1816, and of Bencoolen and Its Dependencies, 1817–1824: With Details of the Commerce and Resources of the Eastern Archipelago and Selections from His Correspondence* (London: John Murray, 1830), p. 60. Emphasis added.

56 Ibid.

57 See James Francis Warren, *The Sulu Zone, 1768–1898: The Dynamics of External Trade, Slavery, and Ethnicity in the Transformation of a Southeast Asian Maritime State*, (Singapore: National University of Singapore (NUS) Press, 2007. First published in 1981 by Singapore University Press), pp. 18–19.

58 See Alexander Dalrymple, *A Full and Clear Proof That the Spaniards Can Have No Claim on Balambangan* (London: Author, 1774), p. 31.

59 L. R. Wright, *The Origins of British Borneo* (Hong Kong: Hong Kong University Press, 1970), p. 35. Emphasis added.

60 British North Borneo Treaties. British North Borneo, 1885. Protocol of 1885. [Madrid Protocol 1885]. Done at Madrid, Mar 7, 1885. file:///H:/Borneo%20in%20the%20Cold%20War/NOTES%20Cold%20War/Colony%20North%20Borneo/Protocol(Madrid).pdf Accessed 5 Sep 2018. Emphasis added.

61 Leigh R. Wright, "Historical Notes on the North Borneo Dispute", *Journal of Asian Studies*, XXV (May 1966), p. 484. Emphasis added.

62 Stephens, who headed UNKO, had initially opposed 'Malaysia', instead preferring an 'independence-from-Britain-first' strategy. However, following his appointment as chairman of MSCC, there was a reversal of opinion: "I found that my fears and misgivings, although quite natural, were unfounded", Stephens declared in his speech at the second meeting of the MSCC in Kuching (Dec 1961), "[t]hat Malaysia was a Plan put forward by an elder brother [the Tunku], who having gained freedom [independence for Malaya, Aug 1957] himself wanted also to see his younger brothers [North Borneo and Sarawak] enjoy the same freedom, and working together as good brothers should be better able to safeguard their future". Text of Address by the Chairman at the Opening Ceremony [Kuching, MSCC], p. 32. Federation of Mal[aysia]. Papers of Sir William Allmond C. Goode, [1960–1963]. GB 0162 MSS. Ind. Ocn. s. 323 (RHUK).

63 "Solidarity Consultative Committee", Malaysia Solidarity Consultative Committee Memorandum Malaysia, CO 947/1 p. 145. (NAUK); and, "Greater-Malaysia-Brunei Aspect", Letter from D. C. White to Mr Eastwood, Colonial Office, 11 January 1962. CO 1030/1012 (NAUK).

64 Meetings of the MSCC were held in Jesselton (21 August 1961), Kuching (18–20 December 1961), Kuala Lumpur (6–8 January 1962), and finally, Singapore (1–3 February 1962).

65 *Report of the Commission of Enquiry, North Borneo and Sarawak, 1962 by the Commission of Enquiry in North Borneo and Sarawak*, Great Britain, Office of Commonwealth Relations, Colonial Office (London: H.M.S.O., 1962), p. 50. Emphasis added.

66 "Penubuhan Malaysia 16 September 1963 [Formation of Malaysia Sep 16, 1963]", (ANM). www.arkib.gov.my/web/guest/penubuhan-malaysia-16-september-19632 Accessed 7 Sep 2018.

67 United Nations Malaysia Mission Report, "Final Conclusions of the Secretary-General", 14 September 1963. Annex 3 United Nations Malaysia Mission Report, Final Conclusions of the Secretary-General. Government of the Philippines (GOVPH) Official Gazette. www.officialgazette.gov.ph/1963/09/14/united-nations-malaysia-mission-report-final-conclusions-of-the-secretary-general-14-september-1963/ Accessed 9 Sep 2018. Emphasis added.

68 Manila Accord. Signed at Manila, on 31 July 1963 Manila Declaration. Signed at Manila, on 3 August 1963 Joint Statement. Signed at Manila, on Aug 5, 1963. Philippines, Federation of Malaya and Indonesia. No. 8029. United Nations-Treaty Series, 1965. p. 348. https://treaties.un.org/doc/publication/unts/volume%20550/volume-550-i-8029-english.pdf Accessed 7 Sep 2018. Emphasis added.

69 Ibid., p. 358. Emphasis added.

70 See *Pelita Brunei*, Aug 1, 1962.

71 See "Greater Malaysia-Brunei Aspects, Report on the Public Hearing of [the] Menteri Besar's Committee on Malaysia", CO 1030/1012 (NAUK).

72 Ibid. Emphasis added.

73 R. S. Milne and K. J. Ratnam, "Patterns and Peculiarities of Voting in Sabah, 1967", *Asian Survey*, 9, 5 (May 1969): 373–381; and, Margaret Roff, "Sabah's Political Parties and the 1967 State Election", *International Studies*, 9, 4 (Oct 1967): 431–451.

74 Marites Dañguilan Vitug and Glenda M. Gloria, *Under the Crescent Moon: Rebellion in Mindanao* (Quezon City: Institute for Popular Democracy, 2000), pp. 2–23.

75 See Cesar Adib Majul, *The Contemporary Muslim Movement in the Philippines* (Berkeley, CA: Mizan Press, 1985), pp. 40–53.

76 "370: Telegram from the Embassy in the Philippines to the Department of State", RG 59, Central Files 1967–69, POL 32–1 MALAYSIA – PHIL. Secret; Priority; Limdis. Repeated to Bangkok, Canberra, Djakarta, Kuala Lumpur, London, Singapore, Wellington, USUN, and CINCPAC. Foreign Relations of the United States, 1964–1968, Volume XXVI, Indonesia; Malaysia-Singapore; Philippines. (NARA).

77 Quoted in 'Sabah! A Game of Diversion' By Senator Benigno S. Aquino Jr. [Delivered "before a civic group" on Oct 5, 1968]. Government of the Philippines (GOVPH) Official Gazette. www.officialgazette.gov.ph/1968/10/05/sabah-a-game-of-diversion-by-senator-benigno-s-aquino-jr/ Accessed 18 Sep 2018.

78 *The ASEAN Report, Volume II: The Evolution and Programs of ASEAN* (Hong Kong: Dow Jones Publishing Co., Asia, Inc. 1979), p. 3; and, Purificacion V. Quisumbing, "International Dispute Settlement in the ASEAN Context", in *Cultural Factors in International Relations*, edited by R. P. Anand (New Delhi: Abhinav Publications, 1981), pp. 279–280.

79 See "The Claim to Sabah: A Historical Perspective", by Kathlyn dela Cruz, ABS-CBNnews.com, Posted at Mar 7, 2013 10:04 PM | Updated as of Mar 8, 2013 11:10 AM https://news.abs-cbn.com/focus/03/07/13/claim-sabah-historical-perspective Accessed 19 Sep 2018.

80 Leigh R. Wright, "Historical Notes on the North Borneo Dispute", *Journal of Asian Studies*, XXV (May 1966), p. 484.

81 Coincidentally the son of Senator Benigno S. Aquino, Jr., Benigno Simeon "Noynoy" Cojuangco Aquino III became 15th President of the Philippines.

82 In mid-February 2013, Raja Muda Agbimuddin Kiram led a 235-strong Royal Security Forces (RSF) of the Sultanate of Sulu and North Borneo laid siege to a small village, Kampung Tanduo in Lahad Datu, Sabah. Malaysian security forces launched an assault on 1 March, killing 56 militants with 10 losses. Agbimuddin, heir apparent to the Sulu sultanate, together with the RSF remained on the terrorist list of the Malaysian government. Ooi, *Historical Dictionary of Malaysia*, p. 390.

83 From the Italian phrase, *vivere pericolosamente*, that Indonesian President Sukarno used as the title of his 1964 Independence Day speech.

84 See Robert Cribb, ed., *The Indonesian Killings of 1965–1966: Studies from Java and Bali* (Clayton, VIC: Monash University Centre of Southeast Asian Studies, 1990).

8   A cauldron of violence

Massacres and guerrilla war

Even if remains only one, we will stick to the struggle.[1]
           Wen Ming Chyuan, NKCP Chairman, October 1965

In his Independence Day Speech of 17 August 1964, Sukarno entitled his address *Tahun Vivere Pericoloso* (The Year of Living Dangerously, shortened to *Tavip*) because of his perception that Indonesia was then threatened by imperialist powers.

> Malaysia is still positioned in front of our door. Malaysia still stands in front of the house of the Indonesian Republic like *the watchdog of imperialism.* Members of military pacts around us. . . . *The imperialists are openly encircling us.*[2]

By "military pacts", Sukarno was referring to the Anglo-Malayan Defence Agreement (AMDA) and Southeast Asia Treaty Organization (SEATO). The former was constituted in 1957 as a security umbrella for the newly independent Malaya; then in 1963, it was re-designated as the Anglo-Malaysian Defence Agreement whereby the UK, Australia, and New Zealand remained committed to the defence of the newly minted Federation of Malaysia. Formed in 1954, SEATO was an anti-communist and collective defense organization with membership from within and without the region, namely the UK, U.S., Australia, France, New Zealand, Pakistan (then included East Pakistan, present-day Bangladesh), the Philippines, and Thailand.

But it was neither imperialists, SEATO, or AMDA that, almost a year later, unleashed a force, a whirlwind of murderous rampage – the GESTAPU (30 September 1965)[3] and its horrific aftermath, the Indonesian Massacres (1965–1966)[4] – across the Indonesian archipelago, whereby hundreds of thousands would perish in its wake. Kalimantan too, to some extent, experienced its wrath but at a later date, viz. October–November 1967.

Meanwhile, neighbouring Sarawak, since the outbreak of the Brunei Rebellion, witnessed a shift in communist strategy from one of a united front tactic with a political party (SUPP) to one of armed revolution. The Sarawak Communist

Insurgency (1962–1990) was a protracted armed struggle of close to three decades that hung like the proverbial Sword of Damocles over this East Malaysian state for the greater part of its early independent period.[5] Military and material assistance undoubtedly came from the federal government at Kuala Lumpur, but it was the local leadership, the tenacity of the security forces,[6] the resilience of the multiethnic peoples that had to confront and endure the daily dangers and adversities of those trying years.

Therefore, between 1950 and 1990, Borneo resembled a cauldron of violence that boiled over, claiming lives, inflicting hardships, and causing fear and panic, anguish and distress. GESTAPU and its aftermath of widespread slaughter and the Sarawak Communist Insurgency were two cases in point. Were the local scenarios a consequence of local decisions and local actions borne from within, or derived from directives from without, the influence and intervention of Cold War players: Washington, Moscow, and/or Beijing?

The GESTAPU Affair

> Early on 1 October [1965], military units arrived at the houses of seven conservative generals to arrest them. Three generals, including the [A]rmy commander [Lieutenant] General Ahmad Yani . . . were shot while resisting arrest, and the seventh, Defense Minister General A[bdul]. H[aris]. Nasution . . . escaped, though his daughter was killed. The survivors were taken to the Halim [Perdanakusumah] air force base in south Jakarta, where they were killed; their bodies were dumped in an unused well. Other troops seized important positions in central Jakarta, and both President Sukarno . . . and the PKI leader, D[ipa]. N[usantara]. Aidit . . . were taken to Halim. The ostensible leader of the coup, Lieutenant Colonel Untung [Syamsuri], who was commander of President Sukarno's palace guard, the Tjak[r]abirawa Regiment, then announced that the action had been launched to prevent a coup by a "council of generals" on 5 October.[7]

This quote succinctly captures the fateful events that came to be referred to as the GESTAPU Affair that developed on the night of 30 September through the early morning of 1 October 1965.[8] As claimed by Untung, ostensibly the leader of the coup, in his radio broadcast to the nation at 7 o'clock on the morning of 1 October, the actions of the junior military officers – members of the 30 September Movement, an Army organization – were a pre-emptive strike against a "council of generals" who were allegedly planning to launch a seizure of power scheduled for 5 October.[9] This so-called council of generals was thought to have been assisted by the U.S. Central Intelligence Agency (CIA) for the prime agenda of toppling President Sukarno on 5 October on the occasion of the commemoration of Armed Forces Day. The broadcast also announced that President Sukarno was under the protection of the 30 September Movement.

The 'military units' referred to personnel from the Tjakrabirawa Regiment (comprising the 'Presidential Guards'), the Diponegoro and Brawijaya Divisions of Central Java and East Java, respectively. Besides Lieutenant General Ahmad Yani, the other two that were shot in their homes were Major General M. T.

Haryono and Brigadier General D. I. Pandjaitan. Three others, Major General Soeprapto, Major General S. Parman, and Brigadier General Sutoyo were taken to Lubang Buaya, a site near Halim, where they were summarily executed. All of the corpses were disposed in an abandoned well. All of the dead generals were members of the Army General Staff. The kidnapping party also shot Police Chief Brigadier Karel Sadsuitubun. It appeared that the coup perpetrators managed to eliminate the 'big fishes' of ABRI, six generals, and the chief of police. But Coordinating Minister for Defense and Security and Armed Forces Chief of Staff, General Abdul Haris Nasution, miraculously managed to evade the assassins, though he lost his five-year-old daughter, Ade Irma Suryani Nasution.

During the night of 30 September, PKI leader D. N. Aidit and Air Force commander, Air Vice-Marshal Omar Dhani, made their way to Halim. Apparently, in the morning (1 October), when he realized the presence of troops in the vicinity of the presidential palace, President Sukarno also headed for Halim.

On the morning of 1 October, some 2,000 troops from the Diponegoro and Brawijaya Divisions took positions on three sides of Merdeka Square,[10] namely on the north perimeter where Army headquarters were located (northeast) and the presidential palace (northwest), on the upper west perimeter stood the building of *Radio Republik Indonesia* (RRI, Radio of the Republic of Indonesia), and its lower part, the Ministry of Defense. Troops were also placed on the south perimeter where were located the government telecommunications building and the U.S. embassy. Interestingly, no troops were deployed on the eastern perimeter, where the headquarters of the *Komando Cadangan Strategis Angkatan Darat* (KOSTRAD, Army Strategic Command) was situated.

At 1 o'clock, three other broadcasts were made by the 30 September Movement: *Dekrit No. 1 – Tentang Pembentukan Dewan Revolusi Indonesia* (Decree No. 1 – About the Establishment of the Indonesian Revolutionary Council);[11] *Keputusan No. 1 – Tentang Susunan Dewan Revolusi Indonesia* (Ruling No. 1 – About the composition of the Indonesian Revolutionary Council);[12] and, *Keputusan No. 2 – Tentang Penurunan dan Penaikan Pangkat* (Ruling No. 2 – About Demotion and Promotion).[13]

Outside Jakarta, the 30 September Movement initiated power seizures across Java (West, Central, East, and Special Region of Yogyakarta [Jogjakarta]), Sumatra (North and West), Riau, Bali, South Kalimantan, and Nusa Tenggara Timur (eastern part of the Lesser Sunda Islands).[14]

Enter Suharto

Undoubtedly, the man of the entire episode was Major General Suharto, then KOSTRAD commander, who, in the early hours of the morning of 1 October, headed for his command headquarters on the eastern perimeter of Merdeka Square. It was within the KOSTRAD building where most of the coup drama unfolded.[15] Having succeeded in gaining support from the commanders of the Navy and the National Police, he attempted in vain to contact the Air Force chief Air Vice-Marshal Omar Dhani and to secure news of the fate of his friend and superior,

Lieutenant General Ahmad Yani. Failing which, Suharto seized command of the Army, issuing orders for all troops to remain in their barracks.

It seemed that supplies of food and drinks were not forthcoming for the troops at Merdeka Square, namely the 454th Battalion, Diponegoro Division and of the 530th Battalion, Brawijaya Division. Capitalizing on troop discomfort and undoubtedly some dissatisfaction among the ranks, over the course of the afternoon, Suharto won over the 530th and thereafter, the 454th, without a shot fired. It seemed that the troops were under the impression that they were affording protection for President Sukarno, who was believed to be in the presidential palace. Likewise, Untung's own 1st Honour Guard Battalion (Army) in RRI also withdrew without a fight. By 7 o'clock in the evening of 1 October, all 'enemy' positions within Merdeka Square were neutralized by Suharto. Two hours later, with Nasution by his side, Suharto announced to the nation over a radio broadcast that he was in command of the Army and intended to destroy all counter-revolutionary forces and save President Sukarno. At the same instance, an ultimatum was issued to rebel troops at Halim.

That evening, it seemed that President Sukarno departed Halim for the presidential palace at Bogor, some 60 kilometres to the south.[16] Following brief skirmishes in the morning of 2 October, Suharto's forces secured Halim. Prior to the seizure by government forces, Aidit departed by air for Yogyakarta, likewise, Dhani for Madiun.[17]

Dramatic as it unfolded, Untung and his fellow coup compatriots, however, were defeated in Jakarta within 24 hours, and elsewhere in Central Java, it was all over for the rebels by the end of the third day (3 October). A special military tribunal, *Mahmillub* (*Mahkamah Militer Luar Biasa* [Extraordinary Military Court], tried the coup leaders and passed the death sentence for key figures including Untung, and gave others long prison terms.

Sweeping the big stage for a new act

Although the GESTAPU Affair only resulted in the deaths of 12 individuals including six senior generals of the Army, the backlash was unbelievably horrific. A bloodbath of officially authorized mass killings began shortly thereafter until the early part of 1966 that subsequently consumed between a conservative estimate of 500,000 lives and an astonishing figure of 2 to 3 million.[18] This wave of wholesale slaughter came to be known as the Indonesian Massacres (1965–1966) that has been succinctly captured in graphic detail by the staunchly anti-communist U.S.-based *Time* magazine (17 December 1965) that objectively presented this exposé:

> Communists, red sympathizers and their families are being massacred by the thousands. Backlands [provincial] army units are reported to have executed thousands of Communists after interrogation in remote jails. Armed with wide-bladed knives called "parangs", Moslem bands crept at night into the homes of Communists, killing entire families and burying the bodies in shallow graves. The murder campaign became so brazen in parts of rural East

Java, that Moslem bands placed the heads of victims on poles and paraded them through villages. The killings have been on such a scale that the disposal of the corpses has created a serious sanitation problem in East Java and Northern Sumatra where the humid air bears the reek of decaying flesh. Travelers from these areas tell of small rivers and streams that have been literally clogged with bodies. River transportation has at places been seriously impeded.[19]

Suharto and his right-wing, anti-communist colleagues in the Army decided on 'sweeping the big stage for a new act' that, once and for all, eliminated their erstwhile rival, the PKI, and ushered in a new order. Hence, the GESTAPU Affair was squarely blamed on the PKI, a convenient pretext for ousting the communists. Black propaganda was initiated. The Army embarked on covert psychological operations in portraying and depicting the GESTAPU Affair as a communist conspiracy to undermine and ultimately overthrow President Sukarno and the RI government. The Army-coined acronym 'GESTAPU' was deliberate, to equate it with Nazi Germany's Gestapo (*Geheime Staatspolizei*), the notoriously repressive Secret State Police apparatus of Nazi Germany and German-occupied Europe.[20] Embellished tales including graphic images of the ordeal of the murdered generals, including being tortured and sexually mutilated (castration), were disseminated to the masses.[21] The black propaganda campaign was convincing and aroused much anger and hatred towards the PKI in particular, and communists and communism in general, among the majority-Muslim population that had hitherto been wary of the atheist communists and their foreign ideology. Compounding the anti-communist feelings, there were added the religious and ethnic factors, the latter targeting the non-indigenous Chinese.[22]

The mass slaughter initiated in Jakarta, commencing from the third week of October, gaining momentum across Central and East Java, and thence Bali. Elsewhere in the archipelago, pogroms were executed in Acheh and Medan in North Sumatra, Makassar, Lombok, and much later, in West Kalimantan.

The Army's involvement was unclear, although in the early stages, undoubtedly military units moved against the PKI. But whether the Army directly 'dirtied' its hands with communist blood or left it to other parties – communal vigilante groups, Muslim youths, local militias, and others – the slaughter in most cases did not begin until the arrival and/or presence of military personnel sanctioning the killings.[23] Thereafter, the pogrom acquired a 'life' of its own to the extent of literally wiping out an entire *desa* (village) or a *pemukiman* (settlement).

Indonesians literally went on a murderous rampage across the archipelago. Central and East Java together with Bali and North Sumatra exhibited the worst scenarios, not unlike that later witnessed in Cambodia's infamous 'Killing Fields' of the late 1970s.[24] The anti-communist pogroms spilt over into religious and sectarian 'settling of scores' on Java, between *abangan* and *santri*, and in other locales, such as in North Sumatra, indigenous against Javanese plantation labour; also targeted were the minority Chinese in Medan, Makassar, and Lombok.[25]

The killings were face-to-face encounters where the perpetrators undertook cold-blooded slaughter that took various forms, viz. from point-blank shooting, stabbing, beheading with Japanese-style samurai swords to more barbaric and sadistic acts of dismembering alive, disembowelling, castration, impaling, and strangling.[26] The weapons employed ranged from machetes, swords, knives, sickles, and ice picks to bamboo spears, iron rods, wires, ropes, and other improvised weapons. Usage of firearms, such as rifles, shotguns, and pistols, was limited.[27]

The bulk of the victims were Javanese, Balinese, and Chinese, all perceived to be PKI members, or known sympathizers, supporters, or associated with PKI, and those directly or indirectly linked to communism and/or the People's Republic of China (PRC), perceived by many to be the backers of the PKI. Black propaganda by the Army paid dividends in reaping unbelievable successes, convincing many amongst the population of the communists as the bogeyman, not only to *Republik Indonesia*, but also to Islam and the indigenous peoples.

Foreign involvement

Intriguingly, Army Intelligence personnel Colonel Sukendro claimed while in Beijing that he received a name list of the assassinated generals prior to the GESTAPU Affair from the Chinese government.[28] Upon his return, when his mention of the name list was made public, mobs attacked PRC consulates in Medan, Banjarmasin, and Makassar, culminating in the sacking and razing of the embassy in Jakarta on 1 October 1966.[29] Consequently, diplomatic relations were broken in the following year. This alleged complicity of Beijing later turned out to be a fabrication, undoubtedly a part of the Army's black propaganda.[30] The damage, however, had already been done.

Complicity of the Western democracies in the GESTAPU Affair remained clouded in mystery and in embargoed archival materials. Nonetheless, a recent scholarly work, published in 2018, unreservedly revealed the hitherto *known* scenario:

> The exact role played by the United States in the genocide remains unclear, as US government archives relating to Indonesia from the period remain sealed. *It is known*, however, that *at a minimum*, in addition to openly celebrating Suharto's rise to power, the United States supplied money and communications equipment to the Indonesian military that facilitated the killings, gave fifty million rupiah to the military-sponsored KAP-Gestapu[31] death squad, and provided the names of thousands of PKI leaders to the military, who may have used this information to hunt down and kill those identified. The United States, Britain and Australia *additionally* played an active role in "black propaganda operations" in Indonesia during the genocide, including broadcasting clandestine radio broadcasts into the country. These broadcasts repeated Indonesian military propaganda as part of a psychological warfare campaign to discredit the PKI and encourage support for the killings.[32]

This claim has been corroborated by various other scholarly studies, academic as well as journalistic exposé, some more explicit than others.[33]

In the Cold War context of the early and mid-1960s, the involvement of the Western powers, in particular the U.S., was entirely understandable, even expected. In 1965, American direct involvement in Vietnam was escalating: the execution of Operation Flaming Dart (February) and Operation Rolling Thunder (March), followed shortly thereafter by the landings at Da Nang of the 3,500 men of the 9th Marine Expeditionary Brigade, the first U.S. combat troops on Vietnamese soil.[34] Washington was wholly committed to ensuring that the frontline 'domino' of Indochina, namely Vietnam, was not going to fall.

Hence, the Sukarno presidency, that was increasingly leaning towards the Left, the PKI, the latter apparently backed by Beijing, posed a *real threat* to the U.S. in Southeast Asia. If the rear 'domino', Sukarno's Indonesia, was to fall, consumed by the communists, it would jeopardize American interests in the entire region, and Vietnam, in particular. Such an eventuality would realize Eisenhower's 'falling domino' principle that he had pronounced a decade earlier.

Therefore, the Johnson administration (1963–1969) had to ensure that the Indonesian 'domino' did not fall:

> Washington did everything in its power to encourage and facilitate the [A]rmy-led massacre of alleged PKI members, and U.S. officials worried only that the killing of the party's unarmed supporters might not go far enough, permitting Sukarno to return to power and frustrate the [Johnson] Administration's emerging plans for a post-Sukarno Indonesia. This was efficacious terror, an essential building block of the neoliberal policies that the West [*read*: U.S.] would attempt to impose on Indonesia after Sukarno's ouster.[35]

Then, on 17 October 2017, "a cache of previously classified telegrams sent from the US Embassy in Jakarta provides *new and damning evidence* that the US is no stranger to the dark arts of covert regime change".[36]

> The new telegrams confirm the US *actively encouraged and facilitated genocide in Indonesia* to pursue its own political interests in the region, while propagating an explanation of the killings it knew to be *untrue*.
>
> The new telegrams, published by the National Security Archive (NSA) [Washington, DC], show Embassy staff were aware [of] systematic mass killings, which they describe as a "slaughter", were occurring throughout the archipelago, from West Papua to Sumatra.[37]

The declassified telegrams further revealed falsehoods that were propagated then to instigate and fuel the "slaughter".

> US officials co-opted media outlets to actively spread military propaganda accounts of the killings both inside and outside Indonesia. This propaganda account described the killings as the result of a spontaneous uprising by "the

people" and alleged that the 30 September Movement – a failed internal-military action that was used by the military to justify its own attack against the PKI – *had been masterminded by the PKI and China.*

The new telegrams confirm that US Embassy staff were aware PKI members around the country appeared to *have no prior knowledge* of the 30 September Movement. They also reveal the Embassy knew that news reports republished by the Indonesian military *claiming Chinese involvement in the 30 September Movement were "a hoax"* that had originated in Hong Kong.

As [US Ambassador to Indonesia Marshall] Green [t. June 1965–1969] explained on 4 May 1966, *allegations of Chinese involvement had been manufactured to serve "the propaganda needs of the moment"*, namely to deflect blame for the [30 September] Movement away from Soekarno. He [Green] had then stated bluntly that "we [US Embassy staff] do not think the Chinese were a primary factor in the September 30 Movement". This did not stop the US (and Green personally) from repeating these claims. In both cases, the Embassy's willingness to circulate what it knew to be "fake news" helped to incite the killings.[38]

Without a shadow of a doubt, Washington was in cohort with anti-Sukarno and anti-PKI elements, and all parties involved wished to have both Sukarno and the PKI eliminated.

Emergence of Orde Baru (New Order)

The covert Western backing in the toppling of Sukarno was an unqualified success. Sukarno's part in the GESTAPU Affair, the particularly damning appearance of him with Aidit of the PKI at Halim on that fateful night of 30 September, to a great extent sealed his fate. The public perception then (September/October 1965) of Sukarno, the revolutionary hero and political strongman, was of a president who had overtly leaned towards the Left, and had in recent years (from the 1960s) displayed tendencies of increasingly empowering the PKI, for instance, the sanctioning of the creation of a 'Fifth Force', a PKI militia.[39] Real or perceived support and in favouring the PKI was detrimental to Sukarno, as the Army under Suharto's command had squarely laid the blame of the whole GESTAPU Affair on the communists, their supporters and sympathizers. Sukarno literally was condemned in the public sphere among the masses. The Army, on its part, instigated and encouraged KAMI (*Kesatuan Aksi Mahasiswa Indonesia* [Joint-Action Union of Indonesian Students]), an anti-communist group constituted on 27 October 1965 comprising largely Muslim and Christian (Catholic) undergraduates and ex-members of the proscribed *Partai Sosialis Indonesia* (PSI, Socialist Party of Indonesia),[40] to protest against President Sukarno for his complicity with the GESTAPU Affair. Within a span of three years (1965–1968), the fortunes of Sukarno declined, and conversely that of Suharto strengthened, the waning of the 'Old Order' and the emergence and rise of a 'New Order' or *Orde Baru*. Table 8.1 traces the transition over a timeline of the shift in the locus of power.

Table 8.1 Demise of *Orde Lama*, Rise of *Orde Baru*

Date	Event, Developments
17 Aug 1964	Sukarno delivered his *Tahun Vivere Pericoloso* (The Year of Living Dangerously, or *Tavip*).
30 Sept 1965	The GESTAPU Affair
2 Oct 1965	Major General Suharto entrusted with the immediate task of restoring security and order in the nation.
c. late Oct 1965 to c. early Mar 1966	The Indonesian Massacres (1965–1966)
13 Feb 1966	Commencement of *Mahmillub* (*Mahkamah Militer Luar Biasa* [Extraordinary Military Court]) trials.
11 Mar 1966	President Sukarno signed *Supersemar* (*Surat Perintah Sebelas Maret* [Order of Eleventh March]), that authorized then Army commandant Lieutenant General Suharto full authority to restore order during the Indonesian Massacres (1965–1966).
12 Mar 1966	PKI and its various mass organizations were proscribed.
June 1966	*Majelis Permusyawaratan Rakyat (Sementara)* (MPRS-S) [(Provisional) People's Deliberative Assembly] strips Sukarno's title, 'President for Life of Indonesia'.
11 Aug 1966	Indonesia signed a peace agreement officially recognising Malaysia, and formally concluded *Konfrontasi* (1963–1966).
28 Sept 1966	Indonesia officially returned as a full member of the UN.
12 Mar 1967	MPRS-S impeaches Sukarno as President of Indonesia; appoints Suharto as Acting President.
8 Aug 1967	Indonesia together with Malaysia, the Philippines, Singapore, and Thailand sign the ASEAN Declaration that hence establishes the regional intergovernmental organization of ASEAN (Association of Southeast Asian Nations).
27 Mar 1968	MPRS appoints Suharto President of Indonesia.

Sources: Robert Cribb, *Historical Dictionary of Indonesia* (Metuchen, NJ, and London: The Scarecrow Press, 1992), pp. l-li; M. C. Ricklefs, *A History of Modern Indonesia since c. 1200*, 4th ed. (Houndmills, UK, and New York: Palgrave Macmillan, 2008), p. 295; Adam Schwarz, *A Nation in Waiting: Indonesia's Search for Stability*, 2nd ed. (Crows' Nest, NSW: Allen and Unwin, 1999), p. 2.

Public opinion worked against Sukarno, in part due to his apparent knowledge of, and sympathy for, the events of 30 September, and for his tolerance of Leftists and communists, whom the Army assigned blame for the coup attempt. Student groups, such as KAMI, were encouraged by and sided with the Army against Sukarno. On 11 March 1966, Suharto secured a presidential decree (known as the *Supersemar*), which gave him authority to take any action necessary to maintain security.[41] Using the decree, the PKI was banned in March 1966 and the parliament (MPRS), government, and military were purged of pro-Sukarno elements, many of whom were accused of being communist or communist sympathizers, and summarily replaced by Suharto advocates.

A June session of the newly purged MPRS banned Marxism-Leninism, ratified the *Supersemar*, and stripped Sukarno of his self-proclaimed title of 'president for life'.[42] In August–September 1966, and against the wishes of Sukarno, the New Order ended Indonesia's confrontation with Malaysia and re-joined the United Nations. Parliament re-convened in March 1967 to impeach the President for his apparent toleration of the 30 September Movement and violation of the constitution by promoting PKI's international communist agenda, negligence of the economy, and promotion of national "moral degradation" via his womanizing behaviour.[43] In March 1967, the MPRS stripped Sukarno of his remaining power, and Suharto was named Acting President. Sukarno was placed under house arrest in Bogor Palace; little more was heard from him until his demise in June 1970. In March 1968, the MPRS appointed Suharto to the first of his five-year terms as President.[44]

PKI, the Army, and Borneo

With a largely rural, agricultural peasant population with an insignificant prole-tariat, Kalimantan was no breeding or nurturing ground for communist ideology, and no Mao Zedong figure arose in its tropical midst. The outcome of the 1955 Parliamentary and Constituent Assembly Elections demonstrated the less than lukewarm reception of the PKI, at the bottom tier vis-à-vis other political oppo-nents in West and East Kalimantan (Table 6.6). In South Kalimantan, PKI achieved a fifth placing among the ten parties in contention. Overall, PKI did not have a strong base in Kalimantan as a whole.

Interestingly, Amar Hanafiah (Abu Amar Hanafiah), a cleric from West Sumatra, helmed as First Secretary in the *Comite Daerah Besar* (CDB, Provincial Commit-tee) PKI South Kalimantan. Although a party member in a senior position, Amar Hanafiah still steadfastly undertook his daily prayers, thereby drawing the com-ment that he "has not yet fully [understood] Marxist ideology".[45]

Nonetheless, his active personality and oratory skills distinguished Amar Hana-fiah at the Sixth PKI National Congress (7–14 September 1959) in Jakarta, where he projected the plight and poverty of the peasantry of Kalimantan, South Kali-mantan in particular, to the top echelons of the party.[46] He revealed that in South Kalimantan, there remained remnants of feudalism in the form of land monopoly by landlords and the foreclosure of peasant land owing to default of debts that placed the peasant as slaves vis-à-vis landlords and loan sharks.[47] He lamented that despite the fertility of the land, "there is not enough food to meet the minimum needs of the people", and he claimed that, "The people live in a state of half-starvation".[48] But with the intervention and proactive activities of the PKI, though at the "preliminary stage", they already "offer[ed] hope" to create "whereby mud rice fields fertilize rice and PKI, farmers unite, struggle [and] to sing and dance".[49] Despite the optimism displayed by Secretary Amar Hanafiah, the reality was far from the picture that he painted.

As has been demonstrated in the electoral results of 1955, PKI was not popular in South Kalimantan as elsewhere across Kalimantan. But, from the PKI per-spective, the villain of the piece was the Kalimantan war hero, Colonel Hassan

Basry. At the conclusion of *Revolusi Indonesia*, Hassan Basry embarked on an education quest, firstly pursuing religious studies at Al Azhar University, Cairo (1951–1953), and thereafter, at the American University (1953–1955). In 1956, he was elevated as Commander of the 21st Infantry Regiment/Commander of the VI Territorial (Army) of South Kalimantan. Three years later, he assumed as Commander of KODAM X/Lambung Mangkurat.

During the early part of 1960, the PKI was active with a slew of activities and establishing mass organizations. The staunchly anti-communist Colonel Hassan Basry issued a 'freeze letter' dated 22 August 1960 that prohibited all PKI activities and its mass organizations. For this action, he was reprimanded by President Sukarno, but as head of the South Kalimantan Regional War Authority, he disregarded the president's admonishment. According to a local historian, "That is why Pak Hassan [Basry] is a figure that the president [Sukarno] does not really like. Because he openly disagrees with the Nasakom concept".[50] But 'Pak Hassan's' defiant action in freezing the PKI and its mass organizations prompted his counterparts in South Sulawesi and South Sumatra to act in similar fashion. The recalcitrant act came to be referred as the 'South Three' – South Kalimantan, South Sulawesi, and South Sumatra, all taking an anti-PKI stance. It was an exemplary show of defiance to Jakarta.

His recalcitrant act notwithstanding, Hassan Basry was elevated to the rank of Brigadier General and took up the appointment as Deputy Regional Commander between Regions of Kalimantan (1961–1963). His successor as Commander of KODAM X/Lambung Mangkurat was Brigadier General Amir Machmud.

GESTAPU, pogroms, and Borneo

While the drama unfolded at Merdeka Square and Halim, across the Java Sea in Banjarmasin on the Friday morning of 1 October 1965, Brigadier General Amir Machmud summoned all his officers for a discussion following the RRI broadcast by Untung of the 30 September Movement. There was understandably some confusion and uncertainties as to developments in the national capital. Communication channels then were not as advanced or efficient to elicit confirmation from Jakarta to faraway Banjarmasin.

According to the RRI broadcast at 1 o'clock, *Keputusan No. 1 – Tentang Susunan Dewan Revolusi Indonesia* (Ruling No. 1 – About the composition of the Indonesian Revolutionary Council), Brigadier General Amir Machmud was named as one of the 45-member *Dewan Revolusi Indonesia* (Revolutionary Council of Indonesia).[51] Apparently non-PKI members who were named to the *Dewan Revolusi Indonesia* were clueless of G30S and were unlikely to be supportive of the movement.[52] Brigadier General Amir Machmud was likely too in the latter category. However, PKI's Secretary Amar Hanafiah urged Brigadier General Amir Machmud not to disregard his appointment, as it was supported by the top PKI leadership in Jakarta; the latter, however, strenuously declined. Moreover, Amar Hanafiah strongly demanded that a local *Dewan Revolusi* be established. Such a demand was also summarily dismissed by the Commander of KODAM X/Lambung Mangkurat.

Finally, at 3 o'clock (local time), the protracted deliberation among Brigadier General Amir Machmud and his officers came to a conclusion that it was *not* an internal matter of the Army *per se* but a coup d'état by young Army officers.[53] Shortly thereafter, upon instructions from Brigadier General Amir Machmud, RRI Banjarmasin broadcasted two statements, viz.:

a   Brigadier General Amirmachmud and Kodam X/Lambung Mangkurat remained loyal and obey the orders of His Excellency the Honorable President/Commander in Chief Bung Karno [President Sukarno];

b   All ranks of Kodam X/Lambung Mangkurat to remain calm and alert and remain in their respective posts.[54]

The radio announcement was followed by instructions from the Governor/KDH (*Kepala Daerah* [Head of Region]) South Kalimantan, Lieutenant Colonel (Infantry) H. Aberani Sulaiman, to all Heads of Level II Region and the Mayor of Banjarmasin to keep calm and lend full support for President Sukarno and take firm action against treason. At 7 o'clock in the evening (local time), the *Deputi Komander Antara Daerah* (KOANDA, Commander-in-chief All Regions), Mandala II Kalimantan Region in daily orders to the populace signed by KOANDA Chief of Staff Brigadier General Moenadi stressed that the people should "only obey orders through the hierarchical channel from authorized superiors, and immediately take firm action against elements that stirred the peace in general".[55]

On 6 October 1965, various political parties and mass organizations and Sekber Golkar (*Sekretariat Bersama Golongan Karya* [Joint Secretariat of Functional Groups])[56] convened for discussions. At the close of their consultations, a unanimous demand was for PKI to be disbanded because PKI and its various mass organizations were masterminds and perpetrators of the September 30 Movement. Ten days later, on 16 October, Brigadier General Amir Machmud, who was also PEPELRADA (*Penguasa Pelakana Peperangan Daerah* [Executive Authority of Regional Warfare], declared PKI and its mass organizations to be dissolved throughout South Kalimantan.[57] The pendulum in Kalimantan had shifted, from loyalty to Sukarno to alignment with Suharto.

Unlike post-GESTAPU mass killings of PKI members, sympathizers, and supporters in Central and East Java, Bali, and North Sumatra, Kalimantan was spared the onset of the Indonesian Massacres. Neither were there massacres of ethnic Chinese, like the slaughters in Makassar, Medan, and on Lombok island. Other adverse developments, however, impacted on the Chinese populace, the bulk of which settled in West Kalimantan, in the late 1960s that, to some extent, had ties to G30S and its aftermath.

Maverick West Kalimantan: remnants of the PKI and the Chinese Massacre

While the GESTAPU Affair unfolded and thereafter the Indonesian Massacres were unleased across Java (Central and East), Bali, Sumatra, Makassar, Lombok, and other corners of the archipelago, West Kalimantan appeared to be in *status quo* until mid-1967. Against the backdrop of *Konfrontasi*, the Army continued its assistance and cooperation including military training of anti-Malaysia elements that comprised the SCO and remnants of TNKU. PGRS (*Pasukan Gerilya Rakyat Sarawak*, Sarawak People's Guerrilla Force [SPGF]), the guerrilla unit of the SCO, and PARAKU (*Pasukan Rakyat Kalimantan Utara*, North Kalimantan People's Army [NKPA]), the military arm of the NKCP (North Kalimantan Communist Party),[58] were active and in partnership and with support of the Army undertook raids and engaged in skirmishes along the Sarawak-Kalimantan border region.

When Malaysia was finally realized on 16 September 1963, Jakarta's response was *Konfrontasi*, for all intents and purposes as far as the Army was concerned, simply marked by a series of occasional, low-intensity raids into neighbouring Sarawak. Military units along the Sarawak-Kalimantan border was not the elite crack battalions but lesser units of the Army, which were tasked in undertaking such piecemeal raids. Besides Army personnel led by commanders who were less than enthusiastic about the idea of *Konfrontasi*, alongside the regular soldiers were the *sukarelawan*, the 'volunteers', a hotchpotch fighting force comprising PGRS (mainly of SCO cadres), PARAKU (remnants of TNKU), and PKI (chiefly those who had fled the pogroms on Java and the followers of Said Achmad Sofyan,[59] head of the West Kalimantan branch of the PKI). No less than 5,000 *sukarelawan* were directly involved in *Konfrontasi*.[60]

During the tumultuous period of the mid-1960s, members of the SCO held an important meeting in Pontianak, a fortnight prior to the GESTAPU Affair in Jakarta.

> The Pontianak Conference of 17th-19th September 1965 was the foundation stone of the Sarawak Communist Movement. However, none of the attendees was communist; they were only the members of the [Sarawak] Liberation League [SLL] and the "O Members" of the [Sarawak] Advanced Youths Association [SAYA]. Although they had discussed about forming a communist party, they had no time to do so, because the situation was very tense and the rumour of a putsch was spreading wild, and so they dispersed hastily.[61]

The Conference was the one and only important gathering of the SCO. Hence, when the NKCP was formally inaugurated in 1971, '19th September' was chosen as the official date of its formation.[62] Interestingly, where or who was the source of "the rumour of a putsch was spreading wild"? Was it referring to the GESTAPU Affair that was yet to explode on the scene in faraway Jakarta? If so, this advanced notice, though only a "rumour of a putsch", to be known in distant Pontianak some two weeks prior to its execution, was uncanny indeed.

A recent study offered another version of the Pontianak Conference that *appeared* to be more conclusive:

> In 1965, relations between the Indonesian government and Sarawak guerrillas improved, and on 19 September 1965, some Indonesian government officials,

[A. M.] Azahari, and the leaders of the Sarawak guerrillas held a conference in Pontianak, the capital of West Kalimantan. On that occasion, they declared the establishment of the North Kalimantan Communist Party. This happened immediately before G30S.[63]

The presence of "some Indonesian government officials" at the conference was indicative of Jakarta's support then. But the date "19 September 1965" for the "establishment of the North Kalimantan Communist Party" is inaccurate.[64] Nonetheless, following this Pontianak Conference, developments from afar were to alter the local situation in West Kalimantan and neighbouring Sarawak.

After the gathering in Pontianak, Wen Ming Chyuan, leader of the SCO, together with Azahari, departed for Beijing to attend the National Day ceremony on 1 October.[65]

Before the GESTAPU Affair in Jakarta, Kuala Lumpur officially announced the separation of Singapore from Malaysia on 9 August 1965, after 23 months in the federation, to become an independent and sovereign state.[66] The implication of this separation initially heightened the hopes of the SCO. Relations between the SCO and Singapore's *Barisan Sosialis* (Socialist Front) was unclear. Apart from sharing the anti-Malaysia stance, the latter might have provided some moral and material support to the SCO. But between 1963 and 1966, the fortunes of *Barisan Sosialis* had increasingly diminished, commencing from Operation Coldstore (2 February 1963), the first of a series of government crackdowns on Leftists utilizing the Internal Security Act (ISA) that allowed detention without trial. Such actions by the Malaysian authorities, and after 1965, the Singapore government, increasingly debilitated the strength of the *Barisan Sosialis*, perceived to be a communist-infiltrated or communist (united) front political party. A weakened *Barisan Sosialis* was of no benefit to the SCO. The latter only had the PKI.

The GESTAPU Affair and its horrific aftermath, the Indonesian Massacre, witnessed the wholesale slaughter of members of the PKI, its supporters and sympathizers throughout the archipelago. But for Kalimantan, because of the weak position of the PKI that generally failed to garner local support, there were scant incidences of witch hunts and pogroms of the PKI, known communists or Leftists, and/or their sympathizers or supporters. In West Kalimantan, the 'aftermath' was merely postponed, only to play out some 24 months later in 1967.

As has been pointed out, PKI did not possess either an elite following or grassroots support across Kalimantan, as demonstrated in the electoral verdict of 1955 (Table 6.6). As a result, anti-PKI forces focused their attention and resources on 'red' areas (communist-infested) on Java, particularly the central and eastern provinces, and elsewhere like North Sumatra, Makassar, and Lombok. Kalimantan, however, located in the outlying areas, was given less than urgent priority by the Army that was bent on eliminating the 'red' menace. Despite West Kalimantan harbouring the bulk of the Chinese population, it did not translate into pro-PKI support. The Chinese community adhered to a pro-Beijing stance more of ethnic and familial ties rather than support for the CCP regime. Moreover, in West Kalimantan, good relations between the PKI and the local Army unit were pivotal for the delayed murderous 'aftermath'.

Sofyan, who led the PKI in West Kalimantan, enjoyed a more than amicable relationship with Brigadier General H. Mussanif Riyakudu (Ryacudu), commandant of the Tanjungpura Regional Military Command (KODAM XII). The latter was a known supporter of Sukarno, and it was not surprising then that he too was indulgent of the PKI. But the Riyakudu-Sofyan tie was akin to a patron-client relationship, with mutual benefit for both parties. Sofyan courted Chinese support; his unqualified success among the Chinese youths of Pontianak went to the extent of him being accepted as *Tai Ko* or 'Big Brother'. Not only was the PKI's cultural arm, Lekra, allowed to utilize the pro-Beijing *Angin Timur* (East Wind) theatre facility, but also the PKI collaborated with a Chinese labour union, and various other associations, to establish and run adult night schools (*Lembaga Pendidikan Nasional*), where undoubtedly communist propaganda was disseminated besides imparting the rudiments of literacy, the 3R's (reading, writing, arithmetic).[67]

Meanwhile, in exploiting his father's reputation as a highly regarded *kiyai* (*kepala distrik*)[68] in Banjarmasin and his own command of Islamic studies, Sofyan garnered support among Pontianak's Islamic elite. His socializing triumph, whether among the Chinese or Islamic elites, placed him in good stead to assume the fifth membership in the expanded *Tjatuh Tunggal* (regional executive committee) in 1963.

At the same time, there was a conspicuous absence of anti-Chinese feeling among the local indigenous inhabitants. But the Chinese population faced numerous prohibitions, from the proscription of their associations including Baperki, repatriation to mainland China, a compilation of all personnel in organizations to licenses for schools revoked, forced participation in labour programmes (erection of infrastructure, agricultural expansion), and re-location from the interior to the coast.[69] Then towards the end of 1965, the Army ordered the expulsion from West Kalimantan of all Chinese in league with PKI or with other Chinese social organizations.[70] There was an attempt to expel some 45,000 Chinese, those from the interior districts, that did not possess *Republik Indonesia* citizenship.

Against this onslaught on the Chinese populace and anticipated onset of an anti-PKI wave of purges, Sofyan fled from Pontianak to the Bengkayang region with a few dozen followers (Map 8.1). Bengkayang was the hinterland of Singkawang comprising the region of north-central West Kalimantan stretching northeastwards to the borderlands adjacent to Bau on the Sarawak side. In the 1960s, Bengkayang was a rural area dotted with Chinese farming settlements. Here in the interior regions, the Chinese lived in a precarious situation, as the indigenous Dayaks were not exactly amicable about having foreign migrants on their ancestral lands. The PKI stalwarts established a base in the forested interior named Bukit Bara, where Sofyan sought to re-build the PKI through recruitment among the rural Chinese inhabitants and conducting military training at various camps across the vicinity, namely the Sambas and Pontianak districts.[71] This armed unit of the PKI assumed the title of *Tentera Komunis Kalimantan Barat* (TKKB, Communist Army of West Kalimantan).

In April 1967, Sofyan allied with members of the PGRS to create the 'Bara Force'.[72] Between April and July 1967, several newly recruited Chinese youths

Map 8.1 West Kalimantan

Source: Author

from Singkawang joined the Bara Force, where they were given training in guerrilla warfare.[73]

Meanwhile, momentous shifts were developing within the Army in Kalimantan that subsequently led to a change in the commander of KODAM XII. Peace talks were underway between May and June 1966 to end *Konfrontasi*. The Jakarta Accords were ratified by Malaysia's Deputy Prime Minister Tun Abdul Razak and Indonesia's Foreign Minister Adam Malik on 11 August 1966. Thereafter, faced with a communist insurgency in Sarawak, Kuala Lumpur began to exert pressure on Jakarta to implement sterner measures in Kalimantan, particularly West Kalimantan, to wipe out the communist scourge. Then, on 17 February 1967, a secret security agreement was penned by both parties allowing for joint and cross-border operations against the insurgents on the Sarawak-Kalimantan border corridor. Consequently, there was a reorganization of the military command structure (Table 8.2).

The ineffectual seemingly pro-PKI Brigadier General Riyakudu had to be replaced. Despite initiating *Operasi Sapu Bersih I* (Operation Clean Sweep I) with

Table 8.2 Military Command Structure for *Konfrontasi* and Post-*Konfrontasi* in Kalimantan

Military Command	Commander	Remarks
Komando Siaga (Koga or Alert Command); c. Jan 1963	Air Force Vice Marshal Omar Dhani	Vice Marshal Omar Dhani was a staunch supporter of President Sukarno.
Komando Siaga Mandala (Kolaga or Mandala Alert Command); Feb 1965	Air Force Vice Marshal Omar Dhani First Deputy Commander (*Wakil Panglima I*): Major General Suharto	Under Kolaga, the Army had the upper hand: the decision-making power was in the hands of Army Major General Suharto; Suharto was also Pangkostrad (commander of KOSTRAD, *Komando Cadangan Strategis Angkatan Darat* [Army Strategic Reserve Command]).
Kolaga: respective commands for Kalimantan and Sumatra; although covered all military services, it was confined to areas of command, namely Kalimantan and Sumatra; troop mobilization came under KOSTRAD.	Brigadier General M. A Soepardjo (Kalimantan), combat forces *Kopur* II, operational name, *Mandau*; Brigadier General Kemal Idris (Sumatra), combat forces *Kopur* III, operational name, *Rentjong*	Brigadier General Soepardjo was pro-PKI; Brigadier General Kemal Idris, anti-communist and staunch Sukarno detractor.
Koanda Kalimantan (All-Kalimantan Regional Command) established March 1967	Under Koanda, Kodam XII/ Tanjungpura took on military operations in West Kalimantan under Brigadier General H. M. Ryacudu; jointly with Third Infrantry Brigade (Malaysia), Kodam XII launched *Sapu Bersih I* (Operation Clean Sweep I).	*Sapu Bersih I* was in every aspect a failure owing to poor coordination, lack of intelligence, conducted by poorly trained troops, unpreparedness, distraction (involvement in illegal activities), and the nonchalant attitude of the officer corps.
	Brigadier General Witono Sarsono, commander of Kodam XII from 29 June 1967	Appointment of Brigadier General Witono Sarsono rested on his vast experiences in executing anti-guerrilla operations, viz. Darul Islam in West Java (1950s), and PKI in Central and East Java (1965–1967).
	Sapu Bersih II (Operation Clean Sweep I), Aug-Dec 1967, codenamed *Operasi Persiapan dan Pengintaian* (Operation Preparation and Intelligence)	*Sapu Bersih II* possessed two interrelated objectives: (1) relocation of rural Chinese settlements to deprive the insurgents assistance (food, medicine, recruits, etc.); and (2) turning Dayaks against the Chinese in order that the latter removed from the interior to the coasts.

Sources: C. L. M. Penders, and Ulf Sundhaussen, *Abdul Haris Nasution: A Political Biography* (St Lucia: University of Queensland Press, 1985), p. 171; Harold Crouch, *The Army and Politics in Indonesia* (Ithaca, NY: Cornell University Press, 1978), pp. 70–74; Semdam XII, *Tanjungpura Berjuang: Sejarah Kodam XII/ Tanjungpura* [*Tanjungpura Fighting: History of Kodam XII/Tanjungpura*] (Pontianak: Yayasan Tanjungpura, 1971), pp. 261, 270; Harjsa W. Bachtiar, *Siapa dia? Perwira Tinggi Tentera Nasional Indonesia Angkatan Darat* (*TNI-AD*) [*Who is he? Senior Officers of the National Armed Forces of Indonesia – Army* (*TNI-AD*)] (Jakarta: Penerbit Djambatan, 1988), p. 468

the commitment of five troop companies and jointly implemented with Malaysia's Third Infantry Brigade, the overall outcome was ineffective. Although there were *inter alia* various factors for the lacklustre performance, the most telling determinant was that of the military in not taking the insurgency as seriously as it should. The change in command was inevitable, and in late June 1967, Brigadier General A. J. Witono Sarsono was the choice of the emerging strongman, General Suharto. The new commander possessed commendable credentials appropriate for the tasks that lie ahead, notably his past experiences in suppressing the Darul Islam uprising in West Java in the 1950s and the ruthless elimination of the PKI in Central and East Java, 1965–1967.

Perhaps a coincidence, or premeditated as a response to the elevation of Brigadier General Witono Sarsono, a PGRS guerrilla squad, allied to Sofyan's Bara Force, launched an offensive on the Singkawang II Air Force Base located in the hilly terrain of Sanggau Ledo. The assault claimed four casualties – three air force personnel and a guard – and the seizure of 150 weapons.[74] It was a wake-up call to the extent that General Suharto convened a meeting in Jakarta of all the military heads involved in Kalimantan to address the insurgency.[75] First and foremost, West Kalimantan was declared a *Daerah Operasi*, or appropriately, a military Operations Area. Reinforcements were brought in: *Resimen Para Komando Angkatan Darat* (RPKAD, Army Para-Commando Regiment), Paratroop Battalion Raiders 100, and Infantry Battalion 328. The RPKAD, in fact, was the initiator of the PKI pogroms on Central Java that spread eastwards to East Java.[76] Whereas the paratroopers were brought in from Sumatra, the battalion of infantry was dispatched from West Java. It was militarily prudent to utilize forces from without for more objective execution of their duties.

'Of fish and water'

> Many people think it impossible for guerrillas to exist for long in the enemy's rear. Such a belief reveals lack of comprehension of the relationship that should exist between the people and the troops. The former may be likened to *water* the latter to the *fish* who inhabit it. How may it be said that these two cannot exist together? It is only undisciplined troops who make the people their enemies and who, like the fish out of its native element cannot live.
>
> Mao Zedong[77]

Mao was digressing on the classic anti-guerrilla tactic, analogically of depriving fishes (troops/insurgents) from water (populace). By late August 1967, *Operasi Sapu Bersih II* (Operation Clean Sweep II) was underway that attempted to employ the aforesaid tactic to literally and physically remove the 'water', of between 45,000 and 60,000 ethnic Chinese rural farming settlements. Witono sought to enlist the assistance of the Dayaks, the indigenous inhabitants of the interior, by provoking the natives against the rural Chinese. What later unfolded remains shrouded in mystery, but the incidences served the military's objective of inciting anti-Chinese sentiments among the Dayaks, who took action.

Apparently, on 3 September 1967, a so-called *Gerombolan Tjina Komunis* (GTK, Chinese Communist Horde) purportedly kidnapped nine inhabitants of Temu village in the sub-district of Sanggau Ledo.[78] Conveniently, nine corpses were discovered by a RPKAD unit working with locals. Inflammatory and racist remarks calling on Dayaks to avenge the murdered were flashed on the military's mouthpiece, *Angkatan Bersenjata*.[79] In the later part of the month, a Dayak *timang-gong* (traditional leader)[80] was killed in the Bengkayang area. Rumours were rife with the gory tale that the genitals of the deceased were removed and hoisted on a pole with a note in Chinese ideographic characters, literally pointing to the Chinese as the perpetrators. Again, as the previous incident, this disfiguring of the corpse was designed to provoke the Dayaks against their *Tjina* (Chinese) neighbours in the area.[81]

Instead, according to a military report, a series of *upacara adat pemabang* (traditional peace rituals) were staged, participated in by both Dayak and Chinese residents in the areas of Bengkayang, Mempawah Hilir, and Mempawah Hulu.

> Each villager, whether Dayak or Chinese or from another ethnic group, takes vows to unite against enemies who come from outside the community. Anyone who does not fulfil this promise will be subject to traditional law or evicted from the village and Dayak society.[82]

The Army appeared to be ignorant of the close Sino-Dayak relations in and around the Bengkayang, hence the peace rituals as a means to cleanse malignant influence "from outside the community".

Meanwhile, in coastal areas, Witono's forces literally undertook a 'sweeping' of PKI elements and, to some extent, were assisted by turncoat PKI members as informers.[83] In tandem, military operations were executed in the interior regions: Sikukng mountainous areas in proximity to the Sarawak-Kalimantan border; in adjacent areas from Seluas southward to Sanggau Ledo; in Mount Merebuk, southeast of Bengkayang.[84] In the latter location, the military claimed to have killed "twenty-five communist [members of] PGRS".[85] In line with its attempt to incite anti-Chinese hatred among Dayaks, villagers that were massacred by the military allegedly to be involved with the insurgents were blamed on 'Chinese PGRS' as the perpetrators. There were wanton killings, or mistaken identity, that the military admitted; for instance, some were Chinese villages that had no relations with either PGRS or PKI insurgents, and in fact, they were participants of the *upacara adat pemabang* alongside their Dayak neighbours.[86] From the military perspective, those killed were simply victims of friendly fire.

Orchestrated bloodbath

From mid-October to mid-November 1967, within a 240-square-kilometre triangular area with its north point at Bengkayang, west point at Sungai Pinyuh on the coast, and east point at Ngabang, between 2,000 and 3,000 ethnic Chinese were massacred by Dayaks, who were accompanied by the military.[87] It appeared to be a *delayed* staging of Kalimantan's version of the Indonesian Massacres (1965–1966) in the aftermath of the GESTAPU Affair.

Since the launching of *Operasi Sapu Bersih II* from late August 1967, the military had been actively instigating the Dayaks to embark on a Chinese pogrom to the extent of engineering the killings in Temu and the gory murder of a *timanggong* in September, and attempted though in vain, to place the blame on '*Tjina Komunis*'. But success came with the assistance of a Dayak figure, Oevaang Oeray, and the emergence and operation of the shadowy *Lasykar Pangsuma* (Pangsuma Militia).

Oeray's political fortune rose in the immediate post-war period of the late 1940s. The leadership vacuum consequent of the wartime executions of principal personalities across ethnicities excluding Dayaks offered opportunities for the latter. His appointment as head of the newly created *Kantor Urusan Dayak* (Dayak Affairs Office), and as one of the five-member *Badan Pemerintah Harian* (Daily Governing Board) of the *Daerah Istimewa Kalimantan Barat* (DIKB, Special Region of West Kalimantan), headed by the pro-Dutch Sultan Hamid II, Oeray was in good stead to be a part of the administration, an unprecedented position for a Dayak. But Sultan Hamid II's treacherous act of attempting to topple *Republik Indonesia*, in complicity with the Westerling Affair, earned him a decade-long prison term.[88] Oeray was side-lined as well. He was removed from bustling Pontianak, the provincial centre, to Kapuas Hulu district, the remotest corner of West Kalimantan, and later, to Sintang district, where he held in both instances the civil post of *bupati* (district head).

Oeray's re-emergence on the wings of the *Partai Persatuan Dayak* (PD, Dayak Unity Party) in the 1955 general elections (Table 6.6) elevated him to the governorship of West Kalimantan in 1960 in line with Sukarno's favouring *putera daerah* (lit., 'district prince', indigenes or native son). But the incoming *Orde Baru* (New Order) administration saw Oeray as the *Orde Lama*, a Sukarnoist, and he was removed from the governorship in 1966 and transferred to the Department of Domestic Affairs in Jakarta.

Although he boasted decades later that the initiative to remove the Chinese from the interior regions was his brainchild, it was quite likely that the military sought him out, believing that he alone could mobilize the Dayaks for such an undertaking.[89] According to military sources, in the wake of the murdered *timanggong* in the latter part of September, Dayak *pemuka* (leaders) had a four-eyed meeting with Oeray in Pontianak.[90] The outcome was a public Dayak 'declaration of war' on the Chinese populace, and the creation of a Dayak militia, *Lasykar Pangsuma*.[91] This paramilitary organization was strategically and symbolically named after the revered Dayak war hero, Panglima Pangsuma, who bravely fought Imperial Japanese forces, advancing into the interior during the Pacific War and military occupation of Borneo (1941–1945). Despite its occupation, the Imperial Japanese military administration possessed only limited control over the interior, where it remained Dayak territory. The allusion was conspicuous: the interior were Dayak territories hence Chinese settlers should be evicted.

The Dayak *Lasykar Pangsuma* was, from the outset, under 'instructions' from the military, hence, while the keyword of the 'spontaneity' of the Dayak killing spree of Chinese communists was stressed in all public announcements and media reports,[92] it was in reality an Army-instructed, directed, premeditated, and coordinated form of so-called spontaneity. According to Brigadier General Soemadi, who was directly involved in the communist suppression then,[93] the military sanctioned the Dayaks that anyone supporting or involved with the PGRS/PARAKU communists "*dapat dipenggal seperti babi atau ayam* [can be cut/beheaded like a pig or a chicken]" and "*antusiasme untuk mengambil kepala (ngayau) berkobar di mana-mana, dan mereka [pengayau] selalu dikawal oleh tentara* [the enthusiasm for taking heads (*ngayau*) flared up everywhere, and they [head-hunters] were always under military surveillance".[94] Moreover, Army-sponsored head-hunting feasts were held as a means of rewarding and encouraging the Dayaks.[95]

Detainees or refugees?

Despite the killings and brutal harassment, the Chinese peasant farmers did not resist the Dayaks and/or the military.[96] The murderous rampage concluded sometime towards the end of 1967. Thereafter, in the closing months of 1967 and during the early part of 1968, an exodus of Chinese was underway. Like the proverbial sheep, as many as 60,000 Chinese from the interior districts were physically removed southwards and westwards to the coastal towns, the bulk to Pontianak and Singkawang, and smaller groups to Mempawah, Sambas, and Pemangkat (Table 8.3). Their physical deportations were a result of having literally fled for their lives from the advancing pogroms, others being relocated in anticipation of forced removal from the interior, and many more were physically and forcefully 'escorted' out of the interior by the military.

Two groups of Chinese were distinguished: detainees and refugees. Those who were designated as 'detainees' were settled in camps in Singkawang and its vicinity; they were likely to be sympathizers, supporters, or even communists among their numbers. PGRS/PARAKU and PKI insurgents were concentrated in the Sambas areas and further northeast to the Sarawak-Kalimantan border. Camps in Pontianak and its surrounding areas housed 'refugees' that were latter resettled elsewhere on the coast. In contrast, inmates in Singkawang camps were closely monitored, and only a handful were resettled in the coastal towns (Table 8.3).

Table 8.3 Chinese Refugee Camps in West Kalimantan, November 1967 to August 1968

Location of camps	Initial arrival, November 1967	Re-registration, May 1968	Post-resettlement, August 1968
Singkawang, and vicinity	22,662	18,401	17,028
Pontianak, Mempawah, and vicinity	11,519	7,282	758

Source: (Adapted from) After Jamie S. Davidson, *From Rebellion to Riots: Collective Violence on Indonesian Borneo* (Singapore: National University of Singapore (NUS) Press, 2009), p. 75, table 1.

In later years, more Chinese in the interior districts were relocated for military purposes, namely implementing the classic anti-guerrilla tactic of draining the *water* (people) to deny/deprive the *fish* (insurgents). An estimate of 17,000 were removed from the border areas in Sanggau, Sintang, and Kapuas Hulu to southwards towards Pontianak and its vicinity in October 1970.[97] Two years later (December 1972), another 10,000 in the interior districts of Sambas were removed to Pemangkat and its coastal surroundings.

Conditions in the temporary refugee/detainee camps were appalling. Despite the notorious repressive measures of *Orde Baru* in muzzling the media, national newspapers such as *Kompas* and *Harian Kami* bravely defied the central authorities at Jakarta in reporting on the deplorable situation in the Kalimantan camps. A multitude of issues and problems, ranging from overcrowding, inadequate supplies of foods and medicines, outbreaks of diseases (malaria, leprosy, etc.), malnutrition, and mistreatment by the guards appeared to be commonplace, and were faithfully reported by *Kompas* and *Harian Kami*.[98] The latter reported of deaths in the camps, 508 in Pontianak camp in January 1968, and of 1,500 children in April 1968, apparently from starvation.[99] Furthermore, inmates of the camps were singularly labelled with the allegations of being involved with communist insurgents, an unjust attribution. Although it was undeniable that *some* of the rural Chinese in the interior and border regions had succoured the PGRS/PARAKU and/or PKI, it was unfair to brand *all* the Chinese in the interior regions that had been removed to the coastal camps of complicity with insurgent groups. Neither detainees nor refugees notwithstanding, the Chinese were literally at the mercy of the authorities.

'Cold' worse than 'hot'

From the aforesaid scenario, it would appear that the 'Cold War' period was worse than the 'Hot War' and Imperial Japan's military occupation (1941–1945). In West Kalimantan, within the confines of a 240-square-kilometre triangular region bordered by Bengkayang, Sungai Pinyuh, and Ngabang, egged on by the Army, Dayaks slaughtered between 2,000 and 3,000 ethnic Chinese and drove many of the community comprising peasant farmers, traders, and shopkeepers to the coastal areas as the Army intended. The Army accompanied the Dayak killers throughout the entire campaign of killings.

This anti-Chinese pogrom exceeded the death toll perpetrated by the Imperial Japanese Navy (IJN) regime during the military occupation of Kalimantan in the Pacific War (1941–1945). In wartime *Minami Boruneo* (Southern Borneo, namely Kalimantan), the IJN executed 1,500 implicated in the so-called anti-Japanese conspiracies.[100] Such killings were carried out during *wartime circumstances* by an occupying military regime against subversion. But the slaughter of the Chinese by Dayaks in West Kalimantan in 1967 was perpetrated during peacetime, in the post-*Konfrontasi* period on an unarmed community that was not in any opposition to the government of the day. This peacetime, unprovoked massacre was an unprecedented phenomenon of ethnic violence – no more no less, a case of genocide.

If added on to the 2,000 Chinese who died in custody as detainees or refugees, the death toll is even higher, almost twice the number that perished during the wartime occupation. Such a high rate of deaths could not be justified on whatever grounds other than a regime-sanctioned murder. It was indeed a tragic outcome that *Orde Baru* inflicted on West Kalimantan's Chinese minority.

Protracted armed struggle, 1967–1976

It took the Army another seven long years with the implementation of *Operasi Sapu Bersih II* (August 1967 to February 1969) and *Operasi Sapu Bersih III* (Operation Clean Sweep III) (March 1969 to January 1974) to finally conclude the nine-year communist insurgency that had been an irritant to Suharto's *Orde Baru* government. Armed with ingenuity and resourcefulness, Sofyan and his PKI guerrillas managed to survive and continue their struggle against the post-1965 regime that had sought their extermination. Likewise, PGRS/PARAKU, that were oriented towards the struggle across the border in Sarawak, too survived the Army offensives.

Despite killings and surrender and/or capture of insurgents between July 1967 and July 1968, Indonesian military sources admitted that the insurgents' supply line remained functional in terms of food and medicinal supplies.[101] And when *Operasi Sapu Bersih III* commenced from March 1969 with fresh troops from Java that targeted Bengkayang and the northwest sector of West Kalimantan southward along the Sarawak-Kalimantan border to the Sikukng mountainous area, the PGRAS/PARAKU forces suffered losses in their leaders, notably Yap Choon Ho, commander of 3rd Company PGRS, and Yacob of Sarawak Advance Youth Association (SAYA), both killed in battle.[102] Not unlike the tactics adopted by Chin Peng's Malayan Communist Party (MCP) guerrillas on the Thai-Malaysian border in Peninsular/West Malaysia, PGRAS/PARAKU insurgents also operated cross-border when the situation favoured their movements, a typically cat-and-mouse scenario fleeing across to the Sarawak side when pursued by the Army, and back to Kalimantan when the latter withdrew or was attacked by Malaysian security forces. This back-and-forth tactic on the border regions made the PGRAS/PARAKU guerrillas a menace on both sides of the divide.

Meanwhile, Sofyan and his PKI colleagues again switched strategies to follow the *water* (people). According to military sources, the PKI insurgents discarded their guerrilla gear and moved out of the forested interior to mingle among the relocated Chinese at Sungai Duri on the coast between Singkawang and Mempawah.[103]

At the same time, the Army was applying increasing pressure on the insurgents. The military enlisted youths in its anti-communist operations, namely *Kesatuan Aksi Mahasiswa Indonesia* (KAMI, Joint-Action Union Indonesian University Students), *Kesatuan Aksi Pelajar Pemuda Indonesia* (KAPPI, Joint-Action Union of Indonesian Youth and Students), and *Laskar Ampera*, an anti-PKI youth militia, to assist in flushing out communist sympathizers, supporters, and communists themselves (regardless of PKI or PGRS/PARAKU) in coastal urban areas that adversely impacted on the latter's logistical support (foods, medicines, intelligence, etc.). While the Army was active on the Kalimantan side of the border, its Malaysian counterpart across the divide in Sarawak were launching offensives against PGRAS/PARAKU insurgents who were actively garnering support from the Iban and Chinese of the interior districts along the Sarawak-Kalimantan border. Joint operations between the Indonesian Army and Malaysian security forces proved effective against the PGRAS/PARAKU communist guerrillas and nullified the cat-and-mouse border-crossing scenario.[104] Literally, the insurgents were cornered with little room for manoeuvre.

Having successfully compromised PGRS forces with the death of Yap and Yacob, the Army turned to crush PARAKU that were active with bases in the eastern sector of West Kalimantan in the Benua Martinus mountainous complex northward from Putussibau in the Upper Kapuas. With scant options, and many of their numbers agreed on the hopelessness of the situation, peace feelers were sent through intermediaries to the Sarawak government for a peace settlement.[105]

Meanwhile, the Kalimantan side of the border also witnessed some dramatic events. In October 1973, while Bong and his PARAKU comrades 'lay down [their] arms', Sofyan's Chinese wife and their seven-month-old baby were captured by the Army in the estuary of the Sambas. Shortly thereafter, 185 kilometres to the south, on 12 January 1974, Sofyan himself, who had a 500,000-rupiah price on his head,[106] was apprehended and summarily executed at Sungai Kelambu, about 24 kilometres upstream from Pontianak.[107] It was another two years, only in 1976, that military operations in West Kalimantan were formally concluded.[108]

Meanwhile, over the border: Sarawak communist insurgency, 1962–1990

Between the outbreak of the Brunei Rebellion (December 1962) and the conclusion of the Peace Agreement (October 1990), the armed struggle of the Sarawak communist movement to establish a communist republic in Sarawak was played out as a protracted struggle, a 28-year drawn-out affair. Much of the drama and episodes occurred in the thick, tropical rain forest of Sarawak, along the Sarawak-Kalimantan border region, and in West Kalimantan's mountainous interior.

Following the Brunei Rebellion, the Sarawak colonial government launched a sweep of all SCO and Leftist elements, whether real, suspected, or perceived members, supporters, and sympathizers. It forced many SCO members to flee across the Sarawak-Kalimantan border to West Kalimantan for refuge. Then in this perilous period it was prudent as well as inevitable that the SCO shifted strategy from its 'united front' tactic to one of 'armed revolution'. Comprising mainly Sarawak Chinese youths, both male and female, SCO members received military drills and training from the TNI. The physical demands of military training and jungle living took a heavy toll on them, mainly middle school graduates, but their idealism, ideological commitment to communism, and youth fuelled their perseverance and tenacious spirit to function, endure, and survive as jungle guerrillas.

Meanwhile, Azahari, in overseeing his war cabinet of the NKKU government-in-exile, on 21 January 1963 named Ahmad Zaidi bin Adruce as deputy prime minister and minister of defence. Ahmad Zaidi, the then president of the *Barisan Pemuda Sarawak* (BPS, Sarawak Youth Front) and an anti-cession Malay leader who strongly opposed British imperialism and colonialism, was a judicious choice. In this connection, he was 'smuggled' into Pontianak in September 1963, and thence to Jakarta to meet Indonesian Defence Minister General Abdul Haris Nasution. Nasution 'instructed' Ahmad Zaidi, in his role as NKKU minister of defence, to monitor Azahari's TNKU and Wen Ming Chyuan's SCO.

The **Konfrontasi** *period, 1962–1966*

During *Konfrontasi*, as pointed out earlier, the aforesaid Sarawak Chinese young men and women, later as members of the PGRS and PARAKU, served as part of the *sukarelawan* units that accompanied and fought alongside regular soldiers in cross-border raids and skirmishes with Malaysian security forces and its Commonwealth military allies.[109]

With the assistance of Brigadier General Riyakudu, PGRS was established on 20 March 1964 at Asu Ansang (Gunung Asuan Sang), a mountainous region in the northwest interior of West Kalimantan, facing across the border eastward to coastal Sematan in Lundu, Sarawak. Bong Kee Chok headed an 80-strong guerrilla force of SCO members that relied heavily on the Army for weapons and ammunition. Its scope of operation was West Sarawak, roughly what was then the First Division.

Besides PGRS, Riyakudu also created *Komando Perjuangan Sarawak* (KOPS, Military Command for the Struggle of Sarawak) on 25 June 1964 of mainly Sarawak Chinese Leftist elements. KOPS too became a part of the *sukarelawan* (volunteers) units that undertook raids into Sarawak territory alongside the Army.

While Riyakudu busied himself in organizing the Sarawak Chinese youths, his counterpart across the border, Director of Borneo Operations (DOBOPS) General Sir Walter Colyear Walker, was stealthily devising covert cross-border raids. Code-named Operation Claret, Walker's brainchild that had tacit approval from both the Malaysian and British governments, would witness British and Commonwealth forces undertaking clandestine raids across the border into Kalimantan disguised as instances of 'hot pursuit' operations.[110] Both special forces (gathering intelligence) and conventional forces (launching ambushes and/or attacks) were involved with the ultimate aim of putting the Indonesians on the defensive. Nonetheless, Operation Claret was meticulously orchestrated to ensure that it did not inflict too much damage to the extent of the TNI losing face and/or escalating the conflict. Operation Claret was carried out with subdued regularity between July 1964 and July 1966.

In order to bring together all guerrilla forces, irrespective of political ideologies, from Brunei, Sabah, and Sarawak for better coordination and control, the NKKU government-in-exile with assistance from Indonesian Foreign Minister Dr Subandrio organized the North Kalimantan People's Revolutionary Consultative

Committee. The Committee held its inaugural meeting on 16–19 March 1965 in Jakarta. At this meeting, the Committee constituted the United National Revolutionary Front of North Kalimantan as an umbrella and unifying front for all anti-Malaysia guerrilla forces.[111]

Towards the end of June 1965, a tragic incident occurred that had significant repercussions. On the Sunday evening of 27 June, 30 uniformed jungle guerrillas assaulted the 18th Mile Police Station on the Kuching-Serian Road, killing two of the nine resident policemen, including Simon Peter Ningkan, the sergeant-in-charge, and Constable Naing, and wounding the others. The raiders seized all the weapons in the arms case. Upon exiting, they shot and killed three members of a neighbouring Chinese pepper-farming family. Thereafter, the raiders hijacked a lorry, forcing the driver to transport them to the border, where they slipped across to Kalimantan. The murdered Iban sergeant's elder brother was Sarawak's inaugural Chief Minister Stephen Kalong Ningkan. An angry Kalong Ningkan swore that there would be "retribution for the treachery of Sunday night".[112]

A year earlier, an SCO training camp was uncovered by Sarawak's Special Branch not far from the *kampung* (village) at the 17th Mile. Drawing from this discovery, the authorities were convinced that the local Chinese populace in the vicinity were communists, supporters, and/or sympathizers. From investigations and eyewitness accounts of the remaining policemen, the police attributed the raid on the 18th Mile Police Station to be undertaken by foreigners (Indonesians) with local collaboration.

In early February 1965, the State Security Executive Council (SSEC) had discussed a resettlement scheme, the Goodsir Plan, after the Sarawak Acting Commissioner of Police David Goodsir, that was similar in principle to the Briggs Plan that was implemented during the Malayan Emergency (1948–1960) and had reaped positive results.[113] It was the classic anti-insurgency tactic of depriving *fishes* (insurgents) from *water* (populace) in *draining* (resettlement) the latter hence starving the former. Jungle guerrillas, to a great extent, relied on villages and settlements on jungle fringes for food and medical supplies, intelligence and recruits. Resettlement of the populace would sever the guerrillas' logistical support, depriving them of much-needed sustenance. On 29 June, there was agreement for the implementation of the Goodsir Plan and its execution codenamed Operation Hammer.[114]

Operation Hammer (6–8 July 1965) witnessed the forced resettlement of 7,600 people from 1,277 Chinese rural peasant families within the stretch of territory between the 15th and 24th Mile of the Kuching-Serian Road. They were removed and relocated into five temporary settlements. Later, towards the end of the year, they were placed in permanent settlements at Siburan, Beratok, and Tapah on the Serian Road.

When the resettled Chinese peasants moved into the purposed-built permanent settlements,

> Each family had its own home . . . and living conditions were much improved [compared to conditions in the temporary settlements]. Amenities included potable water available from standpipes, electricity, and street lighting.[115]

The aforesaid amenities were a far cry from the makeshift dwellings that the families had on the fringes of the jungle, where water often had to be carried from a river source and kerosene lamps and candles were the only means of illumination in the evenings and nights. But a gilded cage remained:

> the permanent settlements were patrolled and surrounded by floodlit, double security fences, and all the original restrictions on movement in and out of the settlements [imposed at the temporary settlements] remained.[116]

Consequent of the Pontianak Conference (17–19 September 1965), coupled with increasing support from the PKI, plans were underway for expansion through recruitment in the formation of PARAKU. Irrespective of nationality or ideological persuasion, any individual who professed anti-Malaysia sentiments and was willing to take up arms for an independent unitary state of North Kalimantan was qualified and accepted as a member of PARAKU. It was conceived as a people's militia, not unlike the abortive concept of PKI's Fifth Force. Bong Kee Chok, Hung Chu Ting, and Wong Kee Hiu were the founding leaders of PARAKU in the field, headquartered on Sungai Katibas, 33 kilometres south of Song, with its designated scope of operation covering the Second and Third Divisions of Sarawak.

Shortly before *Konfrontasi* officially ended, Malaysian Prime Minister Tunku Abdul Rahman offered an olive branch to the Sarawak insurgents. According to the Tunku, there were "approximately 700 hard-core communists" and "about 2,000 sympathizers", mainly in Sarawak.[117] Therefore, Operation Harapan (Hope) was declared on 22 July 1966 (extended to 11 July 1967) to persuade those that had been misled to lay down their arms, receive safe conduct passes, be given rewards for surrender of firearms, allowed to participate in the democratic and constitutional process in the choice of government, and repatriated to other countries with their families if they so wished. Disappointingly, a mere 41 guerrillas accepted Tunku's amnesty. But of those who gave up the struggle, one Yusuf bin Abdullah, a field commander of the TNKU, was of significance. It signalled the demise of TNKU as an armed military force, once the armed wing of Azahari's PRB that spearheaded the abortive coup.

In less than a month, *Konfrontasi* came to a close, after some three years of cat-and-mouse antics played out on the Sarawak-Kalimantan border area. Finally, on 11 August 1966, Indonesia and Malaysia penned a treaty in Jakarta that brought a formal closure to *Konfrontasi*. British and Commonwealth forces withdrew from Sarawak, whereas the Army, that once trained and fought alongside PGRS, PARAKU, TNKU, and PKI, now turned against these anti-Malaysia elements.

With the conclusion of *Konfrontasi*, and all its attendant threat of foreign intervention and/or invasion lifted, focus then turned inwards as Kuala Lumpur in concert with Kuching attempted to contain and ultimately eliminate the communist menace in Sarawak. The following month, in September, the Malaysian government published a White Paper, *The Communist Threat to Sarawak*, warning of communist subversive elements in attempts to subvert and overthrow the state government of Sarawak.[118] The stage was set for addressing and resolving the communist insurgency from within.

Post-Konfrontasi, *1966–1969*

Of military significance in the immediate post-*Konfrontasi* period was a series of joint military operations by the Malaysian and Indonesian military against communist jungle guerrillas, referred to as 'jungle rats' from Kuching's perspective.[119] From October 1966, Kuala Lumpur and Jakarta sanctioned their respective military forces to cross the border in 'hot pursuit' operations. Three years later, in late October 1969, Malaysian-Indonesian Joint Command was set up. Reflecting on the high level of military coordination, Brigadier General Soemadi, Commander Tanjungpura Regional Military Command (KODAM XII), West Kalimantan suggested, and agreed upon, the setting up of a 'Joint Command' between the TNI and Malaysian security forces.[120] Until then, monthly border security meetings were held in Pontianak between Commander of KODAM XII and his counterpart, Malaysian General Officer Commanding-in-Chief (GOC) East Malaysia. The Joint Command was tasked to expedite the elimination of communist guerrillas operating along the Sarawak-Kalimantan border region.

In mid-October 1967, the Dayaks of West Kalimantan declared war on the PGRS that had the tacit support of the TNI. This declaration coincided and was consistent with the then-ongoing anti-Chinese pogrom by Dayaks backed by TNI in flushing out the Chinese populace from the interior districts, forcing the latter to the coastal areas. Towards the closing months of 1968, the PGRS suffered a heavy blow; 200 guerrillas were killed by TNI and Dayaks in West Kalimantan.[121] Thereafter, PGRS was a spent force. Remnants fled via the coast (Pemangkat) to avoid further engagements that they could hardly afford to endure. About 21 guerrillas who escaped by sea landed at Telok Sabang in the First Division, Sarawak. Following attack by Malaysian security forces at Bau, where three guerrillas were killed, the remainder split into small groups to head towards Lubuk Antu in the Second Division to join PARAKU.[122] As their numbers dwindled resulting from successive successful offensives by Malaysian security forces in Sarawak, the communist guerrillas abstained from killing government informants, native (mainly Iban) members of Border Scouts to avoid offending the indigenous peoples and lose their support, instead switched from guerrilla warfare to re-connecting with the masses (natives and non-natives) as a means of preparing the groundwork for the continued armed struggle.

Meanwhile, on the political front, greater federal–state relations were being nurtured with significant positive repercussions that adversely impacted on the Sarawak communist insurgency. On 8 February 1969, during the celebration of the 48th birthday of SUPP Secretary General Stephen Yong Kuet Tze, Malaysian Prime Minister Tunku managed to convince Yong to engineer a party policy turnaround in recognizing the concept of Malaysia and, in turn, the federal government promised to refrain from detaining SUPP candidates in the forthcoming June 1970 state elections or place any restrictions on SUPP political campaigns.[123]

Acceptance of the concept of Malaysia was incorporated into the SUPP manifesto, a significant step in that SUPP acknowledged the reality of gaining political influence and power was through incorporation with the incumbent ruling Alliance Party of the Tunku.

Across the border in West Kalimantan, the Third Branch PGRS was annihilated at its base in Songkong.[124] In a two-day battle (25–26 March 1969), the TNI ruthlessly destroyed the entire Third Branch, the largest of the PGRS corps, including its leaders, Yap Choon Ho and Yang Chu Chung.

In the wake of the disastrous loss of the Third Branch PGRS in West Kalimantan, the North Kalimantan People's Guerrilla Force (NKPGF) was established on 13 July 1969 at Nonok, and another centre at Matang, both in Sarawak's First Division.[125] With local native Iban support and its swampy environment that greatly compromised troop movements, the Nonok[126] peninsula appeared to be a conducive location for the operation of a 'directing and training' centre for the NKPGF.

By the first quarter of 1969, the Malaysian authorities claimed that armed communist guerrillas had been annihilated in the First Division. Although admittedly there remained some 20,000 supporters and sympathizers, the tide was turning against the SCO.[127] On 10 May, 12 individuals were arrested, a commonplace announcement by the authorities, but the tipoff came from the public, a positive and encouraging phenomenon.[128] At the hideout of those detained, located in the vicinity of the 12th Mile on the Kuching-Serian Road, banned communist literature was found as well as in the possession of those arrested. In crippling the SCO's efforts in propagation that went hand in hand with recruitment, it contributed to the weakening and subsequent collapse of the movement.

Earlier in the year (1969), Malaysian security authorities managed to arrest 78 alleged SCO supporters, out of which 14 were Ibans.[129] This coup of sorts in the Second Division was significantly damaging as it broke the SCO-native bond that marked a breakthrough for the government. Support from the masses, native or non-native, coerced or willingly, succoured the jungle guerrillas in sustaining their armed revolution.

As with most insurgencies, where insurgents operated as guerrillas under the camouflage of the thick jungle environment, engagements between them and government security forces were often short-lived skirmishes. The classic time-tested, hit-and-run tactics were the norm, stirring commotion and confusion on the part of security forces. Often the guerrilla perpetrators had long disappeared into the forest by the time security forces had ascertained *what had happened*, discovered the damage and/or fatalities, or mounted a response. In fact, most engagements were no more than 30 minutes, often within a 15- to 20-minute window. Land mines, booby traps made from jungle materials, and advance signalling systems surrounded pathways to jungle camps and mandatory escape routes when camps were being besieged or attacked.

The following are sample portraitures of camps and hideouts discovered and/or captured by security forces in counter-insurgency operations:

> Further investigations following Operation Kuku (Claw) led to the discovery of an SCO hideout in the Oya Road area, in which the police found 'a

homemade shotgun, a set of printing press and other apparatus and a large collection of subversive documents'.[130]

During Operation Jala Raya (Grand Net) the Malaysian [security] forces uncovered two SCO training centres. One was on the fringes of an area planted with coconuts on the edge of the tropical rain forest, with clear views of the approaches and lookout posts. Evacuation of this site had been orderly and the SCO had left nothing of any importance at the site. *The second training centre was quite near to the Nonok bazaar and normally would not have aroused suspicion.* Demonstrating the ingenuity of the SCO, this centre had an alarm system and even electricity, as it was connected to the electricity supply in the bazaar by cable. This centre was not more than three months old and the occupants obviously had little warning of the arrival of Malaysian forces, as they left behind well-stocked with tinned and dried food. There was a large quantity of empty food cans dumped at the rear of the house, indicating that a number of guerrillas had been staying there. Two underground caches behind the house contained some 82 uniforms, a printing duplicator with printing ink and printing material, an SCO publication dated 2 February 1970, and some other minor items. Malaysian authorities believed that the group had donned civilian clothes and split up to avoid detection.[131]

On 8 March [1971], Malaysian [security] forces mounted Operation Hentam (Assault) in the Sungai Budu Pegong area of the First Division, covering 100 square miles from Bako in the north to Sijingkat in the south. The main purpose . . . was to destroy a heavily camouflaged and well-guarded SCO base discovered about four and a half miles from Kampong Muara Tebas. This base consisted of a three-bedroom, zinc-roofed, wooden house previously occupied by a rubber tapper, over ten temporary camps each accommodating up to four people, a workshop, and ten sentry posts, all interconnected with an alarm system . . . found documents, 'red books', weapons (some of which were homemade), ammunition, armoury tools, jungle green packs and food supplies including three sacks of rice and *ikan kerin*[g] (dried [salted] fish). There was evidence of shotguns and pistols being made at the base, vegetables were being grown, poultry was being reared, and rubber trees were being tapped, with latex sheets being sold to pay for supplies. *All the evidence suggested that the site was a major base used by senior cadres for ideological and military training and arms manufacture.*[132]

The second illustration indicated local complicity and support as demonstrated by the close proximity of the guerrilla centre and the Nonok bazaar. The ingenuity and resourcefulness of the communist guerrillas evoked admiration, as shown in the third sample, but at the same instance, apprehension and anxiety over their sustainability. It therefore came as no surprise that the communist insurgents could sustain such a protracted armed struggle of close to three decades, tying down scores of battalions of the Malaysian security forces.

Developments in the 1970s

Two outstanding developments marked 1970: one military and another in the political front. On the former, in early 1970, intelligence had revealed the existence of 'directing and training' centres in the Nonok peninsula, First Division, operated by 30 communist guerrillas who had crossed the border from West Kalimantan. Moreover, village committees, resembling communist-style commune systems, were constituted among the 1,000 mainly Iban families in the area, through which support was garnered for the SCO cause and struggle. Furthermore, in the recent past several months, more guerrillas had crossed the border into Sarawak to regroup following concerted TNI offensives that had deprived them of hitherto safe havens in Kalimantan. It was also here in the Nonok area that the NGPGF on 13 July 1969 had absorbed PGRS remnants after their routing by the TNI and Dayaks a year ago (1968). In response, Malaysian security forces launched Operation Jala Raya (Grand Net) on 24 February.[133]

The belated Sarawak state elections[134] held on 7–8 July 1970 ushered in a coalition government comprising an alliance of the Malay/Melanau *Parti Bumiputera*, the Iban of the Third Division *Parti Pesaka Anak Sarawak* (PESAKA, Sarawak Native Heritage Party), and SUPP. SUPP Chairman Ong Kee Hui was made a federal minister, and Secretary General Yong became (Sarawak) state minister of communications and works. More importantly, Yong was appointed to the State Operation's Committee, the state's security committee, thereby allowing SUPP a voice in counter-insurgency operations and some influence over the welfare of SUPP detainees (alleged SCO involvement) in the 7th Mile Detention Camp, and relocated Chinese settlers in the permanent resettlement centres of Siburan, Beratok, and Tapah.

The following year, there was a restructuring of the security apparatus in Sarawak in the wake of developments in the peninsula in the aftermath of the '13 May 1969' Sino-Malay riots. In response, the federal government established the Federal National Operation Council (NOC) to enforce and oversee emergency rule in the country. In July 1969, the NOC in turn convened a State Operations Committee (SOC) in Sarawak headed by an ex-federal secretary instead of the chief minister of Sarawak. Local dissatisfaction with such developments was understandable; federal–state relations had always been tenuous at best and even contentious at times.[135] Following the state elections in mid-1970, Chief Minister Abdul Rahman Yakub headed a coalition state government. Appropriate for Sarawak and sanctioned by Prime Minister Tun Abdul Razak, therefore, on 29 April 1971, the SOC was replaced by the Sarawak State Security Committee (SSSC) with the Sarawak chief minister as chairman. SUPP Secretary General Yong was appointed deputy chairman, who was tasked to administer security matters in the First and Second Divisions, whilst the chairman oversaw operations in the Third, Fourth, and Fifth Divisions.

In February 1972, a government White Paper on security issues in Sarawak was published. As a follow-up to a previous White Paper, *The Communist Threat to Sarawak* (1966), the Malaysian government published *The Threat of Armed*

Communism in Sarawak, which detailed the changes since 1966, thereby allowing the populace to understand and, in turn, support the need to implement counter-insurgency measures to address and overcome the threat in Sarawak. In his Fore-word, Malaysian Deputy Prime Minister and Minister of Home Affairs Tun Dr Ismail Al-Haj bin Dato' Haji Abdul Rahman was unduly frank and forthright in his reading of the current situation in the state:

2   The peace resulting from the conclusion of Confrontation [with Indonesia] afforded time for social and economic development in the State. This, *inter alia*, produced a situation unfavourable to the long-term subversion and armed insurgency plans of the SCO. The SCO was therefore compelled to accelerate its armed preparations in Sarawak in order to precipitate an insurgent situation.
3   Armed terrorism has therefore been launched on an extensive and growing scale in parallel with subversive activities by the SCO towards creating the conditions necessary for the advancement of its armed insurgency plans.
4   Terrorist groups have infiltrated in strength into various parts of the State and contrived to obtain the support of certain sections of the population through intimidation and guile or exploitation of kinship. Murder has been used as an instrument against those who refused to extend support to the terrorists.[136]

Dr Ismail's reference to "afforded time for social and economic development in the State" was consistent with the government's strategy in addressing the ongoing insurgency issue on the peninsula. When the then Malayan Prime Minister Tunku Abdul Rahman declared the conclusion of the 12-year Malayan Emergency on 12 July 1960, MCP Secretary General Chin Peng and his band of hard-core comrades made a strategic retreat to the thickly forested region of the Thai-Malaysian border for refuge and to regroup. Then, on 17 June 1968, an ambush in the Kroh-Betong area of northern Perak saw the killings of 17 security personnel, and the MCP guerrillas easily slipped across the porous border into Thailand. Kuala Lumpur declared the commencement of the Second Malayan Emergency (1968–1989), a longer struggle than its predecessor, stretching over two decades.[137] Despite the continuity in namesake, the strategies and approaches employed were *different* in this second outing.

Hence, instead of declaring another "emergency" . . . which might fuel ethnic tensions, the government of Prime Minister Tun Abdul Razak bin Hussain . . . initiated Program Keselamatan dan Pembangunan (KESBAN; Security and Development Programme). In combining security and development, KESBAN offered the multi-ethnic population concrete benefits of a more stable and secure society that was increasingly prospering from economic development. . . . In tandem, the security forces ensured that the people were protected from the insurgency and its terrorist acts. *Concerted efforts in focusing on rural developments and the alleviation of poverty among the rural population succeeded in denying the MCP all forms of support from the populace.*[138]

To a certain extent, the strategy and approaches that were adopted in the peninsula were also adhered to in Sarawak in countering its communist insurgency. During the British colonial period (1946–1963), a concerted effort had been started to address the much-neglected field of socio-economic development and continuity during the post-Malaysia period.[139]

Between a military solution and a political panacea

There were dissensions with regards to the perception and view of the communist insurgency in Sarawak from within the state administration, a contention between a military solution and a political panacea. A restructuring was undertaken by the Federal government of the administration of the Third Division. On 26 March 1972, the Third Division was designated a 'Special Security Area' under the over-all control of the newly formed Rajang Area Security Command (RASCOM) head-quartered at Sibu (Map 8.2). In adopting a military solution, RASCOM brought the armed forces, police, and civil service under its fold and dealt with both military operations and civil service functions. RASCOM appeared to be an *imperium in imperio* in overseeing the Third Division, mainly the Lower Rajang, and parts of the Fourth Division, including the Bintulu district. Chief Minister Abdul Rahman Yakub personally headed RASCOM.

In contrast, security matters in the First and Second Divisions came under the purview of the Joint Operation Sub-Committee that functioned within the existing administrative setup. Deputy Chief Minister Stephen Yong chaired the Joint Operation Sub-Committee, which comprised mainly civilians with representatives from both the police and the military. Unlike RASCOM, Stephen Yong and his colleagues in the Sub-Committee viewed the insurgency as a political struggle, between democracy and communism. Hence, 'winning the hearts and minds' of the populace, especially those in the rural areas, was prioritized utilizing psychological warfare in addressing the insurgency. Fruits of this approach were evident, as demonstrated in Operation Sri Aman, that had the effect of the First and Second Divisions being officially declared 'White Areas', denoting free of communist activities and threat.

Stephen Yong, who did not subscribe to a military solution to the protracted communist insurgency, instead believed in appeals to the guerrillas to give up their struggle. He put his idea into action in the latter part of 1973:

By 1973, many of the "jungle rats" [communist guerrillas] had given up, but Bong Kee Chok and many diehards (more than 400 of them), were still holding out. I proposed to [Chief Minister] [Abdul] Rahman Yakub to send a message to Bong Kee Chok, urging him and his men to surrender. The only reliable person to carry out this task would be his mother, because no hard-hearted man would kill or harm his own mother. She agreed, but then had to

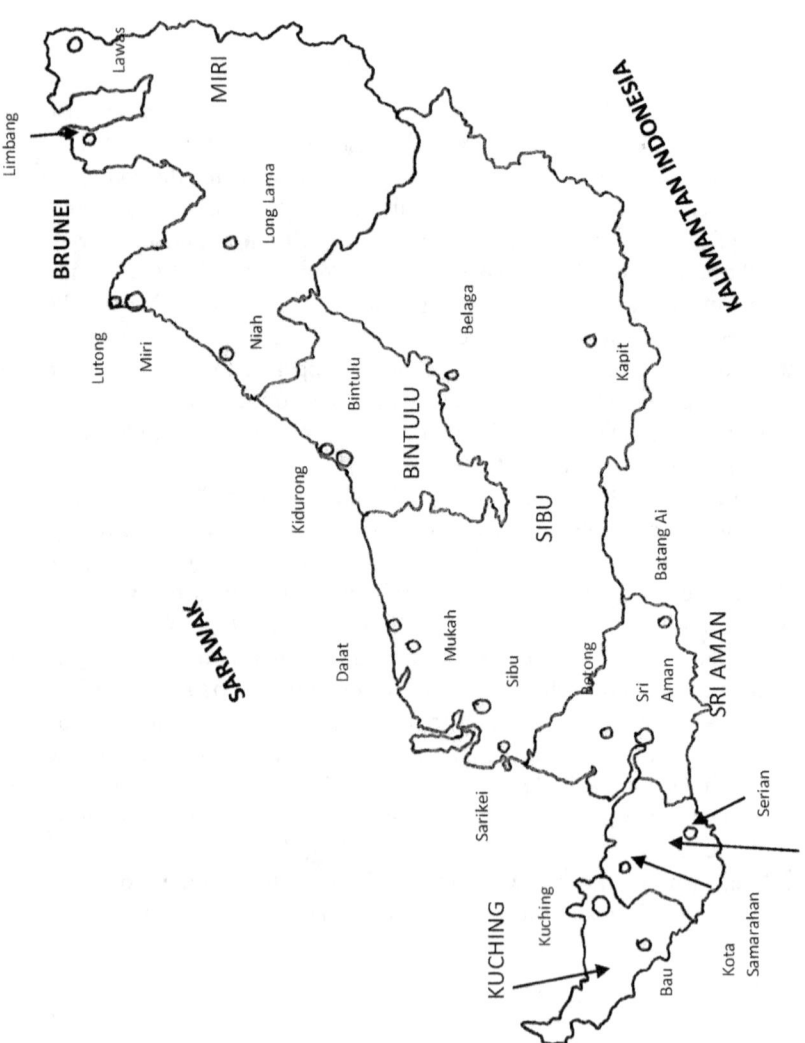

SABAH

Lawas

MIRI

Limbang

BRUNEI

Long Lama

Lutong

Niah

Miri

Belaga

Bintulu

Kapit

BINTULU

Kidurong

SIBU

SARAWAK

Dalat

Mukah

Batang Ai

Sibu

Betong

Sri
Aman

SRI AMAN

Sarikei

Serian

SAMARAHAN

KUCHING

Kuching

Kota
Samarahan

Bau

KALIMANTAN INDONESIA

Map 8.2 Sarawak

Source: Author

abandon the mission because she had a gastric ulcer attack. Bong's father then volunteered, but on condition that he should be given a shop lot in Serian; Abdul Rahman Yakub agreed with this. . . . Despite much searching, which put his life in danger, Bong's father could not meet his son in person. Instead, he left the written message [with a trusted intermediary] for him which Bong [subsequently] received.[140]

By then, Bong Kee Chok, director and political commissar of PARAKU, was ready to negotiate a peace settlement. His penned letter of 10 October 1973 was addressed to "Mr [Abdul Rahman], Chief Minister of the State of Sarawak and Chairman of State Operations Committee, and Mr Stephen Yong, Deputy Chief Minister of the State of Sarawak and In Charge of Operation in the First and Second Divisions".[141] Besides seeking promises and guarantee of "personal freedom and safety" through-out the duration of the 'peace talk', and also in the event "should the peace talk fail", he and his comrades "shall be allowed to leave the control of your army and police", and additionally, he "suggest that all arrangements in the early stage should be kept as top secret and should not be announced nor propagated".[142] This all-important missive was handed to Bong Kee Kien, one of the sender's brothers, who passed it to Special Branch Head Alli Kawi, who in turn had it translated from the Chinese and personally handed it to Chief Minister Abdul Rahman Yakub. Without hesitation, Bong Kee Kien had an audience with the chief minister to make arrangements for a peace talk.

The two-day peace talks (19–20 October 1973) were mutually satisfactory for both parties. Attention is here drawn to two significant points. Firstly, it should be clear and emphasized that Bong Kee Chok and his comrades agreed "*to lay down [their] arms*", and '*not surrender*'. Secondly, the only objection on the part of the government was its adamant refusal to the registration of the NKCP as a legal *bona fide* political party. The Malaysian government's stance in rejecting the communist ideology was non-negotiable.

The 10-point 'Memorandum of Understanding between Ketua Menteri [Chief Minister] Sarawak and Mr Bong Kee Chok, Director and Political Commissar of the Pasukan Rakyat Kalimantan Utara', dated 20 October 1973, was signed by both parties at Rumah Kerajaan (Government House), Simanggang, on 21 October 1973.[143]

Altogether 482 guerrillas, out of which 171 were women, agreed "to lay down [their] arms", accounting for some three-quarters of all communist guerrillas in Sarawak. A total of 398 weapons were also surrendered and subsequently destroyed.[144] It was certainly an accomplishment on the part of the government. The Memorandum was finalized and approved by the Malaysian government on 1 March 1974. As a commemoration of this historic achievement, Simanggang, the administrative centre of the Second Division and venue of the peace proceed-ings, was henceforth renamed Bandar Sri Aman (Town of Lasting Peace).

But it was another six months, on 4 March 1974, before a public announcement was made of the success of Operation Sri Aman that concluded with the signing of the Memorandum of Understanding.

Being hopeful, between 4 March 1974 and 5 July 1974, an amnesty to guerrillas 'to lay down [their] arms' under Operation Sri Aman was in operation: all military activities against the guerrillas were held in abeyance to facilitate free movement and safe passage to those who wished to abandon the armed struggle and lay down their weapons. Despite the grace period being extended four times, demonstrating the government's sincerity and hopefulness, only 7 out of an estimated 120 guerrillas in the Third Division walked out of the jungle 'to lay down [their] arms'. All attempts, including Stephen Yong volunteering to personally meet up with Hung Chu Ting, secretary of the Second Bureau NKCP and political commissar-cum-commander of PARAKU, failed. Finally, the amnesty ended on 5 July 1974.

Stephen Yong's belief in a political panacea paid dividends. He, however, was absent from the significant Simanggang peace negotiations as well as to witness the signing of the Memorandum, as he was at a United Nations meeting in New York then. Despite this momentous accomplishment, he failed to persuade Chief Minister Abdul Rahman Yakub to have this strategy replicated in the RASCOM area.

> I had earlier proposed to [Chief Minister] Abdul Rahman Yakub that I should take over the RASCOM area. I maintained that the Insurgency was a political war, not a military one. Military action could not solve the problem. Only political tact and persuasion could do the trick. *Despite my successful example that culminated in the ceremony at Sri Aman, Abdul Rahman Yakub disagreed with me and as a result, the remnant guerrilla forces in the RASCOM area fought on until 1990: seventeen years after we brought peace to the First and Second Divisions!*[145]

A war of attrition

Between the conclusion of the Operation Sri Aman amnesty (5 July 1974) until the penning of the Peace Agreement of 17 October 1990, the communist insurgency in Sarawak was characterized as a war of attrition.[146] Hung Chu Ting and his deputy, Wong Lian Kui, and their steadfast comrades continued the armed struggle. Their actions were in line with directives from the NKCP Chairman Wen Ming Chyuan, who from Beijing (resident since October 1965) instructed his comrades in Sarawak that, "*Even if remains only one, we will stick to the struggle*".[147] Apparently, Wen had issued instructions to Bong, before the latter signed the Memorandum, to proceed with both overt lawful activities and covert armed struggle.[148] Therefore, Hung and Wong conferred to execute a majority-minority strategy, namely the majority (Bong and comrades) laying down their arms while a minority (Hung, Wong, and comrades) remained in the jungle to carry on the armed revolution.[149] Moreover, weapons handed in to the Malaysian authorities were only their obsolete and homemade arms, whereas modern weaponry such as assault rifles, automatics, submachine guns, etc., were retained by the minority in the field. The majority-minority strategy was a precaution, a fall-back plan, in the event that the government exhibited insincerity and did not honour the Memorandum.

Although the publicized number of 482 guerrillas came out of the jungle together with Bong Kee Chok "to lay down [their] arms", the ones who subsequently returned to the field were never reported or made known to the media and public. One source – but not corroborated by supporting evidence – claimed that a "*few hundred* of the Sri Aman returnees later returned to the jungle to resume the armed struggle".[150]

> That an unknown number, thought to be about 100, had done so, first became public knowledge on 22 October [1974]. On that day, two female Chinese Indonesian guerrillas who had down their arms on 26 May were killed in a skirmish with Malaysian forces. . . . The Chief Minister [himself] quickly rejected a statement on the skirmish by the National Security Council, issuing his own statement to give a 'full and complete picture of the whole incident'. He said that both those killed had been well treated in Kuching, 'but for personal and selfish reasons, they stubbornly made their way back to the jungle on June 8, 1974 to continue the armed struggle'. *This was the first public admission that some former guerrillas had returned to the jungle. No statements were ever issued on the total number who did so.*[151]

According to an official source from the Malaysian government, in the post-Operation Sri Aman period, there were **88** PARAKU armed guerrillas in the field, viz. First Bureau in the First Division headed by Chang Ah Wah with 11 personnel, and the Second Bureau in the Third Division numbering 77 dispersed across the RASCOM area of operation.[152] Leading cadres included: 1st Company, Ling Kee Ching; 3rd Company, Wong Lian Kui (headquarters, Mukah area), Lai Kah Wen (Min Yuen unit, Julau area), Lu Yew Ai (Sibu town), Yee See Tung (one unit, unknown vicinity); 4th Company, Yong Chu Hua (Binatang-Sarikei area). The figure of **88** might represent the core of the PARAKU. The number of guerrillas constantly fluctuated owing to casualties, defections ('to lay down [their] arms'), and new recruits. In 1977, a recorded figure of 138 was given by Special Branch, Kuala Lumpur, and eight years later, there were 76 guerrillas according to the Ministry of Defence.[153]

Deployed to play cat-and-mouse with the PARAKU guerrillas in the Sarawak jungles were the Malaysian armed forces, namely the military contingent of Wilayah II (Sabah and Sarawak) comprising the Third Infantry Brigade (Kuching), the Fifth Infantry Brigade (Kota Kinabalu), military units of RASCOM (Sibu), and nine infantry battalions in the field (jungle).[154] In support of the ground troops were other concomitant units, including Artillery, Cavalry, Engineers, Logistics and Signals, and Field Ambulance. The Royal Malaysian Navy (RMN) based in Labuan and the Royal Malaysian Air Force (RMAF) in Kuching provided necessary support when called upon in the course of the various operations. Paramilitary groups stood in for the Army in routine patrol and guard duties at public installations such as harbours, telecommunications hubs, electricity sub-stations, etc. The Sarawak Local Defense Corps, numbering 350 in 1974, had gone through a three-month military training prior to security duties at strategic installations. The *Ikatan*

Relawan Rakyat (RELA, People's Volunteer Corps) was established (May 1972) in the RASCOM area in the Third Division, Sarawak. By the middle of 1974, 10,000 RELA armed personnel were assigned patrol duties in local areas, *kampung*, and longhouses, guarding against communist infiltration.[155]

Despite the formidable conventional forces against them, the PARAKU guerrillas managed to hold out, and now and then, to strike back with ambushes, subterfuge, the classic hit-and-run tactics of guerrilla warfare. The Sarawak insurgents adopted the guerrilla warfare tactics of Mao's Red Army and creatively adapted to the local environment of thick tropical rain forest and hilly terrain in the interior regions. Like their MCP counterparts in the jungles of the peninsula, PARAKU guerrillas also utilized the rain forest to their advantage.[156] By 1985, the NKCP, with PARAKU as its armed wing, remained intact and active. Information gleaned from the Malaysian Ministry of Defence revealed its formal structure, as portrayed in Figure 8.1.

Momentous events in the East, then in the West

In the East, two ground-breaking events, one in the early 1970s and another in the following decade, impacted to some extent on the communist insurgency in Malaysia in particular and the Cold War in general. China, since the establishment of the PRC in 1949, appeared as the beacon of inspiration and ideological mecca to Leftist elements and communist organizations in Southeast Asia and in the Malaysia-Indonesia context, viz. the MCP, PKI, and SCO/NKCP. Besides ideological inspiration and moral support, it was difficult to believe that Beijing did not contributed some form of material aid to the various communist parties in the region. Given the fact that MCP Secretary General Chin Peng and NKCP Chairman Wen Ming Chyuan had been in residence in Beijing since 1961 and 1965, respectively, the Chinese Communist Party (CCP), if not the PRC government, would have lent material sustenance over the many decades of their armed revolution. Public acknowledgement of such support might not have been diplomatically prudent on the part of Beijing in antagonizing the national governments of steadfastly anti-communist Malaysia and pro-West (post-1965) Indonesia.

Having adopted a pro-West orientation during the premiership of the Tunku (1957–1970), from 1970, under Prime Minister Tun Abdul Razak, Malaysia shifted to non-alignment as its principle foreign policy. Against this re-orientation to non-alignment, Tun Abdul Razak sought the establishment of formal diplomatic relations with the PRC in visiting Beijing in 1974, a 'first' among Southeast Asian leaders. In Beijing, he held talks on bilateral issues with PRC Premier Zhou Enlai and CCP Chairman Mao Zedong. The iconic photograph of Mao shaking hands with Tun Abdul Razak was splashed across the front page of practically all the print media across the region. Following this historic visit, two pertinent issues were resolved, viz. insurgency and citizenship, that had direct impact on the ongoing communist insurgency in Malaysia (in the peninsula and Sarawak). Firstly, Beijing absolved any involvement with the ongoing communist insurgency in Malaysia: "Tun Abdul Razak announced that Zhou and Mao had categorically

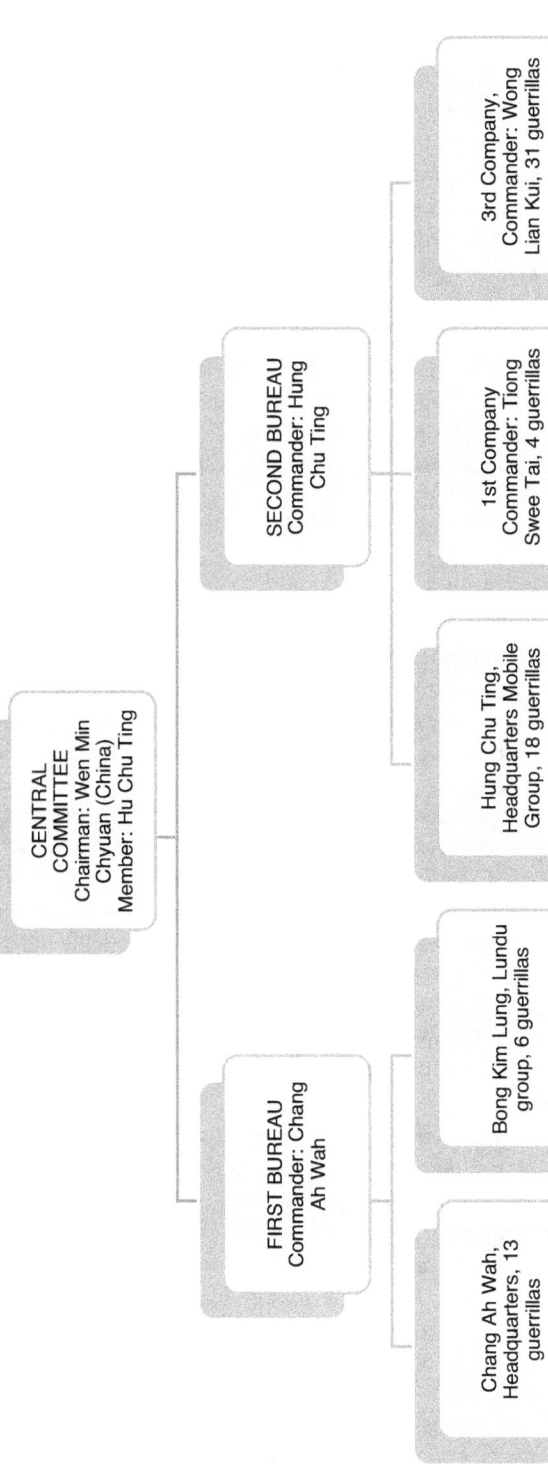

Figure 8.1 North Kalimantan Communist Party (NKCP), circa 1985

Source: *Kementerian Pertahanan Malaysia* [Malaysian Ministry of Defence], 1985 cited in Porritt Vernon L., *The Rise and Fall of Communism in Sarawak 1940–1990* (Clayton, Vic.: Monash Asia Institute, 2004), p. 240.

assured him that they were of the view that the terrorists were Malaysia's internal problem that should be dealt with in the way that the government thought best".[157]

Secondly, on the issue of the nationality of the people of Chinese descent then living in Malaysia, "China maintained its stand that the destiny of the overseas Chinese were intertwined with their home countries and that *they should make every attempt to integrate themselves into the local social fabric* and no longer consider themselves separate from it".[158] Moreover, "According to Clause 5 of the joint communique, both governments of China and Malaysia declared that they didn't recognise dual nationality and that the people of Chinese origin who'd taken up Malaysian citizenship were automatically not Chinese nationals".[159]

A decade forward, in 1981, Chinese leader Deng Xiao Ping, who some 20 years before (1961) had urged MCP Secretary General Chin Peng to resuscitate its armed revolution, hence the Second Malayan Emergency (1968–1989), now encouraged the MCP to seek a peace settlement with Kuala Lumpur.[160] Although Chin Peng did not act then (in 1981), Deng's advice, to a certain extent, indicated that the MCP's armed struggle was beginning to appear fruitless, even irrelevant, against contemporary times.

Developments in the West were equally, if not more, dramatic and certainly invoked positive impacts on the communist insurgency in Malaysia. The global scenario in the second half of the 1980s was experiencing dramatic shifts when the decade ended with the dissolution of the USSR. In an unprecedented move, General Secretary Mikhail Sergeyevich Gorbachev, the eighth and last leader of the Soviet Union, in a public speech in Leningrad admitted the lethargic pace of economic development and spoke of inadequate living standards.[161] As part of his *glasnost* (openness) reform agenda, he sought to initiate the overall restructuring of the country's political and economic systems. The term *perestroika* (lit. 'restructuring') came to represent a political initiative for reformation, the introduction of a series of reforms initially within the Communist Party of the Soviet Union and later, the country as a whole. Instead of helping to contribute positively, the implementation of *perestroika* worsened the existing tensions within the political, social, and economic frameworks.[162] Moreover, *perestroika* accentuated national consciousness and nationalism, spurring the mushrooming of nationalist political parties in the constituent states within the Soviet Union. Ironically, instead of being the intended panacea, *perestroika* – coupled with the long-standing structural weaknesses – created a snowballing impact that subsequently led to the collapse of the Soviet Union, with its satellite states breaking away.

A revolutionary wave – the Revolutions of 1989 – in the late 1980s and early 1990s swept through the Soviet satellite states in Central and Eastern Europe, all seeking to unshackle from Moscow's centralist communist rule. From August through December 1991, most, if not all, the individual Soviet republics, including Russia itself, had either seceded from the Union or had publicly denounced the Treaty on the Creation of the USSR. Finally, on Boxing Day (26 December) 1991, the dissolution of the Soviet Union became a reality, officially granting self-governing independence to the 15 Republics of the Union of Soviet Socialist Republics (USSR). It was a momentous event of the twentieth century, drawing comparison to Victory in Europe Day (V-E Day) on 8 May 1945 that marked the end of the Second World War.

End of the road

Events in the West prompted the MCP and Secretary General Chin Peng (in Beijing since 1961) to consider a peace settlement with its erstwhile enemy, the Malaysian government. According to a Malaysian military source, towards the end of 1989, there remained 1,300 MCP guerrillas spread across three active units, namely the 8th, 10th, and 12th Regiments.[163] Then, on 2 December 1989, 'Agreement Between the Government of Malaysia and the Malayan Communist Party to Terminate Hostilities', or commonly referred to as the Peace Agreement of Hat Yai (1989), was signed and ratified by the MCP and the Malaysian and Thai governments at the Lee Gardens Hotel in Hat Yai, Thailand.[164] This Agreement put to rest a four-decade war.

Observing events in Hat Yai, NKCP Chairman Wen Ming Chyuan, then resident in Beijing (since 1965), sent a message through intermediaries in Thailand that NKCP was willing to negotiate a peace settlement with the Malaysian government.[165] The latter's response was positive, hence led Wen to pen instructions in a letter dated 14 May 1990 to his comrades in Sarawak to lay down their arms as MCP had done, and entrusted all peace negotiations to Hung Chu Ting and his deputy, Wong Lian Kui, the two members of the NKCP Central Committee.

Then, on 16 October 1990, peace negotiations were held at Miri. The terms, conditions, and assurances raised by Hung and Wong were no different from those that their comrade, Bong Kee Chok, made at Simanggang some 17 years earlier. On the next day (17 October) in Kuching, the Peace Agreement was signed between the Sarawak State Government and the NKCP Second Bureau.[166] A total of 50 NKCP guerrillas – 21 from Kanowit and 29 from the Tinjar area – lay down their arms and pledged allegiance to the *Yang di Pertuan Agong* of Malaysia (King of Malaysia).

As in Kuching (1990) and in Simanggang (1973), also in Hat Yai (1989), the communist guerrillas only *lay down their arms*, and neither the NKCP or the MCP were destroyed or annihilated, and *none of them ever surrendered*.

Notes

1 Hara Fujio, "The North Kalimantan Communist Party and China", Second International Conference in Research and Documentation of the Chinese Oversea, Chinese University of Hong Kong, 13–15 Mar 2003, Hong Kong, p. 10.
2 Sukarno's Independence Day Speech, excerpts from. General CIA Record; CIA-RDP78-03061A0003000010027-0. www.cia.gov/library/readingroom/docs/ CIA-RDP78-03061A0003000010027-0.pdf Accessed 19 Oct 2018. Emphasis added.
3 The acronym GESTAPU stands for *Gerakan September Tiga Puluh* (Thirtieth September Movement), also abbreviated as G30S or G-30-S. GESTOK, for *Gerakan Satu Oktober* (First October Movement) is sometimes used. See John Roosa, *Pretext for Mass Murder: The September 30th Movement and Suharto's Coup d'État in Indonesia* (Madison, WI: The University of Wisconsin Press, 2006); Nugroho Notosusanto and

Ismail Saleh, *The Coup Attempt of the "30 September Movement" in Indonesia* (Dja-karta: P.T. Pembimbing Masa, 1968); Sekertariat Negara Republik Indonesia, *Gerakan 30 September: Pemberontakan Partai Komunis Indonesia. Latar Belakang, Aksi, dan Penumpasan [September 30 Movement: Rebellion of the Indonesian Communist Party: Background, Action, and Crackdown]* (Jakarta: Sekertariat Negara Republik Indone-sia, 1994).

4   Variously referred to as the 'Indonesian mass killings of 1965–1966', 'Indonesian genocide', 'Indonesian Communist Purge', 'Indonesian politicide', or simply, the '1965 tragedy'. See Geoffrey B. Robinson, *The Killing Season: A History of the Indo-nesian Massacres, 1965–66* (Princeton, NJ: Princeton University Press, 2018); Jess Melvin, "Mechanics of Mass Murder: A Case for Understanding the Indonesian Kill-ings as Genocide", *Journal of Genocide Research*, 19, 4 (2017): 487–511; Robert Cribb, "The Indonesian Genocide of 1965–1966", in *Teaching about Genocide: Approaches, and Resources*, edited by Samuel Totten (Charlotte, NC: Information Age Publishing, 2004), pp. 133–143; John Roosa, "The 1965–66 Politicide in Indonesia: Toward Knowing Who Did What to Whom and Why", The Southeast Asia Program Seminar, Stanford University, Feb 19, 2015. https://aparc.fsi.stanford.edu/southeast asia/events/1965-66-politicide-indonesia-toward-knowing-who-did-what-whom-and-why Accessed 11 Nov 2018.

5   Being incorporated and a part of the Federation of Malaysia in 1963, Sarawak gained its independence from Britain.

6   Often referred to as 'security forces' that included the police and other paramilitary and militia groups. The preferred term of 'security forces' played down the communist insurgency as *a serious threat* and/or *a guerrilla war*, particularly in public announce-ments and in the mass media (print, radio), for obvious reasons in not giving alarm and concern to the local population, especially the stock market, and the international audience. Any hint, real or perceived, of political instability might adversely impact on the country/state's economic outlook in dissuading investors (local and/or foreign).

7   Robert Cribb, "GESTAPU Affair (1963): Annihilation of the Left", in *Southeast Asia: A Historical Encyclopedia from Angkor Wat to East Timor*, edited by Ooi Keat Gin (Santa Barbara, CA: ABC-Clio, 2004), I: 544.

8   For a detailed chronological development, see Helen Louise Hunter, *Sukarno and the Indonesian Coup: The Untold Story* (Westport, CT and London: Praeger Security Inter-national, 2007), pp. 185–195.

9   Sekertariat Negara Republik Indonesia, *Gerakan 30 September*, Lampiran 1, Letkol Untung 'Cakrabirawa' – Selamatkan Presiden Sukarno dan RI [Republik Indonesia] [Lieutenant Colonel Untung 'Cakrabirawa' – Saving President Sukarno and RI [Republic of Indonesia], pp. 5–7.

10 Presently this site features the *Monumen Nasional* (National Monument), commonly abbreviated to *Monas*, an imposing 132-meter tower that symbolizes the revolutionary struggle for the creation of Indonesia.

11 Sekretariat Negara Republik Indonesia, *Gerakan 30 September*, Lampiran 3, pp. 9–10.

12 Ibid., Lampiran 4, pp. 11–12.

13 Ibid., Lampiran 5, p. 13.

14 See ibid., pp. 103–116.

15 Suharto was the inaugural KOSTRAD commander who served from 2 May 1961 to 2 December 1965. Established in 1961 as a Corps-level command, KOSTRAD was tasked as the main combat unit of TNI with troop numbers of up to 35,000.

16 Roosa, *Pretext for Mass Murder*, p. 59.

17 M. C. Ricklefs, *A History of Modern Indonesia since c. 1200*, 4th ed. (Houndmills, UK and New York: Palgrave Macmillan, 2008), pp. 319–320.

18 For suggesting an estimate of some half million fatalities, see Melvin, "Mechanics of Mass Murder", p. 1; Mark Aarons, "Justice Betrayed: Post-1945 Responses to

Genocide", in *The Legacy of Nuremberg: Civilising Influence or Institutionalised Vengeance?*, edited by David A. Blumenthal and Timothy L. H. McCormack, International Humanitarian Law (Leiden: Martinus Nijhoff Publishers, 2007), p. 80; Robinson, *The Killing Season*, p. 3; and, Iwan Gardono Sudjatmiko, "The Destruction of the Indonesian Communist Party (PKI) (A Comparative Analysis of East Java and Bali)", PhD diss., Cambridge, MA: Harvard University, 1992, who quoted Kopkamtib (Command for the Restoration of Security and Order of Indonesia) (p. 4). Speaking of high estimates, see Leslie Dwyer and Degung Santikarma, "'When the World turned to Chaos': 1965 and Its Aftermath in Bali, Indonesia", in *The Specter of Genocide: Mass Murder in Historical Perspective*, edited by Robert Gellately and Ben Kiernan (Cambridge, UK: Cambridge University Press, 2003), pp. 290–291; "Indonesia's killing fields", 101 East speaks exclusively to some of the Indonesians who participated in the systematic murder of millions. *Al Jazeera*, 101 East, 21 Dec 2012. www.aljazeera.com/program mes/101east/2012/12/2012121874846805636.html Accessed 12 Nov 2018. Also, see Robert Cribb, "Genocide in Indonesia 1965–6", *Journal of Genocide Research*, 3, 2 (2001): 219–239.

19 Cited in Jonathan Marshall, "Hiding the Indonesia Massacre Files", *Strategic Culture Foundation*, 2 May 2016. www.strategic-culture.org/news/2016/05/02/hiding-the-indonesia-massacre-files.html Accessed 13 Nov 2018.

20 The term was attributed to Brigadier General Sugandhi, the director of an Army-controlled newspaper, *Angkatan Bersendjata*. Its maiden appearance was, "*Inilah Tjerita Kebinatangan 'Gestapu'* [This Is the Story of the Bestiality of the 'Gestapu']", *Angkatan Bersendjata*, 8 October 1965. See Michael van Langenberg, "Gestapu and State Power in Indonesia", Cribb, ed., *The Indonesian Killings of 1965*, p. 46.

21 Mutilation of the dead is forbidden in Islam, a violation of one of the ten principles or adopted practices toward the conduct of war as laid down by the Prophet Muhammad (s.a.w.). See Yousuf H. Aboul-Enein and Sherifa Zuhur, *Islamic Rulings on Warfare* (Darby, PA: Diane Publishing Co., for Strategic Studies Institute, US Army War College, 2004), p. 22.

22 Violence against ethnic Chinese in the Indonesian archipelago dates back to the mid-eighteenth century whence pogroms were undertaken by the *Vereenigde Oost-Indische Compagnie* (VOC, United [Dutch] East India Company) that witnessed the massacre of 10,000 Chinese in Batavia (present-day Jakarta) in 1740 during *Chinezenmoord* (lit. 'Murder of the Chinese'). Another xenophobic outbreak of Chinese killings occurred during *Revolusi Indonesia* (1945–1949) against the Dutch; the Chinese were perceived as colonial collaborators, hence singled out for retribution. Since then, anti-Chinese feelings occurred at irregular intervals where Chinese immigrants were targeted for slaughter; for instance, in recent times during the transitional period between 1996 and 1999 following the collapse of Suharto's *Orde Baru*. See Benny G. Setiono, *Tionghoa dalam Pusaran Politik* [*Indonesia's Chinese Community under Political Turmoil*] (Jakarta: TransMedia Pustaka, 2008); Jemma Purdey, *Anti-Chinese Violence in Indonesia, 1996–1999* (Honolulu: University of Hawaii Press, 2006).

23 Robert Cribb, *The Indonesian Killings of 1965: Studies from Java and Bali* (Clayton, VIC: Monash University Centre of Southeast Asian Studies, Monash Papers on Southeast Asia no. 21, 1990), pp. 3, 21; Adrian Vickers, *A History of Modern Indonesia*, 2nd ed. (New York: Cambridge University Press, 2013), pp. 158–159.

24 When the Khmer Rouge (Red Khmer) dominated by the Communist Party of Kampuchea (CPK) came to power in April 1975 in Cambodia under the leadership of Pol Pot, the regime called Democratic Kampuchea (DK) embarked on a utopian plan to return the country to its agrarian origin was forcefully implemented with disastrous consequences. By the close of 1976 when the adverse effects were known, a nationwide purge was undertaken whereby hundreds of thousands were executed for betraying and/or sabotaging the CPK, and others killed were accused of being the so-called class enemies, and many others died of starvation, disease, and exhaustion from forced

labour. The carnage spurred the term 'Killing Fields', referring to the mass graves of the victims, and became the title of a Hollywood movie released in 1984 largely based on the aforesaid horrific phenomenon that befell Cambodia. See David Chandler, *Brother Number One: A Political Biography of Pol Pot* (Boulder, CO: Westview Press, 2000); David Chandler et al., *Pol Pot Plans the Future* (New Haven, CT: Yale University Southeast Asia Studies, 1988).

25 See Adam Schwarz, *A Nation in Waiting: Indonesia's Search for Stability*, 2nd ed. (Crows' Nest, NSW: Allen and Unwin, 1999), p. 20; Cribb, *The Indonesian Killings of 1965*, p. 3; Jean Gelman Taylor, *Indonesia: Peoples and Histories* (New Haven and London: Yale University Press, 2003), pp. 357–358; T. Friend, *Indonesian Destinies* (Cambridge, MA: Harvard University Press, 2003), p. 111; Vickers, *A History of Modern Indonesia*, p. 159; Geoffrey Robinson, *The Dark Side of Paradise: Political Views in Bali* (Ithaca, NY: Cornell University Press, 1995), pp. 273–303. For the Chinese killings, see Mely G. Tan, *Etnis Tionghoa di Indonesia: Kumpulan Tulisan* [*Ethnic Chinese in Indonesia: A Collection of Writings*] (Jakarta: Yayasan Obor Indonesia, 2008), pp. 240–242.

26 Vickers, *A History of Modern Indonesia*, p. 158.

27 Robinson, *The Killing Season*, p. 123.

28 See Syamdani, ed., *Kontroversi Sejarah di Indonesia* [*Historical Controversy in Indonesia*] (Jakarta: GRASINDO, Penerbit PT Gramedia Widiasarana Indonesia, 2001), p. 125. Sukendro, later, was a signatory to *Petisi 50* (Petition of 50), a document dated 5 May 1980 criticizing then President Suharto's abused of the state philosophy of *Pancasila* against political opponents. In regarding his (Suharto's) person as the embodiment of *Pancasila*, any attack on him posed a criticism of the national philosophy.

29 Ibid.

30 See below for discuissions on the declassified telegrams sent from the US Embassy in Jakarta.

31 KAP-Gestapu (*Komando Aksi Pengganyangan Gerakan September Tigapuluh* [Action Command to Crush the Thirtieth September Movement]) comprised a consortium of youth organizations and orthodox Muslim groups. KAP-Gestapu later adopted the new name of Pancasila Front. See Christian Gerlach, *Extremely Violent Societies: Mass Violence in the Twentieth-Century World* (Cambridge, UK: Cambridge University Press, 2010), p. 38.

32 Jess Melvin, *The Army and the Indonesian Genocide: Mechanics of Mass Murder* (London: Routledge, 2018), pp. 9–10. Emphasis added.

33 See Gerard J. DeGroot, *The Sixties Unplugged: A Kaleidoscopic History of a Disorderly Decade* (Cambridge, MA: Harvard University Press, 2010), p. 390; Geoffrey Robinson, "'Down to the Very Roots': The Indonesian Army's Role in the Mass Killings of 1965–66", *Journal of Genocide Research*, 19, 4 (2017): 465–486. www.tandfonline.com/doi/full/10.1080/14623528.2017.1393935 Accessed 14 Nov 2018; Kathy Kadane, "U.S. Officials' Lists Aided Indonesian Bloodbath in '60s", *The Washington Post*, May 21, 1990. www.washingtonpost.com/archive/politics/1990/05/21/us-officials-lists-aided-indonesian-bloodbath-in-60s/ff6d37c3-8eed-486f-908c-3eeafc19aab2/?noredirect=on&utm_term=.def6d002d52b Accessed 12 Nov 2018; Alex J. Bellamy, *Massacres and Morality: Mass Atrocities in an Age of Civilian Immunity* (Oxford, UK: Oxford University Press, 2012), p. 210; David F. Schmitz, *The United States and Right-Wing Dictatorships, 1965–1989* (Cambridge, MA: Cambridge University Press, 2006), pp. 48–49; Syamdani, *Kontroversi Sejarah di Indonesia*, pp. 122–125.

34 See David R. Contosta, *America's Needless Wars: Cautionary Tales of US Involvement in the Philippines, Vietnam, and Iraq* (New York: Prometheus Books, 2017), pp. 102–105.

35 Bradley Simpson, *Economists with Guns: Authoritarian Development and U.S.: Indonesian Relations, 1960–1968* (Stanford: Stanford University Press, 2010), p. 193.

36 Jess Melvin, "Telegrams Confirm Scale of US Complicity in 1965 Genocide", *Indonesia at Melbourne*, 20 Oct 2017, http://indonesiaatmelbourne.unimelb.edu.au/telegrams-confirm-scale-of-us-complicity-in-1965-genocide/ Accessed 14 Nov 2018. Emphasis added. The non-governmental National Security Archives (NSA) based in Washington, DC published all "The 39 documents made available today [17 Oct 2017] come from a collection of nearly 30,000 pages of files constituting much of the daily record of the U.S. Embassy in Jakarta, Indonesia, from 1964–1968". "U.S. Embassy Tracked Indonesia Mass Murder 1965: Newly Declassified U.S. Embassy Jakarta Files Detail Army Killings, U.S. Support for Quashing Leftist Labor Movement", edited by Brad Simpson, National Security Archive (NSA). Washington, DC, 17 Oct 2017. https://nsarchive.gwu.edu/briefing-book/indonesia/2017-10-17/indonesia-mass-murder-1965-us-embassy-files Accessed 15 Nov 2018.

37 Ibid., emphasis added.

38 Ibid., emphasis added.

39 The PKI's proposal of a Fifth Force of armed peasants and workers alongside the existing four branches (viz. army, navy, air force, and police) of the regular armed forces undoubtedly did not receive the generals' approval. In fact, many within the officer corps were uncompromising in opposition, particularly following Beijing's support to the extent of offering to supply the arms for the Fifth Force. Apparently the air force was favourable to such a people's militia, wherein in July 1965 at Halim air force base, 2,000 PKI personnel were undergoing military training. The proposed formation of the Fifth Force, although abortive, to a great extent prompted the GESTAPU. See William H. Frederick and Robert L. Worden, eds., *Indonesia: A Country Study* (Washington, DC: Library of Congress, 1993). http://countrystudies.us/indonesia/21.htm Accessed 2 Jan 2019; and, Robinson, *The Killing Season*, pp. 49–50.

40 The PSI, together with *Masyumi*, were proscribed by President Sukarno in Mar 1960 for opposition to Guided Democracy and support for the Revolutionary Government of the Republic of Indonesia (PRRI).

41 *Supersemar* or *Surat Perintah Sebelas Maret* (Order of Eleventh March) authorized then Commander of the Army Lieutenant General Suharto full authority to restore order during the Indonesian Massacres (1965–1966). This presidential document came to symbolize the transfer of power, from Sukarno to Suharto, or in other words, the demise of the Old Order and the emergence of the New Order. See Sekretariat Negara Republik Indonesia, *30 Tahun Indonesia Merdeka* [*30 Years of Indonesian Independence*] Jilid III (Jakarta: Setneg [Sekretariat Negara], 1985). Also, see F. X. Baskara Tulus Wardaya, *Membongkar Supersemar! Dari CIA hingga Kudeta Merangkak Melawan Bung Karno* [*Supersemar Exposed! From the CIA to Coup D'état That Stealthily Moved against Bung Karno*] (Yogjarkata: Galangpress, 2009).

42 Following his successful engineering of the West New Guinea dispute (1950–1963) that brought Dutch New Guinea (renamed West Irian, later Irian Jaya) under Indonesian administration in May 1963, Sukarno proclaimed himself 'president for life'. It was a presumptuous act executed at the peak of his presidency, power, and influence.

43 Sukarno was a non-apologetic womanizer *par excellence*. He was rumoured to have flirted with contemporary beauties the likes of Marilyn Monroe, Elizabeth Taylor, and Jackie Kennedy. One commenter noted of his 'womanizing behaviour': "it is universally agreed that Sukarno was an incorrigible flirt. He had nine wives. In his own words, Sukarno liked looking at beautiful women 'not just out of the corner of his eye but with all his eyes,' behaviour Indonesians call *mata keranjang* (basket eyes, like a shopper)". 'Flirting with Marilyn'. www.expat.or.id/info/flirtingwithmarilyn.html Accessed 7 Jan 2019.

44 Through a series of re-appointments of his presidential term, Suharto remained as president of Indonesia until 1998, a three-decade hold of almost absolute power as strongman-dictator.

45 "Menelusuri Riwayat Partai Komunis Indonesia di Kalsel; Di Kalsel, Ketuanya Saja Masih Rajin Salat [Tracing the History of the Indonesian Communist Party in South

Kalimantan: In South Kalimantan, the Chairman Is Still Diligent in Prayer]", PRO KALSEL Pro Kalimantan Selatan, Jumat, 29 Sept 2017. http://kalsel.prokal.co/read/news/11476-menelusuri-riwayat-partai-komunis-indonesia-di-kalsel.html?fb_comment_id=2119148951444654_2120434284649454 Accessed 15 Nov 2018.

46 See "Pidato Kawan Amar Hanafiah (Wakil Sekretaris CDB PKI Kalimantan Selatan)", *Bintang Merah Nomor Special Jilid II, Dokumen-Dokumen Kongres Nasional Ke-VI Partai Komunis Indonesia, 7–14 September 1959* (Jakarta: Yayasan Pembaruan, 1960). www.marxists.org/indonesia/indones/KongresPKIke6/PidatoHanafiah.htm Accessed 15 Nov 2018.

47 Ibid.

48 Ibid.

49 Ibid.

50 "Menelusuri Riwayat Partai Komunis Indonesia di Kalsel".

51 Sekretariat Negara Republik Indonesia, *Gerakan 30 September*, Lampiran 4, p. 11.

52 See ibid., pp. 120–121.

53 Ibid., p. 114.

54 Ibid.

55 Ibid., p. 115.

56 Established in 1964, Sekber Golkar was the predecessor to *Partai Golongan Karya* (Golkar, Party of Functional Groups). Golkar only became a political party in 1999. See Eric C. Thompson, "Indonesia in Transition: The 1999 Presidential Elections", *NBR Briefing Policy Report*, No. 9 (Dec 1999): 1–17.

57 Sekretariat Negara Republik Indonesia, *Gerakan 30 September*, p. 115.

58 Although formally inaugurated in 1971, NKCP wore the guises and cloaks of the Sarawak Liberation League (SLL), then became known as the Clandestine Communist Organization (CCO), and later, was referred to as the Sarawak Communist Organization (SCO). All the various manifestations testified to its covert and surreptitious existence and operations. The numerous labels were created by the Sarawak colonial authorities, and from 1963, used by the Malaysian government. See below for the Pontianak Conference, 17–19 Sep 1965.

59 Banjarmasin-born of mixed Arab-Madurese heritage, Sofyan was a key PKI figure in West Kalimantan who had risen in rank to become secretary to the party's provincial central board, its decision-making body. His pro-Chinese stance, as opposed to the Javanese-dominated pro-*pribumi* (indigenous specifically Malay and Dayak) on the matter of recruitment and garnering support, brought Sofyan on a collision course with Bambang Soemitro, chair of the provincial central board. In 1960, Sofyan won and assumed the leadership of the West Kalimantan branch of the PKI. See Jamie S. Davidson, *From Rebellion to Riots: Collective Violence on Indonesian Borneo* (Singapore: National University of Singapore (NUS) Press, 2009), p. 57.

60 For SCO members, see Justus van der Kroef, "Communism and Chinese Communalism in Sarawak", *China Quarterly*, 2, 20 (1964), p. 40; for TNKU, see David Easter, *Britain and the Confrontation with Indonesia, 1960–1966* (London: Tauris, 2004), pp. 35–36.

61 Hon-Kah Fong, "Vernon L. Porritt, 'The Rise and Fall of Communism in Sarawak 1940–1990'", Book Review, *Taiwan Journal of Southeast Asian Studies*, 2, 1 (2005): 187–188. https://web.archive.org/web/20131224123919/www.cseas.ncnu.edu.tw/journal/v02_no1/5.pp183-192書評new.pdf Accessed 20 Nov 2018

62 According to Hon-Kah Fong, NKCP's formation was announced on Mar 30, 1970 by Bong Kee Chok, founder-leader of PGRS. Ibid., p. 188.

63 Toshio Matsumura, "Causes of Lingering Communist Movement after Indonesia's September Thirtieth Movement: The Case of Border Area between Sarawak and West Kalimantan", *Asian Ethnicity*, 19, 2 (2018): 239–240.

64 See Fong, "Porritt, 'The Rise and Fall of Communism in Sarawak'", p. 188; Hara Fujio, "The North Kalimantan Communist Party and the People's Republic of China", *The Developing Economies*, 43, 4 (Dec 2005): 489–513.

65 Lu You-Ai, *Manman qiusuo lu: bei jialimandan geming sishinian tantao 1950–1990* [*Searching for a Better Way Slowly: 40 Years of Revolution of North Kalimantan, 1950–1990*] (Sibu: Bei jialimandan gemin sishinian tantao bianweihui, 2012), pp. 97–98, cited in Matsumura, "Causes of Lingering Communist Movement", p. 240.

66 "Singapore Is Out", *Straits Times*, 10 August 1965.

67 See Angkatan Darat Kodam XII, *Buku Petundjuk Daerah Kalimantan Barat* [*West Kalimantan Regional Guidebook*] (Pontianak: Sudam V, 1972), pp. 329–330.

68 In Javanese, *kiyai* refers to a respected elder. In Kalimantan, however, Banjar Malay utilized the title, *kiyai* to denote, head of a district, or district officer (DO).

69 See *Kompas*, 3 May and 4 May 1966, 21 July 1966; Angkatan Darat Kodam XII, *Buku Petundjuk*, pp. 333–334.

70 *Antara Weekly Review*, 4 and 11 Dec 1965.

71 See Kodam XII/Tanjungpura, *Pelita 1975* [*Light of 1975*] (Pontianak: Kodam XII/ Tanjungpura, 1975), pp. 62–63.

72 Apparently, there was a split in the PGRS in Singkawang in the wake of GESTAPU over the question of strategy, between a faction favouring going on the offensive into Sarawak and another group that preferred consolidation and strengthening through recruitment. The schism saw between 20 and 30 members of PGRS left their Sikukng hill base in Sanggau to join Sofyan's TKKB in Feb 1967. See "The Origin and Development of the Sarawak Communist Organisation (SCO)", manuscript, Kuching, c. 1974 (SMA), pp. 3–4; Sarawak Government, *The Threat of Armed Communism in Sarawak, White Paper* (Kuala Lumpur: Government Printers, 1972), pp. 2–3.

73 Angkatan Darat Kodam XII, *Buku Petundjuk*, p. 335; Kodam XII/Tanjungpura, *Pelita 1975*, pp. 61–62.

74 See Majoor [sic] C. P. M. Moeljono, "'Laporan Chusus' tentang adanja penjerangan Gerombolan PGRS terhadap LANU Singkawang II di SG. Ledo pada tanggal 16–7– 1967 ["Special Report" about the PGRS Horde Attack on LANU[D] Singkawang II at SG [Sanggau?] Ledo on 16–7–1967"]" (Pontianak: Komando Daerah Militer XII/ Tandjungpura Polisi Militer, n.d.).

75 Semdam XII, *Tanjungpura Berjuang: Sejarah Kodam XII/Tanjungpura* [*Tanjungpura Fighting: History of Kodam XII/Tanjungpura*]. Pontianak: Yayasan Tanjungpura, 1971), p. 260.

76 Davidson, *From Rebellion to Riots*, p. 60.

77 Mao Tse-tung, "On Guerrilla Warfare, Chapter 6: The Political Problems of Guerrilla Warfare." www.marxists.org/reference/archive/mao/works/1937/guerrilla-warfare/ ch06.htm Accessed 20 Dec 2018.

78 See Jamie S. Davidson and Douglas Kammen, "Indonesia's Unknown War and the Lineages of Violence in West Kalimantan", *Indonesia*, 73 (Apr 2002), p. 63.

79 *Angkatan Bersenjata*, 21 Sept 1967.

80 Also rendered as *tumenggong*, not unlike the Sarawak Iban title of *temenggung*, that carried the weight of 'paramount chief' as in the case of Temenggong Koh anak Jubang of the Rajang, who was the first to assume such an exalted title. Originally, a title accorded to a Malay chief in charge of order and security in the kingdom.

81 See Brigadir Djenderal TNI A. J. Witono [Sarsono], *Laporan Pang Dam XII/Tandjung-pura tentang gerakan suku Dayak terhadap GTK [Gerombolan Tjina Komunis] di Kal-Bar (II)* [*Report of the Regional Commander XII/Tandjungpura on Ethnic Dayak Action against GTK [Gerombolan Tjina Komunis (Chinese Communist Horde)] in West Kalimantan (II)*] (Pontianak: Angkatan Darat Komando Daerah XII/Tanjungpura, Dec 4, 1967), p. 3.

82 Ibid., p. 4, translated by and quoted from Davidson and Kammen, "Indonesia's Unknown War", p. 64.

83 See *Kompas*, 9 Aug, 18 Aug, 9 Sept 1967, and 4 Jan 1968.

84 Semdam XII, *Tanjungpura Berjuang*, pp. 270–271.

85 *Angkatan Bersenjata*, 23 Oct 1967.
86 Semdam XII, *Tanjungpura Berjuang*, p. 276. Also, see *Straits Times*, 21 Nov 1967.
87 Others agreed on a figure of 3,000 (Hulten and Jenkins), whereas a conservative number of 2,000 fatalities was also estimated (Peterson). Herman Josef Van Hulten, *Hidupku di antara Suku Daya: Catatan seorang missionaris* [*My Life among the Daya: Notes of a Missionary*] (Jakarta: PT. Grasindo, 1992, trans. from the Dutch, 1983), p. 295; David Jenkins, "The Last Headhunt", *Far Eastern Economic Review*, 30 June 1978; Robert Peterson, *Storm over Borneo* (London: Overseas Missionary Fellowship, 1968), p. 21. Also, see Davidson and Kammen, "Indonesia's Unknown War", p. 68. The military recorded the path of the Chinese slaughter with dates and location, Witono [Sarsono], *Laporan Pang Dam XII/Tandjungpura*, pp. 5–6.
88 See Ooi Keat Gin, *Post-War Borneo, 1945–1950: Nationalism, Empire and, State-Building* (London and New York: Routledge, 2013), pp. 140–142.
89 For Oeray's claim, see Jenkins, "The Last Headhunt."
90 Witono [Sarsono], *Laporan Pang Dam XII/Tandjungpura*, p. 3.
91 For details of this at best shadowy organization, see Davidson, *From Rebellion to Riots*, pp. 70–72.
92 Almost all local media reports (radio, newspapers, magazines) that reported and/or commented on the communist insurgency from the mid-1960s and 1970s were military propaganda of Suharto's *Orde Baru*. See Michael Eilenberg, *At the Edges of States: Dynamics of State Formation in the Indonesian Borderlands, Verhandelingen Van Het Koninklijk Instituut Voor Taal-, Land- en Volkenkunde* [*Proceedings of the Royal Institute for Language, Land, and Ethnology Series*] (Leiden: Brill, 2012), p. 128, n. 26.
93 Commander Tanjungpura Regional Military Command (KODAM XII), West Kalimantan.
94 Soemadi, *Kalimantan Barat dalam Menghadapi Subversi Komunis Asia Tenggara* [*West Kalimantan in Facing Communist Subversion in Southeast Asia*] (Pontianak: Tanjungpura, 1974), pp. 94, 96.
95 Ibid., p. 96.
96 It appeared that the Chinese were rather pragmatic and even stoic about their predicament. According to "One old Chinese man who fled to Pontianak in 1967 said that the Chinese did not even consider or discuss striking back at Dayaks as an option. This was because they were imbued with a philosophy of being a guest on other people's land to become a great trading diaspora". John Braithwaite et al., *Anomie and Violence: Non-Truth and Reconciliation in Indonesian Peacebuilding* (Canberra: ANU E Press, 2010), pp. 294–295.
97 See *Kompas*, 11 Mar 1971.
98 *Kompas*, 7 Dec 1967, and *Harian Kami*, 25 and 26 Mar 1968.
99 *Harian Kami*, 26 Mar and 15 Apr 1968.
100 Ooi Keat Gin, *The Japanese Occupation of Borneo, 1941–1945* (London: Routledge, 2011), pp. 108–109.
101 See *Laporan umum Operasi Saberda, tahun 1968* (Pontianak: Komando Daerah Militer XII/Tanjungpura, n.d.), p. 6; Soemadi, *Kalimantan Barat*, p. 94.
102 Semdam XII, *Tanjungpura Berjuang*, pp. 327–330.
103 Pusat Sejarah dan Tradisi TNI, *Bahaya laten komunisme di Indonesia: Penumpusan pemberontakan PKI dan sisa-sisanya* [*The Latent Danger of Communism in Indonesia: The Overthrow of the PKI Rebellion and Its Remnants*], jilid 5 (Jakarta: Markas Besar TNI, 1995), p. 167.
104 See *Sarawak Tribune*, 31 Oct 1969.
105 See below.
106 See *Harian Kami*, 26 Mar 1968.
107 *Kompas*, 13 June 1975.
108 Ibid., 18 July 1977.

109 Malaya/Malaysia was militarily assisted by the UK, Australia, New Zealand, and Brunei whilst Canada, Thailand, India, and the U.S. supported with material aid. Except the U.S. and Thailand, the rest were members of the British Commonwealth.

110 See Thomas M. Carlin, *CLARET: The Nature of War and Diplomacy Special Operations in Borneo 1963–1966* (Carlisle, PA: U.S. Army War College Root Hall, Bldg 122 Carlisle Barracks, 1994); Raffi Gregorian, "CLARET Operations and Confrontation, 1964–1966", *The Journal of Conflict Studies*, 11, 1 (1991): 46–72.

111 Hara Fujio, "The North Kalimantan Communist Party: A Preliminary Study", in *Borneo 2000: Proceedings of the Sixth Biennial Borneo Research Conference*, edited by Michael Leigh (Kuching: Universiti Malaysia Sarawak and Sarawak Development Institute, 2000), p. 205.

112 *Sarawak Tribune*, June 29, 1965.

113 Ibid., Feb 17, 1965.

114 For a detailed account of this enforced relocation scheme, see Vernon L. Porritt, *Operation Hammer: Enforced Resettlement in Sarawak in 1965* (Hull: Centre for South-East Asian Studies, University of Hull, 2002).

115 Vernon L. Porritt, *The Rise and Fall of Communism in Sarawak 1940–1990* (Clayton, Vic: Monash Asia Institute, 2004), p. 141. The permanent settlements were designed like their predecessor counterparts of the New Village in Malaya during the Emergency. See Ooi Keat Gin, *Historical Dictionary of Malaysia*, 2nd ed. (Lanham, MD: Rowman & Littlefield, 2018), pp. 319–320. Relocating communities that proved supportive and/or sympathetic to insurgents was a strategic counter-insurgency technique that had been practiced by the British government during the Second Boer War (1899–1902). See Thomas Pakenham, *The Boer War* (New York: Random House, 1979), p. 493.

116 Ibid.

117 *Sarawak Tribune*, 23 July 1966.

118 Sarawak Government, *The Communist Threat to Sarawak* (Kuala Lumpur: Government Printers, 1966). Earlier, the Sarawak government had published a sessional paper in 1960 informing the public of the pressing issue of Leftist subversion and the dangers therein. See Sarawak Government, "Subversion in Sarawak", Sessional Paper No. 3 of 1960, July 1960.

119 Coincidentally, no pun intended, Kuching, the administrative capital of Sarawak, literally means 'cat' in Malay, hence the 'cat' (Kuching, representative of the Sarawak government) was determined to eliminate 'the jungle rats' (communist guerrillas) within the state. Analogically, it could be compared to a household cat intended to rid the house of rats, a domestic issue in the post-*Konfrontasi* period.

120 *Sarawak Tribune*, 31 Oct 1969.

121 Malaysian Government, *The Communist Re-Insurgency in Malaysia* (Kuala Lumpur: Kementrian Pertahanan [Defence Ministry], Apr 1973), p. 143.

122 Ibid.

123 See Michael B. Leigh, *The Rising Moon: Political Change in Sarawak* (Sydney: Sydney University Press, 1974), p. 130.

124 See Hara, "The North Kalimantan Communist Party", pp. 201–202.

125 Malaysian Government, *The Communist Re-Insurgency in Malaysia*, p. 143.

126 Owing to the meaning of Nonok in Malay for vagina, a name change to Asajaya was made on 22 February 1984. CIRCULAR MEMORANDUM (No. 14/84), 24 March, 1984. The Administrative Areas Ordinance: Change of Names of – (i) Nonok to Asajaya; (ii) Muara Tuang to Kota Samarahan. file:///C:/Users/w10o16/Documents/4741-swksp-am14-84.htm Accessed 28 Jan 2019.

127 *Sunday Tribune*, 6 Apr 1969.

128 Ibid.; and, Porritt, *The Rise and Fall of Communism in Sarawak 1940–1990*, pp. 176–177.

129 Ibid., p. 177.

130 Porritt, *The Rise and Fall of Communism in Sarawak 1940–1990*, p. 177. Operation Kuku (20–22 June 1969) was launched in Sibu that led to the arrest of 23 suspected Leftist.
131 Ibid., p. 181. Emphasis added.
132 Ibid., pp. 188–189. Emphasis added.
133 *Sarawak Tribune*, Feb 26, 1970.
134 Owing to the 'May 13, 1969' ethnic clashes in Kuala Lumpur and in other towns on the peninsula, state elections in Sarawak scheduled for 1969 was postponed despite the absence of any indication, either overt or covert, ethnic tensions within the state. On the contrary, as the 1970 state elections had shown, Sarawak possessed commendable inter-ethnic relations. The postponement was undoubtedly a precautionary move from the national security perspective.
135 The 1966 Constitutional Crisis in Sarawak was still fresh among most local peoples of Sarawak. It began when Chief Minister Stephen Kalong Ningkan was removed from the chief minister post by the Governor of Sarawak in June 1966, and the former took legal action against his removal and was vindicated when the High Court reinstated him as chief minister, and that sparked a constitutional crisis and intervention by the federal government. See Marcel Jude Joseph, "The Saga of Stephen Kalong Ningkan: The Conclusion", *Borneo Post Online*, 26 Apr 2010. www.theborneopost.com/2010/04/26/the-saga-of-stephen-kalong-ningkan-the-conclusion/ Accessed 7 Jan 2019; Vernon L. Porritt, "Constitutional Change in Sarawak 1963–1988", *Borneo Research Bulletin*, Jan 1, 2007. www.thefreelibrary.com/Constitutional+change+in+sarawak+1963-1988%3A+25+years+as+a+state...-a0179660415 Accessed 7 Jan 2019.
136 Sarawak Government, *The Threat of Armed Communism in Sarawak* (Kuala Lumpur: Government Printers, Feb 1972), p. v.
137 See Ong Weichong, *Malaysia's Defeat of Armed Communism: The Second Emergency, 1968–1989* (London: Routledge, 2015).
138 Ooi, *Historical Dictionary of Malaysia*, p. 271. Emphasis added.
139 For the British colonial period, see Vernon L. Porritt, *British Colonial Rule in Sarawak, 1946–1963* (Kuala Lumpur: Oxford University Press, 1997), Parts III and IV. For the post-Malaysia period, see Amarjit Kaur, *Economic Change in East Malaysia: Sabah and Sarawak since 1850* (Houndmills and London: Macmillan and New York: St Martin's Press, 1998), Part III.
140 Tan Sri Datuk Amar Stephen K. T. Yong, *A Life Twice Lived: A Memoir* (Kuching: Author, 1998), p. 211.
141 The translated English version of this letter, originally in Chinese script (Mandarin), is reproduced as Appendix 9, Porritt, *The Rise and Fall of Communism in Sarawak 1940–1990*, p. 273.
142 Ibid.
143 Appendix 10, ibid., pp. 275–277.
144 "Announcement on the Success of the Sri Aman Operation", *Arkib Negara, Kuala Lumpur*, Apr 3, 1974. http://hids.arkib.gov.my/en/peristiwa/-/asset_publisher/WAhqbCYR9ww2/content/pengumuman-kejayaan-operasi-sri-aman/pop_up?_101_INSTANCE_WAhqbCYR9ww2_viewMode=print Accessed 25 Dec 2018.
145 Yong, *A Life Twice Lived*, pp. 212–213. Emphasis added. It remained unclear for the chief minister's non-support. But shortly thereafter, in April 1974, in a speech at Bekenu on 3 April, Chief Minister Abdul Rahman Yakub proclaimed that *a military solution was not the only way in addressing the communist insurgency, and digressed that RASCOM utilized the concerted efforts of the military, civil administration, and the populace in confronting the insurgency.* See *Sarawak Tribune*, 4 Apr 1974.
146 For a detailed narrative of this 'war of attrition' played out in the Sarawak tropical rain forest mainly in the Third Division between the armed hard-core communist guerrillas

under the banner of PARAKU and Malaysian security forces (mainly military units from West Malaysia), see Porritt, *The Rise and Fall of Communism in Sarawak 1940–1990*, pp. 224–246.

147 Hara, "The North Kalimantan Communist Party and China", p. 10. Emphasis added.

148 Ibid., pp. 9–10.

149 See Porritt, *The Rise and Fall of Communism in Sarawak 1940–1990*, pp. 213, 221.

150 Chin Ung-Ho, *Chinese Politics in Sarawak: A Study of the Sarawak United People's Party* (Kuala Lumpur: Oxford University Press, 1996), p. 145 n. 65, quoted in Porritt, *The Rise and Fall of Communism in Sarawak 1940–1990*, p. 223. Emphasis added.

151 Porritt, *The Rise and Fall of Communism in Sarawak 1940–1990*, p. 223. Emphasis added.

152 Malaysian Government, "Penilaian Ancaman Biro Pertama PKKU [Partai Komunis Kalimantan Utara] [Threat Assessment of the First Bureau PKKU (Partai Komunis Kalimantan Utara: North Kalimantan Communist Party)]", [Kementerian Pertahanan?], Kuala Lumpur, 1984, pp. 2–3.

153 Both figures and their sources are cited in Porritt, *The Rise and Fall of Communism in Sarawak 1940–1990*, pp. 234–235, 240.

154 *Sarawak Tribune*, 16 Sept 1974.

155 Ibid., 12 July 1974. RELA members carried firearms such as handguns, shotguns, rifles in the course of their duties.

156 Drawn from his more than one and a half years' experience in Japanese-occupied Malaya, surviving in jungle camps with Chinese MCP guerrillas, often moving long distances through dense and difficult terrain while often enduring fevers and colds consequent of malaria, British Captain F. S. Chapman learnt (the hard way) that the jungle was neutral. One's resourcefulness decides the jungle's utilitarian attributes that could sustain one's survival or officiate his demise. See Frederick Spencer Chapman, *The Jungle Is Neutral* (London: Chatto & Windus, 1951).

157 Alan Teh Leam Seng, "The Real Story Behind the Historic Malaysia-China ties", *The New Straits Times*, 19 Aug 2018. www.nst.com.my/lifestyle/sunday-vibes/2018/08/403014/real-story-behind-historic-malaysia-china-ties Accessed 8 Jan 2019.

158 Ibid. Emphasis added.

159 Ibid.

160 Chin Peng, *Alias Chin Peng: My Side of History* (Singapore: Media Masters, 2003), pp. 482–483.

161 See Jeremy Smith, *The Fall of Soviet Communism* (Houndmills, UK and New York: Palgrave Macmillan, 2005), pp. 38–72.

162 See Archie Brown, *Seven Years That Changed the World: Perestroika in Perspective* (Oxford: Oxford University Press, 2007).

163 Facts and Details, "Communist Insurgency in Malaysia (1946–1989): The Emergency, New Villages and the Politics of Trying to End It". http://factsanddetails.com/southeast-asia/Malaysia/sub5_4a/entry-3621.html. Accessed 10 June 2019.]

164 For an eyewitness account of the proceedings and signing ceremony, see Rozaid A. Rahman, "History in the Making", *The Star Malaysia*, Nov 29, 2009. www.pressreader.com/malaysia/the-star-malaysia/20091129/283824324651362 Accessed 4 Jan 2019.

165 *Sarawak Tribune*, 9 Sept 1989.

166 Ibid., 18 Oct 1990.

9   Conclusion

. . . to be a fight for social justice.[1]

Nie Kiaw Hong, Sarawak communist guerrilla

Finally, the long-drawn-out, 28-year Sarawak communist insurgency came to a close with the penning of a Peace Agreement on 17 October 1990 in Kuching. Neo Kiaw Hong, one of the 50 NKCP guerrillas who 'lay down [their] arms' thereafter on 3 November 1990, one among the last to do so, recalled her experiences in her memoirs:

> For 22 years, we left footprints in the virgin forests and reforested areas, climbed through mountains, stepped on swampy lands and travelled through the rivers of Sarawak, Rejang [Rajang], Oya, Mukah, Tatau, Kemena, Baram, Limbang to the borders of Brunei and Indonesia.[2]

Nineteen-year-old Neo left her hometown of Sibu in 1968 to enter the jungle with other Chinese youths to participate in the revolutionary struggle, a fight they believed to be "for social justice".[3] Neo was typical of Chinese young people in Sarawak of the 1950s and 1960s, where many were seduced by the idealism of communism and the newly emergent People's Republic of China (PRC) with the charismatic Chairman Mao Zedong as the beacon of ethnic pride, hope, and the future of a 'New China'. For their youthful idealism and ideological commitment to communism and Maoism, Neo and her comrades-in-arms sacrificed the greater part of their prime adulthood in the tropical rain forest of Sarawak enduring severe hardships, unbelievable deprivations, adversities, and being hunted down like 'jungle rats'. Nonetheless, Neo and her comrades remained steadfast to their revolutionary struggle aimed at establishing a communist republic in Sarawak. No one coerced Neo in choosing such a life journey; it was her decision, and hers alone, to voluntarily walk into the jungle as a young woman armed only with her ideological commitment. Undoubtedly, her parents and family were reluctant of her life choices, but ever supportive in whatever manner or form to lend a hand whenever the opportunity arose. Beijing, Mao, and the PRC, however, were but mere inspiration and moral sustenance from afar.

Like communist guerrilla Neo Kiaw Hong, many local (Bornean) personalities and regional leaders (Malaya, Indonesia, the Philippines, etc.), to a great extent, chose paths and made decisions of their own choice based on priorities, interests, and/or commitment, ideological or otherwise. Some possessed nationalistic ends, patriotic aims, whilst others seized opportunities as events unfolded to their advantage, pecuniary or political, or other paybacks or gratifications. Still there were individuals who saw benefits in collaboration with certain groups, parties in the expectation for future gains. Besides, there were proxies, pawns of distant powers, and at the same time, victims caught in circumstances beyond their doing and/or control.

In the context of Borneo, against the backdrop of the Cold War of the 1950s through the 1990s, the intention here is to ascertain to what extent the various players whose decisions and actions had direct, or indirect, impact on Borneo, were independent individuals, and not the puppets, proxies, or running dogs of the major Cold War players, notably the USSR, U.S., or the PRC. And not to be taken lightly, post-war Britain, despite its increasing dependence (financial, military) on the U.S., still possessed a strong agenda in the Cold War era that, at times, was even divergent from the latter despite their 'special relations' as Anglo-Saxon allies. Therefore, in this closing section, we shall take a closer look in re-examining and re-evaluating the agendas, motives, and missions of the actors and players that were featured on the Bornean stage, or made decisions and/or executed actions from afar that had impact, positively or negatively, on the island.[4] Alternatively, could the unfolding developments in Borneo during the Cold War be simply a case of the proverbial mousedeer caught between duelling elephants, as depicted in a traditional Malay expression? Or in other words, were some of the actors simply victims of circumstances, or masters of their own destiny?

A 'hidden hand' behind the Bornean stage?

In other words, were the local actors on the ground, from the Tunku, Lee Kuan Yew to A. M. Azahari, Sultan Omar Ali to Sukarno, A. H. Nasution, Diosdado Macapagal to D. N. Aidit, Wen Ming Chyuan, captains of their destiny, or were they being manipulated by some 'hidden hand' behind the stage? In harsher terms, was the Tunku a 'running dog' of the British, Sukarno as Moscow's stooge, Aidit and Wen, both Beijing's pawns? The relationships between local actors and Cold War protagonists are surmised in Table 9.1.

Tunku Abdul Rahman Putra Al-Haj (1903–1990) was prime minister of Malaya/ Malaysia (1957–1970), a prince from the royal house of Kedah, and a Cambridge-trained lawyer. The Tunku was a Malay aristocrat, unashamedly Anglophile, who was staunchly anti-communist. In terms of the latter attribute, he could rightly lay claim that he had overseen a successful defeat of the MCP in the First Malayan Emergency (1948–1960).[5] In 1961, he mooted the idea of a wider federation, namely Malaysia that would comprise independent Malaya, the British colonies of Singapore, Sarawak, and North Borneo, and the British protectorate of the

Table 9.1 Borneo: Local Players and Cold War Protagonists

	UK/U.S.	USSR	PRC	Unclear/Ambiguous
Tunku Abdul Rahman, prime minister Malaya/ Malaysia	Collusion with the British on the 'Malaysia' concept; serves British decolonization agenda.			
Lee Kuan Yew, chief minister, Singapore	Anti-communist 'Malaysia' serves decolonization of Singapore, and addresses communist threat.			
Lee Siew Choh, chairman, *Barisan Sosialis* (BS), Singapore			Opposed 'Malaysia' as it is anathema to BS ambitions of establishing a communist state.	
A. M. Azahari, founder-leader PRB, Brunei				Opposed 'Malaysia' as it disrupts plans for NKKU, a nationalist agenda.
Sultan Omar Ali, 28th Paramount Ruler and Sultan of Brunei	Initially, keen on Malaysia; post-Brunei Rebellion, declined participation. Opted for *status quo* as a British protectorate.			
Sukarno, inaugural president of Indonesia		Purchase of arms from Moscow in his military campaign related to the West New Guinea dispute.	Influence from PKI, adopts anti-imperialism and anti-colonialism stance.	Leader of the ideology of 'New Emerging Forces'; non-partisan to either Cold War camps; nationalist.
A. H. Nasution, Army Chief of Staff, Indonesia				Anti-communist; staunch advocate of *dwifungsi* of the Army; nationalist.
D. N. Aidit, senior leader of PKI, Indonesia			Support and backing from Chinese Communist Party (CCP).	
Diosdado Macapagal, president of the Philippines				Nationalist agenda to regain territorial claim over North Borneo (Sabah).
Wen Ming Chyuan, head of CCO/SCO, chairman of NKCP			Support and backing from Chinese Communist Party (CCP).	

Sultanate of Brunei. The concept of a wider federation, Malaysia, *fitted too conveniently* into Britain's post-war decolonization plans.

The idea of 'Malaysia', in its formulation, was biased towards Britain, and by extension, its close ally, the U.S. From the Cold War standpoint, the proposed formation of 'Malaysia' was intended to foster and strengthen the Anglo-American camp vis-à-vis the opposing Soviet-led communist bloc, including the PRC. Therefore, initiating from this line of thought and reasoning, to what extent did the 'Big Boys' of the Cold War, namely the U.S. and USSR, have a hand and/or voice in the local developments and influence over or even control of local actors?

Although the public announcement of the idea of 'Malaysia' was promulgated by the Tunku, there was little doubt that Britain, its mandarins at the CO and FO and WO, had a hand in forming this concept as part of its decolonization strategy in Southeast Asia. The Pacific War had drawn attention to the pivotal and strategic locations of the Malay Peninsula and northern Borneo. The post-war geopolitical situation in the Southeast Asian environment further emphasized the importance of the proposed components of 'Malaysia', viz. Malaya, Singapore, Sarawak, Brunei, and North Borneo. Strengthening the region, militarily and geopolitically, ensuring that Britain's former possession (Malaya) and remaining colonial territories (Singapore, Sarawak, Brunei, and North Borneo) remained in the Anglo-American orbit, was of utmost priority as far as the FO, CO, and WO were concerned. Having lent military assistance to Malaya in defeating its communist insurgency (Malayan Emergency, 1948–1960), Whitehall was particularly concerned about Leftist subversive activities in Singapore and Sarawak in the 1950s and early 1960s.

Elsewhere within Southeast Asia, a communist-laden wind was prevailing. A communist ascendancy was evident with the defeat of the French colonialists at Dien Bien Phu (1954) in the First Indochina War (1946–1954). The French defeat prompted a greater involvement of the U.S. beginning with the Kennedy administration (1961–1963). The ongoing Hukbalahap Rebellion (1942–1954) in the Philippines might escalate. Meanwhile, the unpredictable Sukarno of Indonesia, staunchly anti-imperialist and anti-colonialist, appeared to be leaning towards the Soviet Union for armaments in his military build-up for a planned amphibious assault relating to the West New Guinea dispute with the Netherlands. Within Indonesia, Sukarno's Guided Democracy saw the increasing assertion of the PKI, much to the dismay and concern of the Army.

In the meantime, island Singapore that had been granted self-government in 1959 witnessed an apparent rise of the far Left. Adopting its united front tactic, communists infiltrated the ruling People's Action Party (PAP) of Prime Minister Lee Kuan Yew. Like his Malayan counterpart the Tunku, Lee was staunchly against communism, though he advocated socialism. Lee successfully outmanoeuvred Leftist elements from within the PAP, forcing a breakaway group that subsequently formed *Barisan Sosialis* (Socialist Front), a Left-leaning political party. It was undoubtedly the ultimate intention of the Leftists to transform the island into a communist republic, a dangerous and nightmarish possibility from Whitehall's perspective. Therefore, merging Singapore with independent Malaya appeared to be a viable design to counter a communist takeover of the island. As pointed out, the Tunku's concern was of the demographic balance that disfavoured indigenes vis-à-vis the large Chinese population of Singapore, hence the wooing of the British northern Bornean territories to offset the ethnic imbalance.

Such a development played well into the CO's decolonization plans for the British Bornean territories. Several options were explored since the 1930s as a form of strengthening effective governance, and in the post-war period, 'a closer union' of the three Bornean territories was formed for administrative expediency. None of the proposals, however, was concretized and remained at the planning and deliberation stages. Hence, 'Malaysia' appeared to be a probable and viable possibility. Moreover, the indigenous inhabitants of Sarawak, Brunei, and North Borneo could allay the Tunku's concerns of a Chinese deluge in the new federation. Subsequently, on 9 July 1963, the Malaysia Agreement was penned, whereby the Federation of Malaysia would comprise Malaya, Singapore, Sarawak, and North Borneo. Brunei abstained and decided to retain its *status quo* as a British protectorate.

Therefore, the Tunku was from the beginning in collusion with the British regarding 'Malaysia'. The British government was fully assured and confident that its remaining colonial possessions would be handed over to the staunchly anti-communist Tunku, ensuring that the new federation would remain in the pro-Western camp headed by Britain's close ally, the U.S.

'Malaysia', on the flip side, has its share of detractors. The most vocal dissenting voice came from Indonesian President Sukarno. Labelling the wider federation as a neo-colony of Britain, a disguise to perpetuate control and retain influence in its post-decolonization period, Sukarno vehemently rejected such an imperial and colonial territorial scheme. Moreover, 'Malaysia' was anathema to his New Emerging Forces ideology. Philippines' President Macapagal's opposition was on the basis of the Philippines' claim to North Borneo. Manila turned to historical legacy in staking its territorial claim.

But were the commitments and motives of both Sukarno and Macapagal solely of their own volition or was there a 'hidden hand' manipulating their actions? Especially of concern was the involvement of Cold War protagonists, notably the U.S., USSR, or PRC, that had a direct, or indirect, control and/or influence on Sukarno and Macapagal. Indonesia's purchase of armaments from Moscow for the intended military assault on West New Guinea against Dutch forces pushed Washington to intervene at the expense of the Netherlands. Nonetheless, U.S. actions did not endear it to Sukarno, who might still harbour recriminations over the Pope affair. Macapagal's claim over North Borneo, for all intents and purposes, appeared to be nationalistic rather than ideological, thus discounting the involvement of any of the Cold War major players, including that of the U.S., the Philippines' former colonial master.

A. M. Azahari's background in the revolutionary struggle against Dutch imperialism and colonialism on the side of Sukarno's Republicans undoubtedly exhibited his sharing of the ideals of the Indonesian nationalist struggle. He and the PRB were keen on the constitutional path to introduce democratic reforms in Brunei.

But whether impatience or premeditated, constitutional means were discarded for an armed struggle in the outbreak of the so-called Brunei Rebellion. Was the PRB's uprising a 'rebellion'? Azahari envisioned a kind of millenarian vision of a resurrected Brunei of its fifteenth-/sixteenth-century golden age, of past glory and pre-eminence with his envisaged NKKU with the Brunei monarch, Sultan Omar Ali, as the head of state, and himself as prime minister.

From Azahari's and PRB's perspective, the unshackling of British colonial domination hitherto under the guise of the protectorate status appeared to be the 'objective' of the December 1962 armed struggle. Members of the TNKU, the armed militia of the PRB that spearheaded the outbreak, believed that their action was undertaken in the name of the sultan and to rid their sultanate of British colonialists.

The idea of Malaysia was obviously incongruent with Azahari's and PRB's agenda and ambition. Whether NKKU was retrogressive or reformist or modernist in character, scant details were available for a fair assessment. Nevertheless, as far as involvement of major Cold War players was concerned, it was an unlikely scenario. Whether Sukarno had a hand in Azahari's conceptualization of NKKU, there was no clear evidence of collusion or complicity. NKKU could simply be Azahari's nationalistic vision of a rejuvenated Brunei. Nonetheless, Azahari's traditional affinity with Sukarno and Indonesia understandably caused anxiety in London and Kuala Lumpur.

But Sultan Omar Ali, who initially appeared partial to Malaysia, later decided otherwise. His status as supreme and absolute monarch in Brunei would be compromised in the wider federation of Malaysia where there were nine other Malay monarchs, whereby one among the royals was selected to be 'King of Malaysia' on a rotational five-year term. Moreover, Brunei's wealth might have to be shared within Malaysia. 'Thanks, but no thank you' was the sultan's response despite visits by the Tunku. In rejecting Malaysia, it did not mean that Sultan Omar Ali was anti-Malaysia, but only his and Brunei's non-participation in the wider federation. The Brunei Rebellion that broke out on 8 December, to a great extent, sealed the sultan's decision on Malaysia.

Whether Sultan Omar Ali was consulted and/or even aware of the exalted status he would play in Azahari's conceived NKUU was unclear. But what was crystal clear was when the insurrection broke out, the sultan invoked the Anglo-Brunei Treaty (1959), the third provision in particular: '(3) the British Government was only responsible for foreign relations, defence, and internal security'. The British government responded with military contingents flown in from Singapore and dispatched police personnel from neighbouring Sarawak and North Borneo. The TNKU was routed within days.

When the armed outbreak erupted, Azahari was in Manila en route to New York to put his anti-Malaysia case to the UN. His mission was aborted due to his failure to be granted a visa to the U.S. Meanwhile, the British military backlash forced remnants of TNKU to flee across the border into Kalimantan, where they were 'welcome' by the Indonesians.

Despite the non-attainment of his ambitions and visions, Azahari remained a Brunei nationalist, who not only intended to unshackle his homeland sultanate from British colonialism, but at the same time harboured ambitions to expand its domain, viz. NKKU, in reclaiming territories (Sarawak and North Borneo) that were once under Brunei's imperial realm.

Sultan Omar Ali, on the other hand, was more self-serving, anxious to preserve the *status quo* of Brunei remaining a British protectorate and himself securely on the throne. In this connection, he sought British military assistance in suppressing the PRB and the TNKU. In rejecting Malaysia, the Brunei monarch was again self-serving in maintaining his royal status and not being subsumed among the nine other peninsular Malay rulers. At the same time, Brunei's oil wealth was kept within its modest boundaries with scant interest in an expanded realm as envisaged by Azahari's NKKU.

The communists, whether the CCO/SCO in Sarawak or *Barisan Sosialis* in Singapore, were ethnic Chinese that looked to Beijing for support and assistance, and they embarked on an anti-'Malaysia' campaign to derail the formation of this wider federation that, in their reckoning, would be detrimental to their ultimate goal of seizing political power and inaugurating communist republics. The battle against merger, from the perspective of the communists, was a battle for their very existence and survival. The realization of 'Malaysia' would spell their annihilation. Hence, no quarters were given in this ultimate struggle.

Therefore, in the context of Malaysia, the Tunku appeared to be a British 'puppet', being influenced and manipulated by the British for their own ends and designs. The Tunku's pro-British stance was clearly understandable against the background whereby colonial Malaya and newly independent Malaya (from 1957) were able to fend off a communist armed revolution through British military and material support. The Anglophile Tunku, as a prince and gentleman, felt obligated to Britain for Malayan independence and the defeat of the communist insurrection, hence, understandably would be beholden to adhere to British viewpoints and arguments as convincingly articulated by Lee Kuan Yew, Duncan Sandys, and other mandarins in the Colonial Office and Whitehall.

The next actor in this Cold War drama on 'Malaysia' related to Borneo was none other than Singapore's Lee Kuan Yew. We have observed how he, with his persuasive powers and resounding arguments, was able to convince the Tunku on two crucial occasions: on the idea of Malaya-Singapore merger and on the pre-emptive August 1963 announcement. Lee Kuan Yew, it seemed, was a pliable British tool who had served the imperial and colonial design in successfully burying the Maphilindo idea and, conversely, in the fruition of 'Malaysia'.

Or was Lee Kuan Yew a self-serving pragmatist-cum-opportunist? In utilizing the united front strategy, communists had succeeded in infiltrating the PAP, but he had outmanoeuvred the communists, forcing them to move out of the PAP and to set up the *Barisan Sosialis*. The communist threat was real and in uncomfortable proximity, and Lee Kuan Yew sought a solution through a merger with independent Malaya. Having to strike a favourable ethnic demographic balance, the three north Borneo territories with mainly indigenous population had to be incorporated into the wider federation of Malaysia. Sarawak native leaders were amiable to Malaysia except the Chinese-dominated SUPP. Over in North Borneo, Donald Stephens, the leader of the Kadazandusun, the largest native community, was unconvinced with the concept of Malaysia and allied himself with SUPP and Brunei's PRB in opposition. Again, Lee Kuan Yew asserted his charm and argued convincingly that subsequently transformed Stephens to be a pro-Malaysia advocate when he was appointed as the chair of MSCC.

Realizing that Britain was highly unlikely to grant independence in the foreseeable future to strategically located Singapore that would be retained as a colony indefinitely, Lee Kuan Yew was convinced that the practical solution was in attaining independence for Singapore through a merger with independent Malaya. Seizing this opportunity, Lee Kuan Yew worked hard to ensure that Malaysia became a reality at all costs; if the Tunku was wavering over merger, he needed to be convinced, likewise Stephens. Lee Kuan Yew applied his 'very all' to sway both individuals, and attained an unqualified success. Malaysia became a reality, and Singapore, as a component of the wider Federation, achieved independence from Britain. Two years later, in 1965, the Tunku expelled Singapore from the Federation over intractable and insurmountable issues detrimental to Sino-Malay relations. Secession then was a golden opportunity for Lee Kuan Yew as prime minister of an independent sovereign republic of Singapore in charting its own destiny, for better or worse, in the turbulent decade of the second half of the 1960s and beyond. Upon hindsight, Lee Kuan Yew was the consummate pragmatist-cum-opportunist who finally clinched *his* island.

Sukarno was a handful as far as the Cold War protagonists were concerned, particularly the U.S.-led Western democracies. Towards the end of his civil engineering studies at the *Technische Hoogeschool te Bandoeng* (Bandoeng Institute of Technology), whence he attained an *Ingenieur* degree ("Ir.", engineer's degree) in 1926, Sukarno published "Nationalism, Islam and Marxism" in *Jong Indonesie*.[6] He was able to reconcile three seemingly very disparate socio-political ideas. Then, in June 1945, Sukarno made the initial iteration of his *Pancasila* (Five Principles) to the *Badan Penyelidik Usaha Persiapan Kemerdekaan Indonesia* (BPUPKI, Investigating Committee for Preparatory Work for Indonesian Independence). The second iteration of the *Pancasila* incorporated it into the Jakarta Charter that subsequently formed the basis of the preamble to the 1945 Constitution of Indonesia. Basically, *Pancasila* comprised the notions of belief in God, internationalism (civilized humanity), nationalism and unity, representative democracy, and social justice.

Although not the 'father' of the idea of a meeting between African and Asian nations, Sukarno, who hosted the Bandung Conference (1955), gained political mileage and prestige in the international arena.[7] Bandung could be regarded as the precursor to the Non-Aligned Movement (NAM, 1961), and again, Sukarno was one of the founding fathers.[8]

The West/Dutch New Guinea issue (1950–1962) led Sukarno to turn to Moscow for military hardware in preparation for an invasion. As mentioned, after Kennedy's demise, Sukarno rejected Washington's aid that had 'prerequisites' and increasingly turned towards Beijing.

The fundamental ideas of Sukarno were anti-imperialism, anti-colonialism, and non-alignment that synchronized with the commitments of Kennedy, hence the

'good rapport' between them. But Sukarno and his avowed beliefs were on a collision course with the British colonial worldview of the reinstatement of colonial
empires and possessions, failing which, retaining influence and control in collaboration with local leaders who were British assets. Hence the idea of Malaysia was
anathema to Sukarno, who in turn responded with *Konfrontasi*.

Notwithstanding arms purchases from Moscow, or increasingly leaning towards
Beijing from the mid-1960s, Sukarno was, first and foremost, an Indonesian
nationalist and patriot.

As co-signatories of the Manila Declaration, Macapagal was aghast, like
Sukarno, at the Tunku's turnaround in the 'announcement in August [1963]',
regardless of the UN findings. In response, President Macapagal pressed the Philippines' claim over the territory of North Borneo, once the possession of the Sulu
sultanate, and Manila, as the successor, had the right to seek re-possession. The
British government had assumed possession of North Borneo from the BNBC in
1946 and transformed it into a crown colony, and it seemed had terminated the
annual 'lease' monies to the descendants of the Sulu sultanate, namely the heirs of
Sultan Jamalul Kiram who had in 1878 negotiated the arrangements with Baron
Gustavus von Overbeck. Whether the yearly dues were for 'a lease' or 'a cession',
all monetary transactions ceased since the 1946 British government takeover.

Even before the idea of Malaysia was mooted by the Tunku on 27 May 1961,
then Vice President Macapagal took on the issue of the North Borneo claim as a
central theme of his presidential campaign. Upon elevation as the President of the
Philippines on 30 December 1961, he continued his crusade for the recovery of
North Borneo that intensified: firstly, when the descendants of the Sulu sultanate
ceded sovereignty rights over North Borneo to the Philippine Government; and
secondly, following the Tunku's Malaysia 'announcement in August [1963]' prior
to the UN findings.

Macapagal's actions could be translated as that of a Philippine nationalist bent
on restoring the territorial rights of his nation-state. Regardless of the legal controversy over 'a lease' or 'a cession', the 'Sabah Claim' became an unresolved
huddle in Manila-Kuala Lumpur relations to contemporary times.

UNKO President Donald Stephens initially upheld an 'independence-from-
Britain-first' stance, and after having attained independence, to consider other
available options for North Borneo. But his appointment as chair of the Malaysia
Solidarity Consultative Committee (MSCC), established in July 1961, spurred his
turnaround, and he became convinced of North Borneo's immediate and direct
incorporation into Malaysia and wholly discarded his earlier stance of 'independence-from-Britain-first'. As mentioned, it seemed that the persuasive Lee Kuan
Yew had a hand in convincing Stephens to change his stance. In prioritizing entry
into Malaysia, Stephens literally 'sold out' North Borneo to the British colonial
worldview. Therefore, a collaborator to British imperial designs seemed apt as a
label for Stephens.

Ong Kee Hui and Stephen Yong Kuet Tze, president and secretary general of
SUPP, respectively, unwittingly officiated a legal political party, in fact the first in
Sarawak, that had been targeted and successfully infiltrated at practically all levels

by the SCO through its united front strategy. The SCO obviously opposed Malaysia, as it represented a hurdle in its quest for the seizure of power in Sarawak. Leaders like the Tunku and Lee Kuan Yew would never tolerate communists in their midst, hence the SCO pushed the Ong-Yong moderate leadership of SUPP to adopt an 'independence-from-Britain-first' agenda. Unawares, both Ong and Yong were duped into the SCO's covert scheme.

In fact, SUPP maintained its anti-Malaysia stance until the late 1960s, when the Tunku was able to convince Secretary General Yong to effect a policy turnaround in recognizing the concept of Malaysia. The policy reversal paid dividends when SUPP became a part of the coalition state government in 1970 that allowed Yong, as deputy chief minister and chairman of the Joint Operation Sub-Committee, to oversee security matters in the First and Second Divisions. In the latter capacity, and with the support of Sarawak Chief Minister Abdul Rahman Yakub, Yong engineered Operation Sri Aman, whereby the First and Second Divisions were officially declared 'White Areas', meaning both administrative territories were void of communist threat in the wake of the Memorandum of Understanding between the Sarawak state government and Bong Kee Chok in 1973.

Both Ong and Yong were local-born Chinese whose families had claimed Sarawak as their homeland. Ong hailed from the illustrious Ong family: his father, Ong Kwan Hin (1896–1982), grandfather, Ong Tiang Swee (1864–1950), and great-grandfather, Ong Ewe Hai (1830–1889), all had been invaluable assets to both the Brooke regime and the British colonial administration. Both Ewe Hai and Tiang Swee were Kapitan China, and the latter was the first Chinese nominee to the State Legislative Council in 1937. Yong was from a proletarian background and was a British-trained barrister, who championed the rights of the people-in-the-street as well as political detainees.

Ong Kee Hui and Stephen Yong were undoubtedly Sarawak patriots, but they were unwittingly 'used' by the SCO for its own end. In Ong, Yong, and SUPP, the SCO could claim to have been successful in its united front tactic until the clampdown on subversives in the wake of the Brunei Rebellion that exposed its vast infiltration of SUPP.

Wen Ming Chyuan, Bong Kee Chok, Hung Chu Ting, and their fellow SCO comrades-in-arms were without a doubt hard-core communists, regardless of undertaking covert operations in towns and villages, or functioning as guerrilla fighters in the vast jungle. But whether the SCO, and its later designation of NKCP, was controlled and/or directed by the CCP in Beijing remained unclear. Wen Ming Chyuan, the long-time chairman of SCO/NKCP, had been in residence in Beijing since 1965, and had repeatedly forwarded instructions to his comrades in the mountainous and vast jungle of Kalimantan and Sarawak. Prior to signing the 10-point Memorandum of Understanding in Simanggang in 1974, Bong Kee Chok received instructions from Wen. Again, directives from Wen in Beijing urged Hung Chu Ting and his deputy, Wong Lian Kui, to negotiate the Peace Settlement in 1990.

The fact that SCO/NKCP Chairman Wen Ming Chyuan was based in Beijing made it clear that the SCO/NKCP had the support of the CCP and the PRC government. It was highly likely, even safe to assume, that Wen took guidance for the general conduct of the armed revolution in Sarawak from the CCP and/or the PRC government. Undeniably, material aid did flow from Beijing to the Sarawak jungle.

Unlike the PKI, SCO/NKCP was dominated by ethnic Chinese, male and female, who joined the armed revolution in their late teens. Their indoctrination during their student days in Sarawak's Chinese middle schools in Kuching and Sibu imbued them with communist ideology, Maoist thoughts and teachings, and the emergence and publicized achievements of the PRC under CCP governance. Ethnic pride and ethnocentrism intermixed with Maoist ideology had sustained most of them as guerrilla fighters throughout the trying years in the tropical rain forest of Kalimantan and Sarawak. Within the rank-and-file, Neo Kiaw Hong and her husband, Yii Sie Tung, fervently believed that "Our struggle together with many others had its significance".[9]

Whether they 'lay down [their] arms' in 1990 or earlier in 1974, Neo and her cohort were all *once staunch communist*. Undeniably, the SCO/NKCP guerrillas received nominal material aid from Beijing. But to label them as Beijing pawns or puppets might not be too appropriate. Ideologically driven, the guerrillas sacrificed their lives (as many did) and the greater part of their adult life in the harshness of the thick tropical rain forest, for they fervently believed and were committed, as Nie Kiaw Hong asserted, "to be a fight for social justice".[10]

The GESTAPU Affair and its aftermath, the Indonesian Massacres, that had led to Sukarno's downfall and the ascendancy of Suharto and his *Orde Baru*, though orchestrated by the Army, had ample proof of foreign complicity. The U.S., the UK, and Australia contributed to the Affair in terms of material aid such as communications equipment, monetary aids, a name list of PKI leaders and associates, and promotion and dissemination of black propaganda, all intended to ensure that Sukarno and the PKI were 'destroyed'. Suharto was without apology pro-U.S. The Johnson administration (1963–1969), committed to the domino theory, was unduly supportive of any faction within Indonesia that would bring down Sukarno and the PKI, the latter increasingly becoming menacingly dangerous with its plans for a Fifth Force that apparently had Beijing's support. The Army and Suharto were more than ideal executors of Washington's design that was steadfast to ensure that the Indonesian domino did not fall whilst the U.S. had committed ground combat troops in South Vietnam (March 1965). During the Indonesian Massacres that had consumed at least a conservative estimate of 500,000 lives, though perpetrated by Indonesians against Indonesians, Washington, London, and Canberra all had blood on their hands equally as well through their covert complicity in one way or another.

Although belated (mid-1967), West Kalimantan too had its share of pogroms against the PKI. Like in other parts of the archipelago, anti-Chinese killings were undertaken here by indigenous Dayaks, sanctioned and in the presence of the Army.

Suharto, undoubtedly, was the anointed Cold Warrior for the West who successfully brought down the recalcitrant Sukarno and the decimation of the PKI.

For the Bornean actors, a mixed bag of motives, from ideological commitment to personal ambitions and ethnic parochial interests, pushed them even to the extent of committing mass murders. Said Achmad Sofyan, who headed the West Kalimantan branch of the PKI, was a resourceful Indonesian communist committed to the cause of the PKI, who under trying circumstances in eluding the Army still managed to hit back (Singkawang II Air Force Base at Sanggau Ledo). Owing to the close relationship he had with Sofyan, Brigadier General H. Mussanif Riyakudu, commandant of the Tanjungpura Regional Military Command (KODAM XII), appeared to be half-hearted or even less than serious in efforts at eliminating the PKI in the aftermath of the GESTAPU Affair. The overall performance of his *Operasi Sapu Bersih I* (Operation Clean Sweep I), supported by five troop companies and undertaken jointly with Malaysia's Third Infantry Brigade, produced disappointing results at best.

Oevaang Oeray, and his shadowlike *Lasykar Pangsuma*, that were engaged by the Army to take on the anti-Chinese pogroms and drive the Chinese from the interior to the coastal areas, executed their assignment with zest, as an opportunity to resurrect the customary head-hunting of their Dayak ancestors that had been proscribed nearly a century ago.[11] Oeray thought by cooperating and collaborating with the Army, he could ingratiate himself with *Orde Baru* and enjoy some political position of authority. For the Dayaks, flushing out the Chinese from the interior regions might offer opportunities for Dayaks to take over the local economy hitherto in Chinese hands. Neither result materialized. Suharto's *Orde Baru* was not keen on Dayaks holding key positions, and Oeray went away with nothing to show for his pains. The killings and violence, in fact, literally paralyzed the local economy of the Pontianak and Sambas districts. Instead of replacing the Chinese, the Dayaks lost out to the Madurese.

> With large numbers already in the area, many working on rubber plantations or road construction projects, the Madurese were best positioned to compete for the new "opportunities" left behind by the fleeing Chinese. As they begun to occupy the now empty land, their trading networks threatened Oeray's designs.[12]

Oevaang Oeray was undoubtedly self-serving in his motives. The Dayaks and the *Lasykar Pangsuma* prioritized ethnic interests to the extent of even committing mass slaughter.

Such inter-ethnic violence and killings in the late 1960s was a harbinger of inter-ethnic strife in the post–Cold War era, and especially significant was the Dayak-Madurese killings in the mid- and second half of the 1990s.

Borneo in the Cold War

The Cold War period in Borneo, like other theatres in the world, had its share of spectacle, excitement, as well as tragic events. Although the era spanned over four decades until the early 1990s, the 1950s through the 1960s were the more dramatic, with the latter decade the most tragic.

Borneo in the Cold War period opened with Britain adding on two more crown colonies to its retreating empire, namely Sarawak and North Borneo, and retaining the protectorate over the Sultanate of Brunei. But the colonial administration in both of the colonies were 'caretaker governments', entrusted with the responsibilities of preparing them for eventual self-government and subsequent independence. Post-war British governments with two notable exceptions (Churchill and Eden) were disengaging and hastening the decolonization process, as exemplified in Macmillan's 'Wind of Change' speech in Cape Town. Paralleling political intervention in preparing the ground for granting independence in the foreseeable future, social and economic developments were gathering apace and picking up momentum. Socioeconomic progress was one of the pivotal answers to Leftist criticisms and condemnation of imperialism and colonialism as exploitative agencies of the non-Western world.

When parliamentary democracy failed over and over again in *Republik Indonesia*, Guided Democracy appeared to be the panacea. But the three-way 'push-and-pull' game among the presidency, the communists, and the Army was heading towards an inevitable rupture. In Kalimantan, the play of party politics facilitated the emergence of a long-marginalized ethnic group, the Dayaks.

Communism, particularly the version as practiced on the mainland of China, was gaining currency in the post-war decades across Southeast Asia. In Borneo, the Chinese minority in Sarawak in particular were the most steadfast who translated their ideological commitment to action, namely armed revolution. West Kalimantan too had its share of Leftist elements but with less than widespread support; to a certain extent, there was some piecemeal support from Chinese settlers in the interior districts. The communists in Sarawak were anxious to establish a communist republic in the state.

Dissatisfaction over the feudalistic nature and characteristics of the Brunei sultanate led some radicals to seek a transformation agenda, initially through peaceful constitutional means, failing which, through armed revolt.

But the Bornean drama had yet to begin. The foregoing was simply in laying the groundwork, preparing the stage, erecting and designing the props, the backdrop.

All of the actors were in position, all in costume, each versed in their respective scripts. The props were in place. The stage was set. Most of the audience had taken their seats, some were fidgeting, and others appeared anxious in anticipation. Both sides of the stage awaited the Master of Ceremony's announcement for the play to commence.

Finally, on 27 May 1961, the 'announcement' was made: a proposed wider federation named 'Malaysia'. Although inappropriate owing to the adverse connotation, the first domino was initiated, to kick-start the Bornean drama in many acts: 'Aye's and Nay's to 'Malaysia' '; 'Brunei Rebellion'; 'Sarawak Communist Insurgency'; '*Konfrontasi*'; 'Sabah Claim'; 'GESTAPU Affair'; 'Of Fish and Water, and Bloodbath'. By the last quarter of 1967, the principal drama was almost over. A new play was in session, viz. Sabah and Sarawak within Malaysia, Brunei withdrawing into its adobe, Kalimantan adapting to the *Orde Baru* regime. Only the 'Sarawak Communist Insurgency' had an extended run, which the MOU attained after Operation Sri Aman (1973/1974), the RASCOM period (1970s–1980s), and subsequent to a Peace Settlement (1990).

On hindsight, Borneo in the Cold War was a decisive period for all of the component territories and their peoples, each embarking on a path and direction that, to a great extent, was of their own design. Nonetheless, it could not be denied that there were 'hidden hands' behind the stage prompting the actors to adopt a certain stance, move in a definite manner, and espouse some preferred thoughts and ideology.

Communism and its adherents, supporters, and sympathizers were arrested and eliminated. No 'Communist Republic of Sarawak' emerged, despite the long-drawn-out revolutionary struggle. Neither was Brunei's 'Golden Age' of the fifteenth/sixteenth century resurrected in NKKU. '*Konfrontasi*', ironically, instead of galvanizing the domestic audience to a foreign distracting war, backfired on Sukarno, bringing down the strongman from his self-made pedestal. New players emerged: Tunku of the Federation of Malaysia; Suharto of *Orde Baru* Indonesia; Lee Kuan Yew of the independent and sovereign Republic of Singapore. The 'Sabah Claim', however, remained unresolved.

It was man who ended the Cold War in case you didn't notice. It wasn't weaponry, or technology, or armies or campaigns. It was just man. Not even Western man either, as it happened, but our sworn enemy in the East, who went into the streets, faced the bullets and the batons and said: we've had enough. It was their emperor, not ours, who had the nerve to mount the rostrum and declare he had no clothes. And the ideologies trailed after these impossible events like condemned prisoners, as ideologies do when they've had their day.[13]

John le Carre, British novelist, 1990

Notes

1 Francis Chan and Phyllis Wong, "Saga of Communist Insurgency in Sarawak", *The Borneo Post*, Sep 16, 2011. www.theborneopost.com/2011/09/16/saga-of-communist-insurgency-in-sarawak/ Accessed 26 Dec 2018.
2 Foreword of the memoirs of Neo Kiaw Hong, as quoted and translated from the Chinese in Chan and Wong, "Saga of Communist Insurgency in Sarawak".
3 Ibid.
4 Some of the arguments and conclusions are derived from, and/or expanded from, the various (unpublished) working papers and keynote addresses that were delivered by the present author at various scholarly events and occasions. See, *inter alia*, "Borneo in the Cold War, 1950–1990", Center for Southeast Asian Studies (CSEAS), Kyoto University, 23 July 2015; "Players from within, Actors from Without: The Cold War in Southeast Asia, 1947–1991", Center for Southeast Asian Studies (CSEAS) Colloquium, Kyoto University, Japan, 29 September, 2016; "Twist and Turns for Hearts and Minds: The Cold War in Borneo, 1950–1990", Public Seminar, University of Sydney, 6 June, 2017; "'Malaysia': An Inevitable Creation, 16 September 1963", Persidangan Nasional Sejarah dan Sejarawan Malaysia [National History Conference and Historians of Malaysia], History Section, School of Humanities, Universiti Sains Malaysia, Penang, Malaysia, 14–15 September 2017; "Borneo in the Cold War: Local Concerns or International Interests?", Academy of Brunei Studies, Universiti Brunei Darussalam, Brunei, 25 October 2018.

5 The MCP insurgency on the peninsula was resurrected in 1968 and referred to as the Second Malayan Emergency (1968–1989).

6 *Jong Indonesie* (*Young Indonesia*) was the mouthpiece of a student youth organization of the name established in early 1927.

7 The Bogor Conference (1949), a meeting of the Colombo group, a loose alliance of ex-colonial territories comprising India, Pakistan, Ceylon, Burma, and Indonesia, laid the groundwork for both the Colombo Plan and the Bandung Conference. The concept of the latter was originated by Indonesian Prime Minister Ali Sastroamidjojo (1953–1955), who suggested the coming together of newly independent nation-states from the Asian and African continents. See Jason C. Parker, "'Small Victory, Missed Chance': The Eisenhower Administration, the Bandung Conference, and the Turning of the Cold War", in *The Eisenhower Administration, the Third World, and the Globalization of the Cold War*, edited by Kathryn C. Statler and Andrew L. Johns (Lanham, MD: Rowman & Littlefield Publishers, 2006), pp. 153–174.

8 Besides Sukarno, the other initiators were Josip Broz Tito (Socialist Yugoslavia), Jawaharlal Nehru (India), Kwame Nkrumah (Ghana), and Gamal Abdel Nasser (Egypt). See Natasa Miskovic et al., eds., *The Non-Aligned Movement and the Cold War: Delhi-Bandung-Belgrade* (London: Routledge, 2014), pp. 7, 23–25.

9 Chan and Wong, "Saga of Communist Insurgency in Sarawak". Neo and Yii "married in 1979, stealing out of the jungle for a proper ceremony and a wedding photo shot". Ibid.

10 Ibid.

11 The Dayaks complied with the Tumbang Anoi Agreement in 1874 at Damang Batu, Central Kalimantan that ended the head-hunting tradition. The peace-making ceremony argued against the ancient practice as it had created conflict and tension between various Dayak groups, hence its prohibition. The colonial Dutch authorities had tried to enforce prohibition of head-hunting in the eastern and southern parts of Borneo. Across the border, James Brooke had prohibited such practices shortly after he became the White Rajah of Sarawak in 1841.

12 Jamie S. Davidson, *From Rebellion to Riots: Collective Violence on Indonesian Borneo* (Singapore: National University of Singapore (NUS) Press, 2009), p. 73. Here was the genesis of Dayak-Madurese rivalry, that in the late 1990s and early 2000s turned into inter-ethnic violence and blood-letting.

13 Alpha History: Quotations: Evaluating the Cold War. https://alphahistory.com/coldwar/quotations-evaluating-cold-war/ Accessed 1 Feb 2019. Emphasis added.

Appendices

Appendix 2.1

Cold War Timeline, 1945–1991

Date	Event	Remarks
1945		
4–11 Feb	Yalta Conference	A post-war planning conference between U.S. President Franklin Delano Roosevelt, UK Prime Minister Winston Churchill, and Soviet Premier Joseph Stalin discussed *inter alia* the partitioning of Germany among the Allied powers, war reparations imposed on Germany, the future of Poland, and framework for a world organization (the United Nations).
8 May	V-E (Victory in Europe) Day	The date marked the formal unconditional surrender of the Wehrmacht, Nazi Germany's unified armed forces and the official acceptance by the Allies, namely, U.S., UK, France, and USSR, hence denoted the end of the Second World War (1939–1945) in Europe. The war in East and Southeast Asia, the Asia-Pacific War (1937–1945), continued unabated.
17 July–2 August	Potsdam Conference	The last Allied conference between U.S. President Harry S. Truman, British Prime Minister Winston Churchill (or Clement Attlee, who became prime minister during the conference), and Soviet Premier Joseph Stalin. It formally partitioned Germany and Austria into four zones, the German capital Berlin divided into four zones, designation of the Russian-Polish border, and division at the 38th parallel of Korea into Soviet (north) and American (south) zones.
6 August	The first atomic bomb on Hiroshima.	In order to hasten the end of the Asia Pacific War, the U.S. dropped the world's first atomic bomb on Hiroshima. The death toll was an astonishing 90,000 to 146,000, and almost half the number died on the first day.
8 August	Nagasaki was the victim of the second atomic bomb.	Some 39,000 to 80,000 deaths were reported, of which half the number died on the day of the explosion.

(*Continued*)

Date	Event	Remarks
15 August	V-J Day (victory over Imperial Japan)	At noon, His Imperial Highness Emperor Hirohito read over radio the Imperial Rescript on the Termination of the War. Formal signing of the instrument of unconditional surrender was undertaken on 2 September 1945.
2 September	Independence of Vietnam	At Hanoi, Việt Minh leader Ho Chi Minh proclaimed the Democratic Republic of Vietnam (DRVN) as an independent republic.

1946

Date	Event	Remarks
5 March	'Iron Curtain' Speech	Winston Churchill, former British prime minister, in a speech at Westminster College, in Fulton, Missouri, criticized the actions and policies of the USSR in Europe, and famously proclaimed that, "From Stettin in the Baltic to Trieste in the Adriatic, an *iron curtain* has descended across the continent". His host, U.S. President Harry S. Truman, was present on the platform.

1947

Date	Event	Remarks
12 March	Truman Doctrine	U.S. President Harry S. Truman, in an address to Congress, proclaimed the principle whereby the U.S. would lend support to any country or peoples threatened by the USSR or Communist insurrection. It marked the commencement of the Cold War.
5 June	Marshall Plan	A U.S. programme of economic aid for post-war reconstruction and rehabilitation to Europe. Countries in Western Europe benefited whilst the USSR and its satellite states in Central and Eastern Europe rejected the financial support.
5 October	COMINFOM (1947–1956)	Establishment of the Information Bureau of the Communist and Workers' Parties ostensibly to facilitate information exchange and communication amongst the communist parties of Europe. The primary purpose was to consummate interrelations among communist parties of Eastern Europe to serve Soviet foreign policy, and as an instrument to deal with the independent-minded President Josip Broz Tito (t. 1953–1980) of Yugoslavia.

1948

Date	Event	Remarks
24 June–12 May	Berlin Blockade	In response to the Western Allies introducing the Deutschemark in their sector of West Berlin, the Soviet Union blocked all access (rail, road, canal) to the sectors of Berlin under Western control. The blockade would be lifted if the Deutschemark was withdrawn. Instead, U.S., UK, and Australian air forces undertook to supply West Berlin via the sky, an undertaking referred to as the Berlin Airlift.

Date	Event	Remarks
1949		
4 April	Formation of NATO	The North Atlantic Treaty Organisation (NATO) was established, comprising Belgium, Canada, Denmark, France, Iceland, Italy, Luxembourg, the Netherlands, Norway, Portugal, the UK, and the U.S.
12 May	End of the Berlin Blockade	The Soviet Union lifted the blockade on West Berlin.
23 May	Creation of West Germany	The Federal Republic of Germany (FRG, *Bundesrepublik Deutschland*, BRD), referred to as West Germany, came into being with the merger of the American, British, and French zones.
30 September	Cessation of Berlin Airlift	The Berlin Airlift ended. Altogether 2.3 million tonnes of supplies (from foodstuff to coal) were delivered at a cost of some USD $224 million.[1]
7 October	Creation of East Germany	The German Democratic Republic (GDR, *Deutsche Demokratische Republik*, DDR), commonly styled East Germany, came into being. It comprised the former Soviet zone of occupied Germany, including a part of the Soviet sector of Berlin.
1950		
25 June	Korean War	War broke out when North Korea launched an invasion of South Korea.
27 June	UN involvement in Korean War	UN committed military support to South Korea. United Nations Command (UNC), headed by U.S. and 15 UN nations, supplied fighting units, viz. UK, Australia, Canada, France, Belgium, the Netherlands, Colombia, Ethiopia, South Africa, New Zealand, Turkey, Greece, Thailand, Philippines, and Luxembourg. Five other nations – Norway, Sweden, Denmark, India, Italy – sent military hospitals and field ambulances.
October	China's involvement in the Korean War	The Chinese People's Volunteer Army (CPVA) crossed the Yalu River to lend support to North Korea in response to the UNC crossing the 38th parallel.
1951		
1 February	Peace talks commence	Consequent of a military stalemate in the Korean War, both sides engaged in peace talks.
1952		
4 November	Dwight D. Eisenhower as U.S. president-elect	On a campaign targeting "Korea, Communism, and Corruption", Republican Eisenhower achieved a landslide victory.

(*Continued*)

(Continued)

Date	Event	Remarks
1953		
5 March	Death of Stalin	Stalin dies aged 74. Nikita Khrushchev succeeded him as leader of the Soviet. He served as General Secretary of the Communist Party of the Soviet Union (1953–1964) and as Chairman of the Council of Ministers (1958–1964).
27 July	Truce in Korean War	North Korea and South Korea agreed to a truce, a cessation of hostilities. Korea remained divided with a Demilitarized Zone (DMZ) at the 38th parallel. North Korea continued in the camp of the Soviet Union, and likewise South Korea too remained with the U.S. and the Western democracies.
1954		
21 July	Geneva Accords	Pursuant to the Geneva Conference (20 April–20 July 1954), the Geneva Accords were issued to formally conclude the First Indochina War (1946–1954), and partitioned at the 17th parallel into North Vietnam under Ho Chi Minh with support from the USSR and People's Republic of China (PRC), and South Vietnam of American-backed Ngo Dinh Diem.
1955		
14 May	Warsaw Pact	A counterpart to NATO, the Warsaw Pact was constituted with member states comprising East Germany, Czechoslovakia, Poland, Hungary, Romania, Albania, Bulgaria, and the Soviet Union. The Warsaw Treaty Organization of Friendship, Cooperation and Mutual Assistance was the basis of the Warsaw Pact.
1956		
1956–1966	Sino-Soviet Split	Beginning from 1956 and concluding in 1966, doctrinal differences contributed to a split between the USSR and PRC. Doctrinal divergences were a result of different interpretation of Marxism-Leninism that was influenced by national interests and priority of each country. Henceforth, both the USSR and PRC competed to lead communism in the world during the Cold War era. Moreover, communist regimes and parties turned to the Soviet Union or China for support (moral and material).
23 October	Hungarian Revolution	Initially a demonstration against Communist rule in Budapest, it gathered strength that brought an invasion of Soviet tanks the following day. When the Soviet armoured forces withdrew on 28 October, a new anti-communist government headed by Prime Minister Imre Nagy (t. 1953–1955) took shape.

Date	Event	Remarks
30 October	Suez Crisis	In response to Egyptian President Gamal Abdel Nasser's (t. 1956–1970) nationalization of the Suez Canal (26 July 1956), an Anglo-French force invaded Egypt to regain control of the Suez Canal. The offensive was greatly criticized, particularly by Washington. The Soviet Union, on the other hand, gave support to Egypt. The UN intervened, forcing a withdrawal. A UN Emergency Force (UNEF) was stationed in Sinai as a peacekeeping force.
10 November	Invasion and occupation of Hungary by the Soviet Union	Hungary was occupied by the Soviet Union. Soviet tanks had encircled Budapest since 4 November. Prime Minister Imre Nagy appealed to the world for aid.

1957		
4 October	*Sputnik 1*	The Soviet Union launches *Sputnik 1*, the first artificial Earth satellite, into an elliptical low Earth orbit. *Sputnik 1* was a 58-cm-diameter polished metal sphere featuring four external radio antennas to broadcast radio pulses. Symbolically, the launching heightened the Space Race between the U.S. and USSR.
1 November	*Sputnik II*	*Sputnik II* carried Laika the dog, the first living creature to go into space. It was a half-ton satellite that carried a female dog, Laika, into orbit, an unprecedented feat that shocked and awed the world, especially in the U.S. Laika, however, died a few hours after the launch.

1960		
1 May	U-2 spy plane	A Central Intelligence Agency (CIA) spy plane over Soviet airspace was shot down, and the pilot, Gary Francis Powers, was captured. Powers confessed that he worked for the Central Intelligence Agency (CIA).
16 May	U.S.-Soviet Summit Meeting collapses	The Paris meeting between Soviet Premier Nikita Khrushchev and U.S. President Dwight D. Eisenhower (t. 1953–1961) broke down owing to the U-2 spy plane incident a fortnight ago. Khrushchev's public outburst in dressing-down the U.S. and Eisenhower, the latter was "furious". The U-2 spy plane incident doomed the easing of Cold War tensions.

1961		
12 April	First human in space	Soviet pilot and cosmonaut Yuri Alekseyevich Gagarin (1934–1968) is the first human to journey into outer space when his *Vostok* spacecraft completed an orbit of the Earth. Gagarin's accomplishment was an unqualified triumph for the Soviet space programme, and he became a world celebrity.

(*Continued*)

(Continued)

Date	Event	Remarks
17 April	Bay of Pigs invasion	A force of CIA-trained paramilitary group Brigade 2506 of Cuban exiles with Washington's support launched an invasion of Cuba to overthrow the Communist regime of Prime Minister Fidel Castro (1959–1976). The mission disastrously failed.
13 August	Berlin Wall	Erection of a concrete barrier named the Berlin Wall that physically and ideologically divided the city of Berlin between East and West Germany. It sealed the borders and hence addresses the loophole whereby East Germans crossed over to the west. The Berlin Wall appeared to symbolize physically the 'Iron Curtain' metaphor that separated Western Europe and the Eastern Bloc during the Cold War period.

1962

Date	Event	Remarks
14 October	Cuban Missile Crisis	A U.S. spy plane sighted the building of a Soviet nuclear missile base in Cuba. It prompted U.S. President John F. Kennedy (t. 1961–1963) to execute a naval blockade and demanded the removal of the missiles and dismantling of the base. Tensions were running high, and the world braced for a 'Third World War' and possible nuclear annihilation. Soviet Premier Nikita Khrushchev decided to remove the missiles.

1963

Date	Event	Remarks
22 November	Assassination of U.S. President John F. Kennedy	To kick-start his campaign for a second presidential term, U.S. President John F. Kennedy visited Dallas, Texas, and was assassinated, presumably by a lone assassin, Lee Harvey Oswald. Controversies and speculation were rampant over the number of assassin(s) and the motive, including implications of CIA complicity or a communist plot.

1964

Date	Event	Remarks
15 October	Ouster of Soviet Premier Nikita Khrushchev	Soviet Premier Nikita Khrushchev was removed from office. Khrushchev's ouster was a consequence of his rather erratic and cantankerous behaviour, an embarrassment on the international stage, failures in agriculture, the Sino-Soviet split, and the humiliating resolution of the Cuban Missile Crisis of 1962.

Date	Event	Remarks
1965		
8 March 1965	Vietnam War	U.S. President Lyndon B. Johnson committed 3,500 U.S. Marines to South Vietnam, marking the beginning of the American ground war.[2] General William C. Westmoreland (t. 1964–1968), commander of U.S. forces, advocated an offensive strategy that relied on U.S. and other free world forces[3] to defeat the North Vietnamese Army (NVA). It was a departure from America's defensive posture of the Kennedy administration's insistence that the government of South Vietnam was responsible for defeating the Viet Cong (National Liberation Front, NLF, South Vietnamese communist guerrillas). Hence, the Army of the Republic of Vietnam (ARVN) or South Vietnamese Army was increasingly sidelined. By December, there were some 200,000 U.S. ground combat troops in Vietnam.[4]
1968		
20 August	Warsaw Pact invasion of Czechoslovakia	Warsaw Pact forces (the Soviet Union, Bulgaria, Hungary, East Germany and Poland) invaded Czechoslovakia to arrest the liberalization reforms introduced by First Secretary Alexander Dubcek. The programme of reforms was also known as 'Prague Spring'. Dubcek was arrested. The invasion was in line with the Brezhnev Doctrine, the foreign policy of the Soviet Union whereby when a socialist country attempts to turn towards capitalism, it becomes not only a domestic problem but also a common problem amongst all socialist countries.
21 December	*Apollo 8*	Launching of *Apollo 8* by the U.S. It marks the first manned spacecraft to leave the Earth's orbit, reach the Earth's Moon, orbit it, and return safely to Earth. The achievement of the three-man crew – Commander Frank Borman, Command Module Pilot James Lovell, and Lunar Module Pilot William Anders – paved the way for *Apollo 11* in fulfilling U.S. President John F. Kennedy's ambition of landing a man on the Moon by the end of the decade.
1969		
20 July	*Apollo 11*	U.S. *Apollo 11* spaceflight successfully landed two humans on the Moon, namely mission commander Neil Armstrong and pilot Buzz Aldrin, who landed the lunar module *Eagle* on the Moon's surface. Armstrong became the first man to step onto the lunar surface. Michael Collins piloted the command module *Columbia* in lunar orbit while Armstrong and Aldrin were on the Moon's surface collecting lunar material to bring back to Earth.

(*Continued*)

(Continued)

Date	Event	Remarks
1972		
26 May	SALT I	The Strategic Arms Limitation Talks (SALT) between the United States and the Soviet Union on the issue of arms control. SALT I led to the Anti-Ballistic Missile Treaty. To some extent, SALT I eased tensions between the two Cold War protagonists.
1973		
27 January	Vietnam War	The Paris Peace Accords formally and effectively concluded American involvement in the Vietnam conflict. Formally titled 'Agreement on Ending the War and Restoring Peace in Vietnam', it was a peace treaty to establish peace in Vietnam and end the Vietnam War. Signatories included the Democratic Republic of Vietnam (North Vietnam), the Republic of Vietnam (South Vietnam), and the U.S.
15 August		Almost all U.S. troops and their allies had left Vietnam (both North and South), likewise Cambodia and Laos. Henceforth, the Saigon government stood alone.
1975		
17 April	Khmer Rouge of Cambodia	The Communist Party of Kampuchea (CPK), or Khmer Rouge, seized control of Cambodia. The regime later established as Democratic Kampuchea (1976–1979) was harsh and merciless, implementing genocidal pogroms that consumed almost 2 million lives.
30 April	Fall of Saigon	The capture of Saigon by North Vietnamese forces signalled the commencement of the reunification of the country under Communist rule.
1979		
24 December	Soviet Invasion of Afghanistan	Soviet leader Leonid Brezhnev deployed the 40th Army into the Afghanistan capital of Kabul, where a coup was undertaken killing the incumbent President Hafizullah Amin and replacing him with pro-Soviet Babrak Karmal from a rival faction within the ruling communist People's Democratic Party of Afghanistan, then facing a rebellion from conservative and traditional quarters of the population represented by insurgent groups known as the *mujahideen* ('those who engage in *jihad*'). This invasion marks the onset of the decade-old Soviet–Afghan War (1979–1989).

Date	Event	Remarks
1980		
17 September	Solidarity movement	Solidarity, a non-communist labour union, is established at the Lenin Shipyard, headed by Lech Wałęsa (b. 1943). Its 10-million-strong membership represented one-third of the total working-age population of the country. It utilized peaceful civil resistance to champion workers' rights and social change.
13 December	Crushing the Solidarity movement	Martial law was declared in Poland to crush the Solidarity movement.
1982		
9 May	START proposal	U.S. President Ronald Reagan (t. 1981–1989) makes the initial START (Strategic Arms Reduction Treaty) proposal at his alma mater, Eureka College, and later in Geneva on 29 June, where he suggested a dramatic reduction in strategic forces.
1985		
11 March	Mikhail Sergeyevich Gorbachev	Mikhail Sergeyevich Gorbachev was elected General Secretary of the Communist Party of the Soviet Union by the Politburo shortly after the demise of his predecessor, Konstantin Chernenko. Effectively, Gorbachev became the leader of the Soviet Union, a position he held until its dissolution in 1991.
1986		
26 April	Chernobyl Disaster	An explosion at the No. 4 light water graphite moderated reactor at the Chernobyl Nuclear Power Plant near Pripyat Chernobyl nuclear power plant in the Ukraine. It was the worst nuclear accident where an entire reactor exploded, sending up a massive fire and radioactive plume that dispersed radiation over a wide area.
1987		
June	*Glasnost* and *Perestroika*	Soviet leader Mikhail Gorbachev announced his intention to follow a policy of *glasnost* (openness, transparency, and freedom of speech) and *perestroika* (reformation of government and economy). The latter's intention was to make socialism work more efficiently in serving the people's needs. *Glasnost* was a political slogan fostering increased openness and transparency in government institutions, and encouraged citizens to discuss publicly the problems of the Soviet system and, in turn, propose solutions.

(*Continued*)

(Continued)

Date	Event	Remarks
1989		
15 February	Soviet military withdrawal from Afghanistan	The last Soviet troops departed Afghanistan.
4 June	Tiananmen Square Protests and Massacres of 1989	Called upon by the government, the People's Liberation Army (PLA) ruthlessly suppressed anti-government protests in Tiananmen Square, Beijing. Also referred to as the June Fourth Incident, it was a student-led demonstration seeking political reform to address the issues of abject poverty and underdevelopment and the adverse impact of the Cultural Revolution (1966–1976). The death toll that ran into hundreds remained unverified.
21 August	Poland's first non-communist premier and of an Eastern Bloc state	Consequent of Solidarity being the dominant political force and increasingly gaining power, General Jaruzelski formally appointed Tadeusz Mazowiecki as prime minister-designate of Poland. Three days later, he won a vote of confidence in the Sejm (lower house of parliament.). Mazowiecki thus became the first Polish prime minister since 1946 to be a non-communist, or sympathizer.
23 October	Hungary becomes a non-communist republic	Hungary formally declares itself a republic, advocating a Western-style democracy following four decades of communist rule. Acting President Matyas Szuros made the historic declaration on the 33rd anniversary of the start of the ill-fated 1956 Hungarian Revolution, a pro-democracy mass uprising that was ruthlessly suppressed by Soviet troops and tanks.
9 November	Fall of the Berlin Wall	The Berlin Wall was dismantled following mass demonstrations by East Germans demanding political change.
2–3 December	Malta Summit	U.S. President George H. W. Bush (t. 1989–1993) and Soviet leader Mikhail Gorbachev held summit talks on the Soviet cruise ship *Maxim Gorky* off Malta. No formal agreements were signed. It offered an opportunity for the United States and the Soviet Union to discuss the rapid changes sweeping across Europe with the lifting of the Iron Curtain, that for four decades divided the Eastern Bloc from Western Europe. According to some observers, the Malta Summit marked the official end of the Cold War.
16–25 December	Romanian Revolution	A violent civil unrest that started in Timişoara and spread throughout the country, culminating in the show trial and execution of Communist leader Nicolae Ceauşescu and his wife Elena, hence, ending 42 years of communist rule.

Date	Event	Remarks
17–29 December	Czechoslovakia's Velvet Revolution	Velvet Revolution or Gentle Revolution was a bloodless, non-violent transition of power in Czechoslovakia, from the one-party government of the Communist Party of Czechoslovakia to a parliamentary republic. Popular mass demonstrations ended 41 years of one-party communist rule. It also witnessed the subsequent dismantling of the planned economy.
1990		
3 October	Reunification of Germany	The German Democratic Republic (GDR, East Germany) became part of the Federal Republic of Germany (FRG, West Germany) to form the reunited nation of Germany. Berlin was reunited into a single city.
1991		
1 July	End of the Warsaw Pact	In Prague, the Czechoslovak President Václav Havel (t. 1989–1992) formally ended the 1955 Warsaw Treaty Organization of Friendship, Cooperation and Mutual Assistance and 36 years of military alliance with the Soviet Union.
31 July	START	START (Strategic Arms Reduction Treaty) was a bilateral treaty between the United States and the Soviet Union on the reduction and limitation of strategic offensive weapons. Initiated by U.S. President Ronald Reagan in 1982, the signatories were U.S. President George H. W. Bush and Soviet leader Mikhail Gorbachev.
26 December	End of the Soviet Union	The Union of Soviet Socialist Republics (USSR), or the Soviet Union, disintegrated into 15 separate countries. The disintegration began on the peripheries, in the non-Russian areas. Mass, organized dissent started in the Baltic region, where, in 1987, the government of Estonia demanded autonomy from the Soviet Union. Thereafter, a snowballing effect followed in East and Central Europe, literally across the Eastern Bloc. The Cold War was finally laid to rest.

Appendix 2.2

Vietnam War (1955–1975): Momentous Events and Developments

Date	Events/Developments
Prelude	
February 1930	While in the British colony of Hong Kong, Ho Chi Minh (1890–1969) establishes the Indochinese Communist Party.
June 1940	Nazi Germany invades and occupies France. The Vichy government, a de facto client state of Nazi Germany, ruled over 'unoccupied' southern France and the French colonial empire in Africa and Asia.
September 1940	Imperial Japanese armed forces landed in French Indochina. Upon agreement with the Vichy government, Imperial Japan could utilize French Indochina, especially Vietnam, as a base for the invasion of Southeast Asia.
May 1941	Ho Chi Minh, a Vietnamese nationalist and communist revolutionary leader, sets up the League for the Independence of Vietnam, or Việt Minh, with the main aim of defending independence from foreign rule, French or Japanese.
9 March 1945	Imperial Japan seized control over Indochina from French colonial authorities; declares independence of Vietnam, Laos, and Cambodia.
15 August 1945	Imperial Japan announces unconditional surrender consequent of the atomic bombings of Hiroshima and Nagasaki. The French return to reinstate its colonial rule over Indochina.
2 September 1945	Ho Chi Minh proclaims the independence of the Democratic Republic of Vietnam (North Vietnam). In fashioning his declaration on the American Declaration of Independence (1776), it is intended to garner U.S. support
	There are sporadic clashes between the Việt Minh and *Expeditionnaire Francais en Extreme-Orient* (CEFEO, French Far-East Expeditionary Corps).
19 December 1946	The Việt Minh launches a guerrilla war against the French colonial government. It signals the beginning of the First Indochina War.
12 March 1947	In an address to Congress, President Harry S. Truman (1945–1953) declares U.S. commitment to contain (policy of containment) communism and to defend democracy and freedom in any corner of the world where it may be endangered or challenged. This foreign policy pronouncement is the Truman Doctrine and serves as the guiding principle throughout the Cold War era.

Date	Events/Developments
June 1949	The last Nguyen emperor, Bao Dai (1913–1997), becomes "head of state" (*quốc trưởng*) of South Vietnam. Backed by the French, he suffers the indignity of not being proclaimed as "emperor" (*Hoàng Đế*). Shortly thereafter, he returns to France.
29 August 1949	At a remote test site at Semipalatinsk in Kazakhstan, the Soviet Union successfully detonates its first atomic bomb, code name 'First Lightning'. It took the U.S. by surprise, and hastened the development of the much more lethal hydrogen bomb.
1 October 1949	Having successfully triumphed over the Nationalist Guomindang (Kuomintang, KMT) in the Chinese Civil War, Communist leader Mao Zedong at Tiananmen in Beijing proclaims the People's Republic of China (PRC).
January 1950	The Soviet Union and the PRC officially recognize the Democratic Republic of Vietnam. Henceforth, Moscow and Beijing render moral, financial, economic, and military assistance to Hanoi.
June 1950	Although anti-imperialist, the U.S. favors a 'colonial French Indochina' rather than a 'Communist Indochina', hence military aid is granted to France in its conflict with the Việt Minh.
September 1950	U.S. President Harry Truman sent the Military Assistance Advisory Group (MAAG) to Thailand and Indochina to assist in the training of conventional armed forces and facilitate military aid. In Vietnam, MAAG was to assist the French to fight the Việt Minh forces in the First Indochina War (1946–1954). But the French colonial military force refused U.S. advice, and denied the Vietnamese army to be trained to use the new military equipment supplied by Washington. Truman claimed that MAAG personnel were not sent as combat troops, but to supervise the use of USD$10 million worth of U.S. military equipment to support the French in their effort to fight the Việt Minh forces.
March–May 1954	Việt Minh forces headed by General Võ Nguyên Giáp (1911–2013) deliver a decisive and humiliating defeat to the French at Dien Bien Phu. Consequently, France withdrew from Indochina, ending its colonial rule and influence.
7 April 1954	At a news conference, in commenting on the strategic importance of Indochina to the free world, U.S. President Dwight D. Eisenhower (t. 1953–1961) speaks of the "falling domino" principle. Hence, the implication of Dien Bien Phu (defeat of the French) could lead to a "domino" effect in neighbouring Thailand, Malaya, and the rest of Southeast Asia. Eisenhower's domino principle is influential in U.S. foreign policy, Vietnam in particular, and the region in general, for the next two decades.
21 July 1954	The Geneva Accords partitions Vietnam into North (communist) and South (non-communist) at the 17th parallel. Free elections are scheduled for 1956 for a unified Vietnam; this election was never held. Subsequently, both sides engaged in conflict, viz. the Second Indochina War, or the Vietnam War.

(*Continued*)

Date	Events/Developments
Vietnam War	

26 October 1955	Catholic nationalist Ngô Đình Diệm becomes the inaugural President of the Republic of Vietnam (South Vietnam) (t. 1955–1963). The U.S. lends support to his government.
1 November 1955	MAAG in Indochina is reorganized into country-specific units, hence emerges MAAG Vietnam. It marks the formal commencement of the Second Indochina War, or popularly known as the Vietnam War (1955–1975).[5]
May 1959	Subsequently known as the Ho Chi Minh Trail, it was a supply route through thick forest and difficult terrain from North Vietnam through Laos and Cambodia to South Vietnam. This supply line (continuously being built and re-built owing to U.S. bombings) serves as the main lifeline for guerrilla forces in their efforts to overthrow the regime of South Vietnam and reunite the Vietnamese people and nation.
September 1960	Due to his frail health, 70-year-old Ho Chi Minh stood down to allow Le Duan (1907–1986) to assume the post of General Secretary of the Central Committee of the Communist Party of Vietnam at the 3rd National Congress.
29 December 1960	Viet Cong-san (VC), or its formal title, the National Liberation Front (NLF), is constituted with its militant wing, the People's Liberation Armed Forces of South Vietnam. VC simply refers to Vietnamese communists. With support from North Vietnam, the Viet Cong attempts to overthrow the South Vietnamese regime, and in turn reunite the country.
January 1962	The U.S. commences chemical warfare when launching Operation Ranch Hand, whereby aircrafts sprayed Agent Orange and other defoliants and herbicides over rural areas of South Vietnam to deprive Viet Cong guerrillas of food and foliage cover.
8 February 1962	Creation of the U.S. Military Assistance Command, Vietnam (MACV) to assist MAAG in overseeing advisory and assistance efforts in Vietnam. General Paul D. Harkins (1962–1964) is the first commanding general of MACV (COMUSMACV), also serves as the commander of MAAG Vietnam, and is the most senior officer representing the U.S. in Vietnam.
27 February 1962	President Ngô Đình Diệm escapes an aerial bombing of the presidential palace in Saigon. It was an assassination bid by two dissident Republic of Vietnam Air Force pilots to eliminate Diệm and his entire family. The bombing was to expose Diệm's vulnerability and activate a mass uprising, but this failed to materialize. Neither Diệm or his family members were hurt. It was spurred by Diệm's autocratic rule and obsession to hold power at the expense of addressing the serious threat posed by the Viet Cong. Moreover, his regime's partiality towards the Catholic minority estranges him from the majority Buddhist populace. Anti-government protests and demonstrations are rife in Saigon and other cities in South Vietnam.

Date	Events/Developments
2 January 1963	Battle of Ap Bac, the Viet Cong's first major victory, broke out at a village in Ấp Bắc Hamlet, Định Tường Province (present-day Tiền Giang Province) in the Mekong Delta southwest of Saigon. Despite their five-to-one advantage and the technical and planning assistance of U.S. advisers, equipment, and airpower, the Army of the Republic of South Vietnam (ARVN) 7th Infantry Division succumbs to a smaller unit of Viet Cong guerrillas.
8 May 1963	Commencement of the 'Buddhist Crisis' precipitated by the shootings by authorities of the Diệm's government of killing nine unarmed protestors in Huế who opposed a ban of the display of the Buddhist flag on Vesak, the birthday of the Buddha. Eight people, including children, are killed. Between May and November – the 'Buddhist Crisis' – political and religious tensions were high throughout South Vietnam, witnessing peaceful resistance often led by the Buddhist clergy faced a brutal backlash from government forces.
11 June 1963	Thích Quảng Đức, a 73-year-old Buddhist monk immolates himself while sitting at a major Saigon intersection in protest against Diem's repressive policies and rule. U.S. support for Diem's regime becomes increasingly ambivalent.
2 November 1963	Overthrow and assassination of President Ngô Đình Diệm in a coup staged by the military led by General Dương Văn Minh. Non-intervention on the part of the U.S. Without any credible leader, instability sets in in South Vietnam. Between 1963 and 1965, South Vietnam underwent 12 different governments as military coups replace one government after another. Subsequent governments, such as that headed by Air Vice-Marshal Nguyễn Cao Kỳ (1965–1967) and General Nguyễn Văn Thiệu (1967–1975), relied heavily on U.S. support. In reality, the U.S. had become both political and military power in South Vietnam until its withdrawal in 1973.
22 November 1963	Assassination of U.S. President John F. Kennedy (t. 1961–1963) in Dallas, Texas. Kennedy was in the midst of commencing his presidential campaign for a second term. Vice President Lyndon B. Johnson assumes the presidency (t. 1963–1969).

Full-scale Involvement of the U.S.

15 May 1964	When combat unit deployment becomes too large for advisory group control, MACV undergoes reorganization and incorporates MAAG Vietnam to its command structure. Following this revamp, General William C. Westmoreland assumes command (t. 1964–1968).
2 August 1964	The Gulf of Tonkin Incident (or USS *Maddox* Incident) brought the U.S. to engage directly in the Vietnam War with the commitment of ground combat troops.
	According to the U.S. viewpoint, the destroyer USS *Maddox*, while undertaking a signals intelligence patrol (intelligence-gathering by interception of signals, or electronic spying) in the Gulf of Tonkin apparently was fired upon by three North Vietnamese torpedo boats. The destroyer retaliated. This encounter became an international confrontation. Two days later, there was seemingly another incident in the same vicinity.
	The commitment of U.S. ground forces was commonly taken as the beginning of the Vietnam War, hence 1964–1975.

(*Continued*)

Date	Events/Developments
7 August 1964	The Gulf of Tonkin Resolution passed by Congress empowers the U.S. President unlimited authority to stage military operations in Southeast Asia without any formal declaration of war to aid any country in the region whose government is threatened by "communist aggression".
November 1964	As a reaction towards U.S. actions, the Soviet Union and the PRC step up military aid to North Vietnam, including a team of Chinese military engineers to help erect defense infrastructure.
1964	U.S. Military Forces in Vietnam numbered 23,400.[6]

Escalation of the War

7–24 February 1965	Operation Flaming Dart is a series of retaliatory air strikes over North Vietnam consequent of Việt Cộng attack at Pleiku and at a nearby helicopter base at Camp Holloway, destroying scores of military aircrafts and helicopters. The operation's first phase targeted North Vietnamese army bases near Đồng Hới, while the second wave focused on Việt Cộng logistics and communications centers close to the Demilitarized Zone (DMZ).
2 March 1965	Operation Rolling Thunder begins a sustained aerial bombardment campaign by the U.S. Air Force, U.S. Navy, and Republic of Vietnam Air Force (VNAF) on North Vietnam over a three-year period (March 1965 to November 1968). The main intention is to intimidate North Vietnam to cease support of the Việt Cộng. Focus targets in North Vietnam include its transportation system, industrial bases, and air defenses, and over the Ho Chi Minh Trail to stem the flow of men and material into South Vietnam.
	Meanwhile, U.S. Marines land on beaches near Da Nang, South Vietnam as the first American combat troops to enter Vietnam.
8 March 1965	Landings on the beaches north of Da Nang of the first U.S. combat troops. Conveyed by the USS *Henrico*, USS *Union*, and USS *Vancouver*, the 3,500 men of 9th Marine Expeditionary Brigade under Brigadier General Frederick J. Karch land in full battle gear greeted by Vietnamese girls with leis, local onlookers, South Vietnamese officers, and four American soldiers displaying a large "Welcome, Gallant Marines" banner. General Westmoreland and others in the ARVN were not amused at the theatrics.
June 1965	General Nguyễn Văn Thiệu of ARVN takes on the role as a figurehead chief of state of a military junta government of South Vietnam with Air Marshal Nguyễn Cao Kỳ as prime minister. The Thieu-Ky partnership provides some semblance of political stability since the demise of Diệm.
28 July 1965	U.S. President Johnson orders an increase in U.S. military forces in Vietnam, from the current 75,000 to 125,000, an additional 50,000 combat ground troops.[7] As a result, the monthly draft calls increase from 17,000 to 35,000. The president's call receives support from Congress and state governors.

Date	Events/Developments
14–17 November 1965	The Battle of Ia Drang is the first major battle between the U.S. Army and the North Vietnamese Army (NVA), a part of the Pleiku Campaign (23 October–26 November 1965), whereby this joint operation is undertaken on the principle of 'common operational concept, common intelligence, common reserve, but separate command'. Owing to the thick forest of South Vietnam's Central Highlands, a novel procedure is adopted utilizing helicopters to convey and drop off U.S. ground troops, and likewise troop withdrawal via helicopters as well. Also, the first time that B-52 strategic bombers are engaged but in a tactical support role. Casualties on either side ran into hundreds and thousands. Interestingly, both sides claim victory.
June 1966	The first U.S. aerial bombing of North Vietnamese cities, notably Hanoi, Haiphong, and the port cities of Hong Gai and Vinh. The last mentioned is a staging area for troops and supplies via the Ho Chi Minh trail.
February 1967	Haiphong Harbor and airfields in North Vietnam sustain U.S. aerial bombing.
April 1967	Massive anti–Vietnam War demonstrations are held across the U.S., including huge protest gatherings in Washington, DC, New York City, and San Francisco. They are overall peaceful with occasional skirmishes with authorities.
3 September 1967	Nguyễn Văn Thiệu is elected president of South Vietnam following a new constitution.
3–23 November 1967	In the Battle of Dak To, in Kon Tum Province, in the Central Highlands of South Vietnam, U.S. and ARVN succeeds in staving off an NVA offensive. The primary objective of the NVA is to draw U.S.–ARVN out of the urban areas to the borders as a prelude to the forthcoming Tet Offensive (1968).
1967	U.S. Military Forces in Vietnam reaches 485,600.[8]

The Turning Point

30 January 1968	The Tet Offensive is launched. It is one of the largest military campaigns of the Vietnam War, comprising countrywide and well-coordinated surprise attacks against military and civilian command and control centers throughout South Vietnam. The offensive is engineered by the Viet Cong and the NVA, with assaults across cities throughout South Vietnam including Saigon and Hue. In Saigon, the U.S. Embassy is attacked. The unsuspected assaults were aimed at provoking a general mass uprising, that, however, did not materialize. On the other hand, the offensive startled U.S. officials. Although the U.S. and ARVN managed to stave off the offensive, it marks a turning point. Instead of further escalation as the military establishment suggests then, Washington decides, on the contrary, on a measured withdrawal from Vietnam. 'Vietnamization' is one of the major outcomes.
11–17 February 1968	This week records the highest number of U.S. fatalities during the war, numbering 543 body bags. By the end of the year, U.S. casualties peaked at 15,000.[9]

(*Continued*)

Date	Events/Developments
21 January–9 July 1968	Battle of Khe Sanh in the Khe Sanh area of northwestern Quảng Trị Province, South Vietnam. Two regiments of U.S. Marines supported by U.S. Army and U.S. Air Force, and a small ARVN force comprises the defense of the Khe Sanh Combat Base (KSCB) against two to three divisional-size NVA. Following a 77-day siege, the outcome was indecisive, but both sides claim victory. Whether the battle was a diversion for the Tet Offensive or the reverse or had other agendas remained unclear, a "riddle of Khe Sanh".
February-March 1968	Concerted efforts of U.S. and ARVN succeeded in pushing out Viet Cong guerrillas from urban areas.
16 March 1968	Mỹ Lai Massacre witnesses the cold-blooded killing of between 347 and 504 unarmed Vietnamese civilians by U.S. Army soldiers in two hamlets of Sơn Mỹ village in Quảng Ngãi Province. The platoon was involved in search-and-destroy operations intended to find enemy territories, destroy them, and hasten retreat. This tragedy further flamed the anti-war movement in the U.S. Mỹ Lai was on record as one of the largest single massacres of civilians by U.S. forces in the twentieth century.
	President Johnson halts bombing in Vietnam north of the 20th parallel. Facing backlash about the war, Johnson announces he will not run for reelection.
31 March 1968	U.S. President Johnson orders a complete halt to all air, naval, and military artillery bombardment of North Vietnam, in effect terminating the "Rolling Thunder" campaign. Silencing of the guns is intended to persuade North Vietnam's leaders to return to the Paris peace table.
5 November 1968	Republican Richard M. Nixon wins the U.S. presidential elections on campaign promises of "peace with honor" in the Vietnam War.
1968	U.S. military forces in Vietnam peaked at 536,100.[10]
20 January 1969	Nixon assumes office as the 37th President of the United States (t. 1969–1974).
May 1969	Close to the Laos border stood the Ap Bia Mountain, whereby U.S. paratroopers launch an attack on entrenched NVA fighters. The main objective is to stem NVA infiltration from Laos in an attempt to cut off North Vietnamese infiltration from Laos. The target site was captured, albeit temporarily. Christened 'Hamburger Hill' by journalists because of the 10-day brutal battle.
2 September 1969	Ho Chi Minh succumbs to a heart attack in Hanoi.
1 December 1969	The institution of a draft lottery by the U.S. government that gave young men a random number between 1 and 366 corresponding to their birthdays. Lower numbers were called up to report to induction centers. Possibilities are high that they will be ordered into active duty and sent to the Vietnam War. 'Draft dodgers' were those who fled abroad, mostly to Canada.

Date	Events/Developments

1969–1972	Implementation of 'Vietnamization', a policy by the Nixon administration (1969–1974) to subsequently disengage from the conflict in Vietnam. Instead, it meant the transferring of combat role to the ARVN, and at the same time, scaling down in the number of U.S. combat troops. Brought on by the Tet Offensive (1968). 'Vietnamization', however, did not affect the U.S. Air Force that continued to undertake bombing raids. Likewise, U.S. support to South Vietnam remained unchanged.
	Number of U.S. troops in Vietnam is reduced from a peak of 536,100 in 1968 to 24,200 in 1972.[11]
18 March 1969–26 May 1970	'Operation Menu' is a series of clandestine bombings by U.S. B-52 bombers over Cambodia of suspected communist base camps and supply zones. It is 'clandestine' because Cambodia is officially neutral in the war.
February 1970	Commencement of secret peace negotiations between U.S. and North Vietnam, the former represented by National Security Advisor Henry Kissinger and the latter the politburo member Lê Đức Thọ. A series of high-profile talks and discussions, albeit no press coverage, are held in Paris.
April-June 1970	In a two-phase process, the Cambodian Campaign is launched with a series of military incursions into neutral Cambodia, allegedly targeting Viet Cong and NVA bases and camps. Altogether there were 13 major missions. Between 29 April and 22 July (Phase I), ARVN undertook invasions into eastern Cambodia. Meanwhile, U.S. forces conducted operations from 1 May to 30 June.
	A coup (12 March) that led to the replacement of Prince Norodom Sihanouk by pro-U.S. General Lon Nol further facilitated concerted efforts in the destruction of the border VC/NVA bases.
4 May 1970	The Kent State University shooting witnesses Ohio National Guardsmen using live ammunition on anti–Vietnam War demonstrators, mainly university students at the campus of Kent State University, in Kent, Ohio. There were four student fatalities with nine wounded. The unarmed student demonstrators were protesting the Cambodian Campaign.
	In the aftermath, protests were staged on college campuses throughout the U.S. Activists launched the first and only nationwide student strike in U.S. history, where more than 450 campuses across the country were forced to close. The Kent State campus was paralyzed for at least six weeks.
24 June 1970	Congress repeals the once-popular Gulf of Tonkin Resolution. Controversy surrounds President Johnson's use of it in increasing U.S. commitment to the conflict in Vietnam. The Nixon administration denied its usage, instead arguing that it utilizes the basis of the constitutional authority of the U.S. president as commander-in-chief in safeguarding the lives of U.S. military forces in the conduct of the Vietnam conflict.

(Continued)

Date	Events/Developments
January-March 1971	Operation Lam Son 719 is the incursion of ARVN into southeastern Laos in an attempt to sever the supply line referred to as the Ho Chi Minh Trail. Unlike the Cambodian Campaign, U.S. involvement was limited to logistical, aerial, and artillery support. ARVN failed and incurred heavy losses.
June 1971	The Pentagon Papers is a *New York Times* exposé of leaked U.S. Defense Department documents about the Vietnam War, revealing the U.S. government's unethical and stealth manners in increasing U.S. involvement in the Vietnam conflict. Officially titled *United States–Vietnam Relations, 1945–1967: A Study Prepared by the Department of Defense* detailing U.S. political-military involvement in Vietnam between 1945 and 1967. The most damaging are revelations that four U.S. administrations – Truman, Eisenhower, Kennedy, Johnson – had misled the public regarding their *real* intentions.
30 March–22 October 1972	The Nguyen Hue Offensive or Easter Offensive is a conventional invasion of South Vietnam by the NVA with support from the Viet Cong against the ARVN and U.S. forces. Defenders of South Vietnam had expected an invasion, but were taken aback by the sheer size when faced with a 300,000-strong massive, three-pronged conventional assault with infantry-armor backed with artillery. The invaders gained much territory in South Vietnam, achieved a stronger and strategic position, hence possessing a better bargaining position at the peace negotiations then in session in Paris.
December 1972	Operation Linebacker was the first continuous bombing effort against North Vietnam since Operation Rolling Thunder. It was in response to the massive Easter Offensive. Hence, U.S. President Nixon authorizes the most intense air offense of the conflict. The aerial bombings focus on the strip between Hanoi and Haiphong, where some 20,000 tonnes of bombs were dropped over dense population areas, resulting in untold fatalities and widespread damages.
27 January 1973	Formally titled 'Agreement on Ending the War and Restoring Peace in Vietnam', it is commonly termed the Paris Peace Accords that brought peace to Vietnam in ending the protracted decades-old Vietnam War. The signatories include the governments of the Democratic Republic of Vietnam (North Vietnam), the Republic of Vietnam (South Vietnam), and the U.S., as well as the Provisional Revolutionary Government (PRG) that represented indigenous South Vietnamese revolutionaries.
	Although the Paris Peace Accords offers an honourable U.S. withdrawal and departure, it did not prevent North Vietnam from pursuing the ultimate goal of reunification.
February-April 1973	Operation Homecoming witnesses the release by North Vietnam of 591 U.S. prisoners of war. It is in accordance with the Paris Peace Accords that stipulates the release of U.S. prisoners of war within 60 days of the withdrawal of U.S. troops.
29 March 1973	The last U.S. combat trooper left Vietnam, ending America's eight-year direct involvement in the Vietnam War. General Frederick C. Weyand (1972–1973), the last COMUSMACV, steps down, and MACV is disestablished.

Date	Events/Developments
9 August 1974	In order to avoid possible impeachment, U.S. President Nixon took the unprecedented move to resign after the Watergate Scandal broke. Gerald R. Ford succeeds as the 38th President of the United States (t. 1974–1977).
30 April 1975	Saigon, the capital of South Vietnam, is seized by communist forces, and the government of the Republic of Vietnam surrenders.
	Prior to the fall of Saigon, Operation Frequent Wind saw the hurried and desperate evacuation of U.S. civilians and 'at-risk' Vietnamese from Saigon being transported by U.S. Marine and Air Force helicopters. Altogether 1,373 Americans and 5,595 Vietnamese and third-country nationals were airlifted out of Saigon in an 18-hour operation.[12]
2 July 1976	The formal reunification of Vietnam as the Socialist Republic of Vietnam under communist rule.

By the end of the war, more than 58,000 Americans lost their lives. Vietnam later released estimates that 1.1 million North Vietnamese and Viet Cong fighters were killed, up to 250,000 South Vietnamese soldiers died, and more than 2 million civilians were killed on both sides of the war.

Sources: www.history.com/topics/vietnam-war-timeline Accessed 26 Nov 2017

The Vietnam War: The Definitive Illustrated History, created in association with the Smithsonian Institution, published by *DK | Penguin Random House, 2017.*

The Vietnam War: An Intimate History, by Geoffrey C. Ward and Ken Burns, based on the film series by Ken Burns and Lynn Novick, published by *Penguin Random House, 2017.*

Vietnam Profile – Timeline, *BBC News, June 12, 2017.*

Operation Starlite: The First Battle of the Vietnam War, *Military.com.*

South Vietnam: The Buddhist Crisis, *Time.*

Buddhists – The 1963 Crisis, *GlobalSecurity.org.*

Vietnam, Diem, the Buddhist Crisis, *John F. Kennedy Presidential Library*

The Fall of Saigon, *United States History.*

What Were the Major Battles of the Vietnam War? *The Vietnam War.*

Statistical information about casualties of the Vietnam War, *U.S. National Archives.*

"Feuds and Bad Planning in Saigon Exit Recalled", *The New York Times, May 5, 1975.*

"Nixon Again Deplores Leak on Bombing Cambodia", *The New York Times, March 11, 1976.*

Foreign Relations of the United States, 1961–1963, Volume III, Vietnam, January – August 1963, *The U.S. Department of State, Office of the Historian.*

"The Truman Doctrine Fades", *The New York Times, May 4, 1975.*

Appendix 3.1

United Nations Chapter XI: Declaration Regarding Non-self-governing Territories Articles 73 and 74

Article 73

Members of the United Nations which have or assume responsibilities for the administration of territories whose peoples have not yet attained a full measure of self-government recognize the principle that the interests of the inhabitants of these territories are paramount, and accept as a sacred trust the obligation to promote to the utmost, within the system of international peace and security established by the present Charter, the well-being of the inhabitants of these territories, and, to this end:

a   to ensure, with due respect for the culture of the peoples concerned, their political, economic, social, and educational advancement, their just treatment, and their protection against abuses;

b   to develop self-government, to take due account of the political aspirations of the peoples, and to assist them in the progressive development of their free political institutions, according to the particular circumstances of each territory and its peoples and their varying stages of advancement;

c   to further international peace and security;

d   to promote constructive measures of development, to encourage research, and to co-operate with one another and, when and where appropriate, with specialized international bodies with a view to the practical achievement of the social, economic, and scientific purposes set forth in this Article; and

e   to transmit regularly to the Secretary-General for information purposes, subject to such limitation as security and constitutional considerations may require, statistical and other information of a technical nature relating to economic, social, and educational conditions in the territories for which they are respectively responsible other than those territories to which Chapters XII and XIII apply.

Article 74

Members of the United Nations also agree that their policy in respect of the territories to which this Chapter applies, no less than in respect of their metropolitan areas, must be based on the general principle of good-neighbourliness, due account being taken of the interests and well-being of the rest of the world, in social, economic, and commercial matters.

Source: www.un.org/en/sections/un-charter/chapter-xi/index.html Accessed 21 Dec 2017

Appendix 3.2

Nine Cardinal Principles of the Rule of the English Rajah

In the Preamble to Order No. C-21 (Constitution), 1941, opened by enunciating the Cardinal Principles, edict by Charles Vyner Brooke, the White Rajah of Sarawak on 24 September 1941 known as the Nine Cardinal Principles of the Rule of the White Rajah. Subsequently the Cardinal Principles were set out in the First Schedule to the Sarawak (Constitution) Order in Council, 1956. It was later adopted into the *Report of the Commission of Enquiry, North Borneo and Sarawak*, 1962 as APPENDIX C as the Nine Cardinal Principles of the Rule of the English Rajah, reproduced below.

1   That Sarawak is the heritage of Our Subjects and is held in trust by Ourselves for them.
2   That social and education services shall be developed and improved and the standard of living of the people of Sarawak shall steadily be raised.
3   That never shall any person or persons be granted rights inconsistent with those of the people of this country or be in any way permitted to exploit Our Subjects or those who have sought Our protection and care.
4   That justice shall be freely obtainable and that the Rajah and every public servant shall be easily accessible to the public.
5   That freedom of expression both in speech and in writing shall be permitted and encouraged and that everyone shall be entitled to worship as he pleases.
6   That public servants shall ever remember that they are but the servants of the people on whose goodwill and co-operation they are entirely dependent.
7   That so far as may be Our Subjects of whatever race or creed shall be freely and impartially admitted to offices in Our Service, the duties of which they may be qualified by their education, ability and integrity duly to discharge.
8   That the goal of self-government shall always be kept in mind, that the people of Sarawak shall be entrusted in due course with the governance of themselves, and that continuous efforts shall be made to hasten the reaching of this goal by educating them in the obligations, the responsibilities, and the privileges of citizenship.

9   That the general policy of Our predecessors and Ourselves whereby the various races of the State have been enabled to live in happiness and harmony together shall be adhered to by Our successors and Our servants and all who may follow them hereafter.

Source: *Report of the Commission of Enquiry, North Borneo and Sarawak, 1962* (Cobbold Commission), Cmnd. 1794, London, 1962. Appendix C, p. 101.
    With slight modifications relating to target audience, as it appeared in *Hansard*, Vol. 426, col. 26, 24 July 1946.

1   Sarawak is the heritage of its people and is held in trust for them.
2   Social and educational services shall be developed and improved and the standard of living shall steadily be raised.
3   Never shall any person or persons be granted rights inconsistent with those of the people of Sarawak or be in any way permitted to exploit them or those who have sought Sarawak's protection and care.
4   Justice shall be freely obtainable and the Rajah [governor] and every public servant shall be easily accessible to the public.
5   Freedom of expression, both in speech and in writing, shall be permitted and encouraged and that everyone shall be entitled to worship as he pleases.
6   Public servants shall ever remember that they are but the servants of the public on whose goodwill and co-operation they are entirely dependent.
7   The people of Sarawak of whatever race or creed shall be freely and impartially admitted to offices in the public service, the duties of which they may be qualified by their education, ability and integrity duly to discharge.
8   That the goal of self-government shall always be kept in mind, that the people of Sarawak shall be entrusted in due course with the governance of themselves, and that continuous efforts shall be made to hasten the reaching of this goal by educating them in the obligations, the responsibilities, and the privileges of citizenship.
9   The general policy of the Rajahs, whereby the various races of the State have been enabled to live in happiness and harmony together shall be adhered to by their successors and all who follow them.

Appendix 7.1

Notable Developments in the Philippines' 'Sabah Claim'

Date	Developments
25 Nov 1957	Sultan Muhammad Esmail Kiram of Sulu declared the termination of the Overbeck and Dent lease, effective 22 January 1958. Therefore, the territory of North Borneo was restored to the Sulu sultanate.
27 May 1961	Malayan Prime Minister Tunku Abdul Rahman publicly proposed the idea of 'Malaysia' on the occasion of the Conference of Foreign Journalists' Association of Southeast Asia at the Adelphi Hotel, Singapore. 'Malaysia' would be a wider federation to comprise independent Malaya, the British crown colonies of Singapore, Sarawak, and North Borneo, and the British protectorate of Brunei.
	President Diosdado Macapagal initiated the Philippine claim over North Borneo.
23 July 1961	The Commonwealth Parliamentary Association Branch of Malaya and Borneo Meeting in Singapore agreed to establish the Malaysia Solidarity Consultative Committee (MSCC) tasked to offer explanation to the inhabitants of North Borneo, Sarawak, and Brunei relating to the proposed wider federation of 'Malaysia'.
	Chaired by Donald Stephens, the MSCC held its inaugural meeting in North Borneo in August 1961; second meeting in Kuching (December 1961); third meeting in Kuala Lumpur (January 1962); fourth meeting in Singapore (February 1962).
31 July 1961	Establishment of the Association of Southeast Asia (ASA), an economic and cultural regional association, with the Philippines, Malaya, and Thailand as its founding members. ASA is often regarded as a precursor to the Association of Southeast Asian Nations (ASEAN) (1967).
20–22 Nov 1961	As a result of talks between the governments of Malaya and Britain, a joint statement announced on the creation of 'Malaysia'. Pre-conditions prior to formation of Malaysia, namely (1) necessitated views of the peoples of North Borneo and Sarawak, and (2) that the Anglo-Malayan Defence Agreement (AMDA) of 1957 should cover the new federation.
17 Jan 1962	The Cobbold Commission is formed, headed by Lord Cobbold and comprises representatives of the Malayan government, namely Wong Pow Nee and Mohd Ghazali bin Shafie, and representatives of the British government, Sir Anthony Abell and Sir David Watherston, and H. Harris as the secretary. The Commission's main task is to ascertain the views of the peoples of North Borneo and Sarawak on the proposed formation of 'Malaysia'.

Date	Developments
24 Apr 1962	Heirs of the Sultan of Sulu ceded sovereignty rights over North Borneo to the Philippine Government. The Philippines House of Representatives urged President Macapagal to pursue the claim of North Borneo.
29 Apr 1962	*Ruma Bechara*, the legislative branch of the Sulu sultanate, advised Sultan Esmail Kiram to cede North Borneo to the Republic of the Philippines, without prejudice to such proprietary rights of the heirs of Sultan Jamalul Kiram.
25 May 1962	British Government issues a note to the Philippines asserting its sovereignty over North Borneo, hence declaring that there is no contention relating to the issue of sovereignty and of ownership.
22 June 1962	Philippine Acting Secretary of Foreign Affairs, Salvador P. Lopez, hands a Note to the British Ambassador in Manila asserting the Philippines' claim of North Borneo.
21 July 1962	Submission of the report of the Cobbold Commission to the governments of Britain and Malaya; both governments agreed to adopt its recommendations.
7 Aug 1962	British Government responds to 22 June 1962 Note of the Philippines, again asserting its sovereignty over North Borneo.
29 Aug 1962	*Ruma Bechara* of Sulu passes a resolution that authorizes the Sultan-in-council to transfer his title and sovereignty over North Borneo to the Republic of the Philippines.
1 Sept 1962	A Referendum was held in Singapore on the terms of integration into merger with 'Malaysia'. More than 95 per cent chose 'Option A', viz. (1) Singapore would retain autonomy on matters relating to education and labour; (2) Singapore would retain English, Malay, Chinese, and Tamil as official languages; (3) Singapore would have a reduced representation, being allocated 15 seats in the *Dewan Rakyat* [House of Representatives] in the first post-merger Parliament of Malaysia; and (4) Singapore citizens would automatically become citizens of Malaysia.
11 Sept 1962	The Philippines government formally accepts the transfer of sovereignty over the territory of North Borneo by Sultan Mohammad Esmail Kiram of Sulu.
12 Sept 1962	Philippine Secretary of Foreign Affairs sends Note to British Ambassador, again asserting the Philippine claim over North Borneo notwithstanding the London agreement (between Malaya and Britain) of the incorporation of North Borneo in the proposed Federation of Malaysia.
Dec 1962	Outcome of the Legislative Council of North Borneo election shows overall majority of elected members favour 'Malaysia', a few prefer independence from Britain, and none support incorporation in the Philippines.

(*Continued*)

(Continued)

Date	Developments
29 Dec 1962	Following consultation, the release of a Britain-Philippines Joint Statement:
	"The Philippine and British Governments being vitally concerned in the security and stability of South East Asia, have decided to hold conversations about questions and problems of mutual interest. The British Government have responded to the Philippine Government's desire for talks, first expressed in their note of June 22, by inviting the Philippine Government to send a delegation to London for consultations at a mutually convenient date in January, 1963. Recent developments have made such conversations, in the spirit of the Manila Pact (SEATO) and the Pacific Charter (U.N.), highly desirable".
26 Jan 1963	President Sukarno of Indonesia pledges his support to the Philippines over the latter's claim over North Borneo.
28 Jan–1 Feb 1963	The British and Philippine governments held talks in London over their respective claims of sovereignty over North Borneo. No resolution to the issue was attained. A Joint Final Communique stated both their respective claims.
7–11 June 1963	Discussions held in Manila among the foreign affairs secretaries of Malaya, Indonesia, and the Philippines. A draft of the Manila Accord was the outcome.
9 July 1963	Malaysia Agreement was signed. The Federation of Malaysia comprised Malaya, Singapore, North Borneo, and Sarawak.
	Brunei declined joining the Federation of Malaysia.
30 July–5 Aug 1963	Following a meeting among Malayan Prime Minister Tunku Abdul Rahman, Indonesian President Sukarno, and Philippines' President Diosdado Macapagal, Maphilindo (*Ma*laya, *Phil*ippines, *Indo*nesia), a loose consultative body tasked to resolve mutual issues, is formed.
31 July 1963	Manila Accord is signed.
5 Aug 1963	Joint Statement by the Philippines, Malaya, and Indonesia.
	The United Nations Secretary-General, or his representative, should ascertain prior to the establishment of the Federation of Malaysia the wishes of the people of North Borneo and Sarawak within the context of UN General Assembly.
	A joint communiqué was issued by the foreign ministers of Malaysia, Indonesia, and the Philippines stating that the inclusion of North Borneo in the Federation of Malaysia "would not prejudice either the Philippine claim or any right thereunder".
16 Aug–5 Sept 1963	UN Malaysia Mission (UNMM) undertake assessment of the views of the peoples of North Borneo and Sarawak relating to joining Malaysia. Members of the Mission: George Howard, Kenneth K. S. Dadzie, and George Janecek.
	Observers from the Philippines were invited and were present throughout the UNMM assessment process.
10 Sept 1963	UN Secretary-General's representative, Laurence Michelmore, submitted UN Malaysia Mission's report to UN Secretary-General U Thant.

Date	Developments
14 Sept 1963	UN Secretary-General U Thant, in his final conclusions to the General Assembly, stated that there is no doubt of the wishes of a sizeable majority of the peoples of North Borneo and Sarawak to join the Federation of Malaysia.
16 Sept 1963	Formation of the Federation of Malaysia as a sovereign nation-state comprising Malaya, Singapore, Sarawak and Sabah (formerly North Borneo).
	The Sabah Claim, therefore, has to be pursued with Kuala Lumpur, the administrative capital of the Federation of Malaysia
	The Philippines decided to withhold recognition of Malaysia until it receives formal assurances that Kuala Lumpur would uphold the Manila Accord (July 1963).
	The Philippines intended to resolve its Sabah Claim in the International Court of Justice (ICJ) and had backing from Indonesia.
17 Sept 1963	Despite being party in requesting a UN Malaysia Mission, Manila and Jakarta rejected its report, namely that a sizeable majority of the peoples of North Borneo and Sarawak favoured to join the Federation of Malaysia.
	Consequently, both the Philippines and Indonesia broke off diplomatic relations with newly inaugurated Malaysia.
Feb–May 1964	Third-party mediation involving the U.S. to urge Maphilindo to resolve the Sabah Claim led to a series talks in Bangkok, thereafter Tokyo.
Feb 1964	Meeting between Macapagal and the Tunku in Phnom Penh, whereby the former agreed to turn to the World Court for adjudication if he secured the agreement of the leaders of Sabah for such a move.
18 May 1964	A Philippine-Malaysia Diplomatic Relations is concretized in the establishment of Philippine Consulate in Kuala Lumpur.
19 Nov 1964	The Philippines propose that the dispute be brought before the ICJ in accordance to the adherence to the rule of law and the UN Charter.
9 Aug 1965	Due to a series of intractable issues, the Tunku expelled Singapore from the Federation of Malaysia. Singapore became an independent republic.
7 Feb 1966	Manila again draws attention to its commitment to the Manila Accord relating to its Sabah Claim, and proposes to hold discussions on a mode of settlement for a resolution. Malaysia notes the Philippine proposal.
3 June 1966	Kuala Lumpur in response reiterates its commitment to the Manila Accord as well as the Joint Statement of 5 August 1963.
April 1967	Sabah held elections to its 32-seat Legislative Assembly. Both the Philippines and Indonesia governments were invited to have observers present; the former sent its observers, but the latter did not.
	Thirty-one who were successfully elected stood on the platform of rejecting the Philippine claim over Sabah.
	Indonesia acceded to the election results and proceeded to formally recognize Sabah and Sarawak as parts of Malaysia. The Philippines, however, rejected the elections outcome and continued to pursue its claim over Sabah.

(*Continued*)

Date	Developments
8 Aug 1967	Establishment of the Association of Southeast Asian Nations (ASEAN) with founding members Indonesia, Malaysia, the Philippines, Singapore, and Thailand. The primary objectives basically focus on accelerating economic growth, supporting social progress and cultural development in the region, and promoting regional peace.
18 March 1968	Jabidah Massacre witnessed the killing of Moro soldiers by the Armed Forces of the Philippines (AFP) while the former were undergoing training on Corregidor Island. The entire tragedy was clouded in mystery.
	It was later revealed that President Ferdinand Marcos was training a team of Muslim Moro militants to undertake a covert mission known as Operation Merdeka for infiltration into Sabah in order to destabilize the state, hence lending legitimacy to military intervention. Operation Merdeka was aborted after the Jabidah massacre.
17 June 1968	Talks held in Bangkok between the Philippines and Malaysia. The intention of the Philippines is to bring the dispute to the World Court.
15 July 1968	Malaysia vehemently rejects the Philippine claim over Sabah.
20 July 1968	Philippine President Ferdinand E. Marcos severs diplomatic relations with Malaysia.
21 July 1968	President Marcos advocated that the Philippine claim over Sabah be brought to the ICJ.
28 Aug 1968	Philippine Senate Bill No. 954 that delineates the baselines of the Philippines that indicates "the territory of Sabah, situated in North Borneo, over which the Republic of the Philippines has acquired dominion and sovereignty". Senate Bill No. 954 was sent for presidential approval.
18 Sept 1968	Senate Bill No. 954 receives presidential approval and becomes Republic Act No. 5446.
	Meanwhile, both Britain and U.S. lent support to Malaysia over the dispute.
	In Kuala Lumpur, some 1,000 students from the University of Malaya entered the compound of the Philippine embassy, took down the Philippine flag from its pole, and trampled upon it.
5 Oct 1968	Philippines Senator Benigno S. Aquino, Jr., in a speech before a civic group, publicly criticized President Marcos' actions over the Sabah Claim. Senator Aquino cited the right of the people of Sabah to self-determination, drawing attention to President Macapagal, who in 1963 stated that the Philippines recognizes the principle of self-determination, and this was evidence from the elections in Sabah (April 1967).
15 Oct 1968	23rd Session of the UN General Assembly, the Philippines and Malaysia argues over the Sabah Claim dispute. The former insisted, in accordance to the Manila Accord, that it intended to bring the dispute to the World Court. Malaysia nullified the Philippine claim by drawing attention to the fact that the peoples of Sabah had shown their intention to be with the Federation of Malaysia, and the latter had upheld the British title to Sabah. In short, there is no Philippine claim, and therefore, there is nothing to discuss.

Date	Developments
Dec 1968	Malaysia proposed for the normalization of Philippine-Malaysian diplomatic relations but sets a precondition, namely that the Philippines should recognize Malaysia's sovereignty over Sabah but without prejudice to the Philippines pursuing its claim.
Dec 1969	Consequent of talks between the Tunku and Philippines Secretary of Foreign Affairs Carlos P. Romulo, diplomatic relations between Malaysia and the Philippines was formally resumed.
23 Sept 1972	President Marcos declares Martial Law in the Philippines.
24 Oct 1972	The Moro National Liberation Front (MNLF) launches its rebellion against the Philippines government.
4 Aug 1977	President Marcos publicly announced that the Philippines gives up its claim to Sabah.
	Malaysia, on its part, requests that the Philippines addressed the following, viz.:
	1. Philippines 1973 Constitution on its broad definition of national territory be amended in order to eliminate the clause, "territories belonging to the Philippines by historic right or legal title".
	2. That the Philippines government proceed to repeal Republican Act RA 5446, particularly Section 2.
1 May 1986	During a meeting in Kuala Lumpur between Philippines Vice President and Minister for Foreign Affairs Salvador H. Laurel, Malaysian Prime Minister Mahathir Mohamad, and Foreign Minister Tengku Ahmad Rithauddeen, Mahathir reiterated Malaysia's commitment to settle the proprietary issue of the heirs of the Sulu sultan if and when a single spokesperson is agreed upon with whom the Malaysian government could negotiate.
Feb-June 1987	Talks and discussions over the Sabah issue continues at the ministerial level between the Philippines and Malaysia.
23 Oct 1987	Acting upon instructions from Philippines President Corazon C. Aquino, Secretary of Foreign Affairs Raul S. Manglapus attempts to obtain a united or common stance among the heirs of the Sulu sultanate.
12 Feb 1989	Sultan Mohammad Jamalal Kiram III, one of the claimants to the throne of the Sulu sultanate, unilaterally revoked the resolution of 29 August 1962, and the Sulu ruler transferred title and sovereignty of the Sulu sultanate to the Republic of the Philippines.
11 Jan 1993	Philippines President Fidel V. Ramos establishes the Bipartisan Executive-Legislative Advisory Council on the Sabah Issues. Reconstituted 5 July 1999.
27–30 Jan 1993	During a state visit to Malaysia, President Ramos' proposal, agreed by Malaysia, to establish consulate in Sabah and Davao, respectively. Downplays North Borneo issue. Despite calls from members of the Philippines Congress, he downplayed the Sabah Claim.
July 1993	A Memorandum of Understanding on Joint Commission for Bilateral Cooperation (JCBC) was signed by the Philippines and Malaysia.
6–10 Dec 1993	The First Meeting of the Philippines-Malaysia JCBC discussed the reciprocal setting up of consular offices in the Philippines and in Malaysia.

(*Continued*)

(Continued)

Date	Developments
28–29 Mar 1995	During the Second Meeting of the Philippines-Malaysia JCBC, Malaysia wishes to establish a Consulate General in Davao City.
29–31 May 1995	At the Third Meeting of the Philippines-Malaysia JCBC, the parties agreed to hold regular, informal consultations to address any outstanding problems relating to Filipino workers and illegal immigrants in Sabah.
2 Sept 1996	Peace Agreement penned between the MNLF and Philippines government.
Dec 1996	The Philippines and Malaysia governments signed the Border Crossing and Joint Patrol agreements.
1–3 Mar 2000	Fourth Philippines-Malaysia JCBC. The Philippines express intention to set up a consulate in Sabah.
Nov 2001	Having failed to extend his governorship for a second term, Autonomous Region of Muslim Mindanao (ARMM) Governor Nur Misuari called on the MNLF to wage rebellion in Jolo. It was abortive and failed. Misuari escaped to Malaysia; Malaysian government extradited him back to the Philippines.
10 Mar 2009	Philippines President Gloria Macapagal-Arroyo signs Republic Act RA 9522, amending RA 5446 that removes mention of Sabah or North Borneo in the Archipelagic Baselines of the Philippines law. This move is in accordance with the second Malaysian stipulation of 4 August 1977.

Sources: Manuel L. Quezon III, "North Borneo (Sabah): An Annotated Timeline 1640s-present", March 02, 2013. http://globalnation.inquirer.net/66281/north-borneo-sabah-an-annotated-timeline-1640s-present#ixzz5QEinTtKh Accessed 5 Sept 2018; Nicholas Tarling, *The Cambridge History of Southeast Asia* (Cambridge, UK: Cambridge University Press, 1999), vol. pt. I; A. J. Stockwell, ed., *Malaysia* (London: Stationery Office, 2004); Kevin Y. L. Tan, *International Law, History & Policy: Singapore in the Early Years* (Singapore: Centre for International Law. National University of Singapore, 2011); "Penubuhan Malaysia 16 September 1963". (ANM) www.arkib.gov.my/web/guest/penubuhan-malaysia-16-september-19632 Accessed 7 Sept 2018; Records of the Bureau of Insular Affairs, Record Group 350, Select Documents from file 980. 1920–1969 DFA Papers Collection, Philippines. (NARA); L. Bautista, "The Historical Context and Legal Basis of the Philippine Treaty Limits", *Asian-Pacific Law and Policy Journal*, 10 (1) (2008): 1–31; *The Philippine Claim to a Portion of North Borneo: Materials and Documents* (Diliman, Quezon City, Philippines: Institute of International Legal Studies, University of the Philippines Law Center, 2003); Rolando Quintos, "The Sabah Question: Prospects and Alternatives", *Symposium on Sabah* (1969): 67–85; Pacifico Ortiz, "Legal Aspects of the North Borneo Question", *Philippine Studies*, 11, 1 (1963): 18–64; Diosdado Macapagal, *A Stone for the Edifice: Memoirs of a President* (Ann Arbor, MI: Mac Publishing House, University of Michigan, 1968); H. G. Tregonning, "The Philippine Claim to Sabah", *Journal of the Malaysian Branch of the Royal Asiatic Society*, 43, 1 (217) (1970): 161–170; Agreement relating to Malaysia (with annexes, including the Constitutions of the States of Sabah, Sarawak and Singapore, the Malaysia Immigration Bill and the Agreement between the Governments of the Federation of Malaya and Singapore on common market and financial arrangements). Signed at London on 9 July 1963. Agreement amending the above-mentioned Agreement. Signed at Singapore on 28 August 1963. UNITED KINGDOM OF GREAT BRITAIN AND NORTHERN IRELAND and FEDERATION OF MALAYA, NORTH BORNEO, SARAWAK and SINGAPORE. No. 10760. United Nations – Treaty Series, 1970. https://treaties.un.org/doc/publication/unts/volume%20750/volume-750-i-10760-english.pdf Accessed 7 Sept 2018; Manila Accord. Signed at Manila, on 31 July 1963 Manila Declaration. Signed at Manila, on 3 August 1963 Joint Statement. Signed at Manila, on 5 August 1963.

PHILIPPINES, FEDERATION OF MALAYA and INDONESIA. No. 8029. United Nations – Treaty Series, 1965. https://treaties.un.org/doc/publication/unts/volume%20550/volume-550-i-8029-english.pdf Accessed 7 Sept 2018; Alfredo G. Parpan, "The Philippine Claim on North Borneo: Another Look", *Philippine Studies*, 36, 1 (1988): 3–15; Jose Veloso Abueva, and Raul P. de Guzman, eds., *Foundations and Dynamics of Filipino Government and Politics* (Quezon City: Bookmark, 1969); Arturo M. Tolentino, *Voice of Dissent* (Quezon City: Phoenix Publishing House, 1990); Jeremia Flores, Ciarencia Reyes, and Rodolfo Sabio. "The Legal Implications of the Unilateral Dropping of the Sabah Claim", *Philippine Law Journal*, 57 (1982): 78–103; Erwin S. Fernandez, "Philippine-Malaysia Dispute over Sabah: A Bibliographic Survey", Research Notes # 1, *Asia-Pacific Social Science Review*, 7, 1 (Dec 2007): 53–64; Benigno 'Ninoy' S. Aquino, Jr., *A Garrison State in the Make and Other Speeches* (Legaspi Village, Makati, Metro Manila: Benigno S. Aquino, Jr. Foundation, 1985); P. N. Abinales, and Donna J. Amoroso, *State and Society in the Philippines* (Lanham, MD: Rowman & Littlefield Publishers, 2005).

Notes

1 Roger G. Miller, *To Save a City: The Berlin Airlift, 1948–1948* (Air Force History and Museums Program, 1998), p. 108. https://media.defense.gov/2010/Oct/01/2001329741/-1/-1/0/AFD-101001-053.pdf Accessed 11 Nov 2017; "Berlin blockade and airlift", The Editors of *Encyclopædia Britannica*. www.britannica.com/event/Berlin-blockade-and-airlift Accessed 11 Nov 2017.

2 Robert S. McNamara et al., *Argument Without End: In Search of Answers to the Vietnam Tragedy* (New York: Public Affairs, 1999), pp. 349–351.

3 South Korea, Thailand, Australia, the Philippines, and New Zealand.

4 Robert Dallek, *Lyndon B. Johnson: Portrait of a President* (New York: Oxford University Press, 2004), p. 284.

5 See entry 'Aug 2, 1964' below.

6 U.S. Department of Commerce, Bureau of the Census, "Vietnam Conflict – U.S. Military Forces in Vietnam and Casualties Incurred: 1961 to 1972", in *Table 590, Statistical Abstract of the United States, 1977* (Washington, DC: U.S. Department of Commerce, Bureau of the Census, 1980), p. 369. Quoted in "The Vietnam War: Military Statistics." www.gilderlehrman.org/history-by-era/seventies/resources/vietnam-war-military-statistics Accessed 26 Nov 2017.

7 "Jul 28, 1965: Johnson Announces More Troops to Vietnam", *This Day in History, History Channel*. www.history.com/this-day-in-history/johnson-announces-more-troops-to-vietnam Accessed 28 Nov 2017.

8 Bureau of the Census, "Vietnam Conflict".

9 Ibid.

10 Ibid.

11 Ibid.

12 Bob Drury and Tom Calvin, *Last Men Out: The True Story of America's Heroic Final Hours* (New York: Free Press, 2012), p. 258.

Glossary

Adat lama   old customary traditions, practices

Adat   Malay, traditions, customs, customary law

Adipati   Malay/Indonesian, viceroy, duke; regent or mayor; head of a region in the hierarchy of royal government in Java and Kalimantan

'Andjing NICA'   Indonesian, 'NICA (running) dogs'; derogatory term referring to pro-Dutch individuals during the Indonesian Revolution (1945–1949)

Buitengewesten   Dutch, Outer Islands, outer regions, territories

Bumiputera   Malay, 'sons of the soil'; native, indigenous

Bupati   district head

Daerah istimewa   Malay/Indonesia, autonomous or special territories

Daerah istimewa   special region

Daerah   region

Dalang   Malay/Indonesian, lit. puppeteer; mastermind

Datu   Malay, non-royal Malay chieftains; social elite class of Malay notables that resided on the northwest and northeast coast of Borneo

Desa   Indonesian, village

Dokoh   Indonesian, sultan, native Muslim ruler

Dwifungsi   Indonesian, lit. 'dual function'; refers to the official doctrine of the armed forces of Indonesia, of the military's role as defender of the realm, and at the same time, direct and active involvement in politics, government, and the economy

Eikyu senryo   Japanese, permanent occupation or possession

Federasi   federal state

Glasnost   openness, transparency, and freedom of speech

Gotong-royong   Indonesian, *gotong-rojong*, mutual cooperation for mutual benefit

Guo-yu   Standard Chinese or Mandarin, whereby its written form utilizes traditional Chinese characters; also, Chinese national language; rendered *Guoyu* or *Kuo-yu*

Hsueh hsih   Chinese, a study for action cell; a common communist cell among students

Huaiguan   Chinese, clan

Hui   Chinese, society, association, clan; also, brotherhoods, clandestine societies

Hulu   Malay, upriver, interior; remoteness

Istana   Malay, palace

Jinshi   Chinese, the highest degree in the Chinese imperial civil service examinations; successful candidates might be eligible as scholar-bureaucrats serving in the provincial capital or at the imperial palace

Kaharingan   Dayak traditional beliefs and practices

Kathi   Arabic, *qadi*, that is, 'to judge' or 'to decide'; also, *kadi*

Kerani   Malay, *krani*, clerk

Kiyai   Javanese, refers to a respected elder. In South Kalimantan, however, Banjar Malay utilized it to denote head of a district, or district officer (DO)

Kongsi   Chinese, lit. means to share, a partnership, a cooperative; a Chinese clan house of a shared progenitor, or from the same (common) country or district

Merdeka   Malay/Indonesian, (political) independence

Mujahideen   Arab, 'those who engage in *jihad*'; one who fights the enemies of Islam; spiritual struggle within oneself against sins

Negara   Malay/Indonesian, political states

Orde Baru   Indonesian, lit., 'New Order', Suharto's presidency and regime, 1968–1998

Orde Lama   Indonesian, lit., 'Old Order', Sukarno's presidency or era, 1945–1967

Padi   Malay, rice stalk

Pejuang   Malay, (nationalist) fighter

Pemabang   Dayak, ritual ceremony

Pemuda   Malay, lit. youth; political 'Young Turks'

Pemuka   Dayak, leader

Pemukiman   Indonesian, settlement

Pengayau   Dayak, head-hunters; from the root word, *ngayau*, to take heads

Perabangan   Malay, a Malay social class comprising of male descendants of *datu*

Perestroika   Russian, reformation of government and economy

Putera daerah   Indonesian, lit., 'prince of the region', indigenes or native son

Raja muda   Malay, heir apparent

Rakyat   Malay, peoples, masses; subjects of a nation, citizenry

Sandiwara   Malay/Indonesian, stage play, drama; a pretence

Shengyuan   Chinese, the first or initial degree in the Chinese imperial civil service examinations; individuals attaining this basic degree might be appointed as scholar-bureaucrats in country or district offices

Shu-jin   Chinese, lit. 'life-redeeming', 'blood money'; extortion demand of money by the Imperial Japanese Army

Sook ching   Chinese, purification, cleansing

Swapraja   Indonesian, self-governing autonomous native territories, areas of indirect colonial rule

Syariah   Arabic, '*shar*' literally means 'the way to follow'; one aspect of Islam that lays down guidelines how Muslims should conduct themselves in accordance to their faith; Islamic jurisprudence

Timanggong   Dayak traditional leader in Kalimantan; similar to the Iban honorific, *temenggung*, among the Ibans of Sarawak

Titah   Malay, royal proclamation, decree

Tjina   Indonesian, ethnic Chinese

Towkay   Hokkien dialect, whereby *tow* (head) and *kay* (family) means 'head of a family'. Also refers to a proprietor of a business, shop, mine, or plantation; overall, attributed as an honorific to an individual of social standing and wealth

Tuak   Iban, local alcoholic rice wine

Upacara adat   Dayak, traditional rituals

Bibliography

Primary sources

Archival materials

National Archives, Kew, Richmond, UK (NAUK)

[Acting High Commissioner] C. W. Dawson to [Colonial Secretary] A. C. Jones, Brunei (no. 5) 24 Sep 1949, CO 943/1/18, Item 1, para 3 (NAUK).

The Conduct of Anti-Terrorist Operations in Malaya, 3rd ed, 1958. WO 279/241 (NAUK).

"Greater-Malaysia-Brunei Aspect", Letter from D. C. White to Mr Eastwood, Colonial Office, Jan 11, 1962. CO 1030/1012 (NAUK).

"Greater Malaysia-Brunei Aspects, Report on the Public Hearing of [the] Menteri Besar's Committee on Malaysia". CO 1030/1012 (NAUK).

Indonesian raid on Tebedu Police Station in Sarawak, 1963. FO 371/169739 (NAUK).

Letter from Reginald Maudling (Secretary of State for the Colonies to (Sarawak Colonial Governor Sir Alexander] Waddel, Nov 1, 1961. FCO 141/12701 (NAUK).

McLellan, D. "Notes on Subversion in Chinese schools", Sarawak Government, Nov 5, 1959, CO 1030/422 (NAUK).

Minutes of the 13th Commissioner-General's Conference held in Singapore on Nov 1, 1949. CO 954 5/3 Item 3 (NAUK).

"Political Intelligence Reports from Sarawak and Brunei", Feb 1951, CO 537/7349 (NAUK).

"Political Intelligence Reports from Sarawak and Brunei", June–July 1951, CO 537/7340 (NAUK).

Review of Emergency in Malaya, June 1948–Aug 1957 by Director of Operations, Sep 12, 1957. WO 106/5990 (NAUK).

"Solidarity Consultative Committee", Malaysia Solidarity Consultative Committee Memorandum Malaysia, CO 947/1 (NAUK).

Bodleian Library of Commonwealth and African Studies at Rhodes House, Oxford, UK (RHUK)

Text of Address by the Chairman at the Opening Ceremony [Kuching, MSCC]. Federation of Mal [aysia]. Papers of Sir William Allmond C. Goode, [1960–1963]. GB 0162 MSS. Ind. Ocn. s. 323 (RHUK).

Arkib Negara Malaysia, Kuala Lumpur, Malaysia (ANM)

"Announcement on the Success of the Sri Aman Operation", Apr 3, 1974. Arkib Negara, Kuala Lumpur. http://hids.arkib.gov.my/en/peristiwa/-/asset_publisher/ WAhqbCYR9ww2/content/pengumuman-kejayaan-operasi-sri-aman/pop_up?_101_ INSTANCE_WAhqbCYR9ww2_viewMode=print Accessed 25 Dec 2018.

"Penubuhan Malaysia 16 September 1963 [Formation of Malaysia 16 September 1963]", (ANM). www.arkib.gov.my/web/guest/penubuhan-malaysia-16-september-19632 Accessed 7 Sep 2018.

Sarawak Museum and State Archives, Kuching, Malaysia (SMA)

"The Origin and Development of the Sarawak Communist Organisation (SCO)", manuscript, Kuching, c. 1974.

National Archives and Records Administration, College Park, Maryland, U.S. (NARA)

"370. Telegram from the Embassy in the Philippines to the Department of State", RG 59, Central Files 1967–69, POL 32–1 MALAYSIA – PHIL. Secret; Priority; Limdis. Repeated to Bangkok, Canberra, Djakarta, Kuala Lumpur, London, Singapore, Wellington, USUN, and CINCPAC. Foreign Relations of the United States, 1964–1968, Volume XXVI, Indonesia; Malaysia-Singapore; Philippines. (NARA).

Records of the Bureau of Insular Affairs, Record Group 350, Select Documents from File 980. 1920–1969 DFA Papers Collection. Philippines. (NARA).

Published official materials

Agreement Relating to Malaysia (with Annexes, Including the Constitutions of the States of Sabah, Sarawak and Singapore, the Malaysia Immigration Bill and the Agreement between the Governments of the Federation of Malaya and Singapore on Common Market and Financial Arrangements). Signed at London on July 9, 1963. Agreement Amending the Above-Mentioned Agreement. Signed at Singapore on Aug 28, 1963. United Kingdom of Great Britain and Northern Ireland and Federation of Malaya, North Borneo, Sarawak and Singapore. No. 10760. United Nations – Treaty Series, 1970. https:// treaties.un.org/doc/publication/unts/volume%20750/volume-750-i-10760-english.pdf Accessed 7 Sep 2018.

Annual Report on Sarawak for the Year 1947. Kuching: Government Printing Office, 1948.

Annual Report on Sarawak for the Year 1949. Kuching: Government Printing Office, 1949.

Bevington, E. R. *The Economy and Development of the State of Brunei*. Brunei: Government Report, June 1953.

British Information Services. "General Surveys", in: *Commonwealth Survey: A Record of United Kingdom and Commonwealth Affairs*. London: HMSO, 1949.

British North Borneo. Charter Granted to the British North Borneo Company, Westminster, Nov 1, 1881. p. 6. www.lawnet.sabah.gov.my/Lawnet/SabahLaws/Treaties/Charter GrantedToTheBritishNorthBorneoCompany.pdf Accessed 29 Dec 2017.

British North Borneo Treaties. British North Borneo, 1878. (Translation) "GRANT by Sultan of Sulu of Territories and Lands on the Mainland of the Island of Borneo", Jan 22,

1878. www.lawnet.sabah.gov.my/Lawnet/SabahLaws/Treaties/GrantBySultanOfSuluOf
TerritoriesAndLandsOnTheMainlandOfTheIslandOfBorneo.pdf Accessed 4 Sep 2018.

British North Borneo Treaties. British North Borneo, 1885. Protocol of 1885. [Madrid Pro-
tocol 1885]. Done at Madrid, Mar 7, 1885. file:///H:/Borneo%20in%20the%20Cold%20
War/NOTES%20Cold%20War/Colony%20North%20Borneo/Protocol(Madrid).pdf
Accessed 5 Sep 2018.

Brunei. *[First] National Development Plan, 1953–1958*. Kuala Belait: Brunei Press, 1958.

Brunei. *[Second] National Development Plan, 1962–1966*. Kuala Belait: Brunei Press,
1962.

Brunei. *Ranchangan KemajuanNnegara, 1975–1979* [*National Development Plan, 1975–1979*].
Bandar Seri Begawan: Brunei Government, 1975.

Central Intelligence Agency (CIA). www.cia.gov/library/readingroom/docs/CIA-RDP78-
03061A0003000010027-0.pdf Accessed 19 Oct 2018.

CICRED Series. *The Population of Indonesia*. World Population Year 1974. Paris: Committee for International Cooperation in National Research in Demography (CICRED),
1974.

Circular Memorandum (No. 14/84), Mar 24, 1984. The Administrative Areas Ordinance:
Change of Names of – (i) Nonok to Asajaya; (ii) Muara Tuang to Kota Samarahan.
file:///C:/Users/w10o16/Documents/4741-swksp-am14-84.htm Accessed 28 Jan 2019.

Committee for International Cooperation in National Research in Demography (CICRED),
1974. www.cicred.org/Eng/Publications/pdf/c-c24.pdf Accessed 18 Aug 2018.

Colonial Office, Brunei. *Annual Report on Brunei*, 1952.

Colony of North Borneo Annual Report 1954. London: H.M. Stationery Office, 1954.

Colony of North Borneo: Education Department Triennial Survey 1958–1960. London:
H.M. Stationery Office, 1960.

Colony of North Borneo: The Education Ordinance, Apr 17, 1947. London: H.M. Stationery Office, 1947.

Excerpt from the "Special Message to the Congress on Urgent National Needs, Section IX:
Space", President John F. Kennedy Speaks before a Joint Session of Congress, May 25,
1961. NASA History, May 25, 2004. www.nasa.gov/vision/space/features/jfk_speech_
text.html Accessed 15 Sep 2018.

The Final Declaration of the Geneva Conference: On Restoring Peace in Indochina, July
21, 1954. https://sourcebooks.fordham.edu/mod/1954-geneva-indochina.html Accessed
25 Nov 2017.

"Grant by the Sultan of Sulu of a Permanent Lease Covering His Lands and Territories on
the Island of Borneo", Jan 22, 1878. Translation by Prof. Harold C. Conklin Done in
1946; Original Text in Arabic Script, See "Letter from Francis B. Harrison . . . .", Infra, at
p. 333. Government of the Philippines Official Gazette: The Philippine Claim to a Portion
of North Borneo. www.officialgazette.gov.ph/1878/01/22/grant-by-the-sultan-of-sulu-of-
a-permanent-lease-covering-his-lands-and-territories-on-the-island-of-borneo/ Accessed
5 Sep 2018.

Hepburn, B. A. *The Handbook of Sarawak*. Singapore: Malaya Publishing House, 1949.

His Excellency the Governor's Address to Council Negri on 6th December 1960. Kuching:
Government Printing Press, 1961.

Hukumonline.com.www.hukumonline.com/pusatdata/detail/21733/node/964/undang-
undang-darurat-no-2-tahun-1953-pembentukan-daerah-otonom-propinsi-kalimantan
Accessed 19 June 2018.

Laporan umum Operasi Saberda, tahun 1968. Pontianak: Komando Daerah Militer XII/
Tanjungpura, n.d.

Laws of Brunei: Constitutional Matters I: Constitution of Brunei Darussalam. rev. ed. 2011 [1959]. file:///G:/Borneo%20in%20the%20Cold%20War/NOTES/NOTES.Constitution% 20Brunei%20Darussalam%201959.pdf.2011%20ed..pdf Accessed 28 Mar 2018.

Lee, Kuan Yew. Speech by the Prime Minister, Mr. Lee Kuan Yew, at the Public Forum on "Merger & Malaysia" Organised by the University of Singapore Students Union at the University on Monday, Aug 27, 1962. For Broadcast on Sep 25 at 7.10 p.m. www.nas. gov.sg/archivesonline/data/pdfdoc/lky19620827a.pdf Accessed 16 Sep 2018.

Malaysian Government. *The Communist Re-Insurgency in Malaysia*. Kuala Lumpur: Kementerian Pertahanan [Defence Ministry], April 1973.

Malaysian Government. "Penilaian Ancaman Biro Pertama PKKU [Partai Komunis Kaliman-tan Utara] [Threat Assessment of the First Bureau PKKU (North Kalimantan Communist Party)]", [Kementerian Pertahanan?], Kuala Lumpur, 1984.

Manila Accord. Signed at Manila, on 31 July 1963 Manila Declaration. Signed at Manila, on 3 August 1963 Joint Statement. Signed at Manila, on 5 Aug. 1963. Philippines, Federation of Malaya and Indonesia. No. 8029. United Nations-Treaty Series, 1965. https://treaties. un.org/doc/publication/unts/volume%20550/volume-550-i-8029-english.pdf Accessed 7 Sep 2018.

McLellan, D. *Report on Secondary Education*. Kuching: Government Printing Office, 1960.

Moeljono, Majoor [sic] C. P. M. "'Laporan Chusus' tentang adanja penjerangan Gerom-bolan PGRS terhadap LANU[D] Singkawang II di SG. [Sanggau?] Ledo pada tanggal 16–7–1967 ["'Special Report' about the PGRS Horde Attack on LANU Singkawang II at SG. Ledo on July 16, 1967"]". Pontianak: Komando Daerah Militer XII/Tandjungpura Polisi Militer, n.d.

North Borneo Annual Report 1949. Jesselton: Government Printers, 1950.

North Borneo Annual Report 1953. Jesselton: Government Printers, 1954.

Perry, R. E. *The Colony of North Borneo: A Five-Year Plan of Educational Development for the Year 1947–51*. Jesselton: [Government Printing Office], Aug 28, 1946.

The Philippine Claim to a Portion of North Borneo: Materials and Documents. Diliman, Quezon City, Philippines: Institute of International Legal Studies, University of the Phil-ippines Law Center, 2003.

Pidato Kawan Amar Hanafiah (Wakil Sekretaris CDB PKI Kalimantan Selatan)', *Bintang Merah Nomor Special Jilid II, Dokumen-Dokumen Kongres Nasional Ke-VI Partai Komunis Indonesia*. Jakarta: Yayasan Pembaruan, 1960, Sep 7–14, 1959. www.marxists. org/indonesia/indones/KongresPKIke6/PidatoHanafiah.htm Accessed 15 Nov 2018.

Population Division of the Department of Economic and Social Affairs of the United Nations Secretariat, World Population Prospects: The 2010 Revision, Quoted in "Demographics of Vietnam", https://en.wikipedia.org/wiki/Demographics_of_Vietnam#cite_note-WPP_2010-3 Accessed 25 Nov 2017.

Profil Propinsi Republik Indonesia – Kalimantan Barat [Provincial Profile of the Republic of Indonesia: West Kalimantan]. Jakarta: Yayasan Bhakti Wawasan Nusantara, 1992.

Profil Propinsi Republik Indonesia – Kalimantan Selatan [Provincial Profile of the Republic of Indonesia: South Kalimantan]. Jakarta: Yayasan Bhakti Wawasan Nusantara, 1992.

Profil Propinsi Republik Indonesia – Kalimantan Tengah [Provincial Profile of the Republic of Indonesia: Central Kalimantan]. Jakarta: Yayasan Bhakti Wawasan Nusantara, 1992.

Profil Propinsi Republik Indonesia – Kalimantan Timur [Provincial Profile of the Republic of Indonesia: East Kalimantan]. Jakarta: Yayasan Bhakti Wawasan Nusantara, 1992.

The Provisional Constitution of the Republic of Indonesia. Promulgated on 15th of August, 1950 (Act No. 7, 1950, Gazette No. 37, 1950). www.worldstatesmen.org/Indonesia-Constitution-1950.pdf Accessed 2 Aug 2018.

Pusat Sejarah dan Tradisi ABRI. *Bahaya laten komunisme di Indonesia: Penumpusan pem-berontakan PKI dan sisa-sisanya* [*The Latent Danger of Communism in Indonesia: The Overthrow of the PKI Rebellion and Its Remnants*]. jilid 5. Jakarta: Markas Besar ABRI, 1995.

Report of the Commission of Enquiry, North Borneo and Sarawak, 1962 (Cobbold Commission), Cmnd. 1794. London, 1962.

Report of the Commission of Enquiry, North Borneo and Sarawak, 1962 by the Commis-sion of Enquiry in North Borneo and Sarawak. Great Britain, Office of Commonwealth Relations, Colonial Office. London: H.M.S.O., 1962.

Report of the Proceedings of the Council Negri held in the Main Court House, Kuching, Dec 2, 3 and 5, 1952.

Report of the Proceedings of the Council Negri held in the Main Court House, Kuching, Dec 1, 2, and 4, 1953.

"Sabah! A Game of Diversion" By Senator Benigno S. Aquino Jr. [Delivered "before a Civic Group" on October 5, 1968]. Government of the Philippines (GOVPH) Official Gazette. www.officialgazette.gov.ph/1968/10/05/sabah-a-game-of-diversion-by-senator-benigno-s-aquino-jr/ Accessed 18 Sep 2018.

Sarawak Annual Report (SAR), 1962. Kuching: Government Printing Office, 1963.

Sarawak Constabulary. *Annual Report on the Sarawak Constabulary*, 1947–63.

Sarawak Council Negri. "Secondary Education", Sessional Paper No. 2 of 1960.

Sarawak Development Board. *Sarawak Development Plan*, 1959–1963.

Sarawak Education Department. *Annual Summary for 1959*. Kuching: Government Printing Office, 1960.

Sarawak Education Department. *Triennial Survey 1955–1957*. Kuching: Government Printing Office, n.d.

Sarawak Education Department. *Triennial Survey 1958–1960*. Kuching: Government Printing Office, n.d.

Sarawak Government Gazette (SGG), Dec 1946.

Sarawak Government. "Subversion in Sarawak", Sessional Paper No. 3 of 1960, July 1960.

Sarawak Government. *The Communist Threat to Sarawak*. Kuala Lumpur: Government Printers, Sep 1966.

Sarawak Government. *The Threat of Armed Communism in Sarawak*. Kuala Lumpur: Gov-ernment Printers, Feb 1972.

Sarawak Information Service. *Sarawak by the Week*. Week No. 21, May 24–30, 1959.

Sarawak Information Service. *A Guide to Education in Sarawak*. Kuching: Government Printing Office, 1960.

Sarawak Information Service. *The Danger Within: A History of the Clandestine Communist Organization in Sarawak*. Kuching: Government Printing Office, 1963.

Sarawak Statistics Department. *Annual Bulletin of Statistics*, 1964.

Semdam XII. *Tanjungpura Berjuang: Sejarah Kodam XII/Tanjungpura* [*Tanjungpura Fighting: History of Kodam XII/Tanjungpura*]. Pontianak: Yayasan Tanjungpura, 1971.

Stockwell, A. J., ed. *Malaysia*. London: Stationery Office, 2004.

Sukarno's Independence Day Speech, Excerpts from. General CIA Record; CIA-RDP78-03061A0003000010027-0. www.cia.gov/library/readingroom/docs/CIA-RDP78-03061A0003000010027-0.pdf Accessed 19 Oct 2018.

Titah, 1959–67, kebawah DYMM Paduka Seri Baginda Maulana Al-Sultan Sir Omar Ali Saifuddin Sa'adul Khairi Waddin [*(Royal) Command, 1959–67, kebawah DYMM*

Paduka Seri Baginda Maulana Al-Sultan Sir Omar Ali Saifuddin Sa'adul Khairi Waddin]. Brunei: Dewan Bahasa dan Pustaka, 1971.

Undang-Undang Dasar Republik Indonesia 1945; Konstitusi 1945 asli dan pertama (1999), kedua (2000), ketiga (2001) dan keempat (2002) amandemen. www.humanrights.asia/countries/indonesia/laws/uud1945 Accessed 26 July 2018.

United Nations Malaysia Mission Report, "Final Conclusions of the Secretary-General," Sep 14, 1963. Annex 3 United Nations Malaysia Mission Report, Final Conclusions of the Secretary-General. Government of the Philippines (GOVPH) Official Gazette. www.officialgazette.gov.ph/1963/09/14/united-nations-malaysia-mission-report-final-conclusions-of-the-secretary-general-14-september-1963/ Accessed 9 Sep 2018.

Universal Declaration of Human Rights. Proclaimed by the United Nations General Assembly in Paris on Dec 10, 1948 (General Assembly Resolution 217 A). www.un.org/en/universal-declaration-human-rights/ Accessed 2 Aug 2018.

U.S. Department of Commerce, Bureau of the Census, "Vietnam Conflict: U.S. Military Forces in Vietnam and Casualties Incurred: 1961 to 1972", Table 590, Statistical Abstract of the United States Washington, DC: U.S. Department of Commerce, Bureau of the Census, 1980 [1977], p. 369. Quoted in "The Vietnam War: Military Statistics", www.gilderlehrman.org/history-by-era/seventies/resources/vietnam-war-military-statistics Accessed 26 Nov 2017.

U.S. Embassy Tracked Indonesia Mass Murder 1965: Newly Declassified U.S. Embassy Jakarta Files Detail Army Killings, U.S. Support for Quashing Leftist Labor Movement", edited by Brad Simpson, National Security Archive (NSA). Washington, DC, Oct 17, 2017. https://nsarchive.gwu.edu/briefing-book/indonesia/2017-10-17/indonesia-mass-murder-1965-us-embassy-files Accessed 15 Nov 2018.

Wilford, G. E. *The Geology and Mineral Resources of Brunei and Adjacent Parts of Sarawak with Descriptions of Seria and Miri Oilfields*. Geological Survey Department, British Territories in Borneo, Memoir 10. Brunei: Brunei Press Limited, 1961.

Woodhead, E. W. *Report upon Financing of Education and Conditions of Service in the Teaching Profession in Sarawak*. Kuching: Sarawak Government Printing Press, 1955.

Woods, John. *Local Government in Sarawak: An Introduction to the Nature and Working of District Councils in the State*. Kuching: Sarawak Government Printing Office, 1968.

Worldometers: Indonesia Population. www.worldometers.info/world-population/indonesia-population/ Accessed 11 July 2018.

Published documents

Archer, John Beville. *Glimpses of Sarawak between 1912 & 1946: Autobiographical Extracts & Articles of an Officer of the Rajahs: John Beville Archer (1893–1948)*. Comp. and introd. by Vernon L. Porritt. Hull: Special issue of the Department of South-East Asian Studies, University of Hull, 1997.

Zaini Haji Ahmad, Haji. *The People's Party: Selected Documents*. Petaling Jaya: INSAN, the Institute of Social Analysis, 1987.

Private papers, collections

Wen Ming Chyuan. "A Historical Outline of the Struggles of the Sarawak Liberation League, SLL", (1965?).

Secondary sources

Articles, book chapters

Aarons Mark. "Justice Betrayed: Post-1945 Responses to Genocide", in: *The Legacy of Nuremberg: Civilising Influence or Institutionalised Vengeance?* edited by David A. Blumenthal and Timothy L. H. McCormack. International Humanitarian Law. Leiden: Martinus Nijhoff Publishers, 2007. pp. 69–97.

Ahmad Basuni Haji Abbas, and Dy Hasnah Hassan. "The Legal System of Brunei Darussalam", in: *ASEAN Legal Systems*, edited by ASEAN Law Association. Singapore: Butterworths Asia, 1995. pp. 3–14.

Alpha History: Quotations: Evaluating the Cold War. https://alphahistory.com/coldwar/quotations-evaluating-cold-war/ Accessed 1 Feb 2019.

Anonymous. Flirting with Marilyn. www.expat.or.id/info/flirtingwithmarilyn.html Accessed 7 Jan 2019.

"Bandung Conference (Asian-African Conference), 1955", Office of the Historian, Department of State, United States of America. https://history.state.gov/milestones/1953-1960/bandung-conf Accessed 3 Dec 2017.

Bautista, L. "The Historical Context and Legal Basis of the Philippine Treaty Limits", *Asian-Pacific Law and Policy Journal*, 10, 1 (2008): 1–31.

Beisner, Robert L. "Patterns of Peril: Dean Acheson Joins the Cold Warriors, 1945–46", *Diplomatic History*, 20, 3 (1996): 321–355.

"Berlin Blockade and Airlift", *The Editors of Encyclopædia Britannica*. www.britannica.com/event/Berlin-blockade-and-airlift Accessed 11 Nov 2017.

Billington, Michael O. "Britain's Cold War against FDR's Grand Design: In the East Asian Theater, 1943–63", *EIR Feature, Executive Intelligence Review (EIR)*, 26, 41 (Oct 15, 1999): 14–43. https://larouchepub.com/eiw/public/1999/eirv26n41-19991015/eirv26n41-19991015_014-britains_cold_war_against_fdrs_g.pdf Accessed 10 Jan 2019.

Brown, Derek. "1956: Suez and the end of empire", *The Guardian*, Mar 14, 2001. www.theguardian.com/politics/2001/mar/14/past.education1 Accessed 28 Dec 2017.

Butler, Rhett A. "Diversities of Image: Rainforest Biodiversity", *Mongabay.com/A Place Out of Time: Tropical Rainforests and the Perils They Face*, Jan 9, 2006. http://rainforests.mongabay.com/0305.htm Accessed 3 Feb 2019.

Chan, Francis, and Phyllis Wong. "Saga of Communist Insurgency in Sarawak", *The Borneo Post*, Sep 16, 2011. www.theborneopost.com/2011/09/16/saga-of-communist-insurgency-in-sarawak/ Accessed 26 Dec 2018.

"The Claim to Sabah: A Historical Perspective", by Kathlyn dela Cruz, ABS-CBNnews.com, Posted at Mar 7 2013 10:04 PM | Updated as of Mar 08 2013 11:10 AM. https://news.abs-cbn.com/focus/03/07/13/claim-sabah-historical-perspective Accessed 19 Sep 2018.

Cribb, Robert. "Genocide in Indonesia 1965–6", *Journal of Genocide Research*, 3, 2 (2001): 219–239.

Cribb, Robert. "GESTAPU Affair (1963): Annihilation of the Left", in: *Southeast Asia: A Historical Encyclopedia from Angkor Wat to East Timor*, edited by Ooi Keat Gin. Santa Barbara, CA: ABC-Clio, 2004. I: 544–546.

Cribb, Robert. "Guided Democracy (Demokrasi Terpimpim): Indonesian Style of Governance", in: *Southeast Asia: A Historical Encyclopedia from Angkor Wat to East Timor*, edited by Ooi Keat Gin. Santa Barbara, CA: ABC-Clio, 2004. I: 554–556.

Cribb, Robert. "The Indonesian Genocide of 1965–1966", in: *Teaching about Genocide: Approaches, and Resources*, edited by Samuel Totten. Charlotte, NC: Information Age Publishing, 2004. pp. 133–143.

Curtis, Glenn E., ed. *Russia: A Country Study*. Washington: GPO for the Library of Congress, 1996. http://countrystudies.us/russia/ Accessed 5 Nov 2017.

Davidson, Jamie S. "The Politics of Violence on an Indonesian Periphery", *South East Asia Research*, 11, 1 (Mar 2003): 59–89.

Davidson, Jamie S. "Violence and Displacemnt in West Kalimantan", in: *Conflict, Violence, and Displacement in Indonesia*, edited by Eva-Lotta E. Hedman. Ithaca, NY: Cornell Southeast Asia Program Publications, 2008. pp. 61–86.

Davidson, Jamie S., and Douglas Kammen. "Indonesia's Unknown War and the Lineages of Violence in West Kalimantan", *Indonesia*, 73 (Apr 2002): 53–87.

Derkommander0916. Map of Sarawak, Malaysia. https://openclipart.org/detail/218777/map-of-sarawak-malaysia Accessed 3 Feb 2019.

Dipesh Chakrabathy. "The Legacies of Bandung: Decolonization and the Politics of Culture", in: *Making a World after Empire: The Bandung Moment and Its Political Afterlives*, edited by Christopher J. Lee. Athens, OH: Ohio RIS Global Series, Ohio University Press, 2010. pp. 45–68.

Division of Korea. *New World Encyclopedia*. www.newworldencyclopedia.org/entry/Division_of_Korea Accessed 17 Nov 2017.

Dixon, Paul. "'Hearts and Minds'? British Counter-Insurgency from Malaya to Iraq", *Journal of Strategic Studies*, 32, 3 (2009): 353–381. www.tandfonline.com/doi/abs/10.1080/01402390902928172 Accessed 3 Dec 2017.

Dove, Michael. "Theories of Swidden Agriculture, and the Political Economy of Ignorance", *Agroforestry Systems*, 1 (1983): 85–99.

Dove, Michael. "Swidden Agriculture", in: *Southeast Asia: A Historical Encyclopedia from Angkor Wat to East Timor*, edited by Ooi Keat Gin. Santa Barbara, CA: ABC-Clio, 2004. III: 1284–1286.

Dwyer, Leslie, and Degung Santikarma. "'When the World Turned to Chaos': 1965 and Its Aftermath in Bali, Indonesia", in: *The Specter of Genocide: Mass Murder in Historical Perspective*, edited by Robert Gellately and Ben Kiernan. Cambridge, UK: Cambridge University Press, 2003. pp. 289–306.

Ellman, Michael, and S. Maksudov. "Soviet Deaths in the Great Patriotic War: A Note", *Europe-Asia Studies*, 46, 4, Soviet and East European History (1994): 671–680.

Fealy, Greg. "'Rowing in a Typhoon': Nahdatul Ulama and the Decline of Parliamentary Democracy", in: *Democracy in Indonesia, 1950s and 1990s*, edited by David Bourchier and John Legge. Clayton, Victoria: Centre of Southeast Asian Studies, Monash University, 1994. pp. 88–98.

Fernandez, Erwin S. "Philippine-Malaysia Dispute over Sabah: A Bibliographic Survey", Research Notes # 1, *Asia-Pacific Social Science Review*, 7, 1 (Dec 2007): 53–64.

File:Borneo2 map english names.svg. https://commons.wikimedia.org/wiki/File:Borneo2_map_english_names.svg Accessed 3 Feb 2019.

First Cairo Conference, 1943. Communique Released, Dec 1, 1943. www.loc.gov/law/help/us-treaties/bevans/m-ust000003-0858.pdf Accessed 17 Nov 2017.

Fisher, Max. "The Emperor's Speech: 67 Years Ago, Hirohito Transformed Japan Forever", *The Atlantic*, Aug 15, 2012. www.theatlantic.com/international/archive/2012/08/the-emperors-speech-67-years-ago-hirohito-transformed-japan-forever/261166/ Accessed 12 Oct 2017.

Flores, Jeremia, Ciarencia Reyes, and Rodolfo Sabio. "The Legal Implications of the Unilateral Dropping of the Sabah Claim", *Philippine Law Journal*, 57 (1982): 78–103.

Fong, Hon-Kah. "Vernon L. Porritt, 'The Rise and Fall of Communism in Sarawak 1940–1990'", Book Review, *Taiwan Journal of Southeast Asian Studies*, 2, 1 (2005): 183–192.

"From the Archive: Mr. Churchill on Our One Aim", *The Guardian*, Nov 11, 1942. www.theguardian.com/theguardian/2009/nov/11/churchill-blood-sweat-tears Accessed 1 Feb 2019.

Geographic Guide Asia Atlas. www.asia-atlas.com/southeast-asia.htm Accessed 4 Feb 2019.

George, K. M. "Historical Development of Education", in: *Commemorative History of Sabah, 1881–1981*, edited by Anwar Sullivan and Cecilia Leong. Kota Kinabalu: Sabah State Government Centenary Publications Committee, 1981. pp. 467–522.

"The Great Smash and Grab That Failed . . .", *The Straits Times*, Jan 21, 1963. http://eresources.nlb.gov.sg/newspapers/Digitised/Article/straitstimes19630121-1.2.71 Accessed 24 Jan 2019.

Gregorian, Raffi. "CLARET Operations and Confrontation, 1964–1966", *The Journal of Conflict Studies*, 11, 1 (1991): 46–72.

Gudgeon, Peter Spence. "Economic Development in Sabah, 1881–1981", in: *Commemorative History of Sabah, 1881–1981*, edited by Anwar Sullivan and Cecilia Leong. Kota Kinabalu: Sabah State Government Centenary Publications Committee, 1981. pp. 183–360.

Gunn, Geoffrey. "The Great Vietnamese Famine of 1944–45 Revisited", *The Asia Pacific Journal*, 5, 5, 4 (Jan 24, 2011). http://apjjf.org/2011/9/5/Geoffrey-Gunn/3483/article.html Accessed 24 Nov 2017.

Hanna, Willard A. "Sukarno: President of Indonesia", *Encyclopædia Britannica*. www.britannica.com/biography/Sukarno Accessed 4 Sep 2018.

Hara Fujio. "The North Kalimantan Communist Party: A Preliminary Study", in: *Borneo 2000: Proceedings of the Sixth Biennial Borneo Research Conference*, edited by Michael Leigh. Kuching: Universiti Malaysia Sarawak and Sarawak Development Institute, 2000. pp. 197–210.

Hara Fujio. "Sook Ching: A 'Cleansing' Exercise", in: *Southeast Asia: A Historical Encyclopedia from Angkor Wat to East Timor*, edited by Ooi Keat Gin. Santa Barbara, CA: ABC-Clio, 2004. III: 1230.

Hara Fujio. "The North Kalimantan Communist Party and the People's Republic of China", *The Developing Economies*, 43, 4 (Dec 2005): 489–513.

Hardjono, J. "The Indonesian Transmigration Program in Historical Perspective", *International Migration*, 26 (1989): 427–439.

Horton, A. V. M. " 'So Rich as to Be Almost Indecent': Some Aspects of Post-War Rehabilitation in Brunei, 1946–1953", *Bulletin of the School of Oriental and African Studies*, 58, 1 (1995): 91–103. https://web.archive.org/web/20131224123919/www.cseas.ncnu.edu.tw/journal/v02_no1/5.pp183-192書評new.pdf Accessed 20 Nov 2018.

Hughes-Hallett, H. R. "A Sketch of the History of Brunei", *Journal of the Malayan Branch of the Royal Asiatic Society*, 18, 2, 137 (Aug 1940): 23–42.

Index of /doc/maps www.acls-indonesia.com/doc/maps/PETA_KALBAR.gif Accessed 3 Feb 2019.

"Indonesia's Killing Fields", 101 East Speaks Exclusively to Some of the Indonesians Who Participated in the Systematic Murder of Millions, *Al Jazeera*, 101 East, Dec 21, 2012. www.aljazeera.com/programmes/101east/2012/12/2012121874846805636.html Accessed 12 Nov 2018.

Jenkins, David. "The Last Headhunt", *Far Eastern Economic Review*, June 30, 1978.

Joseph, Marcel Jude. "The Saga of Stephen Kalong Ningkan: The Conclusion", *Borneo Post Online*, Apr 26, 2010. www.theborneopost.com/2010/04/26/the-saga-of-stephen-kalong-ningkan-the-conclusion/ Accessed 7 Jan 2019.

"Jul 28, 1965: Johnson Announces More Troops to Vietnam", *This Day in History*. History Channel. www.history.com/this-day-in-history/johnson-announces-more-troops-to-vietnam Accessed 28 Nov 2017.

Kadane, Kathy. "U.S. Officials' Lists Aided Indonesian Bloodbath in '60s", *The Washington Post*, May 21, 1990, www.washingtonpost.com/archive/politics/1990/05/21/us-officials-lists-aided-indonesian-bloodbath-in-60s/ff6d37c3-8eed-486f-908c-3eeafc19aab2/?noredirect=on&utm_term=.def6d002d52b Accessed 12 Nov 2018.

Kelinman, Peter, David Pimental, and Ray B. Bryant. "The Ecological Sustainability of Slash-and-Burn Agriculture", *Agriculture, Ecosystems and Environment*, 52 (1995): 235–249.

Knight, Bernard. "School Mothers", SG, Nov 20, 1966.

Kroef, Justus van der. "Communism and Chinese Communalism in Sarawak", *China Quarterly*, 2, 20 (1964): 38–66.

Lim Peng Han. "The History of an Emerging Multilingual Public Library System and the Role of Mobile Libraries in Postcolonial Singapore, 1956–1991", *Malaysian Journal of Library & Information Science*, 15, 2 (Aug 2010): 85–108.

Llewellyn, J. et al. "US involvement in Vietnam", Alpha History. http://alphahistory.com/vietnamwar/us-involvement-in-vietnam/ Accessed 25 Nov 2017.

Low, Hugh. "Selesilah (Book of Descent) of the Rajas of Bruni", *Journal of the Straits Branch of the Royal Asiatic Society*, 5 (June 1880): 1–36.

Mao Tse-tung. "On Guerrilla Warfare; Chapter 6: The Political Problems of Guerrilla Warfare." www.marxists.org/reference/archive/mao/works/1937/guerrilla-warfare/ch06.htm Accessed 20 Dec 2018.

Marshall, Jonathan. "Hiding the Indonesia Massacre Files", *Strategic Culture Foundation*, May 2, 2016. www.strategic-culture.org/news/2016/05/02/hiding-the-indonesia-massacre-files.html Accessed 13 Nov 2018.

Matsumura, Toshio. "Causes of Lingering Communist Movement after Indonesia's September Thirtieth Movement: The Case of Border Area between Sarawak and West Kalimantan", *Asian Ethnicity*, 19, 2 (2018): 235–250.

Maxwell, Allen R. "The Origin of the Name 'Sabah'", *Sabah Society Journal*, 7, 2 (1981–1982): 91–105.

McVey, Ruth. "Early Indonesian Communism", in: *Born in Fire: The Indonesian Struggle for Independence, an Anthology*, edited by Colin Ward and Peter Care. Athens, OH: Ohio University Press, 1988. pp. 22–27.

Melvin, Jess. "Mechanics of Mass Murder: A Case for Understanding the Indonesian Killings as Genocide", *Journal of Genocide Research*, 19, 4 (2017): 487–511.

Melvin, Jess. "Telegrams Confirm scale of US Complicity in 1965 Genocide", Oct 20, 2017, Indonesia at Melbourne. http://indonesiaatmelbourne.unimelb.edu.au/telegrams-confirm-scale-of-us-complicity-in-1965-genocide/ Accessed 14 Nov 2018.

Milne, R. S., and K. J. Ratnam. "Patterns and Peculiarities of Voting in Sabah, 1967", *Asian Survey*, 9, 5 (May 1969): 373–381.

Moore, Alan. "Instruction by Radio in Sarawak", *Overseas Quarterly* (Sep 1963): 212–213.

Mujiburrahman. "Historical Dynamics of Inter-Religious Relations in South Kalimantan", *Journal of Indonesian Islam*, 11, 1 (June 2017): 145–174.

"North Borneo", *The Economic Weekly*, Feb 16, 1952, pp. 184–185. www.epw.in/system/files/pdf/1952_4/7/north_borneo.pdf Accessed 28 Mar 2018.

Ooi Keat Gin. "Sarawak Malay Attitudes towards Education during the Brooke Period, 1841–1946", *Journal of Southeast Asian Studies*, 21, 2 (Sep 1990): 340–359.

Ooi Keat Gin. "Education in Sarawak during the Period of Colonial Administration, 1946–1963", *Journal of the Malaysian Branch of the Royal Asiatic Society*, 63, 2 (Dec 1990): 35–68.

Ooi Keat Gin. "Mission Education in Sarawak during the Period of Brooke Rule, 1841–1946", *Sarawak Museum Journal*, 42, 63 (n.s.) (Dec 1991): 283–373.

Ooi Keat Gin. "Chinese Vernacular Education in Sarawak during Brooke Rule, 1841–1946", *Modern Asian Studies*, 28, 3 (July 1994): 503–531.

Ooi Keat Gin. "Prelude to Invasion: Covert Activities of SRD Prior to the Australian Re-Occupation of Northwest Borneo 1944–45", *Journal of the Australian War Memorial*, 37 (Oct 2002). www.awm.gov.au/articles/journal/j37/borneo Accessed 12 Oct 2017.

Ooi Keat Gin. "Calculated Strategy or Senseless Murder? Mass Killings in Japanese-Occupied South and West Borneo, 1943–1945", in: *The Encyclopedia of Indonesia in the Pacific War*, edited by Peter Post et al. Leiden and Boston: Brill, 2010. pp. 212–217.

Ooi Keat Gin. "The Cold War and British Borneo: Impact and Legacy, 1945–63", in: *Southeast Asia and the Cold War*, edited by Albert Lau. London: Routledge, 2012. pp. 102–132.

Ooi Keat Gin. "Borneo in the Early Modern Period ca. Late Fourteenth to ca. Late Seventeenth Centuries", in: *Early Modern Southeast Asia, 1350–1800*, edited by Ooi Keat Gin and Hoang Anh Tuan. London: Routledge, 2016. pp. 88–102.

Ooi Keat Gin. "Borneo in the Early Modern Period, c. Late Fourteenth to c. Late Eighteenth Centuries", in: *Early Modern Period of Southeast Asia, 1350–1800*, edited by Ooi Keat Gin and Hoang Anh Tuan. London: Routledge, 2016. pp. 88–102.

Ortiz, Pacifico. "Legal Aspects of the North Borneo Question", *Philippine Studies*, 11, 1 (1963): 18–64.

Ovendale, Ritchie. "Macmillan and the Wind of Change in Africa, 1957–1960", *The Historical Journal*, 38, 2 (June 1995): 455–477.

Overzicht Nederlandse Grevelden in Indonesie [Overview Dutch Grieved/Deaths in Indonesia], Nov 10 2013. www.1945-1950ubachsberg.nl/site/erevelden.htm Accessed 11 July 2018.

Parker, Jason C. "Small Victory, Missed Chance: The Eisenhower Administration, the Bandung Conference, and the Turning of the Cold War", in: *The Eisenhower Administration, the Third World, and the Globalization of the Cold War*, edited by Kathryn C. Statler and Andrew L. Johns. Lanham, MD: Rowman & Littlefield Publishers, 2006. pp. 153–174.

Peluso, Nancy Lee. "A Political Ecology of Violence and Territory in West Kalimantan", *Asia Pacific Viewpoints*, 49, 1 (Apr 2008): 48–67.

Peng, Shuzi. "The Causes of the Victory of the Chinese Communist Party over Chiang Kai-Shek, and the CCP's Perspectives", Report on the Chinese Situation to the Third Congress of the Fourth International, Aug–Sep 1951. *International Information Bulletin*, Socialist Workers Party, Feb 1952, from Tamiment Library Microfilm Archives, Transcribed & Marked Up by Andrew Pollack. www.marxists.org/archive/peng/1951/nov/causes.htm Accessed 16 Nov 2017.

Pigafetta, Antonio. "Pigafetta's Description of Brunei: July 1521", in: *European Sources for the History of the Sultanate of Brunei in the Sixteenth Century*, edited by Robert Nicholl. Bandar Seri Begawan: Muzium Brunei, Penerbitan Khas Bil. 9, 1975. pp. 10–11.

Podeh, Elie. "The Drift towards Neutrality: Egyptian Foreign Policy during the Early Nas-serist Era, 1952–55", *Middle Eastern Studies*, 32, 1 (Jan 1996): 159–178.

Porritt, Vernon L. "Constitutional Change in Sarawak 1963–1988: 25 Years as a State within the Federation of Malaysia", *Borneo Research Bulletin*, Jan 1, 2007. www.thefreelibrary. com/Constitutional+change+in+sarawak+1963-1988%3A+25+years+as+a+state...-a0179660415 Accessed 7 Jan 2019.

Quintos, Rolando. "The Sabah Question: Prospects and Alternatives", *Symposium on Sabah* (1969): 67–85.

Quisumbing, Purificacion V. "International Dispute Settlement in the ASEAN Context", in: *Cultural Factors in International Relations*, edited by R. P. Anand. New Delhi: Abhinav Publications, 1981. pp. 267–286.

Robinson, Geoffrey. "'Down to the Very Roots': The Indonesian Army's Role in the Mass Killings of 1965–66", *Journal of Genocide Research*, 19, 4 (2017): 465–486. www.tand-fonline.com/doi/full/10.1080/14623528.2017.1393935 Accessed 14 Nov 2018.

Roff, Margaret. "Sabah's Political Parties and the 1967 State Election", *International Stud-ies*, 9, 4 (Oct 1967): 431–451.

Rohrer, Finlo. "What's a Little Debt between Friends?", *BBC News Magazine*, Wednesday, May 10, 2006. http://news.bbc.co.uk/2/hi/uk_news/magazine/4757181.stm Accessed 21 Dec 2017.

Roosa, John. "The 1965–66 Politicide in Indonesia: Toward Knowing Who Did What to Whom and Why", The Southeast Asia Program Seminar, Stanford University, Feb 19, 2015. https://aparc.fsi.stanford.edu/southeastasia/events/1965-66-politicide-indonesia-toward-knowing-who-did-what-whom-and-why Accessed 11 Nov 2018.

Rozaid A. Rahman. 'History in the Making', *The Star Malaysia*, Nov 29, 2009. www. pressreader.com/malaysia/the-star-malaysia/20091129/283824324651362 Accessed 4 Jan 2019.

Rozan Yunos. "Town and Country Planning in Brunei: The History and Development of Planning in Brunei", *The Brunei Times*, 3 Mar 2008.

Rozan Yunos. "Sabah and the Sulu Claims", *The Brunei Times*, Mar 7, 2013.

Schulz, Brigette H. "Cold War", in: *Encyclopedia of Violence, Peace, Conflict*, edited by Lester Kurtz. San Diego, CA: Academic Press, 1999. I: 319–329.

"September 30th Movement: Indonesian history", *Encyclopaedia Britannica*, www.britannica. com/event/September-30th-Movement Accessed 18 Sep 2018.

Shlaim, Avi. "The Protocol of Sèvres, 1956: Anatomy of a War Plot", *International Affairs*, 73, 3 (1997): 509–530.

Stanley, Peter. "Sandakan Death March: A Tropical Hell", in: *Southeast Asia: A Historical Encyclopedia from Angkor Wat to East Timor*, edited by Ooi Keat Gin. Santa Barbara, CA: ABC-Clio, 2004. III: 1172.

"The Suez Crisis: An Affair to Remember", *The Economist*, July 27, 2006. www.economist. com/node/7218678 Accessed 28 Dec 2017.

Sundhausen, Ulf. "Indonesia", in: *The Political Role of the Military: An International Handbook*, edited by Constantin P. Danopoulos and Cynthia A. Watson. Westport, CT: Greenwood Press, 1996. pp. 189–206.

Sun Jieqiong. "14-Year War of Resistance against Japanese Aggression a Consensus among Chinese Historians", *People's Daily Online*, Jan 11, 2017. http://en.people.cn/ n3/2017/0111/c90000-9165703.html Accessed 12 Oct 2017.

Teh Leam Seng, Alan. "The Real Story behind the Historic Malaysia-China Ties", *The New Straits Times*, Aug 19, 2018. www.nst.com.my/lifestyle/sunday-vibes/2018/08/403014/ real-story-behind-historic-malaysia-china-ties Accessed 8 Jan 2019.

"Text of Hirohito's Radio Rescript", *The New York Times*, Aug 15, 1945. https://timesmachine. nytimes.com/timesmachine/1945/08/15/88279592.html?pageNumber=3 Accessed 12 Oct 2017.

Thompson, Eric C. "Indonesia in Transition: The 1999 Presidential Elections", *NBR Briefing Policy Report*, 9 (Dec 1999): 1–17.

Tregonning, H. G. "The Philippine Claim to Sabah", *Journal of the Malaysian Branch of the Royal Asiatic Society*, 43, 1, 217 (1970): 161–170.

Van Langenberg, Michael. "Gestapu and State Power in Indonesia", in: *The Indonesian Killings of 1965: Studies from Java and Bali*, edited by Robert Cribb. Clayton, VIC: Monash University Centre of Southeast Asian Studies, Monash Papers on Southeast Asia No. 21, 1990. pp. 46–61.

Watts, Carl Peter. "The 'Wind of Change': British Decolonisation in Africa, 1957–1965", *History Review*, 71 (2011): 12–17.

White, Timothy J. "Cold War Historiography: New Evidence behind Traditional Typographies", *International Social Science Review*, 75, 3/4 (2000): 35–46.

William, V. Gabriel. "The General State Administration of Sabah, 1881–1981", in: *Commemorative History of Sabah, 1881–1981*, edited by Anwar Sullivan and Cecilia Leong. Kota Kinabalu: Sabah State Government Centenary Publications Committee, 1981. pp. 3–80.

"Wind of Change": A Speech Made to the South Africa Parliament on 3 February 1960 by Harold Macmillan. *South Africa History Online: Towards a People's History*. www. sahistory.org.za/archive/wind-change-speech-made-south-africa-parliament-3-february-1960-harold-macmillan Accessed 21 Dec 2017.

Wright, Leigh R. "Historical Notes on the North Borneo Dispute", *Journal of Asian Studies*, XXV (May 1966): 471–484.

Books

Abinales, P. N., and Donna J. Amoroso. *State and Society in the Philippines*. Lanham, MD: Rowman & Littlefield Publishers, 2005.

Abueva, Jose Veloso, and Raul P. de Guzman, eds. *Foundations and Dynamics of Filipino Government and Politics*. Quezon City: Bookmark, 1969.

Adnan Buyung Nasution. *The Aspiration for Constitutional Government in Indonesia: A Socio-Legal Study of the Indonesian Konstituante, 1956–1959*. Jakarta: Pustaka Sinar Harapan, 1992.

Akashi, Yoji. *The Nanyang Chinese Salvation Movement, 1937–1941*. Lawrence, KS: Center for East Asian Studies, University of Kansas, 1970.

Allen, Louis. *Burma: The Longest War, 1941–1945*. New York: St Martin's Press, 1985.

Alperovitz, Gar. *The Decision to Use the Atomic Bomb and the Architecture of an American Myth*. New York: Knopf, 1995.

Amarjit Kaur. *Economic Change in East Malaysia: Sabah and Sarawak since 1850*. Houndmills and London: Macmillan; New York: St Martin's Press, 1998.

Ampiah, Kweku. *The Political and Moral Imperatives of the Bandung Conference of 1955: The Reactions of the US, UK and Japan*. Folkestone, UK: Global Oriental, 2007.

Anand, R. P., ed. *Cultural Factors in International Relations*. New Delhi: Abhinav Publications, 1981.

Andaya, Barbara Watson, and Leonard Y. Andaya. *A History of Malaysia*. 3rd ed. London: Palgrave, 2017.

Anderson, Benedict R. O'G. *Java in a Time of Revolution: Occupation and Resistance, 1944–1946*. Ithaca, NY: Cornell University Press, 1972.

Aquino, Benigno 'Ninoy' S., Jr. *A Garrison State in the Make and Other Speeches*. Legaspi Village, Makati, and Metro Manila: Benigno S. Aquino, Jr. Foundation, 1985.

The ASEAN Report, Volume II: *The Evolution and Programs of ASEAN*. Hong Kong: Dow Jones Publishing Co., Asia, Inc. 1979.

Baker, M. H. *Sabah: The First Ten Years as a Colony, 1946–1956*. Kuala Lumpur: Malaysia Publishing House for the Department of History, University of Singapore, 1965.

Barber, Noel. *The War of the Running Dogs: The Malayan Emergency: 1948–1960*. New York: Weybright and Talley, 1972.

Barnouin, Barbara, and Yu Changgeng. *Zhou Enlai: A Political Life*. Hong Kong: Chinese University Press, 2006.

Bates, Peter. *Japan and the British Commonwealth Occupation Force 1946–52*. Lincoln, NE: Potomac Books Inc., 1994.

Bellamy, Alex J. *Massacres and Morality: Mass Atrocities in an Age of Civilian Immunity*. Oxford, UK: Oxford University Press, 2012.

Bideleux, Robert, and Ian Jeffries. *A History of Eastern Europe: Crisis and Change*. London: Routledge, 1998.

Bilveer Singh. *Quest for Political Power: Communist Subversion and Militancy in Singapore*. Singapore: Marshall Cavendish, 2015.

Blythe, Wilfred. *The Impact of Chinese Secret Societies in Malaya: A Historical Study*. London: Oxford University Press, 1969.

Braithwaite, John, Valerie Braithwaite, Michael Cookson, and Leah Dunn. *Anomie and Violence: Non-Truth and Reconciliation in Indonesian Peacebuilding*. Canberra: ANU E Press, 2010.

Brown, Archie. *Seven Years That Changed the World: Perestroika in Perspective*. Oxford: Oxford University Press, 2007.

Calhoun, Craig, ed. *Dictionary of the Social Sciences*. Oxford: Oxford University Press, 2002.

Carlin, Thomas M. *CLARET: The Nature of War and Diplomacy Special Operations in Borneo 1963–1966*. Carlisle, PA: U.S. Army War College Root Hall, Bldg 122 Carlisle Barracks, 1994.

Chalfont, Lord. *By God's Will: A Portrait of the Sultan of Brunei*. London: Weidenfeld and Nicolson, 1989.

Chandler, David. *Brother Number One: A Political Biography of Pol Pot*. Boulder, CO: Westview Press, 2000.

Chandler, David, Ben Kiernan, and Chanthou Boua. *Pol Pot Plans the Future*. New Haven, CT: Yale University Southeast Asia Studies, 1988.

Chapman, Frederick Spencer. *The Jungle Is Neutral*. London: Chatto & Windus, 1951.

Cheah, Boon Kheng. *Red Star over Malaya: Resistance and Social Conflict during and after the Japanese Occupation, 1941–1946*. 4th ed. Singapore: National University of Singapore Press, 2012.

Chin, Kin Wah. *The Defence of Malaysia and Singapore: The Transformation of a Security System, 1957–1971*. Cambridge: Cambridge University Press, 1983.

Chin, Peng. *Alias Chin Peng: My Side of History*. Singapore: Media Masters, 2003.

Chin, Ung-Ho. *Chinese Politics in Sarawak: A Study of the Sarawak United People's Party*. Kuala Lumpur: Oxford University Press, 1997.

Conboy, Kenneth, and James Morrison. *Feet to the Fire CIA Covert Operations in Indonesia, 1957–1958*. Annapolis, MD: Naval Institute Press, 1999.

Contosta, David R. *America's Needless Wars: Cautionary Tales of US Involvement in the Philippines, Vietnam, and Iraq.* New York: Prometheus Books, 2017.

Cribb, Robert, ed. *The Indonesian Killings of 1965–1966: Studies from Java and Bali.* Clayton, VIC: Monash University Centre of Southeast Asian Studies, 1990.

Cribb, Robert. *The Indonesian Killings of 1965: Studies from Java and Bali.* Clayton, VIC: Monash University Centre of Southeast Asian Studies, Monash Papers on Southeast Asia No. 21, 1990.

Cribb, Robert. *Historical Dictionary of Indonesia.* Metuchen, NJ and London: The Scarecrow Press, 1992.

Cribb, Robert, and Colin Brown. *Modern Indonesia: A History Since 1945.* Harlow, UK: Longman Publishing Group, 1996.

Crouch, Harold. *The Army and Politics in Indonesia.* Ithaca, NY: Cornell University Press, 1978.

Cumings, Bruce. *The Korean War: A History.* New York: Modern Library, 2011.

Dallek, Robert. *Lyndon B. Johnson: Portrait of a President.* New York: Oxford University Press, 2004.

Dalrymple, Alexander. *A Full and Clear Proof That the Spaniards Can Have No Claim on Balambangan.* London: Author, 1774.

Darity, William A., ed. *International Encyclopedia of the Social Sciences.* 9 vols. Detroit, MI: Thomson Gale, 2008.

Das, Raju J. *Marxist Class Theory for a Skeptical World.* Leiden: Brill, 2017.

Davidson, Jamie S. *From Rebellion to Riots: Collective Violence on Indonesian Borneo.* Singapore: National University of Singapore (NUS) Press, 2009.

DeGroot, Gerard J. *The Sixties Unplugged: A Kaleidoscopic History of a Disorderly Decade.* Cambridge, MA: Harvard University Press, 2010.

Dennis, Peter, Jeffrey Grey, Ewan Morris, Robin Prior, and Jean Bou. *The Oxford Companion to Australian Military History.* 2nd ed. Melbourne: Oxford University Press, 2008.

Digby, K. H. *Lawyer in the Wilderness.* Ithaca, NY: Cornell University Press and Cornell University Southeast Asia Program Data Paper No. 114, 1980.

Dijk, Cornelius van. *Rebellions under the Banner of Islam: The Darul Islam in Indonesia.* Leiden: Koninklijk Instituut voor Taal-, Land- en Volkenkunde, KITLV, Royal Netherlands Institute of Southeast Asian and Caribbean Studies, 1981.

Drury, Bob, and Tom Calvin. *Last Men Out: The True Story of America's Heroic Final Hours.* New York: Free Press, 2012.

Easter, David. *Britain and the Confrontation with Indonesia, 1960–1966.* London: I. B. Tauris, 2004.

Eckert, Carter J., Ki-Baik Lee, Young Ick Lew, Michael Robinson, and Edward W. Wagner. *Korea Old and New: A History.* Seoul: Ilchokak Publishers for Korea Institute and Harvard University, 1990.

Eilenberg, Michael. *At the Edges of States: Dynamics of State Formation in the Indonesian Borderlands: Verhandelingen Van Het Koninklijk Instituut Voor Taal-, Land – en Volkenkunde* [Proceedings of the Royal Institute for Language, Land, and Ethnology Series]. Leiden: Brill, 2012.

Elson, R. E. *The Idea of Indonesia: A History.* Cambridge: Cambridge University Press, 2008.

Evans, Graham, and Jeffrey Newnham. *The Dictionary of World Politics: A Reference Guide to Concepts, Ideas and Institutions.* New York: Harvester Wheatsheaf, 1992.

Feith, Herbert. *The Indonesian Elections of 1955.* Ithaca, NY: Cornell Southeast Asia Program 1957; 2nd printing 1971.

Feith, Herbert. *The Decline of Constitutional Democracy in Indonesia.* reprint ed. Singapore: Equinox Publishing (Asia) Pte Ltd., 2009; first published in 1962 under the auspices of the Modern Indonesia Project, Southeast Asia Program, Cornell University.

Feith, Herbert. *The Wilopo Cabinet, 1952–1953: A Turning Point in Post-Revolutionary Indonesia.* reprint ed. Singapore: Equinox Publishing, 2009; first published in 1958 by Cornell University.

Fell, H. *1957 Population Census of the Federation of Malaya.* Report No. 14. Kuala Lumpur: Department of Statistics, Federation of Malaya, 1960.

Fenby, Jonathan. *The Penguin History of Modern China: The Fall and Rise of a Great Power, 1850 to the Present.* 2nd ed. London: Penguin, 2013.

Fernandez, Erwin S. *Philippine-Malaysia Dispute over Sabah: A Bibliographic Survey.* Diliman, Quezon City, Philippines: Department of Filipino and Philippine Literature, University of the Philippines, vol. 7, No. 2, Dec 2007.

Forsberg, Aaron. *America and the Japanese Miracle: The Cold War Context of Japan's Postwar Economic Revival, 1950–1960.* Chapel Hill, NC: University of North Carolina Press, 2000.

Friend, Theodore. *Indonesian Destinies.* Cambridge, MA: The Belknap Press of Harvard University Press, 2003.

Gaddis, John Lewis. *The United States and the Origins of the Cold War 1941–1947.* New York: Columbia University Press, 1972.

Gaddis, John Lewis. *We Now Know: Rethinking Cold War History.* Oxford: Oxford University Press, 1997.

Gaddis, John Lewis. *The Cold War: A New History.* London: Penguin, 2005.

Gerlach, Christian. *Extremely Violent Societies: Mass Violence in the Twentieth-Century World.* Cambridge, UK: Cambridge University Press, 2010.

Greenberg, Lawrence M. *The Hukbalahap Insurrection: A Case Study of a Successful Anti-Insurgency Operation in the Philippines, 1946–1955.* Washington, DC: U.S. Army Center of Military History, 1987. https://history.army.mil/books/coldwar/huk/huk-fm.htm Accessed 23 Nov 2017.

Haji, Zaini Haji Ahmad, ed. *Partai Rakyat Brunei/The People's Party of Brunei: Selected Documents/Dokumen Terpilih.* Petaling Jaya: INSAN (Institute of Social Analysis), 1987.

Ham, Paul. *Sandakan: The Harrowing True Story of the Borneo Death Marches 1944–5.* Melbourne: William Heinemann Australia, 2012.

Hamzah, B. A. *Oil and Economic Development Issues in Brunei.* Singapore: Institute of Southeast Asian Studies, 1980.

Harvey, Barbara S. *Permesta: Half a Rebellion.* Ithaca, NY: Cornell Modern Indonesia Project, 1977.

Heiferman, Ronald Ian. *The Cairo Conference of 1943: Roosevelt, Churchill, Chiang Kai-shek and Madame Chiang.* Jefferson, NC: McFarland & Company, 2011.

Holland, Robert. *Britain and the Revolt in Cyprus, 1954–1959.* Oxford: Oxford University Press, 1999.

Horton, A. V. M. *Turun-Temurun: Dissection of Negara Brunei Darussalam.* Bordesley, Worcestershire, UK: Author, 1995.

Hunter, Helen-Louise. *Sukarno and the Indonesian Coup: The Untold Story.* Westport, CT and London: Praeger Security International, 2007.

Jackson, James C. *Sarawak: A Geographical Survey of a Developing State.* London: University of London Press, 1968.

Jackson, Robert. *The Malayan Emergency.* Barnsley, UK: Pen and Sword, 2008.

Jarausch, Konrad H., Christian F. Ostermann, and Andreas Etges, eds. *The Cold War: Historiography, Memory, Representation*. Berlin and Boston: Walter de Gruyter GmbH, 2017.

Jones, L. W. *The Population of Borneo: A Study of the Peoples of Sarawak, Sabah and Brunei*. London: University of London and The Athlone Press, 1966.

Jones, Matthew. *Conflict and Confrontation in South East Asia, 1961–1965: Britain, the United States, Indonesia and the Creation of Malaysia*. Cambridge, UK: Cambridge University Press, 2002.

Jukes, Geoffrey. *The Soviet Union in Asia*. Berkeley, CA: University of California Press, 1973.

Jumper, Roy Davis Linville. *Death Waits in the "Dark": The Senoi Praaq, Malaysia's Killer Elite*. Westport, CT: Greenwood Publishing Group, 2001.

Kahin, Audrey R. *Rebellion to Integration: West Sumatra and the Indonesian Polity, 1926–1988*. Amsterdam: University of Amsterdam Press, 1999.

Kahin, Audrey R. *Rebellion to Integration: West Sumatra and the Indonesian Polity, 1926–1998*. Amsterdam: Amsterdam University Press, 2014.

Kahin, Audrey R., and George McTurnan Kahin. *Subversion as Foreign Policy: The Secret Eisenhower and Dulles Debacle in Indonesia*. Seattle and London: University of Washington Press, 1997.

Kang, Hildi. *Under the Black Umbrella: Voices from Colonial Korea, 1910–1945*. Ithaca, NY: Cornell University Press, 2001.

Kebschull, Dietrich. *Transmigration in Indonesia: An Empirical Analysis of Motivation, Expectations and Experiences*. Piscataway, NJ: Transaction Publishers, 1986.

Keenan, George. *Russia and the West under Lenin and Stalin*. New York: Atlantic Monthly Press, 1961.

Kerkvliet, Benedict J. *The Huk Rebellion: A Study of Peasant Revolt in the Philippines*. Lanham, MD: Rowman & Littlefield, 2002. First published in 1977 by University of California Press, Berkeley.

Khasnor Johan. *Educating the Malay Elite: The Malay College Kuala Kangsar, 1905–1941*. Kuala Lumpur: Pustaka Antara, 1996.

Kirby, Woodburn S. *War Against Japan, Volume 5: The Surrender of Japan*. London: Her Majesty's Stationery Office, 1969. p. 258.

Kirkpatrick, Jeane J. *The Withering Away of the Totalitarian State*. Washington, DC: The American Enterprise Institute (AEI) for Public Policy Research, 1990.

Kolko, Joyce, and Gabriel Kolko. *The Limits of Power: The World and United States Foreign Policy*. New York: Harper & Row, 1972.

Kyle, Keith. *Suez: Britain's End of Empire in the Middle East*. London: I. B. Tauris, 2003.

LaFeber, Walter. *America, Russia and the Cold War 1945–2006*. 10th ed. New York: McGraw-Hill Education, 2006.

Lee, Christopher J., ed. *Making a World after Empire: The Bandung Moment and Its Political Afterlives*. Athens, OH: Ohio University Press, 2010.

Lee, Kuan Yew. *The Battle for Merger*. Singapore: Government Printing Office, 1961.

Lee, Yong Leng. *North Borneo (Sabah): A Study in Settlement Geography*. Singapore: Donald Moore for Eastern Universities Press, 1965.

Leigh, Michael B. *The Rising Moon: Political Change in Sarawak*. Sydney: Sydney University Press, 1974.

Lev, Daniel S. *The Transition to Guided Democracy: Indonesian Politics 1957–1959*. Singapore: Equinox Publishing, 2009; first published in 1966 by Cornell Southeast Asia Program Publications.

Levine, Philippa. *The British Empire: Sunrise to Sunset*. 2nd ed. London: Routledge, 2013.

Lim Shau Hua, Julitta, and Hon Kah Fong. *The Intrepid Sarawak Volunteer Mechanics 1937–1945*. Kuching: Author, 2013.

Li Yi. *The Structure and Evolution of Chinese Social Stratification*. Lanham, MD: University Press of America, 2005.

Logevall, Fredrik. *Embers of War: The Fall of an Empire and the Making of America's Vietnam*. New York: Random House, 2014.

Macapagal, Diosdado. *A Stone for the Edifice: Memoirs of a President*. Ann Arbor, MI: Mac Publishing House, University of Michigan, 1968.

MacDonald, Malcolm. *Borneo Peoples*. New York: Knopf, 1958.

Mackie, Jamie. *Bandung 1955: Non-Alignment and Afro-Asian Solidarity*. Singapore: Editions Didier Millet, 2005.

Madinier, Remy. *Islam and Politics in Indonesia: The Masyumi Party between Democracy and Integralism*. trans. Jeremy Desmon. Singapore: National University of Singapore Press, 2015.

Majul, Cesar Adib. *The Contemporary Muslim Movement in the Philippines*. Berkeley, CA: Mizan Press, 1985.

Majul, Cesar Adib. *Muslims in the Philippines*. Manila: University of Philippines Press, 1999.

Mak Lau Fong. *The Sociology of Secret Societies: A Study of Chinese Secret Societies in Singapore and Peninsular Malaysia*. Kuala Lumpur: Oxford University Press, 1981.

Mao Zedong. *Quotations from Chairman Mao Tse-tung*. Beijing: People's Liberation Army General Political Department, 1964.

Mao Zedong. *Quotations from Chairman Mao Tse-tung (The Little Red Book) & Other Works*. Morrisville, NC: Lulu Press Inc., 2017.

McNamara, Robert S., James G. Blight, Robert K. Brigham, Thomas J. Biersteker, and Col. Herbert Y. Schandler. *Argument without End: In Search of Answers to the Vietnam Tragedy*. New York: Public Affairs, 1999.

McVey, Ruth T. *The Soviet View of the Indonesian Revolution: A Study in the Russian Attitude towards Asian Nationalism*. Jakarta and Kuala Lumpur: Equinox Publishing, 2009. First published in 1952 as Cornell Modern Indonesian Project Interim Reports by Cornell Southeast Asian Program Publications, Cornell University, Ithaca, NY, U.S.

Melvin, Jess. *The Army and the Indonesian Genocide: Mechanics of Mass Murder*. London: Routledge, 2018.

Miller, Roger G. *To Save a City: The Berlin Airlift, 1948–1948*. Air Force History and Museums Program, 1998. https://media.defense.gov/2010/Oct/01/2001329741/-1/-1/0/AFD-101001-053.pdf Accessed 11 Nov 2017.

Miskovic, Natasa, Harald Fischer-Tiné, and Nada Boskovska, eds. *The Non-Aligned Movement and the Cold War: Delhi-Bandung-Belgrade*. London: Routledge, 2014.

Morris, Seymour, Jr. *Supreme Commander: MacArthur's Triumph in Japan*. New York: HarperCollins, 2014.

Noakes, J. L. *Sarawak and Brunei: A Report on the 1947 Population Census*. Kuching: Government Printing Office, 1959.

North Borneo, Brunei, Sarawak (British Borneo). New Haven, CT: Human Relations Area Files, 1956.

Notosusanto, Nugruho. *The National Struggle and the Armed Forces in Indonesia*. Jakarta: Centre for Armed Forces History, Department of Defence and Security, 1975.

Notosusanto, Nugroho, and Ismail Saleh. *The Coup Attempt of the "30 September Movement" in Indonesia*. Djakarta: P.T. Pembimbing Masa, 1968.

Ong Kee Hui. *Footprints in Sarawak: Memoirs of Tan Sri Datuk (Dr) Ong Kee Hui, 1914 to 1963*. Kuching: Research & Resource Centre, SUPP Headquarters, 1998.

Ong Weichong. *Malaysia's Defeat of Armed Communism: The Second Emergency, 1968–1989*. London: Routledge, 2014.

Ooi Keat Gin. *World beyond the Rivers: Education in Sarawak from Brooke Rule to Colonial Office Administration, 1841–1963*. Special Publication Series. Hull, England: Department for South-East Asian Studies, University of Hull, 1996.

Ooi Keat Gin. *Of Free Trade and Native Interests: The Brookes and the Economic Development of Sarawak, 1841–1941*. Kuala Lumpur: Oxford University Press, 1997.

Ooi Keat Gin. *Rising Sun over Borneo: The Japanese Occupation of Sarawak, 1941–1945*. London and Basingstoke: Macmillan; New York: Saint Martin's Press, 1999.

Ooi Keat Gin. *The Japanese Occupation of Borneo, 1941–1945*. London: Routledge, 2011.

Ooi Keat Gin, ed. *The Works of Nicholas Tarling on Southeast Asia, Vol. I: The Superintendence of British Interests in Southeast Asia*. London and New York: Routledge, 2012.

Ooi Keat Gin. *Post-war Borneo, 1945–1950: Nationalism, Empire, and State-Building*. London: Routledge, 2013.

Ooi Keat Gin, ed. *Brunei – History, Islam, Society, and Contemporary Issues*. London: Routledge, 2016.

Ooi Keat Gin. *Historical Dictionary of Malaysia*. 2nd ed. Lanham, MD: Rowman & Littlefield, 2018.

Pakenham, Thomas. *The Boer War*. New York: Random House, 1979.

Parkinson, Cosmo. *The Colonial Office from within*. London: Faber and Faber, 1947.

Penders, C. L. M. *The West New Guinea Debacle: Dutch Decolonisation and Indonesia, 1945–1962*. Leiden: Brill, 2002.

Penders, C. L. M., and Ulf Sundhaussen. *Abdul Haris Nasution: A Political Biography*. St Lucia: University of Queensland Press, 1985.

Peterson, Robert. *Storm over Borneo*. London: Overseas Missionary Fellowship, 1968.

Pocock, Tom. *Fighting General: The Public and Private Campaigns of General Sir Walter Walker*. London: Collins, 1973.

Porritt, Vernon L. *British Colonial Rule in Sarawak, 1946–1963*. Kuala Lumpur: Oxford University Press, 1997.

Porritt, Vernon L. *Operation Hammer: Enforced Resettlement in Sarawak in 1965*. Hull: Centre for South-East Asian Studies, University of Hull, 2002.

Porritt, Vernon L. *The Rise and Fall of Communism in Sarawak 1940–1990*. Clayton, VIC: Monash Asia Institute, 2004.

Poulgrain, Greg. *The Genesis of Konfrontasi: Malaysia, Brunei, Indonesia, 1945–1965*. Barthurst, NSW: Crawford House Publishing; London: C. Hurst & Co., 1998.

Purdey, Jemma. *Anti-Chinese Violence in Indonesia, 1996–1999*. Honolulu: University of Hawaii Press, 2006.

Raffles, Sophia Lady. *Memoir of the Life and Public Services of Sir Thomas Stamford Raffles, Particularly in the Government of Java, 1811–1816, and of Bencoolen and Its Dependencies, 1817–1824: With Details of the Commerce and Resources of the Eastern Archipelago and Selections from His Correspondence*. London: John Murray, 1830.

Ramakrishna, Kumar. *Emergency Propaganda: The Winning of Malayan Hearts and Minds 1948–1958*. London: Routledge, 2015.

Rappaport, Helen. *Joseph Stalin: A Biographical Companion*. Santa Barbara, CA: ABC-Clio, 1999.

Rasenberger, Jim. *The Brilliant Disaster: JFK, Castro, and America's Doomed Invasion of Cuba's Bay of Pigs*. New York: Scribner, 2012.

Reece, Bob. *Datu Bandar: Abang Hj. Mustapha of Sarawak: Some Reflections of His Life and Times*. Kuala Lumpur: Sarawak Literary Society, 1993.

Reece, R. H. W. *The Name of Brooke: The End of White Rajah Rule in Sarawak*. Kuala Lumpur: Oxford University Press, 1982.

Reid, Anthony J. S. *The Indonesian National Revolution, 1945–1950*. Hawthorn, VIC, Australia: Longmans, 1974.

Ricklefs, M. C. *A History of Modern Indonesia since c. 1200*. 4th ed. Houndmills, UK and New York: Palgrave Macmillan, 2008.

Roberts, Geoffrey. *Stalin's Wars: From World War to Cold War, 1939–1953*. New Haven, CT: Yale University Press, 2006.

Robinson, Geoffrey B. *The Killing Season: A History of the Indonesian Massacres, 1965–66*. Princeton, NJ: Princeton University Press, 2018.

Robinson, Geoffrey. *The Dark Side of Paradise: Political Views in Bali*. Ithaca, NY: Cornell University Press, 1995.

Roosa, John. *Pretext for Mass Murder: The September 30th Movement and Suharto's Coup d'État in Indonesia*. Madison, WI: The University of Wisconsin Press, 2006.

Sadka, Emily. *The Protected Malay States 1874–1895*. Kuala Lumpur: University Press of Malaya, 1968.

Sarawak Shell Oilfields Limited (SSOL). *Oil in Sarawak 1910–1960*. Kuala Belait, Brunei: Brunei Press, 1961.

Saunders, Graham. *A History of Brunei*. Kuala Lumpur: Oxford University Press, 1994.

Schiller, Anne. *Small Sacrifices: Religious Change and Cultural Identity among the Ngaju of Indonesia*. New York: Oxford University Press, 1997.

Schmitz, David F. *The United States and Right-Wing Dictatorships, 1965–1989*. Cambridge, MA: Cambridge University Press, 2006.

Schwarz, Adam. *A Nation in Waiting: Indonesia's Search for Stability*. 2nd ed. Crows' Nest, NSW: Allen and Unwin, 1999.

Scott, James. *Seeing Like a State*. New Haven, CT: Yale University Press, 1998.

Sebald, William J. *With MacArthur in Japan: A Personal History of the Occupation*. New York: W. W. Norton, 1965.

Senn, Alfred Erich. *Lithuania 1940: Revolution from Above*. Amsterdam and New York: Rodopi, 2007.

Setiono, Benny G. *Tionghoa dalam Pusaran Politik* [*Indonesia's Chinese Community under Political Turmoil*]. Jakarta: TransMedia Pustaka, 2008.

Shirer, William L. *Rise and Fall of the Third Reich: A History of Nazi Germany*. New York: Simon and Schuster, 1990.

Simanjuntak, P. N. H. *Kabinet-Kabinet Republik Indonesia: Dari Awal Kemerdekaan Sampai Reformasi* [*Cabinets of the Republic of Indonesia: From Early Independence Until Reformation*]. Jakarta: Djambatan, 2003.

Simpson, Bradley. *Economists with Guns: Authoritarian Development and U.S.: Indonesian Relations, 1960–1968*. Stanford: Stanford University Press, 2010.

Smith, Jeremy. *The Fall of Soviet Communism*. Houndmills, UK, and New York: Palgrave Macmillan, 2005.

Soutan Sjahrir. *Out of Exile*. trans. Charles Wolf. New York: New Day, 1949.

Spence, Jonathan D. *The Search for Modern China*. 3rd ed. New York: W. W. Norton & Company, 2012.

Stewart, Dona J. *The Middle East Today: Political, Geographical and Cultural Perspectives*. London: Routledge, 2013.

Stubbs, Richard. *Hearts and Minds in Guerrilla Warfare: The Malayan Emergency 1948–1960.* Singapore: Oxford University Press, 1989.

Sundhaussen, Ulf. *The Road to Power: Indonesian Military Politics, 1945–1967.* Kuala Lumpur: Oxford University Press, 1982. KIV.

Suryadinata, Leo. *Elections and Politics in Indonesia.* Singapore: Institute of Southeast Asian Studies, 2002.

Swift, Ann. *The Road to Madiun: The Indonesian Communist Uprising of 1948.* Jakarta and Kuala Lumpur: Equinox Publishing, 2010. First published in 1989 as Cornell Modern Indonesian Project Interim Reports by Cornell Southeast Asian Program Publications, Cornell University, Ithaca, NY, US.

Tal, David, ed. *The 1956 War: Collusion and Rivalry in the Middle East.* London: Frank Cass Publishers, 2001.

Tan, Mely G. *Etnis Tionghoa di Indonesia: Kumpulan Tulisan* [*Ethnic Chinese in Indonesia: A Collection of Writings*]. Jakarta: Yayasan Obor Indonesia, 2008.

Tan, See Seng, and Amitav Acharya, eds. *Bandung Revisited: The Legacy of the 1955 Asian-African Conference for International Order.* Singapore: National University of Singapore Press, 2008.

Tan, Tai Yong. *Creating "Greater Malaysia": Decolonization and the Politics of Merger.* Singapore: Institute of Southeast Asian Studies, 2008.

Tan, Y. L. Kevin. *International Law, History & Policy: Singapore in the Early Years.* Monograph no. 1. Singapore: Centre for International Law, National University of Singapore, 2011.

Tanner, Rolf. *"A Strong Showing": Britain's Struggle for Power and Influence in South Asia 1942–1950.* Stuttgart: Steiner Franz Verlag, 1994.

Tarling, Nicholas. *Britain, the Brookes, and Brunei.* Kuala Lumpur: Oxford University Press, 1971.

Tarling, Nicholas. *The Cambridge History of Southeast Asia.* 2 vols. Cambridge, UK: Cambridge University Press, 1999.

Tarling, Nicholas. *Britain and the West New Guinea Dispute, 1949–1962.* Lewiston, NY: Edwin Mellen Press, 2008.

T'ien, Ju-K'ang. *The Chinese of Sarawak: A Study of Social Structure.* Monographs on Social Anthropology no. 12. London: Department of Anthropology, the London School of Economics and Political Science, 1953.

Tolentino, Arturo M. *Voice of Dissent.* Quezon City: Phoenix Publishing House, 1990.

Tonder, Gerry van. *Malayan Emergency.* Barnsley, UK: Pen and Sword, 2017.

Tregonning, K. G. *A History of Modern Sabah (North Borneo, 881–1963).* Singapore: University of Malaya Press, 1965.

Tuck, Christopher. *Confrontation, Strategy and War Termination: Britain's Conflict with Indonesia.* London: Routledge, 2016.

Van der Bijl, Nick. *The Brunei Revolt: 1962–1963.* Barnsley, UK: Pen and Sword, 2012. Kindle ed.

Vickers, Adrian. *A History of Modern Indonesia.* 2nd ed. New York: Cambridge University Press, 2013.

Vienne, Marie-Sybille de. *Brunei: From the Age of Commerce to the 21st Century.* Singapore: National University of Singapore (NUS) Press in association with *Institut De Recherche Sur L'Asie Du Sud-Est Contemporaine* (Research Institute of Contemporary Southeast Asia) (IRASEC), 2015.

Vietnam War (1960–1975). The *Oxford Companion to American Military History 2000.* Originally published by Oxford University Press, 2000.

Vitug, Marites Dañguilan, and Glenda M. Gloria. *Under the Crescent Moon: Rebellion in Mindanao*. Quezon City: Institute for Popular Democracy, 2000.

Warren, James Francis. *The Sulu Zone, 1768–1898: The Dynamics of External Trade, Slavery, and Ethnicity in the Transformation of a Southeast Asian Maritime State*. Singapore: National University of Singapore (NUS) Press, 2007. First published in 1981 by Singapore University Press.

Wehl, David. *The Birth of Indonesia*. London: George Allen & Unwin, 1948.

Wertheim, W. F. *Indonesian Society in Transition: A Study of Social Change*. 2nd ed. The Hague: W. van Hoev, 1959.

Westad, Odd Arne. *Decisive Encounters: The Chinese Civil War, 1946–1950*. Stanford, CA: Stanford University Press, 2003.

Westad, Odd Arne. *The Cold War: A World History*. New York: Hachette Book Group, 2017.

Wettig, Gerhard. *Stalin and the Cold War in Europe*. Lanham, MD: Rowman & Littlefield, 2008.

White, Nicholas J. *British Business in Post-Colonial Malaysia, 1957–70: Neo-Colonialism or Disengagement?* London: RoutledgeCurzon, 2004.

Williams, William Appleman. *The Tragedy of American Diplomacy*. New York: W. W. Norton & Company, 2009. First published in 1959 by Clevaland, OH: World Publishing Company.

Wong Hoy Kee, Francis, and and Gwee Yee Hean. *Perspective: The Development of Education in Malaysia and Singapore*. Kuala Lumpur: Heinemann Educational Books (Asia), 1972.

Wright, L. R. *The Origins of British Borneo*. Hong Kong: Hong Kong University Press, 1970.

Encyclopedia.com. www.encyclopedia.com/history/asia-and-africa/southeast-asia-history/vietnam-war Accessed 15 Sep 2018.

Yao, Souchou. *The Malayan Emergency: Essays on a Small, Distant War*. Copenhagen: Nordic Institute of Asian Studies (NIAS), 2016.

Yen, Ching-Hwang. *The Chinese in Southeast Asia and Beyond: Socioeconomic and Political Dimensions*. Singapore: World Scientific Publishing, 2008.

Yong, Tan Sri Datuk Amar Stephen K. T. *A Life Twice Lived: A Memoir*. Kuching: Author, 1998.

Yost, David S. *NATO Transformed: The Alliance's New Roles in International Security*. Washington, DC: U.S. Institute of Peace Press, 1998.

Yousuf H. Aboul-Enein, and Sherifa Zuhur. *Islamic Rulings on Warfare*. Darby, PA: Diane Publishing Co., for Strategic Studies Institute, US Army War College, 2004.

Zabecki, David. *Germany at War: 400 Years of Military History*. Santa Barbara, CA: ABC-Clio, 2014.

Zarrow, Peter. *China in War and Revolution, 1895–1949*. London: Routledge, 2005.

Zubok, Vladislav, and Constantine Pleshakov. *Inside the Kremlin's Cold War: From Stalin to Krushchev*. Cambridge, MA: Harvard University Press, 1997.

Unpublished manuscripts

Hara Fujio. "The North Kalimantan Communist Party and China", Second International Conference in Research and Documentation of the Chinese Oversea, Chinese University of Hong Kong, Mar 13–15, 2003, Hong Kong.

Iik Arifin Mansurnoor. "Socio-Religious Changes in Brunei during the British Residency (1906–1959)", 13th Conference of the International Association of Historians of Asia, Sophia University, Tokyo, Sep 3–9, 1994. 16p.

Ooi Keat Gin. "'Malaysia': An Inevitable Creation, 16 September 1963", Persidangan Nasional Sejarah dan Sejarawan Malaysia [National History Conference and Historians of Malaysia], History Section, School of Humanities, Universiti Sains Malaysia, Penang, Malaysia, Sep 14–15, 2017 [2013].

Ooi Keat Gin. "Borneo in the Cold War, 1950–1990", Center for Southeast Asian Studies (CSEAS), Kyoto University, July 23, 2015.

Ooi, Keat Gin. "Borneo in the Cold War: Local Concerns or International Interests?", Academy of Brunei Studies, Universiti Brunei Darussalam, Brunei, Oct 25, 2018.

Ooi Keat Gin. "Players from Within, Actors from Without: The Cold War in Southeast Asia, 1947–1991", Center for Southeast Asian Studies (CSEAS) Colloquium, Kyoto University, Japan, Sep 29, 2016.

Ooi Keat Gin. "The Man Who Would Be King: The Tribulations of Anthoni Walter Dayrell Brooke (1912–2011) of Sarawak", Invited Speaker, 3rd Nicholas Tarling Conference on Southeast Asia Studies, Exalted Heroes, Demonized Villains, and Losers: Altering Perceptions and Memories of Leaders and Leadership in Southeast Asia, c. 1800–c. 2000, University of Malaya, Kuala Lumpur, Nov 12–13, 2013.

Ooi Keat Gin. "Twist and Turns for Hearts and Minds: The Cold War in Borneo, 1950–1990", Public Seminar, University of Sydney, June 6, 2017.

Non-English sources

Dutch

Zweers, L. *Agressi II: Operatie Kraai. De vergeten beelden van de tweede politionele actie* [*Aggression II: Operation Kraai. The Forgotten Images of the Second Police Action*]. The Hague: SDU Uitgevers, 1995.

Chinese

Lu You-Ai. *Manman qiusuo lu: bei jialimandan geming sishinian tantao 1950–1990* [*Searching for a Better Way Slowly: 40 Years of Revolution of North Kalimantan, 1950–1990*]. Sibu: Bei jialimandan gemin sishinian tantao bianweihui, 2012.

Indonesian

45 Tahun Kiprah dan Pengabdian DPRD (Dewan Perwakilan Rakyat Daerah) Kalteng (Kalimantan Tengah) [*45 Years of Progress and Service of Central Kalimantan DPRD (Regional People's Representative Council)*]. Jakarta: Penerbit Indomedia, 2004.

Angkatan Darat Kodam XII. *Buku Petundjuk Daerah Kalimantan Barat* [*West Kalimantan Regional Guidebook*]. Pontianak: Sudam V, 1972.

Bachtiar, Harjsa W. *Siapa dia? Perwira Tinggi Tentera Nasional Indonesia – Angkatan Darat (TNI-AD)* [*Who Is He? Senior Officers of the National Armed Forces of Indonesia – Army (TNI-AD)*]. Jakarta: Penerbit Djambatan, 1988.

Ghazali Usman, H. A., and H. Ramli Nawawi, eds. *Sejarah Revolusi Kemerdekaan (1945–1949). Daerah Kalimantan Selatan* [*The History of Independence Revolution (1945–1949). Region of South Kalimantan*]. Banjarmasin: Departemen Pendidikan dan Kebudayaan, Direktorat Jenderal Kebudayaan, Direktorat Sejarah dan Nilai Tradisional, dan Proyek Inventarisasi dan Pembinaan Nilai-Nilai Budaya, 1991.

Hassan Basry, H. *Kisah Gerila Kalimantan (Dalam Revolusi Indonesia) 1945–1949* [*Guerrilla Stories of Kalimanatan (During the Indonesian Revolution) 1945–1949*], Djilid Pertama: *Kalimantan diachir Perang Dunia II – 1945 sehingga lahirnja ALRI Divisi IV – 1946* [*Volume One: Kalimantan at the end of World War III – 1945 to the Establishment of ALRI Divisi IV – 1946*]. Bandjarmasin: Jajasan Lektur Lambung Mangkurat, 1961.

Hulten, Herman Josef Van. *Hidupku di antara Suku Daya: Catatan seorang missionaris* [*My Life among the Daya: Notes of a Missionary*]. Jakarta: PT. Grasindo, 1992, trans. from the Dutch, 1983.

Kodam XII/Tanjungpura. *Pelita 1975* [*Light of 1975*]. Pontianak: Kodam XII/Tanjungpura, 1975.

Laksono, P. M., Jajang Agus Sonjaya, Ons Untoro, Y. Tri Subagya, Almira Rianty, Aprilia Budi Hendrijani. *Pergulatan Identitas Dayak dan Indonesia: Belajar dari Tjilik Riwut* [*Identity Struggle of the Dayaks and Indonesia: Learning from Tjilik Riwut*]. Yogyakarta: Percetakan Galangpress, 2006.

Matanasi, Petrik. *Para Jagoan: Dari Ken Arok sampai Kusni Kasdut* [*The Heroes: From Ken Arok to Kusni Kasdut*]. Yogyakarta: Trompet Book, 2011.

PROKALSEL (Pro Kalimantan Selatan). http://kalsel.prokal.co/read/news/11476-menelusuri-riwayat-partai-komunis-indonesia-di-kalsel.html?fb_comment_id=2119148951444654_ 2120434284649454 Accessed 15 Nov 2018.

PROKALSEL (Pro Kalimantan Selatan). *Menelusuri Riwayat Partai Komunis Indonesia di Kalsel; Di Kalsel, Ketuanya Saja Masih Rajin Salat* [*Tracing the History of the Indonesian Communist Party in South Kalimantan; In South Kalimantan, the Chairman is Still Diligent in Prayer*], PRO KALSEL Pro Kalimantan Selatan, Jumaat, Sep 29, 2017.

Mohd. Noor Abdullah. *Kemasukan Sabah dan Sarawak Ke dalam Persekutuan Malaysia* [*Entry of Sabah and Sarawak into the Federation of Malaysia*]. Kuala Lumpur: Dewan Bahasa dan Pustaka, 1979.

Nugroho Notosusanto, ed. *Tercapainya Konsensus Nasional/1966–1969* [*Achievement of a National Consensus/1966–1969*]. Jakarta: Balai Pustaka, Cetakan Ketiga, 1985.

Riwut, Tjilik. *Kalimantan Memanggil* [*Kalimantan Calls*]. Jakarta: Penerbit Endang, 1958.

Riwut, Tjilik. *Kalimantan Membangun* [*Kalimantan Rises*]. Jakarta: P. T. Jayakarta Agung, 1979.

Sekretariat Negara Republik Indonesia. *30 Tahun Indonesia Merdeka* [*30 Years of Indonesian Independence*], Jilid III. Jakarta: Setneg [Sekretariat Negara], 1985.

Sekretariat Negara Republik Indonesia. *Gerakan 30 September: Pemberontakan Partai Komunis Indonesia. Latar Belakang, Aksi, dan Penumpasan* [*September 30 Movement: Rebellion of the Indonesian Communist Party. Background, Action, and Crackdown*]. Jakarta: Sekertariat Negara Republik Indonesia, 1994.

Soemadi. *Kalimantan Barat dalam Menghadapi Subversi Komunis Asia Tenggara* [*West Kalimantan in Facing Communist Subversion in Southeast Asia*]. Pontianak: Tanjungpura, 1974.

Syamdani, ed. *Kontroversi Sejarah di Indonesia* [*Historical Controversy in Indonesia*]. Jakarta: GRASINDO, Penerbit PT Gramedia Widiasarana Indonesia, 2001.

Wajidi [Amberi]. "Ibnu Hadjar dan Stigma Pemberontak [Ibnu Hadjar and the Rebel Stigma]", Jan 14, 2012. https://bubuhanbanjar.wordpress.com/2012/01/14/ibnu-hadjar-dan-stigma-pemberontak/ Accessed 20 Aug 2018.

Wardaya, F. X. Baskara Tulus. *Membongkar Supersemar! Dari CIA hingga Kudeta Merangkak Melawan Bung Karno* [*Supersemar Exposed! From the CIA to Coup d'état that Stealthily moved against Bung Karno*]. Yogjarkata: Galangpress, 2009.

Witono [Sarsono], Brigadir Djenderal TNI A. J. *Laporan Pang Dam XII/Tandjungpura ten-tang gerakan suku Dayak terhadap GTK [Gerombolan Tjina Komunis] di Kal-Bar (II)* [*Report of the Regional Commander XII/Tandjungpura on ethnic Dayak action against GTK [Gerombolan Tjina Komunis (Chinese Communist Horde)] in West Kalimantan (II)*]. Pontianak: Angkatan Darat Komando Daerah XII/Tanjungpura, Dec 4, 1967.

Malay

Ghazali Shafie. *Memoir Ghazali Shafie – Penubuhan Malaysia* [*Ghazali Shafie's Memoir on the Formation of Malaysia*]. Bangi: Penerbit Universiti Kebangsaan Malaysia, 2015.

Theses

Iwan Gardono Sudjatmiko. "The Destruction of the Indonesian Communist Party (PKI) (A Comparative Analysis of East Java and Bali)", PhD diss., Harvard University, Cambridge, MA, U.S., 1992.

Muhammad Iqbal. "Kesatuan Rakjat yang Tertindas (KRjT): Pemberontakan Ibnu Hadjar di Kalimantan Selatan 1950–1963 [Union of the Oppressed People (KRjT): Ibnu Hadjar Rebellion in South Kalimantan 1950–1963]", MA thesis, Department of History, University of Indonesia, Jakarta, Indonesia, 2014.

Sanit Seman, M. "Sejarah Politik Pendudukan Belanda dan Perlawanan Rakyat di Kal[imantan]-Sel[atan] [Political History of the Dutch Occupation and the People's Opposition in South Kalimantan]", MA [?] thesis, Universitas Lambung Mangkurat (UNLAM), Banjarmasin, Indonesia, 1972.

Seng Guo Quan. "The Origins of the Socialist Revolution in Sarawak (1945–1963)", MA thesis, National University of Singapore, Singapore, 2007.

Newspapers, magazines, and others

Sarawak Gazette
Sarawak Tribune
Straits Times

Non-English print media

Angkatan Bersenjata
Antara Weekly Review
Harian Kami
Kompas
Pelita Brunei
Suluh Indonesia

Index

For Product Safety Concerns and Information please contact our EU
representative GPSR@taylorandfrancis.com
Taylor & Francis Verlag GmbH, Kaufingerstraße 24, 80331 München, Germany

www.ingramcontent.com/pod-product-compliance
Lightning Source LLC
Chambersburg PA
CBHW071142100726
47908CB00002B/227

* 9 7 8 0 3 6 7 7 8 4 8 9 8 *